EVERYTHING YOU NEED

A. L. Kennedy has published three collections of stories and two previous novels. She has received many prizes for her work, including the Somerset Maugham Award, the Encore Award and the Saltire Scottish Book of the Year Award.

A. L. Kennedy

EVERYTHING
YOU NEED

V

VINTAGE

Published by Vintage 2000

2 4 6 8 10 9 7 5 3 1

Copyright © A. L. Kennedy 1999

The right of A. L. Kennedy to be identified as the author
of this work has been asserted by her in accordance with
the Copyright, Designs and Patents Act, 1988

First published in Great Britain in 1999 by
Jonathan Cape

Vintage
Random House, 20 Vauxhall Bridge Road,
London SW1V 2SA

Random House Australia (Pty) Limited
20 Alfred Street, Milsons Point, Sydney
New South Wales 2061, Australia

Random House New Zealand Limited
18 Poland Road, Glenfield,
Auckland 10, New Zealand

Random House (Pty) Limited
Endulini, 5A Jubilee Road, Parktown 2193,
South Africa

The Random House Group Limited Reg. No. 954009
www.randomhouse.co.uk

A CIP catalogue record for this book
is available from the British Library

ISBN 0 09 973061 8

Papers used by Random House are natural, recyclable
products made from wood grown in sustainable forests.
The manufacturing processes conform to the environ-
mental regulations of the country of origin

Printed and bound in Denmark by
Nørhaven A/S, Viborg

Mo rùn geal òg

1990

*T*hings *could be worse.*

Alone on Foal Island and waiting, Nathan Staples turned on his bed. He forced his chest flat to the mattress with a mild flex at his hips, then settled and calmed his breath. A familiar lack was stitching up his arms and then climbing further to jab at his brain. All psychosomatic, he knew, all self-inflicted, but all inescapable just the same. He exhaled with care, sidestepping the start of a sigh. Audible despair depressed him, most especially his own.

But things could, most assuredly, be worse.

The Persian Eye Cups, for example – they were particularly unpleasant, quite turned my stomach when I read about them, as I recall – they would be worse.

The Persian Eye Cups, yes . . . Person, or persons unknown, but presumably Persian, might whip out a pair without warning and fit them on snug. They'd prise back my eyelids and bed the cups right down against the nice curve of my eye and then they'd buckle all the necessary straps – I imagine they'd use quite a few straps, to stop me clawing. I would try to claw. But then I'm quite sure that they'd have their way with me, irrigate each cup with the correct corrosive dose and watch it bite.

I would naturally scream and jabber while my eyeballs both subsided into froth and the acid gobbled up my optic nerve. Tip back my head and my frontal lobes would swash about like hot, grey margarine. I'd be totally fucked. Eventually, all I remember would gargle clear out of my ears in two repellent streams and that would be that.

Which would be worse – of course it would.

He was waiting and didn't like it. Never had. The wait, this particular wait: it was always so demanding, so predictably calculating and lecherous – give it an inch or a moment and it closed on him in a tingling swarm to his warmer parts. It bit round the cartilage lip of his ears, breathed close to the bare of his neck, it was brazen at his armpits and the quiet joints of his thighs, it made him sweat. His body weight stung down unfairly against his tensing prick, while his thoughts sank and dressed to the left with a stocky tick of blood.

Rubbing an opened wound with living wasps. My wound. My wasps. Worse.

Or stapling my scrotum to the flesh of my inner thighs and then performing Scottish country dances until I feel my socks congeal.

I think that would be worse.

This was ridiculous. He was ridiculous. A figure of no fun at all, waiting for something which would not happen, could not happen, which should not be considered and surely to God had been set and settled a pathetically long time ago – put to rest on the much larger island near which his was fixed. Surely to God this was over with now, surely *she* was over with.

Being sodomised by an ill-tempered man using a plaster model of my own grandmother's arm.

That would be noticeably worse.

He lurched himself up and off his bed. The bare board floor gave the standard, gritty shove at his naked feet and – now he was paying attention – he found he could hardly see. He couldn't remember the sunset, but against the window, here it was – already night.

He felt for the doorway, the slope of the open door and then stepped through and into the other room, peering and wary. Nathan was, as usual, far more accepting of imagined injuries than actual, factual knocks at his elbows or toes. Five steps to his left and he'd avoided the usual vicious clip from his table top, another two and he could safely shuffle forward to palm the wall and find the switch and then sway dumbly under the violent impact of instantaneous light. His dog twitched in its basket, but stayed asleep, eyes ticking and chasing behind closed lids. Outside, the lisp and murmur of the sea became a little more assertive.

Nathan gentled over to his bookshelves, eased a folder out, opened and dipped inside it, feeling for the photograph. There. The slick give of the surface, the catch of a corner, the touch of a border fast and thin enough to cut.

Want what's worse? What's really worse? Then let's come and fucking get it. All the way.

The fully cocked and loaded photograph – tonight, he was going to look at it again. No need to be just sad when he could be truly, thoroughly suicidal.

As if you can choose. As if you can help it. As if you haven't, just to spite yourself, been asking for it all night. No more games, now — if anyone deserves a head fuck . . .

I know — it's me.

*And don't say a little bit of you won't like it. After all, your head is your only private part that still has any chance of **getting** fucked.*

So we part the mind wide open, spread the thinking till it cracks. Take in the view.

A snapshot view he knew so well now that he saw it quite imperfectly: either in rushes of terrible detail, or a kind of anonymous smudge. Here was the beach, still barred with weed and rock; the pale, refractive spill of pools; the green of algae; all aligned to make a neat perspective that slashed away to nothing and the edge of the frame. Lying along the horizon was a sliver of sea, much more confident and solid than the bleachy sky.

Had he ever been here? Inhaled the raunchy, dead salt scent of it all under that wincing sun? Leaned against the cool, fat sea wall? Chucked stones? Chucked anything? It looked like so many uneasy, unwelcoming Scottish beaches that Nathan never could put a definite name to it.

His attention began to scrabble at the image, hoping, in the customary way, that a proper mental focus would make the picture pliable, snap it out into three dimensions and comprehensibility.

Tangibility.

From the Latin *tango, tangere* — to touch. Something tangible possessed the ability to be touched. Nathan had ambitions in that area, even now. Although, quite obviously, he was being touched already, in a way. His own imagination was performing a type of well-informed rape: penetrating him painstakingly with a ghost, with a time past restoring, an unreachable skin.

You've got a nerve complaining. You love it.

It's all I've got.

But you don't have to love it.

But I do. That's what makes it worse.

Even so, he didn't have the heart to look too long or closely at the picture, at its figure, at her. He couldn't bear to pick out the soft curl

5

of her body, pale in the rocks, and would only skip and brush across her, cradling the whole composition by its sides and staring beyond it to his dog, who was, undoubtedly, enjoying the gruff and healthy doggy dreams that gruff and healthy doggies tended to.

'Hey,' Nathan whispered, meaning no harm, 'hey. Rabbits. *Rabbits*,' and his dog's left forepaw shivered once or twice with a tiny desire to chase. Nathan softened his voice, barely murmured, 'Not now, though. Not now.'

Nathan lifted one hand to his forehead tentatively – as if his skull might really be as fragile as it felt, as liable to flatten into uselessly thoughtful mush. When he edged his right thumb over in a minor exploration, its joints began to ache distressingly. He'd staved it a couple of weeks ago, punching Joe Christopher, and it was now a constant reminder that one should never punch one's friends or that, if one did, one should first check the proper positioning of one's fist.

'Nathan, you're not being serious.'

'Am I ever anything but?'

'Nathan . . .' Joe had drolled out his name with an unmistakable note of sympathy. Joe was always full of sympathy and understanding – that was a lot of what made him such an irritating shit. 'Nathan . . . you don't mean it.'

'Of course I mean it – who wouldn't mean it? I don't fucking trust him. Like I don't fucking trust anyone. Actually. Now that you ask . . .' He'd known he was being too loud here – it was the wine and the Sunday lunch – all that starch and protein and gravy-flavoured sweat. 'Jesus.' Joe hated religious swearing, so Nathan had tried that again. 'Jesus fuck.' Joe's mouth had given a prissy little twitch – serve him right for being so uptight. 'I mean – you grow up and you get a bit of common sense, right? Caution.' Nathan's hands had lifted in a kind of wavery, Al Jolson plea and had begun to infuriate him. He'd known he was looking silly and hot and drunk.

'But you're not.'

'Not what?'

'Like that.'

'Like *what*?' Some people went deaf when inebriated. Nathan was not that particular brand of person – he had simply been faced by a man who refused to speak with anything even approaching comprehensibility.

'Untrusting. I mean, you trust *us*. Don't you?' Joe had smiled, gleaming with group solidarity.

And the group had, of course, been solidly there and watching. They'd surrendered their own conversations, the better to gawp: Richard, Lynda, Louis, Ruth: all of them waiting for Nathan to slip into something more florid, aggressive, bad.

'Now, you know I'm not talking about . . .' He'd felt himself obliging them, becoming more idiotic with each unsteadied breath. 'That's just not . . . When you make this to do with everyone else . . .' He'd frowned fuzzily.

'But who *don't* you trust? Here.' There'd been no malice in the question – Joe, being Joe, was never malicious, only implacably and precisely curious. Also, he liked to take hold of a person's thinking and pat it about like butter, square it up into something neat and digestible, if mildly sickening. But Nathan was never the buttery type – that afternoon, in fact, he'd tried steadfastly to suggest he was nothing but bones and malevolent gristle and increasingly bad blood.

'You're mispere . . . misrepresenting me again. It's –'

'Unfair?'

Nathan hated it when Joe interrupted. He did it so generously, as if he'd just slipped in, quite humbly, to remind the other speaker that their sentence had outlived its usefulness.

'And denying us all your trust would not be equally unfair?'

A thuggish impulse had broken out in Nathan and he'd indulged it happily. 'Well, why not. Why not do that? You couldn't stop me.'

'But why on earth *would* you?'

'To avoid disappointment.' Nathan had been trying not to take this personally, but fury had, nevertheless, bubbled up in his torso and made his colour rise. 'Everyone disappoints me in the end.' There was no doubt that he'd started to look irate. He'd felt himself begin to bristle beside his ears. Anyone staring at him – as all of them were – would have assumed he was about to lose it. So then, of course, he'd *wanted* to lose it and fucking show them all, even though he really, probably, hadn't been going to before.

'So you've stopped trusting anybody?' Nathan had heard that comfy purr Joe stroked through his voice when he was winning.

'You don't, for example, trust Jack Grace?'

'Oh, for fuck's sake. Jack Grace? The man is a foreskin with feet.'

'But you trust him.'

'J. D. Grace? Are you serious?'

'Yes. Quite.' Joe had stood, complacent with whisky, smiling companionably and setting out that single, certain syllable again. 'Yes.' He'd grinned. 'You don't have a problem with J. D. – you have a problem with yourself.'

And that's when Nathan had punched him.

The impact had made the disappointing, nothing-too-much-happening celery snap that punching did, while it stunned and shuddered up Nathan's arm remarkably. He had watched the whip of motion in Joe's neck. Then, before a gentle broiling had begun to seize Nathan's hand, he had been able to think, for an instant or two, that he was, almost certainly, going to feel an extraordinary pain in his fist. Then, quite naturally, he had.

He'd tried not to give a toss what Joe was feeling.

Now when he looked at the two of his thumbs together, facing them towards each other across the photograph, they were definitely differently shaped. This was a worry. In his right thumb, the joint near the meat of his palm made a markedly sharper angle than in the left. This wasn't to do with swelling, because all the swelling had gone. No, this was to do with bone. This was permanent.

He couldn't recall if his thumbs had been this way always, or had only recently started to make a bad match. Things didn't look right here, but maybe they never had. Perhaps he had fumbled through all of his life, oblivious to this constant, if rather trifling, manual deformity. Perhaps other people had noticed and never said.

Staring at both thumbs for any length of time proved nothing and made him feel slightly insane – like a cautionary illustration of what ills might befall an otherwise sturdy fellow who turned foolishly to vice – *Thumb Staring*. He shouldn't do it.

But then, Nathan was full of the things he shouldn't do. He shouldn't look at the picture, he shouldn't think until he hurt, he shouldn't sleep flat to the chill of the wall and let it seep into his brain, or hug himself round the small purgatories of an utterly pointless wait. He shouldn't be Nathan Staples, shouldn't be barefoot and demented and comparing the shape of his thumbs.

'Are you betting, then?'
'Naturally. 'Course.'

They were waiting to watch a car burn. Which would start any time around now.

'Yes, but *what* do you bet?'

'I bet this.' Morgan snaked one arm between the incline of Bryn's back and his coat's lining, then angled on down. He dipped inside Bryn's waistband, gently inflicting the cold of his hands.

'You bet *doing* this, or *getting* this? Hm? Mo?'

Warm shirt. Then warmer and maybe a little moist skin, like a broad kiss at Morgan's thumb, making him say quietly, 'Just this,' and press on for the base of the spine, the final, stern nub of bone. 'Just this.' The unbearable smoothness, the guard of small hairs, the hot knowledge of all this and the feeling of utterly hungry and angry and speechless gratitude. 'Just this.'

'Then I've got it already.'

'Then you've already won.'

Morgan paused while a big rock of pleasure swiped through him. Bryn leaned in and smiled against the tuck of his neck, mouthed him, 'You're a daft bastard, man, aren't you? Incorrigible, aren't you? Hm?'

A nice hope rippled and giggled round Morgan's spine. 'I know.' He could feel a cough starting to lift in his chest and made the effort to swallow things smooth again.

'But if you distract us, we'll miss when it begins. And you'll start up wheezing – I know you. Bad man.' They both liked it when they teased, were warmed with it.

'Don't worry. I'm fine, honest.' But Morgan hurried in another swallow to be sure.

'Sssh.'

The first of the evening's rockets had already been loosed – an acid white detonation, ripping and hooping across the black. Valley autumns were always the same now: nights full of random shouting that smeared into screams, into firework shrieks and sudden light storms and noises that might have been shots. In Capel Gofeg after sunset, the air would taste of damp smoke and coldness, and the possibilities of fear. The town dreamed brokenly of gunpowder plots and deaths by fire.

So, at night, Uncle Bryn and Uncle Morgan would climb the southern side of the valley's end and sit in the bracken: partly to hug each other against the enjoyable chill and partly to be up and out of it all, at peace. When they were far enough above their house, they could look at it without concern, without the worry that it wasn't safe.

And whenever a car was stolen, they would climb and watch and wait and make small bets about its burning, because, sooner or later, it *would* burn, somewhere across on the northern slope. The bad boys would have taken it and played with it – badly, worse each time – before torching its carcass on the hilltop, the rest of their preparatory types of fun all done.

The Uncles made an effort to enjoy each fire, as if it were any other pyrotechnic spectacle. Approaching the fifth of November, with pre-emptive explosions rocketing up all around, the burnings even had a kind of context, they almost made sense.

'Ah now, that's a Toyota, Morgan. Definitely.'

Morgan's fingers scampered happily at Bryn, while they both leaned to see the first bruised light seeping above the head of the sharp north slope. Tall shadows stretched and whipped across the glow, before the whole flare of the car plumed up and on to the hill. 'Not a chance, that's a Ford.'

'Never.' The fire leered and rocked while its sounds broke time with its movements, stumbling somewhere in the distance between the Uncles and what they could see. 'The colour's all wrong.'

'You always say that, Bryn. But the colour is about the paintwork, the plastics, not the make.'

'But now what are the paint and the plastics about, apart from the make of the car? I'm telling you, Mo, I can pick out any bloody model by simply observing the shape of the flames.'

10

Morgan enjoyed a sigh of disbelief. 'Go on then, Butt. You know I do *try* to believe you. Even though I know what you're like.' He took the chance to return a compliment. 'Bad man.' Meaning that Bryn was a good man, because he was just so properly bad, their kind of bad, the kind that did no harm. 'Terrible, bad man, you are.'

'You know what I'm like and you know that I'm bad? That right?'

'Oh, yes. That's right.'

They smiled for themselves, listening to the distant burst of a heat-strained window. Without noticing, they had settled into holding hands.

'Toyota Corolla, Mo.'

'Ah now, though, Bryn, you've let me down, because that could never be anything other than a Ford.'

With one last billowing swing, the blazing shell slithered past its point of no recall and started to bonfire rapidly downhill.

Morgan blinked and found his vision numbed by the blaze into scars of light and ghosting blurs. 'It's fast tonight, then, Butt.'

The Ford or Toyota sped into a snap and flurry of sailing heat, showed its glowing back as it bounced, shivered, tacked, bounced once again and kicked into a messy roll. There were echoes of hard cheering before the Toyota or Ford opened in a final impact of cloudy flame.

Morgan felt Bryn flinch against his arm and wanted to console him. He wanted to attend to the whole feline weight of him, from the sweet salt of his throat to the buckle of his knees and to be sure he was all defended and at peace. Then a spasm of asthma strapped in about him anxiously. He wanted to be of an age to protect his loves: to be stronger and younger and full of breath. 'Nasty little buggers.'

'I know.'

'That's Danno's boy.'

'I'd say so.'

'What if they ever choose the other road? Nothing to stop them, is there? One push, either way.'

'If they choose the other road, Mo, then they will hit the post office or Ianetta's bijou and hygienic continental-style café. They got up a good momentum and a couple of healthy rolls, they could carry on down to us, right into the house – ruin the bloody carpet.' Bryn

11

kissed Morgan on his lips to make a shudder of distraction race through their collarbones.

'You don't mind, do you? The way it's all going?' Morgan heard his words sounding fragile, petulant – needing to be needed, as usual. 'I mean you're good at staying happy. Content.'

'It's only like the war again. That stopped. This will, too.'

'You don't remember the war.'

'Well, if *I* don't, I can't see how *you* do.'

'I was born in '28.'

'That's what you're saying.'

Morgan nuzzled him faintly for the compliment. 'In '28. I remember it better than you do – the war – you were just young, you were. It wasn't like this.'

'I know. It was worse. My Dada told me. He had to go to London and teach them how to tunnel out bodies from under the rubble. He taught them how to mine for people.'

'You said.'

'Little babies, all covered in dust. Men and women. Dead. He found one woman without a mark, except that her stockings were in holes and that might have happened before, that might have been nothing to do with the bomb and only her carelessness.

'Dug with his hands, to be gentle. The only way.'

'You said.'

'When he came back, he would see them in the shadows under-ground – the dead ones. Every day. Grey dust on them, not like coal dust, more like plaster, or ash. He said that. I didn't like to listen, but he said. All the time when he was working and then when he slept, he'd see them lying, grey. Never told my mother. And she would have liked to know.'

'Of course.'

'This isn't as bad as the war.'

'All right, then.'

'Well.' Bryn kissed him, as punctuation. 'It's not.'

Down in the valley, the car was settling into a failing blaze, now and then lighting the side of an older wreck, or the mad edge of a door. The dark thickened beyond it into breaks of pine, scrubland, an invisible river dropping to scour at the valley floor. Further east, and house lights began to make a nervous sequence, then looped and

12

chained and finally settled into the thin glow of Capel Gofeg's central, spinal street, its moving blink of cars. The Uncles could have stretched out their arms and measured the shine and pattern of it all between their palms like some bright kind of fish – their home that never got away. Instead they only watched and thought about making a move soon, about heading back to Charter Road and to their house and to Mary Lamb.

The same Mary Lamb who had just left the pub in Capel Gofeg High Street and paused, trying to breathe herself clear of the evening's cigarette smoke and second-hand heat.

Mary stood to face the breeze: the dark, westerly air which, elsewhere, was coiling round Nathan Staples and his island and his wait. She drew the night inside herself carefully, checking every element – burnt rubber, spruce, explosives and the underlying, spacious roar of green from hills and valleys that hunched out beyond her like the weird undulations of brains or crumpled papers.

She heard the pub door open behind her and then swing to, a mutter of feet. She could guess this meant that Jonathan had followed her out. This was good, but now they might well argue, which was not.

There was only a rind of moon. Mary would have preferred the full, grubby milk circle with touches of cloud to pass across it and spin out a haze of diffraction between breaks of open night. She was saving things up to remember and that would have been her first choice.

Mary edged a glance to her right before she crossed the road. Jonathan was there. Her Jonathan: the one whose name could turn in her unpredictably with a nice, cold charge. She reached out her hand in his direction and waited to feel how he'd made up his mind, to feel if he would join her, touch her, maybe mumble a little grievance across her fingers, rub her thumb.

'Are you all right, then? Jonno?'

'Yes.'

They set off together, Jonathan's hand now round hers, but immobile, carefully silent, straining not to ask what he wanted to ask.

Usually he had talkative, well-read fingers, which she liked. And he was a gentle person, which she liked, too. She also liked that he would, very occasionally, agree to sing, producing a light and careful voice with a tremor sometimes in its breathing – a surprisingly insubstantial, delicate sound rising from the density of what she knew was him. She understood his body as something smooth, compact and definite, which she had, for some time, absolutely liked.

Slowly Jonno's fingers tapped down to her wrist. He sighed and then coughed and then began, 'I do know . . . I understand that you . . . you aren't going to. I mean, that you won't.' A small note of hope edged in, 'Will you?' He was pursuing his own little inventory of good things to save up. 'We could, though.' His index finger strummed at the heel of her hand.

'I know we could. Of course, we could. But we won't.'

'But we would have. Wouldn't we? In the end. We would have?' He was trying his best to keep his voice buttoned flat, to sound neat and undemanding. She felt his arm shaking.

'We might have. Eventually. But we wouldn't have done it *now*.' They'd stalled their progress, halfway up the steps to the opposite kerb. Mary stroked once at his back. It was almost impossible to touch him for any length of time and not begin to be persuaded that she should let him collect absolutely whatever he'd like from her – *with* her – because it was easy to feel she would like it, too. It was easy to think she *should* do that thing – should make love, be with him, fuck him, fuck, precisely *because* she was going to leave soon. And because, as he'd said, they might have done it soon, might have done it any day.

They already knew each other, here and there, had already moved along the way. And she didn't have much to compare him against, but he did seem to be good, to have ideas that were good. He would do things to make her thinking wander over words like *pert* and *buxom* until she gripped his head against her and breathed in the warmth of his hair, while her eyes closed and her whole mind crimped and puckered between his teeth. This was a memory she'd collected already, but she wouldn't object to collecting it again.

'Do you have to go?' Jonathan dropped Mary's arm, knowing that he'd asked the wrong question. He let his hands drift miserably into his pockets. Mary didn't like to see him so sad. In all the years she'd known him, he'd been cautious, patiently expecting disappointment, forewarned but clearly not hopeful of being appropriately forearmed. Mary had thought he'd be safe in her hands and that they'd be gentle

14

together. She knew she'd begun with honourable intentions: no thoughts of abandonment. As he scuffled beside her, she looked at his ears, the pale shape of them. They were the only ears she'd ever found worth noticing: small, almost clenched, but also vaguely fragile and a tender pink. They made her have to touch him and feel how he was.

He faltered to a stop when she hugged him. She kissed him *goodbye* and *sorry* and *Idocareonlyitscomplicated* and *sorryIamsorryIam,* but she was still going to leave him and still couldn't quite sleep with him first. She couldn't do it, even when the brace of his back against her hands and the mild push of his stomach, hips, that extra, other nudge called through her. Breathing the smell of his neck and kissing him there, what she felt most of all was his impending lack. He was receding while she held him, her planned future slipping him further and further away.

'Well?' His voice was very soft.

She grew still, unsure if he'd really spoken. A lone firework slapped open in the air, shivered into straggles of light. She couldn't tell if Jonathan flinched at the sound of it, or at the thought of her saying again that she was leaving him.

'Well? Do you have to go?'

Then they tugged and scrambled at each other, rather than let her answer, pivoting about each other along the pavement until they reached the post office doorway and came to rest. Across the street, someone walked by, not pausing. Mary tried to sound loving while she said, 'I think I do. I do. I have to go. I'm sorry. It's such a chance. I've thought about staying here. I mean, I don't want to leave the Uncles –'

'Oh, the Uncles. I see.' He managed to make this sound unmistakably desolate, while holding her tighter, one hand in her hair, apparently impatient for every detail that he was about to lack.

'And I don't want to leave *you,* either. But the letter, when it came, it put the idea in my head that I could . . . that I might . . .'

His hand took the end from her sentence, closed fast round her palm and smothered her sense. His whisper jolted and pattered through her concentration, tickled her cheek. 'You see – you don't know, really, do you? What you'll do when you get there, what they're like . . .'

15

'I don't *have* to know.' She kissed his eyes shut, found their discreet trace of salt. 'I've never known what I wanted to do before. If I *could* do anything.'

'You don't *have* to do anything, you can just *be*.'

'But I've always *needed* something. I can't forget it now that I've found it finally. Can I? Could you?'

'Yes.' He blinked like a man who was waking from a bad dream to a worse, cleared his throat, 'No. No, I couldn't,' and looked at everything he needed: all of her, all there, Mary Lamb.

Her eyes and hair could sometimes seem precisely the same colour. They fascinated, made him think of looking through stained glass into hot, gold places: interiors that curled with fawn and odd, reflected lights.

Wrists, slim but nicely strong.

Thighs, perhaps fuller than she liked them, but perfectly and softly wonderful to him.

Body, so wonderfully hungry when it fitted and formed against him, even though – tormentingly – she frequently seemed unaware of its effects. He would often watch her walk off home without him after one of her more heated goodbyes and she would be apparently quite steady and composed while the whole aching stump of his brain was up and pushing him towards another sleepless night. She made him mad. She haunted him with her promises of skin and her silky-hard, demanding, extraordinary tits and all the other things he couldn't get to, but which coloured his every educated guess.

'Jonno?'

'Yes, I know.' He peeled himself away from her, hearing his voice sound grey. 'The Uncles will be coming home soon and you have to get back.'

His proper absence began to chill her. 'I don't have to hurry, though. You know . . .'

'But there isn't much point in us staying here, now is there?' He sounded sour. 'I mean tonight, I don't mean . . .' and then simply bereft.

'I'm sorry, love.'

'You're doing, doing . . .' he was slumping towards a kind of stammer, 'I suppose, the right thing. *You* think so, anyway.' She found it difficult to bear when he was forgiving.

16

'No.' She gathered him up to herself again and licked his lips. 'No, I'm not.'

'You . . .' He pulled away, stared at her, quiet, and she realised numbly that she'd given him the wrong hope, that even while she tried to love him, she was going to disappoint him again.

'I mean, I'm not entirely . . .' She watched his hurt turn raw again and then cover its tracks.

He edged himself towards a smile for her, but then couldn't make it. 'Not entirely . . . ?' But he already knew what he would and wouldn't get.

'I think one of my decisions was wrong.'

He frowned at her gently for a space, hoping he'd misunderstood, and then caught at her, held her, huddled his face to her neck, her cheek, searching, kissing, wanting to taste her change of heart, wanting to be happy with whatever her change of heart.

She kissed him back, as fiercely as she could, and tried to make this all that they could think of. 'I was wrong to say I wouldn't.' This had to be them together now, just together and playing the way that they liked to and not worried by anything. 'I might.'

She felt the particular movement of the beginning of his smile. 'Might what?' A real smile.

And she knew he'd understood her perfectly well by the small pounce of his interest against her, his curiosity growing plain, near the crest of her hip.

'You know what. I'm saying I will. I would like to. I want to. Yes.'

'You sure?'

'I wouldn't say so, if I wasn't.'

'You weren't sure before.'

'But I am now.'

'Quick decision.'

'Your tongue in my ear must have swung it.'

'Ah. Like I hoped.' A softness in his last word, a touch of panic, washing back.

So they rested, tight at each other, beating with thought, before Mary moved back. She finger-tipped through his hair to set it straighter, leave him neat and shook her head to stop him speaking or making her consider other things that she would like to do right there and then.

'Goodnight, love.' She kissed him carefully.

'I'll see you later, then?'

'Yes. I've said you will. So you will. And I will.'

'That's . . . ahm . . . that's good.'

'Good?'

'Fantastic, great – whatever word you want, whatever you want, altogether. Always.' He hadn't intended that to sound like an accusation, but she felt it, all the same.

'OK.'

'Yes.' He kissed her back, one soft, concluding brush that blurred into more depth than was calming, or conducive to saying goodbye.

'Now don't you start, Jonathan Davies.'

'Sorry.'

'I'm not.' She bent her head to lick along his knuckles. ''Night, then.'

'Yes. Goodnight.'

'Goodnight.' And Mary let the fall of the street start to ease her home, down to Charter Road.

Behind her, Jonathan shouted, 'Goodnight, Mary Lamb.' She turned back to wave and watched curtains twitch in windows above his head. She waved at them, too.

Nathan's window glass shivered and blinked at a knock of rain. It scared him, eased him a little further along his edge.

But it's all right, though. Everything's fine.

Something bridled in him, surprised by this outburst of gentleness with himself. It wasn't like him.

Executioner's courtesy, that's all.

Ssssh, never mind.

Outside, a downpour was downpouring – spinning high, white coils of malevolent water across the little lights his cottage gave into the night. He thought, extremely cautiously, of fixing in his mind the important points to establish, the ones that would make sure that this evening's proceedings wouldn't be focused on killing, or dying, or any kind of suicide. His actions might seem to be that way inclined, but this would be absolutely not so.

Jesus.

All his very personal alarms were tripped and sirening anyway.

Heart's banging about like a bastard. Hardly surprising, but even so . . .

I don't feel well.

Which means I have to take things gently. Means I have to be delicate.

The island's sky had started to rock and howl an hour or so ago – which was, coincidentally, round about when he'd tucked away his haunted photograph and decided he'd try his luck with the Main Event. He was due for another attempt – the pressure towards it had been building in him for months – modest emotional squalls before the proper storm. Now he was almost ready to start and outside a full, raw gale was dumping rain in gravelly armfuls against his western window, shuddering round his stovepipe and clattering his roof into a corrugated bedlam overhead. He couldn't have picked a better backdrop if he'd tried.

But I do need something more before I start – some kind of music – I do.

19

And not a requiem, none of that nonsense. I want something I'd like.

But what? – Lou Reed? The Beatles? 'Ae Fond Kiss'? **What?** *A fine time this is, to find out I'm hard to please.*

Then again, this is the last thing I'd want to get wrong.

Or just the last thing. The last thing.

He decided he'd best pick his soundtrack when everything else had been done. Meanwhile, he'd check his other preparations in the hope they might suggest a sympathetic melody.

His chosen equipment was simple, elegant. In proper combination, every item was absolutely capable of doing what he planned it should. This was something – in a way – to be proud of. This part was all so resolute and clean.

I planned this. I actually sat down and planned out the best way of doing this. I probably **deserve** *to die.*

No. None of that.

Nathan tried not to have an opinion on whether he actually liked or approved of his plan because this might, however slightly, influence its results and everything here must be left entirely and scrupulously to chance. His primary task was to offer himself up whole into the arms of all relevant natural laws and then let them mesh around him as they would.

I **am** *going to do it. I just don't want to think about it first.*

Shivers started in him, rose like beaten birds. He could feel the process kicking in, his commitment lifting and holding him like a kiss. He felt naked, clear and sweet.

And then nothing but terrified, because now terror was completely appropriate. Soon the entire right order of the universe was going to show itself here, in this one event, plainly written out. There would be no good and no bad about it, only the unavoidable and correct.

That's a kind of consolation. But if I need it, I won't be the one it will console. Poor bloody Nathan. Poor bloody me.

He held his hand to his face and caught his own breathing, the dunting of blood in his skull and in his jaw. For a person of his age and experience, he wasn't badly put together – all in working order, more or less.

He gradually widened the spaces between his fingers, so he could see what was coming next.

My equipment. My paraphernalia. My accoutrements.

Panic floundered in him and he rode it down.

All right, then, let's go.

Sash cord. It wasn't entirely easy to get sash cord, but he was worth this little effort to get the right instrument for the job: one continuous length of cord, curling, relaxed on the table and measuring six feet precisely. Not that Nathan needed it precise, it was simply sold that way. All he cared about was that six feet – even roughly six feet – would give him enough slack to work with, would be adequate, would not cause confusion and dangerous loops. He didn't want any unplanned dangerous loops.

Ready.

Low chair.

Looks like the product of a therapeutic exercise: one of those meaningless hospital tasks. Can't ever see it without imagining some hopeless amputee, hacking it into shape with new prosthetics; everything doubly missing at each stroke.

Which is nonsense. So now I'm thinking nonsense – stress-related, I've no doubt. And, then again, nonsense does no harm and I do so very much want to do no harm.

Currently, of course, he loved the hideous chair, because it finally had purpose, *his* purpose. Perhaps, in the end, it might even earn a degree of notoriety.

Ready.

Metal hook. One of eight, solidly fixed through the whitewashed plaster ceiling and deep into a central beam. This cottage had been a barracks block, back in the 1860s. The first line of defence against the Irish. Or was it the French? It didn't matter, either way. A good deal had changed since, but the soldier boys had still involuntarily bequeathed him their quite viable water tank and their eight inexplicably purposeful iron hooks.

Could have been used for hammocks, onion strings, bestial indecency of the homo-erotic sort.

Each to his own. For Nathan's private purposes, one hook was quite enough.

Ready.

Rope.

Shit. Rope. That's the one. Oh, that's the one.

21

He felt a stickiness, a swither coating his ribs: the cling and tease of utter cowardice.

The way it looks, so patient.

But it's here to be helpful. No need to fret.

Rope. A soft, dark drop of jute, falling for exactly six feet five and three-quarter inches. This length he had measured and cut himself, exactly as it had to be – figure-of-eight loop to secure it on the hook and then a running bowline, tied and waiting at its foot. All fine.

Ready.

Time to go, then.

Ssh. I know.

He took off his shoes and socks and drummed softly across the boards to his CD player – his one little luxury. He knew the disc he wanted now, unmistakably.

Glenn Gould – gobbled down his own premature extinction in heart and assorted other types of pill – he's your man. But not because of that: because he will be company.

And so he was. Gould was there for him, as usual: perfect and quixotic as death. Nathan stood, blood climbing and arcing through him like red light, and let Bach clamber in between his nerves. The cool of the sound was such a comfort, such a kind of protection, that it brought on a certain childishness, tearfulness. *The Well-tempered Clavier* – all clarity and distance and order – closed on every mortal piece of him. It squeezed at his sum, at his still breathing total, at his only way of being Nathan Staples, and it started to swing him away from any sense of adequacy or permanence.

As Nathan began what he had to do, Gould matched him, paced him, the ideal accompaniment. Nathan allowed himself a smile at the familiar, faintly recorded murmurings, the ticks of motion while Gould played, the odd hints of exhalation from a dead man who'd added himself to his interpretation, a marked irregularity under its pulse.

All right.

Nathan took the sash cord, tied the live end into a loop and lassoed it – just for now – around his wrist. A minor surge of horror sledged over him and was gone.

The right wrist, because I'm right-handed – so that must be the one that's done most wrong. Although, now that I think, my sins have mostly been ambidextrous.

22

Oh, Jesus Christ.

Nathan had that cliff-top feeling – the exhilaration of space and beauty and the lovely urge to jump. He found he couldn't swallow any more.

And then he set to in earnest because these things become unwieldy when they take too long.

He caught the rope, opened the bowline and snuggled the noose in over his ears and down.

It's like a tight rollneck, a collar, it's nothing at all.

Nathan checked on the final placement of the chair, then sat. Sweat had already soaked through his overalls. There was still a flinch or two of slack in the rope.

Fuck.

His systems were protesting, every damper and safeguard off. His balls tightened: his prick growing not so much hard as live and almost frantically aware. When he braced his legs apart and set his heels sharp under the chair, he felt on the lip of violation. Opened for anything.

When this is done, I'm in their hands. In anyone's hands. I'm meat.

His own hands were soapy with fear; with that big, blank, hot-mouthing, hair-lifting, sexy, sexy fear that he only ever met at times like this. It was already tugging at him, working him up to one single, hard slither – terror as his bit of rough.

Gingerly, delicately, Nathan leaned forward and fumbled at his legs, pushed the sash-cord loop around one naked ankle and then hobbled his feet, as if he might actually try to escape his own intentions. The work wasn't especially hard, but left him panting.

Then, shoulders back and clicking at the strain, he began to fix his arms behind his spine. His body was defeated now, stretched and aching, defenceless while Gould's piano licked round the walls, tipping rhythm out of rhythm, pressing compact breaks of emptiness between sounds.

He finished the last knot at his wrist. Stage one over. Done his best.

He was still then, the noose a light reminder at his neck. He stared at the meaningless white of the wall, the dumb corner of the window, his insane reflection across the rushing night.

My stupid self in my stupid overalls – last things I'll see.

He suddenly wished he was better dressed.

Then he shut up his eyes and let himself fall in the fist of his private chemistries, his intimate construction. Endorphins and adrenalin raced his brain to a smear and all of him rang at every twitch of his little heart, the obedient yawning and clamping of valves, the biddable sway of his ribs. Jesus, he loved the way he was.

I love you.

Thank you.

Now just shut up and go.

Much faster and much slower than he'd expected, he's hauled up and to the right as he topples the chair. Deafening crest of fear, breaking over his shoulders. He would like to gasp, but is bottled somehow.

Lassitude in his hands, very sweet, but he makes them worry, scrabble, twist. Various ripping pains – most especially at one knee. Something on the edge of sound, a kick of sound. Lunging constriction in the cheekbones, over the eyes. Life struggling in the throat.

The fear of never thinking again.

A red blackness – seductive – something drawing him up from the headache and the sweat. Reality shrugs and then licks him whole, salting something dark and raw, in close beneath his skin. He begins to feel softly tempted to waste his time.

He drives to stand, to kick aside the chair. Does it, staggers, flails out for the rope and clings to it an inch above the noose.

He can't fall again. If he does, he's done with.

Fingers pleading under the jute, gouging skin.

He is being washed. Everything but the closing of death and his own tiny nature has gone.

Eye to eye with nothing, he finds that he is dumbfounded by all that he is. The usually sealed essentials of his nature break out and start screaming, surprising him with how much he has a liking for all of that breathing and feeling and moving and fucking remembering he used to do. He wants it, would give the world for it, but wants the world, as well. Boiled down to basics he has a hunger for more of himself, for more of everything.

Noose off. Now it will be fine for him to fall.

Yes.

Yes.

Yes.
Yes.
Yes.

He whooped in air, bucking on the floor, every effort tearing at him while he tried not to retch.

Take it easy. Easy. Haven't broken the neck, crushed the hyoid bone, collapsed the windpipe. I am able to think that I am thinking this and can therefore assume that I haven't a damaged brain. I will suffer petechial redness in my eyes, a purely cosmetic problem, a trouble to victims of strangulation who survive.

Who survive.

Delight coshed up his torso and nearly choked him, while dopamine yammered insanely out through the sap of his mind – the body's Great Again.

Easy.

Christ, it hurts. I am able to hurt. Jesus Christ, I fucking hurt. That's fucking lovely. Yes.

His pulse tumped fantastically in his ears and swirled nauseous pain in tighter and tighter round his skull. Then he was sick – a few mouthfuls of thin, bitter liquid that scorched his tender throat so badly he could only whimper and curl for a while on his side, feet still bound.

I'm still here, then. I'm still here.

The shivering had started, and the shock. His hair was sodden with perspiration, his overalls clammy, his skin like a dead man's – pale and chill – although he was very thoroughly and certainly and demonstrably not dead. Reconfirmed existence ricocheted in every bone. His sternum creaked, trying to contain it, while Nathan quietly imagined himself, incandescent with life.

Yes.

The best of all possible highs, the fix of fixes, joy at the cellular level and then up.

Yes.

And then the aftershock. He knew the form. Having been so close to extinction, it was natural for his anxiety to re-ignite and set his muscles pulsing uselessly, his breath rabbit-punching in his chest. He had escaped and was still escaping and would feel the rush of flight burning in him for the next whole day, maybe more. And he would be a hair's breadth different, permanently, because he had let himself be recast, restarted. He knew he should consider himself lucky.

Nathan coughed without thinking, a spasm of lacerating panic following. It was important to rest at the moment, but he must make an effort soon to get up and take care of himself. The thought of his own care for his own self pushed him into a tighter curl: a slippery, well-meant hug for the engineer of his salvation. This was always a pleasant stage in recovery.

At the moment, Nathan Staples loved and trusted Nathan Staples unquestioningly. His self-esteem didn't ever get too much better than this. He knew that, in the kitchen, he had left out a hopeful little range of treats and kindnesses. This moved him. He hadn't only planned his death, he'd been prepared for his survival and had anticipated some of its most immediate needs. He was cheered by the thought of the sweet herbal tea, set ready and warm in a Thermos; the witch hazel for his bruises; his only comfortable blanket, newly washed; disinfectant for abrasions; soluble painkillers for pains. He'd make someone a wonderful husband – if all it took was slightly obsessive domestic diligence.

The probable tasks left behind in the wake of his demise had not concerned him. They would have been none of his business.

Back again.

A tremor rattled his teeth and he squirmed down to work at the cord round his feet. He needed that blanket now. And the tea.

His head was clear enough to let the Bach fold in again. It had been playing all this while: prelude and fugue, prelude and fugue: but well beyond Nathan's reach. He let it nudge at him for a moment, was careful to be appropriately glad that he'd come back to hearing with something so beautiful.

Nathan understood that his worries would slowly follow the music in and eventually reclaim him. In hours, or days, or moments, the petty considerations that framed his life, his griefs and preoccupations and very personal cycles of hate would rain down predictably and stick. His physical exaltation would fade, the little difference in his make-up that his almostdeath had lent him would become unremarkable to him, something else to disappoint. Only the music would stay good, that he could guarantee.

I'm still here. Fuck.

On the blind wall at the corner of Charter Road, someone had whitewashed a few blurry lines.

A THUG, VANDAL NEEDS THE ROD OF CORRECTION
PROVERBS 23:13–14
A RIGHTEOUS CHILD IS A BLESSING
TO ITS PARENTS AND SOCIETY

Mary supposed the writer must have either forgotten the source for the final quotation, or just made it up – something about it didn't sound convincingly biblical. She also wondered if the painters of texts on walls weren't technically vandals themselves and if she really wanted her street semi-permanently scarred with the fruits of religious mania. Not that she'd be here much longer, but the Uncles would be staying and they wouldn't like it at all.

'Oh, I don't know.'

Bryn was filling their hot-water bottles carefully two-thirds full with slightly less than boiling water. The kitchen welcomed Mary with the oddly spicy tang of rubberised steam.

'I think a spiritual verse or two could add a bit of class to the place. Religious knowledge. I might approve. What about you, Mo?'

'I think it's that bloody maniac Danno again. You can't ever be sure what he'll do.' Uncle Morgan was waiting with a flannelette pillowcase.

'Like you, then.'

The Uncles smiled privately to each other and brushed hands as Morgan reached to swaddle up the bottle and temper its heat.

Mary loved this – the Uncles' preparations for their winter beds – it had always made part of the household's cold-weather routine. The very first night she came here, Bryn had trotted through with a bottle

27

for her while she searched in her case for something she felt she'd forgotten, for some persuasive memory of what had been her home.

Her journey to Capel Gofeg had taken hours, been filled with confusions of stance and platform numbers and incoming and outgoing times and the threat of her mother's temper, leaking out in yanks at Mary's arm, in sentences hissing with secret pressures, too close to release. It had been fully night before they arrived.

And then, on first acquaintance, Mary hadn't taken to the town. Gofeg's streets had been too steep for her and too narrow and had seemed to be impatiently curled beneath the blustery evening, ready to whip at her and snap her flat. She'd stared at herself: a small, wavery figure, being tugged across the peculiar, yellow-screened window of the hosiery shop.

Hosiery. She'd never seen the word before and took it for something Welsh, a foreign secret spelled out above the door with vaguely obsessive perfection in the shapes of warped and elongated socks. The shop itself had also seemed odd, slightly cunning, almost frightening. It had an unmistakable air of the unnatural, perhaps because its glass reflected her own and her mother's shapes in a way that made them squat and lurching, patently ill at ease. *Hosiery:* she couldn't take to it.

Once they were finally warm indoors, Mary's mother had paused in the Uncles' paper- and aftershave-scented house just long enough for sandwiches and coffee. Mary knew that she and her mother never took coffee at night as a rule, but also knew she shouldn't say. She could hear her mother's voice being secretly angry, parts of words coiling and shrinking and other parts running away, but the Uncles hadn't noticed, or hadn't minded, and were asking her yards of questions and filling and refilling cups, as if there was nothing remotely wrong at all.

'You can't wait until the morning and go then?' This was from Uncle Morgan, the Uncle with the red hair and large ears. He'd been looking at Mary, even though he'd been speaking to her mother and then slowly slipping his eyes to the biscuit plate. He'd known that Mary kept looking there, too, and his eyes had been happy about it and very blue. Mary was used to brown eyes, like her mother's and her own. The Uncles' eyes were thoroughly blue.

'Is there anything you need for the journey?'

Mary and Morgan had stared at the biscuits and then at each other, then Morgan had slowly, solemnly picked up the plate and offered them across. Beyond them, the questions pressed on.

'Would you like a Thermos?'

'You aren't tired?'

Mary hadn't been able to take one. Sweet things this late weren't allowed – except for on special occasions and Mary wasn't sure of how special this occasion might be. Sometimes the rules weren't important and could all be giggled away, but this wasn't one of those times, she was certain.

Then Morgan had given her a tiny, apparently understanding nod and had taken a large, round, chocolate digestive for himself, which he posted suddenly into his mouth, entire.

'You've somewhere to stay in Cardiff?'

While Bryn continued the interrogation alone, she had watched Morgan struggle to chew and then swallow. He looked like something from a nature programme – a snake swallowing an egg. And a small, cool idea had occurred to her then – a seductive, ashamed idea – she'd realised that when her mother left her all the rules might leave her, too. The Uncles' house was very obviously run by very different regulations.

Bryn lobbed in another question, 'Aren't you going to tell her goodbye?'

At this, Mary's mother, who hadn't told her anything, had picked her all up and held her, suddenly. It had felt impossible then that they would really part. Mary had tried and been unable to feel how it might be without her. When she breathed against her mother's green coat, she could taste the dirtiness of rainy buses, smoky trains and the smell of wet weather and nothing at all of the house she'd left that morning and wouldn't see again. Her mother didn't smell like her mother and Mary had wanted her to. She'd felt guilty about the biscuits and wanting one. She'd seemed somehow to be wrong for being left here, as if there'd been another rule she'd broken – a serious one that she hadn't known about.

Her mother had set her down, but then hugged her again, quite fiercely, almost made her hurt. Then she'd stroked Mary's hair slowly and pressed her forehead with a feathery kiss. Mary, who always understood touch rather better than words, had felt that her mother was angry but also enormously sad. She couldn't understand which feeling was for her.

And then her mother went away.

Mary had stood in the Uncles' doorway and waved, been surprised when her mother paused and turned fully to face her, waved back. She was crying.

By herself with the Uncles for her first night, Mary had scaled the stairs to her new room. She'd thought of her mother, alone and being rattled into Cardiff on another bus. Mary's mother had told her that she hadn't been to Cardiff in years and years. She might get lost. This was when Mary had started to cry.

Then a small noise had happened behind her – Uncle Bryn was by her bed, dropping her quilt back over a new hot-water bottle, bought expressly for her. Mary had heard its fat, liquid impact and turned a bit to sneak a look at the side view of his face. He seemed all right – big and dark, but not heavy and not frightening. He'd kept pattering his hands at her pillows, flicking the coverlet, but also, she knew, he'd been listening to her crying and measuring how she was. Without looking, he'd said, 'Are you feeling complicated?'

When she didn't say anything, because she didn't know what he meant, he'd breathed out through his lips, one small puff. She would learn to recognise this in him as a sign of distress.

He'd tried again. 'Upset?'

'Yes.'

'That's the bed getting warm, though. Come by here.'

Which, again, she hadn't understood at first.

'Come by here.' He'd sat on the bed and faced her, extending one arm for her to do something with. He'd puffed again and looked a touch worried, but fundamentally contented, comfortable.

So she'd walked up to him and slipped herself in beneath his arm. Neither of them thought of anything more to say, but they both moved in tiny and gradual ways until she had curled herself up at the big purr and beat and murmur of his chest.

'Are we making you unhappy?'

Mary shook her head against the warm size of his cradling hand.

'You tell us if we do and we'll stop.'

She nodded.

He didn't puff.

'Your mother means well.'

She didn't shake her head at this, but wanted to, and then found herself caught by a sob, an odd kick of angriness. Bryn stroked her neck until she had settled again.

'Most people, they do mean well. They do try.'

He sighed in a small way, but was, she was sure, not at all annoyed with her, not even impatient. And Mary decided that she might like the Uncles then, but this seemed – more than anything else – like leaving her mother and home and so she'd started to cry again while Bryn smoothed and drummed her back.

When she'd fully subsided, he'd squeezed her briefly and said to no one in particular, 'Mo and me, we always wanted a girl.'

Tonight in the fuggy kitchen Mary could look at her Uncles and be sure that she wanted them. She stepped close to Bryn, her arms opened.

'Careful . . . the water.' He danced away from her to set down the kettle, so she hugged Morgan instead.

He wriggled. 'Mary Lamb, you are a funnyosity.'

'No other word for her.'

'I have never known another child like her.'

'Nor another woman, either.'

Bryn tried to keep the smile in his voice when he spoke, but they all heard his sentence echo with her growing older, more separate, choosing to go.

'Morgan,' Bryn folded his arms sternly, 'take those bloody bottles upstairs before they get cold.'

'All right, Boss, all right.'

Morgan kissed Mary: precise dry lips at a forehead he now had to stand up on tiptoe to reach. 'Nos da, love.' He nodded to Bryn.

'I'll be up after you. *Trahit sua quemque voluptas.*' Bryn turned to Mary, eyes quick, attentive cobalt, awaiting her response. 'Well? *Trahit sua quemque voluptas.* Hm?'

'Each man is by his special pleasures led.'

'True enough.' Morgan, calling back down the stairs.

'Morgan, go to bed.' Bryn shook his head, hushing breath in between his teeth, enjoying a little vexation and then giving Mary's response its due praise. 'Yes. Correct. Well done. None of them'll know that.' He didn't like to talk about her leaving, but had peppered the last few months' conversations with references to *them* and *over there* and *your lot* – as if she had already built a whole new existence away from his home, an alien place filled with people that she hadn't allowed him to meet. He sometimes could make her feel as if leaving was in her genes, as if that much of her mother was in her nature. Mary knew he didn't mean it and she knew it wasn't true. She might go away from the Uncles, but she wouldn't forget all about them, she wouldn't fail to love them and let them know. She wasn't her mother, she was herself.

Mary sneaked in a shuffle or two until she could nudge against him, attempting to reassure. 'I hope they'll know *some* things. I mean, I would think they'll know *most* things, between them.' But that made them sound far too much like a positive thing, when they were really more neutral, a necessity. 'I'm going there to learn. If they don't know *anything*, I'll just have to come back . . .'

Bryn let his eyes droop shut a little, the way he always did when he knew what she was up to. 'You won't have to come back. The island will be what you need. We'll see the New Year in and then parcel you off and all of us'll have a fresh start for a fresh year. Neat.' Bryn faced her with a watery grin and they slipped into a long embrace, while he rubbed in the usual way at her back and then paused, considering. He stood away from her, hands tracing her face at his arms' length.

'Do you want your hair cut?'

'Ahm, I hadn't thought about it.'

'Maybe you should, you know.' He brushed gently at the ends of her hair.

'You leave my split ends alone.'

'Maybe if you even made it just above shoulder length . . . Maybe something easier to wash and look after . . . What will the facilities be like?'

'Oh, you and facilities – you're as bad as Mo.'

'I am nothing like it. Morgan is the only one in this family who is mad for plumbing and, in that and many other respects, he is quite beyond saving.'

'But we love him.'

'Of course we love him. We love him precisely *for* his manifold

32

peculiarities. We love him for his Ventolin and his Beconase and his inability to take them when he should and for all his different kinds of cough and his slowness on stairs . . .' Bryn was not being as jolly as he'd hoped.

'He's not getting worse.'

'He's not getting better, either. Filling him full of steroids and then leaving him like that . . . He hasn't been right since. I told him – Doctor Morton – I went and spoke to him.'

'I remember.'

'He doesn't listen much though, does he?'

'Mo's not getting any worse.'

'No. No, you're right. He'll outlast me, I'm sure.' He walked to lean in the crook of the worktops, by the stove. 'And we'd have to love him just the same – even if we knew he'd die tomorrow.'

'Don't say that.'

'But I'm bound to, aren't I?' He huffed out a little sigh. 'I'm bound to think it. But I don't *brood*, that's the thing. I think of it and then I move on, try to appreciate him. If he's saying he can't eat pork and that it's never, ever agreed with him when I've been serving him pork for decades without a single breath of complaint and if he cuts up badly about how I'm contradicting him and then refuses to eat a bite except for boiled tomatoes until the weekend – I can still appreciate him, because he is still wonderful and because I *should*. That's how it works, loving people.'

'And you know he hates boiled tomatoes.'

'That too. Daft article. But I wouldn't want him sensible.'

Mary watched him stretching and working his shoulders, deciding to change the subject. He began quietly. 'Talking of the men we love . . .' He crossed his feet at the ankles, easily, elegantly, folded his arms, his sleeves rolled back on his arms to exactly the right degree. He'd always had the best of his generation's grace – the knack of strolling, of handling humdrum objects with unhurried fluidity. There were times, Mary thought, when his age seemed a relaxing fiction, something to ease the pressures on a sporting young man with a left-handed grin and a warm, unpredictable look.

He began again, almost smiling. 'Yes, the men we love . . . That poor, bloody Davies boy. I can't pass him in the street without losing my appetite. He's so miserable. I'm not saying it's your fault, girl, but

33

if your Jonathan was a horse, I'd have shot him by now. Are you going to *do* anything? About him?'

'I'm not sure.'

Now he did smile, but only quietly. 'Yes, you are. We could see it in your face when you came in. Morgan said – *she's decided* – and you know Morgan, never wrong in matters of the heart.' He waited kindly, but with the clean, direct expression of a man who was thoroughly educated in her particular turns and twists. Mary never lied to Bryn with any kind of confidence or success and they both knew it.

She folded her arms and looked away to the freezer, then examined the cupboards and next the fridge and then found herself facing the leisurely line of Bryn's legs, his body waiting, his eyes expecting nothing other than a perfectly honest reply.

'All right. Yes, I have decided.'

'Well, that's a relief, then. See you in the morning, love.' He swung forward to kiss her.

'You don't want to know *what* I've decided?'

He settled a light peck in her hair. 'Oh, we know *what*. We were just waiting for *when*. 'Night.'

'What do you mean – *we know*?'

'I mean precisely what I intend.' He ambled out, pleased that he'd said all he wished to without fuss or embarrassment. Or almost all he wished. He didn't turn in the doorway, only paused. 'You'll be sure and take care, won't you? With him. And with you. Care's the thing. For everyone concerned.'

'I didn't know everyone *was* concerned.'

Bryn creaked towards the upstairs landing. Mary had hoped – as pointless as she knew this hope would be – that her plans for Jonathan might stay slightly private. Now they quite obviously weren't she found that she felt more comforted than irate.

And under the comfort came an easy prickle of something else.

She moved to the stove and lit one of the gas rings, then switched out the light and watched the rose-blue leaves of flame breathe up a shimmer of dark heat. Mary'd learned how to make this happen, almost as soon as she'd managed her first strike at a match. She supposed that if the Uncles had kept a proper, open hearth, she could have settled down, last thing, for a quiet half-hour and been able to stare into that. But the fire in the sitting room only offered combustion that played like a mauvish liquid over plain ceramic slabs.

So she stayed where she was and watched the gas flowering up into nothing and let her mind fill with its tranquil hiss. Mary thought briefly of the Uncles, tumbling each other's locks in their deep, broad bed, and then lifted the concentration that had kept her Jonathan Davies weighed down in unspoken and unspeaking thought. Now she could revive the dogged argument of his hands, the hot tug of his breath, all of the marvellous chaos he could light. Her memory tickled her with him and sucked and whooped and sank, precipitate and slick.

She wondered if she really would – if she really would with Jonno – and was, nicely, almost scared.

And standing, face awash with cool light, she was also lovely. Nineteen, her skin not far off from a child's: the uncomplicated pink of light and blood and young, transparent surfaces. A young man called Philip Bracer had once said she had *kissable lips* and this had made her laugh, but was pretty much right. They were, quite clearly, lips it would be good to kiss. Her hair was thick and did need cutting, really, but in this light it was a soft, dim shadow, threaded with small glimmers of something fine.

Watching her, silent in the kitchen, almost anyone might have guessed that, very early on, Mary had taken her father's breathing and tied it up tight with her own. She couldn't remember him, a man who'd died years ago, but nevertheless it was true that when he'd first encountered her slightly milk and slightly apple and slightly animal scent, she had altered him for good. She didn't know it, but she'd given him a permanent change of heart.

None of which even remotely concerned her when she finally turned off the stove, waited for the pop and flutter that brought things to a stop and eased up to bed, slightly later than was sensible. The house ticked, cooling. Behind the Uncles' door, Morgan's voice was being pleased at something not for her.

Mary prepared herself quickly and shivered into bed. She was all set to pay attention and thoroughly enjoy a night of restless possibilities. A man in her mind to keep her wakeful: she wasn't completely used to that. She couldn't yet predict her dip and duck through quick dreams of great ferocity and surprise.

And she couldn't know that under the same darkness, the same night, she and Nathan Staples matched each other turn for turn under their blankets, heat for heat. Their two bloods ricocheted through hearts that seemed to clatter and then flinch under skins that were nothing more than a moist babble, aching at every sound. In the end, for their separate reasons, they both watched the dawn.

Which blurred in shakily, dry-mouthed or tender-eyed, depending, and bringing very little for Nathan, but a letter for Mary Lamb – a letter from Foal Island and from a man Nathan Staples knew well.

The letter's contents seemed peremptory, rigid, almost cruel. Mary read them out across the breakfast table while the Uncles listened, Morgan's breath whining softly in his inelastic lungs, and she learned than her schedule had been drastically, arbitrarily changed. If she still wished to accept the Fellowship's offer of a Llangattock Bursary, if she still really wanted the distant but luminous promises their offer appeared to imply, then she would have to come out to Foal Island by November the third. She had only days, not months, before she would have to leave behind the better part of all that she'd known as her life. This was not fair.

'It doesn't say why?'

Mary patted Bryn's wrist – he would want to be angry for her now and there was no point. She couldn't not go: Foal Island had been all that she'd aimed at for more than two years. There was no question, whatever the Fellowship did, that she needed them.

Morgan's voice sounded tight. 'Is it the same man who's written? I mean, he's seemed so decent up to now. Does he know what he's asking?'

Now it was Bryn's turn to pat at Morgan.

'All that work she did, sending off bloody envelopes of stories for months . . . Passing all their bloody tests . . .' Bryn stabbed at his toast and Morgan jerked in an anxious breath, a spasm starting to pull in his diaphragm. He nodded, beginning to sweat. Bryn pursued his point, dirtying the butter with crumbs. 'If they want her that much, if they picked her out of so bloody many, then they should show her some respect.'

'It's all right.' She tried to sound as if she actually believed this.

'It's not all right.'

'I know, but still . . . The Chairman – Christopher – he says they

36

can't hold things open as long as they thought they could . . . then he . . . bad weather's coming, in a couple of weeks they'll probably have trouble with the boat and I won't be able . . . Oh, I don't know – it doesn't make any sense.' She lifted her head from the paper and met the Uncles' eyes. They hurt.

Mary started to speak again, inching her words forward, picking them to carry tenderness and weight. She'd never yet worked so hard to build a proper fabric of sense, to set out love. 'I wanted to be here for all the time I could. And if I could learn what they're going to teach me and stay here, I wouldn't ever go away. You know that.'

The Uncles winced, hearing so much of what they needed, feeling so much sad happiness.

'I do want to come down by here every morning and eat breakfast the way you cook it and be with my Uncles, all comfortable, see?' They'd taught her to speak Welshly – she didn't always, but she could. She did it now to please them, to show them where she really came from, to show them she wouldn't forget. 'They'll give me seven years, they'll feed me, house me, keep me and when it's over I'll know, I'll know if I can do it . . . If I'm any good or not.'

She couldn't quite be clear in presenting her hopes for the island. Possible skills and insights she might be given there would dodge in like shadows, real but inarticulate, and she couldn't make them plain to other people. She also had a small, superstitious dread of saying what she actually, irrevocably wished. And all of that wasn't the point now, in any case – the Uncles needed to hear her tell them, 'I love you. I'm sorry for when we've argued and I'm sorry for doing this.' The Uncles swallowed, breathed. 'I love you.' She drove on. 'I'm your girl. You're my parents. You are. And I'm the best-brought-up person I know.'

Morgan shuddered twice against a cough and then couldn't hold it. He started to drag in breaths, fish-mouthing. Looking at Mary, eyes softened with dismay, Bryn took Morgan's hand. 'You can't know many well-brought-up people . . .' His voice had a fracture in the higher tones – it tended to splinter against emotion. She always wanted to kiss him when it did. 'Still. You've turned out well. Just about. That's the way you came, though, isn't it?' Bryn kept looking, appraising, saving up this picture of her, an uncovered need about him. 'We'll be fine, all of us.' Mary could only sit and bear his attention – suddenly feeling uncomfortably adult and alone.

Morgan, ebbing back to himself, ears and face incandescent with harried blood, broke their concentration. 'We love you, too, and we're sure you have to go. We've talked all about it.' He looked up at her.

Mary laid her hands on the table's edge, feeling the draw of the island, a cold, half-familiar tide.

'So . . .'
   'Yes. It's, I suppose . . .'

They were trying to take comfort in each other, Mary Lamb and Jonathan Davies, rushed into all of this. Not that they didn't both want it now – it was only that they wished they hadn't rushed.

If the furniture wasn't here, making me think this is happening in the wrong place.

Mary was looking at her bed and finding it small.

*We couldn't have gone to Jonno's, though, not with Mrs Davies there. Not even with Mrs Davies **not** there. Mrs Davies is frightening.*

God, Jonno, how do we do this?

There'd been plenty of room in her bed for *her* body, but she couldn't quite see it holding the two of them. Although they would be close. They'd be in *that* position; *those* positions; the ones she could almost completely imagine when Jonathan wasn't here, when they weren't actually together, when everything still seemed possible. Now it was simply obvious that he wasn't going to fit.

If I just jump for him, then we'll be started. But I can't. I suppose he can't either. He hasn't, anyway. But then he might not want to. Oh, Christ.

They had kissed, but were now just standing, dismally. Jonno reached and flopped at her jumper, lifted it quick, up and down again, to peek at her in a way that would have been funny, if she hadn't wanted him to see her properly and gradually, but also just turn off the lights and not see anything for a bit.

Until we've got used to . . . things.

Mary was starting to feel slow, almost sleepy, her thoughts and movements clogging with a syrupy unease.

*Jonno – if he gets self-conscious, if he squints, as he does – looking for problems, as if they're **there** and seeable – then he'll break something, he'll walk into something, hell . . .*

He won't hurt me. I know he won't do that. I do know.

Mary tried not to look at him as if she might be checking for a squint.

Then she sat on the bed. It sank beneath her, giving as obediently as ever. The Uncles had sat right here, at other times, had *been* here, indelibly.

It's them watching – I can't do this when everything feels like them watching; the books and the back of the chair and the pictures – they're all looking at me.

Jonathan, from his face, seemed to be on the brink of sneezing, or crying. Mary lay down and said to the observing ceiling, 'If we'd already done this, it would be all right. This wouldn't be any bother if we were doing it *again*. I think.'

Jonno jumped a little at the sound of her. 'You do *want* to? This is . . .' his hand tore idly at his collar, 'something you want.'

'Yes.'

Now he sat on the bed, pressing against her waist with his back. 'Really?'

Her attention screamed to the place where they touched, to the moment after this moment when they would touch more. The sound of his breathing staggered her blood.

'Really? Mary?'

She kept her eyes closed, concentrating on all of the times they'd been nearly at this point and not uncomfortable. 'Really. Yes.'

The reality of his presence, of his complete availability, jack-knifed suddenly in her, beginning to loosen her reservations. She listened while he eased off his shoes.

Knock, knock.

She felt the dip and nudge and then the full arrival of his whole warmth there, stretching beside her, the first stiffness of his arms and then their familiar clasp around her, the first, joint give of their breath.

Knock, knock. Who's there?

And then her speed was back, clock springing under his hands, breaking into an open glaze.

Who's there?

Jonathan Davies.

That's right.

They wallowed in a guddle of clothes, gently rucking about to uncover themselves, their hard facts. For a while, she couldn't believe she'd ever be unpeeled, free and taut inside nothing but avid skin. She couldn't believe the tremor of his arms against her shoulders as he lifted the entire, pale gift of himself to halt above her, one stroke of heat already near enough to touch.

That's right.

Fluid appetite, jerked sound and give and purchase and anxious weight: their first words in each other opened out. There was a snag of hip bones, a failure of their beat, a sweet, raw collapse and then a flurry towards something better, their hands attentive and only a little desperate.

And no pain. Only an instant's surprise, extinguished by monstrous want.

That's right.

And nothing to distract her from biting him until she tasted metal and then straightening her spine for their next fit.

That's right.

They slowed to blink at each other's faces, somehow dazzled. He levered up from her again and he watched her watching the moving gleam of him: the round push and the draw of him and the pout and the cling and the shine of herself, just painting him with herself. They smiled, open-mouthed, making what they wanted and making more want.

She craned up to lick his chest and knew she was deeper than she'd thought. Each fall and oiling, tugging rise proved how well she held him, complete. She could feel herself becoming a pure astonishment.

That's right.

*T*his is the principal problem with living: it's much more demanding than being dead.

Having found himself, once again, entirely unable to exit his own existence, Nathan had work to do. Failure to pull his own head off, or snap his spine, had left him in no state to sleep, so he'd sat up all through a screaming night and played music: filled himself with every available flavour and type, and then dozed through a rattling dawn. Now he was tired, but still glistening with unwilling life and washed and dressed and obliged to go and visit the Lighthouse and speak to Joe Christopher.

That was the deal. Anyone on Foal Island was free to put him- or herself in the way of dying at any time. Their aim should not be suicidal, but should make genuine efforts towards exposure to absolute risk. Joe was always keen that people should try their best. And, having survived, he was also keen that people tell him all about it.

And the really remarkable part, the part that kept Nathan consistently amazed, was that everyone here had, for their own little reasons, unreservedly agreed to this rather more than slightly unusual regime.

We're all fucking cracked.

*I know that **I'm** cracked.*

Joe's personal theory was that Technicolor, widescreen contact with the Beyond would infallibly compose itself into clear, metaphysical sense.

*And seven tries for eternity are supposed to work the fucking charm. If I hear the fucking quote one more time, I will throw up, God fucking help me. 'He shall save thee in six troubles. Yea, in seven there shall no evil touch thee.' Quoting the bloody Book of Job to **me**. Joe's the only bastard who'd even try.*

And anyone after a cure for anything –

*Not that everyone on the fucking island doesn't want a cure for something: loneliness, emptiness, bitterness, illness – any **ness** you care to name.*

Anyone after a cure for anything was intended to find their states of mind and body had been altered by extreme experience. And, if not, it didn't matter – the odd insight or enlightenment was pretty much guaranteed. And it kept them all safely out of other trouble and off the streets.

Joe, of course, really believed in the island cure – he wanted to be a saint.

Nathan, of course, really didn't believe it – he just wanted to be a corpse.

An absolute cure for Nathan – take him all away.

Although, obviously, he lacked the necessary courage to be a single-handed and successful topper of himself. So he'd ended up here, only playing at death, on a rain-asphyxiated Welsh island, living in a demobbed army barracks in a religious retreat and writer's colony. Nathan detested rain, Wales, islands, the army, religion and writers, above all writers. He had a passing fondness for retreat.

Living, Nathan had noticed, was also much more ridiculous than even the most rudimentary Eternal Rest.

'Come on, well.' Nathan tried to be stern but encouraging with his dog – a good dog, a sweet dog, a black, almost Labrador with a gentle, gundog mouth. 'I don't want to, either, but what I want's got nothing to do with it. Eckless, come on.'

Nathan was still feeling the after-effects of his little sash-cord adventure. His throat flinched when he spoke, his head ached appallingly and the whites of his eyes were Bloody Mary red. What a sodding mess.

He patiently wrestled Eckless into his choke-chain and then jumbled at the dog's ears in compensation. Another gallon or two of rain landed flat against the western window.

Eckless was Nathan's health. After his operation he'd bought the dog, because a man who's had one lung removed has to work and run and pant and ache himself into new sufficiencies of breath. The heart op boys take it easy, but the lung boys sweat. So far, he'd spent ten months fighting to swell the capacity of his left lung – the smaller of the two, but all he'd got and certainly better than none. Eckless had helped take the tedium out of dumbly pounding along the Embankment and back, wheezing in bitter handfuls of London air.

Now they were both adjusting to the sweep of an ocean climate, the rasping cleanliness of salt in their breathing, the virtually constant angling of their bodies into barging winds. Nathan knew the summer weather could be splendid here, he'd landed in a quite presentable June, but every waterlogged footfall and slaty morning was making him more certain that whole season had been a fluke.

He and Eckless cut north until they could walk in the lee of the wood – such as it was. Eckless was being precisely and wholeheartedly dogged. From his limpid eyes to his stoic tail and all along the rain-clotted hairs of his back, he made it clear he thought this a thoroughly foolish excursion, but made it equally plain that he would go with his master anywhere, to his last breath: that he loved him obediently, fawningly, utterly and far beyond deserving.

Nathan was setting a cruel pace, hoping to burn off some of the energy his freshly redelivered life seemed quite determined to provoke. He started up a little, splashing trot, jaw tightening with a tiny burn of rage.

He knew what Joe would ask him and he knew what he would say.

'What did you find out, Nathan? What did you bring back?'

'Well, Joe, I might respectfully remind you, this wasn't a fucking day trip to Rothesay – I nearly died.'

'But what did you find?'

Joe always wanted to know that, to rummage around in something which was, anyone would admit, a rather intimate experience. Suicide and self-abuse – both extremely private occupations.

'Not suicide, Nathan. An exercise in humility.'

Yes, indeed: Joe could sometimes be a smug, unnecessary cunt. Every time he'd say the same – as if everyone needed to be humbled, as if some people hadn't actually been humiliated enough.

Nathan kicked out, gasps of air beginning to rip in his tender throat. A thick, crimson feeling began to rise about his head. He forgot his dog and rehearsed the speech he'd like to make at Joe.

What did I find. What did I bring back to tell you? Nothing. Fuck all. Because I do this for me and only me, because who the fuck else is there? And every time I get the same message – the one I got the last time and the time before that. You know and I know, when you're steamed right back to your bone, when there's fuck all else for you to find, then a big, fucking, comfy, intrusive narrative voice will say:

LOVE, NATHAN – THAT'S THE IMPORTANT THING. WHAT YOU DID AND WHAT YOU WILL DO, WHAT YOU HAVE DONE – ALL THAT MATTERS ABOUT IT IS LOVING. DO YOU DO THE LOVING THING? BECAUSE THERE IS NOTHING ELSE. YOU KNOW THERE REALLY IS NOTHING ELSE, DON'T YOU? BUT DO YOU HAVE THE BALLS FOR THAT, NATHAN, OR WILL YOU BOTTLE OUT?

And of course I do. It's not a fucking revelation. Do you seriously think I didn't know that?

*And I **do** have the bottle, I have the bottle every day. I could love for my country, if my country asked me to. I love every day – because, like it says in the Bible, **Love never ends**. Too right, it never fucking ends – and the process resembles nothing more closely than throwing half-bricks down an empty well, or throwing my fucking liver, my balls, my other lung . . . fuck.*

*If I nearly died and then Some Great Big Bloody Something decided to speak up and tell me how to **stop**, how to **finish** loving. Or told me how to get some fucking loving **back**. Then I would say, then I would say . . . I would.*

He let the anger lift him, close his eyes and beat him forward across the uneven ground.

I would say that was a fucking genuine, fucking miracle.

His chest laboured and sucked unevenly, his saliva burned and thickened when he swallowed and his thoughts fell, became dark heats and colours. He outran them, outran himself.

And then he stumbled, twisted down on to spongy grass and roots which were uncannily like veins, he felt his voice snuffed out of his mind and then felt nothing at all.

Before Eckless clattered over him in a shower of momentum and whimpered concern, Nathan fought to sit up and catch at a blurry scrabble of paws. Eckless licked and panted for his face, while Nathan slapped at him feebly, 'You stupid –' and then held him firm. The dog gave a small yelp of discomfort that briefly knotted Nathan's pulse and set him patting at the animal, rocking it vaguely. Then he lay back flat again, with his mouth opened to the downpour, ribs still banging after his sprint and his hands comforted by live, bewildered fur.

Nathan wasn't going to the Lighthouse. He'd decided. Bugger it.

'Joe won't be pleased.' Lynda was in her dressing gown, as usual. She owned, maybe, four of them, all body-hugging, all furnished with strategic gaps and rents, and all silky – if not actually silk. Nathan had never thought it prudent to enquire after the various secrets of their manufacture.

'I don't care. I don't want to see him. There's no point.'

She smiled with a slight forward motion, just enough to reveal her cleavage by another breath or two. 'I'm glad you came here instead.' You couldn't take it personally, she no longer even planned most of her nonsense. 'Can I get you anything?' This said as she sat and crossed her legs with an inevitable shush of naked flesh, that slight bounce of her tits – still good for her age, one couldn't deny it. 'Richard's still asleep.'

'I'm not surprised.' Nathan tried to tinge his look with some sense of masculine sympathy for Richard – a man sucked and fucked and harpied into unconsciousness so often that he now seemed flimsy and barely opaque in certain lights.

'God, what have you done to your eyes, though?'

He'd been hoping, vainly, that she might not notice how red they were. But she slipped up towards him like a floral-patterned seal, heart set on an exhaustive investigation. She was fast on her feet, Lynda – unnervingly.

'Oh, I see.' She slid a knowing finger between his collar and his neck, saw the bruising.

'Well, of course you see, I'm letting you see. And I certainly can't be the first man you've met who's tried to hang himself, so don't make such a fuss.' He fended her off to a workable distance.

'Can I at least mention, Nathan, that you're soaking wet?'

'Now that you mention it, yes, I am dripping where I stand. I'll take it as read that you're only as moist as usual.'

She chose to ignore him and sat again with the tiniest trace of a sulk. 'I presume you came to use our phone. Again.'

'Yes. Will Eckless be all right there?' The poor beast was slumped in a muddy hump on the floor. Not that Lynda would mind the mess – she'd just get Richard to mop up later. 'I couldn't have left him outside in this weather.'

'Well, we wouldn't want that. I could give him a quick rub with a towel.'

'Try it, if you like, he'll be too tired to stop you. But remember he's still a virgin, please.'

'What makes you such a cunt, Nathan?' With a cool, untroubled smile.

'You'd know far more about that than I. Is the phone still through here?'

'That's right. Make yourself comfortable, do.'

Lynda and Richard's cottage was a tubby, slump-roofed building, set near the old rabbit warren and, at one time – everyone liked to assume – must have housed persons concerned with the cultivation and gathering of cony meat. It did not escape Nathan that the wholesale raising and taking in of meat was one of Lynda's principal occupations. Perhaps because of this, the building always put him in mind of some kind of trap. It was stiflingly cosy, choking with fat chairs and ruffled cushions, flouncing curtains and pelmets and tassels and lace and lace and lace. The place invariably made him feel he was close to choking.

Worse than the rope.

But this was where the radio telephone lived and, although he wouldn't talk to Joe, he *was* going to speak to someone, to get at least his voice free and off the island, away.

It was too early in the day to try the work number, so he chanced calling J. D. at home. The receiver was fumbled up in the customary, haphazard way. A cough. A sniffed inhalation. A noticeably para-noid, 'Yes?'

'Where were you?' Nathan, as a rule, felt it right to encourage irrational fears in J. D. Grace with ill-defined, but possibly menacing questions.

'Hm?' It was definitely Grace, the voice sounding newly woken, unhappily dry. 'Nathan?'

'Yes.'

A snuffle of relief crackled in all the way from London, in concentric laps of sound.

'Where were you last week, Jack? Nobody seemed to know.'

'I had to go to hospital, actually.' One violent cough cleaned the voice, brushed it up into dapper BBC. 'Rush job. No time for messages.'

'What?'

'Testicular cancer. Unfortunate, hn? Careless, even.'

'*What?*' Nathan wavered at the brim of compassion.

'And I wanted to know – I wouldn't normally like to ask . . . Once I'm dead, Nate . . . you'd come and see me, wouldn't you? Just a quick visit? Flowers? No? Oh, well, it doesn't matter. I'm fine now anyway.'

'Jack –'

'But I have both my balls in a jar.'

'We were talking about your health, Jack, not your hobbies.'

'Callous bastard,' J. D. enunciated impeccably.

'Where were you? Truthfully.'

'Ah . . . truthfully . . . That would be tricky, actually.'

'Not again, Jack.'

'No, not really *again*. It's just all only a tiny bit unclear. But not *too* bad. I know for sure that I surfaced in Greek Street on Wednesday, but apart from that . . .'

'You haven't a clue.'

'Your guess is as good as mine. In fact, probably batter – or even better. I'm breaking these teeth in for my dog – they don't make a word of sense.'

'You don't have a dog.'

'See what I mean? Oh, yes, and I was – it's gratuitously alleged – in the Poetry Society at some point.'

'My God. Poetry *and* Earls Court.'

'I know, these are the depths of humiliation to which the drinking chap must drop. Then again, some malicious bastard could have slipped me a dodgy clue. They do that, you know. They tell me lies, they spread rumours, they fill my pockets with books of matches from places I could never have visited. They set out quite deliberately to confuse me. This business is full of evil fucks.'

'Try checking your credit card records.'

'Ah, well.' He assumed a tone of solemn dignity. 'That would currently be slightly difficult.'

'You've never considered that your drinking might be quite irrelevant – that you just have pre-senile dementia.'

'Not at all – I simply believe in energy conservation. If two people witness the same event, then why on earth insist that *both* remember it . . . Did you want something, by the way? Or were you calling as an arbitrary expression of your friendship.'

'You know me better than that, Jack. For one thing, I'm not your friend.'

'Well, thank God for that. I feel heartier already – even if there isn't a full bottle in the bloody house.'

'It all depends on how you look at them – positive thinking – half empty, half full and so on . . .'

'No. No, no, no. A completely empty bottle is a completely empty life – I mean, bottle. And that's that, I'm afraid. Maintaining anything else would be severely delusional. Which, of course, I am not. You do want something, though, don't you? I can tell.'

'A couple of things.'

'Fire away, then. And I *will* remember them. I even had a solid breakfast this morning. I am in my very finest operational state.' An audible, liquid swallow pressed between them. 'Tea. In case you wondered. Earl Grey. With Jif lemon. Bergamot, fake citric acid and lovely limy London water. Mmmm . . . the taste of home.'

'I don't want to tour any more.' A faintly rushing silence answered him. 'Jack? I'm not going to do it again.'

'Well, that's your choice, obviously. Might I ask why? Not to dissuade you, simply to enquire.'

'I don't mean to cause you problems, but I can't do it any more. No more promotional tours. I've exhausted my life's supply of diplomacy. No more pastel hotel suites with nursing-home prints, no more fucked-up flight schedules and snow-bound trains, no more ignorant, ignorant, piss-artist fucks that I have to smile at and not eviscerate. No more people who really believe I want to know even the tiniest *thing* about them, that I'm *listening*, that I'm not kneading the bar stool beside me into papier fucking mâché to stop myself flocking the walls with their blood and hair. No more. It is not worth it.'

'Well, I can hear that you're not happy. The last time was . . .'

'It made me ill. The last time made me ill.'

'No.' Grace seemed to hear himself being too vehement, gave a dry little sigh, surprised at himself, and softly began again. 'You *were* ill, I realise that . . . but it wasn't because of . . . that would have been there before and then you had the X-rays and . . .' He struggled between sympathy for Nathan's lost lung and professional self-

49

defence. 'Look, we did make you work too hard, it was too much, it was unnecessary. We agreed that. I made a mistake, I thought we should show the flag a bit, get you out and about . . . it was nervousness on my part . . . I'm . . .'

'Mm hm?'

Grace's cup jittered against the receiver. 'What?'

'Say it, Jack. Go on – *I'm sss* . . .'

A brief exhalation cuffed out – the closest Grace could get to a laugh this early in the morning – '*I'm cccertainly* not going to say that I'm sorry – you know perfectly well I never say that – one has to have rules. Otherwise I'd be apologising all the bloody time. It would be absurd. If not actually humiliating.' He waited to hear if Nathan wished to comment. 'But you do know that I am . . . sssorry.'

'Well, so am I. I'm endlessly sorry about all sorts of things. And I'm sure you'd try to make things better next time, but I won't see it – I won't be there. No more book tours.

'I do not intend ever again to be paraded through cunting book shops full of maddies who have dribbled in out of the rain for the booze and for the quiet seat where they can wank themselves off in the warm. And I won't do those wall-to-wall-Jaeger English Guildhalls: or the muddy, poncey, shabby, fucking festivals. Jesus, I look down from every platform and the air is shivering, *moaning* with middle-aged, married frustration: all those neat, insane well-washed ladies, shifting and sighing above the slightly moistened M&S bikini-style briefs they will never even *try* to show me, but – fuck – the *need* they'll show instead: the bloody awful lives they'll reek of, which I couldn't do a thing about, if I even *wanted* to.

'*My* life, *my* bloody life . . . Nobody gives a toss about *my* life.' Nathan halted, wiped his mouth. He'd made an agreement with himself that every time he lapsed into full-blown self-pity he would sign a cheque for one of three charities. He was already pretty much committed to another serious donation, it would be foolish and tedious to go on. 'You get the idea.'

'There's nothing at all to enjoy any more?'

'The good people are still good. But who wants to meet good people on the run, or standing up and screaming in a pub, or stupefied with weariness, or drunk. You wouldn't know about that last condition.'

'No, indeed – quite unlike the home life of your own dear editor. And speaking of matters editorial – you won't mind if I don't inform my Gauleiter of your decision, just yet. Not that I think you'll change your mind – one simply has to go carefully in these times. Harmless readers and copy-editors are being defenestrated, even as we speak. We live in interesting times . . . fascinating, in fact.'

'*Fascinating* sharing the same root as *fascism* . . .'

'How kind of you to remind me. Oh, shit!'

'What?'

'I've just seen the time. I have half an hour before I'm supposed to welcome number one wife and talk about number three son.'

'Ah, the Charlie Chan lifestyle of the literary Londoner – number one son, number four wife . . .'

'No. Number four wife goes with number two daughter. Bet you're no good at *Happy Families*.'

'You bet right. I am no good at them.' Nathan couldn't help it – that sounded as heavy as it felt. 'I just type about sex and murder. In the absence of either one. I concentrate on making acts of love seem realistic while other people concentrate on enjoying them – it's a lousy job, but some fucker's got to do it. I beg your pardon – some *non*-fucker's got to do it.'

Somewhere in Islington, in the kitchen of a house with dirty windows and a bald, abandoned lawn, J. D. Grace sucked his teeth. 'Sorry, Nate.' His mind changed gear audibly, neatened out his consonants. 'Honestly I am.'

'It's fine. I'm fine.'

'No, you're not – you're pissed off. Perils of the drinking vocation – you will always seem to piss off the people of whom you are quite fond. And I really haven't done too well this morning, have I? First, I give you the cheap crack about cancer when you're hardly –'

'And then I get the man-with-no-visible-family knee to the groin.'

'My unerring instinct for hitting the Achilles heel, if that isn't too mixed a metaphor.'

'Achilles *leg*. Except it's not too bad this morning – only hurts when I breathe. As we authors say.'

The connection waited while they thought of points to raise which would not be sentimental. J. D. first.

'Fine pair we make, hm?'

'We could fuck up for our respective countries.'

'And – to be perfectly honest for once – life at the office is genuinely not good. I could really rather do with being fuck-up free. For example, our illustrious Editor of Editors has just hired his current bit on the side in a mysterious capacity which is intended to be editorial. Although I have known many, almost mythically stupid, self-obsessed and venomous women – number three wife among them – this Medusa, this Ineptitude Event Horizon, this . . . she is beyond even my capacity for blasphemous insult. I pass her office and there she is, squatting inside, gleaming and pulsing like a huge, ripe pustule full of Tipp-Ex and lost manuscripts. If I simply *look* at her, I am seized with the siren desire to grab her by the snatch and then tug up smartly with both hands until I've turned her absolutely inside out. Then I'd staple her labia over the crown of her head and kick her along the corridor, ribs and entrails flapping as she goes.'

'Mmm. I'm sure I once saw a Fabergé egg that captured the lyrical essence of just such a scene.'

'The late, last Czarina's favourite, I believe.'

'And they wonder how she came to be late and last . . . She must have got such a kick out of Ekaterinberg.'

'You twisted bastard.' Grace tried for a mouthful of tea and choked for a moment or two, quietly and politely. Then back to the narrative. 'Of course, I don't have many dealings with Little Miss Hump-U-Like . . . Conversation is almost impossible – she talks so quickly, she sounds like a fax. Still, they're all crawling round her – Parkinson especially. It's always struck me as appropriate that he's named after a disease. My God, he really is a human suppository. Although, naturally, a suppository would have the good grace to dissolve once it was tucked away in an especially receptive executive colon.' Grace paused and Nathan heard a thoughtful snuffle. 'You're not laughing.'

'Yes I am. Inside.'

'Can I ask?'

'Whatever you like.'

'The second thing – you said there were a couple. Is it . . . are you still letting her come? Mary?'

'She wants to come.'

'You're letting her.'

'I'm not dealing with it: Joe is. But we did both change our minds a little. We decided it might be better if she came this year instead of next.'

'There's barely anything of this year left.'

'Two months – you can do a lot in two months. Anyway, it's not about the timing, really. We thought it would be good to test . . . well, not exactly to *test* her, but to try and find out how determined she was to come. If we suddenly changed all the plans and said she had to turn up early and –'

'Ruined her Christmas and generally played with her mind . . . dearie me. What's that really all about them, hm? You just couldn't wait any longer to see her, could you? Hm?'

'Joe thought it was a good idea.'

Nathan listened while Jack cleared his throat, renegotiated his terms, produced his best voice: the gentler, closer one, more scholarship boy than pure-bred public school, more concerned than disapproving. 'Are you going to be all right? With her there? With being a teacher? Have you thought what you'll have to teach?'

Nathan almost let himself think about possible answers to the above before his heart begin to shrivel and chill. There were some things it did him no good to consider.

'Nathan?'

'It'll be fine.' His tongue woolly, somehow, unconvincing and unconvinced. 'It'll be fine.' If he had managed to die, this would have been someone else's problem. 'It'll be fine.'

Mary's bed wasn't really big enough for a couple to get much sleep. Mary had found a kind of rest, once she and Jonathan had giggled and rocked to their conclusions, but her mind had stayed open behind her eyes. She'd wanted to enjoy their lying and being coated in each other, sticky and slick, the sheet she tugged back over them quickly translucent with sweat.

'Here you are, then, tea.'

The feel of being looked at – she'd known, for the first time, how very much she liked that. Drowsing now, she imagined she heard voices, but shook off the thought, the idea of being currently observed.

Nobody here, no bodies but us.

'Tea's the best thing, really. Isn't it?'

Any movement divided her from Jonathan uncomfortably, parted new adhesions, so they clung still and healed together, flesh to flesh, in one hot graft from their ankles to their scalps. Under the stone weight of Jonathan's arm, his thick breathing, her mind had shuddered with recollected skin, with the thought of the feel of fucking him.

Jomathan. Sleepy Jonathan. Sleeping Jonathan.

'Yes. Tea's best.'

Those voices . . .

Silly boy, sleeping and speaking. Daft. Lovelydaftlovelyshaftlovely.

'And cake.'

Recognisable voices.

'From Barr's – the good stuff.'

Goodlovelyshaft.

A little stirring of the house, a give in the mattress and Mary's heart bumped towards something more lively.

'Battenberg. Fresh.'

54

Her blood leaped, warily, but then eased back to let her picture the first dive of Jonathan's head, the stroke of his breath and his newly barbered hair, the pleasant re-aligning of her hips.

'Mary?'

Yes. That's me.

'I think she's still asleep, Butt. Will we leave it?'

'And he's asleep, too.'

Fuck.

She realised. She understood.

Fuck.

The Uncles were here.

They'd padded into her unbuttoned room. They were here with her now, speaking. Finally, their reality yanked her dumb awake.

'Ah, there now, Mary. What should we do?'

They stood, Morgan holding the tea tray, Bryn's hands holding themselves, and each man gently but plainly alarmed by the way they had chosen to proceed. Still, they were trying to do right by Mary, to let her feel at home and approved of, loved. She lurched up and opened her eyes to Bryn's face: his puzzled eyes fighting to not seem lost.

'What do you think? About where to put the tea? Oh, or Jonathan?'

Jonathan came to in a scrabble of panic, first trying to spring out of bed, then recoiling to cover himself with a small whinny of fear. Morgan set down the tea tray on the bedside table, obscuring – perhaps intentionally – the two sloughed condoms lying there.

Everyone paused, unsure of how they might continue, and fell to staring at the willow pattern saucers and cups, the lumpily knitted tea cosy, the slices of buttered gingerbread and Battenberg. Each of them swallowed. Each of them tasted bedroom air, thick with the low-tide spatter of protein and the sweet, shellfish surfaces of Mary's privacy.

Bryn nodded through a carefully presented smile. 'We thought you might want a drink. Or a little to eat. We find that we do.'

'Afterwards.' Morgan drew away from the bed and back towards the door.

Mary and Jonathan lay rigid, sheet drawn to their chins, eyes dumbfounded, like a pair of bad Staffordshire figures – *The Lovers Apprehended.*

'It's as if . . .' Bryn pondered, also moving for the doorway, 'you'd been on a bus trip for a long time, so you're peckish. Something like that.' He blinked at Jonathan, his voice wavering, perhaps at the verge of laughter, perhaps only made unsteady by the strain of the occasion. 'We do wish you well.'

'We do.'

Mary finally found herself saying, 'I didn't know –'

'We were here. No.'

'We weren't. We had gone out. But then we came back.'

'Because you might need us.'

'You know.'

'We were here in case.'

As if they were taking their leave from royalty, Bryn and Morgan backed respectfully away.

'Mary?' Bryn waited until she turned to him, gave him her proper attention. 'We just wanted you to be comfortable. And, um, proud. Your first time should be something to be proud of, because you'll remember it. Perhaps this wasn't the best . . .' He huffed. 'Drink your tea, now, before it gets cold.'

And, because they might as well now, Mary and Jonno took tea.

'Was that all right then, with the Uncles?' Jonathan couldn't manage above a whisper yet.

'I think so. Yes. They say what they mean – so, yes.' She rocked against him, grinned. 'And it was all right with me, too.'

'Oh, good.' And he grinned as well.

The rattle of spoons and crockery in the warm, stunned room was making them feel a little as if they'd become, somehow, delicate, a pair of happy invalids. Then their appetites overtook them and they cleared the plate of cake, then worked crumbs and butter and marzipan and much more of themselves into the sheets.

But now that the Uncles were home, they lowered their voices – to show respect.

Mary made love to Jonno again on the twenty-second of October, because it was her birthday.

'Thank you for the present.'

'Don't mention it.'

And then – avoiding the terrible Mother Davies – they managed again on the twenty-seventh, because they were both intoxicated by the terrible lack of time they still had left and because – having had five long, still days of reflection – they wanted to.

On the thirtieth they wanted to again because they were missing each other and Mary would be gone soon and because she'd passed Mrs Davies that morning in Bethel Lane and immediately needed, more than anything, to be sliding along Jonno's cock, to be wet with him, and making him push his breath against her neck in a way that his mother, Mary guessed, could very probably not imagine.

On the thirty-first they did it by mistake because they had met to say goodbye – the Uncles out climbing the valley – and had both been intent on explaining to each other why having sex now would only make them sad. They had it anyway and *were* sad, but also wonderfully painstaking and intent. And this time, their last time, he could be naked in her: the round, silk push of him. Her period was only a day or so away, already tender in her breasts, and she could safely catch him up and have him all, live, to remember, to be really there.

Mary thought of Foal Island and, cooried warm beside all of Jonno's pulses, she felt increasingly cheap. Tomorrow she was leaving – no more Uncles, no more valley, no more Jonathan. A lock in her thinking turned, cold and surprising, and reminded her of what it frightened her to find she could still want, even here and even now.

Her new future hissed at her, made her blood bolt in a way she hoped that Jonno wouldn't notice, because it was secret, even from him: beyond simple, visible nakedness. This was what she stripped down to, beyond the bone, this odd, free emptiness. And she did believe that she wouldn't have to make herself lonely for ever, she did feel that she would, in the end, come back to Jonathan, live out her future gently with him here. But she was still going to leave him tomorrow. And that did still hurt.

She woke on the first of November, having failed to notice Hallowe'en, and found that every detail of the house was waiting, ready to lacerate and cling. Her sheets breathed Jonno at her and were full of how quickly he showed he was pleased to be pleased. They reminded her of the temperature of his smile.

In the bathroom, here was the stupid pot with the blue plastic lid where Uncle Morgan's teeth swam their nights away and suddenly she liked it and wanted to see it regularly. His spare inhaler, his bottles of pills, the little daily fight to keep him breathing showed itself to her, inescapable. Bryn's thousand–year–old dressing gown, hanging soft at the back of the door, she wanted to touch it, because it was almost him.

Downstairs in the kitchen, the Uncles were doing their best. They played with toast and jam and appeared to eat. They were immaculately brushed and soaped and shaved, both cleaned to an especially startled pink. Morgan's inhalations fretted more than usual under his cardigan.

'All right, then, girl? Thought you'd never get up.'

'I think I was tired.'

Bryn cradled his teacup, 'Well, no wonder.' He stared at the tablecloth – fresh on, this morning, white with blue embroidered flowers. When she sat, he raised a grin to meet her, but couldn't quite persuade it to take.

Mary frowned back a burst of helplessness. 'I'm sorry.' Her voice waylaid her: was not as she intended, not firm, or cheerful, or strong.

'For what, love?'

'I don't know.' She caught herself back, imposed what she hoped was control. 'For all the time . . . I've been too much with Jonathan. I should have spent more time with you.'

Bryn's hand muffled down over hers, his skin always finer than she remembered. 'You were with us, too.' Ridiculous, tender palms, vulnerable fingers for a man to have. 'Don't worry yourself.' That made the final push, broke the whole pain down on her. 'If you do, you'll worry us.'

Mary swayed with the ache of losing them – the two most elegant, good and dependable gentlemen she knew. The Uncles looked on, stuttered into a clasp of hands. The fridge hummed and ticked.

Then Morgan said, for both of them, 'We do love you.' A kindness which mauled through her, making her almost unwilling to listen when he added, 'You have to go, though. We all know.'

'Don't be sad for us. We don't require it.' Bryn swung up and round the table to hug her so powerfully that the pressure made her breathless as well as glad. She wanted to shrink, to regress and be a small person again in his arms, to slip back with him to a place without decisions or change.

He kissed her forehead, light and neat. 'How are you now?'

'Good. Good enough.' Her words were still frail, and also low, to make them privately his. 'Is that a new sweater?'

'Well. It is, yes. We opened our Christmas presents to each other. Cheer us up.'

She hugged him quickly, to ease out the turn in her stomach. 'Now . . . You'll start me crying again.'

Morgan chipped in, 'And my cardigan – that's new as well. Thanks for noticing. Funny colour. Bryn's never been good at colours. Have you, Bryn?'

Which eased the atmosphere enough to let Bryn squeeze Mary's shoulder and trot back to his seat. They all relaxed by a few degrees and tried to be simply a family having breakfast and chatting.

And, of course, they did have to talk about her trip. They ran over the route of her journey again, praised the many sandwiches Morgan had made, exchanged reassurances about her money and her *spare* money, telephoning, letters and all the ways they could think to keep near to each other while they were apart.

When it was time, Mary left the house and climbed Charter Road unburdened. Bryn had shouldered her rucksack before she could stop him and gravely threatened to fight her if she tried to take charge of her holdall. Morgan contented himself with the carrier bag of sandwiches and bottled water.

They processed along flat-fronted streets of houses busy with the signs of redundancy payouts and heavy, pointless time. Woodwork had been painted and repainted, windows and doors replaced, stone cladding and satellite dishes installed. The video shop, the off-licence, the bookie's and the post office, the late-night shop, were all defended with roll-down shutters and grilles. They were living through nervous days.

Under the additions and improvements, the lean, low rows of houses stayed much the same: accommodation built to hold the workers required by a long-failed copper deposit and a web of narrow coal seams, now worked out. Planted without warning in a steep, damp cul-de-sac of green, the town had become accustomed to a rising scale of abandonments.

At the bus stop, Bryn dropped Mary's holdall and twisted out from under her rucksack, inhaling and stretching one arm with relief. Morgan leaned his back against the wall, life whistling between grey lips. 'Duw, you need a bus to *get* to the bus, don't you?'

Bryn shook Mary's hand, darting in with the movement and making a hollowness clamber in her arms.

'You're not going?'

'No. Just shaking your hand.' He touched his fingertips to her hair and briefly tensed his mouth. '*Ille terrarum mihi praeter omnes angulus ridet.* Don't know that one, do you? *That little corner beyond all the world is full of smiles for me.* You're my corner. Always.' He nodded, placidly, agreeing unrepentantly that he was being sentimental. 'You'll knock 'em dead, you know. They won't ever have seen a Mary Lamb. *Hoc vince.*'

'By this, conquer.'

'That's right.'

And the Uncles waited until Mary's bus came, kissed her in a rush, helped with the luggage, gave her peppermints for the journey, a touch more cash, and then waved and waved and waved her a good goodbye.

After she was gone they had tea in Ianetta's, feeling oddly exposed with only themselves there and no one in between. They linked arms gently going down the hill, taking it slow.

Although it was barely midday when they got home, they drew their curtains and went to bed. Then they made quick, despairing love in the manner of the recently bereaved. Morgan used his inhaler. They both slept.

A still dawn. Nathan lay in his bed and felt day bloom around the house in acidic green and dusty, mineral blues.

It's today.

The undiluted thought of her birled in him, tingled his thighs, made him lunge at an unsteady stack of plans for his day.

I could wear the suit. Formal. Bad thing.

*I should be only a little bit formal and much more **welcoming**.*

Welcoming. Good thing.

*The suit without a tie – relaxed **and** welcoming and, really, forget about formal altogether, because, for all she knows, I might look like that all of the time.*

Or I could just wear my overalls. They were good enough to die in.

Joe's taking the boat to get her. He'll bring her in and I can meet her on the jetty.

But I don't have to. Joe's feeding her at the Lighthouse, I could see her then, when she's more settled.

Or in her house. When she's alone. Or any time. I've got years. Pick my moment, get the right one.

*Jesus Christ, will you listen to yourself? This is a four-mile-long island. When she lands, she'll raise the population to a less than magnificent seven. You aren't going to miss her in the fucking crowd. Why don't you just meet her **accidentally**?*

I am pathetic sometimes.

No. I am pathetic quite frequently.

He dressed in his overalls and banged his way through making coffee and eating buttered bread.

No appetite? Butterflies in the tummy? You asked for this, though, didn't you?

Shut the fuck up.

Go and clean her house again – sweep it out. Put a little jug of rustic flowers on the window ledge. Perhaps a little introductory note.

He scowled away the temptation to do any such thing. The place would do fine, without any more work – it wasn't so long since the last occupant had left. It was wind- and watertight. There were no particular signs of mice. Monstrous spiders were, no doubt, lurking in every fissure – that's what you got for living in a field – but she wouldn't die of spiders, might not even be scared of them. He would cut along in an hour or two to set in fresh blankets and sheets. She could make her own bed.

Could she make her own bed?

She's nineteen and not an invalid, of course she can.

Having dealt with the bedding, he walked Eckless further to the north and west and sat amongst the little rocks that edged their favourite bay. The tide was in, as he'd known it would be. Nathan was getting used to the timing of these things. If he waited long enough, the water's breathing calmed him, licked him to a stop, like a patient partner. Looking down to his left, he could watch the oddly slow push of the tide between the Seven Brothers. Forced around and over the seven rough pillars and stumps of rock, the sea produced a gallery of impossibilities: apparently solid inclines, vitreous whorls, flawless sheets and cobbles and dust clouds of itself. He was beginning to love it – being with the sea.

Eckless crab-trotted up to drop into a nap against Nathan's back. The dog settled and nudged, a grumbling but comfortable dead weight – also now used to the rhythms of the bay and the rhythms of Nathan.

Go on, avoid the issue.

I'm not.

You are, you're going to work now, aren't you? She'll wait by the little post office in Ancw, undoubtedly afraid, but you will not go and help her, you will work. Joe will come and get her, make her feel safe and you will work. He'll motor her out and you will not meet her, you will not even watch her arrive – you will work. He'll land her, help her with her baggage and you could be there, too, but you'll be working, won't you? Because you have no bottle, not a drop.

He tried not to feel that he was failing. There was simply some-thing he wanted to finish and he felt he should do it now. He had his notebook and should make the most of this little peace to get something done.

This wasn't running away, or avoiding an issue, this was timing. Now was the best time to be here and do this – he could spend whole years of days with Mary later, there was no need to rush things now.

This was Nathan, keeping sensibly busy with a few corrections to a text, having decided he wouldn't see Mary yet and that he'd be better to wait. He was very familiar with having to wait.

He stared hopefully at his page. Underlined the title.

New Found Land

It was a story that he'd been attempting to write for a stupidly long time, although stories weren't really his forte and he didn't quite know what he'd do with it when it was finished, or who would care.

My arm was around her; not investigating, only resting, slung low on her waist, and the pleasantly heavy meeting of our sides made me feel I could topple at any time. I was, in fact, imagining that I might fall, drop neatly down with her and see what transpired.

I was drunk, of course, but we knew I was drunk and were not even mildly concerned. My particular brand of drinking only ever made me over-deliberate in largely harmless ways and slightly more inclined to touch. This had always been something about me we chose to enjoy.

Behind us I could vaguely hear our party: our friends in our home: our invited guests. We'd abandoned them for a good ten minutes now, but were feeling no guilt. They had their pick of our music, they could talk, they could finish my booze. As long as they kept the noise down, they could do what the fuck they liked – we didn't mind. The only thing we wanted was for them to leave us be and not come to the kitchen in search of ice, or lemons, or cocoa. Or us.

I'd opened the door to the garden, trying to get us some air, and we'd immediately decided, without ever needing to speak, that we would ease ourselves right outside and be with our plants and our dark. We had carefully left our politeness and responsibility indoors and had, quite quickly, become extremely happy.

The night had hugged us up in a high, open breath of green. I'd staggered a tiny bit, tipped back my head and found I was thumped off balance again by the clarity, by the wholly implausible size of the sky. I opened my arms to it all and then faced her, wanted to hold her, did just that.

I can remember this precisely, because I am the remembering type of man. Things are not quite as they should be with my mind. I pay too much attention, pay it in full, to every mortal thing. My future and its aspirations are quick to disappear or to contract, but my memory only ever accumulates. I wake up on many mornings with a heaviness in my head.

But maybe everyone is like this, more or less. Maybe everyone who is right now, like me, walking down Spadina Avenue, is also walking, trapped in thought, down quite another avenue that Spadina calls to mind. It could be that the whole of Toronto is clattering with pedestrians in possession of Russian doll heads, each one helplessly closing the present in shells of the past. Like me, they may conduct a conversation as if it were all they could need, but meanwhile they'll be reworking something from quite another time: a threat they were too shy to utter, a stalled intimation of love: they'll be mending their last botched argument, making it come out right.

I do hope this is so. I would like not to be the only one bouncing through echoes, recollection muscling in to make reality nervous and incomplete.

My arm was around her, around Maura.

Why that again?

Perhaps I miss her.

Not perhaps - of course. Of course I do.

It's nearly Hallowe'en here, I'd forgotten that was coming, lost my place in the year. The shop-window displays are full of pumpkins, painted in God-awful colours and already gently exploding down into mush and pools of pumpkin blood and gentle, fungal fluff. The darker shades seem to last longer. The only one I've seen still perfect was a shiny, undertaker's black. Which could explain the funeral dress code - an attempt at deflecting decay.

I would consider painting my head black and, therefore, escaping corruption of all kinds, if I didn't know that any such efforts would be a decade or three too late. I'm all past saving.

My arm was around her, hungry, like it is now, anxious to clasp and be sure of her. I was pondering the ebb

and swell of her ribs and trying not to cup too hard at
the slight give of flesh above her hip. I loved the soft-
ness of her there, but she would tut and sigh away if
I explored it too much - she said my doing that made
her feel fat.

I said my doing that made me feel lycanthropic with
desire.

'Love?'

Maura didn't answer, simply rocked once, hard against
me and completely reconformed my concentration.

'It's late, love.'

'Mm.'

'I should go back and tell them they want to leave.'

But I didn't. I stayed and put my mouth to the pulse
in her neck, licked it. I felt her muscle tense to meet
me. I inhaled.

She smelled very slightly like a stranger: disguised
with other people's cigarette smoke, the make-up she
would only wear for guests. All the scents of a duti-
ful hostess: my good friends' aftershave and her best
friend's perfume, appropriate kisses and sociable hugs.

'Yes, you should go.' Her small hours of the morning
voice, I hadn't heard it in a while. 'You should.' It
was closer than my thinking, 'You really should,' salt-
ing my blood.

'If I don't, they're going to come and find us.' Me
with a stranger who looks like my wife.

'I know.'

Fucking her in the night grass - I wanted that.

I ought to remember that I never enjoy being this far
away. I'm not bothered so much by the distance, only by
the time. Here, I'm walking out an hour before dinner
and, there, Maura's already asleep. I hope. Unless the
baby got her up.

But the wee one's much more settled now - hardly ever
really makes a scene. At night, lately, she's seldom
ever genuinely cried. It's more that she's curious,

checking to know we're still there. I can just put my head in most times and she'll go off again, satisfied. I mean, it isn't *unfair* crying, it isn't that unreasonable bellowing you hear from other people's kids. That would drive me crazy. That would make me start to think there was something vital I'd forgotten to provide and that my daughter was growing up with some type of lack that she couldn't describe to me yet, not having words.

I'm glad I don't have that problem. I'm glad everything's all fine.

They'll both be sleeping now, I'm sure. Nice and early to bed and then *spark out*... My dad used to say that – *Spark out in no time*. He was usually right and now I am, too. We're good sleepers, my family, it's in our genes.

Maybe next time, if I'm here again, Maura and Kiddo could come out, too. Then, if I wasn't working, we could toddle about, see the lake, the islands. I'd take Kiddo up the CN Tower. I wouldn't bother for myself, but small people – I'd imagine – might really appreciate high places and uninterrupted views. Kiddo certainly adores all that, endlessly wanting to be picked up. Maybe the CN Tower could save my back: let her know that buildings can lift her, instead of only me. Not that I mind all the lifting. Or being thought of as indispensable. Naturally.

I could nip up today and look out on her behalf, be a dutiful dad. If the mist clears. No point if it doesn't. Although her mother would prefer it this way – so many eerily spotless buildings, looming like monstrous art deco ornaments in dove blue and verdigris. Then the skyline hits mist height and fades into white. If I raise my eyes for too long I could believe I'm walking through a decomposing photograph.

I'll tell Maura about it all tomorrow morning – her afternoon – and she'll know what I mean, she has a good eye for the lovely. That's the one thing I like about being apart – it makes us collect up the best of our days to pass on for each other. It probably makes us appreciate things more.

I'd like to talk to Kiddo, but Maura says there's not much point, which is true, she can't really answer yet, I suppose. But I would still like to say *hello*. It would be something to do once I've spoken to her mother, found myself clinging to her voice, searching it for meanings it doesn't intend.

'Nathan, tell me what you want.'

My arm was around her, around Maura, my wife.

'I want you.' I hadn't felt this horny in ages, not for months. Or if I had, it had never seemed such a good and possible idea.

A familiar, anticipating twitch was back in my hands. 'We could manage before they find us.' We were turning back to our old way of being – to the time before the baby and the house full of infant-sized wreckage – to the time when we were only us. 'We could. You know we could.'

'Or we could make them go home. Then not hurry.'

*Which **was** a far better idea, I had to agree, although I still couldn't leave her yet, even if it was with the definite promise of more fun to have later on. 'All right. You tell them to fuck off home and I'll go up and check on Wee Lamb.'*

'No. Leave it.' I felt her body disagreeing much more clearly than her words.

'Leave what?'

'You don't have to check.'

Obviously, we had to stand apart then, just enough to face each other and talk properly.

'I might as well. It won't take a minute – I'll make sure she hasn't kicked off her blankets, made any troubles in store. After that we'll be clear for the night, I'd reckon. She's been good.'

'You'll pick her up.'

'I won't if she's sleeping.' I had to fold my arms

then - it helped me think. I wasn't easing Maura away.
I would actually have liked to touch her very much, but
I needed a little clear-headedness at that point. 'I'll
give her a wee look. No more.'

Maura nodded and turned for the house, half lights
and glimmers disguising her face, shading away her
eyes. I took a last breath of the garden and then followed her inside.

And I'm almost sure she spoke again. 'You'll wake
her.' Her voice quite sleepy, a murmur that I couldn't
truly catch. 'You'll wake her.' I could have been mistaken. 'Then we won't be alone any more.' I might have
misheard her. She might not have said a word.

I want to buy them presents, that's mainly why I'm walking about. This isn't an idle wander, this is a search.
They have beautiful black squirrels here that Kiddo
would love - sleek as you like, lithe and undulating,
the way our red ones used to be, before the grey ones
killed them. Or before things changed and they were
naturally selected, edged out. I'd expected that somewhere would sell me a toy black squirrel, but it seems
there are none to be had.

The people here are very helpful, nonetheless, more
so when I mention a daughter - being the doting dad.
Everyone has tried their best in the healthy Canadian
way: offering me mooses of every type, some ugly owls,
beavers wearing Mountie hats and polar bears that only
compulsive-obsessives could ever keep clean. But no
squirrels. Squirrels are, perhaps, too urban for mass-
market tastes. Tourists may well demand only creatures
from vicious snowfields, or strange forests - more
unmistakably Arctic types.

I'll end up settling for a moose, but I don't want
to. Kiddo would like a squirrel, I know her taste.
Sounds unlikely, I realise. But she is absolutely her
own small person, even now. So I can sometimes understand exactly what she likes.

I'll trot upstairs, softly, softly, dodge into her room. Her nightlight will be in there, whirling away, making the place seem oddly psychedelic, which unnerves me but amuses her. Then I'll watch. Somewhere under the covers her whole ribcage will be dipping and bowing with breath, flummoxed by inhalations in a way that is terrifying but perfectly customary. The fluctuations of life in her hypnotise me.

And lead me to conjure lies against my wife. Because I do pick up my daughter and hold her when I've promised that I won't. I do eel my hands in round her and lift her, still asleep, so that I can sneak her head against my shoulder and kiss the fuzz above the bone above her personality. This is the best close to my days. When she's been screaming tired and shitty, when she's hated her food and howled and spat – which is hardly a shock: I've never tried a jar without gagging, but she does have to eat, after all – when she's been doing all those mind-bending, draining, bloody things that only babies can possibly think of to do, I just imagine her sleeping, giving me peace. And that sees me through. On other, equally random days she will be almost immaculate, gentle, quiet, and she will hint at small opinions she has – for example, that she'd like a squirrel instead of a moose.

I am going to disappoint her. But I think she'll forgive me. I think a moose will be all right.

Maura asked me for an Inuit carving – soapstone and bone and all that – the smaller pieces are relatively cheap. Not that I wouldn't spend money on my wife – it's just that she doesn't want me to. I looked at some little figures yesterday, but I felt there was something about them I didn't like – disturbing. The seals were inverted, or twisted, or slightly human. And there were precarious carvings of bears that danced and slipped too near to being men, while the men slid overly close to being bears. Everything spun, transmuted and was very smooth and beautiful, but unkind company.

Last night, it seemed to upset me: seeing so many peculiar sculptures made me dream unpleasantly. I woke up frightened and wanted to speak to Maura and to sound ordinary and daft, telling her I'd been scared by the thought of myself as a bear and by the empty yowl of snow somewhere in my head. I *could* have phoned: it would have been her morning: but it seemed I couldn't work the time zones out, couldn't focus properly, so I ended up only having a shower to swill off the sweat I was covered in and the memory of fur. I looked at my hands, washing, and I remembered that in my dream, when I'd had bear paws I couldn't touch my baby, my Lamb.

My arm was around her as we faced our guests. I smiled them goodbye and they smiled back before I started up the stairs.

'Don't wake her.'

'No.'

'Please.'

'I won't wake her.'

I could feel our visitors still grinning up behind me, noting the altered Maura, the changed me. We were, conceivably, more endearing as parents than as friends.

The front door chattered open and let in the street air and I climbed without listening to the last of the night's conversations trickling away.

She'd uncovered herself, my daughter, and was sprawled, expansive and relaxed, out for any count, for any spark.

I feathered the blanket over her again and sat on the floor by her head, watching her face through the bars of the cot, the rush of different lights across her. She was racing at sleep, avid: small movements of hunger from her mouth, her fingers bunching and gripping out of sight.

'You can't leave her be, can you?' Maura was in the doorway, dressed for bed, which meant that I'd sat for more time than I'd intended. 'You can't stop.'

71

'No.' Seeing Maura's shape spinning with colours and in a frame of brighter light I had to guess that she was smiling and that I could be honest comfortably. 'No, I can't.'

'No, you can't. Because you're always feeding off people. Always taking notes. You make me tired.'

I remember every part of the night we spent then, Maura and I: her edging away in the bed until I let her be, any hopes upended, spilt. I lay on my back beside her and attempted to breathe unobtrusively.

Sleep caught me on the brink of morning and I dreamed of somersaulting into skies filled with raging shadow and twisting light. And I landed, chill and giddy, in an unforgiving country where I was not known.

Then my daughter woke me, crying, and I went to her.

'I am the Keeper of the Foal Island Light.'

Joseph Christopher, standing with his back to the low winter sun, white hair burning round a shadowed face. He could look quite remarkable, if he tried, and he was definitely trying. He was aiming to inspire a blend of cheerfulness and confidence, but he only made Mary flinch. For an hour and a half, she'd been shifting dully on the post office bench, mesmerised by tiredness and burned-out expectation. Consequently, she hadn't noticed him creeping up from the harbour wall until his shadow fell across her, cooling her face.

Joe laughed.

God, he's mad.

'No, I'm not, actually. Neither of the lights need a keeper, they're automatic. This your stuff, here?' He was only averagely tall, quite slender and plainly on the far side of fifty, but he slipped her rucksack up over one shoulder, as if it were a summer coat. 'Sorry.' He swung out his right hand and caught hers into a oddly hot, dry shake. 'Joseph Christopher, Chairman of the Fellowship. Among other things. We should get moving, if you don't mind. It would be better if we landed before sunset. Safer – speaking practically. Waiting long?'

'I don't reall–'

'Well, that's all done with now.' Joe broke his turn, stopped, twitched his head to one side, the sunlight striking both his eyes into a blind, bright stare, with a tick of dark movement behind. Mary flinched again, felt somehow inspected, touched. She scuffled up to stand and deal with her holdall and then paused. He was still staring, the look shaded now and much more obviously tasting at her, palpably curious. He rubbed his lips with the crook of one finger, almost frowned.

Completely crazy.

*But he can't be mad, he's a novelist. He's a **good** novelist. That would mean he has to be –*

No. Bugger this, whatever he was – she knew there were types of behaviour she didn't have to like. 'Is there something wrong, Mr Christopher?'

He smiled – something he was good at – a broad, immediately reassuring gesture, full of innocence and well-maintained calcium. 'I'm sorry. I'd been wondering what you'd be like. From your stories. And I am glad you've come. So I'm smiling – I do that when I'm glad. You're bringing our complement up to full strength.' He rested one hand on her shoulder, 'You're home now. You do know that, don't you, Mary Lamb?'

'Tell me what it was like?'

Mary wasn't too long awake. She'd been on the island three days now and met everybody but Nathan – Nathan that everyone talked about, but always in slightly evasive ways – Nathan, the man that no one but Joe seemed to like – Nathan, the writer who was meant to be her mentor for the time she spent here: her teacher (not that this seemed likely), her example (this seemed more unlikely still) her encouraging-even-inspiring-person-who-is-not-supposed-to-alarm.

But he *was* being alarming. Knocking the door and opening it in one brisk movement. Standing, vaguely rigid, packed into a long, tight mackintosh and two pullovers, the upper thick-knitted and oily, the lower a softer polo neck to cover, had she but known it, his neckline bruises. He forced out a hand to shake hers and then immediately asked, 'What was it like? – come on, you must remember, you must have been paying attention. That's our First Rule, if we're going to have rules, *Pay Attention*. Because you'll have to if you want to write. You do want to write?' he growled, still standing, not pausing for any reply.

Mary stood the interrogation for three or four minutes, at least, and then turned her back on him smoothly, found and lit a match. She was pleased when her hand didn't shake.

'What are you doing?' Finally, a question which seemed interested in her response. Nathan stopped, breathing audibly, and Mary thought that she didn't like him, that he was almost sweating for not much reason, his forehead already a little repellent, with a moist, uneasy shine. His eyes flittered, evaded, while his hands clamped against each other, fierce and square.

'What am I doing, Mr Staples? I'm going to light the gas. I haven't had my coffee this morning, or anything to eat, but now I am going to because breakfast is the most important meal of the day. If you like, I can *answer* questions once I've made toast. Or you can just keep on asking them – I don't mind.'

They both surprised themselves by almost smiling, both felt a certain settling in their scores.

Nathan refused toast – it was more than a little carbonised, Mary was sad to note – but he sat docilely at her table, still stiff-armed and mildly breathless, bound up in his layers of clothes. She considered the back of his neck, the hard and very slightly lopsided line of his shoulders. He was her first visitor, the first person to call on her *in her own house*. More of a big Nissen hut, really, but her own place with her own things – a few of them – and, she supposed, her own power to ask unpleasant people to go away. That was a comfort.

She listened to the gas, trying to hold the peaceful sound of it close enough to calm her without letting it make her homesick. She crunched at her charcoaly bread, which seemed immensely loud, and then turned out the almost invisible blue of the singing flame. Nathan rang one thumbnail off his coffee mug and then sipped. She went to join him, regretting each anxious creak of the floor.

As soon as she'd finished eating, he swallowed, cleared his throat, and then began to speak again, perhaps more gently. 'All right. Because you were paying attention and because, by definition, first times can't be had again and should therefore be thought of as precious and intense – because of all these things, you should be fairly capable of describing your first evening here, telling me what it was like, as a narrative exercise. When you met everybody –'

'Everybody but you.'

'Mm hn. When you met everybody. Tell me . . . No. Let's start at the start. Your journey from the mainland. Describe it. Take your time and be careful. And please correct any obvious mistakes.'

'What?'

He looked coolly beyond her at the wall. 'Narration, give me some.'

She felt her heart shy, batter briefly, while her stomach gave a nauseous wink. But then she did begin, softly, aware of his thumb, still tapping against his mug.

'I felt excited, even exhilarated.'

'Which? Make up your mind. No one else will.'

'Exhilarated and, because I'd never been in a boat before, I felt . . . I suppose *seafaring*. Childish. Also foolish, I suppose. And I felt safe. Even though the boat was bucking and – possibly –' she looked at Nathan, '*definitely* also swooning under my feet, I felt well and safe. The wake pushed us from behind, very small, eventually delicate, and there was a clot of shadow ahead, pressed in between two different blues.' Nathan showed no sign of being impressed, although she'd quite liked that, as a sentence. 'I knew that shadow would be the island. Eventually it grew, blackened, solidified – even towered – as we turned under the Lighthouse cliffs. Then, for a while, the land lay between us and the sunset, which was beautiful. I think Joe meant it to be that way. There was no real need for us to motor all the way around – other than to see everything.' She dropped her voice, knowing she was being disappointing. 'The lights, the colours, they unfurled.'

'Better. Slightly.'

'I knew I'd never seen anything exactly so large and lovely. And that I had no way of describing it.'

'Yet. There should be a yet there. You have no way of describing it *yet*.' He smiled, not unkindly, but also not for her. 'Good. Honesty. Better than getting poetic and wrong. Poetry being, of course, by its very nature, wrong.' He smiled again, this time at one of her hands, which she then moved back a little, out of his way. Nathan blinked directly at her, offered her a dark little warning look and blinked away again. 'Now. The Lighthouse.'

'I thought it would be a tower – but it's only a big house and the light's somewhere else. Good, old stone, comfortable, shiny, not very nautical – which I'd expected. It smelled of books and Sunday dinners.'

Nathan laughed out loud, or barked out loud – it was hard for her to tell which. 'Yes. Well guessed. We eat, as it happens, compulsory Sunday *lunches* there every week. Keeping the group together – pseudo family stuff. All nonsense. But we will have to go tomorrow, that being the fourth and, therefore, Sunday. Don't worry, there's no need for formal dress. Go on. You were there, they were there . . . all assembled . . . just like the cast at the start of one of those tacky disaster movies.'

'We had batons of vegetables to eat –'

Nathan gave a small snuff of amusement. 'Sorry. Long story. You'll find that batons of vegetables appear a good deal. They're Lynda's favourite and turn my stomach, but that – as I've said – is a long story which you will hear at the proper time.'

'Well anyway, I was trying not to grab the things in handfuls, but I was very hungry and I half-thought that was all we'd get. I wasn't sure. Everyone was fiddling with bits of carrot and looking as if they wanted to talk to each other but ought to talk to me, so no one was saying anything. Joe introduced them to me, or me to them. Both.'

'So. Ruth Alvey?'

'She's plays and poetry.'

'If she says so. Bakes a good loaf, *I* would say. Sorry, do go on.' He offered her a vaguely vulpine smile.

'Very black hair – that iridescent, almost blue colour.'

'And.'

'Soft. She seemed soft.'

'Or saggy, baggy, puffy, loose, much more than normally afflicted by gravity. You don't have to be polite. I want what you saw, your opinion. Your opinion will be right.'

'She is, in my opinion, not a happy shape. And she's pale. She moves as if she has sore hips, or bad shoes, or bad underwear. She's missing the tips of two fingers, but I didn't ask why.'

'Shark bit her.'

Now Mary laughed. Reining it back, as soon as she'd heard herself.

'True. A tiger shark, I believe. She will tell you – at great length – about the curious hissing noise a tiger shark makes when it bites you. It was, obviously, aiming for rather more than her fingers. In fact, I think she lost *them* trying to prise its mouth off her other arm. You can't say she hasn't been plucky, from time to time.'

'My God.'

'It was probably her own fault – she'll have read it some of her bloody tankas, or her performance poetry until the poor beast could do nothing but go for her throat.' This time his smile was more human. 'I'm interrupting too much, but some things you do need to know. And Ruth *will* talk about sharks. You may say to her, "What a lovely dress." (*I* wouldn't, but *you* might.) And she will say, "Yes – it's silk, very smooth. Unlike the fantastically abrasive surface of a

78

Porbeagle shark." Or you may say, "Fancy a chicken sandwich?" and she will answer, "Indeed I would. Cooked chicken, of course, can be almost indistinguishable from properly cooked shark." Or you might say – despairing – something extremely conservative like, "Hello," and get back, "*Hello* – that was the first word I said on that magical day when I swam with the lemon sharks. They're very maternal, you know." You can't win. It's best not to speak to her, really.'

'Thanks a lot. If she ever, ever talks about sharks now, I'll laugh and she'll think I'm odd.'

'She'll be too self-obsessed to notice, even if you're frothing mad. And . . . if you *did* laugh and I was there, then . . . Well, that would be something in the way of a private joke between us. Wouldn't it? If you like that kind of thing. Might I have a cup of tea, do you think? Thanks.' Nathan sprang up and moved for the matchbox and the gas ring before she could stop him. 'It's OK – I know where things are. This used to be Arthur Llangattock's place.' He dropped the matches and began to scrabble for them, sucking air between his teeth.

'The same Llangattock who's paying for me to be here?' Mary felt she shouldn't help him pick them up, that assistance would embarrass him.

'Yes. Well, no. He isn't *paying* – he *paid*. The money is from a bequest. He's dead. Which is why you're living in his house. Otherwise, *he* would be.'

Nathan salvaged the last of the matches, managing to strike one on the floorboards. Rather than let it flare across the others in his fist, he tried tamping it out on his free palm, hoping a cough could cover any audible signs of pain. In the end, he just had to release it and then stamp on it as tactfully as he could.

He lit the ring and turned, relieved to see that Mary wasn't looking, only idling her time away, drawing arcs with her finger in her plate of crumbs. Perhaps she hadn't seen him being utterly ridiculous. Or perhaps she was only sitting and thinking, '*This isn't Llangattock's house any more, this is Mary Lamb's.*' He hoped so.

'Anyway, go on. Lynda Dowding – the Carrot Queen. Your impressions.'

'Oh. I don't know.'

'Nonsense.' His voice sharpened again, darkened, mouth firming. 'Come on. This is the easy stuff.'

'She's very . . . Her husband is frightened of her. He is her husband?'

'He's certainly married to her, yes. That would be the same thing, I'd imagine.'

'Well, she . . . If I'm being honest . . .'

'Painstakingly, please.'

'She worried me. Or not worried . . . she looked so good, but not in a good way.'

'Explain.'

'Her teeth and hair and nails – everything so perfect. You could tell she'd used one of those little make-up pencils to finish her lipstick off, just right. And she must have blended three or four mascaras, taken a good deal of time. I mean, it looked *effective*, but it still looked false and her foundation was settling into her wrinkles, making them worse. You know.'

'No, I don't, you're telling me. With all the splendid cruelty of youth.' The kettle began its whistle and was snatched from the heat, slopping slightly over one of Nathan's shoes.

'Did that burn you?'

'Mm? Oh.' He looked down at his gently steaming foot. 'No. No, it's fine.'

'Well. Good.'

Mary pursed her lips, looking – both at once – remarkably studious and remarkably vulnerable. Nathan concentrated hotly on not boiling his own hand instead of the tea bag.

'I thought she was nice, though –'

'*Nice?*' The one word barged Nathan's voice up through an octave.

'I thought so. She was very –'

'I don't object to your *opinion*, I told you that. I object to the *word*. In a setting like that, it's, it's . . .'

'Meaningless?'

'Worse, but I can't quite think of the proper literary term at the moment. Oh, yes. *Crap*. That's the one I was searching for. Or *shite*. It's a fine line, either way. Quick, redeem yourself with Richard Fisher.'

'The frightened husband. He's the only one who *looked* like a writer. I mean, he's got the lots of hair and the black pullover and the long fingers . . . that's to say, with the left hand, he does.'

'And the right one is . . .? Honesty, remember . . .'

'His right arm is shorter and smaller that the left – it looks like a boy's arm, but he has everything – all of his clothes – cut so the sleeves fit. He looks very dashing.'

'And that would clinch it, obviously – dashing deformity – must be a writer. The fact that he can only cough up genre crime yarns and post-modernist ragbags of Alzheimered tat should not be taken into consideration. Next – Louis Elcho. Our historian.'

'Oh, *that's* what he does.'

Nathan narrowed his eyes, but said nothing.

'He knew a lot about history – he was extremely well informed, not boring. He was . . . he was sweet. A very, very endearing old man.'

'You liked him?'

'I did.'

'Yes, well, he is the grandfatherly type.' Nathan made this sound particularly waspish. 'Joe?'

Mary took a serious breath. 'Amiable, not unlikeable, initially alarming, but, I thought, fundamentally good. He cares a lot about the Fellowship. He seemed fond of you.'

'In a way that the others did not.'

'That isn't what I said.'

'No. You're right. It's not.' Nathan lifted one hand and studied his thumb. 'Are you settling in, is there anything you need, do you have any worries?'

'I think Mr Christopher took care of everything.'

'Yes, well, he's not really in charge of you, though, is he? If you have any problems now, you bring them to me.'

Mary quietly considered whether this wouldn't be a problem in itself.

'Come here.' Nathan flapped her towards him while backing off in the direction of her front doorway. 'Now.' He opened the door, ushered her out into the billowing drizzle and pointed. Joe had shown her this already – a low, long building on a gentle rise, pale against a hunch or two of brush. 'That's where I live.'

'I was told.'

He dropped one arm around her heavily and she noticed a twitch, a shiver, not in his arm, but in his whole body. He was shaking. The damp and cold could make a person do that, it wasn't unreasonable behaviour, she supposed.

'Well, if you have any problems,' he let go of her, smoothed one hand across the top of his head, 'you go there. If I'm not in, wait. Wait inside. I'll be back. Probably, I'll be walking the dog.'

'You have a dog?'

'Well, don't sound so astonished. I am capable of shouldering the occasional caring responsibility. He is a *nice* dog. You have a problem with dogs?'

'No.'

'Good.' He nodded to her, began walking off as abruptly as he'd arrived.

'You didn't drink your tea.'

'You have it.' He span on his heel in the mushy grass. 'The rest of the time, we'll work in *my* house, by the way. It's bigger. Obviously. Ten o'clock tomorrow, we start properly. I love working on a Sunday. God may have rested on it, but we need all the time we can get.'

'Should I bring anything: paper —'

'No, you should not.' He shrugged round into the face of the rain and stamped away, calling as he went, 'Make yourself at home. Oh, and welcome.'

'Thanks.'

If he answered her, she didn't hear.

And she didn't see him, minutes later, clattering open his door, hands still greasy with terror: memory and unwanted tenderness lodged between his fingers and under his tongue like acrid felt. Nathan dropped to his knees and then — Eckless observing, warily — lowered his head to the boards, started grinding his naked crown against the wood. He ground hard, determinedly, while rain spatter from his trench coat trickled up the bared arch of his neck.

Quiet in her new home, Mary cleared her table. She tried to plan out a letter to the Uncles, because she guessed — correctly — that writing it would distract her, make her feel less alone.

Mary emptied and rinsed their two mugs as Nathan breathed queasily round the shameful hollow of himself and imagined the small thrill, the ill thrill, of Mary actually drinking his mug of tea. Even if it was unlikely she'd have taken his suggestion, set her lips to his cup, kissed where his mouth had been, held where his hands had fretted and sweated and been numbed with terrifying hope. Why not?

I thought she would be . . . I thought. Things should all have been quite different.

Quite another way.

But they still can be.

She looks so . . .

They can still be different.

Please.

Mary walked that afternoon. The rain had thickened and sealed the day, started to cup the island in mist and shreds of an early dusk, but she still went out. Nathan saw her from his window, felt her presence prick in his lung before his mind's eye had entirely recognised her – the shape of a new figure on the island, bending into the weather, cuffed and blustered at. She was heading roughly north towards the shoreline, which meant that she would probably pass his bay. The breeze would really hit her there. But there was no point stopping her, no point running out and shouting, waving his arms in the storm that would rip his voice to eddies and nonsense before it reached her. Without his intervention, she would gather her own experience, she would learn. A person should be permitted to learn from their own mistakes.

One of Mary's introductory letters had given her a list of useful items she might bring with her to Foal Island, including

16 Stout waterproof clothing.

18 A warm hat.

21 Wellingtons.

22 Three-season walking boots.

31 Chocolate. (An optional fillip, but something which islanders always seem to find in short supply.)

Before leaving her hut, Mary had equipped herself with items 16, 22, 18 and 31. Her hat used to be Bryn's, a sheep-oily knitted thing, itchy but also cosy and something of his, something that still smelled of his hair oil and his thinking. She trudged, trying to conjure up his company, but she could only hear Mr Staples's voice, slapping at her with questions.

'Tell me what it was like?' That doesn't mean anything — that simply does not communicate. A writer's supposed to communicate. He doesn't. He doesn't even look at you properly — except slyly sometimes, when he thinks that you won't see.

A gull kited ahead of her, tilting and bouncing a little above the level of the shore. It eyed her, lazily, accustomed to reclining on chaos, confident in its support.

He doesn't like me.

I know he doesn't. It's not just the way I'm feeling and being uncomfortable, away from home — he doesn't like me.

She tried to get some muscle into her discontent.

*But then, he doesn't have to like me. And, as it happens, I don't have to like him. As it happens, I'm not impressed by Nathan Staples. I don't care if he **is** famous. Joe's just as famous and he's **nice**. Which is as good a word as any — a nice man is a nice man, so that's what you call him — **nice**.*

Mary wiped the rain from her eyes and stopped, completely stopped. Recollection flared and span around her unannounced. It held her breath. The feel of Jonno kicked and sparked and yelled between her hips. Before she could damp her memory down, she was lit with the need to make him pant, to make his teeth close on her ear, to make him hoarse and spent and hot.

She'd guessed she might cry today, because she'd been hurt, or scared by Nathan, or because she was in a strange place and missed her Uncles, her old life. Instead she stood and wept while she thought of Jonno, while muscle tricked itself into mouthing at nothing, rocked through an aching twitch. She closed her eyes and, in the small pause of dark, watched her need kiss down against him, raw and lipping him to the root.

Then she was cold, she noticed, or at least shivering, which amounted to much the same thing.

'Mary. Good afternoon. If you don't mind me asking, are you all right? This isn't exactly the best day for a stroll.'

She'd walked almost to the island's north-eastern tip when Louis Elcho found her. She'd seen him, weaving his approach between softening flags of rain. Because she had still felt soft, bleary, she had — at first — wanted to simply wave at him in what might seem a hearty way and then move on before he made her stop. But he could crack out a fair pace when he wanted, a remarkable speed for his size. Not a slim man, Louis. He'd caught up with her.

'Settling in well? Nathan seen you?'

Everyone here seemed determined to do nothing but question her.

'You look tired. Do come and have tea.' Before she could stop him, he'd insinuated a stubby arm under her elbow. 'You can't see from here, but I'm only at the bottom of the slope there – one day, I'm sure, I'll slip all the way into the sea.' He led her forward. 'Not that it isn't high time. I've lived far too long as it is. And I've done enough. I find this continued largesse,' he waggled his unrestricted arm happily at the matted grass, the writhing sky, the heaving grey vertigo of sea, 'almost embarrassing. Seventy-four, imagine. No boy ever sits and thinks to himself – *I shall grow up one day into a seventy-four-year-old man.* No normal boy, anyway. I did ask you about Nathan, did I? An odd sort. Still, *poeticam istud licentiam decet.*'

For the first time since Joe landed her, Mary's mind found itself on familiar ground. '*That befits a poet's licence.* But he isn't a poet. Is he?'

'Oh, excellent. Really. Really.' He squeezed her arm. 'No, he's not a poet, strictly speaking – but he does have more lyrical leanings than he'll admit. All that sex and horror – it makes him money, but it's also rather good – rather poetic. And for that, you need a licence. I think we could say his is fully paid up.' He squeezed her again. 'A fellow classicist. Good news.'

'Not really. My Uncles taught me. I just learned things by heart.'

'So you have Latin in your heart. Delightful.' And he began to slip them gently, Mary restraining him, down to the point where his cottage door could halt their progress and catch them both safe inside.

Like Mary, Louis had a faintly threatening, cylinder-fed gas cooker. Unlike Mary he had straight walls, a distinct ceiling, more than one room and a wide range of possessions, mainly books and photographs.

'Death and letters, you see, death and letters. That's all it's about.' He presented her with a thick slice of what turned out to be date and walnut loaf – the taste of it made her feel immediately nostalgic. The Uncles loved their cakes. 'Books, letters . . . immortality, isn't it?'

Mary knew she was feeling less tense, eyeing the cake and

discovering that her walk had made her hungry. Louis watched her settle, happily. He was one of Nature's welcomers. He should have been a hangman, or a dentist – making use of his gift for rendering strangers unwary. Instead, he'd been a teacher and specialised, as Mary could have testified, in putting people younger than himself at some kind of ease. In her case, warmth, a comfortable chair, cake and some Latin tags were all it took. She was a pushover. But he still respected her.

'And the pictures, well . . .' he waggled his hand at his ranks of snapshots and squeezed himself into an armchair, a very round peg in a square hole, 'hardly a soul in them now who isn't dead. Apart from me.'

'Oh.' Mary tried to be sympathetic with her mouth full.

'No, no. Don't worry. I like to remember – I do it for balance – I love balance. Libran. You are, too, aren't you?' He giggled as Mary began a frown. 'Well, we had to get a *tiny* head-start on you: name and preferred genres, date of birth, that kind of thing.'

'You know I don't live with my parents? They didn't bring me up.' She didn't quite know why she'd said that: perhaps because it was a part of her, a part he might not like.

But Louis only looked at her: delicately, but clearly disappointed that she might have felt it necessary to test him. 'The Fellowship was informed. So I know that you're Libran and that you will probably like this idea. Death and language – each is the opposite and complement of the other. What do you think, hm? If you aren't going to die, why bother writing? Why else put all that effort into something that stays behind. How do you understand you're already dying and that others are already dead? Because there is already writing. Extinction and explanation, the theft and the gift.

'There is more of that cake, if you'd like some.' His eyes dulled by a tiny degree – giving away carbohydrates didn't sit easily with him.

Mary had seen the same generously suppressed panic before in Morgan, when he was down to his last wedge or two of cherry Genoa. She knew what to say. 'Perhaps I could swap you for this.' She lifted down her jacket and brought out one of her bars of fruit and nut. 'It might be a bit damp, but I haven't opened it.'

Louis Elcho came as close as he ever would to a look of unbridled desire. 'Oh.' He almost squeaked. 'Item 31. You will think it bad of me, but I did ask that Joe should include it on the list. In case it might mean you brought some. For yourself, of course.' He swallowed softly, 'But you're too kind. I shouldn't,' while his eyes plainly begged.

'No. Please. I don't have that much of a sweet tooth. I prefer cake.'

So Mary settled herself with another slice, in a kind of tribute to Morgan and other times, and Louis teased away at paper and silver foil in a spasm of almost erotic intensity. For a period, they either didn't or couldn't speak.

Then, 'That's Arthur Llangattock, there.' Louis pointed to his mantelpiece and an image of a slightly younger Louis with his arm attempting to stretch around a tall, broad, serious figure, sporting a tweed cap. 'The man who had your place bef–'

'I know, Mr Staples told me.'

'I suppose that Arthur was my best friend here. Yes, I should say that, my best friend.'

'Was he . . . was he ill?'

'Ill? No. Doesn't look ill, does he? No, he was strapping, quite strapping.'

'Then how . . . ?'

Louis peered at her roundly for a moment, then understood. 'Oh, I see.' He clapped his hands once; they made a small, bruised noise. 'He cut his head off. Last year.'

Mary blinked.

'Yes, quite an achievement, in a way. In our workshop. With our circular saw. He was found very early in the morning – by Nathan, in fact – just lying, his head and both hands off. So he must have extended his arms to save himself and lost them first – before his head. We suppose he tripped – there were all kinds of treacherous objects on the floor. It must have happened the previous afternoon, because there were no lights on and no one would be likely to wander about in the dark in a cluttered workshop with an unguarded saw, up and running somewhere close. Behaviour like that would be close to suicide. Remarkable accident, all the same.

'And sad, of course. So sad. I do miss him. I miss them all.'

He popped a square of chocolate into his mouth, as if it might provide a consolation, but then narrowed his lips, disappointed with himself, and sucked glumly on, turning his saliva guiltily thick and sweet.

Mary tried not to look surprised, or puzzled, tried not to look anything.

Poor man. Staying too long on an island . . . I suppose you could get that way.

Louis gave her a narrow, faltered smile. 'I am sorry, that's not a pleasant story, is it? Not one to tell over tea.'

The backs of Mary's calves relaxed. 'It's a story?'

'Yes.'

Her feet relaxed, too.

'A true story.'

And then both of her legs cramped up their length.

'His height, you'll see in the picture, was mainly in his torso – coincidentally meaning that the distance from the bend of his waist to his voice box was almost exactly the same as that from the edge of the saw bed to the blade. Mm.' Louis smiled carefully at the photograph. 'He was a big man, Arthur, but terribly fond of being enclosed. He loved your little hut – called it his *burrow*. Cosy. A sweet, sweet man.'

Louis laced his fingers under his chin, pressed them to his lips and then touched her with a clear, small glance. Mary found she had reached for his hand, was reading the slight bewilderment, the delicacy in his wrist and the stock of his thumb. He pressed her palm just once and then slipped her hold.

'The thing is, Mary, when something I love or care about is taken from me, I do want to know exactly how and, if I can, why. And I do always try to make what I learn into something that will last. A story is never a person, but it can be a record of their love. It can let the dead speak. It can let me speak for them, with them.' He clapped his hands again, matronly. 'I think you should do something for me now. Change of atmosphere.'

He levered himself to his feet and dusted his knees for invisible crumbs of chocolate – Mary couldn't imagine he'd let any fall. She looked up and found him apparently on the verge of giggling, suppressing his expectation by pressing the flat of his hands against his cheeks. He looked like a monstrously inflated, glistening eight-year-old. 'Well? Will you?'

Mary felt she should stand, too. 'Will I what?'

'Hold on, I'll get it.'

And he toddled happily to a cupboard, rummaged and emerged with what appeared to be a fair-sized pottery jar with a close-fitting lid. For a surreal moment, she thought it might be a funerary urn – more evidence gathered from one of his former friends. He cradled it like a rabbit or a cat and then offered it to her.

'Ruth made it. Solid clay.' He gave it a respectful tap with his knuckle and was rewarded with an almost metallic ring. 'You can put something in it now – you have the right.'

Mary continued to stand, puzzled, oddly unwilling to take the jar.

'Oh, I am silly. Bad explanation. I apologise.' He set down the jar cautiously and walked over to scamper his hands about his desk top. 'Here we go.' Again he extended his arms, this time holding a pen and a little square of card. 'Each of us writes a prediction on a card and then we seal the cards in a jar on the first of November, *El Dia de los Muertos*, The Day of the Dead. I personally think of it as an *ofrenda,* an altar, but possibly more to the Future than the Dead. Then again, the Dead have a great deal to do with our future – balance again.

'Either way, after seven years, we open the jar and see what we said, who was wrong and who was right and then we make up the next one, carry on. It's a sort of game, or an exercise in wish-fulfilment, positive thinking, whatever you like. Joe thought it up for us – he likes to keep us entertained. And, of course, if we like, we can use the predictions as something to aim for. The rest of us put our cards in last November and then I . . . naturally, I had to take Arthur's out. It said that he would always think of me with love.'

Mary tried to begin an effort at condolence, but he shook his head. 'Do write something. For luck – yours and ours. We prefer to have seven cards. Joe does like his sevens. A great believer in numbers – number, anyway – and seven is the luckiest. Then I'll seal up the lid again and we'll open it in . . . well, nineteen-ninety-six.'

'That means I'll only have waited six years.'

'Maybe six years will be all you need.' He smiled at her. 'Now, I'll refresh the teapot and you'll think of something, won't you? Hm? Won't you?'

'I'll . . . I suppose I'll try.'

He punched one fist tenderly into its opposite palm. 'Oh, good. Just to confide for a moment, I generally predict that our education system will have declined to new levels of disrespect and disarray. I would like, just once, to be proved wrong.'

But Mary wasn't listening. She was thinking of what she would write, deciding to risk it, understanding – in a hot little burst of certainty – precisely what would be the proper thing.

Not again.

Mary almost shook her head, considered shouting and then storming out. But she couldn't think of anything insulting enough to shout. Nathan was asking questions. Again. Sitting in a T-shirt and denim-coloured overalls, a kind of anxiety braced in his arms and chest, hands smoothing the hairless crown of his head, as if he still had something there to neaten.

'What did you put?'

'What I wanted to.'

'Secrets?' His voice was softer today and he did seem calmer, but no more pleasant, no less bullying. 'That's – yes – that's allowed. If you insist. Although, in the end, it won't be helpful. Writers are compulsive disclosers, didn't you know that? No, you didn't, naturally.'

I'm not telling you, so just fuck off.

'If you're going to be unco-operative, then you can fill me in with more about where you come from. Your Uncles . . . who aren't actually uncles?'

She looked at his hands, crouched there on his table. They looked strong, potentially harmful, ingenious.

'I call them my Uncles.'

'But you told me they're not. Who are they, then? And do try to maintain some kind of style.'

'If you'd wanted me to give you . . . If you'd said you needed style, I could have written this down.'

'No.' His fingers balled, offended. 'You don't write. You don't write anything.' He was being violently precise. 'You don't put down a word until I tell you that you're ready to. No paper, no notes, no jotting, no *dear diary* last thing at night. Do you understand me? Nothing like that. Now. Your Uncles, come on.'

Fuck you.

'My Uncles are homosexual lovers. My mother left me with them when she lost interest in me, but I don't resent it because she did me a favour. My Uncles love me, they have always loved me. And they love each other. They live together because they want to and they fuck. Bryn is my mother's brother and Morgan is no relation to me at all. My mother abandoned me with a couple of poofs. Or a couple of perverts. Which word would you prefer?' She wasn't shouting, she was only being clear, but still, her last word broke open, snagged hard in her throat.

Nathan – apparently smiling, because nerves sometimes made him smile – pulled at the tufts of hair above his ears. 'I wouldn't be, I wouldn't be . . . too hard on your mother. Maybe. Not that I would know. But for your sake . . .' He hadn't looked directly at her since she'd come in and he didn't now, only let his sentence drift and stared at the sky in the window to Mary's left. She was filled with a need to slap away his grin.

She continued to not quite shout at him, 'Well? You don't want to know more secrets? You're actually satisfied? You don't want to know how the Uncles took care of me? You don't want me to tell you all the questions that everyone asked me at school? *Why don't you have a mam and dad, then?* Mm? My father died and my mother left me and my Uncles are better than both. They are my parents. They are the best men I've ever known. What do you think of that? Or don't you answer questions?'

Nathan winced, rubbed at his lips and cleared his throat. He spoke precisely, but he now also seemed tired and almost cautious. 'I do answer questions. Of course. I'm supposed to tell you anything you want to know. That's my job. I will do my job. At the times when I should.'

'Your father is dead.'

He'd made a statement, rather than a question, spoken quite tenderly, but, by now, she couldn't help snapping a reply. 'Yes. Dead.'

'I am so very sorry.' His hand pressed his throat. 'If you really want to know and you're not just being angry with me – then, I think *poof* is an unpleasant word and *pervert* would be inappropriate. In this context, I would prefer neither. I am extremely happy that you were well taken care of by your Uncles. I can, in fact . . . ah, see that they did a fine job. Actually. I am sorry that you are so angry. But probably I would be, too. And I would rather you weren't angry with me. There.'

He pinched at the bridge of his nose and then met and matched her gaze. She realised the hardest part of him was his mouth, that his eyes had a soft look, a flawed defence. He seemed to be quite careful that people shouldn't notice this.

Then Nathan blinked away again and, 'If I could ask another question, because I would like to know . . . You don't have to tell me – the predictions are intended to be confidential – but I would like to know what you put on your card. But you don't have to say.' He frowned, as if a nagging thought had struck him, and set off for his bookshelves, levered down both volumes of his dictionary and started to worry through the bible-paper pages.

Mary listened to the rustle of accumulated vocabulary, to Nathan's breathing and the new calmness of the sea. She allowed herself time to examine his living room: the rugs, the whitewash, the surprisingly meagre collection of books, the slightly more impressive number of CDs and the atmosphere of absence, of lack. Nathan had no ornaments, no clutter, no dust. He seemed to occupy a space determined to furnish no evidence. She started to search out her own word, found it – *lonely*. He had a lonely house.

I couldn't live here. I'm surprised he can. Nathan Staples – funny man.

'You wouldn't tell anyone else?'

'Hm? Oh, no. Of course not. Everything we say to each other is confidential.' He continued to ruffle through successive definitions, page after page, as if he'd forgotten the convention, the alphabetical order for words.

'I . . . This is embarrassing.'

'Don't force it. I don't mind.'

'I put – I put *Mary Lamb is a writer*.'

Nathan laughed – a sudden, hard crack of sound. He might, conceivably, have laughed because he was delighted, or pleasantly surprised – he could have been amused, or astonished, quite as easily as he could have been moved to mock. And he might have been happy, and perfectly able to tell Mary just what he meant, to erase any possible offence. But he never got the opportunity.

'Sorry, I –'

Before he could turn, Mary was leaving, walking away.

I don't have to be here. I don't need him. He doesn't know anything I want to learn. Fuck him. Fuck him. Fuck him. Fuck. Him.

His last sight of her was blurred dangerously across by his own front door as she hauled it shut and sealed him in. The impact of wood against wood flinched through him, while his thinking clattered and fell.

They both made an effort not to cry and were both not entirely successful.

*Y*ou are a fucking nutter. You are off your fucking head.

No one locked their doors on the island.

Lunatic – he'll hear you.

Open access, everywhere.

Nathan had been stern with Eckless, left him at home and set out alone in the damp, muffling dark. He'd panted into the echoing fog and stumbled and slithered his way south to the Lighthouse, knowing he would be able to walk right in, unresisted and unannounced. The journey had taken him almost an hour – falling, missing the path, cutting across to the shoreline and risking the rocks to follow it. His ears were still filled with the rush and swill of uneasy water, licking at the foot of unseen drops. He was fighting hot shivers and a sick sweat and bleeding from one ankle, although he could not remember hurting it.

Mad. You are fucking mad.

But he remained determined, creaking and tapping through the darkened hall, up the stairs and onwards.

Bath. The only fucking bath on the island and I am making it mine tonight. A nice long soak and then we'll see who's a madman. Then we'll fucking see.

Nathan lit the light and set about drawing himself a deep, hot tub of sherry-coloured water. He shed his boots, socks, coat and sweater, overalls, undershirt and – the usual delicate moment – underpants: he was never entirely happy, entirely naked. Nudity was not his state of nature.

He stood, let the steam lisp and paw all over him, breathe on the curl of scar at his back. He felt his various bodily hairs lift a little, tinily disturbed. He tried the water, its soft mouth roasting tight around his hand, and then stirred in a glob or two from his private bottle of scented blue foaming stuff. OK.

Now you get ready. You do what you should have when she came. You play **Better Late than Never** *and hope for the best.*

Nathan parted the water's surface, slipping quietly in and then gave himself a thorough going over. He cleaned between toes and under nails, scrubbed his involuntary tonsure and his remaining grey ruff of hair. Soaped his neck, arms, armpits, genitals.

No more rubbing than is strictly necessary – no need to think of **that** *just now.*

'Nathan?'

No doors locked on the island.

'Nathan?'

Joe Christopher padded in: inquisitive, dressing-gowned. Nathan sat up, slapping his hands into innocent positions at the sides of the bath and lost his soap. 'Thought you wouldn't mind.'

'Of course I don't mind. It's a bit late, though, isn't it?'

Nathan knew that, if he looked, Joe would be smiling at him with fatherly concern. He didn't look. 'I know, but I felt like it. And could I borrow your phone.'

'All right.'

Nathan let himself subside into the mildly cooling water. He didn't want to talk to Joe – talking would, he was sure, cause panic in him, unpleasantness and tears.

'While you're there, Nathan . . .'

He could hear Joe, kneeling by the bath, braced himself for the encouraging pat on his shoulder.

'I just wanted to ask.'

There it went – a manly, fatherly little thump.

'Have you seen her?'

And one brief dab of fingertips at the yellowing bruise on his neck – just to say they both knew what it meant.

'Yes.'

'How did it go?'

'I've seen her twice.'

'Was it all right?'

Nathan swallowed and closed his eyes, weakness singing up the muscles in his throat. Against his will, he reached his hand out, blind, and caught at Joe's wrist. He let himself cling, only for a reasonable moment, only for a while.

Joe let him slip with a flutter of tenderness over his palm. 'You don't make things easy, do you?'

'No.'

And fuck you and fuck you and fuck you. And thanks. Thanks for letting her come here. To me. And fuck you.

Joe left him to finish his bath and then Nathan, cleaned down to an ache, shaved and then dressed himself properly. The suit and shirt and tie and all the proper accoutrements were folded in his rucksack, ready. His father's cufflinks, even.

As if there is any point. She isn't here. She's already arrived.

But it's the thought that counts.

Sympathetic magic. Acting out your good dreams. The ones you never write.

Crap.

And he clacked downstairs in his best shoes and a haze of aftershave to find the lamp lit and the phone ready for him, but no sign of Joe. So he sat, skin still thrumming with cleanliness and the thought of Mary, of her having walked into this room, the turn of her body, the speed of her smile. He thought of how he might have welcomed her correctly, dressed the part and smiling at her, fatherly.

Nathan, you are a fucking failure, fucking nutter. Cunt.

He wanted to tell somebody, to explain. He wanted to say it all until it went away.

'Hello?' J. D.'s home number had yielded no reply, so Nathan called his mobile. 'Hello?'

'Hello, hello.' The liquid enunciation, the night-time Jack – pacy and, in several ways, high.

'Jack?'

'Yes, it is – and who's this? Or do I have to guess?'

'It's Nathan.'

'Oh, my good best friend Nathan. How are you? So wonderful to speak to you. And I'm fine, I'm very well. I'm so well it scares me. You know how I find good health alarming. What time is it?'

'I . . . about midnight, maybe later.'

'Well, well, well, well. So. Do you suppose I'm working late, or working early?'

Jack really was rolling, hardly breaking between syllables for breath. Nathan wondered for a savage moment if he should hang up and forget it, or scream something obscene, or just wait for Jack's chemical energy to drop.

'Working? You mean you're in the *office*, Jack?'

'I am in the office, yes. I do have to be, now and then – expected for earners of salaries. I told her, the secretary, I told her – I can't come in until later, I said, because I'm sick.

' *Sick?* she said.

'Sick, I said.'

He pantomimed across the night, voice tacking rapidly from a lisping, secretarial squeal to a wheezy growl.

'How do you mean – sick?

'Well, I said, I've just killed my sister and then fucked her while she was still warm – wouldn't you say that was sick?

'Hee hee.' Nathan could hear something – possibly a desk top – being slapped. 'Shit, that hurt. Never mind – it's still a laugh. I love a laugh, laughter's a lovely thing: verb: thing. The leavening in the soggy bread of life. Did you know, by the way, this whole building was designed to form a swastika, when viewed from above. That's why it's always so hard to get your bearings – because of those curly, swirly arms. I wish you were here, Nathan. You could be doing this with me. I have such a lot to do. I have *this* stuff and *that* stuff and that *really*, *really* bad stuff and possibly one snuff more of the stuff I had, just before you called. Did I say you were my friend? You are. God, you are. I wouldn't . . . where would I be without . . . I mean, where would I be. Hm?'

Nathan bided his time, while Grace ebbed. 'You *are* my friend? Nate? No one here is, not any more. That young sod, Benedict Kemmler – him, the fucker – he's doing *every*thing I used to and I'm sitting here – tragically unable to recall how I fucking did *any*thing I used to. I –'

Nathan winced against a painful impact as Jack dropped the receiver. J. D.'s voice grumbled, dodged closer, took up residence again. 'Tell me . . . you tell me . . .' But seemed to suggest he might be slumping towards blackout.

'What, Jack?'

Jack sniffed, rallied into a briefly firm awareness. 'Jesus, it's late. Why are you calling me? Something wrong?'

'Nothing. To talk. Nothing.' Nathan hesitated, unsure of what

97

would be more sad – confiding in a man who was barely maintaining his own autonomic functions, or saying goodbye and then being alone. 'That is . . . She's here, Jack. She came. She's here.'

'She's . . .?' Nathan could almost hear Jack's thinking slither past a random slew of recollections, then, 'Oh. *She*. She –'

'Mary.'

'Mary, that's right. Mary.'

'Yes.'

'Your daughter.'

'Yes.'

'Is it . . . ?'

'Awful. It's awful. I – Jack?' Nathan had gripped one arm across his chest in a try for comfort, consolation, touch. 'You listening?'

A moist cough, a scratch through stubble. 'I am. Go gently, but I am. You know I try. I do try, but I'm . . . off duty now.'

'I know, I just . . . Jack, she thinks I'm dead. Maura told her I was . . . How do I get any furth . . . Fuck.' Nathan caught his breath.

Jesus Christ, he doesn't care. Why should he. Tomorrow, the poor fuck won't even remember what I said. But I just want somebody to hear. Any fucking body. Shit.

*I could tell **her**.*

Mary.

Yeah, like fuck I could tell her. She thinks I'm dead. Bitch.

'Bitch.'

'What?'

'I said *bitch*. Maura – she's a fucking bitch. She sent me a photograph, you know?'

'I know.'

'Years ago.'

'Mm hm.'

'No warning, no note. She just sent me the picture, an old photograph – Mary on the beach, sitting on a rock with her knees up, all of her facing to the side, sun on her, breeze just lifting her hair, little summer dress I'd never seen. And I couldn't, I couldn't remember if it was taken somewhere that we'd been together, all of us, before, I just couldn't be sure. And I thought . . . I suppose, I thought it was a gesture, a reconciliation type of thing. I thought that I would see her then, see them both, maybe, that this was the first step and soon we'd be in touch. But it was funny, because, in the picture, she was so young – only a little bit older than when I'd seen her last – but, by the time I got it, she would have been ten.

'And now I keep wondering . . . maybe, in the picture, she already thinks I'm dead. And she looks . . . happy.'

'Nathan, I'm sure, I uh –'

'Now she's just . . . she looks . . . I don't . . .'

'Take it slow now. Come on, Nate.'

'She's beautiful.'

'Mm hm.'

'I mean, she's like . . .'

'Like Maura?'

Nathan gave a start. 'Yes. No, better. No, the same.' He stalled against the tension of competing loves. 'Maybe better. I mean, just wonderful, Jack. Absolutely. The best-looking nineteen-year-old I've ever seen.'

'Sssh.'

'Except maybe for one.'

'Sssh.'

'Maura.'

Nathan locked his jaw, set his lips against the back of his hand and still it came for him: despair hooping out from every bone and shattering under his skin, breath filling and shaking him, but making no sound. He could feel himself, penned in behind his skull, behind his ribs. An old pain opened again, opening him.

'Nathan. Nathan? . . . Well, it's all right, though. She's, she's there.' Jack struggled to construct a reassurance. 'Mary . . . That's a good thing. You'll be fine. I'm . . . not good at this, but I know it'll turn out, even if I don't sound convinced.

'Nathan? . . .

'I could tell you a joke, I just can't think of anything suitable. There's the one about the little girl out in the woods, but it's . . . no, it's not the thing for now. Still, don't be sad. Please. We can't both be sad old bastards.

'Nathan?'

1991

'So. There's this little girl out in the woods . . .' J. D. was ready with their mutual ritual number four, the welcoming joke.

'Is this something I shouldn't be hearing before lunch?' Nathan, out of breath after the stairs, allowed his hand to be clamped between two very smooth, dry palms. Jack tugged him gently forward, and into the office. Nathan sat. He could still feel himself reverberating with X-rays, they always made him seem light-headed, light-bodied, lit. 'Something disgusting?'

'Of course, of course. Some are disgusting by habit or mistake, some are born disgusting, I am disgusting by design. Sit down. Well? Are you?'

'I think so. The hospital's prodded at me all morning and they'll let me know. I *feel* well. I think. It doesn't do to dwell on it.'

'No indeed.' Jack leaned on the edge of his desk, grinning, waiting to be perused. 'And?'

Nathan tried his best to concentrate, to shake off the quiet shock of having been − once again − systematically stripped and gowned and tabled up and photographed down to his bones. He'd spent the last months forgetting the scrabble of powerlessness in his throat at the thought of disease, the sweet ooze of abandonment as machinery ground and clicked about him and he slid and jarred in silence on his slab.

'Nathan, you're not with me. I hope you're, that is, it's very unlikely . . .' J. D. yanked at his moustache. 'Don't be worried, old man, you've been cleared before. Every time, it must be more and more of a formality.' The corner of his mouth ticked with minor embarrassment. 'Not that it will feel that way. But any road up . . .' He smiled more cautiously. 'Look at *me*. What do you think? Of my overall effect?'

'I think lemon bow ties should be illegal, ditto for corduroy suits, especially if they're algal green.'

'*Moss* green, actually.' J. D. brushed his lapels protectively.

'No, actually, that's the green of cow shite. And I still say the moustache is a dreadful mistake. Glad the sideburns went, though.'

'Thanks for your support. Jealousy – I would just point out – is an especially ugly emotion.'

'All right, all right, let me summarise. You're on the wagon and you're chasing a new skirt.'

Jack's grin widened by a sly degree. 'Good guess. Although I have *caught* the skirt. And will be lifting it again this afternoon. I feel twenty years younger.'

'And how many years younger does *she* feel?'

'Eighteen.' Jack thumbed his moustache flat, all innocence. 'Wonderful woman, a real influence for good.'

'I don't know how you do it.'

'I make them want to save me and then they come and try. And – to be serious – the *professional* grip and performance were being lost in a rather too noticeable way. Time to clean up the act – radically reduce my available number of altered states. Because the minor evil conglomerate of which this merry house is part could well be swallowed by one of two major evil conglomerates any day now. And I have to be an asset when that happens – not a liability. I'm too old for retraining and I have an expensive life. So. Fresh start all round, Nathan. I even have a new author – a girlie. That cow up the corridor wants her, but she's mine, all mine. Not much cop now, but I think she'll be good. I am going to *nourish* her.'

'That wouldn't, by any chance, involve bodily fluids?'

'Not at all. I don't want anything to distract her, not even me. And then, if we're really counting assets . . .' his mouth ticked again, 'I always have you.'

'Why, Mr Grace, you surprise me. But perhaps I *could* come to love you, given time.'

'You know what I mean, Nate. They can't argue with your sales figures and they can't cut me loose without offending you. Can they?'

'You get very paranoid when you're dry, you know that?'

Nathan's hand was clasped again. 'You're my lifeboat, Nate. This isn't the world it used to be – they don't want characters in publishing any more, they don't want mistakes . . . fuck it, they don't even especially want grammatical sentences – they want cash and if you prove you can make it, then they want you to make more. I'd be screwed if we didn't have our little contract, our clause.' Jack blinked down at Nathan, trying not to search too hard for a guarantee.

'Jack, how long have I known you?'

'Twenty years, perhaps twenty-two.'

'We're friends. We'll be OK and I'll keep producing what I have to.'

'Blood, fear and fucking for the thinking lady. Your very own niche.'

'Yeah. But I've started to write a proper book, too.' Nathan hadn't known he would say that.

'Fuck. Really?'

An ounce or two of panic hooked in, twisted Nathan's breath ridiculously. 'Well, yes, why not? I've done it before . . .' He heard himself whine defensively, saw J. D. hear it, too.

'So did I, for that matter, a thousand years ago.' Jack checked himself, cleared his throat and found a more diplomatic tack. 'But, but naturally, you can do what you like. It would be interesting. I mean, more than that – great. Really great. Is this, is this because of . . .' Jack lapsed tactfully into silence.

'My daughter? Ahm, I have to say, yes. Yes, it is. I am that stupid, or that sad. I would like to write something she's proud of.'

'When she finds out who you are. When you tell her.'

The hook flicked back and yanked at him again. 'Well, that might not . . . I don't know . . . really, it wouldn't . . . Anyway, I'm doing it. Which doesn't make me a bad person. Or a good one, either, obviously.'

The two men winced at each other briefly, wanting to be compassionate and confiding, wanting themselves to know that they probably *could* be in another time, another place, perhaps when they'd both been drinking and it was late.

'Well, that's, that's fine. Absolutely fine.' Jack tilted himself forward to stand, his suit hanging loose.

'Christ, Jack, you've lost weight. You must have been off the sauce for a while.'

'Um . . . three weeks. And four and a half days. Look, I hate to rush you, but I do – as I've said – have somewhere to go after lunch.'

Nathan patted his arm at Jack's back, felt the gesture returned. They walked out of the office, gently dunting away at each other, providing a small and temporary cure for their separate anxieties. Nathan delivered a fondly heavy blow. 'I'd forgotten, you actually have dry hands when you're sober.'

'Hm. But they won't be dry for long this afternoon.' Jack gave Nathan his very best lucky dog look, with just the correct degree of delighted shame. 'A man has to have *some* vices, after all.'

'You have all of your own and some of mine.'

'But I pay the price – oh, a horrible price. I am by now, for example, completely morally fibreless – utterly invertebrate and decayed. Which reminds me,' he locked into his best, most breathless, story-telling voice, 'this girl's in the woods and it's night-time.'

'I don't want to hear this.'

'Sssh. Indulge me. Little girl and she's there with a pervert and she says to the pervert, *It's very dark in here, I'm really scared –*'

'And the pervert says, **You're** *scared? – I've got to walk home alone.*'

Jack paused, anticipating, and then sputtered with disappointment. 'I'd already told you?'

'I already knew.'

'Well, all I can say in that case, Nate, is that you are really fucking sick.'

Mary was trying hard not to like Nathan's dog. She wasn't managing. This was the fifth day she'd been left in charge of Eckless and they were getting on dreadfully well. They'd met before – often – but never without his master being there. She would trudge up to Nathan's house to be shouted at, or wheedled, or badgered and then sent away again to not write and Eckless would mainly lie in his basket, perhaps lifting an eyelid or an ear. Once or twice he had snuffed and whimpered in his sleep, always producing a moment of softness in Nathan: a hot, little, tender smile that Mary found surprising. She couldn't entirely believe that Nathan had any of the more humane emotions.

But she couldn't deny he'd left a deep impression on his dog – without him, the beast was distraught. Every time they went out for a walk, he tugged and begged to visit Nathan's place: to clatter in and scurry through the rooms, persistently hopeful that Nathan would be there. She hated to see him disappointed, but, of course, he always was.

'Three more days. Then you'll be fine. I promise. He'll be back. So one of us will be happy.' Within hours of Eckless's arrival, she had lapsed into the small stupidity of talking to a dog and then expecting it to understand. Rapidly, their one-way conversations had become entirely comfortable.

'Why you want him back, I don't bloody know. He might be good at dogs, but he's not good at people.' Eckless trotted accurately beside her, offering no opinion, making an effort to enjoy the day. It was a good one: the sea morsing sunlight across the length and depth of the shockingly blue horizon, a water-cooled breeze to make the heat more bearable.

Mary clambered down to the sand of Nathan's bay – the dog had brought her and she liked it, the way it cupped round her, its privacy.

But she tried not to get too fond of it here. She guessed that, once Nathan was back, this privacy would be made his alone again.

She settled into throwing pebbles and sticks and kelp stems to keep Eckless racing and flirting with the tide until his tongue flagged out and he started wheezing. He finally collapsed, as usual, in the shade of her body. Mary sat and tried to write her letters, while he sighed in the more than human way that only dogs can.

Letters are allowed. He can't fucking stop me writing them.

Technically, Mary was – like each of the other islanders – allowed to use the radio telephone once a week. Or she could have one crack at Joe Christopher's phone and hope the old, undersea cable wasn't feeling too skittish that day. In reality, calling was worse than useless. She could never entirely prepare herself for the shock of hearing the Uncles' voices and of realising how far her memory could drift her away from the proper music of their conversations in even a few days. And neither Bryn nor Morgan had ever found themselves entirely comfortable with telephones.

'We're too old.'

'For what, Bryn?'

'For speaking to people we can't see. We're not adaptable.'

She'd heard Morgan in the background adding his own loud murmur, 'Speak for yourself.'

'Well . . .' She'd struggled to avoid their established gauntlet of questions, but still felt herself begin them. 'You're well?'

'Yes, yes. Both of us. You?'

'Yes. And I'm working away.' *Except that's a lie and I'm not, am I? I'm doing bugger all. I'm a dog-sitter. That's all Nathan thinks I'm good for.*

'That's great. You show them.'

Tell him. Tell you want to come home. Admit it. 'Bryn . . . Bryn, if I came back –'

'For another little visit? Yes, lovely, we'd like that. Morgan wants to speak to you now. He's kicking me.'

She'd listened to the Uncles' receiver being clumped from hand to hand and closed her eyes to see the hallway they were standing in. For a moment she could smell it: blankets, cooking steam, the tang of coal smoke, layer upon layer of passing aftershave. Bryn always handed on to Morgan, just when she'd reached the point of wanting to really talk. He always seemed to break the moment.

Now you're being paranoid.

Except that it does seem that way.

I can't blame him, really. Even if I burst into tears, what can he do about it, so far away?

'Mary?'

'Morgan. Yes. How's the breathing?'

'Still doing it, yes. Here, you remember Dilwyn from Ianetta's?'

*Of course I remember, I've only been gone eight months – nine. Shit, nine months. That's nearly a year and what have I done? Read whatever books he's told me to, read them **aloud** whenever he's told me to and talked and talked and talked about myself. He knows more about me than I do. I don't even know why I'm here.*

'Mary?'

'Yes, I remember Dilwyn, of course I do. Mad, isn't he?'

'That's the one. Well, he's filled the caff up with pictures now – his own pictures – bloody horrible stuff. It's all made out of watch parts and plaster and pieces of broken glass. Says it's an art gallery and we can buy them if we like.'

Bryn added, shouting gently, 'While they're cheap.'

'Mary, love, this must be costing you a fortune.'

'No, I've told you, they pay for it.'

'Oh, all right, then. So . . .' Morgan had subsided into silence once again, dumbfounded by the idea of unlimited, gratis conversation. 'You're well, then?'

'Yes. Working away.'

'That's good. That's good. We're well.'

'Yes.'

'Good.'

And they'd jolted into their customary goodbyes, no better informed than when they'd started.

So letters are best.

You would like it here, in the bay. The tide is turning and front after front of water is pushing in. The sea keeps opening, then folding shut in furls and feathers of white. And I'm brown, very brown. I look like a completely different person, healthier I suppose. Not that I wasn't healthy. My palms are pale, and in between my fingers, and the soles of my feet.

She paused, trying to remember she was writing to Bryn and Morgan rather than Jonno. So wouldn't mention her pale shoulders, breasts and that she was not the kind of person to sunbathe naked, or anything like it – that the secrets of herself were covered. Unless, in other times and places, she wanted them otherwise.

Of course, Jonno was harder to write to, anyway. He didn't reply to her any more. He'd said there was no point. At least, he'd written there was no point and when Mary had tried to phone him his mother had answered and told her to stop playing games. But Mary wasn't playing, never had been. So she still wrote to him, *for* him, and for the Uncles, too – words that were as clear as she could make them, uninterrupted, hers. She tried to make a contact out of ink and paper and the slightest impression of summer sweat, she gave them the small and important things, the shapes of emotion and the absence of fear that a person can find and then trap in their own voice, in their own mind and then wish to transcribe. She had begun to make meanings and patterns and sequences that she liked, that she wanted to give to the people she cared about. She wanted to speak out loud but inside other people: inside, the loudest place of all.

Yesterday, I lay in the grass above the sand cave. Everything shone. Down on my stomach, eyes level with the blades, it seemed that colour was inside the grass, sparking out, very young and golden. It is much easier to see here, perhaps because the sky is so limitless and bright. I wish you could come. I would show you all the parts of the island I enjoy, or that I'm enjoying for you. I want you to be here. I miss you.

'**Y**ou *what?*'

Although Nathan knew Jack had not been drinking, he gave every appearance of being drunk – slower, louder, vocally incautious. 'Hm?' Then again, Nathan *had* been drinking, so he might not be ideally positioned to judge.

'I said, I said –' Jack extended a syrupy-slow mock punch to Nathan's shoulder. '*You what?* As in, what did you say?'

'I know, I was simply hesitating. I feel I'm about to be mocked.'

'Not at all. You are my friend. I do not mock my friends. No indeed.'

'I said I miss her.'

'You are a dirty old fucker.' Jack smiled blithely.

'Cunt. I miss my *daughter.*'

'I rest my case.'

'Listen . . .' Nathan put down his umpteen-and-third whisky, vaguely feeling that he had, in some way, been bewitched into this liver-and-lights abuse on J. D.'s behalf. He had definitely been swindled somehow, in a manner he was, as yet, unable to identify. 'Listen . . .' Fury rose and fell in him like stale water. 'There is nothing like that going on. I just . . . I miss her. She's . . . I've been . . . every day she comes and talks to me, because that's the way I'm teaching her. She tells me about herself, her life –'

'Her mother?'

'No! Fuck it.' Having managed to top the level of Home Counties' braying in the bar, he faltered, tried to smile at J. D.'s flinch of nerves. 'No. I keep away from that – I've never really asked about her mother. But I have got used to . . . to Mary being there. I hear her, I mean, her voice still echoes about, even after she's left. When I'm out walking, when I'm with the dog, or asleep, sometimes, I think with her pronunciations, the print of her mouth. *She's* the one

111

who's meant to be learning how she says things, not *me*.

'Shit. Shit, shit, shit.' A crest of melancholy broke over him, trickled down nastily. 'I just like being with her, Jack. I should have *been* with her. All this time. All this fucking time. I'm owed fifteen years of her. I'm fucking owed it.

'And Maura gave her away. She bloody . . . she dumped Mary with her brother and his lover and that was it. Done. Brought up by *uncles*, for Christ's sake. They did fine with her, but *uncles* . . .? When she could have had a *father*. When she *did have* a father . . .'

J. D. slithered down from his stool and wrapped Nathan in a damp hug. J. D. was back to normal, sweating a touch or two more than the average. Nathan allowed himself to be squeezed at, to have his head taken in – he noticed – moderately tremulous hands. Even sober, Jack couldn't keep quite dry and steady for too long.

And Nathan squeezed and held and handshook back while want sliced in his stomach, because he *did* want – because he was full of want – because the touch of any live, whole body was so close to what he needed, so near to a sadly effective consolation. Because he wanted to hold his daughter: each of them knowing they were each other's, loving and beloved. Because he wanted to hold his wife, to resurrect his kisses for her, to find himself at home again with a skin more than his own to take for granted, to take for a miracle and for everything he could want. He wanted what he wanted and anything else was not enough, was just a wholly unnecessary *memento mori*. But, being forsaken by all others, he clung to Jack.

'Nate? I do wish I could stay, but I've only got half an hour to get to Chelsea.' Jack was playing his strongest persona: the supportive editor: quiet, focused, gently optimistic, and currently easing himself politely from Nathan's grip. 'You'll be . . . It'll all work . . .' Jack folded his arms, clipping away inappropriate phrases, before he could finish them, struggling for something opposite, helpfully distracting. 'It was a nice lunch. Really.' He coughed, rolled his eyes a fraction, so that Nathan might forgive his actual *wording* and concentrate on the more general idea of stout, brotherly, fortifying intentions. 'Good to see you. You do – oddly – look well. Sea air and sunshine, hm? And, um, this was nice, a nice afternoon. I do like to check that booze is still available. Even if I don't have any, the idea of continuing access calms me, I find.' He scooped Nathan's hand up from the bar top, held it firm, 'Have to go,' then set it down again.

An unexpected rush of bitterness smoked and coiled in Nathan's lung, made him spit out, before he could stop, 'You'll fuck her.'

'I'll . . .?' Jack's eyes narrowed for a wary instant. 'Yes.'

'You'll fuck her. Of course, you'll fuck her.' Nathan dug in, now perversely eager to stoke up his self-disgust, 'So you make sure and fuck her right. For me. Hm? Will you? For me,' grabbing Jack's elbow and clinging, quite the professional lush. 'Have her all ways. Ride her, do her, whatever it takes. Make her – just make her do . . .' He couldn't think quickly enough of just what a woman *might* be made to do. 'Make her . . .' Fuck. He was being so stupid – annoying his friend, being a shit, 'Make her . . . *do things.*' His voice snapped into a final, thin, appropriately adolescent croak. Even if he wasn't really a shit at heart, he sounded like one.

Nathan didn't want to look at Jack. He had no desire to know how much offence he'd caused. He'd noticed lately that he'd developed quite a knack for turning sympathy into disgust – now he'd probably managed to turn even Jack's stomach.

Nathan realised he'd quite like to cry now, immediately.

'Nate,' Jack was rubbing at his neck, frowning with concern, but still shamingly affable, calm – this was not, after all, an unfamiliar situation. He'd been here before: sometimes the offender, sometimes the offended – sometimes with Nathan, more often without. 'Nate, what I do with her and how will be entirely and precisely my own affair. But you,' he prodded Nathan's shoulder, 'in my opinion you should go back to the island, go back to Mary. And tell her who you are, before it all gets too late and really *difficult.* If you don't mind my saying.'

'No, I don't mind. Not at all, sorry – I mean, thanks. I mean, sorry. I'm going.' His voice losing its footing, falling beyond his reach. 'I'm going tomorrow.'

'Good. And lighten up on the poor girl. All right, old man? If I'm not being presumptuous, I might suggest you take a wise old editor's advice and *leave her alone.* Writers need leaving alone. Let them find out who they are and what they have to say and how they say it and let them be. Leave her alone – with your confidence. Then she'll work like an angel, she'll break her heart for you.'

'Broke mine already.'

'Shut the fuck up and go home.'

Shut the fuck up and go home.
Shut the furcup and gome.
Shuff the fuff, shuffthefuff, shuff.
Shu the. **Shut** *the. Ach God, man. Get a grip.*

The London Underground is never a good idea for the terribly pissed. Nathan had slithered down into the usual clammy summertime shove and fumble at Piccadilly Circus. He had, initially, felt not entirely out of control. After almost a week in the city, his island pace had speeded, his country nervousness had retired, he was – he'd thought – once again, resilient.

So the suddenly hideous progress of the escalator had only scared him for an instant or two. Part of him was now glad to be carried irresistibly forward by a petulant crush of tourists and tourist-loathers and plunged into the whole huge gauntlet of mouse-haunted tunnels and accidents waiting to pounce: death by suffocation in a panicked crowd, death by frying on the high-voltage rail, death by mincing and twisting under train wheels, death by knifing, clubbing, fucking or other molestation at the flailing hands of wandering lunatics, death by busking . . . No, actually, he wasn't glad, he was losing it.

I don't even **get** *claustrophobia – this is sodding ridiculous. I am a capable, rational adult. Also I am rat-arsed and rubbered and fucked. But I am a capable, rational adult who is rat-arsed and rubbered and fucked and this should count for something, surely?*

His voice was slurring in his head, mislaying his intentions.

Shit. I can't feel my leg – some bastard has done something to my leg.

As the doors of his train dragged shut, vacuum-packing him in with Lord knew who, hysteria groped and sweated in every joint.

BREATHE. This is . . . this is . . . BREATHE. I won't die. No. BREATHE. I won't die. BREATHE.

Fat bastards, there are so many **fat bastards** *in England. In this train, never mind England. In here with me – fat, English bastards, stopping me breathing. I ONLY HAVE ONE LUNG, YOU KNOW, AND RIGHT NOW I CANNOT FUCKING BREATHE.*

BREATHE.

Bastards.

BREATHE.

He thudded out on to the platform at Green Park, buttered all over in free-floating horrors and the knowledge that he was audibly sweating whisky reek. But at least both his legs were whole, if not completely working – no one had done them damage except possibly the much-esteemed Mr Jack Daniel.

Good, old Mr Jack. Mmmm hmmm.

Some people, he now found, had a kind of magnetism, a suction that would drag him, wavering, towards them. Ricocheting slowly, slowly along an especially elongated warren, tiled in screaming white, he couldn't stop himself seeing, trotting towards him, healthy and content, a father. A father, happily loaded with a baby in a backpack, a baby in one of those little infant-containing haversacks, securely fastened and safely reinforced. A father, giddied-up by the soft and rhythmic sway of his sleeping child's feet. A father who looked at Nathan and made him know, all over again, that he was a nothing, a no-balls loser, a man who was not a father in any way.

Shut up. *Enough. Enough, you cunting . . . you . . . you just **leave me alone***.

The father met Nathan's eyes, half-smiling, almost seductively contemptuous.

*Yeah, you've got it a-a-a-a-ll now. See trying to keep it? See **possession** – you'll fucking learn about that. And you don't even know what you've got, do you? Do you – you stupid prick? English prick, bastard.*

Between Green Park and Pimlico, Nathan swam up the aisle for a seat, dropped into it like the heavy and very suspicious package he knew himself to be.

Shit. I can't read the adverts. Fucking eyes won't do this business. Don't read the adverts, then you just have to look at the people, the eyes. Look at the eyes, and the people will know that you hate them, they'll turn, they'll rip you to liquid and buttons before you can scream. Think of you, painted against the inside of the windows, pale little finger stumps, swirling a clear space for the last look out through your own gore.

He sponged his forehead with cautious inaccuracy. His extremities had passed beyond the point of even fundamental usefulness. He could only shut his eyes for a little and buckle his arms woodenly round his chest and hope that he'd make it up and out and into daylight again at any point today. Meanwhile, alcohol had prised up his memory's cruellest lids like a reckless chisel end and he sat, rocked by sideways motion and bewilderment, knowing he was now at the mercy of himself, of his own most acidic recollections.

*We were on the Underground, here. I put my hand over hers while we sat and she never stopped me. Jesus, Jesus, Jesus, down all that side of me, it was like sunburn, I could just **feel** her there, shining into me, and we were bobbing and rubbing and everything together with the train taking corners and nice wee accelerations and stops and I couldn't bear to turn, even just glance at her in case she wasn't looking dead happy, like I was looking dead happy – in my reflection, I could see – big mad grin, I had. Two Celts together, wanting to be together, on a subtly, subtly alien train. There I was with my very own '45 Rising: fucking splendidly impatient against an unforgiving button fly. That was all it took to lift me, to set my brain baying down to my balls – the roundness of her knuckles against mine. I told her, 'You shouldn't be on that side, it's dangerous. On that side, you're right against my hungry arm. I have a hungry arm. It likes to hold things, people. It would like to hold you.' Throttled that last bit, swallowed it before it was out, almost, but she still kissed me, she still did that, she still did.*

The platform at Victoria hauled past him clumsily and Maura's absence laced between his fingers and his hips, like razor blades and wonder, delighting him open to the bone.

Bitch. She's still a bitch, though. Bitch.

But I do still . . . I do still . . .

Bitch.

A sour heat fluttered in his chest. He coughed. A spasm of warning arced behind his eyes.

*No. I am not going to. Not when I'm like this. I know better. I do know better. I absolutely will not think about **that**.*

But it was too late – he couldn't help coughing again experimentally. A dark fumble seemed to rise in a treacly bubble under his ribs and then thicken below his throat, threatening.

*This is crap, this is bollocks, this is bad imagination. When there was **really** something wrong, I didn't feel it. Well, I did **feel** it, but not that way. **Really** something wrong – your body tries to tell you . . .*

No. This is shite.

Even so, the awful recitation bucked into life.

There is nothing wrong. If you think there is something wrong, then you will worry. You already worry about Maura, about Mary, about life, because all of them are something wrong, but you can't think they are wrong things, *because you will worry. If you worry, you get cancer. If you worry about getting cancer, you get cancer. If you worry about worrying, you get cancer. If you worry about **having** cancer because of worrying you'll **get** cancer, then you really **shouldn't worry** because, in fact, you'll **know. You do have cancer – you worried until you made it come back.***

So before it's too fucking late, you will think and believe there is nothing wrong.

I can feel it, though, I can feel it. It's in there. I know.

Nathan understood his anxiety was dripping through him, curdling his only lung into alien solidity, death by drowning.

I can feel.

Nathan shut his eyes and breathed gently. He monitored each press and sag of air, the turning of his tides, and discovered no more than smooth normality.

*This is how far you've come, then. Waiting for your breath to stop exactly the way you used to when you were five – lying in bed and **listening** to yourself. Any self-respecting little bastard would have been reading bad things under the covers, eating sweeties, feeling his dick. But you. Not sodding you.*

His hands were clawed up, twitching, Fight or Flight, oozing out all over them. Opposite, a man in an eager business suit was reading a sheaf of photocopied sheets, headed 'Strategy is an Adventure!'

From the look of him it would be, poor fuck. At long last – a sad cunt who is definitely sadder than me.

Having shuffled back along the Embankment against a gritty wind, Nathan unlocked his old flat in the Square. It never had been very welcoming, but now it was positively brusque. Over the months, his cleaning person had slowly re-arranged what belongings he'd left to suit her taste. He didn't live here any more.

But, with a vaguely larcenous thrill, he could take a shower here and watch his first television in months here and then consider rummaging round here to find something edible and possibly also something intoxicating because he did not in any way wish to be hungover until tomorrow morning, thanks a lot.

So Nathan lay on his sofa, wrapped in a clammy towel and growled abuse at news of the incoming Citizens' Charter, vaguely defining civic joys long gone. And he stared at shots of burning oil wells, left over from a grubby little war: photogenically and nastily conducted while he'd been gone. Then he remote-controlled the lot of it to the Land of Gettofuck and drank himself completely cretinous.

Shit.

A wind tumbled uneasily across his windows, trying to feel its way out of the Square. He couldn't find his breath. Swallowing, already choking, choked. Dread with its fist in his throat, twisting, burning.

Nathan fought to sit up against a dark that seemed to be squatting on his shoulders.

Shit.

He stood, finally managing a wheezy inhalation, another, another, until his eyes teared over with the pain and he remembered to reverse the process, stop himself choking all over again with spit and fear and speeding air.

When he stumbled forward, a low invisible something bit him across both legs and he fell to his carpet, still panting and now letting his fingers dabble and panic against his shins, where the first unmistakably sticky welling of blood was under way.

*Jesus **shit**.*

He crawled and tumbled to his doorway and the light switch and blinked back at his traitorous room. Across the fawn carpet –

*These fucking places – always the white carpets, the cream carpets, the carpets designed for people who never fucking touch the ground. I should have changed it, changed it as soon as I fucking moved in, changed it to fucking **black**. Shit.*

*Shit, I thought I was dying, I thought I was **dying** – sleep on your back when you're rubbered, serve you right, I thought that was fucking it.*

Across the fawn carpet were bloody drag marks, suggesting a hideous murder and body theft. These led directly to his legs – smeary with gore from deeply and generously bleeding gouges: one taken out just beneath each knee. Along an edge of his glass-topped coffee table –

*The fucker, the cunt, the Filipino Psychofuckingpath – she is a cleaning woman, not a fucking interior bastard designer – my table never used to be **there**. Why in God's name put it **there** and think I'll **remember**?*

Along one edge of his glass-topped coffee table – a table quite impossible to see in the dark – was an impressive smear of Nathan's

118

blood and even, he thought, a clump or two of his substance.

Great. Sodding, fucking great.

The blood he decided to leave because he was a novelist not a cleaner and a little scare of haemoglobin left behind might be just the thing to teach someone who *was* a cleaner to stick to their duties and no more.

It was one in the morning, he noticed – soon be daylight again. Nathan hated the openness, the sheer exposure of summer days. Emptiness always seemed far more empty when it was well lit.

He showered again, legs pulsing impressively with affronted pain and managing to bleed through four Elastoplasts. Hugging himself in a fresh towel, he plodded damply off to sit on the edge of his bed – that was, at least, still where it should be. He lay back, feet still on the floor, and allowed a dizzy rush of apprehension to paw at him: here were his shattered family, his flagging body, his failing nerve, the fatal transformation of his lung; here, at last, and after all prevarication, was his guaranteed death. He shuddered under it, the warmth of his cosy brain attempting to writhe away from the cold and the blank, the thought of himself as not himself, as voiceless, as not.

Then Mr Jack stepped in. The merciful dregs of inebriation back-washed home with just enough insanity to suggest his best available distraction – self-abuse.

It would be risky, he realised that. He was quite unhinged enough to think of what he shouldn't, of Maura, really Maura, the best ways she used to be – pink, pink nipples, sugar-mouse nipples, cunt hair like tawny, downy, auburny, sphagnummy kind of stuff that could get so wet, so fast – think of it, think of it, think – of pulling down her knickers and a line, a thread of thick, bright, oystery, sex-lubricating, fucking desire would just *be there*, hanging from her quim for nobody but Nathan to lap all up and gather away and suck out more of until he didn't die and didn't think of dying, only ran right into her, right into her, right into her, right into her, right home.

Maura. Maura. Please.

He shivered, chilled, shrank and the weight of the unobtainable rushed in at him from every side – Maura, completely wanted and completely out of reach. She'd made him admit it again, all to no purpose. A slow tear ran from his left eye back along his temple and dropped coldly into his ear. He ought to get up.

Jesus.

Standing, vaguely giddy, his body still anxious for a dream of touch, he examined his bed. His flat was fast becoming a forensic paradise.

'First, Inspector, the bloody living room, where he struggled to open his veins with a sharpened table. Next the spattered bathroom where he soaped himself into a frenzy, teasing at his body hair with multiple adhesive dressings. And finally the bedroom – the dark blue duvet cover particularly frank in its display of air-dried jism. Here the first shot, here the second, here the third, and here the characteristic smearing left by hand and knob-end wiping. Strange that he saw no reason to cover his tracks.'

But why the fuck should I? This is all I've got. The least a man can do is leave his mark.

Jesus, what a mess.

Tired, aching, stupefied with solitude and toxins, he could no longer dodge that sleek and dogged, inoperable thought.

I don't want to be this way. Dear God, don't let me have to keep on being this way. Please. I'll do anything. If you'll only tell me what.

There came, as he'd expected, no particular revelation.

Eckless was beside himself, incandescent with happiness, muzzle resting firmly on Nathan's knee, the better to gently damp through his trouser leg. Although his dog didn't usually come to the Sunday Lunch, Nathan hadn't the heart to leave him behind today. Eckless, in return, was being even more than usually well behaved. He neither snuffed, nor groaned when he caught the scent of meat, didn't make a sound at any time, in fact – he seemed perfectly contented with leaning against Nathan and feeling and understanding that he was back.

Mary passed Nathan the gravy, 'You were missed,' and watched him slop it right over the edge of his plate.

'Missed? I was?'

'Yes, missed. By the dog. Last night he hardly slept, kept waking up with his ears pricked and his little tail wagging and then he'd realise he'd just been dreaming – I suppose of you – and then he would come and bother me.'

'Oh, right. The dog.' Nathan mopped his gravy off the table with his napkin before working out this would make it too wet to put back on his lap. He seemed nervous to Mary, and tired. 'He doesn't have a little tail. It's quite in proportion to his body length.'

She'd wondered how long it would take him to find fault: even if he had *seemed* different when he got back, more pleasant, more comfortable company. As far as she could tell, he'd been openly, simply delighted when Eckless sprinted to him and bounced up to paw and whine and lick and nuzzle at him in a tense, canine delirium of affection and relief.

Perhaps because he'd been so much surrounded with dog, Nathan had seemed positively human then, had even given her a light, darting hug. Eckless had pushed Nathan's back and jolted him closer to Mary for a moment while they were still embraced, but Nathan hadn't scolded, had simply smiled and then turned to settle the beast, no harm done. Still, she should have known it wouldn't last: Nathan being good-tempered. He wasn't the good-tempered sort.

'Unless you meant, by *little tail,* to imply that he was vulnerable, smaller than us, smaller than his own emotions, and an animal for which you have affection – affection you wish us to share. You would, of course, have been right, if you'd used the diminutive for those reasons.'

'Then I was right.'

And fuck you, Nathan. She forked at her carrots with displaced resentment. *I was trying my best to be nice. I actually sat next to you, even though you never really speak to me when I do. Unless it's to get on my case. Not that we can't all play* **that** *game.*

'When you say *we*, is that the royal *we?*'

'Hm?' Nathan was manfully trying to subdue a piece of beef – it was proving to be a ferocious, gristly mouthful: too big to swallow whole and too resilient to bite.

'Your use of *we* – how did you intend me to understand it?'

Nathan stared straight ahead, eyes watering, a queasy shiver in his throat. 'Hmnn?' Mary watched him, the shift of muscle in his patchily shaved jaw, the sinews of his neck that could stiffen so quickly, roping in against emotions she could never quite identify: presumably loathing, irritation, dislike.

And yet, although she found this surprising, she did seem to feel, watching perspiration gather quietly above his eyes, that the island was rather better when he was around. Something about the place seemed less solid when he wasn't here. Not necessarily less pleasant, but definitely less solid. She watched the side of his face and tried to consider how he might actually, really *be*, looking out from that particular, cantankerous, *Nathan* viewpoint.

He knows I'm looking at him and doesn't like it – doesn't like it at all. Shame that I'm not going to stop, then.

It's his own fault – he's always going on at me to sharpen up my powers of observation. So, why not sharpen them on him?

'Now then, you two . . .' Joe, careful as ever of his ill-assorted flock, had decided an intervention was required. 'This is *Sunday*, this is *the Lunch*. We don't want you coming to blows.'

Grateful for the brief distraction, Nathan relieved his soft palate of its burden, quickly depositing on the side of his plate what appeared to be a well-masticated length of especially hairy, cow-flavoured twine.

Mary, for her part, chose to concentrate on her broccoli, aware that Joe was still studying her closely.

Giving me a bit of my own medicine – it's just like him.

He was making her feel guilty, as he often did. Something about his manner, his *shine*, seemed always to render her inadequate or vaguely ashamed.

'Mary?' Rather than force her to ignore him for any longer, Joe called to her – gentle, friendly, something smoky, or floury, about his voice which made it very easy to listen to and, therefore, very effective when it decided to serve up even the gentlest reproach. After all, it seemed to imply, how could she *not* want to face him and chat with him honestly: how could she manage to be so intimidated by his patent goodness when goodness was such a good thing: how could she still believe, however discreetly, that he was mad?

'Mary?'

She did what he wanted: lifted her head and met his eye. He rewarded her with one of his pristine, grandfatherly smiles.

'Ah, there you are. Lost in thought, were you?'

'I, um. Yes.'

'Not working too hard? Nathan pushing you?'

'No.' She hadn't intended to snap that, but had managed to, all the same. Nathan shifted slightly beside her and coughed, while she made a point of repeating, 'No. He's not.'

No, Nathan isn't pushing me. He isn't anywhere bloody near me, would probably rather I never ever wrote a word. I would say he'd be pleased if I went back to Capel Gofeg and left him alone.

'Well, that's all right, then.'

'She's doing very well.' Nathan cleared his throat again and prodded the last of his beef despondently. 'Actually . . . Very well indeed . . . If you asked me . . . That would be what I would say.'

Mary tried not to look as utterly astonished as she felt. *Very well indeed?* She also made an effort not to be pleased, but couldn't avoid it, couldn't avoid the hot, electric inrush of something so fundamentally, privately, thoroughly satisfying that it made her blush. That Nathan, of all people, could make this change in her, seemed almost offensive.

God, Mary Lamb, you're perverse. The opinion that's most indifferent has to be the only one that you respect.

*Although I suppose it makes a kind of sense. If I'm ever allowed to write anything again and Nathan reads and actually **likes** it . . . Well, I'd know it was good, then, wouldn't I?*

'Yes.' Nathan frowned at her briefly, his eyes making their usual scramble to avoid hers, after a small touching, a second's lock. 'Yes, that's what I would say.'

Beyond Mary and Nathan, the Lunch continued, each of the seven guests establishing and then breaking the usual pools and bubbles of concentration, overhearings dominoing from one conversation to the next while cooling vegetables passed like Chinese whispers – never entirely coherent or attractive by the time they'd reached the circuit's end.

'Now, the Seven Brothers. You know about the Seven Brothers?' Mary realised that Louis, tucked beside her on the left, had probably been talking to her for some time. He seemed to have given himself the task of translating the island for her, unveiling all its little histories and dialects.

'Ahm . . .' She blinked her mind into some kind of focus. 'The Seven Brothers – they're the rocks across from Nathan's bay.'

'Yes, excellent. That's them.' Louis speared his ninth, tenth and eleventh potatoes, making sure they were thoroughly glazed with butter first. 'They're a beautiful case of meaning deepening through time. There have been seven rocks for goodness knows how long, of course. But, during different periods, they have been used to define entirely different things. At one point they were the Seith Marchawg, the Seven Riders of the Mabinogion, left behind to steward Britain when the men of the Island of the Mighty sailed to Ireland. This means they all have names: Cradawg, Hefeydd the Tall, Unig Strong-shoulder, Iddig, Ffodor, Wlch Bone-Lip and Llashar.'

Mary nodded and reached to take another potato herself – not to eat, just to fiddle with and pass the time.

It's not that he isn't a nice man: I think he's lovely. But once he gets the bit between his teeth, he doesn't stop. It was the same with Morgan and plumbing – nothing would please him more than a well-turned-out public convenience. Nothing except describing it endlessly.

She noticed she was thinking of Morgan in the past tense and

124

stopped herself. He was still there, still back in Gofeg with Bryn, and his obsessions which, at this distance, seemed almost completely lovable. She took a moment to hope that Morgan – present tense – was currently delivering an encomium on washers. She hoped he was well.

'Of course, later, the seven rocks are the seven deadly sins, cast out of the island by Joseph of Arimathea and petrified as a memorial. That would mean that we are living on an island without sin. Quite a consideration. The Seven *Brothers* – well, I suppose they would be much the same thing – a memorial to sin.

'A planted Tudor lord sacked and burned the monastery that was said to have been founded on this island. Then he drove off the monks and the other islanders and had his men row all of his very finest horses out here to graze. He believed that his horses were far more intelligent and worthwhile than any of the common run of people. And the island was to be a place for his fine mares and stallions to breed even finer stock, safe from sabotage and theft.

'But all did not go well here. The horses turned barren and sick and none of the lord's servants could, or perhaps would, do anything to cure them. Finally, the lord sent his youngest son to tend the horses, but before he could reach the island a thick, white mist rose up and hid him from sight. By nightfall, the mist had cleared as suddenly as it came and the son's boat had drifted back into harbour, carrying all his supplies and even the clothes he had been wearing when he set out, but there was never any sign of him alive again and his body was never found.

'Each day the lord would send another son and each night the boat would be back in Ancw, fully loaded, and the son would be gone. In the end, of course, he had sent all seven of his sons and lost each one. So he had to row out to the island himself.'

'Did he disappear, too?'

'Oh no – although he wanted to, so that he could be wherever his children had gone – he'd become rather softer natured, by this time – it was the shock. But no, he didn't get his wish. He went to the island quite safely and then killed every one of his horses with his bare hands, each animal coming to him with love, lying down and offering him its neck. Then the lord came back ashore, went to his great house and hanged himself.

'The night he died, cries were heard out at sea, like the noises made by injured birds, and there was a great sound of waves breaking, although the sea was still. In the morning, seven rocks had grown out of the waters beside the island and were named for the seven dead brothers, killed by their father's pride.

'Later, someone rowed out to the island and took away the horses' bones and made them into flutes. They had a beautiful tone, but would only play sad tunes.' He bowed his head for a moment, then bobbed it up again with a buttery smile, something about him, as usual, startlingly boyish.

'Which, apart from anything else, is why this is called Foal Island. As a memorial to a great injustice, the island gave up its old name and took on a new one – as a reminder of the foals that were never born and of the impossibility of creation without love. And whether this is factually true, in any way –'

'Doesn't matter.'

He beamed at her. 'Absolutely, absolutely. What matters is that this is how people remember what is important, this is where they are themselves, where they keep what has been stolen, where their words are their own. We always have the stories we make of ourselves, of our topography, our music. That kind of voice, the true kind, will never die entirely, even if it's turned to stone.' He delicately engulfed a new potato and considered her. 'You look sad, dear. Are you?'

'Oh. Well . . .'

'The Lunch makes me homesick. Even though this is all the home I've had for years. It is possible to pine for a time, a condition, as much as a place. Wouldn't you say? Missing your Uncles?'

She was used to the way he asked questions – his curiosity inoffensive, his young eyes disarming. But, even so, when she told him, 'Yes, I think I am,' she hadn't anticipated how she would feel to hear herself being quite so accurate. She was used to the mild evasions, the polite dishonesties, the average fog of the average conversation. People like Louis, people who told the truth and wanted it – got it – back, they were not comfortable. Between Nathan's demands for specificity and Louis's confidence in, if not reverence for, words, she could see her verbal life fast deteriorating into a chain of increasingly uncomfortable blurts.

Or perhaps just a vow of silence.

126

'And . . . um . . . if you don't mind my asking . . .' Louis hadn't finished, wanted more. 'Jonathan? You miss him, too.'

'No.' Mary watched Louis start to frown. 'No, I'm not missing him. There's no point. It seems rather clear that he isn't missing me.'

Louis allowed himself an infinitesimal shake of his head. He believed in balance and many forms of generosity and also believed that no one could love without being loved back. Mary thought this was wishful thinking and wished she could think it, too.

Joe, quite naturally, had his own opinions about love – ones he wasn't sharing over lunch. Instead he sat exactly as he liked to, balanced in limbs and breath, snug between Louis and Richard, at a table with his company of choice but being, in his heart, elsewhere.

He was imagining the desert at evening and walking out and meeting its first kiss: the dissipating rush, the closing tenderness of mineral heat. He was remembering the scent of size, of a scale so monstrous it could strike him free of his personality, made him naked to his blood: the scent of time, or time's distillate – disinterested, arcane and horrifying. He'd loved it, had known he would love it, had been astonished only by the intensity of that love.

With most of his mind away in the desert, he could make himself free enough to appreciate what was here: his eating, his drinking, his body's life.

This is water: the taste of water, the motion of water, its changes in temperature, its seeking out of places in my mouth, its soft accommodation to the shape of my throat.

This is meat: the resistance and spring of fibres, the metallic taste of blood.

Mouthful by mouthful, he fed himself with the nature of things, he was aware.

Which placed his thoughts strangely close to those of Eckless, who was sitting opposite, his chin still on Nathan's knee, his loyal ounces of doggy brain lighting and relighting with uncomplicated – if ardent – life.

MEAT WANT

WAIT STAYBEGOOD

LOVE HERE BOSSMAN

HAPPYHAPPYGOODBOYBOSSMAN

LOVE HERE STAYBEGOOD

Richard Fisher, sallow, a neat and meagre eater, was rather less delighted by his surroundings. He was facing Ruth Alvey with apparently complete attention, but also listening to Louis – just to see if he could. It wasn't that he didn't have sympathy for, or an interest in, Ruth – he had simply heard her story before. Three or four glasses into a bottle, especially of red wine, and she would usually mumble it out, perhaps in hopes of absolution, condemnation, betrayal – he couldn't say. Whenever he was this close to her, he would experience a kind of seasickness. Something about her was so dreadfully hungry, he could feel it jar at the roots of his teeth.

'They were a good group, they trusted me. And they worked very well. At first the staff – you know staff – they said we shouldn't bother with this type of person. They meant non-literate people. But they could all speak, or point at symbols, or sign. They all had something to say. Which is what an institution won't want, of course, clients with something to say, *opinions.*'

Richard nodded, as seemed appropriate, and wondered how on earth Ruth could manage to stay so pale. The island hardly offered a tender or sheltered environment, but from looking at Ruth, you might guess she was normally kept in a box somewhere underground.

'Rob, he was especially able. In the time we were there, you could really see him coming on, getting more confident, taking part. He looked the least . . . what would you say . . . *abnormal*. Really, he was quite handsome. And striking eyes: large and a sort of purple.'

Yes, underground, like a mushroom. Richard tried not to smile, as he thought of her swelling in some moist and nourishing dark, becoming the plump, white object she was now. Just a touch further round the table was his wife – an altogether firmer proposition, altogether more difficult.

'He had this peculiar way of naming things. I'd never come across it before. No matter how anything changed, Rob was inflexible. If the first time he'd been told what water was, it was called *rain*, then it was always *rain*. Trees were made of *spoon*, I remember. And the terms he chose could show you, could tell you bits of his life. Any type of pain was *belt* because his mother had beaten him regularly – had decided that it was his fault he was soft in the head. Any excess of emotion was *medicine* because he'd spent years away from home in a hospital where drugging replaced the belt.'

Richard's wife, Lynda – Richard's lawfully wedded spouse, Lynda – Richard's own to have and to hold was right there, next to Nathan. Richard rarely, if ever, sat beside her at lunch because the custom was that partners should dine separately when in public. Even if they were the only two here who *were* partners.

Richard had never understood the rule. What was the expected disaster it sought to prevent? What was it that couples might do in the presence of food and observers that would be so terrible? What purpose did it serve to make him sit quite so often with Ruth?

Ruth, the mushroom who bit her nails. Richard tried, every time, not to notice and, every time, failed. The obvious pain of it, the voluntary disfigurement revolted him: the small finger wounds, the livid quick, the fraying and crusting of skin. She had no self-control.

She was still speaking. 'I didn't mean it. I'm not saying it was an accident. After the first time, it was deliberate, obviously, but I didn't mean it to cause harm. No one need have known. I think he agreed with that. We spoke about it and he seemed to understand. And he'd never changed a definition before, there was no reason to expect it. Trees were *spoon*, baths were *rain*, I was *Ruth*. Then in the group, on a Friday morning, we were having our tea, everyone all together, and Rob brought over a tray full of cups. "This is for Andy, this is for Steve, and this is for Fuck." Pain was *belt* and I was *fuck*.'

'It must have been . . . embarrassing.' He'd heard the punchline he couldn't remember how many times and still didn't know what on earth he was meant to say. What could one ever say? What was the point?

Ruth stopped, set down her knife and fork. Richard tried to pay more attention, to concentrate, to focus on this part of the table and not any other. Ruth was squinting with fury, her eyes like malevolent currants in rising dough. 'Embarrassing. Hm? Em-bar-rass-ing.' Her whisper arrived with such force that he could feel it in the hair at his temples.

Richard sighed, slipping into place his usual domestic calmness, his most placatory manner. He was very used to being placating. 'Well, I'm sorry. I didn't want to say *nothing* – but there really aren't available words to say. The situation must have been horrible.' Ruth

129

continued to wish him ill, unblinking. He knew that he never did manage to be a good peacemaker – not with anyone but himself. With anyone else, he seemed to stay too obviously absent, not even sincerely insincere.

'I never used to understand why Lynda is the way she is, but you make her very easy to explain.' Ruth had the most vehement whisper he'd ever encountered, soured with wine tannin and beef.

And, of course, thinking of this, and not of what she was saying, was one more example of why he irritated people – his mind would wander away from them, escape into fragments and details and, sooner or later, they'd notice his vacancy. They would want, at the very least, to shake him. He knew this and sometimes wished he could change. But, then again, his disengagement had advantages, a peace dividend that was more than generous.

'Look at her – she's all over Nathan.' Ruth, on the other hand, was all focus and terrier grip.

'It's fine. He's my friend.'

'Can't you see what she's doing. Don't you care?'

'Nathan is my friend. He didn't ask to sit there, it's where he was put.'

'Where do you think her hand is?'

'It's fine. It's fine. It's fine.' Richard thought about Lynda's hands, about her fingers, about how he might buy her another ring, soon – one that would suit her especially well. Why not? Why not the quiet life? Why not?

Lynda's hand was, in fact, on Nathan's thigh. All through lunch, it had stalked him across his chair and now it had caught him, its thumb exploring the seam of his inside leg.

'Lynda.' Nathan tried to sound as weary as he felt, while speaking very softly and not attracting Mary's attention in any way.

'What?' In her innocent, purry, the-devil-made-me-do-it voice.

'You know perfectly well. Stop it.'

'Stop what?'

Her paw continued to fuss at him like some hot, soft-shelled crustacean, erotic as a breadboard.

*Stop **it**, stop **that**. JUST STOP. For fuck's sake, how many times must a person say they don't want something before they actually cease to get it any more? Jesus bloody Christ, can't we put something in her water, can't we just* *sew over her active parts, can't we do* **anything**?

Nathan could have done without this. The backs of his eyes were still miserable after yesterday's hangover, and his journey back to the island had generally not been good. And he'd wanted, fuck it, to meet Mary in his house, not here. He'd wanted to – yet again – once again – start again, he'd wanted to . . .

Sweep her in your arms and tell her, hn? I am your daddy? Hello, my child?

Like fuck.

Or would you just hold her that little bit longer, discover all over again the way she's so small and so tight on her bones and the way that there's nothing about her you wouldn't bleed for and die for and look after until you went stone mad with the effort of it all, hn? Would you stand there and think of everything you'd lose if you told her the truth and she didn't like you, just didn't go for it?

And why would she? Have you seen yourself, lately? You don't look like a father, you look like shite.

A man with less hair every day who couldn't get his hands really steady enough to shave. What was that all about? The hangover or the nerves? The thought of seeing Daddy's little girlie making you jump?

You sad fuck. You can't stop sweating, because your daughter almost said she missed you. **Almost**. *Turned the room round on you, that one, didn't it?*

A man with a prick that'll only lift for a bitch he'll never see again. Practically dead as a sash weight otherwise. If the mad cunt next to you sucked on it all week, she'd barely get a twitch. But if she said the magic word, hn? Maura? Maura? That do it? Maura? Hn?

And, of course, that did start to do it. The simple sound of a name between his ears did begin a nasty lower little throb.

'All right. All right.' Nathan, cautious of Mary and wincing against the clamour in his head, reached out and sneaked a hold of Lynda's hand. She smirked, as he'd guessed she might.

'Why, Nathan . . .'

He pulled gently, insistently, moving her closer under the table-cloth, gripping her wrist, while he arranged another little matter with his free hand. Then, deliberately, he turned his face to hers and watched: saw puzzlement and then disgust and heard the wet gape of Eckless's mouth beneath the table, his soft and curious tongue setting out to lap at Lynda's fingers. He tried not to smile too much while she yanked away her hand.

'Good boy. Good lad.' He patted his faithful hound's head. 'Good lad.'

Lynda carefully wiped her fingers clean on his trouser leg, but Nathan didn't mind. He didn't mind that she whispered, 'You really are a bastard, Nathan. A poor, bloody, limp-dicked shit.'

'Good dog, Eckless. Good boy.'

His dog leaned back against this hand.

GOODBOYHAPPYHAPPYGOOD

When would it stop: the ridiculous toppling in his heart?

Every time.

Surely it wasn't possible – surely every time he ever saw her, the seasickness wouldn't always start, the stomach tensing like a landed fish, airlessly afraid.

Nathan tried not to think of it, not to think of anything. He drifted over to the kitchen window and breathed the roses in. Joe was good with roses, he kept the Lighthouse hip-deep in lazy, blowsy flowers for as much of the year as the island's climate would allow.

*This is good – I can just enjoy this. This is **nice**.*

Her word, Mary's, the one you wouldn't let her use.

*Shut **up**.*

The rose scent was thick. He could almost imagine it slowing his movements, supporting him in some way. Behind him, he could hear Mary setting the trays with seven bowls and seven spoons, quite used to the Foal Island way of doing things now – the shared cooking and shared serving of Joe's dearly-fucking-beloved Sunday Lunches. Outside, parchment-coloured blooms, a dab of watered blood at their hearts, bobbed heavily and swayed.

'Well, I'm ready . . .'

She was, too. Skin caramel brown from the summer, more and more gold in her hair, slimmer than when she'd first come here, fitter – she seemed prepared for almost everything he could foresee. Horribly able already to take on anything without his help.

'Nathan?'

He felt completely superfluous unless he looked at her shoulders and then all was well. She was wearing one of those weird kind of glorified vest things that she liked and which left her arms and shoulders almost completely exposed – the tender dip and curve of her muscle, the fragility of her bone made him want her to be under constant police protection. The beauty of it all made him want her to become a nun immediately.

Right now – keep her safe from all those bastards out there – keep her from harm.

'Nathan, if you're going to dish up . . .'

Get a grip, get a fucking grip.

'Uh, yes, yes. I hadn't forgotten.' And he scampered to the monster fridge and wrestled out Louis's offering – traditional sherry trifle – naughty-little-boy food. 'Lord, they get bigger every time.'

'He gets to take home the leftovers.'

'True.' He dug in and realised how utterly obscene the parting flesh of trifle can sound. Not the sort of thing one's daughter should have to hear. 'Although Ruth's in one of her down moods, I think – that usually makes her eat her own body weight.' Nathan knew that he was blushing and that he was quite powerless to stop.

'Why don't you like her? She's very fond of you. And she didn't like me keeping Eckless when you went away. You didn't tell me that she usually did it. I think she was upset.'

'She didn't give you any bother?'

'No. No, I'm just saying, you mean something to her. You must have noticed?'

Another spoonful left the bowl with a wet, post-coital smack.

She does watch, then, does pay attention, does take an interest. In me? In me?

'Well . . . I know. But . . . it's . . . she's fond of me in a way I can't reciprocate and so I try not to be around her too much.'

'You haven't told her? That you don't like her?'

A gob of custard flopped on to the tray.

'Told her – yes, of course.'

Of course. Because I'm so good at telling things, aren't I? When they don't matter, I'll tell them to anyone. Fuck.

'But telling someone not to . . . I mean, she feels the way she feels. No one can help that. I just try not to help. I wouldn't encourage loving where it wasn't going to get loving back.'

'Isn't that her choice?'

133

'No.' The cream was out of control now – a huge slaver of it landing between two dishes and spattering.

Jism. On the quilt. Blue quilt. Shins still bleeding. That fucking awful bastard night in the flat.

Your daddy's lovely hobbies, Mary. Your sad fuck dad.

'No, it isn't her choice.' Brandy and fruit juice dribble had suddenly, inexplicably, coated his hands. God, he was making a pig's ear of this. 'Nobody chooses that kind of thing. Nobody would. It's just how they're made. They can't help it. They have no choice.'

Yes, yes, all right, she gets the message. The subtext, she will not understand. Just grow up and shut up and don't go on. Always the melodrama, isn't it, you cunt?

He abandoned his spoon, the trifle subsiding, lubriciously aquiver. 'I'm making a terrible mess of this. But if you hadn't put the bowls on the trays first, it might have been easier.'

She looked at him.

'I mean, *eventually*, everything goes on the tray . . .' She was still looking, not the right way. He was correcting her again, even though he knew she didn't bloody like it.

*Enough, you stupid shit. **Enough.***

He attempted to salvage something, said sentences almost at random, but in a more jovial tone. 'But when you're putting stuff out . . .' She keep on looking, eyes blank mahogany. 'I mean, it doesn't matter. Not really, I was only . . .'

*Shut **up**. Fuckwit, fuckwit, fuckwit.*

'I mean, *I'm* making the mess. Obviously.' He made another grasp for the spoon, but lacked the will to carry the gesture through. Then she spoke, softly, softly, every syllable washing him into fears he didn't want to have.

'Nothing I do is ever right for you, is it?'

'I wou–'

'I do *try*. I *have tried*. But nothing ever makes the grade.'

'Tha–'

'I've been here for *months*. I've been here since *November* and you haven't let me write a *word*. And the things I do and the things I say and the way I think – it's all wrong.'

He made a particular effort, didn't correct her choice of verb. 'No, no, it's –'

'*WHY DON'T YOU LEAVE ME ALONE!*'

She screamed. She actually, literally screamed at him: the full, hoarse punch of that. They both started, apparently equally amazed.

'*WHAT'S THE MATTER WITH ME?*' A lacerating yell now, even louder than the first. '*WHY WON'T YOU LET ME WRITE!*'

He felt absurdly ready to run away. She breathed in an uneasy rush of air and he braced himself for another onslaught, another unbearable question, but she stayed quiet, folded her arms, frowned past him, head low.

'I . . .' His voice sounded tiny, shabby. 'I have never intended to make you feel that . . .'

*That what? **What?** Shit.*

He began again, with slightly more hope, 'I've said . . . I did say earlier – you're doing well. I've told . . . Well, the thing is that I've told lots of people other than you, which was – I realise – a mistake and I should also have made sure you understood . . . I've . . . I've . . . I have meant to help.'

'Well, you didn't.'

Oh, for Christ's sake.

'Y, Y, Y–' He'd stammered at school, only ever at school, not since, this was an old, old nervousness. 'Yes, I see that now. If you'd . . .'

If she'd what? Told you earlier? Go on, try to make it her fault – pass the buck and be the man.

'I think I'll just . . .' He sat on the floor, his back against the table leg. This made things better, this seemed to let more blood get to his head. 'Look, I'm sorry, Mary. I've never done this before – this mentoring thing. I was doing what I thought would be the proper stuff and I haven't got it right. If this is the way you feel, then I've ballsed it up. Sorry.' From the dining room next door, he could hear – he was certain – only the eerie quiet of group embarrassment, of a crowd forced to overhear what they'd rather not know.

Please God, let no one come through.

'Nathan, do you . . .'

He turned when she spoke and was hugely, grotesquely flooded with the certainty that being here and lifting his eyes to her – being compelled to gaze up at her – was something he could spend weeks doing, if she'd only like him a little bit.

'I mean, do you want me to not be here? It seems . . . I mean, I don't have to know about you, but now you know every fucking –'

He loved the way she swore – so cleanly – didn't sound like swearing at all.

'– thing about me and I hardly know more about *you* than your name. Three times, you've been away, Nathan – you haven't said why or where. I think everyone else knows, but I don't. I know I'm only the, the –'

She fumbled for the proper word and the quick of his nails ached with love for her.

'– the student here. But do I not count?'

'You count.' He heard himself squeal. 'Of course you count. And you're not – I don't mean to correct you again – but you're *not* the student, you're one of us. Whether you would want to be, I don't know, but you're one of us. If anyone's said any different . . .'

'Nobody's said anything.'

'Well, good. Because I would have set them right. Would you, ah . . .?' He craned up again, for a soft instant found her eyes, tried with a tick of the head to say what he couldn't in words. And she understood, walked nearer, and then sat cross-legged beside him to his left, unknowingly close to his hungry arm.

Thank you.

He stared at his shoes – Sunday best, black shinies – odd how he played along so much with Joe's need to have a tidy family, once a week. Maybe he wanted the same thing, maybe that was it.

'Well, then, Mr Staples. Did you want something? It's a bit uncomfortable down here. Not my first choice for a seat.' But she wasn't complaining, not really. There was the touch of a grin in her voice.

Terrifyingly, he listened to his voice become playful in response. 'At least it's clean. Joe keeps the place spotless. Not many kitchen floors you could sit on and feel so invulnerable to disease. Anyway . . .' Somewhere in his head, a frightened little man was shredding papers and burning books, destroying all he could find marked *Cancer*. But he did have to tell her, because she had asked. 'Yes, anyway. The reason I go away.'

'You don't *have* to tell me. I was mainly making a point.'

'No, you're right. I know about you and you don't know about me. I had you talk so much . . .' Her hand was near his, near enough to be held, taken. Not that it would be. 'It's good for a writer to know her own voice – that's what I thought. Anyway . . .'

*Fuck, how often am I going to say **anyway**?*

He could genuinely taste burning paper, far at the back of his throat. 'I go to visit the hospital in London where they removed my lung. They took it away because I had cancer – well, *it* had cancer.' He didn't hear a reaction from her, more like a deepening of her silence. Although that could have been imagination. 'It's a simple . . . they take out the lung through your back, between your ribs. I lost the right one – that's the biggest, because the heart is to the left and it needs, naturally, a bit of accommodation. Of course, then they move the heart over, in the hope that your left lung will *grow* – which it does, surprisingly. The heart doesn't like to be touched, though, so it stops. You die for a while.'

'Jesus.'

He heard her and felt his heart kick alive, alive, alive.

Thank you.

'But they started me up and running again. I would guess. Something's ticking away in there . . . so I can't be dead. In fact, I'm OK. In remission. They like to test. They like to check. For re-occurrence of . . . of growth. Every three months, I get an MOT.

'Manage to stay above ground for two years and you're doing well. I nearly have, so I nearly am. After that, I'll have six-monthly checks and then yearly and then . . . I don't know. If I can put in a decade without falling under a bus, then I'm probably clear. Of that, in any case. Plenty more things to die of. Obviously.'

There was enough stillness now between them for quite small, distant noises to ease in, a gull mew, the sea's rush, a blackbird in the garden chiming up at some alarm. She touched his wrist, her fingers cooler than his skin, her thumb brushing over the suicide's favourite place: the shy ribbing of tendon and vein and blood, all threaded neatly under the thinnest skin. Her movements seemed, somehow, enquiring. But his scar there was slightly higher, she wouldn't find it without knowing where to look.

'So that's why I go. By the way, thanks for minding Eckless. He likes you.'

'Well, I feel like a horse's arse.'

A barking squawk of laughter coughed up through him. 'Oh.' He glanced at her – now *she* was looking at his shiny shoes. He couldn't

137

avoid a grin. 'A *whole* horse's arse? I mean – you've just had your lunch. You must have an extraordinary appetite . . .'

She didn't smile until sweat had pearled down the length of his spine, but then she wonderfully, wonderfully did.

'There's daft, you are.'

Another parrotty guffaw. 'There's Welsh, *you* are. I keep forgetting.'

'I wasn't born there.'

'Whatever. D'you want to know the Second Rule?'

'The – ?'

'The Second Rule. It's time you knew it.'

'Oh, right . . . the rules for writing.' She shook her head, indulging him. 'At least, I mean, *now*? You want to tell me a Rule *now*?'

'Oh, yes – this is the perfect time. Really. The Second Rule . . .' He leant in sideways, woozy with terror and delight. '*No one can stop you writing.*'

'What?' She didn't take her hand away from him, but gripped, beginning a little thrum of strangled circulation, a little pain.

He persevered – nothing but all of everything to lose. '*No one can stop you writing.* That's the Rule. No one has the right. Not me. Not even you.'

'You w–' She held him with her other hand now, too – leaning over him, squeezing and shaking at his arm, but he pressed on.

'No one will ever have the right to take away your voice, or muffle, or change it, or do anything other than help it to grow. Ow!'

'Nathan, you –' She was genuinely wrestling at him, hauling and twisting and *fighting* him.

'No, ssh.' Trying to ride out the tugging – the grabbing at his neck – the feeling that she might be going to *hit* him, if she worked a hand free. 'People *die* for this.' But he didn't know if she was angry, or something better than that, or something worse. 'To let your life speak, to let *Life* speak.' She had a good lock on his neck, a close hold. 'This is your right. If I ever – ow – if I ever – oh, now, fuck off with that –'

They were knee to knee now, her one hand doing something unnatural to his ear while he pulled at her wrist, his hungry arm curled around her, restraining or embracing, or restraining. He'd never seen her face so close before, the line of his own mouth there, but made finer, better – her eyes fierce, her breath against his throat. She was a surprising thing, this Mary.

She jabbed at his ribs. 'You swore.'

'I do.' He jerked sideways and was rewarded with a little more throttling.

'You swore at *me*.'

He *could* fight back in earnest. 'You were – you *are* hurting my fucking ear.' He *was* stronger than Mary. 'Among other things.'

'I'll stop if you will.'

He didn't feel he *should* fight back, though. 'I didn't start it.' He didn't feel he *could*.

'I'll stop if you will.'

'All right.'

'Go on, then.'

'You first.'

'All right.'

They loosed each other, unbalancing slightly, perhaps rushing too much to be on their feet, to be dignified, separate.

When he straightened his tie, a shirt button fell to the floor.

She picked it up, 'I'm sorry,' with an unapologetic grin.

'Yeah, of course you are.' Her hand lightly against his again, setting the button in his palm. He made a show of sternness, 'The youth of today . . . picking on invalids . . . Still, you do see . . .'

'Mm?' She'd moved to the table, 'See what?' and doled out the last of the trifle, lifted one tray. 'See what, Mr Staples?' She stood, hair still unsettled, but her face completely serene. She nodded to the other tray and he trotted to pick it up as if comfortably shared little tasks had been something they'd always known. She glanced at him, amused by something – probably the mess he was in.

He stood beside her, the two of them all set to face the dining room without any attempt at explanation. 'Your words are your words. It hurts to have them taken from you. So you look after them now.' He kissed the top of her head.

'OK.' She seemed slightly puzzled by that, but pleased.

Listen to her, changing her whole way of life in two easy syllables and she doesn't even know it.

How could I let any child of mine be a writer? When it's such a filthy, fucking lunatic job?

139

Then again, how can I stop her? When she won't make the same mistakes as me. I'm the one who's the filthy, fucking lunatic, after all.

They walked out into an empty room: plates and cutlery piled up ready to be taken away, but no diners remaining. Nathan supposed it was probably kind of them to have gone, left him and Mary. He thought he heard a murmuring from Joe's study and guessed they were all in there – near enough to lend a hand if screams and crashes had broken out. And, of course, the serious drink was in the study – they'd be having a something and soda to round off a curious afternoon.

Which I wouldn't mind doing myself.

'What should we do now? Nathan?'

Eckless woke from under the table, came yawning and wagging up to head-butt Nathan's thigh.

'You set out the pudding and I'll clear this junk away. Then we can call them through. If it's safe . . .' He waited to see if she'd laugh at that.

She smiled, nodded and made to start work, but then cut a half-turn back to face him. 'This is all right, isn't it? There won't be a problem – about us . . . having . . . ?'

There'll never be a problem again. Not ever again.

'No, no, it'll be fine.' He rubbed his neck and found tangibly, delicately raised, a tiny scratch that one of her nails must have left there. Something near his brain stem opened, smiled. 'They'll just have thought we wanted some privacy. There's no problem at all.'

And they went about their tasks: calm, steady, together. Nathan holding on tight round the foghorning joy in his chest.

Oh, Nathan, Nathan Staples.

Goodboyhappyhappygood.

Two in the morning after Sunday night, a phosphorescent silence round the island, nothing in the air but the mild hum of his own pleasant fatigue. This was the way he'd first written: stepping out of other people's time and into his own and then setting down the press of ideas, the excess of emotion, when both were still remarkable, still welcome gifts.

If he rubbed at his face, he could feel the good bristle of masculine concentration: the romantic, important disorder he'd imagined he might grow up to as a boy, watching John Mills pushing that ambulance through the desert, Ray Milland losing his weekend, Paul Newman eating hard-boiled eggs.

Nathan had always been unathletic and shamefully studious: only lying and smoking, drinking and stealing successfully and therefore undetectably, without the usual attendant popularity or praise. He'd watched the other boys, living their lives in public: running and kissing, laughing aloud and he'd known, entirely understood, that his proper excitements were secret, sleepless, interior. In the privacy of paper he didn't just imagine the desirable disorder, the attractive torments and extremities of his heroes – he *felt* them, *made* them, *perfected* them. He could close his eyes and *kiss women, whole women*, be coated in their gratitude and expertise, have his, in reality, untouched-by-female-hands bollocks clench with the breathless complexities of day-dreamed sex and real ejaculation. From the very start, his mental application produced more than its own rewards.

And he'd always realised, somewhere, that he would come to this: the solo sweat through the small hours under a cone of gently enquiring light: man's work being done. Not for the first time tonight, he let his collar chafe very slightly at the scratch on his neck, the wonderful seam where Mary had drawn his blood. It felt just right – *he* felt just right. Palm and knuckles beating time along the table, pulse flirting fast and high, he could find not a flaw in his fabric, not a loose thread, not a doubt, only his delight in the making of something out of nothing, out of himself and what came to get him, what came and asked to be expressed.

Nathan hadn't worked this way in years, but he'd fitted his mind to its disciplines, its charms and shocks, like a hand into water: like a man intoxicated within a revenant's strange embrace.

By now, he'd slammed at his keyboard for more than the usual day's hours, been dutiful in producing the horrors that J. D. had come to expect: the woman who ate her lover's wife and children to keep him from losing his family when he abandoned them for her, the wife who anaesthetised her faithless husband and then engineered his slow awakening at the hands of a hard-core sadist who tied him and flogged him and strung him up while he bucked into ball-gagged awareness of every nerve before his pubic hair was plucked with eyebrow tweezers and his glans was slowly sanded to a cherry tomato

141

of outrage and blood. The usual stuff.

And now Nathan was at liberty to do what he liked.

Here and here only, Nate, you get to do exactly what you want. Aren't you the lucky fucker?

Yes, indeedy. Sssh.

He was up and running, safety catches off and too tired to speak: just like the old days, just like being young and incautiously happy, being wholly alive.

So.

A little line or two for Kiddo. For the girl.

'In the beginning there were no words.' I know she isn't listening, but I tell her anyway. One never knows. The most unlikely items have been known to trickle in – by accident and sideways, there they'll go. I am resting, heavy in my deckchair, comfy with afternoon beer and I am thinking *in the garden of the knowledge of good and evil, here we are. Standard Issue Fatherly Moment, here we are.*

'In the beginning there were no words because everything was together, all in one piece.'

Mary's in the grass, dibbling with her fingers and a stick: making ant roads, or patterns, or simply a change in the status quo. She does this all the time now – sets about things: noises, actions, laughters only she can understand. I am beginning to find my own daughter mysterious.

'There was no Africa, no America, no Scotland: there was only one great, big island with everything in. All very cosy. It was wonderful. Then things broke apart.'

She possibly nods, but this may not be for me. Lying on her stomach, her weight leant on her elbows, back arched from the hips, she kicks up her feet and wriggles her unencumbered toes which are – of course – miraculously filthy. There is a rhythm to her: a kind of undulating confidence which moves her, even when she sleeps. And I can't help thinking this means that at – God willing – extremely distant dates I'll have to make whole shoals of hopeless suitors appreciate how lucky they've been to find her. Or else I'll break their arms and chase them – I am, I'd say, at present undecided.

'You listening? Lamb?'

'Mm.'

'Fibs.'

'Mm.' The shimmer of a giggle trembles her length.

'On this island . . . before it split . . .' I notice a

familiar tone in my voice: a tiny, parental sliver of despair. 'Well, there weren't any people yet, but there were creatures who were going to be people – hairy, scaly, skinny types of creatures – all together and all touching – they all understood each other, how they were and what they meant. It was lovely. Come here.'

She's shaking her head to make me persuade her.

'Come here.' The usual solar plexus crush of wanting to hold her, of wanting to squeeze away something quite clearly approaching jealousy.

Leave that alone now and come and please your poor old dad. Come on.

'Come here.'

Her feet are ticking past each other in the happy air – her whole body is, meanwhile, preoccupied with glad badness. She loves ignoring me, teasing the edge of permissibility.

'If you don't come here quickly the enormous, incredibly slimy, dribbly, hooky-toed crocodile in the bushes will snaffle out and get you for his tea.'

Mary squeals in the way that only a person quite unacquainted with proper horror can: a person of fewer than four years but more than three. She scrambles above the reach of carnivorous reptiles and on to my lap. I am, meanwhile, aware of every actual risk she runs across: the dangers of tripping and piercing her skull on an unlikely stone; of stepping on insects that bite or sting and receiving a dose of venom I could never have guessed would provoke a fatal allergy; or of trapping her toes and fingers in the multiplicity of nipping joints my deckchair offers and then succumbing to poisoned blood some sad time later.

Both our imaginations palpitate around us, wild with inaccuracies, while we work rather hard to discover that we are safe, that she is safe. She rummages around me adhesively, cooing, lightly moist with sun and grass, and fixes to my torso in a quickly breathing hug. She'll hear me now.

'Hello, you.'

'Hello, you.' Businesslike voice she has sometimes, almost stern.

'Were you listening to me at all?' I, naturally, can't be stern back. I always fail to find myself convincing.

'Yes. A bit. Not really. Was it *intreresting*?'

'It was going to be useful . . .'

'Oh.' She is already well aware that *intreresting* is seldom useful and vice versa.

'But it was good, too. I was saying – because we're all parted . . . the words . . . I mean, now we're separate, we need something to speak and something to write and read . . . and it's . . .'

'Oh, *that* . . .' My daughter, the possessor of all knowledge. 'We've already got that.'

'Well, I know.' I love touching her hair. People in shops hover near her and stop to pat her head and I understand exactly why: they are not necessarily perverts, they have simply guessed, correctly, that she feels remarkable. 'I do know we've already got that, yes, but we have to take care of it, we have to remember *why* we've . . . it's . . . important.' When I smell her skin, the whole progress and defence of Enlightenment seem quite superfluous. I no longer believe or entirely remember what I'm saying – so why should she? One last sentence and then I'll surrender, 'It was called Pangaea.'

'That's nice. What was?'

'The island with everything in it. Pangaea – the land of all lands.'

She doesn't try saying this out loud but is, I can tell, tasting it in her head like chocolate. In a day or two, it will be out again: hers. She does adore her vocabulary: having it properly fed. Her personal dictionary grows daily, almost visibly, and is at the moment attractively gangling like a healthy calf.

Maura thinks I am trying to engineer an infant prodigy – this in the midst of my many other sins. She thinks

I am conducting experiments with my daughter, a personality graft from my overstuffed head to her milkily empty one. But really, on most days, I simply hope my daughter will be someone I can *talk* to, for heaven's sake. I also like to think that she may wish to talk to me. Unlike my wife.

And I don't force her, not Mary, I don't ever push. Even at this age, she does what she does, not what I want her to. She reads because she likes it, she learns – eccentrically, it must be said – because learning is one of her things, as much as disliking gravy, or running away from the toilet flush at night, are her things.

I'm saying we both happen to like reading and the feel, the weight, the promises of books. I'm saying our tastes – here and there – do correspond. I'm saying I love this, although it has nothing whatever to do with me. I'm saying I wish that Maura understood the way we are. But I can't force her, either – obviously.

'I brought this.' Mary fishes out a plastic something from the pocket of her shorts. I see it, briefly, being held towards me: a badly moulded monster/animal/troll in alarming pink. It will have both a name and a history, neither of which I know. I believe this is the first time that we've met. She waves the thing for me slowly – as if seeing it from other angles will help me to find it as lovely as she does. 'Look.'

I turn fractionally. Mary lifts the figure to my face and I feel an odd, electric pressure at my lip when a point of plastic catches it. I am mildly confused by this sensation while, in my daughter's eyes, I watch a new emotion opening. A small heat tickles from my mouth down to my chin.

I have seen Mary like this before. I have. This is not remotely new: the silence, the look of amazement, of horrified wonder, and then the pause, the blush. She's going to cry. She's been hurt before, shocked before – now and then – and I have seen her, quite appropriately, crying as a result and I have felt my usual coronary wince. But this today, this here, this right here is my daughter, weeping only because she's looked at me. She is still staring at me, petrified. Braced against my arms and chest, she's whimpering, she's slipping towards a more solid, relentless noise, and she is unpicking me, unbalancing how I think. I feel sick.

'Lamb, Lamb? What's the - ?' She rocks between trying to touch me and attempting to slip down, away. Her toy is tight in the heart of one fist. 'No, Lamb. Sssh. What? What? What have I done?'

I rub my face, reach for her and, for a swooping moment, see blood.

Not hers. Not hers. Not hers, it can't be, that would make no sense.

In a pinkish trace on her forehead, where I've brushed her, I can see what has to be my blood. I am bleeding. My understanding flutters, snatches hold. When the model caught my lip, it pricked me, broke the skin. I can feel now, I am definitely bleeding, it's all right.

*When I bleed, **she** cries.*

She's howling now and I'm trying to hug her and lick at my mouth so it doesn't look frightening. I am trying to love her as clearly as I currently need to do.

*When I bleed, **she** cries.*

Maura will hear this, she will come out and see and then I'll be the villain again, the purloiner of other lives again, and dinner will be silent again and bed will be *don't you dare* again - as if I would - but I don't care, because I am now crying myself and also smiling and kissing and smiling again and holding her in: my daughter, mine.

*When I bleed, **she** cries.*

Please, God, never take me from this.

'What is it?' Mary was watching a butterfly, a neat fold of fawn and silver, thin and still as paper in the leafy heat. She was trying to think of a good way to describe it, how to make the tilt of its tiny sail come in handy for something, narratively speaking.

Who the hell writes adult prose about butterflies, though? Not that I couldn't be the first.

Or they could just be in a background . . .

I think that Nathan wouldn't like them. I think he'd be looking for something else – more human. More animal, possibly. Less flimsy. Not that I'd be writing to please **him**. *I want to please* **me**. *But even so – butterflies – not promising.*

'What is it – that one? Joe?'

Joe stabbed his hoe between the hollyhock spikes and glanced back. In his shirtsleeves and moleskins, white hair blazing against an almost mahogany skin, he looked startlingly horticultural, slightly too good to be true. 'What's . . .?' He also seemed luminously content. 'Oh, that's a grayling. We get a few of them. I let the nettles grow up round the compost heap to encourage the prettier ones – not that there *are* ugly butterflies, in my opinion.' He waggled his fingers towards a pair of ornate creatures, jigging nervously through the air above the carnations.

'Red admirals.'

'You're as bad as Nathan.' He blinked away briefly, sighted down his hoe shaft to his dark and lively earth, thinking, but perhaps not of butterflies. 'No, those are painted ladies. Red admirals are redder, less fussy pattern, more chocolatey kind of brown. You'll know one when you see one.'

Oh well.

Mary was beginning to suppose she'd been wrong about Joe. He was undoubtedly peculiar, but what was unsettling about him wasn't

148

madness, it was only his weird, continual *goodness* – the intensity and consistency of his personal atmosphere.

Always too good to be true.

If she reminded herself that this was only unusual and not harmful, then she could enjoy his company. He was gentle to be with and unworried by long silences.

Or mistakes.

In fact, with Joe, being wrong could be oddly pleasant – or at least as satisfying as being right. Mistakes and inaccuracies seemed to give him a kind of access to her thinking. She could almost feel him, tinkering under her scalp, setting things right – not as he might prefer them, but unnervingly close to the way that she might have chosen them to be, if she'd thought about it. Of course she rarely *did* think about it – but Joe, he was always thinking, always there.

'Anyway, knowing the name isn't knowing the thing. Is it?' He stroked at the mad tower of blossom next to him, it wagged in reply. Mary had never been able to take hollyhocks seriously: the crumpled tissue flowers, the overbearing height: they put her in mind of floral Brussels sprouts.

'*Red admiral* or *Vanessa Atalanta* – which tells you more?' He grinned at her, almost teasing, waiting to see.

And she decided she might as well take her cue – make Bryn proud of her classical training. 'Atalanta was the huntress, the woman who ran everywhere. No man could beat her in a race and if they couldn't beat her, they couldn't marry her.' She could feel Joe listening, his concentration a small disturbance round her forehead, like the movement of a moth. 'Hippomenes tricked her. He set down golden apples in her way and she stopped to pick them up and lost the race. So he made her his wife.'

Joe glistened with satisfaction. 'And, knowing the woman, perhaps we guess that the butterfly's a racer, barely rests. Or perhaps we remember that determined women can be vulnerable, too. Or that no one can run for ever. Unless, of course, they're young.' He grinned through her, nudging out an aspiration or two, tweaking at a need. 'You're writing, Mary Lamb?'

'I'm starting.'

'Well, that's the thing to do.' He set down his hoe and the garden relaxed, shivered back to its tight, lush perfection, defended from salt

149

and gales by careful walls draped in honeysuckle, clematis, climbing roses, trained plums. Joe loved his garden and – generously, apprehensively – it loved him back. 'Well now. Would you like me to prove how mad I am?'

He idled away a moment in brushing nothing at all from the knees of his trousers and then went to sit on his bench. Crossing his legs at the ankle, he winked.

He always does that, catches at what you didn't intend he should know you'd been thinking. Like Mr Kingston at school – going on and on about **the educated guess**.

'I never thought you were mad. Not really.' Joe coughed politely, giving her time to prepare a proper admission of guilt.

Oh, all right, then.

'How did you know?'

'I guessed.' He came very close to a smirk. 'And, to be honest, most people think I'm mad, these days. Do join me.' He patted the bench and she couldn't help but stroll towards him, rose scent coiling apart and then closing round her. 'So.' His eyes were Bunsen burner blue. 'We're in my oasis, you know that?'

'I suppose . . .'

'I am terribly fond of it here – all this green and fertility and . . . gloss – but I do enjoy imagining that over the wall there's a desert, that I can walk to the front of the house and feel sand slipping underfoot, furnacy dust on my skin and biting light – that kind of thing. Desert places, they tease – they tell you terribly firmly that you have no business being there and meanwhile they freely show you paradise annealed and hungry for trespassers. They are completely, complacently welcoming, like death. Ever been?'

He knows I haven't.

'No, I haven't.'

'But you may yet. My first time was in the Sinai when I was younger than your Nathan.'

He's not mine.

'In fact, I was just thirty – newly turned another decade and wasn't liking it a bit. Which is why I'd gone, as biblically as I could manage, out of Egypt, towards Jordan, which took a while and was, I suppose, very, very faintly hazardous. There were three of us initially, in a jeep: all linguists, all sadly keen to trot out our Arabic. We drove down through mountains apparently formed from boiling milk, congealed blood and flows and curves of tawny rock that were unmistakably corporal, almost erotic, hypnotising. I'm not a good driver at the best of times and, on that journey, my concentration wandered considerably.'

Mary's mind struggled away from contemplating Joseph Christopher and the erotic in the same breath. The conjunction bordered on the blasphemous.

'And, of course, we had to cross a desert, my first. I even got us moderately lost in it because I wanted us to stay there just a little longer than we should. Then my friends and I went our ways – they travelled on to Amman, they had some Nabatean tablets to translate.

'They had their plan and I had mine.'

Joe stopped, leant his head back to catch the sun and closed his eyes. He sighed into a smile while Mary listened to a boat engine moving somewhere which sounded close, but could have been beyond the island's sight. On days like this noises could travel and twist surprisingly. She examined Joe, not sure if he'd finished, or only paused. He twitched his nose, began again, eyes remaining shut.

'Yes, I had a plan. This always makes Nathan laugh, by the way. He says he can't imagine my ever contemplating something so devious. But I did.' He reached and stroked Mary's hand, made her jump, just a touch. 'It was dark when I got to the mountain. I'd taken out most of my clothes from my pack and put them on, but I was still freezing. The stars had that almost painful blue edge they only get in high, chill air and the moon was bright enough to light whole turns of the path. I laughed for a while, on and off – nerves – and I was finding the mountain silhouettes around me ridiculous – they were straight out of the *Children's Illustrated Bible*. But, naturally, they preceded anyone's Bible, anyone's account of local incidents. They were the facts – massive, solemnly crested like lizards and distinctly unforgiving.' He brought his head forward again, still voluntarily blinded. 'I climbed much faster than was prudent – but I just couldn't stop myself. I trotted and gasped past camels, skeins of pilgrims, solitaries like myself, what seemed to be a terribly old woman supporting herself with a gentleman's black umbrella.

'Mount Sinai, I was *on* Mount Sinai, I'd begun the first step. After an hour's walking the ascent took off up a vicious slope chicaning away across a sheer scree that ended with a drop on to rocks. It was the perfect place to take a tumble, so I did.'

'What?'

Joe laughed and sent a blackbird ringing out of the fuchsias in alarm. 'I took a dive. A calculated risk. If I didn't break my neck, I might get what I wanted and I did want what I wanted very much. You'll understand that.' He gave her a small grin – one writer to another.

'Well . . .'

'Sssh. You gave up a great deal to come here.' He squinted at her for an instant with one bright eye, then muffled himself away again. 'And you imagine you have a great desire to write . . .'

'Yes.' Mary wished her affirmation hadn't sounded quite so tentative, but – allowed their head – her hopes in this area seemed at least as confusing and embarrassing as they were intense.

'And, with respect, I will say that you don't know the half of it. You are willing and – if you think about it – volunteering yourself to take charge of the medium that governs and lies, that defines and dreams and prays, that witnesses truth and condemns to death. And, naturally, such a large thing will take charge of you. It will give you appetites you've never known.' His voice thinned, hardened, made her glance at him, his face showing a tiny jerk of something like discomfort, before he smoothed himself calm again. 'Which is only indirectly a part of this story. As I say, I decided where I'd take my fall, leapt off into the necessary tumble, and managed things rather better than I'd hoped – broken arm, dislocated shoulder, cracked ribs and one magnificent dent in the skull. I only recall the first bounce or two and watching the light from my torch spin down in a blade ahead of me and then snuff out.

'Apparently some conveniently sturdy Irish nuns took charge of me, carried me down the hill and then took me to the monastery – the only obvious source of help for miles. This constituted step two.' He coughed modestly.

'By the time they'd dragged me down the mountain, it was almost dawn, and the monks in St Catherine's were blowing out the candles at their icons as the first light stepped in at their windows. How do I know? Because, in the end, I saw it, because it happened every day. Just as every day they baked bread and then gave it away to the poor, just as every day Brother Stephen – or at least his mummified corpse – guarded the bones of their dead in the ossuary, just as every day all seven living brothers guarded the oldest library in the world.

'Which is why I fell.' He gripped her hand now, as if he were falling with her, into what only he could see. She felt a tug of inertia in her thought before it tripped forward to join him. 'There was no other way to reach it. I had to hope I'd be brought to St Catherine's and taken in, that I would be well enough to live, but ill enough to lie there for a while. In fact my fever rambled on for more than two days in Greek and Aramaic, Latin and English and Welsh, Hebrew and Arabic. Something I hadn't counted on, that – the way my head unravels, once vigorously tapped. By the time I'd recovered, they already knew that I was a scholar and that we shared certain beliefs. I confessed my plan and they forgave me and granted me access to their books – access at a price.

'Think of it; a collection founded before Alexandria burned and they allowed me seven days to read it: one day for every brother I'd tried to deceive: just enough time to fully understand how little I would learn before they sent me on my way, no coming back. They made my pleasure my punishment. A little trick they learned from God – Nathan would say.' He smiled, almost drowsily.

'They let me drink from Moses' Well and they let me study in the building that anchors Jacob's Ladder, which was centuries old before the First Crusade. Every morning, I would walk past a cutting taken from the burning bush and realise I now believed everything and nothing. I will always love them and never forgive them for what they offered me, hour after measured hour spent reading and reading and keeping away from sleep. I read the true Book of Zerubabel, I read unknown psalms from the Essenes, I read texts I could hardly imagine, that I promised I'd never name, and I read the only existing full manuscript of the *Sefer Yetzirah*.'

The heat of his grip was almost unpleasant and Mary felt her concentration turning, beginning to protest.

'The *Sefer Yetzirah* – it's the manual for creation. Other copies exist, but they are incomplete. It states, among other things, that there are thirty-two paths necessary for the making of heaven and earth, of life and hell. These paths are the twenty-two Hebrew letters and the numbers from one to ten. Which means God *wrote* all reality and numbered its parts, just as any author would. The *Sefer Yetzirah* explains this. In fifteenth-century Prague, Rabbi Yehuda Loew ben Bezalel used it to make the Golem. And before him, R'Hanina and R'Oshiya used it in the fourth century. They made a calf with three heads.'

Joe faced her, open-eyed now, assessing. 'How long did you believe me for?' He swallowed a laugh. 'Mm? For a while, surely. For a while?'

'For as long as you were believable.'

'Ah, well.' He beamed and squeezed most of the feeling out of her palm. 'We always have to rely on the author to make truth credible.' Another laugh glimmered in his throat and subsided. 'Of course, there are some aspects of the truth which are consistently unfeasible. The thing to remember would be . . .' Joe couldn't resist a wink. 'No really, this *is* true – or something to think about, in any case, and is what I actually *intended* to tell you today . . .

'In the desert you'll never quite know what things are, not at first. The absence of scale and the presence of heat will tend to mislead you: one man standing might just as easily be a rock, a truck, a camel, a tent: you can't tell. Unfamiliar elements will beguile you, but your best course is still to proceed. You'll only know if you go. And see. Then everything will show you itself, will tell you its nature, when you're close enough.'

'This is a metaphor, right?'

'If you'd like, Mary Lamb, if you'd like. Or a small token of my esteem on the occasion of your making your start with words. A clean, indoor job – you might like it – writing.' Joe freed her hand into the relative cool of the sunlight and offered her an almost melancholy grin. She realised she trusted his touch – it had none of the anxious reserve she found, for example, in Nathan's pats and wincing hugs at her.

'Not that you need these things from me. The man who picked you out will be more than adequate.'

'The man who . . .?'

'Picked you out – Nathan. We all agreed, from your work, that you should come, but he was the one who first suggested you. He didn't say?'

'No.'

Too fucking right, he didn't.

'Well, he can be shy.' Joe punched his voice up to a mild shout. 'Can't you, Nate?'

Nathan, easing through the kitchen door, let loose a small squawk of surprise. He was finding himself unsteady, unhandy: a young child with its legs clipped round his waist, its fingers footering behind his neck. Eckless sleeked around his feet and past, gentle as a shadow.

'Now, if you tickle, I'll drop you.' Nathan sounded, he thought, pitifully keen to play the part of The Man Who Often Carries Children, something of shame and eagerness combining to make him bolt and mumble phrases. 'You're too big for this.' The girl answered with a spine-jangling tightening of her multiple holds. She sighed happily with a series of minor, but instantly familiar motions that made him want to faint. This was how daughters felt. Always.

'Nate?'

Mary watched, amazed, as Nathan spun cautiously to face the bench, hands cradling a little girl. His face seemed vaguely shocked and he almost flinched when he recognised both of the garden's occupants.

Nathan met Mary's eyes, suddenly, almost ominously, breathless, and wheezed out, 'Not mine,' as the girl slipped to the grass and ran for Joe.

'No. Mine.' Joe took his daughter's hands. 'My Sophie.' Father and daughter paused to enjoy a mutual smile, a mutual appreciation, while Nathan swayed beyond them, rubbing inside his collar with a fretful hand. Then Joe scooped Sophie up and they made themselves completely busy, completely closed inside all the patterns of noise and touch that let them know each other, claim each other.

Without any formal agreement to do so, Nathan and Mary withdrew. They drifted until they could both stand and stare at the rowan, which grew near the bottom of the garden. Mary felt Eckless nudge a greeting at the back of her knee, before he sat at Nathan's side.

Mary made the first assault on their silence, aware of the shudder faintly visible in Nathan's arms.

That can't be just from carrying her. Unless he is really ill, more ill than he says. He doesn't much look it, though. I'd have said he was quite fit. Nervously fit.

'Who is she?' Mary noticed she sounded almost aggrieved when, in fact, she wasn't aware that she cared if Joe Christopher had a daughter.

'His daughter.' Nathan was trying for something more bullish, the manly deadpan.

'Well, I'd worked *that* out. But I wondered . . . you know . . .'

'As clear as ever in your use of language.' But he smiled at her quickly, to soften his meaning. 'Joe gets to see her in the summer – "when the island's safe" – as his ex tends to put it. She's called Sophie. The daughter.'

'Already knew that. Needless repetition.'

Nathan grinned in earnest. 'Yes, it was. To continue, I've just brought her over in the boat. She'll be staying for a while. She's a good kid. You'll like her. She's the one who pruned my dog's name.'

'How do you mean, then?'

'I mean that Eckless used to be *R*eckless – a perfectly adequate name for a dog. But when they met, last summer, Sophie wasn't overly good at 'r's. So now my poor boy's Eckless – which doesn't even make sense.'

'But Reckless . . .'

'Yes?' Nathan tugged at one of the dog's ears, scratched under its chin.

'Well, did that make any more sense?'

Nathan kept his head down, now just holding Eckless, his voice constricted somewhere. 'It might have done. It might have.' He straightened, began to move back to the house: a heaviness, tiredness producing a strange resistance to his progress, as if he were wading through water. 'Call a dog Reckless often enough, maybe he'll be that way.' He clapped at his leg and Eckless came faultlessly to heel. 'We had high hopes for both of us.'

Mary watched them both slip inside, neither of them attempting a goodbye.

I didn't mean . . .

Well, go, then, I don't care. But I didn't make you. I didn't do a thing to make you go.

Behind her, Joe and Sophie were singing something. She didn't recognise the tune.

Mary was lying in sand, held by it, enjoying its slightly warm support from her skull to her heels. A handful of hot, salt sky was visible through the cave wall above her head, but otherwise there was shadow, old rock forms tongued by long-departed seas, the reddish surface of a high and dry, glacial beach. Llangattock had found the place first, widened the entrance, shored it up and fitted it – no one knew why – with a short, blue-painted door.

If she looked left, she knew, chips and sparks of light would be squeezing in around the door frame, but the seal was still more than adequate for her. Llangattock had paid for her to be here – she felt she should also inherit his cave.

If Bryn caught me here, I know exactly what he'd say. 'Lovely day like this – you should be out.' Every summer, the same thing, he's up and standing in the garden still wearing his dressing gown, trying to decipher any clouds, or to feel if rain is lifting, or thinning out, or to check if immaculate skies will stay that way. 'You can never overestimate the benefits of sunshine. **Nec solem proprium natura nec aera fecit nec tenues undas**. *Sun, wind and waves, girl, made for everyone – Ovid, knew his stuff.'*

But Morgan hates it all. He only ever sits out in it for Bryn – to keep him company while he turns himself as brown as Cary Grant. That's the shade he says he aims for, anyway. Poor Morgan, I have a photograph of him sitting outside on one day in a desperate heatwave with a handkerchief over his face, his hands clenched together, trying to squeeze his mind away from the nagging of sweat and the pain. There's a livid triangle showing where his unbuttoned collar has left his neck exposed and the sun has crept down and scorched him, same as ever. But he's doing his best, all the same, sitting it out and staring at his personal white cotton sky and – I suppose – imagining sunset and camomile lotion and asking Bryn to help him smooth it on.

Then she realised.

No, that isn't a photograph I have. They've kept all the pictures. I should get some, the next time I'm back.

Mary listened to the gla-gla-gla of seabirds close by the other side of the cave wall. She was high in the cliff here, east of the Lighthouse, surrounded by rabbit holes full of shelducks and a squabble of fulmars and gulls. The air she breathed was moistly warm, comforting, private and she now hoped that tucking herself underground in it with her notebook and clearing her mind would mean that she could write. She had been almost certain this would work.

*But not to panic if nothing happens immediately. It makes sense, it's only natural, to be expected that now you're **allowed** to write, you don't want to.*

Can't.

*Never mind can't. Don't want to. It's because I'm used to speaking. Nathan made me speak and now **I** have to make me write and that takes a bit of getting used to, that's all.*

A quiet fear settled in her chest. It itched and snipped her concentration, itched again. She had the brief and sickening impression that her head was no more than a bony goldfish bowl – that nothing inside it could catch a grip. Information seemed to float in ugly clots behind her eyes while little flicks of life mouthed by, too short of memory to be anything more than consistently and moronically amazed.

No. I'm here to learn. They don't expect me to know what I'm doing, yet I'm here to learn. This is a change, that's all, another change. I just have to get used to making paper speak to someone who isn't there.

Which must be one of the more ridiculous things that anyone would want to do.

She tried to find something positive to sustain and found herself quoting Nathan.

He said I was doing well. I think he meant it. I don't think he lied, there would have been no point.

Her thoughts eddied and pooled. She let them, hoping this would drift away her island preoccupations. Having Nathan too clearly in her mind seemed to make her embarrassed, shy of breaking out in an ugly sentence, in some sign of her inadequacy, of her unsuitability, or of whatever other sad quality he seemed to search her for, almost every time they met.

She made a move for kinder company.

The Uncles – they say they're fine when I ask them, and I do want them to be fine without me . . .

Really?

Yes.

But are they fine? Are they both all right?

Foal Island drew her back.

Will the Fellowship send me away if I'm no use?

***Am** I no use?*

Shut up.

*Does Nathan **really** hate me?*

*Does Nathan really **like** me?*

*Does Nathan ever really like **anything**?*

If I can ever do this – write –

The clarity of the verb flooded her for a moment.

*If I ever can, if I am ever any good, will I be good **enough**? Will I be better than other people? Will I get away with it?*

Will I succeed?

Do I want to succeed?

Of course.

And then, frictionless, irresistible, came the questions beneath the questions – their gentle shapes and then their stony impacts, waiting to repeat.

Is he with anyone now?

Does he still love me?

Did he then?

Why do I want to know any more? Why is this still any business of mine when there's nothing I can do to change things? Why not accept that it's totally stupid to care? Why not understand that Jonno isn't here? That I'm not there?

A filming sweat of need hugged at her, kissed her forehead, mouth, both palms. There were still whole passages in seemingly random days when the air around her buckled and ached for him in a way that was so real it could start to persuade her that, finally, they would have to be each other's, that this was intended. She hated it, the smart grip of involuntary fantasy. But worse was the moment when it left her, when the hot choke of frustration seemed lovely, because what came later was always simple and unbearable despair.

She wanted his small, irreplaceable, unimaginable facts. She

159

wanted now, exactly now, more than at any other now, to just hold his hand.

No. I want him to hold mine. Just the good surprise of that.

Men on the brain, that's what she had: Nathan watching her, Jonno lying down in wait: the two bookends between which she could not think, or safely dream, or write. Somewhere, she knew, was the understanding that she could give them the slip if she really wanted to, but to feel herself alone with no more than her words would make her too lonely. She couldn't face it.

She shifted against the dead sand and hoped that she might cry, but this particular pain was too quick and changeable for that. Reflectively mineral powders hung in the narrow thrum of incoming light and the sea breathed, tireless, far below.

And perhaps Mary thought herself close to a sleep, or perhaps she was dazzled by a pursing memory of Jonathan's lips, or perhaps her attention had simply crept away without her – Mary could only be sure that, when Lynda disturbed her, she felt both guilty and unreasonably exposed.

'Hello. Hello?'

Initially, she didn't quite understand the voice. Her heart jolted with faint surprise and she blinked herself a little more awake. Raw day was ripping down into the cave from the opened doorway, Lynda's shadow the only relief from a blast of illumination that made Mary's skin hurt.

'Mary? You are still *here*? Aren't you?'

Lynda. This was Lynda's voice and so this was, therefore, Lynda. *Fuck.*

It wasn't that Mary didn't like her – not exactly. Lynda always tried to be friendly, forthcoming – Mary couldn't fault her on that. Unless it was to wish that she should *try* less and either be more genuine or not bother. Every time they met, Mary could guarantee, Lynda would nip in with a slightly barbed compliment. If Mary was leaning through a wet gale, wearing Foal Island-issue wellingtons, three jerseys and Bryn's hat and hadn't been able to wash her hair all week, Lynda was sure to say how pretty she was looking with perfectly eloquent insincerity.

*Pretty, clever, little – anything she can think of that'll fit with **girl**.*

*This time it'll be, **Well, how clever of you to find such a nice little***

160

cave and how pretty you look in it. *Well, what about –*

Mary sat up, reached for her notebook, as if it might represent some kind of defence.

– fucking right off?

'Oh, there you are.' Lynda turned and then peered towards her, shut the door with an odd, small stammer of hesitation. The dark clapped back in about them both, disorientating.

Oh, thanks a lot. And what the hell are you up to by the way?

'I had hoped –' Lynda stumbled on the uneven floor and Mary heard a hollow, plastic impact. 'Shit. Dropped the torch.'

'You won't need it. After a while you get used to the darkness.' Mary saw, almost felt, Lynda's shape move nearer and then stoop to sit. A tight silence settled, Lynda seemingly unwilling to break it.

So now I have to make small talk. Fine. Just fine. I might have been writing by now, might have really, suddenly felt like it, but fine . . .

Mary began, 'When the sun sets . . .', *by which time you'll have gone.* 'When the sun sets, the colours fall in here . . . and it's remarkable – red sand, red light, red walls. Red. You know. Red. In large amounts.'

Oh bollocks. Talk like that around Nathan and his liver would probably pop out and club him unconscious to save him from death by narrative despair.

Lynda switched on her torch. At once, the cave shrank down, coarsened: its potentials redefined in a cheap, sallow glare.

'I wanted . . . You don't mind, do you?'

Mary attempted a sociable half-smile. 'No, of course,' *like fuck,* 'I don't mind. Is there, is there . . .' *careful now, she might answer,* 'something wrong?'

'I know we don't . . .' Lynda firmed the torch into the sand, let its light boil up through the dust in a tunnel of glinting air. She seemed uneasy, even unwell, her make-up was having to work harder than usual, especially round her eyes. 'We haven't really got to know each other. Not that we have to. The last thing you want in a madhouse like this is to *know* everybody – guessing is bad enough.' She seemed to pause and consider laughing, but decided to simply go on. 'But I did, *do* want, or would like to be your friend. I notice you make all your phone calls from Joe's place now. Hm?'

Mary felt as shabby as she was intended to. 'I hadn't thought about it really. I suppose I talk to him quite a lot, so it seems . . . convenient.'

'Yes. It would be. I'm not criticising, not really. God knows, I'd rather talk to a man than a woman, every time. And not for the obvious reasons. Really.'

Mary tried to look uncontradictory.

'I seem to have more in common with men — attitudes. I can't stand all that passivity, the moaning and fussing about details you get with women. Women fuss. And they want to be your friend before they do anything else, which makes it impossible to work with them. Quite impossible. You feel the same? A little?'

'I suppose.' Mary noticed that the cave had filled with Lynda's perfume — something dry and tinted with sandalwood, but with a richer, warmer aftertaste today, a flavour that was softly rank.

'You can't *make* someone your friend. *Make* them like you.'

'No.' *Where are you going with this?*

Something clattered inside the wall behind Lynda and she lost her thread, tugged absently at the collar of her blouse: silk, something pale between peach and pink.

It's lovely. Too lovely for here, for the island, for us. She always has to try too hard with everything, doesn't she? Always that extra effort.

'Lynda, I —'

'I know. I've walked in on you and you'd like to know why.'

'Well. Yes, I would. Probably.'

'I thought I would add to your education. Or mine.' She brushed her hair back from her shoulders, hands careful, attentive, holding her picture together, although no one was taking it. 'A thing that you'll find as you go on, if you take up our line of work, is that writing is like wishing. You'll notice this. At first, you won't mean it, won't completely realise that what you choose to write about will come and seek you out. What chooses your fiction can choose your reality, too. Which makes a kind of sense, don't you think?'

'Ah, it could do.'

Lynda gave a neat, closed laugh. 'Yes. It could. And you'll catch on, you're bright, you'll see. Quickly or slowly, coincidences will happen: faces, phrases, tricks of speech, foreign cities, accidents — you'll see what you dreamed, what you thought out of nothing, what you wrote. Not too precisely, but enough for you to recognise it, enough to tease. You know what happens next, of course.'

'I suppose you would want to —'

'Control it. That's right.' She treated Mary to a slipping little look of complicity, something faintly repellent about it. 'You really are one of us, aren't you? It's only a matter of time . . .'

Mary made an effort to find this opinion pleasant.

'Yes, you try to control it. You try to make the fucking monster that has eaten up your life and frightened away every man you ever cared about and made you a freak in a Boy's Club profession – you try to make that monster give you back what it's taken – even just a piece of what it's taken. You know? No, of course you don't, but you will. You will. And I'm just saying, I'm just telling you, it doesn't work. You'll never get the part you ask for, no matter how often you ask.'

Lynda folded her arms in around herself – brown arms, fine-boned, the skin showing its age after too many sunbeds, too many afternoons at poolsides, on patios, on boat decks: all the fashionable spots for carcinogenic lounging. Mary, for the first time, could imagine her, at ease in the proper setting, cultivating the knowing, cocktail elegance that seemed so pointless here.

Lynda reached a hand forward towards Mary, but then folded it back into her lap. 'And never, ever trust anyone who writes too much about love. You'll find they turn out to be too unpredictable.' She glanced to Mary, gave a brief tilt of the head, checking on her understanding and then deciding to elucidate. 'Because they're in despair. They write love because they don't have it. Not always true, but quite often . . .' She smiled down, swirled her fingers in the sand, watched – quite contented – as they failed to form characters, to mark out any sense. 'Can I show you something? I mainly came here to show you something. I don't know why I'm telling you this. I'm not usually so maudlin. That's Nathan's speciality. If you don't mind my saying.'

'Why should I mind?'

'Why indeed.' The smile faded, locked off something in her eyes.

'You wanted to show me . . . ?'

'Oh. Oh, yes.'

Lynda stood, slowly, with a muted grace. The torchlight caught at her, whitening unexpected edges, deepening folds. She hesitated, hands indecisive, shining, bone pale. Then, carefully, she nodded to Mary and then looked beyond her to the blue break in the wall. Mary watched.

Lynda's skirt unfastened with a single button and unwrapped from her as it fell, almost soundless, round her feet. Then she lifted her blouse above her waist in a strange echo of a curtsy and waited, naked from her navel to her shoes.

A metal glitter shifted incongruously between her thighs, a new bright clasp to Lynda's body, easing and then interlocking again with each change of weight at her hips, each breath – all part of a permanent grip.

Mary felt the skin between her fingers moisten, a crawl of unease in her neck.

Jesus.

That rank scent smothered in closer, made her swallow and then regret it, while she looked and didn't wish to and had to, all the same, deciphering in the half-light, concentrating.

Jesus Christ.

A number of metal rings were piercing Lynda's labia, firmly bright against her lightly stubbled skin.

*No one does this. No one **really** shaves their cunt. And no one, no one does **this**.*

Mary wiped her mouth, resisted the urge to keep it hidden behind her hand, non-committal.

You don't, not to yourself, you don't, do you?

Lynda's flesh layered in softly, from a nakedly sunless pallor, recently shaven, to a narrow furl of deeper, fawnish rose, now pressed between two lines of surgical steel rings, shining as they curved into her meat. And at the site of each penetration was a reddened flare of infection, a dried crust, yellowish, and the heavy, weirdly fascinating smell of injury and decay.

'It's gone wrong.' Lynda let her hands meet and touch each other. 'I thought it would be good. A change. I thought. This was going to make it mine.'

'But it . . . it is yours.'

'No, it's not.' Lynda continued to stare at the wall above Mary's head. 'Everyone's having it done now, all of the people who have fun.'

'Lynda, why don't you . . . if you . . . Get dressed.'

'I know. I know, it's horrible.'

'No, I didn't mean –'

'It's horrible.' She stooped, knelt, drew the skirt back round her waist and then found herself foiled by the button, fingernails stuttering. She let out an arid laugh and tumbled on into sobbing: irresistible, but quiet, contained.

'Lynda. Lynda. No, really now . . .'

God, Mary Lamb, you are a stupid cow sometimes, you are.

There being no other way to reach her, Mary moved to sit beside Lynda, to hold her, to feel a disarmingly frail body shiver with poisonous discontent, struggle against spasms of something darker, something that Mary did not wish to know.

'You'll be all right, girl, you'll be all right.' Words from the Uncles, words she'd only listened to, never said, words that sounded thinner, shallower in her voice. She pushed, eased Lynda into a slow rock, a rhythm that might fit something other than despair. The torch fell, laid a hot line pointlessly away across the sand until its reach failed, diffused. 'You know it's just . . . when you don't feel well.'

'It hurts.'

'I know.'

I don't, I fucking don't, I haven't the first idea.

Nathan was hung in the thick of the sea, each huge shrug of motion round his body making him, as usual, aghast. He hated swimming, particularly in the sea. The vertigo of suspension above unpredictable depths left him simply afraid, while the supernumerary horrors – submarines, sewage and toxic wastes, tangling net drifts and unreasonable creatures – could mean he was very literally seasick before he could even flail for the shore.

Swimming through your own puke, terrific.

Still, it's all good for the lung, the capacity. I suppose.

And good for the dog.

In fact, Eckless hated the water more than Nathan. He seemed unable to understand its nature – too giving to be ground, but too solid for air. It pained Nathan to see the beast so unsettled, unwilling to paddle or even to swim, albeit fairly pointlessly, after stones thrown into the waves. Other dogs would race into the foam and plunge about, but Eckless was positively phobic.

At least partly to give himself company, Nathan was training

Eckless, along with himself, to trust the water. He wanted to build their characters. After two summers of salty experiment, the animal would follow him as they moved beyond both of their depths. They would then pummel anxiously at the water, heads held improbably high and trying, at any point, to enjoy this.

Eckless's excursions never lasted long. After a minute or two he'd abandon Nathan, withdraw to the beach, shake and – in passing spasms of alarm – bark for Nathan's return, or the sound of his voice, yelling reassurance.

'I'm still here! It's all right, you big daftie.'

Eckless was already done with his dip and lying in the sand today, patiently despondent, while Nathan bobbed, then struck out for the good of his lung and then settled to bob again. The glare from the wavelets and the high sun was beginning to give him a headache. He shoved himself forward through another fifty strokes and then swayed at rest, his heart clumping in his ears like an increasingly weary man climbing wooden stairs.

That's exactly the sound – like hard shoes on a thin carpet, climbing the height of my spine, labouring away towards the point where I can kick myself in the head.

He slapped both hands down on the lightly iridescent surface.

Nathan Staples, you're not allowed the miseries today. No more complaining, not now. Sophie's here and you can borrow her as much as you want. The weather is gorgeous, you can't deny it. Nothing like sunlight and green stuff to relax you. Your tests are all clear again. There is nothing wrong.

Beyond the usual.

Nothing wrong.

An especially solid lunge of liquid crested against him and he felt the usual aftershock, the wash of heat, sweat, his own salt breaking round him. Nathan decided to take the hint – it was time to head for shore. He had things to do.

J. D. – if I phoned him, he would understand. If I asked him, he would understand . . . **Post this letter for me, will you, from anywhere in London you would like. For me. A favour. I don't often ask.**

Jack wouldn't need to know what the letter said.

Then again, why not? I wouldn't mind saying.

In fact, I'll tell him before he asks: it's a letter to Mary.

Jack'll understand.

Of course, first I've got to write the fucking thing.
Shit.

He staggered up and out of the water, feeling his own weight bear down on his bones, his beached clumsiness.

If I start with something neutral, anonymous – not because I'm scared, just . . .

Because I'm scared.

But I do need to be careful at first, to not take any risks, not shock her, not the first time.

Jack'll do it – the man for the job. I'll just post him the letter in a stamped, addressed envelope and all he'll have to do is stick it in a pillar box, only that. A London postmark – far away from here. I don't want to give away clues, not yet.

I want to be gentle. I've waited this long, there's no rush.

Mary wasn't exactly rushing.

Bloody hell. Jesus bloody hell.

More like taking a fast walk.

Fuck.

And it seemed perfectly natural for her to aim her fast walk at Nathan's house.

What did she want me to do?

Jesus, it looked . . .

*And all I could think of was to tell her **boracic acid crystals in water, they're very gentle**, as if picking the right antiseptic is going to solve everything.*

Bloody idiot, I am.

Mary must have waited for something like half an hour after Lynda left, before she'd climbed out of the cave herself and headed up over the heart of the island, past the little lake and home. Or almost home – she'd see Nathan first and clear her head, tickle at Eckless's ears for luck.

Her shadow was spilling away from her, striking out further and further across tussocks that threw up their own increasing shade. The whole island, peatily hot, seemed to camber under the sun while she trotted and stumbled on, silencing the crickets in a watchful hoop around her as she went.

Within sight of Nathan's cottage, she turned and sat, blinking into the sunset. The turf gave softly underneath her, like coarse fur, reassuring.

Bloody woman. Poor, bloody woman.

Mary tried not to reconsider what she'd seen, not to taste a trace of it. She dropped her head to ease off a nasty tug of light-headednesss.

Shit, I should be telling Joe, I should be going and telling Joe. Not Nathan – he'll only be . . . the way he is.

She mopped at her face with the hem of her T-shirt and knew that she was not presentable: hair sticking to her forehead, tacky hands and sand still sticking to the backs of her legs below her shorts. And her throat felt too dry to swallow easily, or speak well.

But she would still speak, and to Nathan, because he was a habit he'd made her form. She actually missed their daily interviews, now they'd been halted to let her write. Or, rather, she missed the occasional times when she could just sit in Nathan's house, drink the water that came from his cistern – the coolest the island had – and know that he was about the place, or on the point of pounding in from one of his runs. She was used to him: the small, but constant fluster in his eyes, his hands digging in the pockets of his overalls for objects he never found, his sudden, elegant sentences, his reliable physical clumsiness and discontent.

'Well, now, yes – but you're guessing, aren't you? Guessing wrong.'

Mary could hear Nathan's voice as she came down the path. At first, she thought he was talking to himself and was – weirdly, briefly – pleased to think her absence might have left him still snapping and griping at thin air. Unless, of course, he'd always done this and her presence had imposed a kind of rational interlude.

'I know I *said* to guess, but I didn't say to guess with *this* one.'

He was grumbling, as usual, but his voice, as she followed it in, was unmistakably different. Nathan – although Mary found this unlikely, even absurd – was sounding *young*.

'That's right – it's like *parcel* – the "c" beside the "e" goes soft – so that sort of ties up the "e" and it can't touch the "i". You know? So *notice* gets to say *noteiss* and not *not ice*.'

Eckless padded out to greet her, tail lashing, and she knelt to hold his head in her hands and fuss under his chin and behind his ears. He could take any amount of fuss – perhaps groaning a little in his throat, if the pleasure proved particularly sharp.

'Well, I know you know now, but you didn't a minute ago.' Nathan broke off for a noticeably jolly shout, 'Eckless? Who've you got?'

Mary presented herself in his doorway only slightly before he reached it.

'Ah. You.' He grabbed at her hand and shook it in a kind of polite spasm, while smiling at somewhere slightly beyond her head. 'Um, that is – not to sound so awkward – great. Lovely. What a surprise.' He managed to make *surprise* sound almost as welcome as *hand grenade*, or *boils*.

Mary was aware that her fingers were inadvertently coating him with dog saliva and old sweat.

'Come in, you look . . . Are you . . . well? Do you want to sit down?' His voice had narrowed again, aged, was suddenly showing more than the average strain. He led her inside, almost guiltily, to where Sophie was sitting at his kitchen table, swinging her legs on one of his high, hard chairs. There was a picture book opened flat in front of her. Her glass of milk faced his cup of coffee: a saucer of biscuits in between.

He never had biscuits with **me**.

'You've caught me in the act, then, Mary.' Nathan dodged back to his sink, began washing his hands and confessing in the general direction of the taps. 'I have – um – another student.' He wiped his hands on the front of his overalls, grinning – half for Sophie, half for her.

'Eeaugh.' Sophie responded as it seemed he'd hoped she would. 'You should use a towel. That's horrible.'

'I don't have any towels.'

'Yes, you do.'

'Well, my overalls are cleaner than my towels.' He handed the soap to Mary without her asking, startling her a little with its sudden give and slip. He rolled his eyes and stage-whispered in a moist lunge of breath, 'Honestly, she's such a tumshie.'

'No, I'm not.'

'Aye, you are, if I say so. Who's the boss here, in any case?'

'Me.'

169

'The cheek of her – you were going to read me that next line – so on you go.'

Sophie performed an elaborate sigh and looked down at her book for a moment before studying Nathan again. He turned to Mary, with a frown barely restraining an expression of unmistakable happiness. 'Joe should be here any minute to fetch her home – there'll be no more sense got out of her today. Not that she isn't doing fine.'

'You sound . . .' Mary let the water shiver her arms clean from her palms to her elbows and back.

'Sound what?'

'Scottish.' She was beginning to feel almost unbearably tired.

'Well, I am. That's where I was born.'

She cupped the flow and held it to her lips, drank and then leaned against the sink, hands dripping. 'A cat that's born in an oven isn't a cake. That's . . . Uncle Morgan always said that.'

'I come from a long line of cats. All born in ovens. Are you all right?'

The light from the kitchen window needled at Mary's temples, bruised her eyes.

'Why doesn't she dry herself, Nathan?'

'Why don't you mind your own business, Sophie?' Somewhere outside, Eckless barked a welcoming bark. 'That'll be Joe – you should go and meet him.'

But Sophie was determined. 'She's got your overalls, why doesn't she – ?'

'Oh, for goodness' sake.' And Nathan took Mary's wrists, swinging her a little towards him with surprising strength, and gently patted her hands against his chest. The cotton was soft from frequent washings, a dark blue darkening to black where the moisture coloured it, and behind it was the muscle of his body, its hard heat, the slightly unnatural movement of his inhalations. As usual, he smelt very vaguely of soap and, today, a trace of salt, but with nothing beyond that – no scent of his own, or no scent that she could notice, that was significantly different from her own.

He sighed beneath her palms, his breath sweet with biscuit, and the heaviness at the back of her skull billowed up in reply and unsteadied her.

'And her face. She has to dry her face.' Sophie slithered down from her chair, then ran to Nathan and hugged his legs as he loosed his hold on Mary's hands and then tucked one arm at the small of her back and drew her the necessary inches in. For the first time since they'd fought in the kitchen they made a kind of embrace.

'And her face.' Sophie fumbled their knees together, enthusiastically.

Mary found herself quite malleable, foggily willing to have Nathan's hand rub her neck, nudge her until her cheek was firm against his sternum, his soft resilience under cloth. Her breathing scrambled, climbed, started to beat in a way which meant she must be crying, although she only felt exhausted, not sad.

'Aahm . . .' Nathan swayed a little, his palm setting a quiver of pressure against her neck. Eckless clattered in across the boards and what must have been Joe's footfalls closed towards them gently, slowed, paused. There was a tautening in Nathan's spine, where, Mary realised, she was now holding him, hugging him back.

'No. Not yet. I don't want to go yet.' Sophie's clasp was eased away from them.

'Ssssh.' Joe was tactfully determined.

'OK.' She released them. 'Bye, Nathan. Bye, Mary. Bye.'

Sophie's farewells receded as Joe left the cottage with her, absenting himself as quietly as he'd come. And perhaps Nathan smiled goodbye to them both over Mary's shoulder, or exchanged significant glances, or winked, or perhaps he had his eyes closed the way she did, she couldn't tell. She heard Eckless slump, huff and settle for a doze.

Nathan cleared his throat. 'They've gone.'

Mary slipped her hands from him and began to step away. His arm twitched in around her waist, 'Which is . . . no . . . but that doesn't mean,' and then released. 'Unless you want to – of course – want to stop, or . . . do you want to, to . . . Tea? In case of emergency, make tea. Ha. Yes.'

She was cold where each of his different pressures had lifted and gone.

'You should sit, Mary. Shouldn't you sit? Or lie? There's the sofa . . . Are you not well? What's wrong?'

Questions. He can't help it, can he? He always has to ask. Except he means them now.

He was craning his left hand to scratch his right ear and wincing with concern.

But I can't tell him. Not something that's so . . . when I think of . . . I shouldn't have come.

Nathan rushed water into the kettle, splashing his legs. 'Oh, for fu–. It seems I'm not intended to be dry at any point today.' He showed her a little grin. 'Look, you go through to the other room, have a seat and we can finish the biscuits. That's one of the good things about Sophie – she makes me get biscuits in. I don't have them otherwise, because I just eat them.'

'Well, that's what they're for.'

His grin repeated, warmed. 'Nobody loves a smart-arse – away in and sit down.'

Once Mary had told him what had happened Nathan waited, folded his arms and waited.

Easy, easy.

Closed his arms and waited.

Nothing hasty – blow this and you fucking blow the lot.

*She came to **me**. Told **me**.*

Maybe everyone else was out.

He rubbed one eyebrow and noticed that it was shedding hairs – quite a lot of hairs. Just what he wanted – to go bald in the eyebrows while she watched.

Fucking concentrate, come on.

That stupidfuckingbastardfucking – Jesus Christ, what kind of an arsehole psycho is that bitch? To do that? To do that to my fucking daughter? To make her look at that.

Be calm, be calm.

*Fuck, I worry about the boys on the quay in Ancw, the way they look at her, just **look**. Never mind when I see people **hugging** her. Trustworthy people in the Fellowship, hugging her.*

*I mean, even **me** hugging her, for Christ's sake, is slightly, slightly a worry, because of how I should try to do it – not knowing the right way – because of her not knowing who I am, because she really shouldn't trust people who are men and not her father and because she thinks that **I** am a man and not her father and it's . . . too difficult.*

*But **women** – bloody women dropping their kit and flashing their bastard* *piercings, I hadn't even **begun** to worry about **that** . . . Jesus – that's the kind of thing to make her go away.*

Shit.

Lynda, you cunt, you com-plete cunt.

'You're . . .'

Mary jerked him out of his private rant, nodding to his hand: the way it was fixed around hers in what must have become – quite a while ago – a painfully tightened grip.

'Oh, shit – sorry. Sorry. I was thinking.'

Look at it, you've left marks, even. Good God, you shouldn't be allowed out on your own. She'll leave, she'll go away back to Capel Whatever and it will be your fault – playing at Daddies with someone else's kid, instead of paying attention to what might be happening, keeping an eye out, taking care – you fucking fuckwit.

He felt his saliva thickening, somehow, making it difficult to talk. 'I am sorry. I've hurt you. Are you all right, though?'

'Yes – you just got a bit firm, there, for a while.'

'No, I mean with the . . . Lynda thing. It hasn't made you want to . . . You *are* safe here. Lynda, she's . . . she won't have intended to upset you.'

'She didn't.'

'Oh, well, that's . . . good.'

But you want her upset, don't you? Falling back into your arms again, patently alive and there and needing you again? Someone who'll let you save them. Someone to stop your fucking eyebrows falling out.

*And you're calling **Lynda** a psycho.*

'It was just all very . . .'

'Strange?'

'Yes, strange.'

Nathan felt his heart rattle with satisfaction.

Congratulations. She agreed to your end for her sentence. Big sodding deal.

The rattle stilled and somewhere near the root of his tongue he caught a rising sourness. He punched, inappropriately but gently, at her shoulder and found it difficult to control his vocabulary.

'I'll, um . . . This has . . . You're all right?'

'Yes. Now.' And she did look much better, less pale – she was made of resilient stuff.

Shame it doesn't run in the family.

173

She faced him, eyes a calm, sugary brown with movements of copper and gold to tug him in. Maura, in their beginning, could look at him through just the same colours and tourniquet his every thought to a throbbing stop. She blinked. 'Is there anything we should do? For her?'

'Um?' The walls seemed to shutter in at him, then skip back. He could smell a perfume that he hadn't met in years.

'For Lynda.'

'That's something, something – look, I'm a bit – ah – angry about this, so I'm . . . I'm going to step outside.' He snapped to his feet and immediately regretted it, a watery sweat blooming on his face and hands. 'Yes. Right. But don't go. Yet.'

I can make it, I can make it, I can make it.

And he did – he made it outside.

Oh, God.

Where he proceeded to throw up.

Oh, God.

Two custard creams and one digestive biscuit, one sandwich of (tinned) ham and (baked by Ruth) brown bread.

Oh, God.

He crouched in the shadow of his house and let nausea press him empty until he could only shiver and cough – keeping things as quiet as he could.

Oh, God, Maura. Dear God.

Back in the kitchen, he sluiced over his neck with water and swilled out his mouth.

'Better?' Having slipped in at his back, unnoticed, Mary brushed his shoulders with her hands and shrapnelled him through with the thought of himself as an altogether different man: someone domestic, cared for, caring, gentle-minded.

In your fucking dreams, you sad, old git.

His eyebrow twitched. 'Yes, I'm fine. I went for a –' He was going to suggest that he'd been for a run round his only available block in a manly exorcism of righteous rage: but he knew it would be plain to both of them he was lying, so he settled for, 'Yes, I'm fine.'

'You should look after yourself.'

'I do.'

She smiled at him, forced him into a yelp of justification. 'No, really, I do.'

'Well, I'm going home now.'

'You're –'

What?

I knew it, she's going, she's fucking going. She's leaving me.

Shit.

'Back to my bunker.' She pointed to the Nissen hut and Nathan shut his eyes for a moment as his panic shook and then dropped him, stalked away.

'Good, good. I mean, not good that you're going, but good that you *can*, that you feel able . . . But if you're disturbed in any way, at any point . . .'

'I know where to come.'

You do, you do, you do.

And we can both have another therapeutic hug.

*Women are lucky, they're small – smaller. We grow. We lose the possibility of being embraced and **feeling**, properly **feeling** that we are cared for, surrounded by another's care. We get alone.*

Shite.

Tell her that and she'll start to realise how truly unwell you are.

'Oh, yes, absolutely. I know where to come.' She glanced out at the grass, now mainly in the shade of a long dusk. 'But if Joe's out, I can always come to you.'

Nathan produced an especially ugly whinny of laughter before he could stop himself. People were only cheeky when they felt secure – so she must feel secure and that was good.

'Well,' his voice sounded as if he was smiling, smiling far too much – then again, she was smiling, too, 'if I've got nothing better to do, I might let you in. Meanwhile, you might want to get your finger out and slip me a manuscript. Or two.'

Is that the right tone, the nurturing tone, the supportive one? Fuck.

'I am trying.'

'Oh, I know. I'm sure. I'm not hurrying. Just teasing. In fact.'

Bearing in mind that if you're teasing but you have to explain it, then you're not teasing, you're just ballsing things up and being a fucking thug.

He tried a more sincere approach: because that's what he *was*, for goodness' sake, sincerely sincere. 'But I would really like it, if you'd give me a piece to read. I like reading. Now and then.'

'Soon. I am trying. Soon.' She began stepping out into the evening, into the smell of relaxing vegetation, a somnolent sea. 'Soon.'

'And you're sure you're all right?'

She turned and, over her shoulder, as casual as you like, and he *did* like, she called, 'Yes, fine. And you're all right?'

'I'm all right, yes. I'm all right.'

Yes.

For two weeks out of every year, a funfair would set up in Ancw – just along from the quay. On the island they would hear it in the evenings, waltzing and screaming up into blurry life – all nauseous lights and unlikely fortunes and rolls full of mysterious, scalding meat. Nathan found himself – at this distance – rather fond of the whole sad, fraudulent and shoddy swing of it.

Like the Lammas Fair – except that was autumn, probably autumn, always bloody raining, anyway – strings of little, pearly white light bulbs gusting in and out of focus through the mist – the stink of burnt onion smoke and diesel and wet wool – and seeing what I could knock . . . the best . . . I think my best theft was that pocket knife with a Highland soldier's picture on each side – it slipped in the palm of your hand, just as easily as your thumb – made for the taking.

And then I felt guilty about it for weeks, couldn't use the fucking thing. In the end I buried it somewhere, I think . . . can't remember. I can only clearly recall the guilt. I knew I'd have to pay for it, that's the thing, I knew I'd eventually have to cough up the going moral rate for all of my sticky, shitty, prickly sins: even the ones I hadn't liked. I knew it. I just wasn't sure of when.

If religion was good for anything, it would tell you: never do a bad thing when you're young, because God has no intention of sending you to hell, he will just wait – as you may have suspected – to fuck you around for the raw entirety of your adult bloody life. Petty theft, kicking, deceit and petulant wanking: enjoy them while you can: the fee will be desolation, middle-aged foolishness, getting your prick into just enough cunt to miss it, crave it, howl for it in each of your clammy dreams until senility finally pisses out your fire. Put that in the Bible and you'll catch everybody's attention – and fuck who begat who.

Fucksake, stop whingeing. You've got the girl here, haven't you? You're with your daughter. And you never thought you would be. Well, did you?

177

Mm hm. Miracles happen. Ha ha ha.

Shut up and enjoy it. I mean, things are going fine, finer than they have in ages. Be reasonable, man.

He kneaded his scalp and then webbed his fingers behind his neck, flattened his pillow, threw off his sheet.

Why? Nothing else is reasonable, why should I be?

The signs weren't good. He'd already lost his sense of humour and it probably wasn't even midnight yet. It made a kind of sense – he was tired enough to feel more than a fraction unhinged – overdoing it lately. Under cooler circumstances, he'd be deep in his preferred condition: unconsciousness. But tonight the humidity was broiling him awake every time he dozed and, if he couldn't actually sleep, then he had to think. And the last thing he should do while unattended in a darkened room was *think*. Unless his mind could be deflected, be persuaded to soften its edge until exhaustion finally came and smothered him.

Mary's looking well.

Good start.

Looking like Maura.

Sssh.

The way Maura was.

Sssh.

*The one I **can** see looks so much like the one I **can't**. Oh, Christ.*

A salt choke welled in his lung. He made a studiously courteous effort to negotiate the threat away.

Please now, that's enough. Please.

I always know I'm fucked when I get polite.

But, even so, let's give it a rest. Tears after bedtime – that's not what we want.

Fuck, I sound like a district nurse.

Look, just get yourself sorted. If you wanted to see Maura, it wouldn't take you long to work out how. Well, would it?

*But I thought that she would have wanted to see **me**. I thought she'd hear, that she'd find out where Mary was going, who she'd be with when she got here, and then, surely to God, she'd have . . . Anyone else would have tried, would have made the effort to get in touch. A message. Just a fucking note, even. Anything.*

Christ, she's a cunt.

Using the daughter as bait for the mother. You haven't a moral muscle in your body, have you? Hm? So who's the cunt now?

He turned on his stomach, mashed his face to the mattress, forgetting that the motion would mean his mouth had, inadvertently, to make a kiss. He forced his brain to shout the first words of any comfort it came across.

MARY LIKES ME.

And I like her.

Love her.

Love.

The bleak imbalance of this equation plummeted in him, left him with the tearing sensation of having landed badly inside his own skin.

And then, in a moment's incaution, he remembered, like a sweet, lancing flare, Maura's hottest smile. He twitched against the ghost – not this, not now – of the first, magnificent time she pushed her lovely, slipperied middle finger in all the way to her final knuckle up his grateful, astonished, grateful, grateful arse. He relived the shudder of his thighs: the bowstring slap of lust from the base of his spine to his neck: the blush of penetrated, tensing sweat: his whimper at her cheek.

God help me.

Not that He will.

Rolling again, he reached for his water glass and poured out its tepid contents across his shoulders and chest – jolt himself out of it.

Oh ffff– And now I've got a wet bed, on top of everything else.

Under everything else.

Shit.

He flopped himself back against his soggy sheet which was, at least, now cooler and counted his breaths, tried to feel himself hammocked beneath them, relaxing, swaying in his own breeze. He started to fix his concentration on the few topics he was safe to consider after nightfall.

Ruth. She'll be asleep now and dreaming of sharks, the weird hiss of the tiger shark, shutting its car-boot jaws around her . . . around her what? Which part would she actually favour? What would she like? The warm throat closing on one of her legs? Or both legs, with those cheeky, sharky teeth just hugging her tight at the waist? Or the whole of her body sucked sexily in with only her head snipped off like a troublesome button and freed to bob and stare, chiffoned with blood? She'd like that – a body without worries, without memories, without shame. I'd like that myself.

Beyond Nathan's cottage the muggy air swaggered faintly with sideshow music: insistent, mechanical and clashing through the jolly syncopations of melodic insanity.

Mary heard it, too, filaments and rags of drunken nursery tunes and bad pop, working in between the trees around her. She listened to the dodgeming refrains, along with all the rest of the encoded night: the nervous leaves and twig snaps, the starting of rabbits, the visible silence of owls and the reckless crash and snuffle of her local hedgehog rooting for a feed – the usual animal and vegetable hubbub, seasonally adjusted, and then amplified by the saturated dark. A fraction of moon spiked behind sails of hot cloud, while half echoes caught in the wood fell stickily against her as she tried to understand why they all seemed different tonight. When she walked, patterns of muted light and sound seemed to ebb away and then close again behind her, thickening towards sense.

Nathan rubbed his face, coughed, rubbed again.

*Richard will be swabbing at Lynda with the antiseptic liquid of their choice. They'll agree that he should use his full-size arm for this, because his other one is why she married him, his point of interest. Which, of course, he decided to tell me when I didn't want to know. And I don't actually want to remember now. His life is not something I wish to consider – his unhappy childhood, his unhappy schooldays, his fucking unhappy Shakespearean withered arm – but he always does manage to slip in and tell me about it all, in any case. Why me? What the fuck would suggest I'm the sympathetic type? One minute he's business as usual – the Virtually Invisible Man – fucking fascinated by the middle distance – and then he's tight beside me, concentration breaking out all over him like lice, and I know why he does it, I fucking know – because it makes my skin crawl. Because I ought to be sympathetic, but I can't. He isn't another poor bastard, buckled by grief, he isn't my cunting soul-mate – he fucking **enjoys** it. He fucking loves the suffering.*

And I don't.

I'm sure I don't.

I am fucking sure I don't.

But there he'll be tonight, in exquisite despair, dabbing and sponging at the heart of Lynda's charms and doggedly keeping his shortcoming in the shade, because that and only that about him turns her on, and Lynda won't want a turn-on when she's in no state to fuck.

Although maybe she'll want to feel sexy, attractive, and maybe he'll want to help. This could all be the kind of arrangement that they make: their own kind of sweetness. United in pain. Uncovering unaccustomed passions.

Fuck.

Imagining them shagging is the one thing I know that can douse my libido no matter what state I'm in. Those two, they don't bear thinking about. Like right now – he could – in fact – be at her, could be taking his conjugal pleasures, exercising his husbandly rights, bouncing off her pubic bone until he opens up her wounds.

Now there's a little picture we shouldn't paint.

Mary had written for most of the evening – building paragraphs and then scrawling them flat again. She had made a kind of start, had produced one or two scraps that were almost saying something, but they still weren't enough. Out of doors now, in an effort to stroll her head clear, she passed by the stone wall of the old rabbit warren, Richard and Lynda's house not too far away.

Mary's literary situation appeared to be frighteningly plain. She was not one of the people who could do this. She did not come from the right kind of place, she had not been brought up appropriately, she had not lived in the proper way, she did not naturally use the acceptable range of words, she was not a womanly enough woman and certainly not a manly enough man and her stupidity was constantly, horrifically deafening – she didn't, couldn't ever, know enough. All the ideas she had ever been going to have had already occurred to her, there were no more. This was the time to give up, to let go.

Louis . . . You can never be sure with Louis – I'm not even convinced that he sleeps. Although he could, of course, be tucked up now with a head full of saints and martyrs, dormitory feasts, the ghostly tickle of Llangattock's eyelashes, sideburns, tongue.

I saw his pyjamas once – old Louis's – proper Chinese silk with piping, the sly dog.

Nathan's heart tried to skip aside on him, to summon up Maura and coax him hard awake, but he ignored it. He pinched the skin on both his forearms as a distraction and continued his internal Foal Island tour.

*Collating us, our deaths and near-deaths — that's a job **I'd** leave until after dark, perhaps Louis does, too. Yes, I feel that he may be archiving us while we're asleep and can't feel him fumbling at our lives, at our attempts to end them.*

Mary began to work back towards the hut, trying to fix out a form of words that would let her say goodbye to Joe without her crying. What she would say to Nathan, she didn't want to consider yet. She noticed, when she walked, that her tiredness had finally deepened into a kind of intoxication — she was amiably unco-ordinated, disconnected from her thoughts and oddly easy with the prospect of abandoning her total sum of hopes. Even the surprise her indifference lifted in her was distant and irresistibly ridiculous.

And I never can imagine Joe, not in any way. I could almost be persuaded that he won't let me. Somewhere, I suppose, he's shining away to himself, praying at us all until we're better than we are. No wonder I don't sleep.

When she reached the rise, Mary sat. From here she could see four different lights, ticking out their particular hazard warnings: one on a count of seven, two on two different counts of four and one scything up from below the horizon, a brief wag of illumination for one second in every five. They measured against each other, skipped their different beats and then, somehow, locked.

Mary felt the instant fasten round her, fit her, inside and out: finally, massively, shockingly articulate. This one shrug of blood, valved in her heart; this one taste of breath, its fractions of sea rock, grasses, earth, a note of honeysuckle, a note of pine; this one black and dove sky, flesh hot; this one lighthouse twitch; this one blink of absolute comfort when she started to stretch, to swallow and then *know* this one exponential scream of unconfined generosity, possibility, life. It changed her mind.

Then the ordinary flow of time tipped over her again and, for a few moments, reality leaped from a standstill to a rush and then centred itself while she attended to the sensual creep of an almost sexual understanding. Her skin shuddered against the static rub of it while she raced with information: this was hers, this part of this second, and then this and the next; everything was hers, things of which she had no comprehension were still hers, would still come to her and speak. The possible scope of her inspirations was so thoroughly beyond her that she felt completely unafraid: there were no details here to alarm her, only the first real hook of hunger, growing in, and setting up a charge in her that meant she wouldn't sleep until the sun was almost risen and she was home and sitting at her desk and tired beyond herself, but not beyond imagination, not beyond the finished pages she'd been driven to produce.

And by that time even Nathan was dreaming: splinters of conversations he'd never quite had, of near-completed meetings and the clear idea that he ought to be touching somebody.

And, over in Ancw, the fair was quiet now, closed away.

And, about half a mile beyond it, resting in the gorse that grew by the sea-front path, were a pair of children's trainers and a purple T-shirt. A tourist would notice them there in the morning at around nine o'clock, think nothing of it and walk on.

And at nine, or a little after, in Bethesda Street, in Ancw, Darren Price's mother, tired of shouting upstairs to wake him, would climb to his room and discover he wasn't there. She would hunt through the house, imagining that he was hiding, calling his name. Then she would search the street, her nearest shops. Later, she would regard this as time that she had wasted – as a betrayal of her son and all later attempts to find him and bring him safe home.

And at ten, or a little after, Mary would already have surprised herself by being entirely awake and walking in on the end of Nathan's breakfast to set a slim handful of papers on his kitchen table and walk out. He would choke on his toast and only be able to nod his head in acknowledgement before she slipped away. This would be the last he was able eat for some hours, his digestion baffled by the onset of pride and pleasure and critical unease.

And at 15.28 Darren's shoes and T-shirt would be found in the gorse, followed at 16.10 by the discovery of his tracksuit bottoms, stuffed in a waste bin outside the public lavatory. It would become much harder to picture him still alive.

And at 18.07 that evening, Mrs Price, supported by her husband, would appear for the first time in a televised appeal for information, for Darren's return, for a power that could stop her knowing he was gone.

And later on Foal Island, without the intrusion of televisions, newspapers, or recreational radios, Nathan would spend the same evening reading and then re-reading the work that his daughter had given him. There was no mistaking – it wasn't good. He would read the pages over and over, trying to like them, until it was dark.

And when the night was drawn full in, Mr and Mrs Price would occupy it in uncovering one of God's hidden gifts to them – unlimited resilience. In utterly separate ways they met pain, surpassing pain, surpassing pain, surpassing description and still they didn't die.

And through the next day they continued to live, even when a policewoman solemnly told them the story of their boy – their adventurous, outgoing, very often smiling boy – of his slipping down out of his window to visit the fair, of his being seen by neighbours, cousins, friends – who were, all of them, at that time, somehow less than capable, rushed, called aside at vital moments, temporarily rendered unable to ask why he was out so late, out all alone, and then out with a man they had never seen before – a man Mrs Price can now smell under her fingernails, taste in her cigarette's smoke.

And at lunchtime that same day, Nathan would smile at Mary, at her newly confident face, and lie to her, saying that he had not read her stories yet. This would seem important to him, this small keeping of his child from harm.

And at 17.05 a policeman and his dog would find Darren Price in woods twenty miles from Ancw, apparently asleep and snuggled up in leaves. Curled on his side, his shoulder naked, Darren – from a distance – was only wonderfully pale. For a few, remarkable seconds, he seemed flawlessly strange, not dead.

And later, a little later, Mrs Price would not remember when she screamed. She would be given sedatives.

And quietly, tenderly uneasy, Nathan would walk to his daughter's home and see her through the window for one beating instant, sitting in consideration of a page. He would look at her face: clear and solemnly open, as if it were tilting into the moment before a kiss: and he would know they were made of the same thing, he would know they were both – quite willingly – at the mercy of their minds. He would know how much she was his daughter. He would watch all the sense of his life, turning with the paper beneath her hands.

And officers undertaking to reveal Darren's body entirely would be the first to see his wounds. They would be careful to think of him with respect, but also as a body, not a little boy. They would find this strategy relatively unsuccessful. Within months, one would ask for counselling and another would leave the force.

And Mary would listen to Nathan while he ceased to stammer, fumble, cough, while he told the truth. They would sit elbow to elbow and be together in the imperfection of her words, in the gentle drum and murmur of his voice, and she would be angry and then ashamed and then both disappointed and overjoyed – what she had done was good enough to be wrong, it existed enough to be fought with, to deserve someone else's critical assaults. Mary would be pleased, in a bruised way: she would, for the first time, think that in writing she need not always be alone.

And all around them, minds of every cast and inclination would continue to mark out fantasies, futures, hopes. In thoughts as free as children, bright as knives, acts would be rehearsed and then created irrevocably.

And no one would be caught for killing Darren and no blame would be lifted and no mercy would come with time.

And Mrs Price took her pills and slept and wished never to wake.

Two days after a murder he knew nothing of, Nathan used Joe's telephone, and – still fretting over Mary's manuscript – called Jack for advice. As is perfectly human and natural, he had a great capacity for entertaining worries that were focused on very personal, but really rather minor points.

'Her material, it's not . . . it's not *finished*. It's really remarkably . . . bad. Compared to what she wrote before she came here . . . I mean, I think I've managed to make her *worse*. Jack?'

'Mm.' J. D. breathed too close to the receiver. 'Well, she'll sor . . . sort it out. If she's writing, then she'll learn. And it's much better to make mistakes than to get it right. More educational.' He tried for a laugh, didn't make it. 'Anyway, you've got more on your plate than that . . . Do you know?'

'You're drunk.' Nathan tamped away the usual disappointment, tried to judge if the conversation was worth continuing.

'I said, did you know you'd got more on your pla –' Jack's flow stalled, re-adjusted. 'Yes, I'm drunk. I left her. Lovely girl.'

'You *left* her?'

'You know . . . left her . . . pre-emptively buggered off – things on the cards – not good. Don't make me think about it, Sport. This Mary stuff – you talked to her about it? Did you? Her work? Hm? Nate?'

'Well, I . . . she was . . . I was so fucking scared – not to blow it, you know. And then,' Nathan decided to take the confessional tack; there was a kind of pleasure in confessing to a drunk, knowing the recording angel was firmly out to lunch, 'at first . . . at first, I know she didn't like it – what I was saying, but then, then I altered my . . . Christ, Jack, it's all so fresh with her – she likes doing it so much – it's all so . . . young.' He paused to allow himself the total foolishness of a grin, the quick peppering of memories from last night: the first

186

time she'd argued back, the first time she'd giggled and he'd known it would be all right, the easiness falling on him when they really kicked in to work and then when they'd finally called a halt, stretched, had a coffee and a good, tired hug. 'I couldn't bear – I mean, when I had to go, because it was late, because we'd finished, because . . . I had to go. I didn't want to. I almost told her, I almost said, about . . . who I am.' Nathan heard the quiet muffle of a hand across the receiver, blurry noise. 'Jack. Jack? Are you all right? Did you really leave her?'

Jack's voice grappled closer as, not far from his receiver, came the sound of something hollow falling. 'Do leave it be. And . . . and . . . Let me tell you the news, *your* news. It's shit . . . it's all shit – all of *my* news is shit, you should know that by now, so should I – but this, this stuff is different shit, far worse. Fucking country we live in, Nate, how does anyone live in it sober? Mm? How?'

Nathan concentrated, stared at the brass of Joe's table lamp while J. D. stumbled through an explanation of Darren Price's small chain of events. At first Nathan thought he was listening to some kind of drinking nightmare, recited. Then he believed, recalled the left-handed boy who'd liked to look after the Foal Island boat when it moored at the quay. And then, of course, he *couldn't* believe. Violent death did not happen to old-fashioned little boys who liked feeding gulls and coiling ropes up neatly.

'Nate? You there, Nate? All right? Don't be quiet.' Jack sniffed, might even have been crying, it was always hard to tell. 'I've had enough of people being quiet. Nate?'

'I'm here.'

'It's all fucked, you know? There's only us who isn't – aren't. It's fucked.'

'Yeah.'

'In the office – quick bastards, they are. Clever, clever fucks. Bright at things – some things, anyway. All day I could hear them, sniffing at the secretaries, same as ever: pushing the comments, the stories, seeing how much it took to make them squeal. Today's best line? Did I tell you? Latest joke? "I hear the fair's dirt cheap in Ancw, this year – Prices slashed." And I laughed, too, Nathan. I'm one of them. I laughed.'

'Go to bed, Jack, get some rest.'

187

'No. Fuck it, I didn't laugh, I'm lying again. I always lie. I didn't *laugh* – I *said* it. I fucking said it. I'm such a cunt.'

'Go to bed.'

'Can't – when no one else is there, it scares me.'

'Did it ever occur to you, Jack, that I know that.'

'Well, fuck. Don't be like that. Please. Not now. Nate? Nate? I would, if I could, apologise. Nate?'

'I know. Goodnight, Jack.'

'No. Not like –'

'Goodnight.'

1992

Nathan had cut the top off one of his fingers. Not in fun: just by accident. He'd been dicing potatoes and had let his knife and attention slip. So the soup for the Sunday Lunch had gained a gout or two of inadvertent thickening. He'd chosen not to mention the addition – Foal Island soups were an ugly enough proposition at the best of times: normally Lynda's speciality, allowing her, as they did, extensive contact with cylindrical vegetables.

I'll have to tell Mary, eventually. Difficult to phrase it with delicacy, though. 'By the way, we all go a little bit carefully with Lynda's veg. We tend to be guided by shape – the carrots, zucchini, parsnips, Chinese radish, cucumber, yams – they're generally the ones to watch. I mean, a cucumber isn't a vegetable – of course – but then, Lynda doesn't pay much attention to classifications, she mainly picks her ingredients for their dimensions, for their fit. You know what I mean . . .'

Except Mary **won't** *know. At least, I hope she won't.*

No, she will, of course she will, she's not a child. Not any more. Of course she'll know. Probably. She's a grown woman, after all.

The removal of Mary, her theft, the whole years of her lost to him, made their usual incision and scored the bone at the base of his skull. He shook his head and changed his subject back.

What would be the best way to put it? Mm? The fatherly way. 'Look, we tend to be a little bit hesitant with Lynda's cooking because . . . because we know it all comes out of her smallholding, as it were. Not that her holding's so terribly small, by most accounts. Really, rather well-used.'

I'll sound like a dirty old man.

'Pretty much anything, really, she'll have a go at it. Even with turnips and potatoes, you can't be safe because what she can't fit up her snatch at the first time of asking will end up trimmed and whittled until she can. She has no mercy. And no intention of not confessing her violations at intimate length – Lynda, the sly seducer of roots and shoots. I myself find our separate

191

appetites are mutually exclusive. Although I have been known to gag down whole platefuls of carrot batons, just to spite her, just to stop her bullying. Or reducing us all to scurvy by sullying our access to Vitamin C.'

No. Why turn her stomach? She'll only worry about what she's already swallowed, unknowingly. And we can't have her worried, not Mary.

Mary. The thought of her lips, of her mother's lips, of his women's lips, eating, closing over warmth, neat – it hurt him, hurt in his blood.

As did Mary's current absence. Just now she was away from him, his only daughter, she was visiting her Uncles on the mainland. Her absence made him feel naked somewhere, psychologically exposed. It happened every time – she would make a little trip away and he would have to realise, all over again, how much she softened his reality. Everything seemed to sit more easily around him when she was there. She was his defence.

He sighed and leaned back in his chair, looked about the room.

'Why shouldn't I be able to?' The Monthly Business Meeting was grumbling along without him: Ruth in especially whining form. 'I have a right to say whatever I like about whatever I like.'

Nathan wanted to walk, let the lunch settle, be with his music for the rest of the day, let it sluice him down and get him away from Business. Business was one of the many things that could be guaranteed to niggle him into a rage. Nathan was not a person who took naturally to committees and processes involving compromise.

'Well, don't I? Isn't that the point of being here? That we're all free? That we write what we want?' Ruth simply wouldn't let her point drop.

He pressed experimentally at his raw digit through its layer of sticking plaster and was rewarded with a warming, jangling hurt. Nippy, but controlled enough to be almost pleasurable.

'Well, you've made your views very clear now, Ruth. Perhaps someone else would like to comment. Nathan, what do you think?' Joe leaned forward, his head showing dark against a window blanked out with white autumn mist. 'Mm? Not like you to have no opinion.'

'He's sulking.' Lynda grinned. 'No little Mary to play with.'

'Fuck you. At least I still *have* recognisable emotions.'

*No, don't fight. You want to go for a walk, you want to get **away**. Shut up.*

192

'And you *have* a daughter. I would have thought someone with *recognisable emotions* might have told her she had a father by now.'

'Well, you would have thought wrong.'

Joe was gathering himself to intervene while Ruth glared mournfully about her – no longer anything like the centre of attention. 'Aren't we forgetting – ?'

Nathan lost his temper, felt it slither clear out of his grip and bounce away, nastily. 'Aren't we forgetting what, Ruth? Anything of importance? You, for example? The whole tragic fucking balls-up that is your tiny, tiny mind? What is it you want to do, again? To exercise your free speech over? Oh, yes, I remember – you want to write about the Price boy, you want to rummage around in his death, see what you can take.'

I'll regret this, I will.

'You want to steal his life all over again, piss in his parents' hearts and give his murderer a handy little volume to toss off with for hours at a time.'

But I don't fucking care.

'This from a woman who fucked her way through the halt, the lame and the hard of thinking until no one would employ her except the sodding prison service – a woman who hangs out with rapists and murderers for a year, does a runner and then starts coughing up tacky verses based on confessions weaseled out of the incarcerated. Tell us, do – when did you decide to come here for the good of your art? Before or after the boys from Category A found out how to phone you at home? Mm? You're not a writer, you're a fucking body-snatcher. Jesus Christ.'

Oh, you are a bad boy, Nathan. Oh dearie, dearie me.

Oh, yes-in-deed.

Ruth was scrabbling in her pockets, Nathan guessed, for a handkerchief. Richard appeared to be grinning very slightly: perhaps amused by the spat, perhaps preoccupied with something else entirely as he reached for his wife's hand. He seemed hazily surprised when she touched him back, pattered an investigation round the pale, fine fingers of his smaller fist. Lynda herself was watching Nathan, waiting to see if he'd drawn enough blood to be satisfied, to stop. She was, therefore, just as surprised as he was when Ruth halted the search of her pockets and threw two biting showers of hastily gathered loose change at Nathan's face.

'Christ, ya fu–' He tried to sound adequately angry while maintaining a cringing position; he'd always had a particular fear of losing his sight at the hands of some random maddie, chucking things. 'What do you – ?' And now could well be the hour.

Ruth lurched to her feet and he braced himself for another, more personally projectile attack. To his left he could hear an unmistakable snuff of nervous laughter from Louis – that man had no bottle at all.

Not that you do. Look up and meet her eye, at least. You're in the right, remember. You're only saying what all of them think.

Ruth wavered above him, looking more than usually bloated – her doughy face marked with two little thumbprints of furious red on either cheek.

You hit the spot, then. Really pissed her off.

Tee hee.

And if you grin now she will kill you. She will snap your back, rip out your spinal cord and go skipping down the stairs with it. Do not even consider grinning, not even a hint at it.

Tee hee.

Sssh.

'Nathan,' she sounded tired, unpleasantly vulnerable.

Oh shit – she's pulling that old trick, is she? So now I'm supposed to feel sorry for her. Fucking women – they always do that, bend things round until you end up hitting yourself. Well, not today.

'Nathan, I'm very happy for you. It must be great to have never made any mistakes in your life. You must be really happy and content. And you must love always knowing what people are going to do and why, always thinking the worst of everyone.'

She walked out of the room in exactly the kind of embarrassed, but vaguely impressed little silence that Nathan had known she would try to generate. Sure this was a bad idea, he nevertheless called after her, 'That hurt, you know. Throwing things at people . . . that's, that's not . . . safe.' He sounded as much of a prat as he'd thought he might. The remainder of the Fellowship studied him.

OK, then. Stare at me, you fucks. I'm not storming out. I'm staying just exactly here and when you start up Uncle Joe's little psychic circle: all the good, wee writers united: all letting your brains flap out together in the rosy, cosy silence, well, I will still fucking be here and I will concentrate on nothing

194

else but screwing up your vibes.

'Nathan.' Joe, sneaking out his best placatory voice, which actually was quite placating: not a stain of admonishment in it. 'Nathan.' Calling him back to his better self.

Well, sod off, I don't want to go. I've never liked my better self.

'I might suggest that our Business Meeting has concluded. Or almost concluded – what would you say? Nathan.'

*I'd say **fuck, wank, bollocks, Jesusfuckingchrist**.*

'I'd say whatever you like, Joe. Whatever.'

'Anything for a quiet life? That's not like you, Nathan.'

Nathan could feel the room congeal around him – the audience all set for a turn or two of badger baiting and here he was, stumbling and growling: the mad, bad badger again.

'Not like me to be agreeable, you mean?'

Joe smiled, almost tenderly, 'No. Not like you to compromise,' spun a glance across at Nathan and held it, glinting, testing him out, ready for a serious dig, a proper excavation of his head. 'What would you have said to Ruth? What did you want to say? Really.'

'I said what I wanted to. I always do.'

'All right. Then what would you have said to Mary? About the Price boy.'

*Get the fuck away from that, just get the fuck away from that – Mary is **my business**.*

'Nothing. I would have said nothing. Talking about it upset her. I don't try to make her upset.'

'But you must have prepared something. What would you have said, if you could? What would have been the principle of the thing?'

'Oh, for fuck's sake!'

Joe didn't even flinch, only waited, working to reel in the words he wanted from Nathan – his patience was tangible, like a cold stroke at the side of Nathan's neck.

And Nathan dropped away from the grip of his intentions, acquiesced. Joe always got what he wanted in the end, so why fight? Why not let him shake out the last bloody syllable and be sure you were fully expressed – as if that were ever really a good idea. 'Joe, I would have told her, *will* tell her, that she can never take away anything she hasn't the power to put back. Writers *write*, they don't *steal* – we *make* something. We only have the right to rob ourselves.

Break the rules if you want to, but then don't complain when they break you back. But I think,' he swallowed round a dipping swell of something terribly like pride, 'I think she's fine, I don't think she'll have any bother with that. I think she's . . . fine.'

Joe watched on, still avid, still looking for another sliver on his pound of flesh.

All right. You want more, you can have more.

'Unlike me, Mr Christopher, and unlike you, she is fine because she is still a normal human being. I mean look at you – look. You're fucking insane. You keep it nicely covered, but we both know it's true. Hauling out opinions, establishing principles – you still think it's *important*, don't you – what any of us thinks. You think it matters what *you* think. Because for all of those fucking-multi-media-prominent-opinion-forming-leading-British-fucking-novelist years, every time you had a really interesting new idea, every time you squeezed one out in the morning with the first crap of the day, you'd call up the fucking *Guardian* or Radio pissing Four and some stupid cunt would let you tell us all about it. We just *had* to know. As if a *writer*, as if a fucking professional *typist*, a cunting *typist* knows any fucking thing about anything. But you fell for it. They all told you that you mattered and so you believed that it was true. How long did it take for you to work out who was wanking who?'

Joe was wincing, only very slightly, but Nathan still knew he'd bitten him squarely on both Achilles' heels. He allowed himself a grin while Joe swallowed, rubbed his thumbs against his palms. 'Everyone matters. There's nothing masturbatory about that.'

'But you wanted to matter more than most.'

'Yes.' Joe was never slow in admitting his faults. Nathan tried not to find this admirable, but usually failed. 'It's good you've reminded me. Yes. For a long time, I forgot my priorities. Lost perspective. You saw me do it, I know.'

'Our words are our right, but they're also our privilege.' Nathan heard his tone soften the way it always seemed to in the face of honest regret. 'Mm? You've said it often enough to me since.'

Joe smiled to himself: entirely, but self-effacingly, penitent. 'Yes. So now I have no say. I've used all my words. That's why I'm here – no more public statements, no more writing, no more of all that.'

A silence settled. Louis gently offered, 'And our island would be the perfect place for that kind of retreat. Even when barely a trace was left of the monastery – Foal Island was seen as a place of sanctuary.'

'That's a shame.' Nathan could feel himself snarling, which was never a good sign. 'A leper colony would have been so much more appropriate.'

Joe only nodded mildly and reached out to take Nathan's hand. As ever, his clasp was drily overheated. Nathan felt his fingers start to sweat, a pang of salt pain under his injured nail.

Shit.

He hated when Joe did this: hand–holding, waiting to meet the eyes and then scouring back through the uneasy charges firing in his brain.

'What do you want, Nathan?' Joe giving him that long, long look.

Not now.

This was the end of the Business Meeting and the start of the Meeting proper – Joe's idea of therapy for them, or of bonding, or of worship, or of fuck knew what. Nathan didn't like it – their sitting and waiting and being silent. It was too much like being alone with himself, like closing the door on all his efforts at peace of mind.

'Nathan, what do you want?'

The old refrain, Joe's favourite enquiry, lobbed out precisely whenever Nathan had no wish to answer it.

'Nathan?'

*Shit. Fuck. **Shit.***

Joe asked the others questions, various questions, questions of all kinds, but with Nathan it was always the same, the exact same one.

'Nathan, what do you want?'

'The unattainable. OK? The unattainable. That's what I want.'

Never another question and never another reply.

Like holding a wary, edgy electricity, like walking on rice-paper, water, an unbalanced hope, Mary found her expectation of him shadowed her whenever she went outside. Jonno.

'Now, girl, we did think we should say,' Bryn had told her, Morgan nodding agreement, gently stirring his unsugared tea. 'Well, you see, he's left Gofeg. He's working in Cardiff. Got a job there in graphic design.'

'Computers. You know Jonno and computers, loves them.' Morgan had bitten at his thumb, regretting his choice of verb and eyeing Bryn, who, in his turn, had looked to the fireplace and puffed out softly worried breaths.

'So he's not here.' Mary had let them off the hook, cultivating, for all their sakes, a tone of something approaching indifference. This news of his departure had left her feeling simultaneously hollowed and freed.

Which now made walking unexpectedly difficult. She seemed noticeably lighter than she was used to being, more liable to topple or be blown adrift. A lock of tension had settled, triangulating fierily between her two shoulders and the tender vertebrae that moulded the give of her waist. She looked, had anyone cared to observe her, slightly sleepless, preoccupied: one hand intent on keeping her hair from her eyes when it fanned in the uneven breeze.

She kept moving, threading her observation along familiar streets. *Not yet, then. Not yet.*

Mary was still waiting for that one trip she'd make back to Gofeg when everything would seem smaller and further away. The trip that would mean she had properly left, or properly arrived, somewhere else.

I don't know why it hasn't happened yet.

But Gofeg had refused to shrink for her – instead it had simply decided to prove her more and more irrelevant. Each time Mary came back, she was the one who seemed to be shrinking. On this visit she discovered the supermarket had, once again, renewed its façade. All but one of the remaining chain stores had withdrawn – temporary charity shops now squatting in their abandoned premises. The garage and the post office had started to sell increasingly inappropriate, hasty-looking goods. It was all changing without her. After her second or third return to Gofeg, Mary had begun to reassure herself by referring to the distant, more permanent conformation of hills, the limits of the landlocked sunsets, the fists of pigeons, opening and turning, closing again for home.

Home. Now there's a word. Where the work is. Where the house is. Where the heart is. Difficult to pick.

She did this more and more, she'd noticed – gabbling away to herself, easing her nerves, or passing the time, or practising narrations she'd never remember or want again. This was, of course, a good way of avoiding any genuine thought, of dodging proper contact with the lick of chill that came when she paused at words like *heart*.

Hearts. Hearts and flowers. Broken-hearted. Broken. Broken down.

You don't know when to stop. Do you?

Hearts and flowers. Birds and bees. Fucking.

You just don't know.

The way he was.

She pocketed her hands more firmly and remembered to nod at the faces who nodded, to smile at the people who smiled, to look away when anyone gave her the small, brutal stare that was meant to make her feel ugly for having gone, got away from Gofeg to something better, or at least something else. And they blamed her for leaving Jonno, she knew that. She did, too.

Jonathan.

The taste of him ran at her, made her falter, stand considering a section of pavement, the base of a wall, the warm unfocusing of her vision. Her past broke against her while a part of her was finally, loudly bewildered.

This is Gofeg, he should be here. He shouldn't have gone without saying where I could find him.

'What's the matter? What's wrong?' Nathan had pounced a little too savagely for the phone and sent a lamp skating perilously close to the table's edge. 'Sorry, sorry. That's not what I should start with. Ah, hello.' Joe had walked across with a message to say that Mary had called from Gofeg and wanted to speak to him.

She's ill.

She's decided to stay there and not come back.

She's coming back early, coming back home to me.

She wanted to speak to me.

'Mary?' He had started to shiver with possibly terror and possibly joy, apparently more out of breath since he'd stopped running and had to sit waiting on one of Joe's creakily leather armchairs while Joe himself tried to hover helpfully and offer hot and then finally alcoholic drinks. The last of the sunset had slipped down behind the horizon before she rang.

'Yes, hello. Nathan.'

'Mm . . . that's, yes, me.'

'Good. Good.'

Oh, Christ, she sounds nervous. She's delaying, working up to saying something bad. I knew it, I fucking knew it. The Bad News Pause.

He said, 'Mary, is everything all right?' when he wanted to say

*I'm sorry, I know I've done everything wrong, whatever the problem is, it's all my fault, which means that I can fix it. Absolutely, that will be my responsibility. I know you appeared to be happy when you left and I managed to totally miss all the signs that should have told me that you weren't, but I **will make you** happy, I will make everything the way that it should be and you'll be great, just fine, and so will I – **we'll** be great. We will. I promise you. We will.*

But he only begged, in under his tongue, where no one could hear him.

Christ. No spine at all.

'Nathan?'

'Yes?' *Anything, yes.*

'Well, this is silly really. I wanted . . . I love talking to the Uncles, it is wonderful to see them, it is – I just . . . tell me what's happening there.'

'I . . . hu, um, I'm afraid mainly the usual things.'

Fucking magnificent – anyone would guess from that what you do for a living – gifted with words – a born storyteller – in your blood.

In your arse.

'Eckless misses you.' *Me too, me too.* 'Ah, very badly.' A pulse had dropped to pummel round his stomach and he thought he might be sick quite soon if he didn't really concentrate and only swallow carefully, now and then. 'That is to say, he misses you very well. He's the best misser of things I know.' *The **dog**? You have nothing better to tell her about than the bloody **dog**?*

'Yes, he is, isn't he? Is it raining?'

'Is it? . . . Oh, no. It has been, but it's dry now and I think we'll have a frost. Did somebody, I mean . . . upset you?' *Because, if he has, I will maim and then kill him and eat his bones.*

'No, no. At least, the person I used to know here.'

Knew it – that fuck. What was he called, Jim? John?

'Oh?' He tried to clamp the waver out of his voice.

'He's gone. It was finished ages ago, I think I said . . . but he's moved away now, away from Gofeg, and it's . . . should I write about it?'

'*What?*'

'Should I write about it?'

'No, you should feel sad like any other normal human being.' *You witless moron, show some tact.* 'If you, if you *do* feel sad then, then what to do is,' *do everything I don't,* 'you should talk to people – which you are doing – and, um, be kind, be gentle with yourself, do nice things, eat nice things – except you won't have any appetite, I suppose, hm?'

'Not really.'

'But the Uncles'll see you right, won't they?'

'Oh yes, oh yes – they're . . .'

*Try not to say **wonderful**.*

'They're wonderful.'

Thanks.

'That's good, then. You're in safe hands.'

'But I don't . . .'

'What?'

'I don't want to feel this way. So I started to, to put it down, to write it, and it doesn't make any sense – it's just no good as a piece of work at all, but it makes me feel . . . it makes it easier. I just, I know that what I'm writing isn't mine, I know that part of it is *him* and that's . . .'

'Look, if it makes you feel easier in your mind then do it. It's not as if you're producing a kiss-and-tell memoir or anything, is it?' He felt her tiny inhalation, far beyond his reach, and he understood that *kiss* had sprung the trap and tipped her into crying – the silent, private kind of weeping he knew altogether too well. 'You'll work out what you feel comfortable saying, when it's time. This is about, about,' *saying this will only make things worse,* 'the relief of pain. Everyone has the right to relieve their pain.'

Congratulations, you have made things worse.

Nathan listened to Mary's unsteady breath, jolting in, shaking her, telling her – as if she wouldn't be aware – that grief had a hold of her now and would – for a while – enjoy moving her as it wished. He wished he could explain that this was a type of rest, the forgiving brand of sadness that would beat itself out of her while it stopped her thinking and made her tired enough to sleep. Instead he closed his eyes and resisted his own tears. He was rewarded with an increase of pressure behind his eyes.

'Mary. You do whatever you want to, whatever feels right and you'll come through. And you can . . . you can call me at –' *Any time.* 'Any time. Any time at all. Joe will get me and I'll call you right back and then soon you'll be, well, soon you'll be here again and I'll,' *not expect you to be delighted that you're back – although I'll want you to be – but anyway,* 'I'll make you work like a slave and give you no time to think. Ha.' He never was able to reproduce laughter effectively when he especially needed to. 'Unless you want to take it easy, in which case, you can. You know? Rest? We're here for you.'

*No, **I'm** here for you.*

But I can't say that, because of so many deficiencies I am too sickened to recite.

'That's, that's good. Thanks, Nathan.'

She sniffed, perhaps wiped her face, her eyes: that's what he imagined. Did she carry a handkerchief? He couldn't remember, which seemed absurd. She would need one, from time to time, obviously – but, really, paper ones were better – disposable, more hygienic.

She'd be flushed: the emotions of the fair-skinned, always more visible.

Except at those terrible times when you don't catch them. With Maura, when it really mattered, I couldn't tell what she was feeling at all.

'Mary? Are you OK? You've gone all quiet.'

'I couldn't think of anything to say.'

She was steadying up now. Good girl.

'That's all right.'

'I'd better go.'

'No.' *Don't squeal, you stupid fucker. Think about somebody else, for once in your life.* 'Unless you want to. I mean, that's fine. You'll be back on Saturday, then?' *As if you could forget.*

'Yes.'

'I'll have the boat ready. If you don't mind my seamanship.'

'You're a good captain – fine.'

'Not as good as Joe.'

'But more . . . stimulating.'

'Yeah, right, OK.' A grin firing up from his knees and rocking him. 'I'll see you then. Bye.'

'Yes, thanks, Nathan. Really, thanks. Bye.'

He kept the receiver, rested it on his stomach for a while and thought of nothing, allowing himself to be content.

'You should tell her.' Joe slipped round the doorway, angled his head an inch or two, enquiring. 'Don't you think?'

No rest for the wicked.

'I will. In my own way, in my own time. We're only just . . . comfortable, don't make me have to – don't make me do anything to make it go away.'

'You'll never be made to do anything here, Nate. That's not what we're for.'

Nathan replaced the receiver, officially ended the call. 'No, it's not. So you'll keep to your business and I'll keep to mine.'

I know what I'm doing here. She didn't call you, she called me.

When Mary came back to the living room, the Uncles were studiously relaxed. Morgan lay along the sofa, perhaps asleep, his head pillowed on Bryn's lap, while Bryn read from one of his favourites, *The Universal Home Guide*.

'If a husband is detained in an institution for those of unsound mind and becomes a charge of the poor law authority then the wife can be forced to support him.' He loved the sections on *Law* and *Etiquette*, especially. 'A husband has to pay for his wife's funeral, but a wife cannot be compelled to pay for his. There's complicated for you, Mo. Silly old things, marriages.'

Morgan simply bedded the back of his head a little more firmly against Bryn's thighs.

Mary turned off the light by the door and eased over to her seat. She hoped that, in the dimness, no one would notice she'd been crying. They all adjusted to the dim, slightly fleshy light of burning gas, the motionless, patchy red of ember-effect moulding.

Mary could hear Bryn's hand slowly stroking at Morgan's hair. Since she'd left, the two men seemed to touch each other more. Sometimes she thought this was to do with their need for comfort in the face of a diminished family and sometimes she thought that her presence, for all of those years, must have restrained them, kept them apart from the ways they wished to be.

'Mary?' Bryn's whisper seemed remarkably loud. 'We thought you were over that – we thought the thing with Jonathan was –'

'I know, so did I.'

Bryn sighed faintly. 'We're sorry. So sorry. *Amor et melle et felle est fecundissimus.*'

'Love is both generously sweet and bitter.' She'd heard that one from Louis, too.

Morgan cleared his throat carefully, paused in case this sudden movement of his breath would cause him complications and then spoke. Mary tried not to notice that, alone in the dark, his voice was unmistakably older, its melodies stiffening. 'We've been lucky though, Bryn and me. We always had the sweet of it, really. Not so good before we found each other, but then – then we were dancing.'

Bryn leaned and kissed Morgan's forehead, motherly. 'Couldn't have been happier, we thought, and then Maura brought you.'

'Surprised us.'

'Surprised *me*. I hadn't heard from her in years, didn't know she was married. And then she calls up, out of nowhere.'

'Out of up in Scotland somewhere – Perth.'

'Out of nowhere. And she says she's bringing you.'

'And we realise the only thing we've ever wanted and never had.'

'You.'

'We've been happy.' Morgan seemed about go on, but had to cough. Mary knew that, in the black and blood-coloured shadows of the room, Bryn was concentrating. He would feel each shuddered opening of Morgan's throat, each retching closure as he held Bryn while he coughed. They both tried to take these things lightly and to wish them over quickly, the peace unbroken.

'Easy, Mo. Easy.'

Morgan sat up and swayed, arched, bowed forward and stilled, Bryn still cradling him while his breath was sandbagged, clotted, slashed. Mary wanted to go and kiss them both, but knew this series of sweats and spasms was theirs now – another thing they did together without her.

'Easy.'

'Bryn, I think . . .'

'Don't you think at all. You go upstairs and take your stuff and I'll come and annoy your recovery later. Go on.'

The Uncles cupped each other's faces, shared a battle-fatigued kiss, and then Morgan edged himself out and upstairs, minding his pace. Bryn patted the sofa and Mary came to join him, to hug him, to hear the panicked rhythm breaking in his heart.

'Never worked a day down a mine and still he's like that. Doesn't make sense really, does it. Not right. Something about it not right.'

Mary could think of nothing to answer him.

'Gives me an excuse to walk out with him, arm in arm, though. Happens all the time here – old miners, old cripples, old couples – some mornings the High Street seems like, seems like – I don't know – a dance hall, a place where you do want to look in love.' He closed his hold on her until a tremor ran in his arms. 'And we are.'

'And you are.'

'It was National Service, you know. In Palestine. A hotel blew up

205

in '48 and caught him. After that, he couldn't breathe right. And they've never paid him a penny, they've never said it was their fault – making him go there. Like the bloody work camps they made you go to before the war. Trying to keep the boys busy, teaching them how to sing hymns, join choirs, sweat away like bloody slaves. They never say sorry, they never do better. They never help.

'And they buried my Morgan alive and ruined him.' He cupped her neck with one hand, kissed her forehead and reminded them both of how many times in how many years they'd been in this position, done these things, belonging to each other.

'Is he? It doesn't seem too much worse?'

He swallowed, dropped his arms from her, smoothed both palms across his face. 'I don't know. Sometimes he's fine, lovely. But when he's taken badly, then – well, I can see he's frightened. He has to fight more to get out of it.' He rubbed his forehead again. 'I should go up to him, or he'll be asleep. It makes him tired.' He brushed at her, found her hand and briefly caught it hard in his. 'You should be happy. A woman like you: clever, pretty. You should be happy. None of this other nonsense.'

'I try.'

'I know. We all do.' He counted along her knuckles with his thumb. 'Will you sleep, do you think?'

'Maybe. I've had a cry. That's meant to be good, isn't it.'

'I find so, yes.'

Something wavered near Mary's solar plexus at the thought of Bryn ever having to cry. 'We'll manage, won't we?'

'No choice, really.' He leaned into her shoulder, attempting a playful bump. 'And none of it's so terrible. Look at you – off doing these wonderful things. There you were on the telephone, just talking to a novelist, a novelist you can cry to. Not something you'd get in Gofeg.'

'I think he was embarrassed. I know I was.'

'But he's good with you? You've settled down? The people there are treating you the way they should?'

'Bryn, I've been telling you that since the first day I went.'

'But you were lying at the start, so we wouldn't worry.'

'I was not.' She felt him grin at her. 'I was a bit, then. Only a bit.' He grinned more. 'They're OK. I could happily drown Nathan, sometimes. But he's too good a swimmer. And he's not so bad. We make a sort of family, I suppose. An odd sort of family.'

'Oh, you'll be used to that.'

'No. I'm used to the best sort of family.'

He kissed her again. 'I feel it best to leave a room on a compliment, if this is ever possible. So I'll go now. Don't stay up late.'

Mary waited until she'd heard him leave the bathroom, open and close the bedroom door, the small hum of conversation, a break of coughing, conversation again. Then she got ready for bed herself, thinking all the time that she hadn't noticed the point when the skin of Bryn's hands began to smooth and thin. He had an old man's touch now, delicate.

Sleep, when it had made its peace in her, was cloudy and dank. Anxiety flared in randomly unpleasant scenarios: searches for people she'd never met, lost items of immense importance, fatally missed appointments and dumb-struck telephones. Waking with the clear impression that she had been running all night, she then washed through the usual, four-second time lapse of drowsing amnesia, before the full weight of her awareness could stab into place. She was not a happy sleeper, because she was not happy awake. Her bed, the bed where she'd fucked him, burned her skin.

So once again, she took a clumsy breakfast with the Uncles. Each of them had their own reasons for listlessness, stammering hands, the stupid clatter of a fallen knife. But their lack of rest gave them reasons for tenderness, too. Bryn helped Morgan through the pitfalls of combining water, crockery, milk, sugar, tea, the balance of spoons. Morgan helped Bryn through the carving of bread, toasting, the clutter of possible accompaniments. Mary made them their porridge, almost as thick as she liked it, far thicker than they preferred. And they rubbed each other's shoulders, kissed ears, exchanged and held slow glances, leading to smiles. They were moving forward, regardless of obstacles, supporting each new moment with the last. Nothing much was said.

Washing-up completed, Mary stepped out to wander up Charter Road. Later, she would meet the Uncles in Ianetta's and drink bad coffee and not accept the customary offer of a dairy-smelling meat pie, freshly heated with the steam from the cappuccino nozzle. Now, she would just walk, liking the gentle cold, the sourness of old leaves in the air, the release of even a little exercise. Off the island, she realised, she was increasingly restless – deprived of the scrambling and plodding and dog-walking her body had grown to expect. Her body was like that – constantly fixing habits, asking for more of the same again.

There.

She didn't believe it when she saw him, there was no twist in the stomach, no shock.

But it is.

The image was simply not credible.

Him.

Jonno, turning the far corner. Jonno, heading directly for her. Jonno, wearing a different jacket but the same old scarf. Jonno, the angle of his shoulders, the whole pitch of him showing that he was thinking, not ignoring her, only preoccupied.

God, it is him.

They were, by this time, already too near to take evasive action and then, perhaps, both hypnotised by their simultaneous, unlikely presence, they simply advanced. Jonathan's expression moved from puzzled to neutral and back to puzzled again, no obvious trace of pleasure showing. About a foot apart, they stopped.

He looks well, he looks better than me.

'You look well.'

He shrugged, slipped a look across her and into the air beside her head. 'I'm . . . I think I'm sickening for something actually – fluish. I thought, you know, last night – it's Friday tomorrow and I'm not well and I'm coming back Saturday in any case – for a visit – so . . .'

'Take the day off.' She felt the start of a sick shake in her spine, his proximity lighting a sweat on her wrists.

'Yeah, that's right. You . . . ? You're well?'

'Fine.' It was no good, she could feel it: the whole of the situation, dribbling away. She could hear him speaking with that terrible gentleness of someone who has been closer, but who isn't, who won't be now. Her own voice sounded much the same: tired and wary. 'I didn't expect to . . .'

You should ask him . . .

Ask him what?

208

'I thought you'd be in Cardiff.'

'I was.'

*Come on. Say **something**.*

'Do you like it?'

Christ.

'No.'

For an instant, he met her eyes and she could almost believe this was his way of beginning to say that his life was discontented without

Me. Me?

'No, I don't like it.' He looked away, 'But it's better than nothing,' and let his balance shift, getting ready to go.

'I, Jonno . . .' She needed to touch him, to settle the emptiness in her limbs, to tell him good things, to punch his head for being so quiet and bloody sad and out of her reach.

'Yes? What?' Now he seemed impatient.

Slap him, slap him now, see what he does.

'I just wanted to say goodbye.'

'You already have.' He moved forward, as if to pass her, but set his hands quickly on her shoulders, tugged her in and brushed his lips near her temple. The scent of him, his recognisable heat, made her close her eyes, made her want to weep, made her turn for him unsteadily when he was already clear and pacing away.

Minutes later, Mary became aware that she too had started walking, heading off at surprising speed and taking a route of which she was now unsure. She came to rest in a small, modern street on Gofeg's western edge: part of an aborted development scheme. She found she had no recollection of ever having been there before.

Eckless was looking disappointed. Someone who didn't know him well might have missed it, the signs were small: a vague listlessness in the tail, something heavy about the ears, a tendency to stare. But Nathan noticed.

He's my dog. So I look out for him. I look out for the things that are mine. If I can.

He clapped at the dog's shoulder, ruffled the fur along its back, but got barely a response.

'It's no good.' Nathan straightened, faced himself slightly more squarely into the breeze, and shrugged across to Louis.

'Hm?'

The sea between them and the Head was chopping and ghosting with spray. The Head itself waited out the race of air and water about it, belligerently solid, spiked with cormorants.

'Eckless – he really can't settle around you at all. He just associates you with chocolate and biscuits and not getting them.'

'You don't want him to have them. I'd be happy to treat him sometimes. Bearing in mind my own fondness for things that are sweet.' Louis eyed Eckless with the air of a fellow sufferer, another slave to chocolate.

'I know. It's my fault, but you get the blame.' At which, the animal flopped down into the wind-snaking grass and moaned briefly, just to underline the point. This marked a move on the Eckless Scale from Huffy to Despairing and meant Nathan was due for an unsettled night full of whines and glowering. Usually he would unload the problem on to Mary, but she wasn't back yet.

Soon, though, tomorrow. Off I'll go and fetch her – just as we agreed. I'll pick her up from the quay.

The quay with the Price boy's shadow still drifting at the edge of vision, still kicking at nothings, still eating chips and letting one fall now and then for the gulls.

*You have to remember **every detail**, don't you? Can't leave anything be.
Passed the mother in Ancw, last week. It hasn't left her be.*

'Nathan?' Louis was holding the peak of his cap down, to keep it
from taking flight.

*Naturally aerodynamic, caps. And – perhaps more importantly – they
make you look a total prick. Although Louis, I have to say, does wear his
well – it's the spherical head, helps to carry it off.*

'Nathan? Can I speak to you?' Louis reached out his hand, palm
open, and Nathan took it, held it, a fraction discomfited by the
commitment this might imply. Louis turned squarely to face him,
while making an effort to seem quite casual. 'In confidence?'

'Always, Louis. You know the way it works – tell your secrets to
an antisocial bastard and they'll never go astray.' He squeezed Louis's
soft, fleshy little fingers, he hoped reassuringly. 'What is it?' There
would be a point when he should let go and he would miss it. He
always made his move just too late or too early, whichever would
cause the most offence.

'I wanted, if it wasn't an intrusion, to ask you about Mary. I feel
she's progressing well?'

'I think she could be . . . that is, there's promising stuff there.
Almost.'

'Proud of her?'

Nathan's throat shied at the thought of it, but 'Yes' croaked
through, nonetheless.

'Told her?'

'Told her what?' A gluey defensive edge in that – something
grubby about his pronunciation.

'That you're proud.'

'Ah, that. I've, I've . . . in a way.'

'Not good at talking, are you?'

'No.'

'But you'll have to talk to Mary eventually, about everything.'

Nathan nodded, feeling ten again and stupid. Louis could reduce
him to this in moments – he had the teacherly knack.

'She's working? Progressing? Reading?'

'She's doing everything she should. I couldn't stop her, even if I
tried. She wants it – whatever *it* is. And whyever one should want it.'

211

'Maybe *it* wants *her*.'

'Don't pull that crap on me. Yes, writing is something that happens to us. Fine. Yes, it is quite astonishingly beyond our fucking control and if anyone really knew how little charge we have over our vehicles, they would deprive us of them at once. OK. But don't read any more into it than that. I type for a living, I'm not on a mission from God.'

This is ridiculous, I can't stand hand in hand with someone and argue effectively. Although, God knows, with Maura, I tried.

'Look, Louis, sorry. But you know the way I am. No offence.'

'None taken. I'm only saying this because, perhaps later, I will be unable to.' Louis couldn't help taking a tiny glance down at the sea.

Nathan struggled for the right, oblique question. It wasn't done, on the island, to pry into anyone's plans in the risk-taking area, but even so, 'You're going to try it?'

He's too old, he won't make it. It's his own choice. But he's too old. Fuck, by his time of life, you're risking death just getting up in the morning – trying not to slip in the bath. His own choice, though.

'I do feel I have limited time in which to make another attempt. And this would still only be my sixth. And seven's the lucky number, isn't it?' Louis extracted his hand, leaving an imprint that chilled. 'You've become a fine swimmer, haven't you, Nathan?' He smiled to Nathan, an uncharacteristic tick of melancholy in his eyes.

'I'm adequate.'

'That cuts down your possibilities, surely? For this kind of thing?'

'Not necessarily.'

'Yes, of course, you're right. Because you still couldn't, for example, swim up here between the cliffs and the Head, without expecting to drown? The undertow, the general turbulence is too great. And I speak as one poor in the water and quite elderly.'

'Don't.'

'I beg your pardon.'

'I know, I'm not supposed to say it, but,' he re-grasped Louis's hand, 'I would much rather you didn't try to leave us. Or not that way. Your chances of survival would be almost nil. It would be suicide, not . . . not what we're meant to do.'

Louis slipped free and trotted forward, the harshly downward slope of the hill seeming to trundle him dangerously near an immediate rendezvous with his intent. He sank gently out of sight, and it seemed that, when he finally came to a halt, he had no more to do than pick his time for the final, tiny move into the drop. Louis snatched off his cap, rolled it, and put it into his pocket, safe. Something about the gesture, its neat finality, gave Nathan's stomach a twist and set him running down towards the limit of the slope.

I'm not supposed to try and stop him, but, then, he's not supposed to try and make me watch.

Nathan slithered into Louis and felt a retching horror grip him – he detested heights. His momentum clattered both of them far too close to the uneven line where the slithering grass ended and the greasy sky began. For both their sakes, but primarily for his own, Nathan toppled their already winded bear-hug over into a tangled but minor impact. He realised that he'd wrenched his back, perhaps seriously. Eckless was woofing with alarm and making ready to gallop in, but Nathan yelled at him to sit, to stay away. The last thing he needed today was to find himself shoved off into a watery grave by an over-enthusiastic canine.

'You know,' Louis shifted under Nathan, extricated one arm with a tiny wheeze, 'I think you're quite correct. Going over this particular cliff would be quite unwise.'

First, *the Christopher Credo: we believe, like a number of lunatics before us, that if we have been in a place beyond the reach of all but divine intervention seven times and if, seven times, we have been kicked back into this existence, then we become special. We become holy, blessed, Grail-keeping, generous to nuns, fairly pleasant, unlikely to spit in the street, who the fuck really knows?*

Nathan's mind was wandering again. He changed his pen from his writing hand to his arsing-about-and-tapping-the-table-with-it hand.

*If we don't get seven natural absolute risks, then we're allowed to make them. This is a wee bit cheeky on our part, but apparently God doesn't mind. Frankly, it makes Him look better – He's already admitted that the only way of getting His attention is to **die at Him.***

Second, the Actual Credo: we are tired and we are lonely and we don't want to have to do this any more. If we could, we would chuck it all in today, but we haven't the balls we were born with, so we'll play little terminal games with ourselves and, if we're lucky, they will kill us and, if we're not, they will at least distract us from all this bloody misery.

He tapped and settled his stack of paper so that its edges exactly matched. He stared at it. Then changed pen hands again.

Tomorrow.

A tight pilot of excitement stretched up into a flame. Mary would be here tomorrow and he would meet her, help her home and then tell her the news, the news he hadn't passed on to Louis or anyone else – no indeed – because it was theirs, his and Mary's.

Slightly unethically, about three months ago, he had posted off two of her stories to a halfway decent magazine. No, actually a fucking good and demanding magazine. And they'd accepted one of them. Because it was a belter and they couldn't do much else. (In Nathan's opinion.) And (also in Nathan's opinion) there was nothing worse than sending things off and then waiting and then maybe getting rejected, so he'd just saved his daughter all of that.

She'll have to go through it every other time – this one's on me.

He hoped she'd be pleased, delighted, ecstatic, chuffed – something along those lines. She needed cheering up and this would be just the thing. For once in his life, good timing had broken out spontaneously. He would tell her the news and she'd be happy, simple as that.

*I know **I** am. Christ, I wasn't this happy with **my** first acceptance. Even though I've been a bit underhanded, not asked permission . . . Even though . . .*

She will be happy, won't she?

He was beginning to panic in earnest. He'd tried lying on his floor near the stereo with both its speakers on his chest and playing 'Bat Out of Hell' into his torso until the shadow of his stolen lung ached and banged just as hard as the one they'd left him with. Sadly, this had no particular effect – worry was still fisting in his heart. He'd shelled discs of Gluck, Duke Ellington, Lou Reed in and out of the player to no tangibly quieting end.

So here he was with pen and paper instead, ready to numb the brain with scribbling. If this didn't work, he'd have to use the whisky – but he was trying to save this last bottle for a real emergency. He readied the hand, the wrist, the fingers: the black Pilot pen, fine nib, the way he liked them: to make writing small enough for hiding his meaning from everyone but him.

And the person I might want to read it – Mary has wee writing, too.

Golgotha

*Think of how high we are – miles. I'd say, at least five.
It would take you more than an hour to walk the distance we are currently above ground.*

I want to say this to my fellow passengers. I want to
set them straight.

*If, through malign intervention or some innocent mis-
take, we should find ourselves sucked out through a window breach, or displayed like rows of bleeding seeds in
the savagely opened pod that was our fuselage – if we
are simply catapulted skyward by explosives, far beyond
the shards that, until very recently, constituted our
fold-away tables, our lavatory tissue dispensers, our
floor – if we lose all those little niceties that cradled our lives aloft and discover ourselves, still conscious and in individual flight – do you realise how many
minutes it will take us to fall?*

I want to stand and make my own little safety
announcement, one based on common sense.

*In what way do you imagine the illuminated gangway
lights will help you as you plummet, still strapped into
your seat and neither dead from injury, nor shock, only
bracingly conscious of your hurtle towards a kaleido-
scope of gross dismemberment? Have you pictured yourself, finally, slowly dying in your personal impact
crater – no more than a breathing, thinking pouch of
jelly and tubing and grit. You will lift your eyes, perhaps, to nearby trees, garlanded with luggage and
unjointed limbs, or maybe you'll have just the time to
blink into the face of a passer-by, ambulance worker,
journalist and fill them with a lifelong need for
therapy. I mean, have any of you **thought of this**?*

Every time I board an aircraft now, it's the same: my
compulsion to wander the aisles, playfully squeezing
shoulders and tousling youngsters' hair and saying what
I need to, which is – *these things used to concern me.*

216

Before even the shortest journey I would take super-stitious steps: cleaning my house, so that, later, when the policemen came, responding to the sad news that was me, all would be trim and shipshape and suggestive of an exemplary, sorely missed life. I would read no news-papers, for fear of jinxing headlines and articles that mentioned death. As I boarded, I would always peek down through the gap between the gantry and the body of the plane, to glimpse my final, solid horizontal: saying goodbye to my natural home.

You may have similar rituals, quieting similar fears, but you must know, you really do have to understand – **nothing remotely unpleasant is going to happen on this flight. You will be FINE**. You are safer right at this moment than you have ever been. Smile, relax, don't worry – all is well.

Because **I want to die. I want to crash and burn. I want to be hacked to pieces by random metal, reduced to fibres, roseate rain.** And let me tell you on the best authority – destruction courted becomes coy. Today there will be no windshear, no sabotage, no trace of turbulence. For as long as you're in here with me, you need have no fear.

She needs cheering up, my Mary, something to make her smile. So I suppose I could give her this, if I wasn't scared to. All very well her handing over work to me, but I can't realistically contemplate the reverse. I am forced to admit that she is braver now than I have ever been. I would like to feel proud for my genes, but I'm certain my genes have had nothing to do with it.

And maybe, after all, this wouldn't amuse her. I suppose the material is, quite fundamentally, unfunny. Suicidal impulses and wholesale death – with me they'd almost always raise a laugh – but not with everyone, I know. Not with healthy, happy people, I do know.

So. I should concentrate more on my early days in literature: the touring, one of the perils of the writer's life, of which Mary ought to be a touch forewarned, being well on the way to writerhood herself.

The woman who meets me at Ben-Gurion smells of halito-sis and depilatory cream. She tunnels a way ahead of me through the airport crowds as if she has done this very often, which - quite probably - she has. She speaks English with an English accent and Hebrew with a Hebrew accent and I am impressed, but also careful to angle myself so as not to face her mouth. I try to think of her with sympathy, as someone condemned to tangential conversations and brief, but smooth-thighed relationships, only flourishing while her partners suffer head colds. Or I imagine she may be suffering with bad teeth. Although she doesn't look unhappy, or in pain.

Which I am beginning to detest in people - the unmistakable evidence of general content.

Nevertheless, I am polite with her and apparently interested: responding to questions and producing anecdotes as civilly as I can, weaving manfully out to her car, still feeling mildly assaulted after the flight.

She is a jerky driver, concentrating only in spasms on the dangers of the road ahead. I remain tranquil when forced, for the third time, to make a sudden, close inspection of the arse end of the car in front. Giggling inappropriately, she tells me she can't think what's wrong with her today.

I can.

But do not tell her so.

I look out of the queasily blue-tinted window at an alien motorway and very familiar sleet and she apologises because the sun is not shining and I tell her this is not her fault and she laughs in a way that lets me understand I am making her very nervous. I am very glad.

Which isn't the proper mind-set - not by a long fucking way. Not for coming into Jerusalem. Not for Nathan the prophet, riding into Jerusalem.

Nathan the cunting prophet. What did I ever know that everyone else hadn't worked out years ago?

Nevertheless, the *idea* of Jerusalem, the density of the word, does strike a light. I let my eyes droop closed while my lungs, my currently untouched pair of lungs, my sleek-in-the-chest-like-twin-pink-oven-mitts-and-never-really-loved-enough lungs, sparkle with a blush of adrenalin. I hear myself sigh and feel an answering jolt in my escort's steering.

Jerusalem, and if it were possible . . .

I can't finish the thought, but it's there, like a soft growth under the skin: the hope that I am – in spite of myself – a pilgrim, that I could have earned a pilgrim's reward.

Please, God, I've come here. Now take all the bad things away. Although, of course, one of the bad things is probably me.

And I've hardly had a rigorous journey: free flight here and back again and a fee for a brace of readings and one lecture – as yet uninvented. A thoroughly cushy number, as penitential travails go.

Except I paid for this before I came. I'll go home to a house which is not my house, which has in it nothing left for me to love and nothing I know that can love me. You've taken my wife and daughter, God. You've made me live seven years without sight of them. I have paid, I have paid to the bone.

I want to hope that if I've got here, no matter how, then I have made it and no questions asked – a deal's a deal. I find myself surprised by my desperation and my willingness to believe even a fraction of the nonsense Joe Christopher's tried to feed me for fuck knows how long: this being only a fraction of the nonsenses available that mention Jerusalem.

Miss Mouthwash leaves me at my hotel after the usual courteous stammering around the check-in desk. I believe that she wanted to go with me into the lift, to check the room, to aid my unpacking and I don't want to picture what else, but I was having none of it.

Big room in the American pastel motel style, very reminiscent of a private hospital: aggressively concrete flooring underfoot and an air-conditioning bulkhead above the bed which will roar all night and keep me awake with din and dehydration. The bathroom is showily clean, the usual sachets of this and that. I have a great temptation to piss right around the circle of surgically sterilised tissue they've left on the toilet seat to defend my tender buttocks from leaping disease. Maybe on the day I leave . . .

I now have two hours to 'be refreshed' before she will come and collect me and expect me to prove myself the performing bear I am.

Why is it always two hours? Just long enough to get sleepy but not to get a sleep. Just long enough to dis-cover the vital item you haven't brought with you but not to go and seek out its replacement. Just long enough to feel abandoned, but not to find relief.

In case of emergency, check mini-bar.

2 midget kosher white wines and 2 red, 2 Beefeater gins, 1 Angostura Bitters (as ever, suspiciously caked and old), 4 Johnny Walkers, 2 Camparis, 2 (for God's sake) baby champagnes, 3 Cokes, 3 beers, 3 mineral waters, 2 orange juices and 2 bottles of something vodka-looking called Silent Sam. 2 boxes of fancily smoke-flavoured nuts and 2 Toblerones.

Which taste a bit soapy but sugar is sugar and that's what I need. I will deepen my acquaintance with the rest of the range when I get back tonight, having feigned tiredness and avoided the clutches of my orally chal-lenged chauffeuse. I feel she will proffer clutches at some stage and my refusals always cause offence.

What I want now is a cup of coffee. Not in the bar or the restaurant or on a room-service tray, but made by me. After a run of cheap one-night gigs – distraction for the lonely man – I am still fixed in the B & B frame of mind. My expectations are based on the standard British triangle of second-class comforts and perks: the bed and the portable telly and the little nest of coffee powders, tea bags and UHT milks out of which will grow a kettle and perhaps two shortbread rounds. The tiny rooms and their tinier showers and their teeny admonitory notices and their total fucking lack of alcohol - the thoughts of a forthcoming audience to please when I can no longer remotely please myself - they break me every time to the brink of weeping.

But, predictably, I miss them when they're gone.

Like everything else.

Nathan pressed the heels of both hands against his eyes, sucked in a breath while the image of *her* hands against his pages unfurled in his vertebrae, along with the consideration that his words might speak in her mind, that his beat could take her breath and coax it out however he wished. He felt afraid to continue and desperate not to stop, as if there were someone palping each thought already, examining – or as if he had only this last chance to impress.

*But impress who? Who is this for, really – do tell? Not the daughter, surely? Not ever anyone but the wife. Maura – who never liked to read you, even when you lived with her, even when you weren't tossing off formulaic gore – a bit of splat and trickle for the ladies. Even when you wrote proper novels, she never did want to know what you wanted to say, unless you were **saying** it. Sometimes not then . . . Why the fuck don't you jack it in, Nate – **there's no one listening**.*

Nathan considered smiling. At one time he couldn't have let himself think this way. Now, he knew it didn't matter *what* he thought. Understanding that he wrote without a purpose or effect had no power to prevent him from scrawling on and on; the alternative was being left alone inside his head with nothing to defend him from his memory, as it sliced and burned – his inadvertent homage to Hieronymus Bosch.

*But Mary **will** read me. In the end, she'll read me and she'll know what I mean, because we're like each other. She'll take in what I give her and she'll add herself and we will fit.*

When I wake up all my skin feels gritty - too much MTV and hospitality, swilled down with the sterling Silent Sam. But I've earned my free day in the Holy City, the Centre of the World and, now that my ears are also conscious, I realise I've been roused by the sunrise call to prayer: the cheaply amplified wonder of somebody singing at God.

I have already been warned that such apparently holy messages can be clandestinely vicious and subversive. Similarly, someone in the corridor, some woman I almost fell into on the long stagger back to my room last night, hissed that I should never eat Arab falafels because they're cooked in the dirty oil the Jews force them to buy. This is a city full of genocidal gossip.

But inside this city is *the* City and what I want. Or, *perhaps* what I want. I'm not sure now – if I ever have been. My need is not articulate, it is only need.

In through the Damascus Gate, and the walls fold round me, charged. Under the puddled cobbles and behind the dripping stalls, there seems to be a press of credulity, certainty, insanity. Perhaps because it is something so little a part of me, I am sure that I can taste a haze of faith. Between the tang of damp leather souvenirs and kerosene stoves, there's a nagging flavour of horribly long-standing belief, I can feel it roping in to shorten my breath.

I find I am almost running in a kind of atheist alarm when, as they say, the heavens open and too much water falls out of the sky for me to continue. I wait things out in a clammy cafe, sipping sage tea and eating three pieces of something not unlike a sugary omelette with cheese. I am not hungry or thirsty, only anxious for something to do. I could buy a packet of cigarettes, but I have recently given them up and this doesn't seem the time to fall from grace.

Although I am trying not to, I recite in my mind Jerusalem's map of agreed impossibilities: here an ascent into heaven, here the sweat mopped from God on earth, here prayers slipped into cracks in a wall like letters to Father Christmas, like notes to a secret love, expected soon. And I am afraid. I am a trespasser. An unbeliever lapsing back to superstition, because he can't get what he wants any other way: I shouldn't be here, I shouldn't be allowed.

*But you **are** here. So you might as well go all the way.*

222

*And, by the way, you **are** a believer, remember? You believe you're damned.*

My head is still delicate when I start my ascent, the previous evening's excesses making my neck wince at every flux of beaten blood. The omelette is giving me a not unwelcome sugar rush.

And on we go. 'He who would true valiant be' . . . And so on and so on.

Twice I miss the entrance and think of giving up, going back. Done my best, no point in pushing it, get down to the hotel bar, have a hair of the dog and then a kip . . .

*I mean, you have no **logical** reason to be here.*

So who said there should be anything logical about want?

Doubling back yet again, I find the archway, the court-yard, the stack of abandoned crosses like a bad joke. This is, through the ragging drizzle, the Church of the Holy Sepulchre, the one place on earth where there might be a miracle, even for me.

Through the doorway and I can't believe the noise: the unsanctified crush, the puzzle of lamps and chapels, scaffolding, pillars and steps and, here at my feet, a plump girl kissing a stone. Everywhere, people are kissing, touching, rubbing special places already greased black with adoration. I let myself bounce and drift with the crowds, the backs of my legs sweating and my spine braced, as if I were balancing at the verge of some dreadful event. Around me, mass intoxication has boiled up over the years into forms I cannot recog-nise as Christian, they are too garishly eccentric, too admirable and devout.

In the end I have to do it - what I promised myself I would - climb the stairs and queue beneath the baubled, crouching ceiling, unable to see the altar until that penultimate step when the woman in front of me drops to her knees and there it is: Golgotha, the place of the skull, overwhelmed by gold and marble.

And then it's my turn, the sweat on me really serious at this point, embarrassing. I kneel under something approximating a little fireplace, one hand already resting on a circle of polished metal surrounding a hole. I lower my head, my shoulders, and I actually do kiss something very cold, although I'm not sure what because my eyes are closed. I feel no pressure to hurry. Here anyone can do almost anything - we are all creating our own rituals as we go, every move has the weight of potentially supernatural prompting. Nevertheless I decide quite quickly that I will put my hand into the hole.

There is nothing there.

I clench and stretch my fingers in blind air.

I don't feel a thing.

Stumbling now, hot, I scramble to my feet and dodge around the line of worshippers, sink into the crowd again.

All you had to do was reach for it, touch it. But you couldn't, you were scared.

I lunge out into the thickening rain, lean against a wall of some antiquity and wonder if vomiting here will be considered blasphemous. A bell explodes into action somewhere above me, beginning a peal of raucous, dangerous clatters.

What did you think would be down there? The grab of another hand? Teeth? God tugging the cuff of your shirt?

I go back inside and climb to the altar, repeat everything as I have already done and make for myself the Ceremony of the Second Chance. And this time, this time I drive my arm all the way in and the palm of my hand hits Calvary: cool, clean stone.

And I prayed that I could see her again for even only one more time. I asked if I could be with her, but I couldn't use a name. Maura or Mary – any choice was a betrayal. So I hoped that God would understand me, that he would let me have them both. On my knees with my arm in a hole through the floor, I begged for that.

Then the following morning, I remember, when I woke my clothes still smelt of incense and had perfumed my room. For a while I took this as a sign.

'D'you know why people like tennis?'
Jack Grace was trying a new line. Really, it was going to work best during Wimbledon Fortnight, but confining a goodish opener to only two weeks of the year didn't seem an efficient application of intelligence. At least it didn't tonight. Trouble was, the bloody club was so noisy – it made screaming *de rigueur* – and you couldn't just bawl this kind of thing at a woman and hope to get a promising result. You needed to be able to *modulate*.

His current target peered at him through the semi-darkness, possibly a little revolted, possibly a touch bemused, and then shrugged away to join the press of slightly less desperate guests. Now that he looked, she had a fat arse anyway.

'And fuck you, dear.' He consoled himself with a perfectly unslurred enunciation of his favourite phrase, 'Fuck you,' which evaporated inoffensively into the din.

Out in the evening and two streets to the west, Mary was being surprised by Soho, but not in the way that she'd expected. In the dark it seemed remarkably unseedy: neon shivering across the pavements with every drive of powdery rain, the illusion of warmth from lit and misted windows flickering with diners and drinkers, the fact of warmth clasped in doorways, or sprinting for shelter. It was too early in the evening for anything more malign and, perhaps, too cold.

Nathan padded beside her, quiet as he'd been since he'd taken her off the island. She'd fully expected him to be the kind of man who didn't talk on public transport and he hadn't let her down. Not that his silences were unpleasant, they were almost companionable in a way, peppered with bursts of instructions when he escorted her through transfers, took charge of her bag, paced off doggedly in search of sandwiches or drinks. He'd simply never really explained to her why she was coming to London – beyond suggesting what was going to happen here would be educational.

She had allowed him to deposit her at an obviously pricy hotel and had then been uplifted again, two hours later, by a Nathan she'd never entirely encountered before. This was a man, rather carefully brushed and polished, dressed in a black suit just slightly too stylish to match his face. But, then again, even his face was a little different: closely, closely shaved and firmer, somehow, more confident than she'd known it. His very blue shirt made his eyes seem also very blue. This was the professional Mr Staples, a person who actually looked as if he might be a novelist. Mary was glad she hadn't met Nathan earlier – he would have been completely, instead of mostly, unapproachable.

And now here he was, leading her into Soho. Here he was, unfamiliar, but gradually proving himself to be fundamentally unchanged. He stopped abruptly up ahead, turned, and then stared, slightly off balance, into his reflection in a blacked-out window stacked with explicit videos. With a little inhalation of impatience he twisted further round through all the degrees required to halt directly in front of Mary. He then frowned down at her with such intensity that she almost felt afraid – not for herself, but for him.

He's . . . what's wrong?

He seemed startled, concerned by something, but she couldn't tell what. The slope of his shoulders under the rain seemed – ridiculously, in such a muscular man – frail. He was managing to form a range of vulnerable slopes.

Nathan nodded, eased the tension round his eyes, lifted her hand, shook it and then set it loose again.

'Congratulations.'

'What?'

'Congratulations. I was going to say this before, but then I heard about this party and I thought . . . I thought. Two birds with one stone is what I thought.'

'What?'

'Sorry.'

He smiled, practically sniggered and she realised that it would take only a few small, similar changes in his behaviour to make him seem unmistakably peculiar.

*Sorry about **what**, for crying out loud?*

'Sorry. I couldn't think of how to tell you. Which means I've dragged you all the way to the evil city, dumped you in a strange hotel –'

'It's not strange, it's just expensive.'

'You're not paying, so don't fret.'

'But I do fret.'

'Well, *don't*. Please.' He swallowed. 'This is all part of the learning process. Sometimes . . . if you are a published author . . .' he grinned unguardedly, 'people may – now and again – do things for you, buy things for you – food and drink mainly, as if you were a trained seal, which isn't too far from the truth – and you will accept these things because they are part of the Great Good Cloud of Free Things that circles the world and discharges itself here and there, but rarely where it would serve any practical purpose. People – for example – who have no proper clothing are never given free designer suits. People who have too much clothing often are. All of which has nothing to do with us now. What is important is that *you* are now a published author.' His grin returned, obviously settling in for the night.

'What?'

'You can't just keep saying *what* all the time. Others who do not know you as I do will think you are simple-minded. You are published. Going to be, anyway. You know "The Lines of the Hand"? That story?'

'My "The Lines of the Hand"?'

'Well, of course, yours.'

The shower was firming, also settling in for the night. Mary was aware they were getting substantially wet. And there was something else, a rushing in her skin.

'*My* story?'

'Yes. Which *I* sent away and which a magazine has said they want and if you want them to want it then you can write back and say so and all will be well. If you want. It's your thing. You can do what you like with it. They'll pay you.'

'They'll . . . You sent away something of mine?'

The rush increased, seemed to rummage underneath her scalp and scamper round her larger arteries.

Nathan swung to the shop window, peered, realised what he was

227

peering at and swung back again, discomfited. 'I know: I should have asked. But I thought, maybe, if you had no expectations that would be better than if I suggested that you should . . . This seemed a way of . . . This seemed –' He wiped an accumulation of water from his brow with one hand. 'We are going to have . . . fun now. At a party.' A slight grimace signalled how unlikely he found this both as a concept and as a sentence he might pronounce. 'You can come and look around – see where you'll finish up. Once you're a published author. If you're very unlucky.'

'We're going to a *writer's* party?'

Her breath was altered now, thinning and speeding.

'No. We're going to a *publisher's* party, that's something completely diff . . . Well, you'll see. It's a place to visit. You don't have to stay.'

'Now we're here, though . . .' She couldn't think of how her sentence might end. She'd stopped listening to what she was saying. More and more of her attention was withdrawing, anxious to repeat what he'd told her, to whisper it inside the sudden racing of herself.

Published.

Nathan continued, 'Really, we can stay as long as you like. Until it gets ugly. Not that it absolutely, necessarily will. Obviously.' He swabbed his eyebrows free of water. 'You look nice. Did I say?'

'What?'

'You will have to stop that. 'Really.' He bleared at her through the damp – not exactly relaxed, but certainly more jolly than she'd imagined he could be. 'It makes conversations very tiring and you know I'm not fond of conversing in the first place. Come on. It's too wet to keep waiting about.'

Nathan gave her his back and squelched a few steps up the lane while she closed her eyes and exhaled, enjoying a shudder of something new.

Published.

'Mary. Mary?'

She tried not to smile when she faced him, but couldn't manage, her delight oozed out. It was tapping at the underside of her finger-nails, almost lifting them with a kind of fuzzy heat – the same heat that seemed to be smoothing something in her head, then moving it somewhere better, more suitable, opening an unexpected room.

'Mary.' He was also trying, and failing, not to smile. 'You're like a cow looking over a dyke.'

'I'm?'

'A wall – a cow looking over . . . it's an expression . . . one with little or no heterosexual meaning outside Fife and, therefore . . .' He folded his arms and then shook his head at the pavement. 'May I assume that you are happy?'

'Yes.'

Oh, yes.

'Good.' Quickly, entirely serious now. 'Then I am happy, too. Come on.'

PUBLISHED. Oh, yes.

The street outside the club was full of music: there was no room for it anywhere else, the interior pressure of voices being too great. Melodies drizzled down three storeys of gaping windows in layered attempts at Latin abandon, finally washing away to ribbons in the pavement cracks.

'Is this it?'

Nathan nodded. 'This is it.' One high, terraced house, picked out from a squeeze of others by rebarbatively colourful paintwork. 'This is, absolutely, it.'

And do I really want to bring my only daughter here? My only lung? My only anything? Too fucking late to balk now, though, of course.

Subsiding from the head of the stairs, taking two at an unsteady time, came a short man: another man, much taller, draped across his shoulders like a python with rubber false arms. As they stumbled through their descent both were talking softly, but not to each other.

Nathan took his daughter by the elbow and steered her into the first available room. The usual fog of anxiety and cigarette smoke, fear and cleverness, rolled him in its twitchy embrace as if he'd never been away. Part of him loved it: the pale faces in the dark, the drive to be warmed, incautious, helpless, connected and accepted before the drink and the time and the sympathy ran out.

Sssh. You've been here before, you know how it always ends – less Byronic, more moronic – and weepings and gnashings of teeth pretty much guaranteed. You're not fit for it, remember? They can scent it on your skin,

229

the sweat of your particular weaknesses — **man holding emotional fire sale, stand well back**.

He concentrated his attention on shaking off the nevertheless inevitable buzz, the wily desire to drop into it all and disappear.

Not tonight, though, not tonight.

Tonight he was going to be responsible, but not heavy-handed, letting Mary circulate, while still keeping his attention inconspicuously edging round her, just for safety's sake.

Which doesn't stop me feeling like a fucking puppy-killer — leaving her alone in all of this. And Jesus, did she have to dress like that? I mean lovely — really, truly lovely — but she's far too attractive: too much like blood in the water after dark, calling up the appetites with the tide.

He introduced her to a safe, gay, untalented poet and meanwhile thought of all the things which should be said by a proper parent when in charge of an innocent child, but which couldn't be, for fear of said parent then losing it utterly and for fear of said parent also creating unpleasant fears in aforementioned mainly fearless child.

Or, let's be fair, I might just as easily make her laugh. When I tell her to look at them: their sweating, their fumbling, their imperfect secrecies. When I tell her to remember what they're like, so that when they offer her the nice lies, the convincing flatteries, she won't recklessly accept them, won't believe them the way I did. The way we all do, always, because, having sold off our dreams, having raised them up for slaughter and printing, we want to think they can still be wonderful and living and our own. We don't want the truth: to feel lost and cheap and emptied and superfluous.

If I could, I'd just say to Mary, **Examine those stares, those taxidermist's window stares, those kisses that are not kisses and those smiles that do not smile and consider that most of these people used to love words and now they only try to own them, which is not at all the same thing.**

But absolutely above every other thing, I want to tell her: NEVER FUCKING EVER TRUST A MAN WHO WORKS WITH HIS MIND ALL THE DAY, FIDDLING AT PUNCTUATION AND SHOVING HIS IMAGINATION TIGHT UP MOISTENED CLAUSES: YOU CANNOT IMAGINE HOW HUNGRY HIS BODY GETS. AND HE WILL NOT BE WELL, HE WILL NOT BE HEALTHY, I CAN PROMISE YOU THAT. I MEAN, WHAT THE FUCK CAN YOU CALL AN OBSESSION WITH

Take it from me, they are monsters. I am their kind of monster, so
I should know. I should explain that they will want to be witty,
polysyllabic and well read, amusing, charming, delicate, clean,
urbane, but most of all they will want to be wearing the gusset of your
knickers across their mouth while they fuck you from behind and prove
unable to remember your given name.

His mouth swam with nauseous saliva while he fought not to
picture anyone, anyone at all, anyone remotely female with her
mouth opened, anything opened for any kind of penetration, for
anything.

No, no, no, no. This is just paranoia. Nathan, you are being paranoid.
*She can look after herself. And they're not **all** maniacs. Fuck, there are even*
***women** here. Not many, but enough to dampen down any overly laddish*
tone. Almost.

*But lots of them **are** maniacs. Him, for example.*

His stomach cramped with fatherly despair.

*Him **especially**, the fucker. That cunt takes more than half a pace towards*
her and I'll squeeze his eyes out slowly through his arse.

'Nathan. Good Lord.'

Nathan found himself clamped in a humid embrace before he
could recognise Jack's voice.

'You old bastard. What are you doing here? Not exactly your
scene.'

'J. D.?'

''Course. Why're you here?'

'Brought my girl to see the animals at play.'

My girl.

A dab of proprietary vertigo tambourined between his shoulder
blades.

That's right, my girl.

Nathan felt the thick, sweet breath of long-term alcohol use curl
at his neck as Jack chuckled.

'*Girl?* You?'

'Daughter. Mine. Remember?'

'Aah. Of course, Sport, of course. I do beg your pardon.' J. D.
relinquished him with a parting slap at his kidneys. 'Fuck. Good to

see you. Bit too drunk to enjoy it.' He nodded severely. 'But, all the same . . . Nice to have company with whom one may actually converse.' Managing a conspiratorial glance about himself, 'This is all shits and slappers tonight. But then, was it not ever thus?' He darted a hand to his inside pocket, 'Know the secret of modern editing?' and reached out a dark, stubby bottle, apparently full.

Nathan supplied the punchline, such as it was, 'Designer jackets and designer beer.'

'Oh.' His wine glass swayed with disappointment. 'I told you.'

'You did.'

'Well, whenever I said it, it's still true. They're in it for the business, for the pissing contests, for the — most of them can't even fucking spell.'

'Whereas you can't even fucking read.'

'No, currently I probably couldn't, 's true. But I can rise to the occasion, if asked politely.' Left hand occupied with its glass, Jack deftly employed his right in manipulating his bottle and unscrewing its top. 'Now then . . .' Frowning with determination, he lightened his glass by a generous mouthful and then topped it up with a reddish, syrupy liquid from his personal supply. 'Mm. Surefire winner.' He swirled the concoction, downed it in one. 'Nectar of the gods, that.' He bared his teeth in a spasm of satisfied pain. 'Port and Benylin.'

'Doesn't that kill you?'

'One can but hope.'

'You're off the wagon, then, can I presume?'

Jack's mouth narrowed with controlled distaste. 'I was never *on* the wagon. Not this time. I've been *in treatment*. And now I am cured. And I am not – apparently – an alcoholic.'

Nathan listened for traces of irony and found none, 'Really. That's good to know,' but didn't entirely manage not to offer some himself.

'Yes, I thought so.' J. D. ignored him, keeping it straight. 'I only have a compulsive and addictive personality, so I'm told. The experts say I can drink as much as I like without worrying. Or anyone else worrying, which was always rather more the problem. My counsellor said she couldn't believe I drank so *little* – given the amount of tress, that is, *stress* under which I am forced to be creative and endlessly fucking flexible.'

'*She* couldn't believe? They gave you a female counsellor.' Nathan

232

watched a low burn of mischief start in J. D.'s eyes. 'Jack . . . you didn't. Not with your counsellor . . .'

J. D. laboriously tapped the side of his nose and winked while repocketing his bottle with a shoplifter's *élan*. 'My counsellor, a fine lady, very fine, good lips – both sets of them, very good . . . she chose to resign for . . . ah, *personal* reasons at precisely the point when the clinic and I also parted company. She has sought employment at another fa-cil-i-ty – shit, that's a difficult word late at night – facility. I have no facility for saying facility.' He seemed about to drift beyond his train of thought, but then he gave Nathan a smirk and reined himself back in. 'I graduated as a non-alcoholic *cum laude* and then I . . . hum . . . I chose to buy her a ver, ver, *very* nice goodbye dinner, before saying goodbye. All's fair in love and therapy.' He seemed to search his memory for something slippery, then, 'And now I have to, um . . . recharging the glass should now take place. Don't you go too far away, though, because you are my friend here, my dear, dear and only friend.'

Nathan watched him swing back for the bar, announcing firmly to a neat young man whose drink he'd spilled, 'I *intend* to be unpopular. That is my *aim*.'

His dear, dear friend, that's me. I don't know which one of us that makes the sickest bastard.

*But it's true. Who else around here do I actually really **know**? It's been a while since I walked out on literature, or since it walked out on me, but – even so – where have they all gone? There are maybe fifteen people here I recognise, the rest are –*

He caught sight of Mary, her hair taking what little light there was and glowing with it, glistening; her shoulders slim under the dress and minorly tense, but elegant, womanly, unmistakably beautiful.

The rest are just as they always were, only younger. Different people, different faces: but the bankrupt eyes the same as ever. But my Mary, she's something special. Yes, indeed.

His jaw clenched as he watched. Maura, her likeness, the form of the woman she'd been, threatened to breach at any moment in a smile, or a gesture of Mary's and to finally make him fall on the floor and howl out loud. But the resemblance never locked entirely, only shimmered at him, gave him gooseflesh and the taste of pain.

★

Patronising buggers. Everyone in black, everyone smelling of money, of London, of knowing each other too well. That's it – they all smell the same, like one thing. Thing being the operative word.

Mary was not exactly having fun.

And where are you from? *Wales.* **Oh, dear.**

And what do you do? *I write short stories.* **Ah.**

Confessing to short fiction was obviously even more distressing than having to be Welsh. So, as the evening progressed, she began to lie.

I'm an undercover meat inspector.

I design sanitary towels.

I'm having an affair with that man over there. No, that one. No, that.

Which had worked twice, but then she'd tried it on a lady key accounts manager, who'd squeezed her hand and told her a number of frankly nasty reasons which explained why that particular liaison could never have taken place.

From somewhere upstairs a cheer erupted and then shattered into bursts of stamping. The voices around Mary faltered and, at her shoulder, a man began to laugh, producing a small, dark sound, taken on the inward breath – when she turned to him, it seemed as if he were eating his own amusement. He glanced at her, evaluating, then shrugged and glanced away as the room came back to itself, re-establishing a level of noise just high enough to knuckle lightly at the bones of everybody's skull.

'D'you know why people like tennis so much?'

A soft weight nudged her side and she spun to face a wetly smiling figure, sweat gathered in alarming patches across his forehead. Having brushed against her, he now stood, completely motionless, deep in the statuary stage of intoxication.

'I beg your pardon?'

He blinked, puzzled, as if he'd only just noticed her and then spoke again. 'Have you ever wondered why people like tennis so much?'

'No, actually. I haven't.'

'It's bec–' His eyelids drooped further into a lazy wince. 'You're new, aren't you. Tonight, I have to be cautious with new people, but I have, at present, misplaced why.' He was directing his voice painstakingly at a point several inches below her chin. 'You wouldn't be kind enough to divulge your name?' Quick as a slap he looked directly at her, eyes as sad as a basset's, moist with an undefined hurt and a tiny, tiny flirt of pleasure, just a tickle that slipped away. 'Would you?'

'Lamb. Mary.' She wasn't sure if she wanted to talk to him or not – he seemed both almost harmless and almost interesting.

'Mary. That's ... that's very melodic. How are you finding literature's great and good? Mm? We could play pin the tail on the novelist – if we could find a proper novelist. Or we could just slip off to somewhere else.' He grinned a grin which almost managed to suggest *this is so sad and so obvious, so much a mid-life crisis type of play, that really it must be something different, more intelligent, more fun – or at least an occasion that we both can rise above.*

Mary grinned a grin which said *nice try.* 'I'm here with someone else.'

If Nathan qualifies as someone else. Or even someone.

Time was, I could have been really here with someone else. Time was, Jonno. Time was.

'I don't see him with you now. And I really do have to go *now* – these occasions have a very limited tolerability.' He beat a clear path through *tolerability* by slowing to a quarter of what was already a creeping rate of speech. 'This is what hell will be like, you know? In heaven there are many mansions and in hell there are many houses – all of them publishing.'

'Publish and be damned.'

You're a tosser, but you're a nice tosser.

'Yes, I'd heard that, too. Shall we go?'

A determined tosser, but don't get annoying – or I'll get annoyed back. I've met better than you back in Gofeg at the Nelson, trying their luck before stop tap and trotting off home to the wife.

'No thank you.'

'Not even to another *room*? If I say please.'

'I don't think so.'

But, fair play, you have certainly managed to be drunker than I have seen anyone get and stay standing.

Something about him was forensically compelling. She noticed she wasn't the only one watching him as he acted out his own little martyrdom.

'But we could . . .' Just what exactly they could tumbled out of his grasp – she could almost see it drop. 'I'm so sorry, but your name . . . ? Was . . . ?'

'I've told you once already. You said it was melodious.'

He sighed. 'Sorry. Really – I'm very sorry.' He dabbed her shoulder with his finger-tips and then recoiled elaborately at such an unseemly physical excess. 'Sorry. Slightly inebriated. But the mind has not yet . . . deliquesced. Splendid word, that – deliquesced.'

'Descended into liquid form.'

Nobody beats me on vocabulary, even if I've had a couple myself. Not that a couple would make any odds, not tonight.

She hid her thinking in a longer than average blink.

Published.

It felt like silver and the moment before a kiss.

'A liquid descent, yes. Wonderful idea.' He tried a roguish smile, but had to settle for a quickly extinguished leer.

*Oh, **fuck off**.*

'Look, my name is Mary Lamb and I'm not going anywhere with you – I'm here with Nathan Staples.'

'Oh, Christ.' He simultaneously drained his whisky glass and dragged his unencumbered hand viciously through his hair. The already disturbed mass of grey settled into an even less happy disarray. 'Oh . . .' A wet cough. 'Dearie, dearie me.' He sucked in air through his canvas-coloured bottom teeth.

*He's blushing. After all the shady moves he's tried to pull, he's blushing **now**? Men really don't make any sense.*

'I . . .'

His glassless hand was extended to her stiffly. She accepted its vaguely gluey warmth, its unhealthy peeling away.

'I should introduce myself, Mary Lamb. My name is J. D. Grace and I'm a friend of your fa– friend . . . a friend of Nathan's.'

'Oh, you're *Jack*? I should have known.' She watched, helpless to prevent Jack colouring further and, despite the gloom, achieving a highly apparent and rather worrying shade of damp cerise. She touched the back of his hand, she hoped reassuringly. 'Not because of what you tried . . . that is . . . he hasn't really told me about what you . . . with women . . .' Mary could feel herself slithering towards charges of manslaughter by shame as Jack swayed away from each tactless syllable. She rushed out a final anodyne effort, 'You publish him.'

'I do,' emerged from Jack as a sort of anguished hiccup. 'I really must . . . I have to . . . I should apologise.' He snatched at her wrist. 'Please don't tell him. Will you?'

'Tell me what?'

Jack's grasp leaped away while two other hands slipped to rest on Mary's shoulders.

Nathan to the rescue – about bloody time. Not that I couldn't have rescued myself.

A neat relaxation rolled through the muscle in her back: she recognised Nathan's voice, even if his touch was a little surprising, even if she wasn't used to him smelling of aftershave, of that particular kind of maleness. She could feel the peculiar weight and vibration of Nathan's chin resting itself on the crown of her head as he spoke.

'Mm, Jack? Break it to me, I can take it. You're my editor, aren't you? – terrible news for me, but I have to say I had already guessed. Is that what you wanted to tell me? Or did you want me to know you'd got rid of your moustache?' The movement of Nathan's laughter nudged softly at Mary's back. 'You look much better without it. And, by the way, why *do* people like tennis?'

'Now, Nate, this is hardly the time or the place . . .' Perspiration was oiling from one of Jack's sideburns and down his cheek – a fat line, gleaming with unease.

'Oh, I think it is, though.'

Jack almost growled, it seemed partly irritated and partly proud. 'All right. With pre-emptive apologies to the lady in our midst. People all like tennis because when the players serve they tend to sound very much as if they've just come. And then there's the matter of all those shorts and thighs and knickers and balls – it's a very sexy game. So now you know.' He cleared his throat. 'You didn't introduce me to your protégé, Nate. You really should have. Safer for all concerned. And much more pleasant.'

Nathan moved to stand with his arm around Mary's shoulders while Jack winked at her politely. She was beginning to feel slightly besieged, even claustrophobic. Jack continued, discussing her as if she had been a particularly wise investment on Nathan's part.

'You have a splendid, um . . . splendid person there in your charge, old man. Quite splendid.'

Just to remind them that I can speak . . .

She eased herself free of her minder's grip. 'Thank you. I often think I'm splendid, too, and,' she could feel the word – *that* word – pushing out, shameless in the air, before she could do anything about it, 'and *published*. I am a published author.'

'Well . . .' Jack winked again, this time at Nathan. 'This is, I may say, not entirely surprising,' then shifted his attention to her, 'you must come from good stock. Not to mention having talent of your own. My heartiest congratulations.' He darted a kiss to her cheek with a delicacy that surprised her and whispered, 'The way you feel now – do enjoy it while it isn't complicated.' She ducked, almost flinched back.

You sleazy old bugger.

Jack raised his hands in shaky surrender, shook his head. 'No, no, no. The way you feel about being published – *that* feeling – it's something you should treasure, very pure.' He twitched a smile. 'That's what I meant.'

Mary found herself patting his shoulder, finding the cloth of his jacket surprisingly soft – made for indoor working, gentle skin, unresilient wearing, an easy life. He was a kind of man she wasn't used to, a kind the club was filled with and suddenly this made her uncomfortably tired.

I want to go home.

'Nathan?'

He'd stepped slightly aside and was staring at her, an odd, fragile stillness in his face.

She tapped at his palm, repeated, 'Nathan? Do you mind if I go now? I think I've had . . . all I want of this.'

He stayed still for a breath, then broke into busyness, searching his pockets for nothing much, rubbing at his neck. 'Of course, of course. I'll come with you.'

'You don't have to. I could get a cab. I have money.'

'I know. But I'm also going – because I've had all *I* want, too. 'Night, Jack.'

The men clapped each other's hands into an interlocking clasp and Mary left them be.

238

She picked up her coat and walked out and under the still falling music and rain. Tipping back her head, she could taste the cool of it. In the shadows of the doorway, when she looked back, Nathan and J. D. were shuffling forward, embracing as they went. Then she could see Nathan talking, handing over a slip of paper or an envelope, the nod of Jack's head and then another longer, tighter hug: both men standing still. Nathan faced over Jack's shoulder, his eyes closed, his expression one of great content.

And not unlike Mary's when, later, in her unaccustomed hotel room, she slid right under the heat of a bubbled bath.

That's that then, really. Here I am, me. The same. Only now I'm a writer.

Blood, heat and nerves sang and creaked lazily in her water-filled ears.

*Only I wrote what I wrote a while ago, so I must have been a writer then. If not before. If I am now. And if I **am** now, then I'll have to keep on being it now. However you do that . . .*

She surfaced with a sealy huff of air.

First thing tomorrow, I'll phone up the Uncles and say. Call them from here. If that's not too expensive. From in bed. Call them from in bed and tell them that I'm a writer, that someone else thinks I am, too, and that I'm going to be published. Tell them that.

Mary giggled and then giggled again at the thought of herself – up to her neck in scented water and so happy at such a peculiar, papery thing. She stretched, leaned her neck against the back of the bath and lifted her toes to rest between the taps. Then she cupped one hand to her forehead, thumb and forefinger laid to fit snug at the hairline and gently rubbing, comforting. She would say she had always done this, that it was a gesture of her own making.

Across the Square in one of the apartment blocks, Nathan stood in his darkened window, looking out at others that were lit and cradling his forehead in just the way that Mary did. Because this was his movement, too – his movement and his bloodline's.

He'd watched it repeat in his father and grandfather, less like a visible gene than a signal, a gift. They'd made a whole alphabet, the family, with their angling of arms, their duration of smiles, their pulling of the soft heart out of bread and the squeezing of it into pills and wafers, smooth on the tongue. They all played with their food, the Stapleses. Their shrugs had, for generations, been slightly too disinterested to be anything but provoking. Their early kisses were often too light. And nevertheless, for generations, they had happily echoed each other and their dead and seen their bodies reflecting in younger and sometimes better flesh.

Nathan watched the night, the scent of Mary still stirring about him when he moved, the shape of her still warm inside his hands, and he braced himself against the salt flare of an unfamiliar thought.

I am enough now, just enough.

'The fucking bastard! The bloody . . . I can't . . . I don't even . . . Jesus!'

'Now,' Nathan sat holding on to his table's edge, aware that it was turning in some way plastic, undependable under his fingers' clamp and fuss. This was going wrong. Had already gone wrong. All wrong. 'You'll need to . . . please . . . please, calm yourself.'

Jesus, I just, I just. **Shit, it shouldn't be this way**.

Eckless stirred in his basket, uneasy, while Nathan watched Mary pace his living room, the sky an unfeeling blank of mist, fixed at the window behind her. She'd folded her arms around herself savagely, letting him see – in case he didn't know for sure already – that he wouldn't be able to touch her, that no one would, that anyone might stand observing, but she was doing this alone.

'I can't believe . . . I mean, do you think it's true? I can't . . . how could anyone have done this, been like this? How?'

Her voice was ragged: the sound of it filled his mouth with the wet, metallic taste of injury and he wanted to cry, but couldn't, wanted to move, but couldn't, wanted to help his daughter, but could not. She looked at him, bewildered, enough dismay in her eyes to knock the breath out of his lung and sting his ribs.

'Nathan, do you believe it?'

Oh God, I'm sorry, I'm so sorry. I am such a sorry fuck.

'Well, I . . . it could be. I don't really – I don't know.'

He considered the knuckles of his hand and attempted to govern his pulse, while she grabbed at a chair and sat beyond his reach, leant her elbows on the table, let her hands fall, wooden with unhappiness.

She rubbed at her hairline – the family gesture – and closed her eyes. 'He says he cares, says he *cared*. But he didn't ever write before now – not in all this time, never let me . . . I don't think it's him. It isn't him. My father's dead, that's what my mother told me. My father's dead.'

No, your father wants to be, only wants to be dead.

'Perhaps –'

'Why didn't he contact me before? He says he, he says he . . .' Her words were beginning to hiccup and break. 'Then why didn't he . . . write? Nathan? Christ, he hasn't even given a return address.'

The room sunk around him while he stayed still, absolutely still and maintained the crawling tension of a body lie: the calmly concerned surprise in his face, the quiet leaning of his spine against the chair back, nothing about him showing a sign of being sudden or desperate. He answered her carefully with words that felt muted and cottony.

'Perhaps he was afraid.' She snapped round to look at him, entirely incredulous. 'I, I don't know, though. I don't know . . . anything, except that if he is who he says then I'm sure that, I'm sure that, having known you myself now for some time, I'm sure that he would . . . have feelings. I'm sure that –'

'But I wasn't even four. At least, I don't think I was four when he, when he left.'

'He would remember. That would have been enough. To know.' His throat closed at the last syllable and his vision smirred.

Shit.

'And why would she tell me he was dead? Why that?'

He could only shake his head.

Which is pretty surprising, really – having done so much damage already, it's strange you can't think of something more hideous to do. Why not just punch her? You might as well.

Shit. It seemed OK, it seemed the best way in the end – J. D. writes the letter, copies out exactly what I gave him – like the good man he can sometimes be – he posts it from Islington and then . . . I thought she'd be pleased. Find out you've got a father, find out that he loves you, that he always, always did – that would make you, wouldn't it, pleased?

She had lowered her head now, one hand nestled over her eyes, so that it didn't matter if he cried because she wouldn't see him, wouldn't know.

Good thing, too – because you're not crying for her, you're crying for yourself. She hates him – hates you. Look. Look at what you do to her by simply being you, by simply announcing that you exist.

*I did think of explaining properly: I did think about doing that – setting out the whole of the final arrangement with Maura, what it meant – but then I decided I should just say what mattered: that I **am** somewhere, that I **am** loving her, that more will follow, if she wants it.*

Wrong. All wrong.

He stood – almost surprising himself with the movement, dizzy – and stepped to wait behind her, hoping some change in the fret of her breath, some particular motion of her unease would tell him this was just the time when he could rub at her shoulders, lay his palm on her neck's heat, be usefully, noticeably, helpfully with her. But nothing altered – he stayed unnecessary.

'Mary. Mary?'

Oh, shut up and leave her alone, can't you?

No. I can't.

'Mary, thank you for coming to me with this.'

She steadied a long inhalation. 'There's no one else I can come to.'

'Well. I suppose. If you say, then that's true.'

'I don't want to worry the Uncles.'

'No. Of course.' Everything he could see had started to slide and spangle from the edges in. 'This will be fine, though. It will work out.' She stayed silent while he tried taking frequent shallow breaths for fear of blacking out. 'It will.'

'You don't understand.'

'I . . . No. That's right. I don't.'

Nathan hugged himself and felt sweat, came close to staggering when she pushed back her chair to almost clip his shins and walked out: not a word or a look for him. He heard her break into a run outside, her footfalls softened by turf, but still clearly anxious to leave him behind.

For a sickly moment his mind filled with the scent and image of his mother, a memory of her raging at him and – unheard of, this – slapping him inefficiently for some particularly imbecilic crime. He realised strongly that what he wanted most was for her to swoop at him, alive and pallid with anger again today, to clatter him with her forearms and her hands until his marooned lung shuddered and rattled in the over-large bell of his chest. He needed her to hit him unreasonably hard and confirm his total understanding that he was not grown enough to be responsible or capable in any way.

It was a terrible cliché: going to the Lighthouse for help, making a floundering ship of himself and then limping on into safe harbour – but Nathan had exhausted all other options, pretty much. He'd listened to Piaf and Jacques Brel, dredged up some Cajun social music until they sawed out 'Un Homme Marié' and reminded him of Maura and his whole fucking, bloody life and everything and then he'd played Philip Glass for mindless hours before the incessant twiddly-diddly of it drove him clear outside. He'd sprinted then with Eckless to the point where both of them were shaking and pole-axed in the chilly grass. He'd watched the sea split and cup and ride itself down, his dog whining in polite concern beside him, trotting up to lick between his fingers, stealing salt.

She hates me.

Mary's voice was hot in his mind, still hobbling his thoughts and translating them into bleak distances, unexpected hurts. The sea breeze had kicked up a gnawing pressure in his sinuses and he'd attempted to build the consoling fantasy of swinging in the current, dead to all worlds, fish-nibbled and bloated, the skin of his hands slipping off like malignant gloves. It hadn't worked, so he'd had to come here, to the Lighthouse.

*Bloody Christopher, he sets us up for this: the Lighthouse. It couldn't be the coalhouse, greenhouse, shit-house – no, it has to sound illuminating. **We look to the Lighthouse, from whence doth come our aid**.*

'Nathan, I didn't expect to see you here.' Ruth burst up from a chair in the darkest corner of Joe's sitting room, surprising Nathan and reminding him strongly of some medically repellent growth, swelling palely towards a time-lapsed lens.

'Oh, right. Hi. Joe around?'

Ach, shite. Why this morning? Why you?

'No.'

244

And shite again.

She smiled at him warily and he allowed the bookcase to catch his eye – nothing more convincingly fascinating being available. 'Away out then, is he?'

'For a while. He left a note in the kitchen. He was expecting me' – this given the pointed delivery she seemed to hone by another barbed inflection each time they met.

'Whereas I'm not expected at all.' He remembered not to look at her finger stumps – once he'd started doing that, he could never quite stop.

'Well, no. No, you're not.'

Ruth prodded herself down into the chair again and stared at her knees. Still feeling bloodied after Mary, he found himself moderating his distaste and relenting slightly when he looked at the bow of Ruth's head. He was suddenly anxious to practise even one unwieldy expression of tenderness, one gesture out of the many he seemed to keep in pointless storage, flaking to dust.

'I, uh . . . Would it be an imposition if I asked to wait?'

She blinked at him, suspicious – as he often was himself – of his courtesy. 'Wait if you like. It isn't my house, I don't have a say in who stays here.'

'I was –' He blocked himself. Primed to talk to *someone*, he knew he might just go off and blurt out his horrors over *anyone* instead.

No call to give her ammunition when she can already snipe away without any assistance. Should the mood take her.

Not that, to be honest, she seems in that mood currently. No chucking coppers at my eyes today. And she does look, for wee moments, I have to say, as if she were twelve, or eight, or some age equally unlikely and inappropriate for a woman of her size, but nevertheless unmistakable in its expression of vulnerability. That's what I most detest about her – the way she'll make you want to play caretaker for her, the way she'll be so invitingly sad.

'I was – I've had trouble with Mary.'

Why *am I saying this?*

'It's all quite difficult. It's things I'm not good at.'

Why? Because I'd say this to Joe's desk lamp if I had to. I just want it out and away. Not solved, just away, just for a while.

Ruth chipped in, glumly, 'I never had children.'

*She always does that — talks about herself in the past tense, as if she was already over. Even **I** don't do that.*

She folded her arms tightly, inadvertently allowing Nathan to notice she must be wearing too small a bra. Under tensed layers of cloth, the limits of size B containment were plainly impressed on two rises of size D flesh: the outline of her breasts faced him, plump and unnerving, like unhappily transected baps. He made an effort not to find them grimly fascinating, wary of purely professional interest being misconstrued, and jerked back to consider the wreck of his fatherhood. 'Well, I haven't exactly had my child for any length of time.'

'But I'm sure you're doing what you think is best.'

'Recipe for disaster, every time.'

She gave a not disagreeable chuckle and then shook her head. 'I'm sure that isn't true.'

'But then, you don't know me very well.'

'No, that's right, I don't.'

A mildly electric silence began to strap itself out between them and Nathan scuffled his feet, burning off a number of seconds in which he could think what he should do. 'You know —' He turned and faced her with, perhaps for the first time, his entire attention. And there she was: Ruth Alvey, reeking with loneliness, eyes frozen for however many years in a type of perpetual flinch and with odd varieties of anger, keeping up a twitch and snag in her lips.

You don't notice, because of the way she is, that she does have a fine mouth: essentially sensual. Shame.

Nathan watched her, watching him, and knew that, in other circumstances, this might conceivably be the beginning of something. But with this particular Nathan Staples and this particular Ruth Alvey, here on Foal Island on this particular afternoon – or, let's face it, in any other place or time – this was the beginning of nothing, nothing at all.

'Ruth . . .'

She adjusted the collar of her uncomplimentary blouse, pulled it a fraction further clear of her uncomplimentary sweatshirt. The air around him seemed to kick softly, like the surface of dark water, disturbed. His prick woke with a minor caterpillar spasm of unease.

'Ruth . . .'

246

At the backs of his knees and in the taut line of his neck, he recognised the instinctive creep of free-floating need, untimely as ever.

Lonely people, dry people, people who would prefer to be untroubled by any more hope: they really ought to fit. It should be possible to match them together quite arbitrarily: two minuses making a plus, two unloveds making love: but, of course, it doesn't work that way. Despair doesn't lead to compromise, that's what makes it so despairing.

Slick and limber, like a mist against his skin, came the memory of forming an embrace: the second-nature daily ease of that and of drawing in air to the crest of a breath, the turn of a breath, and then holding, squeezing Maura fast against him while he sighed away his brain and his heart unbolted fearlessly and everything was fine.

I know exactly what I want and nothing else will ever do.

*And Ruth, I suppose, I **hope**, thinks much the same.*

He glanced away, broke their contact, and discovered he was feeling seasick and a touch unclean.

'Ruth?'

A dusty flare of warmth showed in her face before she could smother it.

'I . . .' He rubbed at his cheek with the heel of one hand. Under his palm, a muscle began to tick. 'I think it's best if I left this till later. I'll come back when Joe isn't busy.'

'You don't have to.'

'Mainly, I needed the walk – you know? Here and back? It's done me the world of good. Really. So I'd better head off. And,' he measured the words out, careful they should have no more meaning than he meant, 'it was nice to see you.'

'OK, Nathan.' Ruth nodded, gave a bruised grin, as if she'd just heard a bad joke at her expense – the one that she'd been expecting all along. 'Nice to see you, too.' Her voice emptied to grey.

'Yeah. Take care.' Which sounded to Nathan the most stupid thing he could ever have thought of to say.

At first Mary couldn't think of what was missing, of what small thing was gone. Morgan lay, as he always liked to, in the middle of the bed – a terrible, greedy sleeper, that's what Bryn called him.

Morgan's usual range of nonsense was set on the cabinet, waiting for the night's possibilities: small inhaler, luminous alarm clock, folded handkerchief, two peppermints, a water glass, the tub of Vaseline. His clothes were draped ready across the chair, his shoes settled underneath it. His favourite picture of Mary was leant on the mantelpiece where he would see it if he just sat straight up and looked straight ahead. Things were as they should be, very orderly, the bedroom full of the dry, sleek scent of Bryn and Morgan, Morgan and Bryn: their blankets, their sleeping, their skin.

She looked at Morgan again, slowly, avoiding the brief, tender fan of his red hair, perfectly legible against the pillow's white, trying to slip her gaze over the soft close of his eyelids, the hard gape of his mouth.

No.

Bryn, she knew, was behind her: more ready for this by now and perhaps more accustomed. Mary reached out one hand to him and, almost at once, Bryn burrowed it safe between both of his own. Neither Bryn nor Mary spoke.

No.

And then she realised what was gone, what her eye couldn't help expecting, even in the teeth of common sense. There was no more rise and fall in Morgan's chest.

Look at him.

No, I don't have to.

I don't know what I'll see.

But, of course, she did have to look.

She stood, sensations bleeding away, her body becoming a kind of pause, and she looked at a face close to being his face, but entirely strange. And the dark of one smooth thought began to pierce her, gently irresistible: she wasn't seeing *him* any more, she was seeing *it*. This theft of Morgan, his replacement with something false – she tried to believe that it meant he'd had a soul, a soul that had moved him, a soul that had left her behind now while it turned and settled, still living, in an unthinkable elsewhere.

She had never thought of death before as such a closed and selfish space. And she had never thought that absolute absence would offer such a savage consolation: this lunge of bloodied faith, choking her with a need to believe in continuance, in life after life, before her confidence failed her and abandonment spindled out, cutting everything to weeping threads.

But in the undefended corner of her eye, the soft back to her mind, she was still waiting to see him breathe, still knew that he would breathe, was still quite certain that he would breathe. Or else why continue to love him, why be unable to call a halt? Why let herself be tipped into a future charred and silted with emotions which already had no point? For the first time in her adult life, Mary understood she'd made too many plans.

'You don't have to, if you don't want.' Bryn's voice sounded improbably, garishly alive. 'I already started, I could go on . . .'

His hands pressed hers and then he held her, arms needy, his breath breaking in her hair. She hugged him back. 'No, I'll do it. We'll do it together. So they don't have to.'

'They wouldn't –' He drew in a tentative measure of air, shifting against her delicately. 'They wouldn't do it right. Not the way he'd like it.'

'No, not the way he'd like.'

So they parted and faced Morgan and did what their separate loves required.

Mary padded round the bed – as if here she might still be able to trouble a sleep – and lifted the whole armful of his clothes, lifted the feel and smell of him in one cool and insubstantial weight and carried it to the bed. Where Bryn had quietly drawn the covers back to show her Morgan, his skin blue-pale as watered milk and his limbs too thin; Morgan, for both of them, lovely, only ever beautiful. Morgan's body wore his black dress socks, a fresh white vest and boxer shorts in dove grey silk.

Bryn's eyes ticked to her. 'He loved silk, the bad man. And I always liked grey.' The horror of his own likings and what they now meant snatched his voice and left him swallowing, frowning gently, quiet. Then he extended his open hands to Mary, steadier, ready to begin.

She passed him a new white shirt and, while he struggled with its wrapper, she set Morgan's things at the foot of the bed and moved in closer. Then, one on either side of Morgan – his overly heavy head, his too-light limbs, the terribly meaningless touch of his skin – they dressed him.

'Handkerchief, he'd have a handkerchief.'

'But in the trouser pocket, not the breast.'

Remembering him back to life.

'That's right.'

They made themselves busy fulfilling the needs he no longer had.

'That collar, it's too big. I should take it back . . .'

'It's fine.'

'He never wore a tie, nearly never.' Bryn gave a tiny huff of concern and then pursed his lips, trying to stem his usual sounds of unhappiness. They were inadequate.

'I know.'

'He looks better with one on, though. I always said so, but he wouldn't be told.'

'He looks –'

But she couldn't think how Morgan looked. Except that, dressed, he was both closer and further from himself. Still, she wanted him, more than anything, to be handsome and comfortable. Mary wanted to know for sure that he was completely comfortable.

Bryn brushed Morgan's hair, fastened on the wristwatch and eased the arms to a proper rest.

She felt herself say, 'His reading glasses.'

Bryn seemed bewildered for a space, almost afraid, but then moved to the dresser, opened a drawer and there were the glasses, among the socks. 'I just . . . put them in the first place I could . . .'

'I know, I know.'

They met each other's eyes, surprised again by the newness, the headiness of their pain.

Morgan's inside pocket took the glasses and all was made straight, tugged and tucked and smoothed, and then Bryn and Mary stood, suddenly smothering inside the certainty that this had been everything there was to do.

Later, Mr Howells would come with the coffin – they didn't have to say this, it was understood – but Bryn would stay with Morgan until that happened, he would keep watch. Alone. So Mary kissed the body that had been Morgan and told it goodbye, then she kissed Bryn, lightly, lightly. Both of them shivered at the touch of warm lips.

'He read your story, the one about the hand. They publish it yet?'

'Not yet, no.'

'He thought it was very good.'

'Mh hu.'

'So did I. Proud of you. Both of us. Proud.'

She let go of Bryn's hand as she moved towards the bedroom doorway and didn't want to hear about stories, or writing, or the way she'd abandoned Gofeg and the people that she loved for a great deal of typing, a great deal of paper and dead ink.

Mary eased the door closed and crossed the landing, careful not to hear Bryn sobbing, the soft, deep impacts of grief.

And when everything important had already been done, Mary attended the funeral service of Cyril Iolo Morgan, a man who had been her uncle by mutual consent. Howells the son drove the hearse and Howells the father walked in front, and both took responsibility for moving Bryn and Mary between the crowds, the quiet jostle of condolence, the unrehearsed theatre of it all. Beside Mary in the chapel, Bryn could sing none of the hymns he'd chosen. She put her arm around him and felt the jolts of misery, wrenching silently under his back.

But they got through, finally staggering a little like marathon runners approaching the end of their course. They made it home. Back to a house full of loping shadows, stabs of memory, and the paralysing reassurances of strangers. Mary wandered the afternoon away in a house made not their own, crowded with the dark of mourners, the susurration of their proper concern and the guilty crack of their laughter, that healthy, pointless noise.

Every conceivable surface was unruly with plates. Mary drifted to a stop in the kitchen doorway, mildly confounded by the impenetrable clutter of sandwiches and pork pie slices, napkins and cakes and glasses, teacups and unsteady, dirty knives. Someone passed behind her and she felt the now usual nudge and stammer of acknowledgement at her elbow.

'We saw him off well.'

'Yes.'

They all said that, or something to that effect. As if there had been the possibility of seeing him off badly, with hatred, with contempt.

But I suppose it happens – sometimes it must.

*This isn't for him, though, is it? This is for **them**, to see him off, to be seen well.*

Danno Buys and Sells Anything, Mrs Danno, the Cennards, Dilwyn Ianetta and all of his tribe, there were so many people here, so many mercifully indistinct faces, as if she were seeing them at speed, or through a barrier of salted glass.

And Mrs Davies, Jonathan's mother, had turned up for a while. Mary was sure she remembered a thin kiss at her cheek and then the back of a pious raincoat making for the door, duty done.

'That story, Mary . . .'

Irene and Mildred from the hosiery shop caught Mary in at either shoulder and steered her along the passage towards the front room.

'Poor Morgan showed us.'

*So he's **poor Morgan** now.*

'Clever old thing, you are, aren't you? He never stopped telling us.'

Their voices pecked at her, left and right.

'Just stopping by in the mornings and telling us all about it – how you were getting on.'

Not this, not now.

'So pleased when you were published, he was.'

'I'm not yet.'

'But you are *going* to be, he explained.'

'You made him very happy.'

'Yes, you did.'

'No, I didn't. Not enough.'

They clutched at her, all soft arms and softer bodies, while she cried, suddenly caught by a vaulting hurt. She gasped inside their little atmosphere of 4711 and inquisitive kindness and lily of the valley talc.

'You'll be fine, lovely.'

'And if you need anything ever, you just ask.'

'Write to us,' Irene suggested, her eyes faintly anxious to make the right offer, to indicate securely that everything would go on, that Mary should do what Mary did best and that time would move forward: this being a process requiring no consent.

'Yes, do,' Mildred scooped up the inspiration with relief, 'do that,' before they dabbed her with kisses and steered themselves away to the shuffle of conversations near the sideboard. The clock chimed its first quarter after four and Mary wished them all gone, every one.

Except for Jonathan.

She only knew for sure that she'd been waiting for him when he was standing there.

'I'm sorry I missed the . . . I only heard last night.' He brought in the damp of the afternoon, pearled in his hair, and slipped chill fingers quick against her palm, the unforeseen man: Jonathan. 'You didn't think I'd stay away?'

She could feel him assessing her expression and was powerless to know what he'd find, how she looked, what she thought.

'I mean, as soon as I – I'm very, very sorry – he was such a . . .'

All around them, the house's attention was audible. Sticky little currents of curiosity were already trying to eddy them closer and then witness the return of . . .

What? What do they think will happen? What do they think we can be? God, Jonno, what am I . . . what are we supposed to do?

'It is good to . . .' Rather than finish the sentence, she moved inside his arms, accepted the rain-frosted give of his coat against her cheek, then the nudge of foreheads, his hands at the small of her back while the hunger for comfort screamed in her blood like a circular saw.

Because she was like all the other mourners, really just the same: they were each one of them avid for life, heat, touch, for any indication that good could come of this. Any sign of youth, of liveliness was being coddled up today with an almost unbearable, angry appetite. Children were being pointedly indulged, unremarkable babies passed in wonder from lap to lap, anything would do, any temporary foxing of loss.

'This is –' Her voice seemed unpleasantly intrusive, so she pressed away her sentence as they gathered each other in.

'Come on. Come outside.'

'Mm?'

'Just come on. I haven't got long.'

'What?'

'I haven't got –' He kissed her hair and the room gave a small inhalation of approval. 'Come on.'

Jonno led her through the house, it seemed, for hours, while she gazed at his cheek, his mouth, the loose thread on the collar button of his shirt, and wondered if he was absolutely, genuinely there. Far below her thinking, her body was being drawn into an edgy run, as they stumbled to catch each other's pace, dodged furniture and observers, broke out through the kitchen into the good, cool prickle of outside air. Then they clasped together again beside the back door, a robin watching them from the wall, unwilling to sing.

'Now then, let's have some sense.' His first kiss opened on her, tested and parted her teeth with his tongue, pushed her into an old dream she'd thought she wouldn't see again. They fell into the old silk pattern of flutter and flex and tense, the breaks and beats of feeding. And she did want this. She did, very naturally, want this – but not in one hard crush, while his fingers unfastened her jacket and one hand worked around, puckering up her skirt until he could palm at her knickers and then slip in, as if this was his body as much as hers. Which wasn't true, which wasn't true.

He tried for a firmer contact, running the obvious furrow, while a mist of rain dampened the backs of her legs, chilled her fully into her senses again.

'No.'

'Mm.' He was trying to ignore the resistance in her thighs, her arms fending off now, thumping.

'No.'

He swung back from her, wiped his mouth with his hand and was held for an instant by the scent of her, fresh. He paused, almost started back to her, but then caught her eye and folded his arms instead. 'Well, fuck, what the bloody hell *do* you want? Jesus, I was trying to make you happy, I came to make you happy. When I saw you, the way you looked – sad – I thought –'

'No, you didn't. You didn't think.'

He dropped his head, appeared to be listening for something

254

interior, some private advice. Then he scowled out, 'My mistake then, eh? Forgot what you were like there, for a minute,' already turning, buttoning his coat, clawing his hair back into order, 'but I won't forget again,' and striding for the gate, grabbing it open and shoving it closed behind him. A sliver of old paint dropped from the hinge. Mary went and retrieved it, unthinking, and crushed it in her hand until it splintered, hurt her palm. Jonathan reached the lane's end, turned and paced out of sight.

Inside, the house was emptying: people off home, or up to the pub. Some of the women had stayed behind and were tidying and washing up.

But what about this evening? Without the mess to deal with, what'll we do?

Bryn stood, halfway down the stairs, staring at something above the movements of the house, as if he'd only just been lifted down from a hilltop, some scything perspective he'd been surveying, a place to still the bone. He was elegantly motionless, only the sheen of his eyes trembling faintly, broken, the rest of him dapper and dashing and pinned to a moment outside any moment she could reach. Mary had never seen him look so fine and so terrifying. Old Carmon had given him a haircut this morning and a proper barber's shave to clean and pink his skin. He seemed very well. He gleamed. His throat was delicate and smooth above the stiff white fit of a new shirt, the twin of Morgan's. The one that had gone with Morgan to the grave. He was wearing his best suit – heavy wool, brushed and pressed to a perfect darkness – and shoes with a shine like new oil and the proper clapping ring of leather about them to sound out, whenever he stepped.

Dear Christ, he's like a bridegroom.

She felt the stumbled fuss of the passage slew and shudder, almost halt around Bryn, before he took a breath and turned to face her. Life going on.

No more sleeping in the parlour, no more sofa now, I know. I saw him setting out the sheets. He'll go upstairs tonight and back into their room. His first time lying in the empty bed.

'All right, then, girl?' He sounded frightened.

'All right, yes.' So did she.

Nathan had brought Mary gently back out to the island and had been glad this was the first day when summer had finally seemed to be taking hold and had been delighted when she rested her head back and let her face just catch the evening sun, had wanted her so much to be a part of things again, reachable – even if only by light. But he naturally hadn't told her anything like that, had mainly kept silent and perhaps touched her hand or shoulder, now and then.

He'd left her to settle her things, but had found himself unable to rest away from her and had strolled past the Nissen hut loudly with Eckless, just before the last of the sunset, in the hope that he and his dog might both find themselves invited in. He thought, sidling round the door, that this had been a good idea. And, sitting with the daylight fading round her, cradling an unread book, it seemed that she could have been expecting him.

'Oh, Nathan. Right. And Eckless, my lovely boy.' She knuckled at the dog's ears until he groaned. Something about her movements was muted, automatic, her will and attention elsewhere. 'How are you, boy? Grand dog, yes, you are. Yes, yes.'

Eckless, like the lovely boy he truly was, only nuzzled lightly at her hands and then quietly submitted to being stroked at as a distraction.

'He's glad to see you.'

As am I. As am I.

'He's a good dog.'

Nathan hared silently through conversations he might conceivably begin and discovered nothing satisfactory. But Mary was quite willing to talk without assistance.

'It was odd, you know . . . I thought of you – at the, um, funeral. Because of that party you took me to.'

She seems calm. Which isn't good. I mean, that kind of loss, it should show more. Unless it's so deep that it can't.

He tried to avoid the greasy whisper which promised she would never miss him as much as this.

But at the funeral, she thought of me.

'Of me?'

'Yes.'

She smiled in a way that made him want to insist she slept now, or had a bath, or took a sleeping pill of the type that wouldn't harm her – not that there probably *was* such a thing – or that she maybe should just lie down for a while and let him relearn across her shoulders the way that he'd once been able to massage her mother to sleep.

'Yes, I kept thinking it all reminded me of something and then I realised – it was like that party in Soho. So many people, all dressed in black.'

'Well, that's . . .'

Go on, tell her. At least keep her company in all this shit.

Nathan wanted her to be looking at him while he said this, but she kept facing the window, eyes closed.

'I used to wear black all the time. For business. I was in the habit of dressing in black for signings and readings and, naturally, parties. It seemed to make things better – because it's the invisible colour, the one that lets you be less there. That's my theory, anyway.

'When my father died, I was already quite . . . established as a writer. He was the last of my family to go, so I must have been – well, older than you, anyway. And I attended his funeral, of course. But all the way through I was thinking, *I'm dressed for work – the writer and the undertakers, we're all just dressed for work.* I was never so fond of the black after that. In fact, for a while, I couldn't seem to wear it.'

Do you want me to hug you? Do you want to cry? You can be safe with me. Let go, break down, touch me and call me whatever you like, whatever makes you happy: Nathan, Uncle, Dad.

Except she doesn't like her dad.

Through the lining of his trouser pocket he pinched his own leg, attempting to shock his thoughts into decent order.

Mary rubbed her neck, let out a quick breath. 'And do you know what everyone talked about? While I was there?'

'Ah, no.'

'That fucking story. He'd told everyone about it, Morgan – Mary Lamb from our valley going to be published, his Mary Lamb.'

'If it made him happy, that's . . . nice.'

'Some people had seen a copy of it – read it – they came up to tell me so. But why talk about *that*? Why act as if it's made me any different? Why not . . . oh, I don't know.'

She stood up, startling Eckless out of a doze, and then – it seemed – could think of nothing better to do than fidget and sit down again. Nathan's heart writhed tenderly with the hope that he might, for once, be able to tell her something useful now. An insight.

'You remember my rules?'

'Your?'

'Rules for writing, or for being a writer, or for staying a human being while being a writer – those rules. I believe that we'd managed to reach Number Two.' He waited for her to agree, but then went on in any case. 'Number Three, if this is really the right time to say it: and I think it is . . . Number Three would be *Disregard*. However much they single you out and give you attention: *disregard*. It doesn't matter. The good and the bad opinions: *disregard*. What anyone else is doing, or has done, or will do: *disregard*. All the rosy fortune-telling about your wonderful, promising career: *disregard*. You are who you are already, *that's* what lets you write, defend it, keep it simple and . . . clean.' He glanced at her, felt the wise and encouraging smile ooze from his face like the facile, greasepaint effort that it was.

Shit.

'Clean?'

Shut the fuck up.

He swallowed clumsily with a flustered little gulp. '*Clean* would be the word, I suppose.'

'I see.' She was almost whispering, but still there was a dark edge in her tone. 'So you think that I'm getting above myself, that I should know my place.'

Something unwieldy started to twist from his stomach to his throat. 'No, I – primarily I'm remembering all the mistakes that *I've* made.'

Save it. Save it, you cunt, you witless, fucking cunt.

'And it's – you know, Mary – I only mentioned it to make sure you could take the pressure off yourself. You need to be able to relax and to be free . . . That's all, I . . .'

Please. No, please.

The flat muscle over her jaw was flickering as she turned and started to stare him down. He babbled on, finding it almost impossible to inhale. 'I wanted . . . you should know you're free of all the crap. Because when you write, when people examine your thinking – read you – it can have an odd effect. Uh.' Lack of air choked him to a merciful stop.

'Thank you for letting me know what you think of me. I hadn't realised I went to Morgan's funeral to have my ego enlarged.'

'No.' An involuntary whine. The noise of a hapless man.

'Do you think you could go now?'

He frowned for a sliding moment, fumbling around her meaning, as if it would turn into something he could accept. Mary clapped Eckless a quick goodbye, filling the beast with brief, wagging hopes of a walk outside, and then went behind the partition that hid away her bed.

Having nothing else to do – nothing he could think of – Nathan knelt rather clumsily in front of Mary's kitchen table and then cracked his forehead as hard as he could against its edge. Pain spattered whitely across his closed eyes and he guessed he had bitten his cheek when his mouth began to thicken with the sweet, salt metal of himself – of the red inadequacy stuttering up his veins.

He waited. Cracked his head again.

And again.

He waited.

He swallowed blood again.

When I bleed, I cry.

She didn't come back to him.

He knew she wasn't going to.

1993

Atlantis

I am absolutely certain.

This is the finest water in the world. It is, most likely, full of tractor oil and sheep's piss and is probably radioactive or so acid it's corroded all the frogs, but I love it very deeply, all the same.

It is running off the moor in a tawny sprawl over rocks and then dashing down the last few feet to the path in a gently pummelling fall. Under which I have placed my shoulders and my head. Doing this feels better than anything has since we left the hotel, since we left our room.

Thinking of which – and I do in a brief, hot stammer of happy blood – several things felt very good this morning, back in our room.

It's the different sheets, at least partly: taut and ferociously clean and proper against your skin. Makes you feel dirty. Makes you feel pleased that you do. And I can touch her, smell her so clearly when she's some- where I don't know: first the haze of her warmth in the dark and then the brush, the contact, the turning her over to kiss from the back of her knee to her arse, tenting up a starchy roof above us when I crouch. Cosy.

I still reek of her, it's wonderful. Even if I did make a show of scrubbing round my face, my hands, main- taining an air of decency at breakfast, Maura's still in my hairline, she's here at the flat of my wrists and live under my tongue. This morning I ate carefully to be sure I'd keep her there. Her taste. And mine. And her taste with my taste, worked together and spread into what we make together and at no other time, ingrained again in a night.

Christ, I'd missed it. Missed her. That of her.

The water is numbing my skull and, when I straighten, it fingers down my back and chest underneath my T-shirt, then dams and oozes at my belt. I rebalance my weight.

Bastard. My feet, my bastard, bastard feet. My ankle bones have worked out through my heels – it's the only explanation for that particular fucking pain. Jesus, shit.

This almost isn't worth it. There's no view to speak of, the glen one sullen scoop of green below me, no more arresting from five thousand feet than it was from fucking four. Brief cloud shadows scull across the distance and the sun buckets down unseasonably and I find it all less inspiring this minute than I managed to the last. And the path, I do not wish to mention. It is an exercise in unremitting inclines and false summits – we have hated each other now for several hours.

This is meant to be fun. I could be at home, trepanning myself, but, instead, I am having this fun.

But then the stillness catches me. The high, deaf weight of silence kisses in, makes my ears rush and whisper, bewildered with nothingness.

Which is why I come, remember? For the peace, for the lovely miles of emptiness, whorled out from the bones of the head and then – when I'm finally sore and knackered enough – the lovelier miles of emptiness, whorling in. Up here I can almost cease to think.

A small breeze trembles at my face, licks my sweat cool, fades. My legs jar down through the opening steps of the next bastard stage, setting off again. I scuffle, rush, drag to find my proper rhythm and then tick-tock on, kidding myself forwards with illusions of being mechanical and therefore beyond afflictions of any kind.

I am good at such tricks. Soon I will uncover completely – as if it was ever in more than a shallow grave – the tedious part of my nature which makes me entirely unable to give up. Although most of me will wish to sit down, lie down, curl in the grass with my boots off and go to sleep, I will not. My mind will tease and blackmail, bully and promise and possibly hypnotise, to keep my one foot following the other.

This isn't a bad thing about me, my determination. If I'm courting, for example, I will chase you like the Grail until I get you, then stay faithful as a stalker, come what may. Maura knows that, she understands. No matter how much I have to travel now: doing readings, lectures, all that crap: she can be absolutely confident that I am, as they used to say, true.

True and, every now and then, blue.

*Maura. In our room tonight – that's what to keep stamping on for – **us**. Us. Tonight. No interruptions. We really should do this more often. Now Mary's older, we can get away for husband and wife stuff whenever we like, we need to remember that. It's easy to let things deteriorate and have distances intrude, but we're setting that right.*

Us. Tonight. I'll slip up and be cribbed in her and we'll play and play and play.

Naturally, single-mindedness helps my work. A book demands my utter concentration, so I do concentrate utterly. I spend a good deal of time with imagined people, I'll admit, but that makes me need my real ones even more. I love when Mary runs up and sees me in my study. I have no objections to that at all.

If I'm too busy, she'll sit right in under my desk and draw – she can last for an hour or so like that, quite contented. Then she'll start to sneak pencils down into my socks and I have, perhaps foolishly, agreed that when she's run out of pencils I have to tell her what I've written and see what she thinks. It's a harmless bargain that helps us both. Of course, here and there, I censor, keep her safe, but this is still a good thing we do together: it makes her happy and it keeps me clear, lets me know what I mean. I would say nothing beats telling Mary, for helping me see what I mean. I find it quite hard when I have to work without her, although Maura prefers it if I do.

Maura. Us. Tonight. A little bit further.

Maura. Us. Tonight. A little bit further.

265

I have no more spit. My breath is hacking, kicking, thick in my throat and my hips are beating with gravelly, penetrating aches.

It's my own fault, I shouldn't have rushed my start. Maura says I'm too competitive, that I always have to race, but that isn't true. Not entirely. Everyone, in the end, has a separate, comfortable pace and any party on a trek like this will straggle out and settle in a natural order. It so happens that I will most usually be at the front.

Bollocks. I fucking cripple myself every time, just to get away. A little bit further. Not to win, just to be clear of people. No small talk to wheeze out, no exchanges of encouragement, no fury as some tottering couple jams up an ascent – a little bit further – only peace and a free path ahead.

Maura's not so far behind me, she's always been fit. She just happens to like her walks sociable, which is her choice. The last time I saw her she was breaching above a rise with, I think, that German bloke beside her. I took a few mouthfuls of water and a square of chocolate, watching her, until a sly little prod of lust began to light. I thought of waving, but something about the motion of that never fails to leave me sad.

A little bit further.

The path is unmistakably falling now. It denied me a definite peak to celebrate and only eased and tilted sur-reptitiously into descent – but I am willing to forgive it because it is sloping towards home. Unused to the new angle, my calves have started to shake.

I'm fucked.

But I'm still moving. I'm still here.

A little bit further.

Maura's in the bath – I said she could have first go for not completely generous reasons. I plan to slip in round the door soon and soap her and see what we'll think of next, because although she enjoys being clean for such occasions, she sometimes appreciates it if I'm not. She'll whisper against the salt crease of my thighs, then breathe and blink and smile and generally torment, tight where the hair is already moist, already heated, my skin shining, greased for her tongue.

Time enough, time enough.

I barefoot across the woolly lawn of carpet to the window, trying to stop my concentration from unfurling too rapidly. The chill near the glass is pleasant against my skin, as is - unusually - the minor exhibitionist thrill of being naked in front of clear glass. Not that there's a soul around to see me, only a tussle of crows, flopping and ragging through a modestly bloody sunset. I do like this place: an ugly, pretend Scottish castle, squatting in genuine Scottish grounds with rhododendron thickets and a tiny, kidney-dish, outdoor swimming pool, completely empty.

I've told Mary all about it here - my daily phone fix, checking she isn't having too much fun without me.

'I'll . . . we'll be back tomorrow.'

'Mm hm.'

'Don't sound pleased, then.'

'Is your book really finished?'

'Yes, it's done.'

I could hear our neighbour's children bouncing and whining in the background. Mary likes staying with them, but I can't think why. I don't like other people's children, I find, at all. I only like what's mine.

I added, I hoped not too plaintively, 'I missed you.'

'I missed you. It's my birthday soon.' She scrambled her hand across the receiver and I knew that she was laughing.

'Really? I thought that was more than a month away, which is ages. You might have been turned into a coelacanth by then.'

More giggles. 'That's silly.'

'I wonder if anybody will buy you presents.'

'Yes. Somebody will.'

She really is the most definite child I know, unshakeable. Unlike her father.

'Oh, that's good. I won't bother then.'

'*No-oh*. You're the somebody.'

'Ah.' She is a clever one, this Mary Staples, and may already have weaseled out my best gift from where I've hidden it. A walkie-talkie set - a hurtfully expensive one that actually works. I will admit this is something I pined for hopelessly until I hit twelve and began to find women a little more enticing. Nevertheless, I have bought the set because it will please *her* - no retrospective treats for Daddy here.

And now we'll be able to talk to each other from anywhere in the house. No interruptions, no one to intervene.

'You be good until I'm back and then we'll see what happens.'

'I'm always good.'

'Except when you're not good, I know. Get on with you to bed now. Scoot.'

I hung up, feeling - as ever - a minute but unmistakable pang of amputation.

Still, it's get on with *me* to bed now, or places to that effect. Yes, indeed.

The bathroom is huge, all chipping gilt taps and sepia *faux* marble with a bath which I hope and believe could accommodate two.

I creep in. 'Hiya?'

Maura's head is resting on the lip of the tub, her body, stretched and glimmering under the peat-stained water. I've drunk too much of that stuff on the hills today, I notice, my mouth tastes of smoke and iron - like whisky without the kick.

'Maura?'

I wonder if she may be sleeping and if I may be able to wake her gently, perhaps by kissing the curve of each breast where they're proud of the water, coyly buoyant. But then she turns and looks at me, fully awake, and makes me wonder if I shouldn't have worn a dressing gown. I wish I had pockets, then I'd know where to put my hands.

'I'm almost finished.' She's seen that I'm slightly risen, slightly hard, but she doesn't smile, doesn't meet my eye again.

I feel I should say something and manage, 'I'll be . . . outside, then. Obviously,' without sounding too ill at ease. For the first time since we've come away, I can smell our house. I can smell the fug of all the arguments we hiss at each other like baffled lizards, pretending we're making sure that our daughter won't hear.

I start to go, the bathroom seeming bigger, cooler than before.

'No, don't. I want to talk to you.'

I can't currently think if this is a hopeful sign. My stomach winces in any case. 'You want to . . . all right.' I kneel by her head. My already dwindled prick pats the side of the bath and shrivels completely at the chill. 'Is there something wrong?'

'Oh, for God's sake, of course there's something wrong. That's why we're here.'

'But we're here because we want to work it out.'

'No. We're here because you've finished your fucking book and you felt like a break and a bit of a ride.'

'You know that's –'

'I've had enough, Nathan. Enough. Jesus, you couldn't even bear to be near me on the walk. What were you doing? Making notes for something else?'

'I'm a fast walker.'

'Well, now I won't be there to hold you back.'

'Maura, please. You know I'll do –'

'Anything but change. This is it, Nate.'

My knees are aching against the floor, but I can't move. I'm staring at my wife, my wife naked, the everything I know about that, the redness of all of her hair – she can't be leaving, I'm here with her naked. She can't be leaving, she's my wife.

She stands up: suddenly, numbingly streamed and fluted with water, makes a long, arched step out, level with my face.

If I kiss her. If I kiss her, if I kiss her cunt, if I remind her, if I hold on to her, beg. If I tell her that I'll die. That I will die.

She wraps herself up in one of the bathrobes that came with the room - two of them, a robe for each half of a pair.

'Nate?'

I think I'm curled over, I may well be bent right over with my forehead on the wet linoleum.

'Nate, I do love you.'

Something in my head bursts.

She sounds as if she may be crying. 'But where's the point in that?'

I realise that I am crawling, squatting, hugging my shins. 'Maura.' I can't tell if I've said this or only thought it. 'Please. I mean, what about Mary?'

'I can take care of her. I usually do, if you'd ever notice.'

'I'll have to . . .'

My Mary. If I see her, then I see you. If I see you, we can start again.

'I'll have to . . . I can't not . . .'

Mary. How will we tell her. Christ. How can we tell her what we've done.

'We'll have to work out times when I can see her. Maura?'

'No.'

What?

'Or you can -'

'No.'

'Well, then how -'

'You won't see her. You'll go away before her birthday and you won't come back.'

'What?'

270

In my chest. Something must be bleeding in there.

'You'll go away and you won't come near us. After a while we'll move – move away from London. You won't find out where we've gone.'

'Maura, are you fucking crazy?'

'I can't see you, Nathan. I love you. If I see you, you'll get back. I know you. And we have to stop.'

'But Mary –'

'You're not the way you should be with her, she isn't an adult, she isn't a writer, she isn't in one of your plots. Why can't you just leave her alone? I have to make sure she grows up . . . like a little girl. I'm sorry, I should have done this before.'

'This is a fucking joke, right?'

'If I don't do it this way, I won't be able to leave you at all.'

'Then don't!'

'I have to look after myself, Nathan. And her. And I have to be able to breathe.'

I'm standing now, quite close to her – I don't remember how I came to be here. 'I'll take you to court. You can't do this. No one would let you do this.'

Her hands are shaking – one holding the other and both shaking. 'You'll let me, Nathan. Or I'll tell them you've . . . with her. I'll say . . . I'll tell any lie it takes to get us free of you.'

'I would never, you know I would never do anyth–'

'Of course I know. So don't make me say that you have. Let us go, Nathan. Let us go.'

I hit her now. I watch the long swing of my hand, before it compacts in a jarring blur and I hear her breath come – a terrible, hard sigh of breath – and then she is screaming and running and crashing the door and I am saying *sorrysorrysorrysorrysorry*. Back on my knees again.

I wait and rock until there are no more sounds from our room and then I wait more. I understand that she has gone and I do not expect her to return, I am just

271

waiting, I don't know for what.

Please.

In the end, when I walk to the bed, the clock dial is shining out 01:23. I want to ring Mary, ring my neighbours, ring the police and say there has been an emergency. But I don't. It's too late, entirely.

This isn't true. None of this is true. Please.

I go back to the bathroom and lie in the cold of the water that Maura left. It makes me cry.

Then I dress and go out through the quiet hotel. The night is clear, at the edge of a frost, and I'm shivering very deeply, helplessly. I cut over the grass and then trample across a flower bed, crush out the last of the late blooms, I don't know why.

And I come to the palely blue-painted curl of their swimming pool and scramble in. It's warmer down here, peaceful: the floor all soft puddles and scatters of last year's leaves. I work my way past hazy, graded markings from the shallow end to the deep and then I stand. I can feel the ghost of drowning, closed over my head.

S ophie was watching him, Nathan wondered why.
  'What is it, love? Mmm?'

'Are you all right? Have you finished?'

He glanced down at his paper, his story, and then remembered, couldn't help but sit and keep quiet while the memory of it all jolted out in him, broke. Working these things through, forming them for other eyes, it never helped.

And you say you want to write a proper novel – get one last crack at legitimacy. Some fucking hope.

'Uncle Nathan?' She slipped her hand into his and he knew she would find his palm unpleasantly clammy, greased with unhealthy thought. 'Are you . . . ?'

He was disturbing her – no doubt looking almost as desperate as he felt.

Shit.

'I'm only – I was thinking about losing things. That's all. What time is it?'

'Time to go for Lunch.'

'God, already? I'm sorry – I shouldn't have worked while you were here, it's made me go and forget the time. Sorry. Go and have the Lunch, then.'

'You should come.'

'I can't – Mary's going.'

'You used to like her.'

'I still do like her. We're just not speaking, so it's easier for everyone if we go on alternate weeks.'

'Joe says it is *counter-productive*. And he made me look up *Pyrrhic* in the dictionary and said it would help me to understand what you're doing.' She reproduced an adult look of exasperation. 'I don't think it did, but I know that he wanted me to tell you about looking it up.

So I have.' She nudged her head against his arm. 'You shouldn't hurt yourself.'

'Well, I want you to tell him that you're going to go back and look up *inappropriate*.'

'I already know what that means.'

'I know.' He tried to grin, but a tremor started in his lips and he had to cover them with his hand.

'Is it Mary you lost? Because she isn't – she does still talk about you. If you wanted to know what she says . . .'

Oh, Christ, just go, just go away, you don't want to see the way I'll be now. Just go.

'Yes. No. I mean, I've lost lots of things. Her, too. But lots of things.'

***Hold it together**. Say something, say any fucking thing to get through the fucking time until she goes. Don't go to pieces on her – talk.*

And so Nathan talked, talked until the veins stiffened near his temples, talked until he almost believed himself. 'I've lost, I've lost – no, **we've** lost the way it should be. You know the Aztecs thought paper was sacred? *Amatl* – it was an offering for the gods. And in ancient Egypt, the word was the deed, it was powerful in itself. The naming of life, it's in the Bible, it was man's first duty. All this was ours and we lost it. The life we lived in ourselves, the power of that, the way we made it speak, it was taken away.'

He could tell she wasn't understanding this, wasn't even sure that he was himself.

'Nothing *means* anything any more – the less we know the better, the less we can shape our future, remember our past, the less we can be free, the more everyone seems to like it. We get fed tiny, tiny pieces of monstrous, monstrous facts and fantasies to fill the space between them. But *real* fantasy, *real* fiction – the kind with power, the kind that we're born with, that's our right – we're not supposed to want that any more – we have to be helped with our minds, we have to be prevented from letting them go too far. You know, I have a friend, Jack, and I used to think he was wrong about life, but he was right – the only way to do it now is drunk, stoned, as far away from feeling as you can get. Be easy, be malleable, be interested in your substances and nothing else – let anyone do anything and don't give a . . .' He caught her eye before he swore. 'Don't care about

274

anything as long as you get your stuff. That's the way. The only way.'

Sophie hugged his arm and he knew his first choke of pain was rising and that he should have kept his fucking mouth shut.

'I could not go to Lunch, if you wanted. We could go for a nice walk.' She frowned at him, worried.

'Not at all. You have to eat, or you'll grow up as silly as me.' He swallowed, made a tentative, floundering breath. 'Off you trot. Go to Mary's house and she'll take you – you know the arrangement.'

'I'll tell Pa to come and see you.'

'Don't worry him, it's OK.' He nudged at her, trying to reassure.

'No. I will tell him and he will come.' She considered him, very serious, thinking her words through. 'He is responsible for you. That's what he says. You are his responsibility.'

Nathan only nodded, accepted her kiss at his cheek, waved and fussed her away, his ribs clenched.

And when she had closed his door, it all came bad, all fell away – his life, pissing blood before his eyes. The hurt of it beat through him, noiseless and tight: not a release, only another demonstration of his powerlessness.

God, what the fuck do you want from me?

God, enough. Just enough, enough.

I miss her.

*We haven't spoken for a fucking year now. A year. I wasn't at her twenty-first birthday, I won't ever get that again. **We** won't.*

A year. One whole blank, fucking year. It's enough.

Why let me have her near and then take her away? Why only bring her here to hurt us?

We've never done anyone any harm. She's never done anyone any harm. This is enough.

Please, God, let it be enough.

1994

'Nathan. Nathan!'
    Nathan had hoped that, as his swimming got better, his sleeping would, too. The lunging out into gluey sweeps and dips was the same in both cases. There were similar treacherous depths.

'Nathan. Please!'

And, every night, syringing in under his better judgement, came his will: the witless drive that made him strike out through every dream to dive for traces of Maura, Mary: Mary, Maura. Sometimes –

'Nathan!'

Sometimes he'd break his head above unconsciousness, the last fish gasp of his mind still glistening with Mary's voice.

'Jesus, Nathan. Come *on*.'

He sat up, his mind following a moment later, the room wheeling as he squinted about.

Thank you again, God – You never can resist the chance to kick me while I'm down and out.

Waking into disappointment, the stealing away of dreams, he was used to that. But then he blinked and swallowed, shook his head and stared and stared at the genuine, real-life hand tugging at his shoulder. It really was Mary: Mary's hand dunting him awake, her breath near his temple, flurrying, and naturally, absolutely, of course, her voice, all mashed up with *Abbey Road* – he'd kept the CD playing on repeat next door to keep him company, like an audible nightlight.

'Hmffu?'

'Nathan, I need you. You have to come now.'

She was standing by his wide-awake bed, plainly, but softly illuminated by the dawn glow that was creeping along his windows, January pale. His skull thrummed with blurry alarm.

'Are you all right?' He didn't know whether to pull up the covers further and hide himself, or to simply sit there, obviously rumpled.

'Yes, yes. But Ruth isn't, come on.'

'Well, that's,' if he'd thought this was going to happen, he'd have changed the sheets, 'that's . . .' changed his pyjamas, taken off his hideous cold-weather-in-bed sweater, 'yes, I'll come.' Jesus, he must just seem to be nothing more than one great lump of shoddy, male neglect. He bleared up at her, 'If you could . . . perhaps step into the other room.'

And out of this one – away from the lonely man's bed.

'Oh. OK.' But she didn't move, only looked at him, enquiring.

'Ah. Ah, yes.' And he realised that he'd reached out, caught her arm and, no doubt, also treated her to an inadvertent waft of bedding-flavoured air. 'Uhm, nice to see you. It's . . . it's –' The less reliable portion of his brain began to shudder but he thumped it into shape. 'It's been a while.'

'Yes.'

He tried to read her expression and failed.

'Yes, it has,' and she left him.

He grazed and stumbled his way through dressing.

She said, 'Yes'

through his living room, Eckless following . . .

'Yes,' that it was nice to see me . . .

through his kitchen, Eckless following.

Or 'Yes,' that it's been a while, because it has been a while, it's been a fuck of a long while, but that's OK, it's OK, she's talking to me, she's back now – she's outside, she's waiting for me, I hope she's waiting for me.

and then, with his dog beside him, he battered outside to meet her, stepping and grinning straight into a still, hard cold that stripped him down to the skin again in seconds, made his eyes sting – lack of sleep, there was almost nothing like it for making you raw.

As soon as they were all together, his daughter, his Mary, his own and only daughter Mary, simply beckoned and ran ahead, Eckless beside her now, barking just a little. So Nathan ran too, catching up: heart clanking, breath ducking and plunging against gusts of light-headedness.

'What's the . . . What's wrong? Something's happened to Ruth, did you say?' His pulse was slamming his blood far beyond what he felt were its healthy limits. Lack of sleep and lack of caffeine, that was the problem. If he'd drunk even one cup of coffee before they set off, he would have been sprinting like a deer. Or, more likely, just wallowing along beside her, exactly the way he was now, feet jolting and sliding stupidly, as the shock of her, the lovely shock of her, wrecked his co-ordination wonderfully. He tried another wheezy question, 'What's happened?'

'I said – it's Ruth.' She was only a little out of breath – quite fit, his girl. 'Louis found her clothes in a pile at his door this morning. He said that she's tried swimming across to the Head. He came over to my place and now he's on the way back there to keep a lookout.'

'To look . . .? Oh, OK.' He was coming to slowly as he pounded along, 'And did he . . .' gradually feeling almost unpleasantly aware, 'did he suggest that you came to, to me? Louis?'

'We both thought that I should.' She upped the pace, sighting Louis's form moving with surprising speed up ahead.

'Uh hu, uh hu, makes sense.' On his left side, his hungry side, he could feel her presence, her sudden return, scalding into him, neat, like antiseptic on a wound.

'We both thought it. I just said it first.'

Nathan could have sworn that she almost smiled as she spoke.

They caught Louis up and hurried three abreast over the tussocky grass. As they went, Louis explained the situation, gleaming with excitement, his arms milling and flapping about, until he might almost have been a rather portly boy, running and scaring up crows. 'I saw, yes, indeed. Saw her quite clearly. In the rocks at the foot of the head. Just above the high tide line. She saw me and waved. *Waved*, for goodness' sake.'

Nathan considered, once again, the ways in which Louis would always be one of the youngest people he would ever know. 'Is she waving now?'

'*Precisely* now? Well, I couldn't be certain, of course. She had fallen still when I left the cliff.' He turned to Mary. 'My dear, would you mind? I left some blankets in my house. If you rushed ahead and had them ready . . .?'

Mary glanced at Nathan and then nodded, pushed on and took Eckless with her.

'Well, well . . .' Louis breathed, happy. 'Together again. Mm, Nathan?'

281

'Precisely *now*? No. You've just sent her off.'

Louis gave a glancing flap at Nathan's arm. 'But together again, all the same.' He beamed – Louis was like that, happy with other people's happiness. Nathan, on the other hand, always found it vaguely threatening: as if the good fortune of strangers would leave even less for him.

'Yes, all right. Together.' He thumped on, the Head now clearly visible, a huge thumbnail of shadow, rising from the sea. 'This business with Ruth – was she trying for it . . . taking another step, or just . . .'

'I wish I knew, Nathan. The risks are very high.' He snatched in a breath. 'Beyond the currents and the tide . . . is the danger from exposure. Which is why we're running to –'

'Save her.'

'Yes, to save her.'

'Even though we wouldn't have stopped her swimming out . . .'

'Oh, I don't know about that, Nathan.' He waved to Mary, who was standing in his doorway, arms round a bundle of blankets. 'More and more, I'm of the opinion that death comes soon enough.'

'Told Joe that?'

'Of course.'

'Of course.' Louis, Nathan knew, would never think to lie, would never even try to tuck just a touch of the truth aside for private purposes. 'Tell me something.'

'Yes?'

'Do you have a toasting fork? I bet you have a toasting fork, don't you?'

'A toasting fork?' Louis studied him briefly. 'Well, yes, I do.'

'And you actually use it? Muffins in front of the fire and all that?'

'Yes, Nathan – and all that.'

'They really don't make them like you any more, Louis. Maybe they never did. You're like . . . a different species.'

Louis peered at him, benevolent. 'No, I simply try to live a comfortable life. Certain ways of behaving make for comfort, certain others do not. It's only common sense.'

'A different species.' Nathan would have said *different fucking species*, but swearing at Louis, even in fun, was always remarkably hard.

Louis laughed, gulped for air and laughed again. 'Nathan, Nathan, Nathan. First it was the children, now it's you.'

'What do you mean?'

'You keep the mind busy. Keep me young.' Louis grinned at him without a trace of irony. Nathan could only shake his head.

The two men juddered to a halt in front of Mary while Eckless bounced around them, delighted by his unexpected outing and – perhaps – by the chance to be with Mary and Nathan, both at once.

Louis bent forward with his hands on his knees. 'Dear me, I can't do this too often – not built for rushing about. You go on now, Nathan, and I will feed your dog – I'm sure he's had no breakfast. Then Joe should be alerted.'

'Yes. Good. Yes.' Nathan kneaded one of Louis's shoulders in a way that he hoped suggested affection and then faced Mary, much of him anxious to hug her, rub her arm, shake her hand, make contact. But, of course, he only angled his head very slightly, looked at the cliff edge and told her, 'Come on.' A slim breeze snuffled round them as they walked.

And there it was.

Shit.

The evil little ladder pinned and bolted to the lip of cliff and then darting straight over it.

I'll be sick.

Straight over and down to the shifting, speckled black of the sea. Ruth must have used the same ladder last night, climbed the same way in the dark.

She's got more bottle than I have. Or more despair.

The rungs, the uprights and their restraining fixtures all seemed corroded beyond any reasonable doubt and down below, apparently several miles away, there bobbed the minute and elderly boat that Louis kept moored to the ladder's final sea-gnawed foot for other, less pressing, offshore jaunts.

How the fuck he gets down here, I'll never know – just drops and bounces, probably, giggling all the way.

Nathan knelt and turned his back on the mercifully calm, but still horribly distant, sea that breathed and waited below him.

'OK.' On his knees, he raised his face to Mary and lifted up his

283

hands, hoping that nothing about him would seem to shake. 'Give me the blankets now and I'll go down.'

'No. I'll bring them. I've tied them up properly, it'll be easy.'

He fought to sound reasonable: respectful, but firm. 'Look, I've been down here before, it's tricky and the blankets will be heavy. I may seem indecently old and feeble, but I am still stronger than you. Come on now.'

She looked down at him, completely and quite naturally concerned. Her attention clamped his breath and he focused on not feeling dizzy all over again.

'Are you sure you'll be all right?'

'I'll manage, it's not a problem.' He almost believed himself. 'No bother at all.'

He went down on all fours and then backed unbravely towards the ladder's start, fear oiling out from his kidneys, vertigo painting the backs of his legs, his armpits, feet.

*You will do this, because you are a **father** and a good father can do anything, anything at all.* ***Any fucking thing.*** *ALL RIGHT?*

He moved himself over the edge and on to the ladder, got his one hand firm on an early rung and then eased his load of blankets down. The weight of them yanked at his shoulder joint and whipped through him in a way that made his whole surface slither with horrors. But he steadied himself, thought of Mary, began his descent.

Should be easy, really easy — after all, you've never had any problem sinking, only with getting back up again.

His right hand began to twitch against the blistering cold of the rungs, the emptier cold of the air, and his left tried to manage the blankets. His mind showed him good and bad visions of falling. No: bad and worse visions of falling. But he still kept his grip and kept his feet and kept on going, working beyond his palsied confidence, his watery bone.

An unexpected ring of motion clattered his arms. 'Now what the fu– ?' Mary was following him down. 'No. You stay up there.' This was not in the plan, this was the kind of bone-marrow terror with which he could not deal: the fear of the fall of his daughter, far worse than any drop that he might take. 'Get back up – go on. It's not safe.' He was yelping, he could hear it.

'You'll need me. To help.'

'It's not safe.'

'I'm not going back.'

Jesus, woman, don't make me proud of you **now**. *Not* **this** *way . . .*

But, of course, she did, while his nerves pitched and yawed with the need to keep her safe. He fixed his eyes on the wet rock ahead of him and went on, rung after rung: the catching and loosing, the sickening moment of balance and then the catch again. Below him the water clopped and hissed and the deep, sea cold began to rise and seize his legs. The ladder shuddered as he moved and his daughter moved and both of them edged their way down.

Jesusfu– wha– ?

An ugly tap came at his heels.

Bastard, bastard, bastard.

Calm. Be calm. Look round. Look down. It can't be anything bad.

The tap came again and a little creak with it this time.

It was the boat, already nudging him. He must have come down faster than he'd thought. Not that he wouldn't have shifted even faster if he could.

Not that I wouldn't have clamped the old ankles to the outside of the uprights and then slid down the whole fucking ladder like a fireman if I'd thought it would impress. (And not kill me.)

Not that I want her here to watch me. But I'll not argue, not now – it's bad when we argue and I can't bear it being bad.

'Mary? Stay where you are for a bit, love, I've come to the boat. And don't look.'

'I'm not scared of heights.'

'Well, don't look anyway. I'll just get in and then I'll give you the word. And be careful. Because I can't be careful for you.'

'I don't need you to.'

'Yes, well, OK. OK.'

He tried to position himself to board the wobbling boat.

Have I offended her, did she sound offended, is this going – fuck.

He put his foot neatly through the aged tarpaulin that covered what was, he had to admit, a glorified sodding punt and not in any way a convincingly sea-going craft.

But we'll give it a try, in any case.

Mary stepped aboard with such quick and easy neatness that he had no time to feel sickened on her behalf.

Out on the water, the morning was icy still. Nathan hauled the outboard to life and then pressed them out over a deadened sea. They slid forward insubstantially across a dense, silvered surface, leaves of black turning across it in long, patient rolls: sinews of motion and light. Locked above them was a layered sky, nothing but blades of colour, horizon upon horizon, slicing away. Try as he might, Nathan couldn't find this calming. The tranquillity seemed watchful, impatient: the nervous futter of their engine and the furrow of their wake struck him as incautious intrusions above a swell of intelligent emptiness.

And alongside his unease, there oozed something equally familiar – the knowledge that he was being ludicrous. Hand on the tiller, reading the tug of nasty currents, eyes intent over the prow, his daughter looking on, perhaps admiring . . .

My Errol Flynn phase. Ha, ha, ha. And all too late in life. Ha, ha fucking ha.

Ruth was huddled on the thin gravel beach, a few feet between the rock face and the sea. She was wrapped in the kind of foil insulation sheet beloved of marathon runners and outdoor types.

Must have folded it inside her swimsuit – I presume she is wearing a swimsuit? Please, God.

Good thinking on her part – it would keep off hypothermia for a while – make it a more even bet that someone would find her alive. Body weight would be in her favour, of course: tubby wee seal that she is.

Ach, Nathan – just hush and leave the poor woman alone. She's harmless.

And I have a daughter and she does not.

Ruth watched them beach the boat with the intoxicated smile of a person still very pleasantly surprised by her own continuance.

Mary sprang impressively ashore while Nathan sucked his teeth, trying to fix on the proper remark.

What would be appropriate? **Well done? How was it for you? What were you thinking of – you could have been killed? Although, of course that was, quite precisely, what you were thinking of. And give me a clue, Ruth, were you going for enlightenment, another step forward to the Grail, or were you just paddling off to eternity? Suicide or sanctified risk? Hm? Do tell.**

Not that she will – we never do. We all keep our Russian roulette wheels muffled here.

Ruth stood, revealing herself to be unsteady but apparently sound and dressed in a businesslike one-piece costume. University colours? College? Surely not school? Nathan saw – and at once regretted seeing – the prickle of inch-long hair at her inner thighs, the unmistakable harsh regrowth after bikini-line shaving. And there was the scar of shark teeth on her arm, the other on her thigh, from earlier salt-water jaunts. She'd got off lightly this time, apparently.

As Mary swaddled her with blankets, he wondered how Ruth had thought she would be found, how she'd wanted her body to look, why she'd decided that this was the way she would offer herself to death.

Making her mind up and then rushing here before sunrise, stroking out across the dark water for the fuck of her life, the deepest one we ever get, the one that leaves us slack-jawed, comprehensively gaping, without breath.

The women swayed together over the stones towards him, apparently overwhelmed by one huge woollen toga. Ruth lifted her head, luminously pale and cowled in grey. 'Nathan. It's all fine. Isn't it? There's nothing wrong.'

Mary squeezed at Ruth's bundled shoulder, parcelled her up more tightly. 'No, nothing at all. You're fine. We'll get you back and you'll be fine.'

'No.' Ruth kept to Nathan's eyes, 'It's all right. Everything is all right,' and Nathan swallowed, understanding jigging at even his cynic's pulse.

*She doesn't mean **she's** all right – she means **everything** is all right. She means the universe has knelt down and kissed her on the soul and told her that **every fucking thing** is guaranteed to be completely fucking all right. And she believes it – she's in the glory. For now.*

Ruth stumbled aboard and swayed forward into his arms as he reached to greet her. She felt too soft for going out in the sea alone, too much alive. She shouldn't try this kind of thing again. 'Hey, Ruthie. Good morning.' He patted her somewhere near her elbow, kissed above one of her eyes.

'Morning, Nate. I'm glad it was you – that came.'

'Mm hm.'

'It's all right, you know.'

'Yes, OK, love. I know.'

He disengaged himself then stepped into the bite of the water, delighted by this minor recklessness with his shoes and socks. He dragged the craft afloat again while Mary helped him with a shove at the stern. She climbed in and sat with an admirable maintenance of balance, and he even made a fairly agile job of boarding himself. They could all go home now.

'Mary? Sit close in the blankets with her, will you? Body heat. Don't want anything nasty setting in.' He grinned while she did as he asked, exactly as he asked, because it was a sensible request and correct and possibly might also show that, when the emergency chips were down, he was a person upon whom one could rely. That's what he hoped. 'And no going to sleep, Ruth.'

'I won't sleep for a week.' She beamed, post-coitally.

'Just stay awake for the journey – that's all we'll need.'

The motor hacked to life and he began steering round to the west, heading for the jetty. Mary kicked at his foot as he settled to his task.

'Mm?'

'You said it was nice to see me.'

Anxiety lapped between his shoulder blades. 'Yes? Um. Did I?'

'You did.'

He couldn't think where this was going, almost didn't want to know.

'You don't like *nice*. You think it's a bad word.'

'There are no bad words.' He risked a look at her – got no clues. 'And I'm never all that eloquent when I'm semi-unconscious.' But there was a growing softness about her mouth, he could see that. 'And it *was* nice. It was –' A Calvinist tickle in his throat prevented him from completing a full confession of pleasure without a readjustment, a little break of tone. 'It was – I'm sorry – very nice.'

'You're sorry it was nice?'

'No, I'm not sorry . . .'

She was smirking. Cheeky, fucking, lovely wee woman: she was cuddling Ruth and also laughing at him. In a *nice* way, laughing.

'No, I'm *not* sorry. I'm not sorry at all.'

And the motor ran and the tide drew and together they were rocked in the sea's lap and Nathan faced Mary and Mary faced him back, quite quickly serious, but liking him, he was almost certain, quite probably liking him.

★

And, in the days that followed, the island maintained the shine it had taken when Ruth was trundled up the jetty and into the surrogate grip of her Foal Island family. Joe, above all, bristled with contentment: another trial volunteered for and passed, one of his flock ascending a whisper further towards their state of grace, intact.

Nathan tried but couldn't find all this ambient glee offensive – he currently had too much of his own to care. By the time the whole crew of them made it to the first full-complement Lunch in more than a year, Nathan considered himself to be dangerously happy. Every time he opened his mouth, he expected an adolescent squeal to emerge like the sound of bad bicycle brakes, or of a man inclined to speak and act unwisely when under the influence of delight. It had been so long since he'd really felt this way, he suspected his condition might actually be something far less pleasant – perhaps the onset of some disease.

'Nate, don't look so worried.'

Joe, pink-handed and generally moist, passed him another plate to dry. It was their turn for the washing-up.

'I'm not worried.' Nathan was enjoying the dewy fug of the kitchen and the pleasant strain of too much food, eaten slightly too quickly. If he stayed this jolly much longer, he'd get fat.

'Ah.'

'What do you mean *Ah*?'

'You're the only person I know who would find not worrying, worrying.'

Nathan fought not to produce the rictus with which he always seemed to receive this kind of manly wordplay. He hated male bonding, he detested the merry ribbing of hearty chums, in fact most of the elements of friendship – now he thought of it – made him vaguely sick. Or maybe it was just Joe's particular way of being pally that filled him with the need to gag. The man was like a walking Public Safety Announcement – too much common sense and trustworthy, kindly charm.

Yes, that's it – I look at Joe and I want to use power tools badly, take parcels abroad for strangers, smoke cigars in petrol stations and swallow chewing gum. I want to run down steps with my hands in my pockets and stare at the sun.

'Nathan. You're not paying attention. And you're going to dry the pattern clear off that plate.'

Nathan attempted a leer. 'You know me – keen on vigorous rubbing. Made it my life's work.' But it was no use. There was no shocking or distracting Mr Christopher – all you could hope for was his *immensely patient but slightly disappointed that you've let yourself down again* look.

'Do stop rambling, Nate. I want you to consider that, now we are all together again . . .' He gave a murmur of a grin and Nathan couldn't help but grin a wee bit back. 'Now that you and Mary are – approximately – as you should be and with Ruth having . . . taken another step forward, as we might say . . . I think the time is right for Mary to attend our Meetings. She ought to get to know us properly.'

Nathan played for time by putting down his plate and starting to wring the tea towel's neck. 'I . . . You wouldn't tell her *everything* . . . ? You wouldn't . . . not all the . . . death stuff, yet. Or, even – I don't, don't think she need *ever* know *that*.'

'Nathan, she can't be surrounded by people who, now and again, do ostensibly suicidal things without eventually knowing why. Or at least wanting to.' He set both hands on Nathan's shoulders, allowing suds to ooze quietly through his shirt. 'But it's all right – I only intend she should know the important things. I only want her to be really one of us.'

'And it'll make the numbers up to seven.' Nathan partly teasing and partly hoping to imply *you may well be the boss with all of this numerology, mystical pathway shite, but she is **my** daughter*.

'Well, you know, I am fond of sevens. There are meant to be seven heavens, if you believe a certain brand of mystical thought.' Joe's look flared a moment, quietened again. 'Nathan, come on, what do you think? I say we should tell her and I think we should do it today.'

Mary wasn't sure if she ought to be angry or not.

*Not a business meeting. That's what they've been having – Not Business Meetings. Ever since I came here, they've been having **Not** Business Meetings. Or, **um, well, Not Quite Business Meetings and you'll see what we mean today**.*

*Which is to say that I'll see what they've actually been doing all this time while **telling** me that they've been doing something else – now that they feel like telling me. Now that I can be trusted. Or they can be bothered.*

I mean, if it's not my place to know, then all right . . . not all right, really, but better than being lied to. I mean, lied to, even by **Nathan**. *I mean, he's shifty, but he doesn't lie . . . or, at least, very clearly he does, but I don't notice.*

And now he's being – especially now – he's being . . . oh, I don't know, he's being . . .

Nathan was being incomprehensible. He'd spent more than a year looking past her and seeming incredibly pissed off and he'd made it just impossible to talk to him, sort things out, but now he was – she still couldn't exactly put her finger on it – but he was different. Extremely different.

Watching me the way he always has, that almost creepy way, but he's now making sure I'll notice. And, all the time, seeming about to speak, but then saying hardly anything. And why did he lie, or not lie, exactly, but never mention this – the Not Business Meetings? Not a word – nothing but **Oh, it's just that we all tend to meet up after the Lunch, organise things to keep the Island running, administration – you know. You're well out of it***. Yes, and I* **was** *well out of it, wasn't I? Nathan kept me out.*

He wants me in now, though. He wants me in.

Which let her realise what his greatest alteration was since they'd started speaking – the one that had really thrown her off.

He **wants** *me there with him. He isn't pretending, or making a joke of it, he doesn't mean to say something else. He's admitted that he wants something – something from* **me**.

This was probably the only reason why she decided she would do what he asked, go along to their Not Business Meeting and not make a fuss.

He's a daft, big bugger. But, fair play, there's no harm in him. And if he **wants** *me to be there, then I suppose I might as well.*

At which point, Nathan gave her a quizzical nod, eyes slightly preoccupied, mildly demanding, wanting to see her decision: for or against. She nodded back *yes* and he glanced away with an odd, shadowed snap of emotion, turning to her again with an almost fragile smile, something altogether tentative about him.

Still, tentative or not, he'd got his way. Mary smiled herself now, firmly, thinking that this was how the private, careful people usually got their way. Because whenever they really did creep out and declare what they cared about, their vulnerability was difficult to resist.

'You'll, uh, join us today, then, hm?'

When he was nervous, she could hear that he was Scottish: he didn't have much of an accent at other times. He sounded very Caledonian this afternoon.

'Yes, I'll join you – whatever that means. No one seems willing to say.'

'Aye, well, sorry about the reticence – we've never had a Fellowship . . . scholarship . . . you know – a person like you before, so we weren't sure of what to do, initially. We are now, though.' His face calmed, began showing something like sadness, or tenderness. 'Come here.' They paused. 'Up the stairs. Then left. It looks like a cupboard door – but it's not, it leads to a room.'

A room which was surprising. Whatever she'd expected, it wasn't this: a banal little space with a low, uneven ceiling, one dormer window, a fireplace modestly supplied with fire, seven bentwood chairs: five of them occupied, two waiting. A roughly cubic space, packed in between stripped floorboards and plastered walls that were painted a fawnish pink. There was nothing else.

The fire creaked gently, Nathan sat and then, like the rest of the Fellowship, leaned around to face her. Louis, Ruth, Lynda, Richard, Nathan, Joe: everyone seemed anxious to see her claim the unoccupied seat. And there was something else: a pressure, a touch in the air that watched and waited, too. It was all more than enough to make anyone pause.

'Mary. We're so glad you felt like coming.' Joe winked at her like a large and possibly peckish cat, but his tone was apologetic. 'I know, I know, we could have asked you before . . . Still, you're here now – that's the thing. And we –' He tilted his head, his voice unmistakably playful, but under the words a purr of determination, fixed intent. 'Do sit down.'

Mary thought she might like to, but not yet, not until she knew what it meant. She had the feeling that making any move here would be like signing a very blank cheque.

Louis, perhaps to ease matters, suggested, 'You have to remember, Joe, that Mary has received a proper education – she knows about these things. The one chair in the strange room, invitingly empty – it could be the Siege Perilous – sit in it when you're, shall we say, *unqualified* and death is your reward.'

292

'Oh, for fuck's sake!' Nathan scrubbed at the flesh between his eyebrows: his other hand, a tense fist on his knee. 'Less of the hocus pocus.' He flushed, mumbled. 'She deserves better.' Mary caught herself wishing the empty place was next to him.

Well, why not? At least I'm used to him. And he seems my safest bet. Or something like that.

Joe elbowed Nathan softly. 'Would you like to explain?'

'No, you explain – it's your thing. I only deal with the typing and related affairs. This stuff is none of my business. Just do get started.'

Mary continued to stand.

My safest bet, I'd guess.

And I will have to guess, if nobody's going to tell me what the fuck is going on.

'Just to let you know . . .' Joe met her eyes, calmly daring her to wonder if he really did always know what she was thinking. 'Just to let you know what's going on. Several years ago, when some of us were starting the Fellowship, we decided that we should spend time making communal business decisions.' He stopped and grinned. 'And at this point in my narrative, I can say, without having to look, that Nathan will have rolled his eyes, but really everyone in the group *does* agree with the choices we make, or we simply don't make them. In Nathan's case, he'll disagree with disagreeing, which amounts to much the same, but is easier for him.'

Mary was trying to keep her patience. 'But you said this was *not* a Business Meeting.'

'Mm hm. There is an additional element, yes.' He studied her. 'This is where we practise . . . being open-minded. So that, as writers, we can be ready to –' He paused and looked to his side. 'Nathan, *you* do this. Please. I think, under the circumstances, that you should.'

Nathan coloured and scratched his ear. 'Oh.' Folding one arm behind his head, he began to palp at his shoulder and neck. He kept talking, but addressed himself primarily to the floor. 'Well, this is different for everyone and I'm really not the best one to describe it, but we all come here, I suppose, to shut up. We stop the words. We do pretty much clear our minds, and some of us may even wish to wedge them open. And then we wait – as if there isn't enough of that in my life.' He stopped, flustered, and then slowly lifted his head, something in his eyes unclasping, deepening. 'We're all here to do what writers do, that's what this island is for, that's what we are for. And this is where we get ready, properly ready, to work. If that means not moving, not speaking and trying to not think in words, even in syllables, even in sounds, then that's what we do. Sometimes, I will admit, it can feel good, when we're in here all together: not acting, not pretending, not having opinions, not being in our own fucking way – just getting ready to be as we are at heart, feeling the shape of that.

'Although sometimes, I have to say, I just sit back and think about shagging. It's non-verbal, very suitable – shagging and nothing but. Then again, maybe that's the way I am at heart.' He glanced at Joe. 'Anyway, I close my eyes and let the action slam and slap away – nothing I can do about it. Of course, there never *was* anything I could do about *that*.' He winced, impatient with himself, and went on.

'Or sometimes I'll imagine murders: lengthy, elaborate, nasty, messy, unrepentant executions. And, now that I come to mention it, in my fantasies I'm hardly ever the one having sex, but I am without exception the one who kills. Funny how the thinking runs. At heart.

'And I could do as much at home if I wanted – in fact, I have done and will do again, but when I'm here . . . When I'm here, there are occasions . . .' He sighed out an unamused laugh. 'There are occasions when I end up feeling better, happier, like a good man. I'll sit, finally empty-headed, in this company and then I'll suddenly, without my doing anything . . . It's hard to explain – it's a kind of energy that comes, an anticipation, a not unpleasant need. The only not unpleasant need I have.'

Mary wished he would stop because she now felt she was intruding and also wished he would go on because she had never known him be like this before. Quietly, she took her seat.

'And Joe tells me that it all should make me peaceful, but in fact it does nothing of the sort. It makes me awkward, difficult. Because it makes me believe absolutely that what I do – that my state, my way of being and my power to describe them are all *mine*. This in my head, this is my own. This particular quiet is my own. This particular noise is my own. This choice of words, this meaning, is my own. Anyone can steal words, forget them, remould them, deny them, but their shadow and the way to make them is still here, a part of me.'

Nathan wiped his mouth, considering. Mary thought that he might be calming himself, but when he began again he sounded, if anything, more overwrought.

'Joe finds it extremely amusing that this makes me believe in truth, this memory I have for words. But I do. I do believe in a universal right to truth. And, when I'm out in the world, I know that I am a *passenger*, not a *customer*; a *patient*, not a *client*; a *man*, not a *consumer*. And I don't want to be *informed*, I want to be *educated*, and I don't want to be *enabled*, I want to be *helped*, and I don't want something *new*, I want something *better*, and I don't want to be *offered choices*, I want to be *free*. I have spent a great deal of my life learning to love what words *mean*. Especially the bad ones, the ones that need careful watching. Assassination, removal, termination, problem-solving, taking out, euthanasia, cleansing, special handling, natural wastage, merciful release, killing, murder – I do understand that these are all very much the same thing. Offer me a euphemism, a circumlocution, a truth economy, a fucking lie, and I will be moved to pulp your brain, to lop off your hands, to draw out your fucking tongue with pincers and roast it before your eyes – because you are not using what you've been given properly.' He glowered at his own hands. 'So. That's the way I am, at heart. Joe is a man who has spiritual aims, mine are a matter of principle, or just of anger. I like to recall, now and then, that language belongs to me, to the individual, to each and every individual – that anyone who wants to *own* it is trying to own *me*.'

He pressed his fingertips against his forehead, blinked hard, and then quickly, gently looked at Mary. For a moment he seemed to search her face and then withdrew, stared down at the floorboards again. She realised, too late to smile at him, that he'd been checking for her approval.

When he started to speak again he was almost whispering, 'Sometimes, at the heart of me, there won't fall a word, there will be nothing but the wait. But then it comes, it speaks, it's there for me and I am there for it. We give ourselves to each other, we each possess the other, we agree. And after that, nothing can stop us. Not even me.'

He sighed, sat back, at rest, and met Mary's eyes again in a slow flinch of pre-emptive shame. And now she could smile for him and did and, at once, he smiled back, in some way younger, more tired and more alive. He muttered, perhaps swallowing down on unaccustomed pride, 'The job can actually seem worth doing if I think of it this way. In writing I am part of something – I get it and give it away. I can speak myself to life, speak my future and what I want. I generally don't get it, but if I couldn't even say . . .' He ginned at her again. 'I disagree with hope, I think it's a cruel thing and predicting the fulfilment of my needs, even simply stating them, does give me hope. But hope is generally better than emptiness.'

Nathan cleared his throat and shut his eyes, folded his arms very tightly around his chest. His breathing seemed louder than usual and, with his body so forgetful of itself, Mary noticed that he'd let his right shoulder drop. This puzzled her and then she thought it through: without a constant effort on his part, the lack of his lung would make his torso sag. She looked away, ashamed for having pried.

Then, true to Nathan's word, peace lapped in and took the room.

Mary shifted in her seat and tried to let the quiet take her, too.

This is . . .

This is . . .

Sssh. You're meant to be quiet.

But poor Nathan. To be the way he is. He ought to be able to be happy. That shouldn't be too hard. Ssssh.

A breeze sang in the chimney. Unwieldy seconds passed while her mind whirred out into unfamiliar territory, confronted by too much space.

Shagging – he said he thought of that. Naturally, anyone would think of . . . But I won't . . . not his name.

Jonathan.

Nothing apart from his name.

God, this is hard.

She tried to think of her breath, of its to and fro and nothing more, but it couldn't hold her attention for long. She gave up, let her voice back in again.

The letters.

There are four now. Four. He doesn't write to me for fifteen years and then I get four letters – one every six months – one about every six months. What does that mean? That he's interested, but not too much?

*And I don't know who they're from. Even if they **are** from my father, I don't know him. He's a stranger.*

*And if they're **not** from him. Then my father's dead. The way I thought he was. But when I thought it before, it didn't hurt me.*

That thought did send her quiet for a space.

Four letters with nothing definite to say, nothing of him. He only ever writes about me. He tells me he remembered it was my birthday and to have a good day. He tells me I liked reading, I liked beaches, I liked bread. He tells me that I was a person I can't remember.

And I can't picture him – when I try he just gets mixed up with other people. People I want to be like him. People I want him to have been like.

I wouldn't know him now.

I wouldn't even know my own father – that's what he's done to me.

He tells me he loves me.

Considering this made it hard to swallow.

But he never says he wants to see me.

A knock of pain climbed in her, nothing to stop it ricocheting right around her skull. The benefits of clearing the mind.

I'm not going to cry.

A thin recollection billowed forward, curled behind her eyes: being small and held and lifted, swung *up*. She'd loved to be swooped *up*. And here was almost the touch of hands: an exact, concerned pressure, a tender force to keep her safely high and then move her into the ghost of a scent, a firm temperature, something maybe fatherly and so long ago she had thought that it couldn't be wanted, missed.

She'd never had a photograph of him and couldn't imagine his face, but the shape of him being near to her and looking after her shape, that hadn't ever gone from under her skin.

I'm not going to cry. This is ridiculous. I have no reason to cry about him now.

She eased a look at her watch. Only five minutes gone.

I don't think I want to keep doing this. I don't think I can.

Nathan's chair complained as he recrossed his ankles and Mary found herself watching him. He seemed to feel her attention, met her eyes and offered an uncertain frown, followed by a still, clear look that she couldn't hold, or entirely understand.

297

All right, you want me to stay here. I know. You want me to sit it out.

She folded her arms, liking the grip on her ribs, the security of that.

I'm not going to cry.

Morgan's aftershave came to her in one electric breath, loss reaching out to loss all around her, but she steadied herself.

I'll stay. If that's what Nathan wants, what they all want, then I'll try.

She tried to lean into the rhythms of her unease, the peaks of pressure and the gradients of release. Now and then an unexpected current took her, but she fought it, governed her breathing, closed her eyes. She pictured herself drifting out in a disinterested sea, nudged and tugged by mobile salt.

Head for home, head for home. It'll be all right.

This was the life. Nathan was actually quite hungry but was throwing his sandwich away to a pair of gulls. They peered at him with critical, yellow eyes, pacing tidily beneath their folded wings and anxious for his next gift.

'You're just going to chuck it all to them, aren't you?' Mary, beside him on Ancw's sea wall, dug placidly at his side. 'You know you get bad tempered when you're hungry.'

'Not at all.'

One gull lowered its long neck and started to mew, finally flinging back its head and screaming, its sharp little rose-grey mouth opened like a shell. The noise was pleasantly appalling. Its mate webbed earnestly up to join in the din.

Nathan laughed, producing a gullish squawk himself – not exactly pretty, but not too bad, either. He was with Mary, he could relax, he could even be a little bit ugly and not mind.

'I don't know which is worse – you or the birds.' She stood, allowing him to look up at her, squinting against the surprisingly warm spring sun. 'That's my bus in. So I'll have to go.'

'Unless you want to miss it.'

'Which I don't.' She smiled and made a half step back, the angles of her body opening a touch, unmistakably inviting a hug.

They'd established this little routine with each other quite quickly. After a couple of months in their new acquaintance, their goodbyes hardly ever happened without it. So he stood, set himself in her embrace, let her body close against him, slight, full of little strengths and softnesses, her head snug at his chin. She always began with the left arm, then the right, then shut a flicker of contraction round him. He patted his response, while a small metallic area in his chest shone hotly, possibly proudly, for a breath.

'Off you go, then. Need a hand with your bags?'

'No.'

And she left him with the chill of her withdrawal and a pointedly independent grin.

Nathan nodded in lieu of waving while her face at the misted bus window pulled away. Then he took himself on up the hill into Ancw for a wander. He had an hour to waste before he could catch his own bus and start heading for London. And he enjoyed the stone echo there was to walking about here, the slightly hollow bang of his feet, bouncing in the narrow spaces between flags and walls. It made him feel bigger, more substantial and snug.

Which meant that he was smiling and unwary when he walked past Richard Hooker: a softly moving shadow in the shadow of the chapel wall.

'Ah, Nathan.'

'Ah, Richard.' *Fuck it, he's got that look – he's got that* **Nathan, let me tell you something** *look.* 'Everything fine?' *I don't want to know. I am being happy and that's taking all my strength.*

'It's still there, then.' Richard nodded to the chapel noticeboard.

Nathan squinted at it briefly and saw that – yes, indeed – Ruth's inevitable, ragged verses on the Price boy's death were still there, rustily pinned and yellowing.

'Mm hm. As if people hadn't enough to put up with. They have to get blurry doggerel inflicted on them as well. I can only assume no one's taken it down because no one wants to touch it.'

'Maybe they appreciate the gesture.'

'Well, it makes me want to reciprocate with a gesture of my own.'

Richard produced the injured, but indulgent smile that always made Nathan want to stab him in the throat. In the absence of offensive weapons, Nathan kicked at nothing in the gutter, watching the toe of his shoe as it scuffled uselessly.

I know, I know – you've had a shitty life and you're not angry all the time, you're not offensive the way I am, I should do better, I should keep my mouth shut. Then again, you're being fucked insensible on a roughly daily basis. Just exactly how sorry am I meant to feel for you?

Nathan tried to think of Mary, to let her calm him, while what was left of her hug in his memory was shredded away from around his ribs by little pangs of fury. 'How's Lynda?'

Richard made another smile – this time, the nervous one. 'Oh, you know . . .'

'Yes.' Nathan couldn't think of even one more suitable word, 'Yes,' but started serious work on the casual intake of breath and the shifting of weight, the relatively chummy nod that would lead up to his leaving, to his neat get-away. 'Yes, yes.'

'I was just telling her . . .' And Richard stopped him. Five words, that was all it took.

*Shit. The sly fuck. I was going, I was practically, officially, to all intents and purposes fucking **gone**.*

'I was just saying – I think maybe a week ago, possibly more.'

There was something in his tone, something quite literally compelling which made Nathan wonder if Richard didn't fake his vagueness, his distraction to save them all from having to hang on his every word. *God save us from that.*

Richard allowed himself the small, dry preface of a cough. 'I was just letting her know . . .'

Don't ask him for more, don't ask him. 'What?' *Bollocks, he gets me every time.* 'Letting her know what?'

Ach, let it go, though. Why not let him? Where's the harm?

'Mm?' Richard blinked, as if Nathan were suddenly a puzzlement, but then he dropped slickly into his story, speaking softly, keeping Nathan eye to eye. 'I told her about the time that I ran away. I wouldn't have been much older than the Price kid. I sneaked out at night, too – the way that he did. A summer night. And I walked and I walked and I ate all the food that I'd managed to take with me and I didn't sleep very well and I got tired and I got scared. I got more scared of going on than I was of going back.'

Nathan nodded, grim: strenuously holding his imagination back from any depiction of the early Hooker household. 'You went home?' *And it was terrible, they beat you, they locked you in the cellar, did things . . .*

'Yes, I went home.' Richard licked his lips, examined the sky. 'And nothing happened.'

'Nothing?'

'Nothing. It was like dying.'

'Hm?'

'Like dying and finding out that you aren't missed. Not in any way. I came back and everyone's life was continuing. They hadn't

301

searched for me, hadn't called the police. They'd wanted me gone. They'd got rid of my things.' He looked at Nathan, puzzled again, 'They got rid of my things, Nathan,' asking for an explanation, for sense.

Christ, the pain in the world. Jesus Christ.

And Nathan gripped Richard's hand, the smaller frailer one, and held it and nodded and peered at the chapel wall, the pavement, the street, anything other than Richard's face.

'You listen well, Nathan.'

No, I don't.

Richard shrugged his fist free. 'And you're good with Mary.'

'That's . . .' Nathan realised that Richard had been watching when he'd said goodbye to Mary. 'You . . . ?'

'I happened to see.' Richard blushed very slightly. 'You hugged her.'

'Yes.'

'That's the kind of thing you do. A parent, hugging his child. That's the way it should be.'

'Yes. Yes, I suppose it is.'

And Nathan shut his eyes and hugged Richard and tried to make the contact unquestionably firm and caring and humane and in any way a compensation for an aching childhood, for a marriage without children, for a lack of honest or of loving touch.

Jack was under his desk. He hadn't fallen, hadn't even been pushed – he was not there by accident, but by design.

'I am not here by accident, but by design.'

'Well,' Nathan had stopped worrying about J. D. – there was no point. Nevertheless, he couldn't quite think of him without a yank of something not unlike concern at the back of the throat. 'Well, could you possibly get up by design? I want to talk to you. Or are you having one of your episodes?'

'I am perfectly chemically unaffected, thank you. I am looking for my pen.'

'No, you're not.'

'I am if anyone comes in. Or, no – I am sitting on the floor because I have sciatica and it's more comfortable for me here.'

'Jack, do please make sense. I have come rather a long way to have this conversation, which will relate directly to a book which – degraded and genre-bound though it be and very far from the proper novel I do promise I will eventually produce – is still, nevertheless, a volume you have undertaken to publish.'

Jack raised his head until his eyes could peer across the desk top and flitter about the suspicious crannies of his new office. 'Christ, you're pompous when you're pissed off. Come round here.'

'What?'

'Come here and help me to look for my pen.'

Despite himself, Nathan sank to his knees and then all-foured it to where Jack was crouched: the modesty panel between them and the door. 'I bet you say that to all the girls.'

'Not any more, they just laugh. Hello, Nate.' Jack was going through one of his portly phases, beginning more and more to resemble the late Margaret Rutherford. His eyes gave the impression that he had been recently shocked out of sleep, but he was not otherwise dishevelled. In fact his orangeish tweeds, his tattersall checked shirt and cautious manner, almost gave him the air of a country squire, lurking in a covert for the game to beat by.

And if ever a man seemed in need of a 12-bore, it's Jack. Not that anybody sane would let him near one.

'So. What the fuck is this all about?'

J. D. smirked and then straightened himself. 'Now, old Sport, I must point out *tout d'abord* that you shouldn't say I'm being paranoid because, quite frankly, you don't know, you do not fucking understand what things are like here.'

'Since the move?'

'Since the move, since being taken over, transported and possessed, since being bought out by Rex Mundy and his evil cohorts, since being stuffed into this cupboard as if I were an unwanted ironing board . . .' He knuckled away a dot of splenetic spittle. 'Since then, everybody knows what I'm doing, what I've said, what I'm fucking *thinking*, for God's sake. And the last thing you want these shits to be sure of is *that*. I might as well fax them all death threats every morning.'

'I thought you did.'

J. D. rolled his eyes into his sleepiest, most psychotic stare. 'That was an isolated incident, a very long time ago. And meant as a joke. But this, really, Nate, is most disturbing: my plans, my tucked-away promising authors, the bastards know about them all. I couldn't work out why and then I realised – it's the new building.' He paused, a tight, nodding smile inviting a gesture of agreement.

'Ah . . . the building?'

Jesus God, don't have lost it this much. Please. You're so good when you're good – just get your bloody head in order.

'Yes.' An unnerving urgency was starting to twitch at Jack's arms, while flattening his voice to a wheezy growl. 'The *building*. Rex Mundy Ltd – it's like any other conglomerate now – it wants to check up on its staff. And how do they do that? – with pinhole cameras, video surveillance, CCTV. All illegal, but what do they care? I'm telling you . . .' He knelt closer, his breath alcohol-free but vaguely dank. 'We are being watched. So the only way to keep a secret is to work, rest and play under here.'

Nathan knew he was now smiling like a maniac – his usual

304

response to people who quite plainly *were* maniacs. 'You don't suppose they might know all about you because you'll tell people almost anything once you're tired and emotional? And that you then don't remember doing it afterwards? Perhaps?'

'Blackouts, you mean?' Jack frowned, apparently pondering.

'Well . . .' Nathan tried to keep it casual, 'maybe . . .'

'Yes, blackouts would explain a lot – I see what you mean.' An uncomfortable pause elongated uncomfortably.

Before Jack's smirk widened and he chuckled himself into a full, tubercular laugh. 'Oh, Nate. Fuck me . . . You're getting slack. Surely you didn't *really* believe your old editorial chum was *that* far gone?' He wheezed and made a pretence of dabbing his eyes. 'Ah, you did, though. Poor old Nate – you're so gullible, it's almost no fun gulling you.'

'But only almost.' Nathan shoved his hand rapidly forward and grasped Jack's throat. 'You shit.'

J. D.'s eyes gave a bewildered shudder while he recoiled and thumped his head against the underside of his desk. He opened his mouth, then thought better of speaking, but left himself gaping in any case.

Nathan, on the other hand, had something to get off his chest. 'You manipulative, shoddy, fucking bastard.'

Jack forced a swallow past Nathan's constricting thumb and tried to nod. Then Nathan snatched his grip away, giggled. 'And *you're* even more gullible than *me*. Surely you didn't imagine I'd *really* garrotte you, my old editorial chum?'

J. D. managed to rasp, 'Ha, sodding ha,' scuffling to his feet. 'All right, let's get out of here. And you can tell me what it's like to be speaking to your daughter again.'

'I didn't say –'

'Didn't have to. It's painted all over the backs of your eyes, shines out like daylight through a dirty screen door.' He was going for a Bogart drawl.

'Mm hm. Don't give up the day job. But, yes, we are . . . back.' A nuzzle of pleasure stretched his spine. 'Back the way we should be.'

'She spoken to you about letters? From her father?'

'Only the one you sent for me . . . Letters?' Jack was looking both smug and shifty: this wasn't a good sign. 'Jack, what have you done?'

'What you would have, if you'd been thinking sensibly.' He gave a tactful cough. 'Nathan, I may be a highly unsuccessful father, but I do know what fathers are supposed to do. Writing to your daughter once, after fifteen years of silence, and then not ever writing again isn't on the list of recommended behaviours.'

Nathan's imagination turned clammy. 'Jack, this is another wind-up, isn't it? By which I mean, it had better be.' He realised that he was still on all-fours and got up to argue his point from a position of dignity.

Jack withdrew a pace. 'Calmness, Sport, tranquillity . . . keep a grip. I do, after all, know your style – the way that you like to put things, your common usages. I simply dropped her a few more lines, now and then, signed them *Your Father*, as we agreed, and that's that.' Jack rested his arm across Nathan's shoulders. 'Don't worry, Sport – I just told her what you've told me, the stories, the places you'd been – this and that about the way she was. I told her you loved her.'

'You had no right to do that,' Nathan was saying this and trying to sound outraged while shame creaked and broke in him, soured his mouth.

'No, Nathan, I would say that you had no right not to.'
Bastard.

Braced against his own justifiable fury, Nathan was, in fact, simply swamped by a sudden, caustic need to weep. He stumbled forward against Jack, treading on one of his feet, and completed a clumsy, slapping hug. 'I suppose,' his voice sounded ridiculously breathless and bleak, 'I suppose I should thank you.'

'Yes, quite probably. But we could probably take it as read – don't you think? And I do have another foot, but I'd rather you didn't dance about and try to flatten that one, too.'

They stood back from each other, examined the room and hunted their pockets softly for distractions.

Bryn had always been elegant, but now, Mary thought, he had an edge about him. He had become striking. His hair had turned completely, startlingly white and was cut very short on the rise to the crown and then allowed to finish in a longer, almost military, brush cut. This had the effect of elongating his face, lifting him, somehow.

When Mary visited, he seemed younger, was, in actuality, slimmer and had a tightness or tautness about him, traces of an unfamiliar energy, pent up for undisclosed, close work. As any widow might, he had taken more to dark colours and absolute black, but he'd also developed a taste for brilliant waistcoats: ember red, butter yellow and one in velvet, electrostatic blue.

'Well, you know, love, when you're by yourself, you can please yourself. You can do things that, before, you might not have, even if perhaps you have to like them differently. You know?'

'I think so.'

They were dawdling along Roberts Street, arm in arm – a way of walking they'd only developed recently. A dusty blue van was parked in the lane on their left, its motor idling and Brian Perry leaning on its steering wheel, seated beside a very much younger woman. They were hot in what seemed, behind the windscreen condensation and billows of exhaust, to be an extremely unpleasant conversation.

'Is that who I think it is?' Mary tried not to peer, while Bryn stared across, proprietorially blatant.

'Yes. Brian Perry with Tracy Williams – they've been going on like that for months and thinking no one knows it. But I see them. I see everyone. There's not much else to do here, except for having extra-maritals. And the drinking, I suppose. *Facito aliquid operis, ut semper te diabolus inveniat occupatum.*'

'The devil makes work for idle hands.'

''Specially when no one else will. Still, it's better than the way it used to be, I suppose – the work schemes, the camps in the country – I've seen men start up crying, just thinking about them. Billy Marsh, you remember him. They sent him off digging ditches, officer-types screaming at him, humiliating him. Never had the same heart in him when he came back. Dead now, of course. Most of those boys are. All too long ago. Billy Marsh, he went to London, lay down in the road to make people see that he mattered. You wouldn't have thought it, looking at him, would you? That he'd go and do a thing like that. The things inside of people that they never say – always surprising . . .'

Mary thought she should change the subject for him, but he brightened without her help.

'So, yes – Brian and Tracy. Not happy, but doing their best and Mrs Perry not too much the wiser. It all started with the fuss about the pigeons. Someone tried using stolen dets to kill the peregrines. Brian and another boy, they strapped them on to the pigeons, set them flying, and hoped that the falcon would take them, get blown up. Didn't work – well, not often. And people, including Tracy, said it was cruel. In the end, she made Brian agree – with that and lots of other things – and, true enough, nobody wants bits of pigeon coming and landing all over their wash. Now that I think, you know, it was Mrs Perry's wash one of the times when it *did* work. Hasn't had a lucky year, that woman.'

'You're the neighbourhood watch then, are you?' It was strange being out with him, exploring a town that looked shabbier, more rattled, every time she came back, with a man who only looked glossier, more assured. His confidence, his air of ownership, was almost embarrassing.

'Well, you know the valley, though, don't you, love? Very fond of watching itself.'

But under his shine, this burning of some part of himself, she wasn't sure how he was. At the end of a climb, his leisurely pace could seem enforced, not chosen. Sometimes she watched him making the simple movements he always had – slicing bread, filling the crossword, pulling down a book – and deep in the motion she thought she could see a fugitive tremor of tiredness, or doubt.

Perhaps he's like Nathan now, always a part of him working to keep himself in the right shape.

Bryn and Nathan, they had the same feel when she hugged them: a tiny flinch of withholding, a physical secrecy. Without thinking, she squeezed Bryn's arm, rested her head towards his shoulder for a moment.

He smiled, slightly puzzled. 'You all right, girl?'

'Mm.'

Maybe I feel the same way. The way people do when they want to touch more than they can, when they miss it, remember themselves being other ways.

She didn't want to consider how Bryn might be missing Morgan, how she was herself, how both of them still listened to the random noises of the house and almost caught the sound of Morgan, just about to pop downstairs. She heard herself speaking to fill up whatever unhappy space might be threatening to slip between them. 'Bryn, I've had some letters.'

'From Jonathan?'

She hated that his name could still flip that chilly switch in near her breastbone. There seemed to be no defence. 'No. No, they're from – well, he says they're from my father.' Another flip.

Father. *What does that even mean?*

'Who said they were from your father?' Bryn stopped, brushed his hand to her face, gave a small huff of worry. She hadn't meant to disturb him, only to ask what he knew.

'No one said . . . I mean, whoever writes them said.'

'How long has he been writing?'

'Ah, a while. I didn't mention it before, because . . .'

*Because I didn't want to upset you the way I'm managing to now. It's not that I **needed** a father, it's just that if I had one . . . I think I'd like to know.*

'Anyway, he's kept on writing and . . . I wanted . . . do you know anything? That's what I wondered. Does it make any sense to you?'

'Oh, love. Oh, love.' He started them walking again, their sides pressing together and easing back, a soft, soothing motion. 'I wish I knew anything at all. You know that Maura and I, we never saw each other much. As soon as she could, she left the valley – Mam and Dad and me. I couldn't have been more surprised, more beautifully surprised, when she brought you to us.' He hesitated minutely as he heard his own voice saying *us*. 'I never met your father. All Maura told me was that he'd gone.'

'Gone?'

'The way she said it, I though she meant dead. I suppose she didn't make it all that clear. Fair play to her, but no one ever really knew where they were with Maura. She wasn't so much cold, but very, very determined. I was her big brother – by a long way – old enough to be a father when she was born. We always said she was a nice little accident to have happened, a late surprise, but I could still have known her like my sister . . . She didn't want that, though. She was her own person, straight off. Still, to lose touch with you the way she did, I couldn't understand her doing that . . . We tried our best, two old wives bringing you up, but even so –'

'You *were* the best. I don't even . . . I don't remember her very much.'

'Look, I don't know . . . perhaps it *is* your father. You could ask her – Maura – she would tell you the truth if you asked her straight. She's a very honest woman. You can't fault her on that. Too honest altogether, I'd say. Go and ask her to her face.'

'I don't know if I could.'

'You could.'

Would Nathan come with me?

No, I don't need him.

But it would be better with him there.

'I'll see how I feel.'

'You can do anything you want to. You're our Mary and we brought you up to be that way.'

'Well, I'll see. I'll see if it's anything I want.'

'I am going to leave my body to domestic science. You will remember, won't you? That is my wish.' J. D. was lying on Nathan's sofa, arms funereally crossed. 'You will see to me, look after my *post mortem* needs?'

Nathan was half-curled in one of the armchairs, trying not to feel in any way alarmed.

This is my flat, I own this, I can do what I like here.

Nevertheless, a part of his brain was still on its best behaviour, still anxious for furniture and fittings that were too unfamiliar to be his own. This room, for instance, seemed far too clean and delicate to be anything to do with him. He kept catching himself, stamping about on the carpet, adoring the sensation of something so soft under his feet. In fact, he thought he'd just get up and have a wander round again.

Jack sighed, 'Jesus Christ, what is the matter with you, man? God knows how many years of celibate living and finally you're reduced to getting off on shag pile – the name is enough.'

'Leave it, Jack. I'm being happy tonight.'

'Happy? What a dreadful thought. Start being that and who knows where it'll end. Of course, I'll never know, with bastards like you refusing to promote their books . . .'

'I said I would give one interview. That's already one too many.' He wriggled his toes and scanned around for the whisky bottle. It was, naturally, standing on the floor within reach of J. D. – its spiritual master. Nathan sighed, trying to avoid becoming discontented. 'I've heard myself talking about myself for a fucking decade, almost two. And I don't believe me any more. It's like . . . it's like.' He couldn't remotely think what it was like. 'Well, first I thought I was a tart because I was working for money instead of art and then I worked it out. I'm a tart because you sell me and other

311

people get the fun and I'm in the fucking middle, not even feeling when I get screwed.'

J. D. lightly adjusted the crotch of his *Country Life* tweeds. 'Lovely. Mummy always said I'd grow up to be a pimp.'

'Tell them I've become a hermit – that'll be an angle they haven't tried.'

'Bastard. But never mind.' Jack hugged himself inaccurately. 'My protégé still loves me. And this year she won the *Crapbutpromising Prize* and the *Provincial Underdog's Consolation Award*. She didn't get the *Shitforbrainsgirlie*, but, then, that's always such a fix. And the Chairmaness of the judges doesn't like me – because of an incident in her kitchen. With her au pair.'

'Her au pair and *you*, that would be?' Nathan decided that the carpet would be even more pleasant if he lay down on it immediately. He set about doing precisely that.

'It was a boring party, what else was I to do?'

The fibres were curiously soothing against his face. 'Ah, the wonderful world of literature. One day . . .' Nathan yawned and then closed his mouth on rather more of the lovely fibres than he'd have liked. They tasted of dog. He missed his dog. 'I shall go back to it all. One day.' His blood, he was sure, was turning soupy, slippy, somnolent. Already, he was far too soluble and heavy to get up.

Heavy water – that's me.

'I thought you *were* going back – doing me a proper novel instead of forcing me to rely on all these dreadful children that everyone's touting about. My God, last week I was offered fifteen pages of a book that doesn't exist, by an author of no visible previous work and then asked to *bid* for it.'

'And you did biddeded – bidded – did you?' While Nathan's tongue rattled fatly in his mouth, total anaesthesia was coming like a mallet, he could feel it dropping.

'Mmm. Had to. Semi-autobiographical, children's home, sex abuse, *rites* of passage saga from some Mancunian slapper. Didn't *look* as if she'd been regularly sodomised by fully qualified care staff, but who can tell? I bidded. But I didn't get it. Fuck, publishing's all so revolting now – it disgusts even me. Give me a *good* book, Nathan. Hm?'

Jack's hand paddled out for the whisky and knocked it over.

Nathan was distantly aware of a liquid chugging at his ear as the bottle started coughing out its load.

'Shit.' Jack snatched it up. 'Nearly a disaster there, Nate.

'Nate? Write me a book. A real one. Go on. I'd do it myself, if I had the time. I *could*. I won the *Crapbutpromising* myself, remember? A hunner, hunder, hundred years ago. But I *did win*. Only, only . . . you know I've never had the energy to do more writing since.

'Nate? My novel. Did you like my novel, Nathan? Nate?'

But Nathan couldn't hear him, because he was already faster and faster asleep.

Good God, that's quite remarkable. I'm dead.

Nathan's imagination was flopping like a wet moth on elastic, some distance above what was undoubtedly his corpse.

Nice suit. Fuck, that's so bloody typical – the best suit I've ever had and I'm dead – can't go out and show it off or anything.

At this, his awareness sank into his body with a thoroughly nasty shudder and was able to peer out from one of his eyes as if it were a wide-angle spy hole in a door.

His coffin was set on trestles, not in a chapel of rest, but at the front of a respectful audience, all seated on folding chairs. Some of them were reading his books.

Well, if they're expecting a performance, I'd say they're a little too late.

Although he suddenly realised, with a spasm of rigor-mortised outrage, that nobody's attention was fixed on him. Sober and perhaps ten years younger, here was Jack Grace, immaculately tricked out as a Victorian undertaker, sweating discreetly beneath a crêpe-ribboned top hat.

'Of course the cadaver has been dressed in the traditional McAbre tartan – black checks on a black ground – according to the wishes of the deceased.'

I am not deceased, you pillock. Quite plainly, I am not.

The tiny, phlegmy presence which was Nathan's soul scrambled the length of his body for a point from which he might signal his continuing consciousness. No luck. He knew that his heart would be kicking and bucking by now if it could, and that he might also quite like to scream, if his mouth were able.

'I shall now,' J. D. swept an authoritative arm towards Nathan, 're-veal the very latest process of embalming. Allow me to demonstrate.'

Will this hurt? Because I'm still here, you know. Fully aware and conscious and sensitive and quite emotional, actually, and I'M STILL HERE.

This probably will hurt.

Fuck, this is unreasonable.

But then Nathan, suddenly freed from his stiffened flesh, looked down in bewilderment at an entirely different room: vaguely culinary machinery lounged against white tile walls. Somewhere an engine ground. This did not bode well.

This does not bode well.

Broiling with demonic energy and in no way resembling Margaret Rutherford or any other well-loved British character actress, Jack swung Nathan into the air by the heels and gave his body a single, unlikely snap which left his limbs and torso peeled while his skin shuddered to the ground like a clammy diving suit. Not content with this, Jack, now in bloodied shirt sleeves and panting with delight, began to twist and pull the meat from Nathan's bones as if he were tearing the shells off giant prawns.

That's not the way, that is not the way, I mean that really is not the way you do embalming. Really not.

Nathan's dismay thumped impotently back against the tiles as his flesh was tossed in handfuls into a mincer, his miraculously spotless bones were clattered into a grinder and the whole of his fabric reduced to two colours of slurry in what seemed rather more than jig time. Jack then capered about a vat of curing solution in which he was stewing Nathan's skin. This finally emerged, steaming gently.

*Oh, bollocks. This is patently disrespectful and inaccurate. He knows **nothing** about embalming. The man's a fraud.*

Dripping and tanned to the colour of wallet leather, there was his skin. It creaked expensively. Nathan now guessed with nauseous certainty that he was going to be stuffed.

But if he's ground up all my bones, I'll just be floppy. I don't want that. How will I do things? He evidently hasn't thought this through.

Then again, who'll notice – I won't exactly have a giddy social calendar underground.

At which juncture Jack emerged from a cupboard with an enormous sack of cotton wool. Feet slithering in Nathan's gore, one fist suddenly covered in a latex glove, Jack advanced on Nathan's defenceless epidermis.

Jack Grace, I don't think I will ever forgive you for this.

But with no more time, even to flinch, Nathan's mind leaped forward again to find itself jangling nervously over his casket and his body, restored within. As polite applause scuttled about the room, he saw that – reasonably enough – the tanning process had left his face and hands looking dashingly bronzed. And rather than seeming limp he was, if anything, far more rigid than before.

Good man yourself, Jack. You must really have jammed that wadding in there tight. In there. In me, in fact. You really must have jammed it in me tight. Which is, I suppose, what friends are for.

Jack was taking his final bows. A humble smile flickered at his lips and from time to time he managed a self-effacing shake of the head.

Well you may efface yourself. You couldn't have done it without me, could you, eh?

Nathan's soul wasped forward, contemplating an attack.

If I could fly in through one nostril, then I'd kick him right between his frontal lobes.

But then an odd detail drew Nathan's eye, a terrible discrepancy. He gazed down at himself, at his wonderful suit, at the slight jut of his shirt cuffs, at his shaved wrists and then on.

The fuck. The cheapskate little fuck. The bastard.

There were no fingers on his hands. Presumably they'd been too troublesome to stuff.

Cunt.

All that was left were Nathan's palms, like squarish paddles, poorly oversewn at the edges to keep their filling in.

Bastard. Bastard. Bastard.

How will I write?

'What?'

The floor of his own apartment swayed uneasily below Nathan and he lurched up, causing a matching sway at the backs of his eyes. 'Oh.'

'Who are you calling a bastard?'

The sound of Jack's voice brought on a rush of sour perspiration and Nathan checked him quickly to see if he was still in his embalming costume or not. Not.

'Bastard? Ah . . . a publisher . . . I dreamed about a publisher. A bastard.'

'Absolutely. They're all bastards, every one. I myself, of course, am *not* a publisher. I am a taker of empty bottles –' he waved the, by now completely drained, whisky bottle by way of explanation, 'and I fill them with wonderful messages and send them off. Think of it – in all the ocean, a fragment of mind held in glass. And perhaps not every bottle of mine will be shattered or lost or drowned. Perhaps . . .' He swung into a seated position and then breathed pensively. 'You don't mind if I have a minor vomit, do you? No need to fret – perfectly capable of reaching your lavatory.' He slithered down to his knees, punched Nathan reassuringly in the kidney, then shuffled up and off.

'No, I won't fret. I won't fret at all, Jack. No.'

Nathan settled himself back to the horizontal, one elbow resting in some kind of soggy patch. He licked his lips and found them remarkably salty.

Jack called through hoarsely, 'Don't let your daughter on the page, Mr Staples. Mmm?' A choked snigger followed. 'But we'll keep her from the worst of the bastards, won't we, Sport? Ah, here we go.' There came the sound of what could only be a toilet seat clanking up.

Nathan pondered Mary's future, pondered his own, while listening to his editor throwing up comprehensively.

Love. He'd quite forgotten that it was, beyond all the gloss and brimstone, a kind of very wonderful sleepiness. Being with your person, whoever that was, would bring an immediate inrush of easy peace: an insulation from torments, large and small. That person, your person, simply could not annoy you. Even if they endlessly repeated all their most potentially dementing habits, affectations, ticks, they would leave you not only unmoved, but even happier with their essence, their presence close to yours. And the dreadfulness of the world was no longer dreadful and your limbs had a pleasant, unlooked for, certainty and your lung (should you happen to have just the one) would feel light and efficient and healthy in all its transactions with the satisfying air. My God, love could make simply *breathing* a splendid thing.

Nathan footled with the papers in his pocket and tried to avoid bursting rashly into song.

Jesus wept, you've got it bad.

I have a right. I've waited nearly twenty years to get it bad again.

Mary was standing among the rocks with her back to the breeze and, therefore, her face to him. He was glad he'd brought her over to the Head again – this was absolutely the best place for what he'd been planning, not to mention the finest time. Then Mary sat on a little boulder, slipped her feet up and hugged her raised knees. Nathan observed.

Dear God, I never thought . . . So I get that, too. After all of this time.

Without even considering what effect this might have, he moved round a few degrees to his right and looked at her again.

Oh, Mary.

Recognition gently filleted his heart. She'd adopted exactly the pose he knew from his haunted photograph: different beach, different decade, same Mary Lamb. But no camera here to steal this from them, to make them share this with anyone else. No one to see her now but him. Overturned longing, then joy, then tenderness flayed him entirely alight.

'Oh, Mary.'

That surprised them both – he hadn't meant to say it out loud. And now matters might have a tendency to get upended, to go astray. If he didn't take care, his intentions could work quite seriously adrift. So he should really start getting on with what had to be done.

Fuck, she was amazing, though. Amazing and right here.

'Yes?'

For an instant, he couldn't think what she was asking him. 'Ahm, yes, I . . .'

*That buggering **sleepiness of love** bit doesn't last, though, does it? Doesn't come with a guarantee. One minute you're dozy, the next you're all poker-worked in to the bone with fucking confusions and fright.*

He cleared his throat and grappled with his composure, hoping that it might consent to be composed. 'Ah, yes, indeed, I thought we might talk through the bits and pieces you gave me and then we could climb up and look round off the top. You should see the top. You've never been up there?'

'The beach is as far as I've got.'

He wondered if she was enjoying herself. It was, maybe, a little chilly for this kind of jaunt, but she did look as if she was happy enough. In fact, she appeared – he swallowed hard but the thought still remained – she appeared more than averagely pleased to be with him.

'Nathan?'

'Hm? Oh. Right. Well . . .' Nathan pulled out the fold of papers, checking his hands for signs of nervousness, but – no – he felt safe to proceed without any tremors or reservations. 'Bit of a mixed bag, aren't they? I mean this one –' he waved a portion of the sheaf, felt a nudge of sea air inspect it cursorily, 'is perfectly acceptable, really fine.'

'I know.' She frowned, uncomfortable with having been so definitive. 'I mean, it got published. It must be OK.'

Mary gave him a watchful look. Its acceptance and publication had, of course, happened while they weren't speaking. But he could say, 'I know,' which would, he hoped, translate as *I did still take an interest, I kept an eye on you.* She nodded with a tight, good, little smile.

'And then you go and give me *this*,' he waggled another, less happy sheaf, 'and Jesus – it's God-awful. I'd never have thought you could *be* so bad.' The thing about doing this kind of talk, he hoped, was to drive on in, make it sharp, but with any luck amusing and useful and nothing personal. 'And that thing about the woman and her pets. *Fuck*.' He was taking the right line, here. Apparently. She was still sort of smiling, agreeing with her eyes – he *thought*, agreeing – so no need to worry at all. 'I picked it up and read it and it was like . . . like having maggots fall out when you tap a biscuit. Not a proper handful in any way.'

'I'd have thought that was what you wanted.' She wasn't going to take this completely lying down, which was all right, too. Very healthy. 'The kind of stuff *you* write, I would have thought a fistful of maggots was right up your street.' The light of a grin just flitted behind her eyes.

'Mm hm, *A Fistful of Maggots Is Right Up My Street* will be the title of my autobiography.'

'If it is, I'll demand a percentage.'

'There's no copyright on titles. Not a chance.' Teasing. Such a good thing to do. Bit of banter to sharpen the brain. 'And what were you thinking of with . . . hang on . . .' He shuffled the pages until he found what he was looking for. 'Here we go – "the sun, like God's bleeding arsehole" – *God's bleeding arsehole?* Do tell me what possible kind of excuse you could ever come up with for that. Concussion? Pre-senile dementia? Ergot poisoning from one of Ruth's dodgier loaves?'

She giggled and frowned simultaneously. 'I said I knew that some of it was crap. All I needed was for you to agree and then I was going to go back and work on it again. Or burn it – obviously.'

'I know.' He nodded his most understanding nod – *this is just the game we're playing, this is just a bout of sparring, a proof we are safe with each other, even when we come to blows*. 'I remember what you told me when you handed it all in. No pre-senile dementia *here*.' He tapped at his skull, finding it shockingly easy to endorse his own thought process.

'Really?'

'Yes, really. Meanwhile I'm still waiting for you to justify your hideous sunset.'

'Oh, good grief, fine.' She stood up, shaking her head with – he knew – mock impatience. 'I was trying to reflect the protagonist's state of mind in my description of his surroundings.'

'Ah, I *see* – so he's a verbally challenged lunatic deprived of his medication. All is clear. Or else he's bow-legged with monstrously gory piles that go unmentioned in the rest of your narrative.'

Mary pursed her lips, solemn, and bent to pick up a largish, flattish stone. Almost at once she began to swing her arm back, still holding its burden, in a movement that suggested, for one astonished breath, that she might be about to brain him, there and then. He let out a whinny of alarm as she flung the rock wide of him to land flatly in the sea with a cracking slap. This sent up a hard, broad tangent of water that thoroughly drenched his leg. As she had, no doubt, assumed it would.

'Ach. You *fucker*.' Nathan danced vainly across the gravel as if he could retrospectively avoid the impact. His shin was chilling already. 'That was completely unnecessary.' He enjoyed how plaintive he was sounding. And how attractively triumphant she looked.

'It shut you up, though, didn't it?'

'I was actually on the brink of dealing very admiringly with some of the excellent sections in the good stuff. I was going to lavish you with unreserved praise. Before you made your characteristically highbrow contribution to the debate.'

'It wasn't a debate, it was a mugging.' And then, as a milder afterthought: 'Are you very wet?'

'Not really.'

'Damn, I'll have to do it again.'

She began casting about her for another stone while, intoxicated with the whole proceedings, he dodged and slithered like a fool and made small bleats of protestation.

Perhaps I am a masochist.

No. Not possible. If I were basically masochistic then most of my life would have been just nothing but concentrated fun. Every time I woke up, bleeding from my heart and soul, I'd find myself barely able to hide my joy.

I'd be adoring every moment. Like I am now.

They reached a giggly truce and decided to abandon this stage of the proceedings. Nathan led her to the point where the gravel narrowed and then disappeared, crushed between the water and the cliff face. Here, just before they ran out of ground, was the start of an uneven staircase, cut into the rock, its steps hollowed and pitched with long usage.

He let her go ahead, hoping this would give her the comforting sense that, should she slip back, he would catch her.

Not that we wouldn't just both break our necks, to be frank, but it's the thought that counts. And nothing unpleasant will happen today. It can't.

He bawled forward to her, trying to be a good guide, 'The Head is one huge cylinder of basalt – a volcanic core.'

'I'd noticed that it was a cylinder, thank you. And that it's got bloody steep sides.'

'Shut up and fucking listen, I'm being educational.'

'Well, that doesn't happen often.'

'Ungrateful cow. Shush. The steps you're climbing are extremely ancient. Probably pre-Christian. The only reason they aren't worn completely away seems to be that people didn't come here very much.'

'I can't think why.'

'Or that, once they had come, they stayed.'

Then the climb took over and they panted their way to the sudden clarity of the summit, a slightly rounded oval, hunched under the moving air, risen out of the sea's horizontal imagination. Mary wanted to sit for a while in the wiry grass, but Nathan shooed her on. 'You can rest in a minute, it's just a little bit further – go on.' He loved this part: the gentle ascent across the softly domed surface here always made him think of walking over a tiny planet, his own space. 'Now. There. What do you think of that?'

Just where the apex of the rock should be, there was instead a steep-sided hollow perhaps twenty yards across and flat at its base. And lifting in the turf of the base like pumped veins were ridges – beautifully defined – marking a path that whorled in and in concentrically to the island's heart. Mary stood at the lip, silent, looking from Nathan to the pattern and back again. When she spoke, she whispered – people often did once they got up here, 'God, it's lovely. What is it?'

'Oh, a variety of things. If you're Christian, you step into the spiral there, where the opening lets you in, and you walk until you get to the centre and then back, perhaps in your bare feet, perhaps fifty times, perhaps a hundred – some number of times, anyway – and that would be the equivalent of going to Jerusalem – no need to head off and stab any Saracens. Or, indeed, risk being stabbed.'

'I'll bear it in mind.'

'Or maybe it's only a model of the alchemical pathway to material transformation. Or maybe it's Celtic and the path leads to the sun, to life, or through life.'

'They used to put mazes on tombstones to keep in the dead.'

He resisted the temptation to say *well done*, but was – nevertheless – impressed. 'That's right.' Pointing her way to the start of the path, 'And here the dead are our speciality,' following her, wanting to go in and round the track with her, to be there with her, 'On you go,' right at the final curl of it, inside with her.

They slithered down the bank and started the walk, single file – all the marked channel would allow. The grass was short, mossy and oddly giving, it took the sound from their feet. The breeze faded, the sea below them was struck dumb and their progress continued, noiseless. Above them, the air thickened and smoothed, almost gave the impression of sinuous walls, grown up about them to keep their course safe and unvarying.

Nathan touched his hand quickly to Mary's shoulder and murmured, as if they were in a hospital, or a church – some place demanding his respect, 'You know that, at one time, the sailors in Brittany paid no taxes to the king because of their unusual duties. At night the new dead would come to them and would ask to be borne out of life, would wait to be taken to sea and so, after sunset, the fishermen would sail them northwards to the Island of the Dead.'

'North? That would take them to Britain.'

'Yes, they were heading here, for Britain. And people have occasionally said that their proper destination was precisely this point in Britain. Because Ancw is pretty much a Welsh way of spelling the Breton name for the dead. What's the matter?' Mary had halted in front of him. 'Hm? What's wrong?' He stroked her back and she shivered her shoulders in response.

'Wrong? Don't know . . . Walking on the gate of the Under-world . . .'

'It only is if we say it is.'

'Make you feel like you're being watched.' She shook herself again. 'Uff. Like an invisible camera crew, or something, an intrusion.'

'Sorry. Didn't meant to . . . It's just a story, after all.' Their words, he noticed, emerged compacted, vaguely watchful, slipping between them as if they were bolting for cover. 'Do you want to go back?'

'Oh, no. Not at all.' She didn't turn to him, only started on again. 'This is all part of the package, isn't it? The experience.'

'What experience?'

'The one you've planned to give me. Oh.' And now she did turn, having reached the centre of the maze and caught sight of what he'd known she would.

'I haven't planned anything,' he feigned ignorance, in a way that let her see he wasn't ignorant at all. 'Not really. This is just something I thought that you might like to know about.'

They smiled slowly, met each other's eyes, almost bashful, then found the fit of the look and held it, calm, while high silence raged on every side.

Then Nathan blinked. 'You said *Oh*. You saw the carving, then.'

'Mm? Oh, yes. It's wonderful. I think that's the right word. A bit mad, but wonderful.'

'Now and then people have said the same of me.' It felt right to tell her that, it wasn't boasting, or stupid, it was OK.

Mary smiled again and knelt to look at the midpoint of the maze, the little stone-sided box sunk into it, the basalt sculpture set there, staring up at them. It was a man's head, darkly sleek, streamlined to an almond shape, a little as if it were some stranded seafaring creature, and not a head at all. Its eyes were wide, the pupils deeply pierced, and its mouth full open, brimming with gathered rain. Other details might well have been worn away, but it looked exactly right as it was, as if this was the way it intended to be.

Nathan crouched beside her. 'Every time I see him, he makes my own head smooth. I mean, he's soothing. And the opened mouth, for singing, speaking – that's a sign of life.'

'Or death. The dead can't close their mouths.'

He could hear it, she was hurt. Nathan felt the sourness of that close on his mind before he even understood her words. When she

323

hurt, he had to make it stop. When she hurt, he hurt also.

He began to straighten, edging his palms under her elbows, finding she gripped his arms in return and used him to help her stand. From there it was easy to hug and think of nothing for a while, to be smoothed.

Go on, go on, go on. Follow through for once in your life.

God, she's a good wee woman, deserves better relatives than me.

Go on.

'Mary. Another story you don't know . . .' Love broke, folded in his chest – it was the same each time: a clean sheet taken, stretched and snapped and pressed into layers of heaviness, into a pack of frightening, complicated weight. It shortened his breath.

He made his decision – backed away from the one *big* story, set another that was merely important in its place. 'There's supposed be a library here, buried, cut in the rock: books from Alexandria, from Mistra and Bessarion, the Pythagorean Brotherhood, the Gnostics and the Alchemists; unknown Vedas, Mayan Codices, a new Homer, a more dangerous Bible; things that even Crowley wouldn't read. And the antidote for gunpowder; the constitution of a perfect state – anything you'd like, kept here alive.' She was still in his arms, listening, light against him. 'I have my personal wish list. I like to think of it, sneaked away under our feet. And I'm never going to try and find out if there's anything really here. Not that it would matter, anyway.'

'Mm?' She frowned up at him, her chin resting sharply on his chest with a nice little pain.

'No, really, it wouldn't matter. We could make them all again, if we had to. What matters about them is still here, in us, we just have to notice. I mean . . . I mean.' He kissed her forehead, neither intending nor expecting to have done so, and then stepped a half pace backwards, but reached in to hold both her hands, continue the touch. 'I mean . . .'

Shit, I'm losing it.

Mary squeezed at the roots of his thumbs. 'You mean that . . .' She grinned, 'Let me think if I can think what Nathan Staples would mean. That . . .' and let herself be, tenderly, quite serious, 'well, I've always thought we were like the Masai. You know? Maybe you wouldn't say this, but I would. The way that the Masai see it – all of the cows in the world belong to them, cows are their thing. All of the cattle, all over the world, are theirs by right. And all of the words in the world belong to us.'

'Oh, no.'

Shit.

He hadn't intended to be so loud with that. She flinched, withdrew from the comfortable look she'd had and dropped his hands.

He went on in any case, whatever damage he'd caused already done, 'No, that's the point, that really is the whole, important point. They *don't* belong to us.' He dodged forward slightly and held her shoulder, loving, just loving, just loving, that they could talk about this, be together in this – his work, their work, the work that they'd both do now. 'That's, that's . . . the words, you see – you can't wish them here when they're not, you can't stop them when they are: they'll fill your life, make your life, *eat* your fucking life. They can't belong to anyone. They're like land – it's not in their nature to be *owned* by anyone and if you try it, they'll choke you – in the end they will choke and skin and bury you. A writer sells what a writer owns – the skill and the effort and the time – not the words. You don't own words. Things will all go *so* wrong if you even start to try.'

'Is that a Rule?'

He tried to tell if she was cross with him, or not.

'Um . . . ach, all right, then. Yes. Yes, if you want, that's Rule Four. *You do not own your words.*'

'If you say so. OK.' She folded her arms.

'Really?'

Fuck, that was easy.

'Yes, really.'

'Because otherwise, for one thing, when people like your stuff you think they like *you* and when they hate it, you think they hate *you*, and then there's that arrogant thing people get when they assume that the whole thing's their right and a sign of their being a fucking genius and –'

'It's OK. I'm agreeing.' She grinned, shaking her head at him in a good, in a positive way.

He grinned, too. 'And I hope you notice that when I tell you your description of the sunset is immensely repellent shit . . .' he waited while she rolled her eyes, 'I say that because I care about the words and I want them to be their best – I'm not getting at you – I want to find the words the shape they need to say what's closest to their intention, and to leave the right spaces around them, because *God's bleeding –*'

'Enough. You know how I get violent.'

'I'm only trying to explain –'

'Really, Mr Staples. Enough.' She was enjoying being stern with him, darting close to kiss his forehead and slingshot his whole future through him, clean up from his heels, extremely bright.

Oh, Mary.

That sleepiness was seeping in again. He closed his eyes, swallowed. 'Let's walk out of this thing and get home. Go on, get a move on. I don't know . . . bloody writers . . .'

'What did you call me?'

He opened his eyes, looked at her. 'You heard.'

*M*aybe *I should start to smoke. Drink more. Or I could be healthy. I could run. Nathan runs . . . All the time, every day, he runs.*

Mary wanted a habit. More specifically, a bad one, but any one would do. She sat in the sand cave, a spring scurry of wind jostling the door and Eckless bellyflopped into a quiet dream near her side, and she felt the need of something.

Everybody has habits, for goodness' sake. Beyond dog-walking and short stories. People get obsessed. That's a thing they do — it's a part of their normality. And I haven't got . . . not properly. I mean, bloody hell, if I laid out a map of my current life it would have gaps all over it. Whole countries unaccounted for. Sodding continents. . .

She'd hated missing Jonathan, but not missing him was worse. Now, when she tried to move her mind across the form of him or the part of herself that had grown to answer him, there was no response. Her emotions had become evasive, callused over, deafened by sudden, sucking depths.

But, still, there was a need in her for *something* — it was quiet, but it was there. She should find it a focus before it turned on her, before she ended up like Ruth and Lynda: baking and pining and swimming and piercing their lives away.

But you can't have any fun without knowing what you would want to have fun with. Or who — who you'd want.

Her thinking stalled, became clotted with an oddly attractive unease.

*But if you **do** know. Who you'd want . . .*

She stroked the sand and stared beyond her lamp's light into the permissive dark. Something was turning, gloved in her chest, spreading its fingers slowly with a soft, smooth heat. His giving against her, a kind of admission in the pressure of his arms, a change: the mildly peach-skin nap of the skin between his eyebrows when she kissed him: unlikely things to think of and to find so good.

Nathan.

'Is this wise?' Unusually, it was Richard who sailed her over to Ancw. He rarely left Foal Island, but apparently he'd needed a trip today – had specially asked to take Mary across, to take himself away. His touch with the boat, she found, was appreciably subtle, gentle. Not taking silence for an answer, he shouted to her again, across the engine din. 'I said, do you think this is wise?'

'I don't know. Really. I have no idea of why I'm doing this.' Which is much the same thing she'd said to Bryn when she asked him to find out her mother's address. 'But there are just . . . things happening, changes going on and I want to – to sort things out, I suppose.'

Richard navigated onward, his expression on the doubtful side of non-committal.

*Well, I **don't** know. I'm not going to lie. But it feels right, with so much going on . . .*

She sidestepped what exactly the goings-on might turn out to be.

I have every right to see her. Bryn agreed with that. She is my mother.

A tiny spike of anger nudged at the back of her throat. This didn't bode well for the trip. She tried to reassure her thinking.

*Nothing is anyone's fault – not mine, not hers. I'm just going to go and finish things. Or start them. Or both. It won't be a problem, we don't know each other, we don't **need** each other.*

She had to swallow again.

I'll go and I'll ask about my father. Definitely that. And then maybe . . .

Romantic advice from a woman who wished her husband dead and forgot about her child.

Oh, fuck, why am I doing this?

Richard watched her calmly and fiddled at his chin with his good hand – he was growing a beard again and the new hairs were troubling him. 'My mother and I didn't get on too well.' It seemed strange for him to have to yell this, but he appeared quite happy, confiding at the top of his voice. 'When I hit thirty – funny age, thirty, the point where a great many types of shit start to hit a great many fans – I went home to see mine – my mother. We hadn't been estranged or anything, we'd simply spent a couple of decades being excruciatingly polite. While she ice-picked me in the back at every turn. Politely, though – of course. So I turned up, confronted her – she was laying the table at the time and didn't stop, which annoyed me more than almost anything else she'd done.' He halted, perhaps drawn into one of his habitual distractions, perhaps remembering. Mary found her patience was shorter than normal.

'What happened?'

'Hm? Oh, nothing. I didn't feel any better and she didn't change. It gets too late to change, sometimes, and one shouldn't try. Same thing with my arm – a condition not amenable to alteration.'

She nodded, not knowing why, but feeling some response was needed, although Richard's attention – apparently – was now fixed on a high, milky blossom of cloud to their south.

Bryn had told her not to get her hopes up, too: his voice sounding impossibly distant, which was only a trick of the line, but still set her bellowing that she loved him and hoped he was fine. She found that she didn't like raising her voice to say personal things. It seemed to make them mean less. Bryn had said he'd caught a bit of a cold but was all right now. They'd told each other their respective weathers. She'd wanted to touch him.

To touch who, exactly?

A flare and swim of need took her briefly, tightened her jaw.

Bryn? Who?

Nathan hadn't come to the jetty to see her off – he'd said he was expecting a call and would have to be at Joe's place. He'd listened to her plans, smiled quickly, said that she ought to do what she felt was right and then explained that he had to rush.

She'd wanted something more. She had undoubtedly wanted something more.

Nathan, penned in the Lighthouse, but awaiting no kind of call, felt Mary out at sea, withdrawing, hauling his nerves along with her until they tore. She'd packed up his logic and taken it with her.

She'll love Maura better than me. Maura will tell her bad things. She'll come back hating her father, fucking hating me.

Shit, don't let me lose her.

His mouth tasted of burning and of fear.

Don't let me lose her.

He folded his arms around his head, didn't drink the drink that Joe had left him.

Don't. Just don't.

Bus from Ancw, train to London, Underground to the Elephant and Castle and then the bus to Peckham Rye.

Maura had explained it – the best route to take – patiently, precisely, as if she'd expected the call. And Mary had known the voice at once, recognised it completely with a soft turn in her blood. And years of quiet Christmas cards and cheques sent at her birthday had opened and split back to the days when mother and daughter must have spoken, when they must have known each other well, when they must have had things in common, of which Mary now found she had barely any convincing memory. At the end of the call, she'd kept holding the dead receiver and wished that she could cry.

From Peckham Rye on foot.

A short walk by streets she'd tried to teach herself, according to Maura's instructions and the *A–Z*. Mary didn't like to go round London with a map in her hand: an opened indication of bewilderment and muggability.

She was nearly there.

This'll be fine. This'll be fine. I don't need anyone with me. This will be fine.

I would like somebody with me.

This will be fine.

It surprised her that she wasn't feeling nervous. In fact she seemed unable to feel at all. She passed patchy, stringy gardens and loose, Sunday afternoon children, running down shallow perspectives of repeating window frames and doors, and might have been numbly on the way to meet any stranger. Walking through small, harassed streets, brick terraces, she could have been in Roath, or Canton, or Capel Gofeg, or a daydream of her own.

But I'm not, I'm in London, in Nunhead, in the street where my mother

*lives . . . I ought to be able to **be here**. I ought to be **aware**. Or at least*
ready. *I can't even tell if I'm **that**.*

After all this time, she's still taking things away, leaving me empty.

I should just go back now. I should just go home.

Checking numbers now, searching for twenty.

I only want her to tell me that I won't be the way she was. I want to know
that I can marry, can be normal, can have children that I'll like.

The gate, the path with the dusty hedge to either side.

But nothing is anyone's fault. Not hers. Not mine.

The door. Her mother's door. Maura Lamb's door.

Not mine.

An urgent lash of panic shivered her breath, made her realise that
she was sweating, made her hand unsteady when it reached for the
bell, made her disbelieve the sound of footsteps closing, as her heart
flinched and then there was only numbness again.

'Underwear, that was the thing. To be honest.' Maura took a hissing
sup at her cigarette, not looking at Mary. 'He started buying
underwear for me – the silly, uncomfortable things you might
expect. I let him. Why not? But then he wanted to buy it *all*. He only
wanted me to wear things that he'd chosen, nothing else. Then he
suggested I should change my hair to please him, when – as it
happened – the style he was after would never have pleased *me*. I
started to get a feeling of suffocation. Ownership.' Another drag, this
time less fierce. 'And then there was that whole thing of being the
professional man's wife. Not myself. I lost my name. I'm not saying
he *intended* I should disappear, but in the end it seemed that he really
didn't mind if I only existed by way of him . . . As if I was someone
that he was imagining.'

Maura didn't speak with malice, only in words that seemed slightly
over-rehearsed, or as if she were giving her explanation cautiously,
avoiding too much conviction, or unpredictable heat. Then she
faced Mary, something fragile in her eyes. The hand holding her
cigarette wavered before she could rest it on the arm of her chair.
'This will all sound very petty . . . a list of things to rise above. I do
realise.'

Mary shook her head, but had nothing to say – it seemed, nothing
to think. All she could do was watch her mother: the eyes that were

almost Mary's eyes; the hands that were her hands, but slightly fuller, the nails more cared for, but – here and there – nicotined; the face like a somehow more finished version of her own, more settled, more dismayed.

'Do you always stare?' Maura crushed out her cigarette, smiling, not unkindly. 'You're thinking I look like you, aren't you? When, actually, *you* look like *me*. Of course, if we knew each other . . .' She pondered the ashtray, as if she'd forgotten what it was. 'If we knew each other, we wouldn't notice the resemblances. We'd only be ourselves.'

'But we don't. Know each other.' Mary saw the quick break in her mother's expression, and then the tidying away of pain.

I didn't want to do that. I don't want to hurt her. I don't. I don't want to be angry.

I don't want to be angry out loud.

Maura had cupped her hands in her lap and was peering at them hard, head low. 'I had to leave, Mary. I had to leave both of you. I didn't want to. I've always thought of you . . .'

Mary shut her eyes while the words tugged in her, twisted something loose.

I didn't want to I didn'twanttoIdidntwanttoIdidnt.

She wanted to hold someone, but only sat and clenched her fists and listened while Maura's breathing caught and then steadied. 'I always knew Bryn and Morgan would be great as, as parents. Better than me.' It seemed that she almost paused for Mary to comment, but then changed her mind and pushed on. 'I wouldn't have been good with you. After the divorce, it took a long time to be – I don't know – over with him. And I did have to leave him. There was no other way.' She blinked up at Mary, having plainly cried just a very little, quietly, beneath her words. 'You didn't ever think it was your fault? I didn't leave you thinking that?'

At once, Mary felt a grey, hollow kick in her chest. The tears of strangers did not usually affect her.

A stranger who's my mother.

The hollowness turned live in her, raw. 'I . . . No, I didn't think it had much to do with me. It even seemed . . . normal. Maybe because I was so young. I mean, I'm sorry . . .'

I'm not sorry. You should be.

She couldn't prevent herself from causing a little hurt. 'I don't really remember the way things were before the Uncles – not really. And you can't, well . . .'

'You can't miss what you can't remember. I know.'

And then she couldn't prevent herself from wanting to take it away. 'I didn't ever forget I had a mother. But the Uncles were the ones who were there. They were very good.' Her breath failed at the last word, thinking of Morgan, while she saw Maura try to be pleased at being so easily replaced.

'I didn't forget you, either. But in the end, it seemed wrong to keep coming back and unsettling things. You made Bryn so happy.' She shut her lips quickly, glancing away. 'And, when I left your father, everything seemed very hard to do – I hated to go out, I couldn't stand noises, I was afraid of my own temper, I –'

'I know you don't want to say . . . but what was he – was he very . . .' Mary couldn't think of any word to say other than *bad*, which seemed an entirely ridiculous choice.

'He was very himself.'

They both paused to consider what that might mean and Maura lit another cigarette, hungry-mouthed.

The silence seemed to swell and then recede against Mary. Twice she felt ready to speak and then couldn't quite catch the rhythm of the room, the dodge and press of tension between them. She waited, sighed back a rush of stage fright. 'Is he alive?'

'What?' Again Maura's face masked over, hid everything but the first light of fear in the eyes.

'Someone is writing to me. He never gives his name, but he says that he's my father. He seems to know me. Is he alive?'

Maura crushed her cigarette before it was half-smoked. 'I did intend to tell you –'

'Is he?'

'But then it didn't seem possible.' She frowned. 'He couldn't ever have come back to us. I couldn't have stood it if he had.'

'Is he alive!'

They each recoiled a little after her shout. Mary folded her arms: a quick, strong thought of Nathan coming with the hug of her own arms against her. She lowered her voice, 'I only want to know,' but she believed it already. 'He is, isn't he? Alive.'

334

'Yes.'

The pressure that had built between them darted away. Mary thought she felt it rock at her spine as it left them. 'Did you say yes?'

'Yes.' The air juddered, paused again, but Maura said nothing more.

'But you aren't going to tell me who he is, where he is.' Mary understood already, this could only be a statement, not a question.

'He'll tell you. If he's written to you, he'll tell you when he thinks it's time. If he hasn't done it yet, it's because he's . . . nervous. He can be that way. And I can't . . . do you see that I can't contradict him?'

'No. No, actually I can't.' A wordless pulse rose behind her eyes when she closed them, the colour of old bruising. 'I cannot see why neither one of you will tell me my own father's name.'

'Have you written back to him?'

'He didn't give his address. The postmark is always from London, that's all.'

'From *London*?'

'Yes. Wouldn't it be?'

'Oh, there's no reason. No, no reason, I suppose. I just didn't know we were in the same place. Not that London isn't big enough for us to miss each other.' A twitch of a smile appeared at that – *miss each other*. 'Look, I took us away from him. I had to. If I had the choice again, I . . . Well, there's no point thinking about it. The choice I'm making now is that I don't want to take this from him, too. He will tell you in his own time. I know him – he doesn't give up.' She smiled more, then covered her mouth with her fist, her look briefly fierce and then emptied. 'He really doesn't ever give up.'

For the first time, they met each other without reservation.

Maura nodded, eased out a breath, began, 'When I met him in the beginning, he'd write me notes. We didn't really speak. Because he wasn't good at speaking and I didn't want him to be. I was already in a relationship – nothing deep, but nothing unpleasant, either – and I had no need of anything more, but he kept on – your father – he wouldn't let it drop. I've never known anybody be so perseverant – so obsessive, actually. Obsessive would be a better word.'

The evening had dimmed, but neither one of them made a move to switch on a light. Mary guessed that for both of them this would make things easier – to be nothing but voices inside a thickening dark.

The end of Maura's cigarette glowed. 'Not that it isn't attractive when somebody puts that much effort into . . . nothing but you. And he wasn't, I suppose, unattractive in himself – very funny when he wasn't nervous, bright – but very, very serious, too. Everything mattered a little bit more than it should. The things he cared about . . .' She stumbled to find the word, or to avoid it. 'The things he *loved* had to be his, absolutely his.' Maura broke off again with a short sigh, apparently impatient. 'And even that isn't so bad. It can feel very good to be wanted so much. Feeling *owned*, that's different. That stops you being a person any more. He would have to take trips away and then I wasn't needed and I wasn't supposed to need him. Or he'd be working, typing all night upstairs – or *not* typing, just thinking of typing – either way . . .'

'Typing?'

Maura seemed startled. 'Oh, yes. Of course, you wouldn't know. When I met your father, he worked in a publishing house. He was a reader, assessed manuscripts to see if they were fit for publication – him and this lunatic friend of his. Then both of them wrote a book. Your father's was the less successful one – I think it was too literary, a bit obscure – but he kept on going. That determination again . . .'

Maura turned to her, examining Mary's face, seeming to search her for traces of the man she couldn't name. 'I suppose I might have expected you'd write – the house was full of it: books, papers, the people they attracted.' She might have been describing any unpleasant infestation. 'I gave birth to a daughter, but he gave birth to books, one novel and then another – something far more important than a child. He never gave you his time, not properly: it was all about the books – one way or another, it was always about the books.'

She was studying the air beyond Mary's face, peering softly at a point where it seemed she might soon begin to see some final satisfactory explanation of the past. Mary realised that Maura, completely, unusually, still like this, was

lovely. Odd word to use about your mother. But she is. Lovely. You could look at her and be lost.

So we're not alike.

I'd have noticed if I had that – that loveliness.

'Sometimes . . .' Maura broke Mary's dream, speaking it away, 'some days, everything seemed natural – the way that a father and a daughter ought to be – but then I'd see his eyes, and I'd know he was still working, studying you, writing you somewhere, out in the back of his mind. Even when he was playing with you – he was sort of waiting, too – until you were old enough to be like him. By the end, he was already reading you pages and pages of things you couldn't understand, things you *shouldn't* understand, sometimes until you'd fall asleep. You were happy enough, but you were changing – he was starting to make you serious – his kind of serious. He wouldn't let you stay a child.'

'You told him how you felt?'

I don't remember any of this, not a fucking thing. I mean I just see a lawn, sometimes, maybe, sunshine, but . . . not really anything.

'Yes, I told him. And he promised that he'd change, relax more *around his character*, take it easy – really, he would say anything I wanted – but he couldn't keep the promises. He couldn't just be easy with you. He wasn't an easy man.'

Maura leaned forward and pressed the back of Mary's hand. 'He wrote more and more and lived less and less. I didn't want to leave him, but he'd already left me. I was tired of him getting up in the small hours, or coming to bed when I was asleep. The noise of his bloody machine, batting away. I forgot what he was like. Or I decided it was better if I tried to. We started fighting all the time. I had to go. Sorry.'

'I'm sure you did your best.' That didn't sound as if she meant it.

Maura stared across at her with a flat, cool look. 'Have you ever made love to a man and been absolutely sure he wasn't thinking of you? Better than that, have you been completely certain that he was comparing you to a woman who didn't exist, a woman he'd made to please himself, a woman he spent every day with? Or did you know that he'd take all the best of you and then tell it to somebody else?'

'I didn't mean –'

'I hated it when your father's friends came round to visit. One man in particular, his eyes on me always felt too well informed. I felt as if I'd been sold to them.' She breathed a laugh. 'And, I suppose, I had.'

337

Mary knew she was flushing slightly, but couldn't slither back from asking, 'He didn't . . .? I mean?'

'What?' Maura laughed. 'Oh, no. There was nothing . . . triangular going on. Except for in our minds.' She laughed again – this time a narrower, cooler sound. 'But then, with your father, the mind was everything.'

Mary shut her eyes – one weight too many loaded on and the balance of calm betrayed. A hope she hadn't known about was falling, spinning and splintering in her as it lanced down. She'd wanted better, something cleaner, or something neater than this.

'Mary. Mary?'

She wanted to raise her head when Maura called her, but couldn't. A breath shivered in her throat.

'Mary, I didn't mean to say that he wasn't a good man. I didn't ever mean that. He was very . . . he loved you.'

Mary shook her head, wishing she could cry now and not caring if it showed, but being – instead – pressed, throttled by an arid pain.

'He loved you. You mustn't think he didn't. You don't know. I told him that he couldn't see you and I made him agree. Because *I* couldn't see *him* – not without taking him back. Even with everything so wrong, I would have taken him back. He was, he was – he was so close to being worth it. He was almost worth anything.'

Mary let her hands be lifted, held.

'You have nothing to be ashamed of in him.'

They talked until the last of the evening had gone, until the room was yellow with street light. Mary found herself growing calmer, more assured, while Maura grew more anxious, attentive, motherly.

'I should go now, it's getting late.' She didn't know what to call her – Maura, or Mother.

'Have something to eat.'

'It's late.'

'You can stay here. I have a spare room. It won't be any bother.'

'No, really, I'm fine.'

'I haven't done this well, have I?' Maura stood, turned on the lamp and frowned at Mary through its unaccustomed glare. 'Have I?'

'No, you've been . . . This has been . . . what I needed.'

'I meant that I haven't done any of this well . . . this being a mother.'

'You've . . . I –'

'It's all right. I know.' She lifted her second pack of cigarettes and shook it – empty. 'You're sure you won't stay?' worrying her hair away from her eyes. 'No, of course you won't.' She looked immensely tired.

'Nathan – from the island – he got me somewhere in Pimlico. Somewhere I can stay.'

'Nathan.'

'Staples.'

'He's looking after you well?'

'Yes.'

'Does a good job?'

'Yes.' A small flare of nice awareness prickled through her slowly – not enough to disturb her, she was too tired – just enough to feel good. 'Yes, he does a great job. I'm very . . .'

Fond of him? Close to him? More? Feeling the kind of thing you would tell your mother? If you knew your mother.

'You're very . . . ?'

'I'm very pleased.' Mary picked the word randomly, but it seemed to serve.

'Good. Then I give him my best.' She met Mary's eyes – one deep catch of enquiry, almost of need. 'If you wanted to tell him that, it would be OK – that I give him my best.'

'All right. I will.'

Mary went back to the Square in the minicab her mother paid for with a quick, determined press of too much money, folded into Mary's hand. Sitting back, in motion, half-watching unknown streets and lights, Mary sensed herself beginning to be clean, somehow, scooped out and settling into a slightly different form. She thought she might be happy quite soon, doing what she wanted and – perhaps – in love. The idea, the temperature of loving slipped in thin as paper while the journey rocked and nudged.

I think he loves me back. I think.

If he did, I would love him.

Passing the Square's embankment façade, she noticed that part of the ornamental ironwork made exactly the shape of the wicked queen's crown from *The Lion, the Witch and the Wardrobe* – exactly the pattern of something that she hadn't known she knew. Somewhere she must have seen an illustration. Somewhere, when she was younger, still a child.

She went to bed certain, as she realised she'd always hoped she could be certain, that in her father she had nothing to be ashamed of, and that he was, tonight, hers and alive. She slept for fifteen hours, quite dreamlessly.

Nathan dreamed of eggs. They were impressively large eggs, above knee height, and sitting up on end together like a huge clutch of accusing Humpty Dumpties. He was pacing round them, mother-hennish, adjusting the warm, blood-soaked towels that they were draped in and trying to figure out just how many of these oddly incalculable objects there were.

When he woke, sweaty and unnerved, he was still desperately trying to count. Because – it was achingly plain to him – the eggs were his books. They were the secret of his books, they were the number of books that he would write, all swaddled up like threats and promises in a sticky fug of his own blood. And he couldn't help asking

What if I've used them all, written them all away? What if I've got nothing left?

God, you're a sick fuck.

*Yes, well, never mind all that. Have breakfast, take out Eckless, get yourself established in the day and then go and see her. She didn't come round yesterday and she **was** back, Joe went to fetch her and then, later, I could see her light. But she could have been tired, or just feeling antisocial, there could have been lots of reasons for her not popping in to see me, many of them unalarming. She didn't phone me while she was away, which was disappointing, but possibly quite understandable – her being busy and all that . . .*

He glowered again at his new mobile phone. Everyone on the island had one now. Joe had decided that they should all embrace a convenient touch of technology. God knew what the point was in Nathan's case. Now and again he would check if it was working, if he'd got the bloody thing turned on, but Mary hadn't called him in all of the time she was gone. And, to be honest, neither had any other bastard.

Dressed a little more presentably than was strictly necessary, he made a pot of tea and some rounds of toast and then set them out with the usual accompaniments before staring at the whole assembly until it was cold and congealed and completely beyond consumption.

I don't know how she'll be.

I don't know.

My wee woman, I don't know how she'll be.

Later in the day, anxious to keep himself busy, Nathan walked Eckless inland, close to the lochan. This was asking for trouble, he knew, because the place was always a bedlam in the spring: neurotic birds bickering thickly on the tiny central islet, like a huge, soprano, dysfunctional family. If anyone came near them, especially Eckless, the whole crew howled upwards into a ragged funnel of outrage, dingy bodies spinning like flakes of ash above some huge, invisible blaze.

In response, Eckless bayed and leaped, leaned himself against his unaccustomed leash until approaching strangulation and excitement made him cough. Although, Lord knew, even running loose, he'd do barely any damage. Nathan had seen him cowed by a single herring gull before now. The dog lacked the will for killing. But he did like to pretend.

Like master, like dog.

'Enough, though, you silly bastard, calm down.'

Not that Nathan was calm himself. He only ever came here for badness, for the joy of annoying already cantankerous gulls and being in the midst of a chaos that was in no way threatening. Although he would occasionally be dived at – all part of the fun.

'What on earth are you doing?' Richard's approach had been masked by the uproar. 'They're breeding.'

'Lucky them.'

'You shouldn't disturb them.'

'I don't. Often. Anyway, you're here too. Being disturbing.' He noticed Richard looked even more haggard than normal. 'What's up?'

'She's leaving.'

'What?' Nathan truly was surprised. He'd never imagined Lynda and Richard's marriage as being anything other than purgatorial, but he'd also never imagined them apart. 'Permanently?'

'America. She says she can't stand it here – too cold, too much like a madhouse.'

The feathery squeals and shrieks about them were shredding their sentences. Nathan found himself carefully mouthing, 'Well, for once, she's not wrong.'

Richard gripped Nathan's arm with a thin snarl, its sound ripped away. 'She won't say if she's coming back. But you don't give a shit, do you? You never fucking think of anyone but yourself. My wife is *leaving* me. You, of all people, might be expected to understand . . .' He panted quietly, through bared teeth.

'Yes, OK. It's only nerves, you know: trying to laugh through the crisis – it's the way I'm made.' Nathan checked Richard's expression, tried not to look sympathetic, but only like a man who did, indeed, understand. 'I take it you've been up all night.'

Richard nodded, winced his eyes shut.

'Then you should go home.' Nathan patted at Richard's arm and felt him shiver. 'But you could head over to my place instead. I've just replaced my emergency whisky again – you might as well get into that. Give me a couple of hours and I'll probably join you. In the end you will have to feel it, but I am of the opinion that if you want to be numb with exhaustion, or alcohol or self-inflicted pain or any other fucking thing you can think of, then you should just go ahead. You have every right.'

They began walking seaward again, Eckless tugging to play some more, a single scouting bird braced in the air above them, crying their position back to the lake.

'If she's going, *I* should go.' Richard was sounding more and more punch-drunk. 'I don't know why we ever came here.'

'Because Joe asked you, like he asked me, like he asked everybody.' Richard snapped him a look. 'All right – we came here because we're not fit for anywhere else. That's why we came and that's why we stay. At least, that's the way it is for me.'

'And that's why we kill ourselves.' Richard let out a nasty laugh. 'What did Joe tell you would happen if you managed the seven steps? If you actually didn't die. What did he say would happen that would be so fucking good?'

'He doesn't say – you know that.' Nathan fumbled around the vague nausea that always came when he found himself defending Joe.

343

'We stay here . . . because here there are people like us. We can belong and hate each other lovingly – like a family. And we can get . . . whatever's wrong with us right. Or make it not matter, or whatever the fuck we're after, or think we're after. We can get what we need. Apparently.'

'You believe that? That we'll get what we need?' Richard stopped. Nathan turned to him and recognised the look he must have had himself for years – the look of a man fighting lacerating appetite.

Richard couldn't help himself reaching for hope. 'Well, do you? Do you believe that?'

'I don't believe anything else.' Which was certainly fucking true. Nathan was an empty enough man to stay here and give Joe's craziness a try. And the island had given him Mary: Joe had given him Mary, he couldn't argue with that. A small and pleasant combustion unfurled in his lung – he'd be off to see her soon.

I'll find out how she is. What she heard about her father.

The combustion flared, anxious, dropped again.

'I . . .' Richard rubbed at his eyes, tiredness visibly stroking over him, numbing his mouth. 'I would like to – thank you – come back with you, but I won't. I can't. She'll, she'll still be there. You know – at ho . . . I have to . . . be there, too.'

'OK. I understand.' Nathan thought of saying more, of giving the poor fuck a hug to speed him on his way, but Richard stumbled round, surprisingly quick in an unsteady way, and trudged back towards the lochan, taking what wasn't remotely his quickest way home. Nathan didn't call him back, let him step down to the first anxious spinning of wings, the outbreak of visible madness, screeling and gyring in the air. Best place for him.

He didn't mean to watch. At first, it didn't even feel like watching – only a glimpse of something and then the natural turn of his head to find it out.

Nathan had dawdled home, trying to think of how he should be, how best to slip in on Mary casually. Eckless, still leashed, had given up tugging out Morse reminders of his unwillingly tethered state and mooched along beside his master, washed out with a good morning's baying and quite possibly lost in wolfish daydreams of dominated feathers and freed blood.

344

They passed by the back of Nathan's house, his bedroom window, the skip of shade behind it, someone inside.

Mary?

Perhaps if she'd noticed he was there, hadn't been so intent, it would never have happened. And he would never have found himself observing, his heart like a frog on a spike, kicking and twitching clammily.

Mary had moved to stand with her back to the window, facing the head of his bed. Something about the quality of her pause, the tension plain in her spine made him pause, too, and only look – not trot up and knock the glass, smile his hello.

Then quickly, smoothly she knelt near his pillow, her hand at the pale angle of open sheet where he'd left his covers back. His breath furrowed and locked while she leaned forward, rested her head where his had lain and waited – he knew, waited – until her skinheat raised his scent from the cloth, until it felt right to ease her fingers between the sheets, push in deep to the wrist.

No.

Wax-mouthed, he braced himself against the touch of her thinking, the crawl at him of her wanting the man he wasn't, couldn't be: of her taking and crumpling his quite different colour of love to nothing but the new, grey sweat that covered him.

No.

Pulling Eckless up out of his slump, Nathan backed, staggered, almost fell away. He didn't stop going until the cottage was blinded to him, no windows in sight, and then he dropped to the grass, sick pain in his legs and hands.

Her eyes had been closed. Of course. He knew the drill. All through the bad days at the end, he'd lain on her mother's bed every single afternoon and done the same: aching and shifting and breathing Maura's separate sleeping in, right in, eyes always shut to keep out any traces of impossibility. It must be in their genes: like father like daughter: their capacity for longing.

Eckless whined, confused at being so close to home without going inside it. He gave a single, pettish bark, quite loud enough for Mary to hear him in the house.

Which is the way to do this. The only fucking way. To warn her of my arrival, make her stop.

Shit. Just, shit. If I'd told her, this would never have happened. If I'd just fucking said who I was.

He clapped at Eckless, dunted his neck, mock wrestled him by the front paws until he was fixed in a happy frenzy. Then he let the dog loose. Eckless crouched and stared for a moment, wondering whether to run or stay and play.

'Go on. Go home. Go and get Mary. Mary. Where's Mary?'

Which did the trick. Eckless clawed across the grass and disappeared around the house. He would then either huff and clatter in, one solid black excitement, or he would thump himself at the door until someone unlocked it. Until Mary unlocked it. Whichever way he arrived, he would disturb her. He would stop her, he would make her stop.

'Hello, anyone there?' Nathan couldn't help it, he had to say something, break the air.

She was sitting at the kitchen table. Eckless – his paws on her knees – was lifting his head to her for strokes. 'Yes. Only me.'

Nathan caught her smile and felt all his gathered solidity shudder and slap. Nothing else about her would have told him what she'd done, except that softness, the almost lazy, secretive close of her lips. So like her mother.

'Only you, eh? So. Back then.' He could tell she was trying to catch his eye, but he couldn't let her. He sat, lumpish, the table between them. 'It, ahm – you don't have to say – but did it . . . It went well?' He rested his forearm along the table top as casually as he could, then saw that his muscles were shaking from his elbow to his fingertips. Too late now, though, to move it back. 'You found out . . . anything . . . enough?'

Or perhaps she found out everything.

Perhaps that's why she came here. Perhaps that's . . . No.

She reached to cup her hand over his knuckles and sent a fear he'd never contemplated rifling up his neck.

'I found out that my father was . . . not a bad man.' She stopped, apparently discontented with the way that sounded. 'I think I believe that he was good. No. I'm sure I believe that, because I –'

She paused, waiting, silent until he ground his head round and finally did face her: swallowing too much, thoughts scattering. There was no denying that she looked fantastically well.

'Because you what?' His voice whimpering out, small and woolly.

'I miss him.'

Under her palm, between their two skins, he could feel the start of a mixing sweat. 'You?' He coughed, wheezed down an uneasy handful of breath, his past bursting under his skin.

'I miss him. I never – are you all right?'

'Mm hm.' He made sure he didn't cough again.

'I haven't missed him before, really ever, I don't think. Or not for a very long time. I can just about remember, maybe, that I imagined he was away travelling. He was a story – a little man walking in something like a desert – so hot that no aeroplane could fly there and the post wouldn't ever get through because it would burn and no one could ever see him. I hadn't thought of all that in years, but – coming back on the train – I realised the story had started out by explaining why I never heard from him. Or maybe why he died. Or it could have been a dream I had. He was so long ago. But now I miss him.'

'I'm sorry.'

Jesus Christ, let go my hand. Please, fuck, because I'll move, I'll move and I'll touch you, I'll touch you back and mean what I mean, and only what I mean, but what you'll misunderstand.

Now it was her turn to falter, drop her gaze. 'It's, it's not bad really. I should be taking notes, mm? Of the feelings.'

'You should be feeling them – the notes will take care of themselves.'

'Only teasing.'

Her last word shivered across the table at him, made them both shift slightly. She lifted away her hand and settled it with the other in her lap. 'Only pulling your leg. Nathan?'

Her voice round his name – it used to be such a good fit.

'Nathan – knowing he's alive, it seems to have made everything more . . . more definite. What I feel about all kinds of things . . .'

Shit, she's going to tell me.

'I went to see my mother for two reasons – not only to ask about my father. I wanted her to know about something that was happening here, on the island, but then I didn't tell her. Silly, really, because I could have. Only I thought I might talk to you first, I thought –'

He rushed in hard, voice over-loud, 'That's good, that's very good. Great. And we *will* talk, but, you know, I have to go and see Joe. Now. Right now. In fact, I'm a bit late. I'd intended to just leave Eckless here and then go straight across. Do you think this could be postponed at all? Hm?' Nathan attempted to crank up a breezy grin.

'Oh.'

She seemed, for an instant, slightly stunned and he wanted to be able to hug her and make them both feel better uncomplicatedly.

But he kept himself reserved, pacy, 'You don't mind?' and also – he was quite certain – rather obviously mad-eyed.

'No. No. We've got plenty of time.'

'That's right. Absolutely right. Look, I'm really so glad that things turned out well – about your father.'

'She never said who he was.'

'Hm?' He'd been about to stand, to escape, walk her outside, shut the door very firmly and get them both away – away to quite separate places. 'She never . . . ?'

'Said who he was.' She looked at him, 'But she thought he would tell me in the end,' like cold water over his scalp, 'she told me it was up to him to say,' like a kiss on each eyelid, each palm, 'oh and she gave you her best,' a crochet hook finding his spine.

'That's . . . she . . . ?' He did stand now, nerveless, beyond thought.

'She asked if you were looking after me and I said that you were and then she told me to give you her best.'

'Well . . . well. Good. I have to go now. Yes.'

Her best. My God, her best.

'Her what?'

'Her *hand*. Jesus fuck, there's nothing else that sounds like hand – her *hand*.' Nathan was beginning to see the point of his mobile phone. It meant he could call from the cliffs above his bay, lie and feel the grass around him being ruffled, combed in the wind and wish that his brain could be ruffled and combed, too.

'In your bed . . . *Her* hand in *your* bed.' J. D. sniffed in the manner of a man for whom brisk inhalation was a favourite pursuit. 'And all the rest . . . that's . . . hold on.' Nathan could hear a vaguely chiding voice, muffling out something to Jack. Then an equally disgruntled reply, 'Well, I can't help that, I haven't done it yet. No one could have done it yet. Tell him . . . tell him it's the next thing on my desk and I will stay late this evening *again* and I will then leave it on *his* desk before I go home in order to come in early and do something else which has nothing to do with my job description. OK?' A wounded mutter bounced back. 'OK. I know it has nothing to do with you. I do quite heartily wish that it also had nothing to do with me.' Another unhappy murmur. 'Fine.'

Nathan felt he should suggest, 'I could ring you back later.'

'I'd still be here. And still working. It doesn't matter. Well, it only matters to me. Christ, I'd rather do anything than this job. We used to be gentlemen in publishing, we used to burn out sedately in our sixties, having quite possibly made some good books. We had time to care. My superior is fifteen years younger than me and if he promotes me any further sideways I'll be strapped to the side of the building in the window cleaners' cradle with a queue of young Turks all wrestling each other to fray my suspension cables. Sorry – you had a problem. Ah, yes . . .' Jack breathed carefully, brought his voice a little closer. 'It's a problem of your own making, of course. Apologies for saying so, Sport, but really . . .'

'I know. I should have told her. I thought that if I liked her, she would understand I was liking her – well, loving her – in a fatherly way and then she would like me and then, when I felt it was right, I could tell her and nothing would go wrong. Fuck, J. D., I've waited so long – I can't have it not work . . . when I finally say what I have to, things have to be all fine. I couldn't bear it not being fine.' Nathan stared at the ease and curve of the waves, hoping it would pace his breathing.

'Nathan.' Jack rolled out his smoothest, calmest voice. 'Nathan, this is me you're talking to. I know you. I've been tinkering with your manuscripts for – what – twelve, fourteen years? So I know you. Some days I've been in your head far more than I've been in my own. You'll manage this. You've got good old Uncle Jack to help you and difficulties of this sort are my speciality.'

'*Making* them, yes.'

'And then leaving them rapidly. I can be out of a relationship in the time most men would take to tie their laces. Trust me – you know you want to. And when all of this is settled, I'll let you in on my plan to retire and corner the market in vanity lamination. Imagine it, all those sticky little poems for dead babies and those single ladies' odes to their cats, or their cakes, or their cunts – the muck even pay-per-view presses won't take . . . I shall go forth and gather it up and turn it into plasticised mementoes – especially suitable for graves. Which would prove handy because I feel I might end up shooting a fair number of my clients through the eyes. Just for fun. And let's face it, who'd miss them? Not me, obviously. Or, if I did, I could always fire again.' Jack brought himself to a halt. Paused. 'Nathan. Lighten up.'

'Then tell me what to do!' He hadn't meant to sound so bereft. 'Please. I'll lighten up when I've got a solution. Really, I will.'

'All right, all right, relax. You don't have to tell her anything directly. You don't have to have a scene. Just arrange to be otherwise and rather off-puttingly engaged.'

'But I'm not.'

'But you will arrange to be. Temporarily. As soon as possible. Tonight.'

'I can't get somebody *tonight*.'

'Of course you can.'

'I can't do it.'

'Think of the alternative, Nathan – then you'll find that you can.'

Jonathan, he meant what he meant. He was straightforward. Most of the time he was, in any case.

Mary was trying to read a note. She wasn't having much success.

Nathan, he can be lovely one day – a bit of a bugger, but fine – and then the next time you meet him, he'll have locked himself down again, won't even give you a smile.

The folded paper had been slipped underneath her door while she was out and now she held it, almost glared at it, in an attempt to pay any attention to what it said.

This didn't work.

I love the way he laughs, though. As if he doesn't want to and it's taken him by surprise. He'll tuck his hands in his pockets, or he'll fold his arms and duck his head, avoiding it. But then he'll let go. Sometimes, he'll really almost hoot until he's wiping his eyes and unsteady, supporting himself on the furniture, on people, on me. Then he looks the way you'd think he could be all the time – like a man who knows how to be happy, who stands well – lean, tight muscle in his legs, good hips.

It was difficult to read with a mind full of tripwires and ribbons, all of them straggling off towards Nathan, or parts of Nathan, shades and ideas of him.

The smell of him, it's delicate, faint: more like a temperature or a touch than a proper scent: but on his pillow, it was there. I found it.

Her stomach gave a small, electric twist.

I could find him, really find him. If that's what I wanted. Maybe. I could find him. If that's what he wanted me to do.

Once again, she concentrated on the note. This time, it caught hold and told her that Lynda was leaving, that she should come over to her cottage this evening and say goodbye.

Nathan wanted to know where Richard was, but Lynda wasn't

351

telling. Given the circumstances, this was a more than minor irritation.

'He's around.'

'*Around.*' He pawed at his cheeks nervously. 'As in *back soon, around*? As in *bursting through the door any minute full of outrage* around? As in *taking a swing at Nathan* around? You couldn't be specific?' He let go of his face and started to massage his neck while he shook his head. 'Oh, shit, I can't do this anyway, I don't know why I'm asking. Bollocks.' He continued to plod out a neatly oval course between the sofa and the fireplace. It seemed prudent to stay on the move.

'Nathan, I said I would help you and I will. I am already doing you an extraordinary favour. At least try to be even remotely courteous, because there *were* other things I would rather have done tonight. And, just for the record, I think you're insane.'

'Where's Richard?'

'Oh, for Christ's sake!'

Lynda briefly seemed to be on the point of slapping him and he found the prospect curiously comforting – at least one thing this evening that he might understand.

But then she restrained herself, hissed in a breath and sighed it out again. 'Anything to shut you up. Richard is over with Joe and will be spending the night at the Lighthouse.'

'The *night*?'

'There's no need to squeal. He is staying the night because of *us.*' Nathan could feel himself blanch, but listened while she made herself clear. 'By which I mean the Richard and I *us* – not the you and me *us*. As if there ever was such a thing. The thought of you being here overnight is enough to make me gag.'

'Thank you.'

'I just wanted to make it clear. There'll be no need for you to stay here a moment longer than is strictly necessary. Now will you *sit down.*'

'I don't want to.'

Lynda clicked her tongue, shot him an elaborate look of impatient contempt and then settled back in her armchair with a magazine – her dressing gown falling open to her knee, in a slithering little threat. Eckless grumbled in the corner behind her. He was in a huff, unsure of what was happening exactly, but certain that it was some kind of stupidity.

352

And he's right, poor bloody dog. They're both right – I am insane. I am completely off my fucking head. And this isn't going to work, I don't know why I'm even trying it. This will only make everything worse.

Fuck, I need a piss.

'I need a piss.'

'Thank you for sharing that. *Another* piss?'

'Yes, another one.'

Eckless raised one eyebrow at his master balefully and sighed.

Lynda only smirked. 'Nervy, aren't we?'

'Yes, yes, yes. Fine. Yes. Nervous. Yes, I am.'

He sprang up, agreed himself viciously across to the bathroom, stepped inside, threw the bolt, and at once felt a fraction of the evening's torque easing out from his vertebrae. His pathetically self-conscious bladder doled out a token trickle while he tried to hold his dick with a properly disinterested air: as if he were not thinking of Lynda thinking of his holding it and thinking of her thinking.

Christ.

Then he washed his hands. A lot.

I am a grown-up. I am the **man** *in this situation. I am a grown-up man. And I am doing what I have to do. She's only helping.*

So I should be in charge. Or at least an equal. At least a fucking equal.

God, help me get through this with any dignity. Let it all be as simple as Jack said.

For fuck's sake, I'm relying on Jack Grace – this is absolutely an all-time fucking low.

Lynda yodelled charmingly from behind the door. 'You're taking your time. Having a quickie before we start?'

'You know, you could try to enjoy this a little less. I know you *want* to humiliate me.' He clumped back out into the room. 'But I am about to do that, all by myself.'

'Oh, cheer up, for God's sake. You don't even need to feel guilty, I told Richard all about it.'

'You what!'

'He *is* my husband – for the moment – I did think that he should know. And, because he is mature and has a backbone, he understands. He said to tell you it was fine.'

Nathan was about to argue that Richard wasn't mature, or especially vertebrate, only in shock, when she reminded him, 'I told her to be here at seven-thirty. It's not far off that now. We should be ready.'

She stood and slipped off her dressing gown before he could speak. Then she turned to him, revealing the full-frontal view of the traditional, time-dishonoured adultery kit: basque and matching knickers, stockings with seams at the back. He was immediately washed with an awful desire to snigger and then a slimmer, more robust inclination to take an unspecified but degrading advantage of all this, to get genuinely, mindlessly sullied and really screw everything right up. She smelt of woman: those particular, undeniable notes of heat.

Lynda eyed him flatly. 'Do you want me in heels, or can we just make do with this? I really can't be bothered going to fetch them.'

'This is . . .' He nodded in lieu of producing a word that he couldn't quite think of right now. 'What time is it?'

'Seven-thirty.'

Shit. I'm not ready for this.

Nathan quietly pictured himself tucked away into a coffin on a furnace-bound conveyor, helplessly propelled towards destruction.

Anything rather than this.

He shuffled himself to within his arms' reach of Lynda as his heart and blood and breath and sweat all betrayed him distractingly.

Lynda entirely neglected to stifle a yawn and scooped her right breast up and over its containment. He noticed her nipple was lost in its areola, flat – completely and contemptuously somnolent.

'Do you think that's absolutely . . .' Again his vocabulary deserted under fire and he tried to stare at her warningly, sure he was appearing only witless, blank. 'You'll kiss me? Be kissing me?'

'I'll be exactly what I need to be.'

'I wish you wo–'

Eckless shifted and stood, stared towards the door, his tail wagging modestly.

If I shut my eyes, I'll make it worse.

No. No, in fact, it's better. Much.

He extended his arms forward blindly. Footsteps closed outside, past the curtained cottage window. His embrace was pushed aside. Eckless whined. And then Lynda yelled out, 'No, we don't have time. I told you.'

Nathan, mystified, staggered back a little at the slap of sound, but then felt something he didn't wish to understand.

*Not **there***. She surely —

The noise of his zip, descending defencelessly. The long lost combination of breathy warmth and opened chill. A hand clasped at the back of his thigh.

Eckless was barking now.

Nathan couldn't help but open his eyes, look down, 'What are you — ?' at Lynda's forehead resting quiet against his belt, while her right hand adjusted his dress more than vigorously, 'No,' and — unmistakably — her laughter pressed in through his gaping flies and cuffed his bollocks with the shock of steam and his prick pricked.

'Oh, Jesus.'

And, naturally, the front door opened and there was Mary as, 'Fuck,' his hands flailed out for balance and gripped at Lynda's head with apparent passion, apparent lust, and his naked eyes (exactly as stupefied as they would have been if this was in any way real) met his daughter's face and he could only gape and whimper, his throat furred up with shame, before she turned and started leaving and he managed to call, 'Mary,' when everything was too late.

Shit.

Lynda sat back on her heels, left him alone.

Shit.

The front door slammed behind his daughter. He heard her footsteps rush away.

Shit.

It was all the way it had to be.

Shit.

A total fuck-up.

Shit.

Just the way it had to be.

The cottage ached with sudden quiet. Slowly, Lynda stood, put on her dressing gown and moved her chair. Nathan folded both hands tight at the back of his neck. 'Thank you.'

'Mm hm. Do yourself up.'

He frowned at her, groggy, then realised his condition and, ludicrously, turned his back to fasten his flies. 'That's it, then.' He faced her again. 'All over.'

'Nathan, you're crying.'
'I know.'

It's his life. Which is good. I wouldn't want it.
First Mary had walked up to Lynda's.
It's his life.
Which is nothing to do with me.
And now she was walking back home.
Just up to Lynda's and then back.
Lynda's.
He was with Lynda.
It was all oddly simple, if she didn't think of why she was coming back.
*With **Lynda**.*
Fuck.
*Not **fuck** – **fucking**. The right word is **fucking**.*
Her brain felt clammy, grubby, jolted somewhere behind her eyes.
Fucking Lynda.
She could still see perfectly clearly, but nothing she looked at seemed able to *mean* anything.
Nathan. Fucking.
The half-clear picture of that made her
Embarrassed. Ashamed for myself. More ashamed for him. The way he looked – so
So
It was a nice evening. She was aware of that. It was clear, so you could see the stars, which was good, even if it meant you might be slightly cold. And the sky was that particular deep and glowing, stained-glass blue that came right before true night. This was Mary's favourite time – had been Mary's favourite time of the day.
So
So scared. He looked so scared and so silly and so old.
He looked so old.
Once she reached the Nissen hut, there seemed to be no harm in not going inside, in just sitting down on the step, in smelling the spring pushing forward to summer, the insistence of green.
I wasn't sure . . . I wasn't . . . I had wondered, I had tried to imagine the way that he would be . . . touching . . . with someone.

356

A blackbird off behind the hut hammered narrow metal notes up into nowhere.

With someone. Not with Lynda. Just with someone.

Someone else. Other than Lynda.

I'd thought he'd look better than that.

It occurred to her that she was tired. She was tired, most especially of missing people, of missing Morgan and missing Bryn, of missing Jonathan, of missing the ghost of her mother, of missing a father who was less than that. And now she was missing Nathan – missing the man she'd supposed him to be. The loss of him seeped round her, thick in the dark like a night blossom's scent.

I could manage without him. I've done that before.

The scent clawed gently in her throat.

He was sad when he saw me, seeing him. That made him sad.

I could manage without him.

I could.

I just don't want to, that's all.

I don't want to.

When she was almost ready to go indoors, the quiet air brought her first the sound of Eckless trotting and then Nathan's slower walk. The pair were going home. If she peered to her left, she could make out the blur of their moving forms in the weak moonlight.

He isn't happy – not if he's shuffling like that.

The idea of his face, snapping round to her – that single, startled look – made her feel slightly sick.

But I would rather have him with me than not.

For the work.

Just for the work.

'Nathan!' Her shout seemed enormously loud after so much silence – she even surprised herself. Immediately, one of the figures stumbled while the other bounced and barked, steered towards her.

'Mary?' Nathan's voice seemed in some way weakened, bared.

'Yes.'

Sod, now I don't know what to say. **Did you have a nice time?**

Something of anger and something of sadness grated in her, faded, and left her simply feeling stupid and too much alone.

'Mary?' Nathan sounded as if he were lost.

'Yes.' Eckless barrelled into her in the dark, winding himself, but

357

springing back: all earthy paws and curiosity, tongue flannelling her hand. She tried to hold him still. 'God, boy, get off. Settle.'

'Mary?' Or perhaps, she now thought, Nathan sounded more as if he were scared she was lost.

'Yes! Yes, I'm here.' She realised that she hoped he would stay where he was – wouldn't come any closer to her now. 'I just wanted to say goodnight. So. Goodnight.'

A soft jumble of noise came to her, unintelligible.

'What? Nathan? I couldn't hear that.'

'Will I come over? Over there?'

'No.' She hadn't meant to say that so firmly.

'Oh. I . . .' There was a space of silence and she wondered if she was, again, missing what he said, until, 'I quite understand.'

'But I did want to say goodnight.'

'Thank you.' Again a weakness, a break in the tone.

'Goodnight, Nathan.'

She stood, nudged Eckless away, but found that he wouldn't leave her.

'What?' Nathan sounded slightly closer, but she couldn't quite tell.

'I was trying to . . . Could you call Eckless? He won't leave me.'

Mary patted the dog goodbye and listened to Nathan, more like himself, coaxing the dog home, and then calling once again, 'Mary?'

'Yes.'

'Goodnight.'

She pushed open her door and he shouted again.

'Mary?'

'Yes. I said, yes.'

'Thank you.'

She could think of no answer to give him back.

'Mary? Are you –'

'What?'

'Are you all right.'

'No.'

'I . . .'

'But I will be.'

'You will be? Will you?'

'Goodnight, Nathan. Goodnight.'

J. D. Grace, Jack Grace, Mr Jack Dowd Grace stood at his office window and pondered the patterns of the night, its glimmers, flares and shades. Stacked above and below him and chaining out to either side there were other office windows, all empty now. And directly ahead of him, caught in his window's glass, a further office shone, its image stammered and repeated by the double glazing. Reflections blurred across reflections of almost the office he called his own. He scanned the phantom bookshelves he'd never rifle, the ghost of a paper-littered desk and the insubstantial image of a tired man whom he did not wish to know: a paunchy, seedy figure, smirred eyes glistening shiftily.

Jack gently touched his forehead to the smooth cool of the glass. The tired man did the same.

Of course, he'd had another dreadful day. Panic had slithered on panic and then everyone came in to scream for a slice of his head. But that was all finished now, the work finally done, his body filled with the cottony, grainy calm of complete exhaustion. Jack turned back away from the view, stretched, tried to think of the last occasion when he'd really worked as he wanted to. He found that he couldn't remember and also couldn't particularly care.

In search of consolations, he slipped in behind his desk and half-filled his coffee mug from the bottle of tequila he'd left sleeping in his drawer. He'd been sober all week, stone-cold sober. Which is how it felt – like being cold stone.

A simple sip or two would just unfreeze him, just let him be human for a while, just let him have a rest before he had to head for Islington, for a minor attempt at sleep. His sleeping wasn't so great, right now: not too reliable. In fact, this was the only good bit any more, sitting here and sipping and feeling the atoms start up dancing in his throat, his corpuscles' ruby shine. In and of himself, with only a little, little drink, he could be his own fireside, his own home away from nowhere in particular that he felt he could call a home.

To his right (he knew and did not really want to look) there were his bookshelves and on them the alphabetically ordered and comprehensive collection of his books, safe in their fold and all the way back to the first he'd ever edited, a thousand years ago. His books. He'd looked after every one of them, brought them to light. At one time they had been able to make him proud.

This wouldn't do. He was getting maudlin and tonight he hadn't the energy for that. He decided to make himself happy with a recitation of one of his lists. He had any number of lists, all cheering: the names of all the people he'd kill slowly one fine day, the types of unnatural death he'd prepare for them, the types of unnatural act he had performed and in what places, the types of unnatural act he still wanted to perform and with whom he would like to perform them. All good, all good.

But what he needed now was his Shorter Catalogue of Hate.

Jack tipped back his chair and swung up his heels to rest them on his desk. Then he began.

He hated each and every particle of this building with a deep and righteous hate.

He hated the air conditioning – its constant, fucking drone, the black, infectious dust that crept out around its grilles, the carcinogenic vapours it circulated, unzipping his DNA with every breath.

He hated the motley furniture, the cheap motel chipboard doors, the ghastly bloody carpet in excremental brown and all the shabby fucking stains thereon.

He hated the papery people, their malign and perverse observations, their slipping and sniffing about, their constant peculiar thirst for ruin and slander.

He hated the empty ache of computer screens, the photocopier's sour breath, the trashy, bitter reek of new paper and too much print.

He hated every fucking bastard agent in every fucking bastard agency. Sly and greedy cunts, cunts, cunts.

He hated every fucking bastard critic in every fucking bastard magazine and paper. Sly and witless cunts, cunts, cunts.

He hated every fucking bastard arse-mouthed no-balled fucker of a lousy writer. Stupid, stupid, time-wasting, greedy, witless, arrogant, self-obsessed cunts, cunts, cunts.

He hated the lunge and fumble of bad writing in his brain – all the time in his brain – the mutter and jump of manuscripts as they jerked off their watery efforts inside his mind, as they wasted his intelligence, as they dry-fucked his privacy, as they made him disappointed beyond bearing.

And he hated himself for not wanting to care any more. He hated the fact that he'd rather not fight for the voices, the proper voices, the new words that still found the old joy and made it articulate. He hated that he longed only to stop. He hated that all he was good for now was hate.

Jack Dowd Grace hated the man that he was and did not wish to be.

And that was enough.

That was more than enough.

Time to go.

As he eased on his coat and scooped up his briefcase, Jack thought of Nathan, of how he was. Nathan his friend, his very oldest friend. The thought of him made Jack happy, which was all that he had ever wished to be.

1995

Party time again.

Outside the club's opened windows, the dark of Soho was slippery with heat: roads and pavements locked into one damp, elbowing, ill-tempered crawl. Inside, as far as Jack could judge, things were pretty much the same. Not that he minded, dear me, no – like this, it was so much more cosy and humane. What better recreation for a gentleman of publishing than to slither and sweat with others of his merry kind while surrounded by emporia of altogether less stimulating perversities.

'Jack, I have no idea what you're talking about.' Lynda smiled in that wonderful *I really don't like you, but I just might fuck you* kind of way. 'Not a bloody clue.'

'Ignore me, then. I'm being happy.'

'That's not like you.'

'It's not like *you* to even be here. You haven't cruised this particular circle of hell in years. In fact . . .' He frowned contentedly, enjoying his mind's random skid and plummet through loose information. 'First you were over with Nathan and that mob and then . . . I thought you'd emigrated. Australia?'

'America.' For the fourth or fifth time, she glanced beyond his shoulder and smiled a greeting. 'But now I'm back. In the flesh.'

'Yes, quite.' He gave her a meaningful look and got one back. This was all starting to seem quite promising. 'But do stop that.'

'What, Jack dear?'

'Dividing your attention. It makes me feel unloved.'

'I was just nodding hello to Benedict.'

'Benedict Kemmler? That shit.' His conviviality briefly threatened to evaporate.

'Now, now. He's no worse than you.' She moved in to clamp one arm around Jack's waist. 'His heart's in the right place.'

365

'No. It's still beating in his chest.' He turned to deliver his best breathy whisper close to her ear. 'If it was in the right place, it would be in my refrigerator.' She shivered against him gratifyingly and he tried to recall unto whom she had given the clap and at what point. He knew it had been a long time ago, back when even *he* was young and when the clap and the pox were the worst you could possibly catch. Oh, and crabs, of course. Happy days. Although, from wife number two, he'd always suspected a low-grade but persistent rabies risk . . .

Lynda dabbed a kiss at his cheek – magnificently insincere. 'Now *I'm* the one who's feeling unloved. You're not thinking about me, are you? And I don't like that – people's minds wandering. If I wanted to be forgotten about, I could just go home to Richard, couldn't I?'

'A thousand apologies. Why don't we . . .' He pondered fleetingly the likelihood of his being already too drunk to get it significantly up. He decided to introduce a small, transitional step along the way to what he hoped might be a pleasantly meaningless experience. 'Why don't we cut a dash through the soggy mass to that suspiciously darkened corner over there? Then you can tell me all about it.'

'About what?'

She was already moving with him, warm, grinding and nudging aside the usual smug little cliques. Tonight he didn't mind them. 'About?' Good movement in her hips. Impressive. 'Oh, whatever . . .' This was good. This was another good thing when he actually already had a few. He was, in fact, on the up and up all round: genuinely back in business. 'Tell me about America. Land of the free.' A couple of truly cracking books lined up for the autumn, a smear of respect here and there about the office and now this – tonight's arguably overheated bonus, the company of a splendidly sluttish, mediocre women's-novel novelist. 'Exactly how free did America mean you could be?'

'You really want to know?'

They were lodged now, Lynda safely in the crook of the silent baby grand and Jack's back to the wall – his favourite position. 'Is it all very sordid?'

'Yes.'

'Then of course I want to know.'

'Really, Jack, has anyone suggested that you're turning into a caricature of yourself?'

'No, no, no – I've always been larger than life.' Jack gave her his most convincingly well-endowed smile, 'Now. Speak to me,' and waited for the grubby press of observation to start on his skin. He was going to be a player again soon – worth gossiping about – so this little scene could get as theatrical as it liked. Onlookers could look on.

'Oh, all right.' Lynda pulled her arm back from hugging his tender kidneys and then reapplied it, having first darted it into the humid space between his jacket and his shirt. 'I went to California, because I needed some sun and some optimism and just some fucking *youth*. And where the hell would I get that in this country?'

'My dear lady, I could not agree more. So you flew off and fucked surfers, hm?'

Lynda eyed him severely. This was the point where they either hit you, or threw wine, applied a swift knee to the testes, or possibly walked off yelling, or else – as she was doing, bless her – simply decided to ditch their dignity and go on. 'You are a prick, Jack, aren't you?'

Speaking of throwing wine, 'Not quite the verb I'd have chosen. I do *have* one . . .' he'd run out. No more wine. 'Do go on.' Which made for an awfully poor show. Lynda, he'd noticed, was still fussing with almost a full measure of the dismal red the bar was doling out. 'But first, let's have our hands unencumbered.' He took her glass, drained it with unfeigned passion and set it aside on the opened piano's strings. It raised a tiny dissonance. 'Mm. Well. That's better, isn't it.'

Almost directly beneath Jack's feet, Nathan was cornered in another broiling room. He had, quite recently, noticed that he was softly treading through any number of abandoned canapés.

Fuck. So this is where they've all got shot of them. I had to sodding eat mine.

The conversations around him jarred along with a clinical cheerfulness which led him to believe he'd fallen amongst a whinny of PR persons.

Whinny *is the correct collective noun, I'm sure. Or possibly a* ***fawning***. *Although it should be a* ***lie***, *naturally.*

367

He shifted oozily over dead sushi and puff-pastry fragments and considered just butting his head against one of the walls.

Or all of them. One at a time. But then the PR persons would rush up and be forced by naked instinct to congratulate me on my butting technique, or tell me how much better my face looked once my forehead was the size and consistency of a rancid cantaloupe. Whatever shite they'll think I want to hear.

Oh bollocks, why did I come? I've been on the island too long now, that's the problem – I can't be with this many people at once any more. Not that I ever could. The problem is really . . .

He tapped the back of his skull experimentally against a low picture rail.

The problem is really that I had contemplated having other plans. Sad fucker that I am. First, get Mary here for the party, another educational trip – show her about a bit, now that her work's getting known – do the needful and . . .

His patience with his self-deception tinned out like the element in an especially low-wattage bulb.

You were going to ditch Mary here and go off, weren't you? You were going to weasel out Maura's address and then scuttle off to see her, see her street, see the shine in her living-room window, bedroom window, how would you really know? You would never have the backbone to knock on her door and find out.

*Or – as it turns out – the backbone to even **get** her sodding address. So you'll just have to stay around here: one more for the evening's running count of soured menopausal men.*

He started to scrape his shoes clean on the skirting board while an aggressively jodhpured young woman stared at him. When he looked up again, she was marching across. 'You're Nathan Staples, aren't you? I love your books.'

'That makes one of us.'

She released a delighted, animal bray. 'No, really . . .'

'*Yes*, really . . .' He had absolutely never been less in the mood for this. Their conversation, Nathan feared, could only end with his grey-spattered figure being dragged from her twitching, headless body – his one fist still deep in her cranium, swinging it round like a hairy bowling ball. Or would it look more like a very bloated mitten?

She giggled and glistened up at him – every inch the sacrificial offering. 'I saw you in the corner there – thinking.'

'I'd hoped it wouldn't show.'

'In fact *I* was also thinking . . .' giggling, she suddenly muffled both his ears with weirdly smooth hands, 'I'd like to . . .' tugging him down to meet her mouth, 'kiss your brain.' She did indeed deposit a wet stamp of admiration on his forehead. 'Your lovely little brain.'

'Um.' He reared back as politely as he could. 'Yes. You haven't seen Jack Grace, have you? I feel that I may need to speak to him. Right away.'

'Oh, I wouldn't bother. Even if he's here, by this time he won't be making any sense.'

'That's fine. I don't want him to.'

'I'd really like you to stay.' She granted him another Campari and cocaine snigger.

'Mm, I know it. 'Bye.'

Jack was finding things difficult to believe. He loved it when reality slopped out of control this way. 'Surely you're not suggesting that you could *accommodate* that – not without reconstructive surgery, at least. Even a *child's* stump . . . if they'd just lost a foot or a hand . . . you couldn't get it in . . . you couldn't take it . . . up you.' Good words, most especially when found together, *up* and *you*.

Lynda smoothed his hair behind his ear and smirked. 'A stump doesn't have to go *up* to be exciting. Even the look of them . . . soft and blind and hard all at once, the pallor, the scarring . . . They're wonderful.'

'You are a very beautifully twisted woman.'

'That's why I'm talking to you.' She whispered, 'But I didn't cross the fucking Atlantic for the amputees. They were only an optional extra – not the main event.'

'Do you think we should sit?' He had, in fact, already started a comforting slide down the wall. His back and head were both, no doubt, leaving a sweat trail as he sank.

'Well, if you really can't keep upright . . .' She descended with him. The leather, or plastic, or rubber, or whatever black and glossy stuff her jeans were made of puckered and distended liquidly.

It was better to be on the floor, J. D. thought, much more private, and much more stable if he started to feel at all strange. Because, it

369

had to be admitted, odd turns did take him, now and then. If he had another drink he'd be settled, absolutely fine, but this wasn't exactly the moment for leaving to get one. He sat with his legs flat out before him and then reached to peruse the length of Lynda's thigh, he hoped with a properly lascivious attention. 'So if you weren't there for the Freudian limb ends . . . ?'

'As I've said, I didn't go for the *amputees*. I went for the *amputators*. I went for the Red Triangle – the zone of optimum risk. I went for the sharks. God's oldest and most beloved and sexiest fucking fish.'

'Mmm.' Something was scrabbling through the nerves at the back of Jack's eyes, but if he pressed his temples fiercely, the sensation almost went away. 'I'm going to prop myself here at an editorial angle – you let it all roll out, darling, just let it all roll out.' His mouth seemed bad again – oily, his tongue finding unpleasant places, soft gaps. The thought of them made him want to retch. But instead he worked his fingers wetly between Lynda's and clung on.

'Ruth Alvey turned me on to sharks – back when I was on the island. Every other bloody sentence you could get out of her was about them – on and on and on – and I thought . . . I don't know . . . why not have a shark of my own? And why not have all the rest – while there was still time, still the physical credibility, why not go and play with the great big fishies and all of those nice Californian boys in the sun?

'They were gorgeous – the boys – new, tight, ticky muscles and that honey skin – they're generally about as bright as honey, too. But then I didn't go out there for conversation. I was tired of having my bloody *intellect* stimulated, you know? Enough is enough.'

'Oh, yes.' He was trying to picture her splayed along some idiot surfer's board, or tugging and sucking at him, kneeling . . . none of it kept back the uneasy tickle of bile in his throat.

'I found my perfect amputee – right hand missing, bitten off. His forearm stopped in just a lovely nub of flesh: tiny, feminine folds there, and the marks of stitches: adorable.'

'Good friction?' He prayed she would get more graphic soon and fingered a sting of sweat away from his eye.

'And good pressure. I'm sure I could feel, when we were really going, the way his radius and ulna moved – their cut ends were free to shift inside his flesh.'

That, Jack *could* visualise and didn't want to, just at present. He was swallowing rapidly to keep pace with his own saliva: its sudden, sullen rush. 'But the sharks?'

'I'm coming to them.' She pushed her hand flat between Jack's legs where they were crossed at the knee. 'My manually abridged young escort had been a diver. He had friends who still were . . . they took me out and taught me how to dive: dropping to thirty, sixty, ninety feet; buddy breathing, signals, orientation, depressurisation, what I should do if I pissed in my suit. The whole deal.'

'Congratulations.' He gripped his thighs together and was rewarded with her knuckles' pleasantly insistent wriggle in between them. Things down there were becoming distinctly unsavoury – one slick heat raising another – and he wouldn't have had it any other way.

'It was all a means to an end, the messing around in kelp groves with sea lions and seals. They're immensely sensual creatures, by the way – so fluid and self-possessed, even flirtatious when they're underwater. They showed off the tucks in their fur where their flippers start, the innocent way they blink, the bubbles in their whiskers, their scars. Sometimes, we'd lie on the cliffs – myself and whoever – and I'd look past the boy and on down to the rocks, the seal pups sleeping like folded pocket knives and the adults hanging, turning, dark in the risen waves, just letting it happen. Watching them made me come fantastically.' She wedged her hand higher, but – sadly – not indecently so. 'Are you really interested in this?'

'Fascinated.' But if he didn't get even a tiny bit harder rather soon, he would pass out. He was getting far too sober, far too fast.

'Well, in the end, all this ducking,' her hand slipped higher, 'and sucking,' and higher, 'and fucking,' and higher, 'paid off. I persuaded some of my companions to get in a boat and take me out where I wanted to go – to the Faralon Islands. To White Shark Heaven. I mean, if you're going to meet a shark, you should meet the best, yes? Abalone divers do it all the time, dip in and risk it: get as deep as they can, just as fast as they can: it's safer that way. And we risked it, too. Went looking for it. Asking for it. Mm?'

He flopped his hands across his crotch and her fingers as she finally reached the spot, palming him gently. 'Hm.' It seemed he could no

371

longer speak. But he could lift his hips just a little and sweat just a little bit more.

'It happened the third time we went out. The way I'd known it would. The Pacific was being pacific and only stroking, stretching up under the boat and teasing me to slip in and part it and find what it wanted to give. So I did. Over the side with a full tank while everyone else was dozing and then out on my own, which is strictly not allowed.

'And he was there, a prickle in the water, a quiet heat. Nothing to see yet, but he was there. And he made me . . . ready. You know how it's possible,' Lynda ran her thumb around the outline of Jack's cock, 'to be made ready. Properly.'

Jack raised a sigh of agreement, hard with the certainty that he would now be perceived as having definitively, absolutely *disgraced himself*. He could feel the gossip washing warm around him. The occasion could only be more perfect if some ignorant bastard tried to intervene.

'Well, Jack. You're a bad, bad boy. Which means you'll understand the way I felt with him.'

She continued to lightly trace and retrace Jack's length. His peripheral vision turned pink. 'Hnuh.'

'I pushed it, went for depth, twisted while I sank. Looking. Clear water right around. And then he was there.' She let her hand rest still, making Jack's whole pelvis jolt with ungodly frustration. 'There's nothing more like itself than a shark. At first I couldn't believe in him – worrying through the bars of light, dappled, as if he were crossing a clearing, all pulse and flex and neat intensity.

'He swung by, above me and to my right, quite far off. For a moment I had his perfect silhouette, the smoothed brow and the tricking out of fins, the sleek shape of his claspers, clearly marking him as male. So languid and so hard – he was perfection. Perfection heading away. And I believed that he was going to leave me then, that we were done before we'd even started and, for the first time since I'd seen him, I felt afraid.'

Jack, no longer remotely circumspect, shut his eyes and listened to the drift and glide of Lynda's voice while moving his hips against her hand. If she noticed the plaintive rub of his crotch, she gave no sign. He ground on.

'His speed, his thrust, they emptied him out of numb blue and he'd barged me before I knew it, torn my hand and my forearm raw. Not with his teeth, with the rip of his skin. Close to, it looks like velvet, from the darkest to the palest grey, and you want to touch it, you do want to touch it, the ruffle and gape of his gills, but just a brush will draw your blood. All I saw was the stripe of the muscles in his side as he slammed in, huge, and then was gone – a fist of angles shrinking out of sight.

'He didn't give me the time for terror, just pushed me through it before I could think. I felt almost sleepy while I watched my bleeding cloud out and streak, greenish in the salt light. I tried to think of my breathing and check my tank and I realised I had no idea of how long I'd been down there. Minutes or days: I couldn't have told you and I couldn't have cared.

'A thick, charged tension at my back made me turn. And, of course, it was him, closing. Again. In the time that it took me to know I was going to die, he didn't kill me. He was there and he let me be. He left me. Every night, I remember everything: the silver preoccupation of his painted eye, blaring, the naked race of his belly above me, and his mouth. His mouth. Powder pink.'

Jack slowed, let his efforts drop, but Lynda's hand took up his rhythm, at him again.

'It was plush, his mouth, and rippled, like the lining of a box. You'd think it delicate, imagine it was warm, a place to slip into: one long, muscular, saline fit. And there to close on you, keep you tight, are the white blade and bristle of teeth upon teeth. I see them in my sleep. Sometimes, I need only blink and I will see them. But they did no harm to me.

'The whole half moon of his gape grazed past me, over my head and he was finished. Away.'

Jack knew he was shrinking fast, failing, nausea punching in his neck. Meanwhile she was scrubbing at him, pinching the head of his prick through layers of cloth, making a fool of him while his mind belched up ghosts of – it seemed – every cunt he'd known and fitted every one of them with infantile, peggy teeth.

'I rose to the surface with a practically empty tank and blood streaming into my eyes. At our last meeting, he'd taken a strip of skin from my scalp. I knew I was in much more danger at the surface, but

I was equally sure that he was gone. I had no understanding of why he hadn't taken me. I was just left without him. To meet so large a life and then have it leave you . . . the want that makes in you . . . I can still feel it.' She pressed her lips to his ear. 'I can still feel it in me.'

A bitter wad of liquid filled Jack's mouth and he gagged it quietly down again. 'Ahm.' He swallowed once more. Coughed. 'You know . . .' There was still a chance for this. If he got out of here, he could still make it. Get a drink and get out of here, that's what he should do . . . 'We really should leave now. If we want to make a night of it.' He made a good effort at a suitably raffish – if rubbery – grin.

Lynda winked back obligingly. 'Oh really, Jack, what on earth made you think that we'd be doing that? Have you looked at yourself lately?'

'What made me think – ?'

'And have you smelt your breath?'

'I have a . . . something with my teeth . . .' A mosquito whine had kicked up in his ears – appropriate for this heat, but even so . . . he couldn't help but object. It seemed an imposition . . .

Lynda stood with an elegance which quite surprised him. Then she leaned down towards him, in a way that he hoped to find encouraging, but which actually only scared him. 'Yes, you certainly do have a something with your teeth. And the rest of you.' She patted his head. 'Go home, darling. Will you? Don't be embarrassing.'

J. D.'s vision cramped with fury, he couldn't breathe, his thinking Stanley-knifed across every word of *fucking cunt* disparagement, every *dyke wanker* denigration, every *knob-loving easy slapper sagging witch ring-licker slack-gapped fuck* invective that he had ever pronounced.

But nothing was enough, not nearly enough, and Lynda was, quite naturally, already absent when he looked up to tell her all of those wicked and wounding things that he couldn't exactly grasp but would any moment, any moment now.

If he possibly rested first, that would do the trick. Unquestionably that would work the magic and then a tiny vodka and then perhaps another and then there'd be plenty of time thereafter to tell her – *bitch*.

*

'I'm looking for Jack Grace, have you seen him?' Nathan was having no luck.

A neat man, discreetly inebriated, stopped and swung sleepily in his tracks. 'Jack . . . I think he *was* upstairs. But I couldn't say. He'll be very, ah . . . *tired* by now, though.' He nodded for no obvious reason and then seemed quite content to stand, awaiting any further enquiries.

Nathan did his best to oblige – slightly *tired*, himself. 'Has anyone ever mentioned how very closely you resemble James Haigh?'

'Mm?'

'The acid-bath murderer – Haigh?'

'I'm sorry? I don't think . . .'

'No, that's fine. Thanks for your help.' Nathan swam himself off up the stairs, the man peering at him as he climbed – clearly trying to decide if he should take violent offence.

'Oh, you. That's nice.' Nathan was working his way round a clotted landing when an unexpected surge to the wall dodgemed him softly into Mary. 'It really is too hot for all of this.'

She leaned into him. 'Yes, I'd like to have some air that no one else has breathed already.' At some point today she'd had her hair cut rather shorter than he would have liked. Not that she wasn't still the most attractive person here. With some difficulty, she threaded her arm through his, nudging him sideways against the crush. 'Still, I suppose it's fun.' Mary hadn't touched him this much since they'd had what he tended to think of – delicately – as their *temporary derailment*. 'I mean, *they're* having fun.' She nodded her head towards the body wall behind him. 'Lots of fun.'

'Some of them . . .' This, while warily squeezing her arm, he hoped in an only friendly way. 'I would imagine there are also people who are *appearing* to have fun, because everyone around them is doing the same. If we all just relaxed we might actually like it here.'

'Like life.' She squeezed him back and made him think he ought to withdraw, perhaps, drift politely away.

*Sod it, if I can't be **with** her when I'm with her, then what's the point? We might as well be apart again if it's going to be . . .*

He staggered slightly, partly in response to a solid battering at his back and partly within the preliminary, sodden grip of a burst of melancholy, late-night thinking.

No matter what happens now, I never will have been with her long enough. And I could die soon . . .

He examined the warm dark, the brandied honey, of her eyes.

*I **could** die. My lung's all right – so they tell me – but anything can happen, these days – I might – even now – for instance, be infected with mad beef . . . my neurones gently unfastening and casting my self adrift. And if I die without having told her.*

*Ach, fuck it, I **shouldn't** tell her. It would just be an imposition. I want her to be my daughter to please my ego, not to please her. Now she likes me because she likes me, not because she feels she ought to.*

*As if knowing I was her father – knowing I was that particular pathetic, uncommunicative shit – would make her feel she ought to **like** me.*

Christ, do nothing, do something: either way, I'm fucked. Like life.

'Nathan.'

Well, look, Mary, I've been meaning to tell you, although this is not a good time . . . He blinked at her, stunned by the sudden clarity of the sentences in his head. Beneath the fog of too much Scotch, circumstances were rapidly swirling together to suggest how simple all of this might be. He was far too, far too drunk. 'Well, look, Mary, I've –'

'Nathan, Lynda's here. Did you know?'

He blinked again, all the sensible parts of his brain apparently now engaged in a spin cycle of some sort: then a hot-water rinse, another spin – perhaps the first signs of incipient beef poisoning. 'Lynda?' And, knowing this would sound imbecilic, he parroted on all the same, 'Lynda? Lynda Dowding? *That* Lynda?'

*Yes, that Lynda, of course, that Lynda – **blowjob Lynda**. Not that she actually blew. Or, for that matter, sucked. And here I am, attempting to even begin to pretend that there might be another one. I have all the moral fibre of a rusty paper clip.*

'She didn't tell you she was coming back?'

He couldn't work out how Mary was feeling about this development: angry, wounded, jealous, sad? Then again, he wasn't sure how *he* felt: shabby, humiliated, embarrassed, ashamed? He was blushing, he realised, while she was only serious, almost blank.

'Nathan? You haven't seen her tonight?'

'No.' He sounded grotesquely defensive. 'I haven't at all. I didn't expect to.' Protesting, way too much. 'We were never really . . .' Nathan could feel Mary staring him down, but now that his mouth had started, it wouldn't stop. 'Despite the, uh . . . appearances, we weren't close. That, um, evening was out of character for us both and came' – he tried not to falter at the choice of verb – 'to nothing. I don't . . .' This was the important bit, though, the point where he'd redeem himself, say the right and useful thing. 'I would never have that kind of relationship with anyone out on the island. There are people there I care about . . . immensely. But not in that way.'

Good man, yourself, Nathan Staples. Good man.

He winced up in time to see Mary look away, approaching a smile. 'I'd hate to see what you do to the people you *do* care about in that way.'

'Now, you –' He scrubbed at his forehead with one hand. 'I can't tell you how hideously . . . I was so . . .' She bumped him with her shoulder. 'Ashamed.' He turned again and, this time, faced her.

She nudged him again to shut him up, apparently, or as a consolation. 'It's all right. I shouldn't have brought it up.' Now she looked away, the almost smile fading. 'Everybody gets lonely.'

'But I wasn't –'

'And I know how they feel. There's nothing like a party to make you feel bereft, hm?' She studied the middle distance, the finally thinning crowd, 'I still miss –' gave Nathan a beat to brace before he had to hear her say a name and then, 'I still miss Jonathan, really. That's who I miss.'

Which, thank you, puts me in my place.

Not that it shouldn't. Not that I would have this any other way.

He tried a small nudge of his own. 'I am sorry. It doesn't seem to be widely understood that being solitary, without other people, can be a very pleasant thing. Being without only one person, the one person you need is . . . well, anyway.'

They fought to reposition themselves and hug.

Please don't resemble me so much. Get into the way of being happy. Please.

Somebody stepped on his heel in passing.

*She feels . . . not thinner, because she **isn't** thinner, but **harder**. That's the way you get when you worry, when you are sad.*

He wanted to kiss her but didn't. A stumbling weight knocked them in passing and they parted, both smiling in the way they might have if they'd been woken from a pleasant nap.

'Oh, and I'm –' She brushed something from his shoulder, made him flinch. 'I'm . . .'

'You're?'

'All right, well, now I've started to say it – I'm writing a novel. I know it's a stupid idea, but I am and you can't stop me so don't try.'

Now he did kiss her, just caught her ear. 'Congratulations. I wouldn't dream of stopping you. About time, in fact.'

'About *time*? You mean you don't mind?'

'Why would I be anything other than delighted?'

'You complete bastard.'

She prodded his arm in mock outrage, while he shook his head, breathless with joy.

'Yes, you are, you are a complete bastard. I had to get this drunk to tell you and you don't even bloody mind.'

'If,' he clasped his hands against her arms, the moment quavering about him, 'if I were your father, I would be more proud of you than I could say. Speaking for myself – as long as you're not going to cough up some dreadful saga, or a whodunnit, or anything remotely approaching the bilious nonsense I write – I am pleased that my tutoring has brought you to this point.'

'Oh, so it was nothing to do with me.'

'You're too young and inexperienced to understand the very subtle and elegant support I've offered you.'

'Deluded old bastard.' She shook him off, but then clasped his hand.

And he wished she hadn't. The fucking heat and all the rigours of the night must have left his touch indistinguishable from that of a cow's tongue. Sure enough, she let him go quite quickly. 'Well, I'd better have another trot round – just to show them. This weird man came up and said he'd read my stories. You believe it?'

'These things happen. Did he try to chat you up?'

'I don't know *what* he was trying. He gave me his card.'

'Come and get me if he gives you any bother.' He stroked her shoulder before she began to glare. 'Any bother you don't wish to deal with yourself.' She nodded, independence satisfied, and nodded once more – *see you later* – but he caught her gently back. 'And, as far as the novel goes, I will tell you the only thing you need to know.'

'When we'll both forget it in the morning. Good move.' She

grinned, but then leaned in to hear him, hungry.

I cannot help but notice that she does always want to know what I have to say. My girl.

'No, no. We'll remember this. *Listen to it.*'

'Listen to it? To what?'

' No. *Listen to it.* Any piece of writing, but especially something as large as a novel can be, will have the power to tell you what it wants to be. Each word will have a say in each word that comes after. Nine times out of ten, your work knows how to go forward far better than you. So listen, have respect, don't fight. Rule Five.'

'How many Rules are there?'

'Don't be so cheeky. *Listen to it.* Rule Five.'

'Pompous, deluded, old bastard.'

'Less of the old. Now, then, where was I . . . Yes. Looking for that fucker Jack.'

Nathan burrowed his way serenely up the next flight of stairs, every inch the quality father and proud, proud man.

'Jack.' He was much plumper than Mary remembered.

Even the bags under his eyes are looking fatter. Funny – he's got wonderful posture and really not bad legs, but everything else is buggered.

'Jack. You remember me. Mary?'

He narrowed his eyes and eased into a vulpine smirk. 'Couldn't forget you, dear girl. If you keep kissing Nathan in public places, by the way, certain parties will get the impression that you're in lust. That particular titbit reached me before you did.' His expression cleared, sobered for a few unnerving seconds and he seemed to search her face. 'Not that you *are* in lust, or in love with him. That wouldn't be quite the thing, would it?'

'No. Of course not.'

J. D. winked sympathetically and sank back into his favourite persona – jovially malign and erudite lush. In either guise, he seemed slightly forbidding, as usual.

I never think he'll be good to talk to, but – in the end – he always is. At least, he's funny, anyway. J. D. Grace – the consistently pleasant surprise. He wouldn't want that to get around.

'Did anyone happen to tell you I'm writing a novel?'

His attention surfaced gratifyingly for a moment. Then he decided he'd rather be uninterested. 'My dear, *everyone's* doing *that*. I'm even contemplating it myself. I've done it before, after all – about halfway through the Precambrian period.'

*But I'm **really** going to do it. Not just talk about doing it.*

Jack drawled on. 'That passed-over journalist there: writing a novel; that man who was raped in his teenage years and just has to tell us all about it: writing a novel; that heavily pregnant doxy: writing a novel; and an alleged Estonian pimp and child molester who will appear in an alleged translation, as arranged by that smack-head agent over there: writing a novel; writing a novel, one and all.' He squinted at her, testing her patience, then relaxed. 'Of course, none of their novels will be any good. Whereas, with yours one never knows . . .'

Mary thought it best to change the subject. 'Nathan's looking for you.'

'Good for him. If he finds me, come and let me know.' He reached out urgently for the piano, found its side and held on. 'Unsteady spasm, there – not to fret. Talking of Nathan – did you know that, on paper, he never lies?'

'I don't understand.'

'Absolute fact – if you ask him to write something down he will be unable to tell you anything but the truth. It makes his letters very interesting. And rare.'

'And short, I would think.'

'That, too. But very precious also.' J. D. beckoned her closer and then covered his mouth with his hand before murmuring, 'Don't mention I told you. He might not like it. But do bear it in mind. Nathan means what he writes. He's like . . .' J. D. shuffled back a pace and coughed to his side, paused, apparently wary of ill effects, coughed again and frowned. 'I'm terribly sorry to say that I shall have to cut along.' His voice sounded thick and preoccupied. 'I do apologise.'

He marched past her, sweat soaked through the back of his linen jacket and bright on his neck.

'Jack Grace.' Nathan was still getting nowhere with his interrupted search. 'Jack Grace?' Half the people he asked didn't even answer him. 'Has he left?' Ignorant fucks.

380

*Oh, bugger it, **I** don't even care any more, why should **they**? I'm tired, I want a shower, and I want to be the fuck out of here. And Jack can take care of himself – none of my business. Right now, he is most likely off having no trace of conscience about things I can't even consider considering – lucky shit.*

Jack Grace, you amoral bastard, I, Nathan Staples, loose you and let you go. You have my full permission to be somewhere else, enjoying I will not contemplate exactly what.

Meanwhile, I will go home and be very happy about my daughter. I'll just ask Mary if she's ready to go. Not that she has to leave with me. We needn't be inseparable. Not all the time.

As he'd half-expected, once Nathan started searching for Mary, her whereabouts became suddenly obscure. And, it was true, not many of the guests were really sure of who she was.

*We'll change all that, though. **She** will, anyway. In the end, she'll have every one of them gagging to meet her.*

The thought of literary London, gagging *en masse*, proved slightly less beguiling than he'd have liked and he decided he'd adjourn to the gentleman's room to freshen himself up – lighten the load. It had been a long night.

The charcoal marble around the sinks showed signs of having served as a surface for assembling neat, small lines of fine powder. Nathan doused his face and was about to move over and stand himself in a stall when he heard what he'd been looking for.

'Aoh, shit.' This was followed by a retching cough, 'Hoagain,' and then a more earnest splash of matter, more coughing, the cistern beginning to flush.

'Is that you? Jack? You all right?'

'Bastard.' It was definitely Jack, only he could lend those two syllables their absolute, perfect weight. A sigh ensued and a scramble of feet.

'It's Nathan. Are you all right?'

J. D. Grace emerged from the cubicle blinking, his chin stringy with dark saliva, his face wet. He had completely undone his bow tie. 'Oh, God, it *is* you. I thought you were some kind of auditory hallucination.' Waving Nathan away, he made quite coherently for the sinks. 'Keep back. I'm unpleasant at the moment.' He dashed the basin full of cold water, braced his arms to either side and then pressed his face down into it, surfacing finally with a walrus sneeze of breath. 'Christ, I think I'm getting gastric flu, or something. It's this bloody heat. Good to see you, by the way. Excuse me for not shaking hands.'

Nathan shrugged his head in dispensation and watched as Jack let the sink drain and then gingerly sluiced his mouth at the tap. The first ejected mouthful of water was grainy brown, thickened with purplish matter. By the end of the process, the liquid was pinkly clear with the odd translucent streak of red.

'Jack,' Nathan eased forward, rested one hand at Jack's clammy shoulder, 'are you bleeding?'

'Mm.' J. D. smiled narrowly and shivered off Nathan's touch. 'It's nothing unusual – someone took a couple of my teeth out. They haven't quite healed. It's a bit of a trial, throwing up across open sockets.' He started a grin, covering his mouth with his hand before it could break. 'Sorry. Even a man of your tastes probably didn't want to know that, hm?'

'I could quite probably have done without it, yes. But what do you mean by *someone* – a dentist, I hope?'

'As it happens, not exactly a dentist, no – but a good man, all the same. Mary tells me she's starting a novel . . .'

'Don't change the subject. What's going on?'

'Nothing alarming, I promise. And I will explain, old Sport, but not tonight. I'm not entirely feeling at my best and it will make for a long and rather nasty story. Some other time.'

'Will I take you home?'

'No, you will not. Go and be paternal to your daughter, if you want to indulge your caretaking instincts. And then how about *you* writing a novel – I mean a real one? The one you keep promising. I can't wait for ever.'

Nathan slid his hands to either side of Jack's face – the skin of J. D.'s cheeks was remarkably soft, almost feminine, but very chill. 'Look me in the eye, will you, Jacky.'

'Ooh dear, he's calling me *Jacky* – pet names, not a good sign.'

'Look me in the eye.'

Jack conceded, completed the look, his pupils hungrily wide. 'And . . .?'

'You're not going to die on me, are you?'

He swallowed. 'Of course not.'

'You're quite sure about that.'

'Yes.' Jack shook his head gently against Nathan's grip. 'Come on now, Nathan. We should hail our respective cabs and get home.'

'Because it would be much less pleasant to work without you.'

'Hm, well.' His lips stayed closed across a short, wincing smile. They met each other's gaze again. 'I'm quite sure I won't be shuffling off for a good while yet. No need for worry, there. I promise.'

'Never trust an editorial promise.'

'That wasn't editorial, that was me.' He clasped Nathan's wrists. 'You can let go now.'

'Don't you dare waste yourself, Jack.'

'I fucking won't. OK? So don't you waste yourself, either. Write me a book.'

'All right. All right.'

Nothing further to say, they stood, still holding each other, for perhaps half a minute more until a slim young man in a repellent velvet suit walked in on them. They separated quickly, with a kind of tender shame.

Under Mary's hands, the dough was turning, as she'd been told it should, towards the consistency and temperature of human skin. Behind her, the open doorway was breathless, curtained with warping air.

It's finally happened, the island has been so hot for so long that the whole place is just going to melt down and vitrify into something weird. As if today isn't weird enough. All change, that's what today is, all change.

Off in the distance, grass hollows flickered, heat-silvered. Reality seemed to be growing a kind of somnolent, fluxing intelligence, while she jolted the bread into properly textured life. Sitting outside, against the wall, Ruth and Lynda were talking, sipping root vegetable wine: their respective personalities, apparently liquefied and waxing into each other, transfusing. Ruth talked about sex, while Lynda did not. Lynda talked about sharks, while Ruth did not.

'He was one huge flex after another, so unremitting and precise. I remember his fin dragging up beneath the surface for a moment, barely moving it: only raising one, big, silk ripple . . . And his eye –' Mary couldn't quite hear, but guessed that Lynda probably sighed. 'His eye was just like a writer's. The way a proper writer is inside. You know? When you meet the real thing? A real, fucking bastard writer who'll look at anything, sleeping or waking, curiosity with no brakes, no moral judgements, just appetite.' She paused again. 'It's odd – for all that Richard has missing, all his fucking hollowness – he's still got that eye.'

Mary set the bread aside to prove, aware that it was already, almost visibly, rising, spurred on by the feverish day. She wanted to go to the sand cave now, where the cool was guaranteed and she could think. As of this morning, she had a great deal to think about. Her news hung, trembling above her, like a water drop waiting to break.

The two women continued to murmur beyond the door,

seemingly more and more sleepy, less and less cautious of being overheard. Ruth yawned and, 'When he swam at you, when you thought you were going to die and then he didn't kill you, did it feel . . . was it . . .?'

'Intensely. The most intensely sensual, sexual . . . every other time I've almost died, it hasn't been like that. Before it's been pretty businesslike, in a way – cold, a kind of official appointment with a very large disinterest. Whereas this *was,* quite literally, a meeting with something large and disinterested – but when he was there, he was so *alive* . . . For days, once I'd come ashore, he made everything seem a part of everything else. What he was extended into everything and made it want to touch. I'd never known the world be so . . . urgent.'

'Did you tell Joe?'

'Could hardly avoid it, could I? He does always have to know.' Lynda turned her head muzzily as Mary came to the door and peered out, but then continued with a remarkably loud whisper, 'Actually, I *wanted* to tell him. Before, I've resented the intrusion – him crashing in on it all like a fucking vulture – but everything about *this* step has been so much happier . . . insane word to use, but has been much more contented, more something to share around. Mad old bastard – he's got me sounding like him.'

'You've tried how many . . .?'

'Four. Same as you.'

'It's a good number.'

'The best so far.' Lynda stroked Ruth's arm ruminatively and then appeared to remember that Mary was there. 'How're you doing?' She did seem more relaxed, contented, than Mary had known her.

'Fine. If anyone thumping dough about in a heatwave can be fine.' Ruth giggled. 'I am sorry. It's my job, of course, but I just couldn't face it today. You are a dear to have done it.' She giggled again. 'Actually, I'm not that sorry. It's a bitch of a job in this heat.'

'Yes, indeed it is. Thanks for pointing that out.' Mary shook her head at them, parentally. They made a strange pair: Lynda deepening her, no doubt, all-over Californian tan, while Ruth turned a scalded crimson. 'If you two don't mind, I'm going to sit round the side in the shade for a bit. Sorry for interrupting you – know how you like to obsess about death.'

Lynda answered quietly, 'I don't think we're obsessing.'

Ruth agreed, 'And we're talking about living, not dying.'

'Oh, *dying*.' Lynda's tone suggested it was something on a par with putting up shelves – a humdrum, survivable, practical chore. 'Yes, that's hardly the issue.' She patted Ruth lightly on a patch of not-too-inflamed skin. 'I think we'd better go inside before you combust.'

Mary made herself as comfortable as she could on the shaded turf at the cottage's side. She lay on her stomach across browned grass, the earth roasted to an ungiving surface beneath it. Resting her cheek against her folded arms, she finally let her thinking creep forward and unlock.

He's coming here.

Why would he want to? For me? For him?

While her mind tumbled through doubtful combinations, her body nudged and softly shifted into a muscular understanding: Jonathan was coming to Ancw. Her Jonathan.

He'd be working with a local firm, starting things up from scratch, advising on their choice of computers, their software, setting things up.

Starting things up from scratch.

He never mentioned how long he'd stay here, how long it would take. He only asked if I had objections.

'Objections? Even if I did –' and she'd been going to say – *it would be none of my business*, but that had seemed, perhaps thuggish, perhaps inaccurate. 'Why would I have objections?'

'I thought that you might. Do you not?'

Her breathing had picked this point to change with the shock of hearing his voice. Her inhalations had become flimsy and unhelpful. 'I have,' words lumbered and stuck, 'I have no objections. No. But why are yo–'

'Good. I'll put you back to Bryn, then – his phone, isn't it? Don't want to run up the bill. 'Bye.'

'But *I* called *him* – it isn't his bill . . . Jonathan? Jonno?'

But Jonathan had already gone – receding into the small shapes of ambient noise, the ticks, the perfect pitch of footfalls to let her know that she was listening to Gofeg, to Charter Street, number eighteen.

'There you are, then, girl. I told you I'd got a surprise.' He could be a sly one, Bryn: sly and romantic with it.

'You could have told me it was him.' She could hear herself sounding breathless, absurd. 'And what are you up to, anyway? Is he still there?'

'That's right.' His voice had the hearty informality of one who was being overheard.

'So even if you were ever going to tell me what your cunning plan was – you wouldn't do it now.'

'That's right.'

Mary didn't want to be fully angry with him, there would be no point and Bryn was already sounding wary, if not hurt. She calmed her air supply and eased out, 'Do you think this is a good idea?' wishing he could tell her, that either of them could really know.

'It could be. Taken gently. Up to you.'

'Oh, listen, if you're going to have to talk in code, maybe I should call you back later, eh? When he's gone?'

'Yes, you could do that. Although, now I think about it . . . No, you can't.'

'Going out on the town, are you? Off with those two from the knicker shop.'

'No, no. I forgot to say. I'm paying a visit. For two nights, or three.'

'What do you mean *paying a visit*?'

'Never you mind.' Bryn was beginning to puff, here and there, with anxiety, or rather – she supposed – embarrassment. 'I'll be down in Cardiff. And I'll call you when I get back. I don't know how long I'll be there, it depends how we get on.'

'Are you going to tell me what you're up to?'

This is all right, this is good. He should do things. Make another life.

'I'm passing the time, love – you know the way things are – anything I can do to pass the time . . .' Almost as soon as his mood had dipped, he brightened himself. 'But you can pity me going to Cardiff. Cardiff: it's not even –'

'Bloody Wales.' She finished his second favourite joke. 'I'm going to come and see you soon.'

'Yes, all right, love. You just think about that other thing, now.'

'What – Jonathan?'

'You think about that.'

But she didn't have to think about him, she could feel him, the threads of connection still there, winding and tugging through the heat.

Nathan had finished his first swim in six days. Sophie had been visiting again and his nerve always failed him when he considered letting her anywhere near the sea. So washing away the interminable glare of everything on the island in a bit of tepid swell had been impossible. Until today.

Now he and Eckless lay, painted across the sand, with barely the energy to grunt, proud of their exertions and subsequent healthy sufferings.

He did well today – was a good, old dog. Came out as far as me and seemed to like it. We do both still rush a bit, though, when we're on our way home.

'But it's normal to panic when you're on your way home, isn't it, pal?' He pressed at the dog with his knee and got a sighing groan in reply. 'Suit yourself.'

Nathan reached into his bag for his water bottle, took a few judicious sips and made an effort at swilling his hands clean of the usual post-dip mineral friction. Next, he rooted round for the towel and his shoes and shorts.

Sand removal from in between bollocks and toes, followed by the imposition of decency.

He was settling nicely into the work, shorts and left shoe on, when his mobile phone chirruped from where he'd forgotten it in his bag. Eckless's ears flagged a slight interest. 'Somebody loves us, then, boy. But I can't think who.'

'You took your bloody time.' Jack delivered a familiar polished growl and then a burst of tense, snuffing laughter.

'If I'd known it was you I'd just have let it ring.' He whispered an aside to his dog, 'As you were, nobody loves us – it's only Jack.'

'What? Are you in company? Is this a bad time?'

'When has that ever stopped you. And what have I done to deserve this. Which guardian angel brought me to your thoughts?'

'None, I hope. I'm working from home – dreadful migraine this morning, couldn't go in – and I thought I'd have a break and a chat. Over my tea and Bath Olivers. You don't object?'

'No. I'm just sitting on the beach. The way you do.'

'The way I _don't_, dear boy. Do you know when I last had a holiday?'

'No.'

'Neither do I.' Another few dabs of breath came at the receiver, perhaps indicating amusement. Silence leached in.

'Jack, are you all right?'

'As I'll ever be. Beast of a fucking headache at the moment, but _this too shall pass_, as they say in the good old AA.'

'You're calling to tell me you've joined Alcoholics Anonymous? Surely some mistake.'

'Do I _sound_ like an arse? Of course not. Although I did get corralled into one of their prayer meetings at the clinic – you remember when I went to the clinic? The whole thing was a blurry pantomime, of course – the nice little circle of doped-up patients – an occasion filled with the most astonishingly puerile sloganeering I've ever encountered. And I've been going to marketing meetings for decades. What was I saying? Oh yes, _this too shall pass_ – the most irritating AA motto of them all. What the hell _won't_ pass and why should I care, in any case?

'Anyway, I wanted to chivvy you about the book. The one you haven't written yet.'

'I've got lots of those. Which book I haven't written yet do you mean?'

'Now, Nate, this is actually quite important to me. A personally professional, professionally personal type of thing. I think it's time to step away from the, the . . .'

'The pulpy horror shite.'

'No. It's not pulpy – pulp_ing_, perhaps – not pulp_y_. It's very good. But we always said that, one day, you'd go back to something . . . perhaps less immediately commercial, perhaps not . . . Something with your heart in it. You know.'

'Why now?'

'It's time. I really am quite sure that it's time.'

'Why?'

'Because I'm a literary editor, fuck it. I _know_.' It wasn't like him to be so unmistakably committed, to let belief loose in his voice. 'Because I'm quite good at my job, because I have functioning instincts, because if you don't do it now there won't be any literary fiction *in* publishing – ten years' time it'll all be dead. Virtually is now.'

'Jack, I . . .' Nathan wished he weren't lounging under an incandescent sky, wished he couldn't hear good water and birds – he wasn't in any condition to be this serious. 'I respect you professionally. You know that.' And on the phone it was so hard to tell what a person meant, or to be adequately comforting. 'But I don't know if things are as bleak as you feel . . . Even if they are, you of all people know, you can't hurry that type of writing. And you can't hurry *me*. I don't respond well to it.'

'But will you write this book for me.'

'Oh, for fuck's sake, I'm writing it. OK? A little bit here and there. But it's slow – slow work. I'm trying to get it right.'

In London, a sigh pressed at the receiver. 'You've really started work? None of that *making a few notes* crap? Actual work?' Jack's delivery calmed, almost purred.

'I'm making more than a few notes.'

'But not anything else?' The purr stopped.

'There are some short sections finished, but I'm not sure about them. They might belong somewhere else. What I could probably do without is pressure on this. Explain to me why there's a hurry – are they threatening to fire you again?'

'No. No, I'm quite the flavour of the month now. That girl I was hand-feeding for a while – she's coughed up a wonderful novel, *Doctor Dee's Table*, did I send you it? No, I forgot. Well, I will. It'll come out in September, but everyone loves it already. So all is well. And next time it'll be you. Tell me.'

'If it makes you happy – next time it'll be me. And while we're playing question and answer, *you* tell *me* what you've been doing with your teeth.'

The pause for thought was slight, but clear. 'Only the usual. Mastication and all that.'

'Jack, you're not a good liar, remember? Hence divorces one, two and three. What are you up to?'

'No good. What am I ever up to apart from that?' There was a fumble of movement, a sniff, an exasperated breath. 'I was going to tell you. But not now – it's all experimental now. I . . . Nate, this is embarrassing. Really.'

390

Nathan tried to think of any horrendous activity that J. D. hadn't already confessed to with complete equanimity, if not quiet pride. 'No need to be shy, Jack. This is just us.'

'Well, I should hope so. I'm simply anxious that you shouldn't misunderstand my position. This will sound far more peculiar than it is . . . I'll be talking about a hobby here, that's all. Understood?'

'Fine. Do go on. Please.' A brief sea breeze ruffled over him, cool enough to feel clean.

'All right, all right. I've been having a problem. I like to relax – you know I like to relax. I like to sleep, to relax, to have fun, unwind. For all of those things – like many other reasonable people – I find I need a drink, just to get things rolling. Recently, that's been getting rather difficult. I think age is catching up with me. And I may have an ulcer, or something, I don't know . . . What it all comes down to is that I don't get quite properly drunk any more, or that the speed is wrong, my speed. After the first few glasses, I'm very nicely adrift – rather more than I would have expected to be – and then . . . and then I just seem to stall. I don't seem to get anywhere. I don't progress in drunkenness, I simply feel more trapped. And I'm throwing up too much, these days. I hate that. I have never, ever liked being sick. And I'm being sick all the time.

'And needless to say, my condition was becoming a bit of a drag. But then I met Oscar. Then I was *introduced* to Oscar. And things have been much better ever since.'

Eckless, recovered from his swim, sat up and leant against Nathan sandily. Nathan shifted the phone to his other hand. 'This would be Oscar the dentist.'

'This would be Oscar whose profession I do not know. What matters is that, in his spare time, he's a Top. That is to say, the dominant partner in arrangements of a sado-masochistic nature. Homosexual arrangements.'

'And does he wear leather and have a handlebar moustache?'

'Ah, the good Scots' homophobia will out. No, he is clean-shaven and, with me, he wears a suit. I met him through an attenuated series of acquaintances.'

'You always did know the best people.'

'Quite. And Oscar, in this instance, is the very best person I *could* know – because he's . . . well, as one might expect, he has an extensive experience of many physical procedures and is – among other things – more than happy to administer colonic irrigation.'

'*Irrigation?* He must be quite a guy – the most I could manage would be . . . say, half a gill.'

'If you're not going to take this seriously, I won't continue. You know perfectly well what I mean.'

'That he gives leisure-interest enemas to people who find that their kind of thing. OK. What does this have to do with teeth?'

'I'm *trying* to tell you. Usually, Oscar meets men of compatible interests, takes them home, goes through the usual tying up and thumping stuff and gives them enemas. He's very responsible and careful about it – it's in his best interests to keep his partners safe.

'And he's very strong on hygiene . . . And . . . and, the point is,' Jack began to rush his words, 'there were only two ways of taking alcohol I hadn't tried. I could have injected it, but doing that is almost always fatal, so it didn't recommend itself. The other way was to dilute it to the proper degree and then absorb it directly through the lining of the gut. This is also dangerous – even with a mild dose, it makes you terrifically drunk almost immediately – and you can't do it yourself – you need someone on hand. I pay Oscar to take care of things, to be on hand. He keeps me safe.'

'This is a joke, right? Jack?'

'This is a problem I have solved.'

'But you don't need –'

'Yes, I do need. You have no idea how much I do need. You are not in my position. Oscar does nothing to me – I mean, nothing beyond what I want – I bring my own enema bag and my own Bardex tubing that no one else uses and I get the job done. It's like having a massage, Nate, it's a therapy. I undress, I lie on his table, curl up on my left-hand side – that way we get the benefit of gravity, because the gut curves round first to the left – oh, the things you learn when you're having fun – then he sets things up, inserts the tube, and I get the sweetest, deepest blackout I've ever known. When I come to, he's cleared up and I'm human again – I can go and get on with things. Even the hangovers are nicer, you wouldn't believe . . .' His sentence trailed off, wistful.

'The only downside is the payment. There's no sexual transaction and he won't take money – judging by his house, he has quite a lot of that. All he asks is that I allow him to do the one thing he's always wanted and that no one else has let him try. So each time I go, while I'm under, he pulls out one of my teeth.'

It wasn't that Nathan hadn't guessed what might be coming. It wasn't that he was squeamish by nature. What was making it so difficult to think was simply, perhaps, the confirmation in reality, in that voice, from that damaged mouth: his friend's voice, uncomplaining, soft.

'Nathan?'

Nathan's own mouth slicked with nauseous saliva.

'Nathan, don't over-react about this. You're over-reacting, I can tell. Speak to me. It's temporary. I mean, it has to be, for heaven's sake. I'm hardly going to stand for someone pulling *all* my teeth. He's just clearing out the molars – the ones nobody sees. I'll find another solution later – something better. Nathan? Speak to me.'

'I don't know what to say.'

'Jesus, you've imagined far worse things – written them down.'

'But I haven't *known* far worse. I don't understand how you can be so . . . vicious with yourself.'

'I'm no crueller to me than you are to you. In fact, I'm kinder – I only hurt my body and my body is just a body, it takes its medicine and goes on – I don't damage anything important – I'm still intact in heart and mind. And, now and again, I get to relax, to really, genuinely relax.' He halted, eased his tone. 'Look, we shouldn't argue, especially not about this. You work on the book and look after Mary and everything will be fine. I promise you.'

Clutching for anything positive he could mention, Nathan suggested, 'Mary likes you.'

'And I like her back. And if you're going to say that she'd want me to be careful, I can tell you that I am. And I can also tell you that you certainly shouldn't worry her with this. And I can also tell you that there are two things I'd like to see by the end of the year: your first draft and her with an identified father. Think I'll be in luck?'

'I don't know, Jack. I really don't know.'

They hung up with the usual courtesies, a little more gently delivered, more consciously meant. Nathan set his phone down and lay back in the sand. A gull turned in front of the sun, its shadow disappearing into the brightness faultlessly.

★

That evening was a slow, broad falling of fire. Dusty heat rose, lazy, from the ground while the burning of the sea and sky commenced with peach and egg yellow and ended with sparking iron, bright mercury and blood that cooled to a thickening, ashy dusk.

Under all this, Foal Island kept its peace.

Ruth and Lynda still talked amiably together, slicing fresh bread to have with their soup for supper while Richard made his slow way to be with them, considering – in spasms – the reprieve of the life that he'd thought he had lost and the new, taut happiness in Lynda. He watched his shadow reel away beside him, a steady accompaniment, never stumbling or showing a sign of each vision that clipped him open, daubed him with the feel of his wife, spread and then fitted hungrily to so many other men. Rhythmically, he cleared his mind, kept walking.

Louis was reading from one of his favourites – *Meditations from Marcus Aurelius* – and eating a single chocolate truffle, one nibble at a time, as an aid to concentration and because it was fun. He whispered to the honey-coloured dust, caught and drifting in the block of light from his window, 'He who has seen present things has seen all, both everything which has taken place from all eternity and everything which will be for time without end; for all things are of one kin and of one form.'

Joe was sitting in the Meeting Room, letting his mind loose in dunes of light. Had his thoughts been running in the shape of words, he would have concurred with Aurelius.

Mary slept, the sand cave shifting to absolute dark around her as the day closed down. Sleeping, she stood at the foot of broad, red stone stairs, staring up at Jonno. He poured milk out from a basin, laughed, and then looked down at her. There was a heat about him that she would taste and need when she awoke.

Nathan sat at his desk with his dog slumped, warm and snoring, across his feet. Having tried – and failed – to doze for a while himself, having tried to concentrate, to be clear in his mind, to be contented, he'd given up and settled for watching the sky. For the eighth time this evening his phone rang, but he didn't answer it – the heat was affecting the signals again, twisting and evaporating calls. Phantoms were talking to phantoms, bristling Eckless's fur.

Ancw, across the water, was all decked out to celebrate the anniversary of a thoroughly popular war. The three pubs were garlanded with sandbags, windows crossed with blast-resisting tape and their foulest beers were offered at a roaring forties' price. The Church of Wales had red, white and blue bunting on its porch, the Methodist and Baptist chapels – not being established – did not.

Nathan supposed the retrospective enjoyment of so much distant death helped to paper over the stain of the Price boy's individual, more recent, extinction. It was said the killer's total of children might now be as high as twelve, no one could be quite sure. But it was not improbable that, for years, he or she had been working through Britain, making a personal celebration of lives ended arbitrarily. But there were, it seemed, no governmental plans to make this smaller war a cause for widespread delight, or the sentimental/political distortion of those values assumed to have once made Britain Great.

Bugger it, there's nothing I can think of tonight that isn't going to make me sick. My own fault – I shouldn't have parboiled my head on the beach all day – I can feel my brain adhering to the inside of my skull like a burnt poached egg.

He knew it would ease the pressure if he wrote, but as soon as he started he would hear Jack's voice, seeping in, describing actions he had no wish to imagine now. Or ever.

Bloody man.

Poor, bloody man.

A man who wants a novel from me, but I can't give him that.

Nathan picked up his pen, leant his free hand to his forehead, tried to look like a writer preparing to write.

But I'm not writing for fucking Jack. Not this time.

This is for Mary.

Although there's hardly any point – I'll never show it to her, she'll never know.

Ssssh. When I'm ready, I'll hand it all over, every word. I will.

And this time . . . this time I want to show her something happy, somewhere good.

He reeled himself back to the point where he first began thinking for two. As soon as he'd known she was on the way, his Mary, he'd started saving things for her – for when she was ready, when she was older, and then, later, for the time when he prayed he might meet her again.

And now she was here, she was with him, and he still had notebooks full of the places he'd described for her, the photographs he'd taken, the postcards he hadn't sent.

But there had always been a choice of what would make the best offering: which part of Milan? – the Inquisition Torture Museum or La Scala, risotto Milanese? The holocaust mass grave in Budapest or the soft oases of sunlight between trees, the secretive, green court-yards in the Jewish Quarter? The beauties of the European railways or the slipping along complicit tracks that once led to body pits, to the European types of war? The first sight of day through the windows of the Sainte Chapelle in Paris, or the spot in Orléans where Dr Beaurieux held up a freshly guillotined head, called it by name and saw it look at him? Should he show her the way to the Grail, or the holy bloodshed, the dead or the living word – he'd never been sure of which map would serve her best.

In the end, his decision was easier than he'd thought – he simply picked the only place that he could bear considering.

Hyperborea

I can see the sun. Low, at the far, pink edge of an
April sky, it is twirling as suns never really should
in nature, but, currently, I do not mind. I am inhaling the live and vegetable damp of opened countryside
and also listening to my radio, to the cheerfully Gothic
porno funeral music of – if I'm not mistaken – the
Doors. And I have all the time I need to think that I
very much like the Doors.

The road is delirious with light, casting up great,
aching slaps of reflection that make me blink, while my
arms are content to marionette away from me, to flap and
judder in time with my feet, in time with the road, in
time with the sun, in time with my car as it rolls
impossibly slowly through thick-as-liquid air, in a
clamour of metal and frightened engine, to my right and
to my right and to my right and then on down a small
embankment, where it tips to slither sideways, wheels
quite pointless, creaking with unaccustomed momentums,
and finally rocking soft and neat to a mildly angled
stop, righted, still.

And this is delight. Entirely and unmistakably, this
is delight. I was always sure I'd know it, when it came.

I turn off the final mumble of engine, blurrily amazed
that any gesture of mine has even the slightest effect.
Somewhere behind me something tiny and metal snaps.
Otherwise, there is no sound. And almost no sensation
beyond the baying of joy round my skull, the lick of
irresponsibility inside my veins and the touch of my
wife's fingers between my fingers, our warp and our weft.
Under my skin, or her skin – our whole, proper skin –
there skips the minute and continuing pounce of life.
We smile at each other and at ourselves, stone drunk
with survival.

'Jesus Christ. Sorry, love.' I squeeze at her hand
until I can feel the pleasant bite of pressure in my

finger bones. 'I don't know what . . .' As far as I can tell, I have no other pains. 'I really don't . . . know what to apologise for.' I snigger for no good reason beyond the amusement suddenly, plainly inherent in existence.

Maura shakes her head, equally unscathed and close to laughing. 'I know.'

Beached at the edge of what we think is a potato field, we try to patch together the train of our unlikely events. A number of minutes ago we were driving at moderate speed on a perfectly clear and even, rural, Scottish road. A rather smaller number of minutes ago a slapstick burst of nothing we can understand flipped the car into a birl of helpless motion, somewhere in the midst of which I thought it more useful to hold Maura's hand than to clutch at my redundant steering wheel. She thought this much more useful, too.

We unfasten our seat belts - our wonderful, tried and not-found-wanting seat belts - and we hug, we kiss. We agree that our mouths make sense, although nothing else does. Then Maura feels, and I could swear that I feel also, the deep, weird dunt of our almost child against her body wall: our nearly infant, elbowing in.

'Oh.' My wife says this, always, as if our baby had precociously tapped out a private and slightly surprising piece of entirely coherent news. 'Oh, my God.' Maura draws back from my arms.

'What? What?' The day starts to crumple round me, while I search Maura's face, try to translate her expression, and glide one hand - tenderly, witlessly - over the taut, new shape of her stomach. 'What?' Her body is different again from last week, altered from the week before.

'I think,' she folds her own palms over mine, 'I think he liked it. Our little sideways trip.'

'He's all right?'

'Oh, yes.'

'You're sure?' Relief already levering my joints,

cooling a flush of sweat I hadn't noticed rising.

'Oh, yes.'

'And he's a he?'

'Or a she.'

'Which do you think?'

'Which would you like?'

'I think I'd like one or the other.'

'Liar. You want a girl, don't you? I know you.'

And I realise that she's right, that I do want a girl, a daughter. Before I can stop it, a raw drag of need plunges in me at the thought of being only months away, only inches away, from *having* a daughter.

I hold Maura as gently as I can, wincing against the onset of tearfulness and trying to appreciate how dreadful things will be if all my preferences are really this decided, but I end up with a son. Of course, I will try to love him, encourage him, tell him the things that only a man can say to another, smaller, man, but *I want a daughter*.

I do my best to be concerned by this possible ghost across my future, but I fail. Because I know, re-embracing my wife, I fully understand from each part of the shining, soft/hard, unnerving body she is building for herself, that she *is going to have a daughter*. In there, inside Maura, more inside than I'll ever be, is a girl. Enjoying today with us, flexing, waiting, is our daughter, I am sure.

'Nathan?'

'Hm?'

'Am I right? You'd prefer . . .?'

'Uhm. Well, could be . . . a girl. What do *you* want?'

'I shouldn't say. But probably the same.'

'It's listening, though. Tell it we love it, in any case – whatever.'

'Oh, it knows that. It's clever, already. Extremely talented.'

'Ah, I see.' This sounds wholly reasonable: in fact, to be expected. My daughter, the bright girl.

399

'And it's noticed two men are coming to rescue us – look, from behind the bank. Do we want to be rescued?'

'I suppose we might as well.'

I turn and watch our pair of saviours, who are, indeed, high-stepping towards the car, over the earthed-up potato rows and plants. They are wearing muddied boots and overalls, clay-coloured caps and padded jackets and – as they close on us – seem increasingly aged and stooped.

Unsure of accident victim etiquette, we do nothing but sit still and watch until the first man halts at my door, leans into an even lower bend and taps my window. I wind down the glass, absurdly close to simply asking directions for somewhere and then winding shut again.

But he pre-empts me. 'Are you hurt, ken?' His words are unfocused and have an almost singing quality. I realise that he is deaf. He stares into the car, bluntly inquisitive. 'Are you?' I shake my head. At this, he summons his companion – an even older man, who looks to be his brother – and they exchange a flurry of hands and noddings. Then he dips his head to face me again. 'Come away out then, eh?'

We do as we're commanded, finding ourselves quite able to move and walk as usual, but with limbs a touch lighter, more sensitive than before. I feel we may float off soon and leave our escorts trudging ahead of us, unaware.

The brothers – they must be brothers and are both, apparently, quite deaf – take us into their farmhouse and feed us the slightly leathery, sliced white bread I had forgotten it was still quite possible to buy in Scotland. This is accompanied by margarine and an unidentifiable variety of oily broth. We are then given one slab each of whisky-damp fruit cake, which we eat in silence, as we have done everything in silence since we came indoors. There is no radio. There is no television. There is no telephone. There is no question, as the last of the light leaves the evening, that we will do anything other than stay here tonight.

I look across at Maura and cannot help but see that she is one breath away from giggling like a maniac, unstoppably. I am, myself, in exactly the same condition. The younger brother solemnly doles out tea the colour of molasses and I whimper with wicked, ungrateful hysteria. Maura sighs unsteadily and I cover my face with both hands, hiccuping towards a state beyond any assistance.

We are saved when the younger brother lifts away our emptied cups and carefully pronounces, 'Good night.' His senior then pats me on both shoulders and indicates that Maura and I should follow him now up the lean stairs.

Having climbed, we are left in a yellowing but not unpleasant room, dominated by a high, dark double bed.

Maura manages, in a breathy squeal, 'Oh, Christ – it's their parents', isn't it?'

'As long as they're not still in there.'

'Fuck, Nathan. I mean . . .'

We stumble together and then giggle against each other for a time.

'*We'll drive up to Scotland*, he says. *I'll show you where I come from – it'll be great.*' She squeezes me sharply, once. 'Nathan, I will never, ever take another holiday with you.'

'This isn't where I come from – the food's too good.' I mouth her neck for a moment, thinking. 'And we'll sort this all out tomorrow. It'll be fine. I promise.'

'It's fine already. Bloody peculiar, but fine.'

'And our offspring?'

'Is enjoying it too. I can tell. Now, what's that place . . .?' She kisses me on my left eye and my right – something which always removes any trace of my independent will. 'What's the name of that place in the north where everyone's happy?'

'Easy. Scotland.'

'*No*. Really – the classical place, the Greeks had a name for it . . .'

401

'Ah, *right* - the place where everybody's happy *without* penalties and guilt . . . that's um . . .'

'Hyperborea. That's it - land of happy people in the north. Here we are.'

'Yes.' I am astounded by my certainty. 'Yes. that's right. Here we are.'

We undress as if we are, somehow, surprised by the fastenings of our clothes and then mountaineer bravely up into the monster bed, where we lie, pressed beneath the clammy weight of fuck knows how many blankets, all topped off with a frayed mauve satin quilt. We wait, anticipating our next moves.

'Nathan?'

She knows *I'd* like to. I nearly always do.

'Maura?'

And now I know *she'd* like to, although this is becoming unusual in these expectant times.

And if *she'd* like to and *I'd* like to, then we ought to. So we do.

In the soundless dark, we position stealthily: Maura crouching on elbows and knees, because, for pregnant ladies, this is the sensible way to be, and not at all because it slackens my jaw to even think of her, curved here against me, my thighs beginning to press at the slightly cool and upturned flesh of her arse and having its brain-glazing smoothness press me back. I hunker up tight behind her, reach round and play, find her heat and kiss her spine: the lovely bone that guards all her motion, her every nerve. And, of course, finally, finally I am sinking, driving, praying in - being held and muscled in, deeper than want.

Maura is the first to speak. She whispers, mutters, then almost chants a wonderful succession of appalling obscenities. I am puzzled for a throbbing moment and then realise, join her, gamely narrating my way in and out of her cunt while she growls from the back of her throat and I hold her hips and we work up into a fast, wet smack of fucking, the sound and feel and scent of

402

which sets me jabbering every carnal thought I've known, a red pressure closing both my eyes and Maura even – in a way that makes me come – actually, fully screaming at each jerk of me.

We cool, heaped softly together, in the deafened house.

'*Fuck*, Nathan.'

'I think we just did.' I begin to cover us, settle us in. 'You are a shameless woman.'

'No, I'm not – I'm your wife.'

This information rings through me, makes me kiss the damp beat of her throat. 'That's right.'

'Mm hm. But I've got to pee. I'll be back soon.'

'You be careful out there.'

'I will.'

I listen to her fumbling into – very probably – my shirt, covering it in the process – I hope – with the smell of her, wet and traced with me. Something lovely to get up for in the morning.

My thinking mists and snatches as I wait for her to be back here again, beside me. I think I recognise the first dip of her weight on to the mattress, returning, but already I'm losing hold of the night, its sense quietly folding away.

When I dream, my mouth still tastes of Maura, her sweet salt, and the sun is once again spinning, numbing my mind's eye.

Nathan capped his pen and set it down, then rested the side of his head against the desk, the cool of paper at his cheek.

How was it for you, then, you stupid fuck?

A trill of lust was nagging the small of his back and he wished he would just go away and leave himself alone.

And why the last two paragraphs? You don't need them. You're imposing a false circularity on a story with nothing circular in its nature – all to avoid putting emphasis on what should be the final line. All because you can't stand to end with **Something lovely to get up for in the morning.** *You can't handle the wholesale fucking impossibility of that. So you've bottled out.*

*You've even lost your **narrative** backbone now.*

Nathan straightened, frowned, hugged himself round a yawn and then, sleek and quick and mortal against his arms and neck and chest, he could feel Maura, exactly Maura, as if she'd lifted from him, no more than a smile ago. And then, of course, came the acid scald of loss.

He hugged tighter, self against self, jolted again by the shock of his own nature, the reflex that would always kick him into writing the very things he would like to leave lie, into staring where he shouldn't even look, because that's where the life was. There was never a genuine choice involved, never the chance to skim out the hurt and leave the joy, to edit his commitment – there was only his mindless, nerveless appetite, the knife-point compulsion to make all of everything speak, no matter what – to always try for that. If it would make for a better sentence, he knew, he'd consent to anything.

I have a backbone, I have more fucking backbone than I can bear.

The following morning, when Nathan was lying in and grimly clinging to unconsciousness, Mary was up and breakfasted and even attempting to work. She was drinking her fifth cup of coffee and trying to think very hard in the general direction of her novel when the telephone rang. The beginnings of her book were tending to stodge together palely and then grease away again like so much over-animated pasta. Prolonged consideration of her ideas seemed only to fire them with an incomprehensible spite, so she was glad of any interruption – even if this was no more than yet another false alarm, another trick of the unremitting heat.

'Mary.'

It still surprised her how little it took for her to know him: the beat and curve of his voice through her name, his inhalation before speaking, that one, small opening breath.

'Jonathan?'

'Yes, I . . . Yes, it is. Sorry, I didn't mean to . . . are you? What are you doing?'

'Just now? I'm worki–'

'Oh, I'll call you back, then.' He failed to hang up.

'No, no. Don't do that.' Her hearing tensed, still anticipating disconnection. 'I'm working at this . . . umm.' *Novel* really did seem a hugely misleading and silly name for a couple of dozen sheets of worried paper. 'This, ah . . .' But it did seem to summarise what she was trying to produce.

'Book?'

Which is, of course, the other word — the one I could have used, if I'd wanted to show I had any control over my language of sodding choice. 'That's, yes — a book.' *Not that I can even currently control my **pulse**. Fuck, why is it so bloody easy for him to do this, to make me feel him, to make his voice touch?*

*Because I want it to be easy, because I want it, full stop. His voice, his touch — the way they are — **were** — when we were together properly.*

And, Jonno, what are you thinking, man, while I'm thinking this? It would all be easier if I knew.

She heard him sigh. His mouth always softened when he did that, the way it would before a kiss.

'I did think, Mary, assume, when you were . . . in my mind . . . I had guessed . . . you'd be ready for that — I mean, *doing* that, by now — writing a book. Or that you'd maybe have *written* a book.'

He's breathing too loudly — nervous.

He swallowed audibly, beginning to slide towards desperate small talk. 'What kind of book is it, then?'

'Just now? Very short.'

*That sounds like I'm taking the piss now. And I am, but out of **me**, not him.*

'It'll be good, though, Mary. I'm sure it'll be good.'

No, this is fucking nonsense. We can't start discussing bloody literature — Jesus Christ.

Even so, I would like him to think it was good — what I write — if he ever saw it. Which he knows. Clever bugger. Clever, complimentary bugger.

She tried to be firm, no nonsense: to talk very casually about what so happened to be her job and then move on. 'I'm not really even started, love. Really — I spend half my time staring at nothing and the other half walking about.'

'What did you call me?'

She played for time, 'Hm?' surprised by how quickly her words could bolt ahead of her, dodging caution.

His voice nudged closer. 'What did you call me?'

She shut her eyes. 'Love. I called you *love*.' The admission drummed patiently under her ribs. 'I – it felt, it felt like what I should say.'

'That's . . . good.'

They lost themselves in a hot pause, until Mary attempted to ease the tone, to keep it light. 'I should have said *cariad*, shouldn't I? Now that it's fashionable to be Welsh.'

'Cariad. Gwn.'

'I don't know, though. Wyddoch chi, pam dylwn I ddysgu Cymraeg?'

'Why should you learn it? Why *really* learn it, beyond what you get at school? Who knows. Pwy a wyr? Because it's part of who you are. And if it's not, you should leave it alone – it's done you no harm. Cardiff's full of fashion-victim Welsh – Welsh is where the money is – so that's all you hear when they're talking: *arian* – cash. Or people trying to be what they're not. But then, you get that everywhere, I suppose. And I don't honestly care much about it, or at least I don't want to, right now – Mary?'

'Yes?'

'When you called me . . . what you called me . . .'

'Love.' The syllable knocked at her again, always a slightly unexpected pressure, new each time.

'Yes.' A gentle push of breath. 'What did you mean?'

And that was a question to answer at once, or not at all, but she couldn't reach a wording – the answer wasn't in words.

'I see. That's what I thought.' He sounded slightly too brisk now, and brittle. 'You meant nothing much.'

'No. That's not true.'

'Then speak to me, for Christ's sake. Please.'

He was upset now – she hadn't meant to make him upset. 'I'm *trying*, but . . . Fuck, if I was good at speaking, I wouldn't write. I mean, if you – if you come by here . . . *when* you come by here, we'll be able to *see* what we *both* mean, we'll *feel* it.'

'*Feel?*'

Oh, shit, I know – he's going to tell me that the last time he felt me, it didn't exactly go down too well. God, is there really any point to this? Are we ever going to reach a place where we don't just offend each other all the time?

'Yes, *feel*. If we can be – oh, bloody hell, I don't know.'

'You were going to say *gentle*. If we can be gentle.'

406

'Or careful, or – yes – anything like that.'

'All right, then – careful. And I'm sorry for having been anything else.'

'That's . . . yes. Me, too.' Hope settled in her, airless and breakable, but definitely there.

'Look, I'll call again before – before I see you. If you don't mind. Bryn gave me your number and said you wouldn't mind.'

'He was right.'

'And I should do the same favour for him, really. Give you his number.'

'What do you mean?'

'I know he told you he was going off somewhere and was all mysterious. Well, he's down here in Cardiff, having tests.'

'Tests? What kind of tests?'

'See? – he said you'd worry. But I thought it would be better if you knew, because then you could ring him and stop him getting bored. He's gone into the hospital for a sort of medical, I think, but don't say that I've said so, that he's joined a private insurance scheme and now they're checking him over. But it's embarrassing his socialist principles. Not that I blame him at all. I mean, what the hell can he really expect to still get from the National Health? Anyway, I'll give you the number and then you can ring and cheer him up.'

'Of course.'

And he darted in, quietly, as if this was of no significance, 'And I could give you my number here.'

'Yes. Yes, you could. And I could ring you, if that would . . .'

'Yes.' Mary could hear that he was smiling. 'That would . . .' She recognised the mumbling, humming laugh he sometimes made when he was finding himself ridiculous. 'It would make me happy to hear you, Mary. It would.'

A memory teased up over her and pushed in: the turn and the smooth heat of licking his tongue: the need that would balance between her hips, the first ache, the way in.

For the rest of the day, Mary tried to keep working: the thought of the taste of Jonathan, here and there, spilling in when her concentration ebbed. Perhaps in an effort to resist this, to be professional, she drove especially hard at her opening chapter and found it surprisingly amenable to sudden discipline. By the time she leaned back in her chair and discovered she was hungry, there were five new pages to flop on to her tiny stack.

And this was the very thing she could phone and tell Bryn – the day's achievement, something they'd both like.

She searched for him, 'Bryn, Mr Lamb, Bryn Lamb,' through a chain of women's voices, all speaking from different departments, different wards, and it seemed to Mary that a hospital should be more careful, should keep a better check on who was where. The last transfer left her listening to a phone as it rang out and rang out, until, finally, with a concussion of noise, the receiver was rattled up.

'Oh, yes, Mr Lamb. Come in and see him today, did you?'

'No, I live away.'

'Ah, well, then, maybe tomorrow. He's asleep now – bit poorly – but we'll tell him you called. His daughter?'

'He doesn't have a daughter.' Which it felt untruthful to say: as if he were really her father, now denied. 'I'm his niece, I suppose. Yes, that's what I am. He's asleep? – Bryn?' Something about this seemed unlikely, made it temptingly reasonable to demand that he should be woken and brought to the phone, or else that the phone should be taken to him, that her uncle should be allowed to speak. That she should be allowed to hear him.

'That's right – he's sleeping. You're the one who writes, aren't you? He said.'

'Yes, I . . .' Mary couldn't ignore how very tangibly inappropriate this particular admission seemed. 'I write.' And although this also seemed somehow shameful, she heard herself add, 'I suppose, if you wouldn't mind, you could tell him *five pages* and then I'll explain what I mean tomorrow. At least, he'll *know* what I mean already, but I'll explain more . . .' But she wanted to be talking about Bryn, and *to* Bryn, not about her job. The dumb space left after her sentence petered out seemed to suggest that what she was saying hadn't really registered and wouldn't be passed on. 'Is that all right? You'll tell him?'

'Yes. Lovely. 'Bye, then.'

The emptied line dropped into place, Mary feeling bullied, aggrieved. The woman had sounded unhealthily breathless, older, careless, stout – not the sort of nurse that Bryn would like.

408

*If she **is** a nurse − she could have been a cleaner, a porter, someone just passing in the hall − I wouldn't know.*

She gave a small huff of concern, just as Bryn would have.

This is silly. He was right, Bryn − I do worry. Even if there's no need. And I'll be speaking to him in the morning. He's bound to be awake in the morning, I'm sure they wake them up at the crack of dawn.

'Oh, yes, he's awake, but he's not here. Mr Lamb, was it?'

Mary thought this wasn't the woman that she'd spoken to before.

'He's having a procedure this morning.'

Her tone was firmer and she sounded slightly Irish − actually, the voice was quite different.

'A procedure?'

'Yes. But if you came in this evening, he'd be . . . You're his niece?'

'Yes. Mary.'

'Yes, he talks about you all the time. If you come in this eveni−'

'I live away, though.'

'In the valley?'

'No, further than that.'

'Ah, well.'

Mary could taste the disapproval in both words.

'Do you want me to . . .' A dark chill came at her, surprising and knowledgeable, exposing the balance of her day. When she spoke, her words seemed just enough to fray reality. She couldn't quite believe her situation any more. 'Should I come . . .? I mean,' absurd idea, this, completely absurd, 'is there something wrong with him?'

'He's a bit poorly. Perhaps if you call later. Could you do that?'

'Of course.' Mary had started to feel tired, now, and chill. 'I can. After six? Or later?'

'Probably later. Say, eight.'

'Well, that's fine. OK. Eight.' And she walked herself over to Nathan's house, still holding her phone, and her faith not entirely convinced when she gazed at the tilt of the ground, the fall of light, the structure of her hand.

Joe and Nathan were both leaning, shirtless, against the cottage wall. Nathan noticed her first, smiled and then made a little spring forward. If he was, as he appeared to be, slightly concerned, she

409

could find this only distantly interesting – nothing touched.

'Mary? Are you OK? You look . . .'

'Yes. I'm fine. Well, just worried. I think I'm worried. I shouldn't be, though. I have nothing to worry about.'

Eckless woke up from the grass when he heard her and came forward to prove himself wholly convincing beneath her hands – the big bone of his head and the bump of warm, sleepy fur.

While Nathan flustered behind them, Joe set his arm at Mary's back and steered her indoors, clear through and into an armchair in the living room. Nathan battered about domestically in the kitchen, keeping close to his kettle. Joe knelt beside her, methodically listening: his hard, hot palm arched above the back of her hand on the armrest. He smelt of earth, she noticed, of a greenery that had been dried out from everywhere on the island but his garden. Something in his always very obvious health, the strength of life about him – a kind of shine on his skin – made her calmer. She almost didn't need him to speak, although he did in any case, reassuring.

'*Poorly* could mean anything. Hospitals have a whole range of their own infections, he might have picked something up while they did their tests. Ah, here's something to set us right.'

Nathan paced carefully in with a tray of tea things and irregularly sliced bread and butter. Mary noticed his left thumb was bleeding at the knuckle – fighting with the bread knife again – and saw a faint, pale line across his forearm, the sign of some old injury. He set down the tray, smiled at her and backed away, only turning quickly once he was safe in the kitchen again. For a moment, he showed her the thick, curved scar beneath his right shoulder blade. Her resistance broke: the thought of him hurt, of him opened and then worked at in the hard glare of an operating theatre, made her have to cry for him, for Uncle Bryn and for herself.

Joe stroked at the back of her neck. 'You're tired. Too much work going on, I think. You don't have to write everything at once.'

'But this week, I mean, these last days, it's been a way to not have things on my mind, you know? Like a place to go to.'

'Don't do that.' Nathan was back in the doorway, now wearing a crumpled T-shirt, a plaster on his thumb. 'I always do that and it's no use. Most of the things that I always do are. Don't do it. You start off

410

avoiding awkward moments and you end up just typing over your life.'

'This isn't an awkward moment.' She was surprised by how angry she sounded.

His face trembled into a frown and he trotted to her, took her free hand and – apparently unsure of what gesture he should make – kissed it. 'I know, I know. This is you being frightened for someone you love. I know. I'm sorry. Another thing I always do – say the wrong thing.'

Joe, for almost the first time since she'd met him, seemed hesitant when he spoke: or rather, seemed to be shaping what he would tell her far more carefully than usual. 'I never want the people I love to be harmed. All I ever wanted for the island was that my friends should come here and be well. Getting well, getting better: that can be hard and terribly slow. But then, the progress is precisely as important as the goal. And you, Mary Lamb, you *are* better. You *arrived* better. You're here to have all the best things we can give. Here you won't ever come to any harm. I promise.' He kissed her forehead and then spoke with what she couldn't believe was anything other than complete authority. 'You will always be looked after, that's your nature. I happen to know.' He glanced at Nathan, then stood abruptly. 'And for now, Mr Staples will be doing the looking after until you can make your telephone call and find out what's what. Eight o'clock and you'll know. It'll be fine. All right, Nathan?'

'Of course. Of course, it's all right.' Nathan kissed the top of her head now, pulling back after, clearing his throat vaguely, wandering off to fetch a chair, bring it closer and sit. 'You know, I . . .' Nathan rubbed his hands together, stared at his nails, while both of them heard Joe, easing the front door shut, leaving them alone. 'I hate hospitals. Even before I had anything much to do with them myself, they never seemed a great idea – not somewhere that I wanted to be.'

He was trying to distract her, they both knew, trying to tell her a story that might name and then defuse her fears. Mary wanted to thank him, but felt that if she tried to, she might start up crying again. So instead, she joined him in talking the bad things away. 'Well, you wouldn't want to be in hospital because you wouldn't want to be ill.'

'Mm. But then, being ill always seems less serious than *being ill in hospital.* The operation . . .' He swallowed, let the taste of the word make contact again, while she wished he would look up and let her smile at him and that, perhaps, he would move again to come within her reach. Nathan simply carried on, 'Going in for the operation worried me more than the cancer. The thought of lying under their hands, letting them cut at me, spill my blood, allowing them to part my ribs – it seemed far less natural than having a cancer turn me into something else. Cancer – that's not an unreasonable way for a writer to die. We spend our lives trying to be a growing medium, after all.'

'But you must have wanted to live. You let them operate.'

'Oh, yes. I . . . did have a couple of reasons for wanting to stick around. But it wasn't pleasant – the anticipation. The only way I found to deal with it was by learning the process, knowing exactly what they'd be doing in the absence of my conscious mind. It's still here in my head, all catalogued: Guedal airways, Essex or McKerson face masks, the pluses and the minuses of the various makes of gas, sectional operation tables, antiseptic protocols, padded straps and pillows for holding a body adrift from its will, the function and form of scalpels, catgut packs, the size of needles and the closures they might use – mattress, or blanket stitches, or figures of eight around pins – the washing and polishing of organic sutures cut and spun from the intestines of New Zealand lambs. I learned it all.'

'And did it help?' She wanted to touch him.

'Not really. I still had to put myself in order, be ready to go under and not come back. They still cut out my lung. When they touched my heart and stopped it I still died.'

'But then they brought you back again.' She wanted to touch him and break his concentration, allow him to be less alone.

'Me, or somebody like me.'

'No, I'm sure it was you.' It felt odd to say, too personal. 'I mean, I'd hope it was you.'

Nathan lifted his face to her with a sudden, hungry stare. 'Then probably it was.' Then he gave her a tentative smile, slipped his look away, shielded her from it. Or shielded it from her. 'Probably it was me. It's, it's . . . um . . . difficult to kill people, actually. I mean, it seems quite difficult to die.'

'Do you try to die often?' She'd intended that as a kind of joke, but instead it sounded insensitive. 'Sorry, that's a stupid question.'

'No. No, it's not.' But something about his manner had retreated, cooled. 'And really I wasn't making myself clear. It simply surprises me sometimes that I'm not dead. I should have been killed in a car crash I had once and then there was the time when I ate untreated kidney beans and was terribly, ridiculously ill – could have checked out then. Or the cancer could have got me, or they could have failed to start my heart again on the operating table. There was a time I almost kind of choked . . . I'm actually rather used to preparing myself for the worst. And then it doesn't come. At least, not in the ways I'd expected.'

And now she did touch him. Standing and walking to him, she kissed the slightly downy, warm skin at the crown of his head and set one hand on his back, feeling the muscle beneath his T-shirt give a single tick. 'It's all right, though. Isn't it? Nathan?'

'Being alive?' He leaned forward, his voice thinning, turning frail, tense. 'Oh, it's fine. Just here, just now – it's fine.'

Mary felt a large breath lift and then leave him. She realised her palm was resting on his empty side.

'Yes.' He reached, took her wrist and then tugged her round to face him. 'Yes, it's fine. But *I* was supposed to be cheering *you* up, wasn't I?'

'I think we're both doing OK, in actual fact.'

'Well, I suppose . . .' He formed a mildly anguished grin and then nodded, she thought, rather solemnly.

I wish he wouldn't be so uneasy – I don't know many people who are better at being caring, fatherly. And I'm not . . . I don't want . . . there's nothing I want from him any more.

Nathan made a little meal for her to pass the time, demanded she help him, picking the shells from slippery, hot, boiled eggs, dyeing her fingers with beetroot blood, keeping occupied. They both made a show of eating, until the room burst in at her softly with the scent of Bryn. Her heart pitched while she breathed his hair, his skin, his washing, shaving, waistcoat and cotton warmth. His touch walked through her, caught her neck with the unmistakable dab of his breath.

When she could move again, think again, she looked at Nathan. He was staring at her, swallowing, fingertips stalled in tearing

413

forgotten bread. 'Are you . . . Is it . . . ?'

She let him stumble up and round the table, reach and hold her, the press of his arms, for the first time, uncomfortable, a poor fit – she wanted to be holding Bryn.

'Mr Lamb. Bryn. I'm his . . .' Calm as marble, the certainty settled in her – who she was didn't really matter any more. 'How is he?'

Nathan watched her while she asked the question, the evening's heat thickening round them, but leaving them both cold, almost shivering. Mary wasn't sure, but thought he must feel – as she did – that this was a game they were playing, all pointless now, after the fact.

'He's quite poorly.' Another new voice.

'What do you mean *quite poorly*?' As if the meaning wasn't perfectly clear now, wholly translated.

'I'll go and fetch the doctor.'

The distant receiver was clacked down, still live, and offering her the mumble of a corridor, soft-soled shoes passing, trolley wheels.

After too short a pause, 'Miss Lamb?' A man speaking this time. 'Is this Miss Lamb?' He sounded English and young.

'Yes.'

'You were calling about Mr Lamb?'

'My Uncle Bryn. Yes.' She wanted to hear his proper name.

'We think you should come in and see him. Tonight, or tomorrow if you could. You live on an island, I understand?' As if this were a self-indulgent and unsupportive eccentricity on her part.

'I'll come tomorrow. He's quite poorly? Is that right?' Repeating the numb phrase, 'Quite poorly.'

'Yes. I'm –'

'I'll be there tomorrow, as soon as I can. Thank you. Can you tell him?'

'Of course.'

'Thank you.'

So he can still be told, then.

She jerked the next thought away, kept talking, 'Give him my, you know, my love. And tell him I'm on my way. Thank you.' She didn't want to say goodbye. 'Yes. Thank you. Thank you.'

This is what we do. This is what we do. This is what we do.

Nathan piloted Nathan, propelled both himself and his daughter through the dumb cogging of events.

He took them across to Ancw, the boat engine echoing wearily inside a thundery, bruised dusk. He would drive through the darkness, have her there by dawn.

He hired Radio Stevens's car, pushing an uncounted fist of notes into the man's unwilling palm.

'Nathan, I don't want the money. You just take the bloody thing.'

He was too far beyond himself to argue. 'For petrol. Damages. For fuck's sake, just take it. Be offended if you like.'

Mirror, signal, manoeuvre. Remember the way it all goes.

What the hell kind of cunting gearbox is this, anyway?

He was glad of the sweating concentration that driving took. He hadn't done this in years, had forgotten the patterns his body used to make, his natural seat position, the knack of keeping an uncramped grip on the wheel. Behind him, Mary lay on the back seat, perhaps sleeping. He hoped, sleeping.

He wound across Wales and into England, searching out wider, faster roads, then cut south under a sudden break of blinding rain. For a moment he felt the car slewing across the road, while his one hand fumbled stiffly for the windscreen-wiper control. His scalp crawled with quiet alarm. A paired smudge of lights rose and closed ahead of him, temptingly.

And then he thought of Mary, curled behind him, in his care, and eased his steering back to responsiveness, safety, set the wipers swiping at the viscous depth of water across his windscreen and was in command again. A shiver tightened in his spine, outside, the temperature falling in the dark.

He drove out of the twenty-fifth of June and on into the twenty-sixth. He drove his daughter into morning: into the early, empty grip of that.

'Mary? That's us. Come on, love. Wake up.' He led her into the hotel – an ugly block of modern brick that loomed beside the shopping centre. 'You get yourself fresh and then we'll go.' Her face was sleep-creased. 'I asked them to give us rooms that were on the same floor.'

As if that will be a help.

God, Kiddo.

We'll be OK, we'll be OK.

Waiting for her in the foyer, he knew he should have brought a jacket. The morning was cold, almost blacked out with rain, no place for shirt sleeves.

Then she was standing, ready, pale. He took her hand, delaying, although there was nothing to stop them leaving now, setting out for the hospital. 'Do you want to phone first?'

'No.' She kept hold of his hand, but started walking, 'I don't want to know,' leading him outside. 'I just want to see him. That's all.'

The curtains were closed around one bed. Mary noticed that as she came in.

The staff on the ward kept her walking from one nurse to another and then on, leading her down a corridor, saying nothing as they went, and letting her into the cream-coloured office, where the doctor sat and asked her to sit, too, and then quietly, precisely told her that Bryn was dead.

But she'd known that already, because of the curtains, the way that they were closed around one bed.

She'd forgotten how naked his pulse could be, so clear in his body when she held him that she caught his beat, raced with him while they lay, tight in one still ache, not moving, because this was all they wanted for now, all that they could stand. Mary and Jonathan, safe and folded away in her hotel bed. Quiet, for the sake of Nathan, asleep in the next room.

'Mary?' Her name made another, softer rhythm in his torso and his throat, against her torso and her throat.

'Sssh.'

'OK.'

She found herself tensing against him, as she gathered him closer, hard in, past the point where it hurt, and all the time she was thinking of Gofeg, the whole of Gofeg, halted as the hearse went by, and the sweep of Old Howells' top hat as he bowed to the coffin and then walked ahead, his coat as black as dignity, as black as respect.

Mary pressed her forehead to Jonathan's, felt him breathe, allowed the warm shift of his leg, moving in between hers, while the hollowed house in Gofeg – Bryn's house, left for dead – sang out all the way to Cardiff, found her, recited the list of furniture and the little time it took to clear: the bin liners heaped full of blankets, linen, clothes. And then there were the boxes and the cases full of everything: photographs, glasses, a cribbage board, the scent of one afternoon in a small, easy summer when she'd stared at the sweet peas in the garden until their colours fixed, stained everywhere she looked when she ran inside.

And in her palm and fingers she still held the final, indelible touch of Bryn's hand, laid flat on the hospital coverlet, cool and emptied of all memory. She thought she'd seen a little bruise behind his knuckle, but couldn't be sure – the way the light fell had been strange, misleading.

'What the fuck are you talking about?'

Jack was confusing Nathan and Nathan was loving him for it, laughing really rather too much, because right now, any sign of life – no matter how unnatural – was exactly and positively what he wanted.

'I'm talking about a new and anointed beginning for me and perhaps for you. My son.'

'The only way you'll anoint me will be under general anaesthetic.'

Jack gave a sputtering giggle. 'I wanted you to be the first to know. That's all. And now your lack of proper reverence is wounding me to the quick.'

'What on earth would be the proper degree of reverence to show? You – possibly the least God-fearing, most blasphemous, devotedly substance-abusing, manipulatively libidinous –'

'Any cunt in a storm.'

'Any *port* in a storm.'

'Well, a good glass of wine does go down pretty pleasantly, too . . .'

'Which just goes to demonstrate exactly what I mean – you are a completely and irretrievably depraved and sorry wreck of a man – and now you're trying to tell me that you've just received your ordination.'

'As a Christian minister. Yes. And I am now – for a moderate fee, paid in dollars by post – entitled to all the rights, privileges and benefits accorded thereto, including the possible foundation of my own, pleasantly informal, church, affording me easy access to the ardent supplications of as many tantalisingly vulnerable parishioners as my lower back can stand. The Church of the Second Coming. Hallelujah and Amen.'

'Seriously, though, why've you done it?'

'Because the aphrodisiac effects of my recent professional successes were beginning to wear thin. Or because I do have the fear of God in me somewhere and this seemed an appropriately threadbare response to it.' This having, perhaps, tickled a genuine nerve, he paused. 'Oh, I don't know. It amused me. And I have always wanted the Benefit of Clergy.'

'That just stopped you being hanged if you could read and write.'

'As good a reason as any. Literacy going the way it is – I can see it making a comeback. Or maybe they'll start hanging people who *can* read and write.' He sniffed, straightened his diction. 'I thought I might also call and ask how Mary is. And, by implication, how you are. Did you go to the funeral?'

Nathan wandered to his kitchen window and studied the drizzle outside, the summer broken, something in the slant of the day to make him chill. 'Yes. Yes, I did. And Mary got through very well. But then she had her . . . her . . . The boy she used to go out with, he was there.'

'Oh.'

'Well, there's no need to say it like that. He did well, too.'

The sly little fucker.

I mean, he was concerned, I could see that. And he did seem genuine. But even so . . . the way that he touched her shoulders, said he was there to help. I don't have to have liked that. I do not.

'A touch of paternal disapproval in there, Nathan? Hm?'

'I haven't the right.'

He had her. That last night in the hotel, I'd bet my lung he came back once I'd gone to bed and had her. The way she looked in the morning, the way she slept on the drive: there was something there as well as the sadness. And I could swear that I heard . . .

Not that I'm saying it wasn't the best thing she could have done.

A good act on his part.

A good act. Although if it was only an act I will, of course, kill him.

Having waited for him to say more, Jack chipped in, 'And since when did not having the right to feel something ever change the way you feel?'

And then in the service station, when she cried and held me and cried again – she smelt of him, of what they'd done.

'Nathan, you've gone quiet.'

419

And I'd have done the same, in their place — just the same.

But if that bastard Davies thinks he'll take advantage, get his feet in under the table while she's vulnerable . . . when he comes to Ancw . . .

Pre-emptive anger churned at the base of his skull.

He'd better make her fucking happy.

'Nathan? This is your friend, Pastor Jack — speak to me. What are you thinking?'

'That he'd better make her happy — this Davies bastard — that if he hurts her in any way I will peg him out in the field behind my house using the sharpened ends of his own long bones.'

'But you didn't tell him that?' Jack making an appeal on behalf of sanity — something new.

'No, I didn't tell him that. But I did . . . I did . . .'

Jack allowed a tiny sigh to escape him. 'But you did . . .?'

'I did look at him. I did look to the back of his eyes, where all of the crap gets tucked away, the shiftiness — you know?'

'Oh, I know. Yes, indeed.'

'And I did ask if . . . I did say that . . .' Nathan's throat was closing over, either with jealousy or fear. Or both. He bolted on: 'I told him that lots of people were fond of her — very fond of her — and anxious that nothing should hurt her. Ever.' The plaintive dizziness of the moment was tugging at him again.

'And . . . ?'

'He met my eyes.' *The bastard.* 'Said he understood.' *The fuck.* 'Said he would never let anything harm her if he could help it.' *The unmitigated cunt.*

'That's OK, then.'

'Yes.'

'Sound as if you mean it.'

'Yes.' Nathan could hear it in his voice — the sound of a man becoming superfluous.

Jack nipped in gently, trying to calm the mood, playing the pacifying pastor — playing the friend. 'How is she now?' Being the friend. 'How's Mary?'

Nathan moved to the other window — looking out to see no light in Mary's window, no chimney smoke. 'She's . . . I don't know. She sleeps all the time, Jack. I go down and see her — take her sandwiches, I even make her soup, for Christ's sake — and sometimes she's up to eat a little bit, but most of the time she's not.'

'It's shock.'

'I know, I know. That's the worst thing about it – I'm absolutely sure it's shock, because we both take it the same way. You remember how I was after Maura . . . I don't want her to have to feel that way.'

And now that I've said Maura's name, he'll ask me because he can't help it. And I'll tell him, because I can't help it either.

'Was she there? Nate? That is, I'm assuming that she wasn't, because you would have said, but –'

'No. Maura wasn't there.'

'Her own brother's funeral? And she didn't go?'

'Mary called and told her what had happened. I think they both agreed that it would have been hypocritical for her to turn up at the funeral when she hadn't seen him living for so many years. And neither of them wanted the gossip it might have kicked up. And I think Mary wanted to be sure it was Bryn's day and no one else's. She wanted to be there by herself. And with this Jonathan . . .'

'And with you.'

'Anyway, Maura didn't come – she wasn't there.'

*Not that you didn't hope, just the same – eyes trailing over the pavements, picking through the crowd and **finding** her – fuck it – finding her all the time – catching at the angle of a shoulder, a glancing face, and then the turn of your heart breaking in at you again, and the jolting blood, even though your common sense is saying all the time **don't look for her, don't look, she can't be there, don't look.***

Except I didn't listen because I am a stupid, stupid man.

And, of course, she wouldn't have been there. She wouldn't have wanted to be with me.

Nathan swallowed, keeping his voice controlled, 'If she'd been going, I would have stayed away,' but everything was starting to waver and fray. 'Listen, Pastor, I really should go and check on Mary again.'

'I quite understand. Give her my best. Or, possibly, your best – that might be better.'

'Hm? Oh, yes.' He could feel the whining throb of circulation at his temples. 'Well, I'll give her yours and mine both. That should be enough for anyone.'

'I'm sure you're looking after her perfectly, Nate – you're a good father.'

'No.'

'Don't argue with nature, Nathan, it doesn't become you. And look after yourself, too. And . . .' a smirk crept into his delivery, 'God be with you, my son.'

'And also with you.'

Nathan set himself to slicing bread and then buttering it – building sandwiches again. He couldn't think of a good filling this time: perhaps some tinned salmon and lettuce. With no tomatoes, she didn't like tomatoes.

My Mary – I wouldn't want her to have a thing she doesn't like.

This, Nathan hadn't expected: the music transecting his skull, a soft clatter in the meat of his thinking, an old lyric pushing his tongue's root, swinging up and under his scalp in a warm diameter of sound. He recognised 'Come Together', felt it pressing in and making him certain that he'd been an altogether different person when he'd heard it last.

Somewhere level with his spine, almost – weirdly – from behind him, his hearing was fingering in a cymbal spill, the pad of drums palpable in his right ear, and, tamping at his left, the private, hallucinatory reality of a voice. He looked about himself slowly, a minor elation ringing in his ribs at this new, almost perfect, secret din, unveiled at the back of his eyes.

'Do you like it? I hoped you would.' Mary was studying him where he sat. Her face was thinner, firmer and he couldn't resist thinking that, in these last weeks, she'd finished her growing up. This could mean she was moving beyond him – which, naturally, he didn't want, but might accept – but mainly she looked as if she was growing much closer to the way he was when he wouldn't wish the way he was on anyone. Genetic sadness, something you shouldn't pass on.

'Do you? Nathan?' She touched his cheek and then lifted his chin, as if he were her child, and he peered up at her, soaked with his own past.

'Like it? Yes. Yes, of course.'

She smiled for him while a shudder of time made him shake his head. 'I haven't heard this in years. It came out in what? – sixty-nine, seventy? Before you were even born. *Abbey Road*, Jesus . . .'

'And something new to play it on. I was surprised when you said you'd never had one.'

Another love song opened and caught Nathan's mind. He found he could smell the kitchen in their first house: the one Maura had forever referred to as her favourite. She'd been fond of the Beatles, Maura – especially George, because of his seriousness and spirituality. And the sad eyes.

There was a bewilderment in the words now, a certain tenderness, and he remembered singing them once in Maura's kitchen, their kitchen, and knew he couldn't listen any more. He disengaged the little earpieces gingerly and let his head clear, rubbed his neck, 'Hm. Yes, that's . . . Thank you so much,' and half-stood to kiss her, his lips dabbing her slightly awkwardly above one eyebrow before he subsided again. 'I hadn't thought of getting one. Just because I've never met somebody using one and not loathed them at first sight – all that hissing percussion. But this is lovely. Thank you. Really. You shouldn't have, though.'

'I don't see why not. I have money now. A bit. Bryn . . . Uncle Bryn, he kept quite a lot in the house – a silly amount, really, it wasn't safe – and then there was some other . . . even after the expenses . . . I mean, my mother didn't want any of it and I don't want it either, but there's nowhere else that it can go. So I can buy presents. If I want.' She sat on the floor, leaning against the side of his armchair. 'And I do want.'

He reached down and let his hand rest on her head, the fine heat of her crown. Her hair was washed, brushed – such things being taken care of again, a sign she was coming back to normality. 'Well, I'd say you should do precisely what you want. You bought one for yourself, too, I hope?'

'Mm hm. Joe brought them both over from Ancw with the flour and the post and things this morning.'

'Good.' He slipped his touch back until he was cupping Mary's neck, rubbing very lightly, in exactly the way – he remembered with a leap of fear – he had liked to in the evenings sometimes when they were together before: together in his other, former, better life: together inside the same family, father and child. With some stupid detail like this, the repetition of some triggering incident, he might unwittingly slip into recognition, being known.

You wish . . .

Her head shifted towards him, pleasantly needy. 'No, don't stop. It's relaxing.'

424

Of course it's relaxing, it always was relaxing, that's exactly what I mean it to be.

'I used to do this for my wife.' Which was true, but he had no call to say it.

Too late now.

'Your wife?'

Mary tried to turn and look at him, but he maintained the pressure of his palm and kept her softly, unresistingly in place.

'I didn't know you had a . . . I thought I'd heard . . . but then . . .'

'I was married. A long time ago. And then I lost her. And our child.'

This time she did turn and he didn't prevent her. 'They . . .?'

He let her face him, although he couldn't, now, entirely meet her eye. 'They went away.'

She kissed his hand and he rested his head back in the chair, stared and winced and stared again, the first blur of tears rising up at him, the sting of a coming collapse, quite plain on the roof of his mouth. 'The point to make . . .' speaking for the sake of speaking, his voice thick, 'the important thing, the serendipitous . . .' and her fingers at his wrist now, tight. 'I started to love music. It filled the space. For quite a while, once I'd lost them, I really couldn't leave my house, because I needed the sound of the music so much – to hear something clean in my head, something without my voice, without their voices.' He felt her grip on him grow fiercer, fastening him to this island, this moment, this daughter, this here and now. 'It's a good present. And it might suit you, too.' He understood she wouldn't let him go. 'Thanks.'

They sat quietly after that, Nathan with his eyes closed, his future open and babbling.

*She is a wonderful girl. Really, very wonderful. I would say that, because I'm her father – but she is, in any case. And she'll make her way through this bit – she **is making** her way through this bit – and I'll help, here and there – and then we'll be ready and I'll tell her and she'll be my daughter. She **needs** a father now, she's got the space for a father now. I'll tell her. I will tell her.*

We'll be here together.

We'll write our novels together.

Separately, but together.

425

Close in a way that won't be cloying, only very natural and something to admire. Quiet articles in the press.

No. No press. Fuck 'em. Just us with each other.

All good things to those who wait.

I'll have her back, get her back, and then, and then Maura. Why not? No reason why not.

All good things.

And he slithered towards a doze, jarring quietly in and out of the warm awareness that his daughter's cheek was rested on his arm, that her hand still held him, that he was safe.

'Yes. Yes, I know, love. Sssh.'

Nathan, his mind unfastened in sleep, was taking an embrace, keeping it, closing it round him until it stroked his stomach, cupped his balls and mouthed them with want.

'I would like that. Jonno . . . that would be lovely.'

His dreaming thumbs trembled at the fastening of a bra he could not possibly have deserved to recall in such excruciating detail.

'I can't say that – not just now . . . because I'm not alone, Nathan's here, sleeping. In a chair.'

Hooks and eyes: they were always so temperamental just precisely when co-operation was required. But any minute now, the first, hard suckle, the hot urge to bite . . .

'I can't say that . . . Because . . . because, I wouldn't – even if he wasn't here.'

Some kind of spasm locked his fingers while Maura's body roared against his skin. He wished that she would help him. He knew that, if she wanted to, she could.

'It's different *then* . . . I would say it *then* . . . Yes, when there's no need to.'

His consciousness was fighting to surface, while his imagined fists punched it down and then stammered back to his wife more slowly than he could bear. He felt that he was running out of time.

'Oh, bloody hell, man, OK – I want you to lick me there. Where d'you think?'

His mind was cramping, getting the bends.

'All right, all right . . . There. My cunt.'

A sharp, fast breath elbowed him closer to consciousness and jerked him away from his last chance at a kiss, left his thought craning forward, anxious and bereft.

'My. Cunt. There, now. Satisfied?'

He frowned out blearily at the room, unwillingly aware. The lights were on now, the night settled outside. His hands were cold and his mouth clammy. Mary's voice, tactfully compressed, was perfectly audible, murmuring behind the curtain that hid her bed.

'I know that, I know . . . You do cheer me up. You're very good . . . And I'll see you . . . quite soon. I'm just going to stay here for a while now – Nathan's looking after me . . . No.' She started a gentle giggle. 'No, he's not like that. Not with me, anyway. He's . . . he's a good man.'

Nathan swallowed at that, feeling it warm away a part of the yawning loss he'd woken to. The chair, he noticed when he stretched, had moulded a needling ache into his side.

'Yes. Yes, I will. And you take care, too. Yes. Love you.'

Now, now, now . . .

A sweet twist of jealous happiness made Nathan grimace and begin to stand.

No, then she'll hear me and think I've been listening. Which I have. But not much. Not too much . . .

Maura's ghost rose in him again and his dream of her crept back under his fingernails, hurting him. He attempted to shiver it off and work himself into a suitably somnolent pose.

I know she was saying something, I'm just not sure what. The usual young love stuff, I suppose. Young love, Jesus.

But she should have it, she really should have it in spades – the best of everything. Nothing standing in her way.

Beyond his convincingly closed eyes, he could hear her moving, walking closer, halting and leaning close enough for him to recognise her scent, the smell of her hair.

'Nathan? Nathan? Are you awake?'

He allowed himself a tiny intake of breath, a moment of apparent confusion. 'Mm?'

Lying to my own daughter.

Not exactly lying – avoiding embarrassment.

He stirred, yawned, massaged his forehead and peeked at her while his fingers were still in position to partially mask his face. 'Mary?'

She smiled at him with a long, straight look.

Bugger it, she knows I wasn't sleeping.

'Naturally Mary – who else?'

'Indeed. What time is it?'

'Gone seven.'

'*Seven?* Shit. I must have been tired. Sorry.'

'It's OK.' Another overly intelligent smile. 'You were no bother. While you're here, can I make dinner? Pay you back for all the sandwiches?'

'You're going to cook at me?'

'Like I said – pay-back time. Omelette do you?'

'Omelette would be fine.'

So she cooked and he cleaned up after her until she told him to go away and just sit down. They ate slowly, even exploring a bottle of Louis's fatal potato gin, before abandoning the washing-up.

'I'll just throw the dishes away in the morning.' Mary thumped down into a chair and felt about for her glass.

'Quite right, although I usually give mine to the dog and he licks them clean.'

'You know, I almost believe you.'

'You can always believe me.'

And I mean that – and you can see that I do – so now we both know it and everything's fine.

They smiled at each other until Nathan had to drop his head, an even broader, uncontrollable grin, welling dangerously. He tried to cough it away, but heard himself giggle instead. 'Hm. Yes. Well. That was lovely. Thank you. I've had a good day.'

'Oh, I am sorry, Nathan.'

He narrowed his eyes, made his best suspicious face while she tried to stay deadpan and nearly managed – only showing a twitch at her lip.

'And why are you sorry, exactly?'

'For making you have a good day – goes against your nature, doesn't it?'

Nathan produced a vaguely strangled laugh, thoroughly delighted to be mocked, but also tasting something of his own blood. 'No, it doesn't go against my nature – it goes against my luck.' That sounded too solemn. 'I don't know – I spend years imparting the mysteries of my craft to her and then all she does is take the piss.' Better.

'But she doesn't mean it.'

'Of course she doesn't mean it – he understands that.'

But he'd disturbed her a touch and she was standing now, moving to the desk, the sadness that had gone from her all evening seeming to mist in again. She rummaged in a drawer. 'I want to show you something. If you don't mind.'

'Of course.'

She was holding a photograph, walking towards him, offering it out. 'This was them years ago, on Barry Island. I took it – that's why I'm not there, not in the frame. This was them.'

Dear God, love, don't. You'll hurt too much.

He took the picture: two studiously smiling faces, summer shirts open at the throat, behind them, a sunny blur. 'This is . . .'

'Bryn.'

'Then he's Morgan.' He stumbled towards an effective comment, a believable truth. 'They seem fine men.'

'They were.'

He tried to offer back the image, but she wouldn't take it, only leaned one hand on his shoulder and spoke again, very gently. 'I kept this with me after Morgan died and it never seemed right – that both of them were there, when one was really gone. Then I took it out last night and now . . .'

She stroked at him, brushed at the lobe of his ear in a way he could guess she would have done with one of the Uncles, the other fathers in her life.

'Now it's . . .' she sighed in, 'now it's OK. In the picture they seem to be together again, looking out from another country. Somewhere else they went.'

'Together.' The beautiful, terrible word.

'Together. Yes.'

'Give us a shag, Nurse Collins.'

'Once you've grown up, Mr Grace.'

'Eleven inches, Nurse Collins. Possibly more.' Jack's voice seemed, somehow, more painstaking than usual, more deliberate.

'But all of them flaccid. No use to me.'

'You are a cruel woman, Nurse Collins.'

'But you can call me Anne.'

Nathan edged his chair in closer to the bed as Nurse Collins brushed past him crisply. He gave her the bashful nod of a man apologising for his sex and intending to distance himself from the boorish and recidivist behaviour of others. She rolled her eyes and marched from the room, frighteningly dignified, sensible shoes squealing softly away along the corridor outside.

'Well, this is nice,' Nathan lied and inhaled another mouthful of hospital: the stifling clamp of cleaning fluids laid across all those other troubling traces of bad stew, strayed body fluids and accumulated sweat.

Jesus Christ, I hate these fucking places. Being ill is the least of your problems, once you're here.

'You've got your own room and everything . . .' Nathan peered round at the buttermilk walls, the pastel blue floral dado line, the bewildering accretion of Yuletide flora, dangling near the door, and the solitary Russell Flint print, to say nothing of the solitary patient. 'It's very . . .'

Jack Grace was reclining in sea-green pyjamas, blankets to his waist, surrounded by a scatter of watchful equipment and tubes – one of the monitors was tinselled.

It's only November, for crying out loud – is this leftover festive spirit from last year, an early start for this, or just a general urge to make things sparkly? Jesus Christ, it's all appalling, whatever.

Jack was currently connected to no particular device, although a shunt was fixed in the back of his hand, discreetly taped. He had the air of a man who had just put the finishing touches to a major work of art – or, perhaps, of a man who had just become one.

J. D. smirked. 'It's very . . . like hell. Pas-tel hell. God knows how anyone could stand it if they didn't have a private room. Health insurance, Sport – got any?'

'With my medical history the premiums would be fatal.'

'Ah.' Jack nodded, slightly chastened, but brightened again. 'I wasn't joking, you know.'

'Mm?'

'About the inches. Want a look?' He leered, delightedly. 'You can touch it for a fiver. I'm thinking of becoming a religious icon.' He twitched at his coverlet teasingly while Nathan shook his head.

'What the fuck are you on about? Or is this something that only a pastor would understand?'

'Yes, that was a laugh – they asked what religion I was when they wheeled me in – I told them *my own*. I think they counted that as Protestant – which isn't far off. I do only ever contact God to make complaints.'

'Jack, how many drugs are they giving you?'

'Far too few, old man, far too bloody few.' He slowed, rocked his neck back and forth for a moment to ease some unspecified ache. His skin had a yellowed tinge with undertones of green and looked slightly more transparent than it should have been. Other than that, he seemed to have put on weight. 'It is good to see you, Nate. I've had every sodding member of all my families trooping past for the last two days – much more than mortal man can bear. The age range my children cover is truly alarming. It could be worse, obviously. Better than no visitors at all. But what I want is *company*. Nothing like the family to make you feel alone.'

Nathan's brain writhed silently for several seconds, trying to find some cheerful observation. In the end, he could only cough out, 'And are you all right?'

Jack spluttered into a bray of laughter. 'Well, obviously bloody not. I'm in hospital.'

'You know what I mean.'

'Just the usual stuff, really. Pancreatitis grumbling, liver not too happy, kidneys whingeing and the heart not one hundred per cent. Very dull. The best bit is the water retention. If you hadn't been intent on rejecting my advances, I'd have shown you . . .' He winked lugubriously. 'Below the waist, I am reaching quite awesome proportions.'

'Not *only* your dick, surely?'

'Sadly no. Not that it wasn't a fine old thing in the first place . . . No, no, all of me's depressingly waterlogged, I'm afraid. I'm just hoping the tide won't rise any further. Queer way to drown, wouldn't you say? From the inside out.'

'That isn't likely, is it?' Nathan tried not to sound alarmed.

'No, not very. Strange, though . . . At the moment my bollocks look for all the world like a pair of infants' heads. Viewed from above.'

431

'But without the ears.'

'God, you're a pedantic shit.'

'You wouldn't fancy telling me how you got here.'

'You mean you haven't heard the story?'

'I mean I haven't heard it from you.'

'Ah well, then, I suppose . . .' Jack sniffed and settled himself into a more narrative position. 'Haven't got a drink on you, by any chance? Just before I start?' His eyes wheedled just a little too long before he shrugged and cleared his throat. 'Uncaring bastard.' He gave Nathan another look, softer this time, and very still. 'Then I'll begin. Once upon a time there was a promising young editor who loved his work and the look of his future and his books . . .' He paused to rub his eyes.

'Perhaps we might skip a few years, Jack? Till we get to last week.' Nathan felt an absurd urge to pat at Jack's hand, along with an equally strong and opposing conviction that he didn't really want to *touch* Jack, right now, at all – that his flesh might be clammy, or sticky, or something worse.

Which wouldn't be his fault. But should still be his own business. No need for me to intrude.

'What are you thinking, Nate? About me, isn't it? I can tell. You needn't worry, you know. I am perfectly all right, really. For a hospital case.' Jack paused, solemnly waiting for Nathan to agree.

'Fine, OK, I'm convinced.'

'Good. So stop worrying. You look repulsive when you're worried.'

'Just because you're in bed, that doesn't mean you can just insult me indefinitely.'

'Sign of affection, though, isn't it?' Jack skipped his gaze towards the window and frowned slightly.

Nathan scratched his ear for no good reason. 'Mm. Yes. No doubt.'

'But back to our hero Jack . . .' J. D. folded his arms, yawned and made a proper start. 'Well, as you know, *Doctor Dee's Table* did terribly well. My girl and I – surprisingly – won *Themiddleclasswankers Thankyoufortrying Award* (sponsored by Gubbins and Muggins Electric Shock Batons Inc.). We were both of us rather chuffed.'

'Yes, congratulations.'

'And then we were long-listed for the *Headfuck*.'

'And then short-listed.'

'Yes, indeed. Which meant we had to bib and tucker up and go off to the dinner, eat our humble crow and Armageddon pie.' He sighed. 'I went once before, a thousand years ago. But it hadn't been to do with me, then – I'd just been an observer, not taking it personally at all . . .

'Either way, I'd forgotten what it was like. Everywhere you looked, we were all of us, visibly, shaking apart – nervous ticks and tremors, stumbles and fumbles and defects of speech bursting up out of nowhere. The whole place looked like a psychiatric ward in evening dress – one with inadequate access to Largactil and ECT.

'And I'm in there, just like the rest, another bundle of mutating superstitions and indecent sweat and I'm fighting to keep the glass full and the smile in place and the hands as they should be and not gripping my own or some other fucker's throat and above the whole shivering ruck of us there's a haze of pure alcohol, just roiling up from every inch of skin as the pressure of undiluted professional terror simply fucking evaporates every drop we can manage to drink.

'Then, when they've trotted us round the parade ring for a lifetime or so, we're herded in to sit up nicely and dine. And eating your own offspring in a floodlit slaughterhouse would be really much more pleasant and entertaining . . .' Jack grinned balefully, wiped his mouth.

'So I'm holding my author's hand now under the table – not even attempting the gluey dessert – and Benedict fucking shithead tosser Kemmler is sitting at the table opposite because *he's* got a punter up for it, too – God piss on him in purgatory for ever – which means there are two books short-listed from the same infernal house, Christ help us – and he grins, he grins right fucking at me, the poisonous shit. The sleazy, bastard fuck. And, by now, this is not about winning, not even about being taken apart by whoever does fucking win, this is not about my book, or anyone else's, this is not about trying to keep myself from weeping, or crying out, or just replacing that smug fucker's eyes with my nicely polished, family heirloom cufflinks – it is simply about not dying, about getting through the

433

next fifty minutes of nationally televised blood sport without dropping down fucking dead.' Jack's colour was rising, taking on an unusual orange blush. He shook his head, continued.

'And that is the point, the exact, fucking moment when you understand, very clearly, that what you are watching is the death of language and of truth and of whatever, at one time, might just have felt a little bit like your soul. And you sit, like a hollowed apple, rotting quietly beneath the lights, while the cameras close on another table – that opposite table – that may-you-baste-eternally-in-your-own-fucking-body-fat-right-in-the-heart-of-the-darkest-turd-in-the-arsehole-of-hell table – and you work out the winner before it's announced – *Last Seen Heading Athwart* – Kemmler's book. Kemmler's fucking punter. Kemmler's fucking book. The fucking winner is Kemmler's piss-fucking-poorly presented homage to fucking catatonia, his post-modernist colostomy bag of self-referential pus, his roman-à-no-clef-needed-it's-about-my-ex-wife wank, squeezed out of possibly the most ungrateful and boring typist to ever have spewed on a waiter at the Groucho Club. Fuck. Fuck. Fuck. Fuck. *Fuck*.

'I got annoyed, Nathan. I really did get quite annoyed.

'And my girl was very brave and then went down to the ladies for a cry and came back looking dreadful when she'd been genuinely prettily turned out and had bloody well deserved to win and maybe, if anyone had liked her editor, she might have. It was shitty for her – not what she deserved – and I didn't know what to say, didn't know how to help her. She wrote a good book, Nathan – she broke her heart to write a good, straight book. The way it *ought* to be done, you know?'

'I just about remember.'

'No. You know. You're the type that does. And you're going to do it yourself for me soon.' He winced, breathed, reined himself in a touch. 'Sorry. Sounding rather shrill there. I do apologise. Where had I got to . . . Ah,' spiring his hands to his mouth now, obscuring a smile, 'my final downfall, yes. Well, of course, the house had hired out that ghastly place in Soho for their aftermath party: Mr Kemmler borne off to it shoulder-high, with a special wave for me as he was leaving. *His* charge was off being grilled by the universe's press and *mine* . . . ? What the hell could I do with mine? Couldn't haul her off

434

to the same bloody party – someone else's victory party – that would be altogether far too grisly. In the end she told me she just wanted to go home.'

Nathan couldn't help but grin mildly.

'Not at all, Mr Staples, don't even think it – she went to *her* home, by herself, back to her grubby hubby. I won't say I didn't consider an offer of serious consolation, but then – surprisingly – I found I didn't have the heart. So she jumps in a cab and I take another and I did absolutely mean to go to the bash myself, to walk in and face them all – do the sporting thing and fight another day: having lost the battle, try for the war: get up and keep running and be a good boy and so on and so on and so on . . .' He glowered at the bloated shape of his legs under the blankets.

'But I couldn't. I caught a cab all right, got to the place, made it almost to the door, but then I heard them laughing. And, of course, it was very probably not laughter aimed at me, not even remotely referring to me, but it felt as if it *was* and I couldn't go in, Nathan. I could not go in. They beat me, then. I let them win. That was precisely the point when I let them win.

'And so I went to see Oscar, Oscar my personal dentist – why not? – to get myself properly, thoroughly loaded, to turn out all of my lights. He has a flat in Frith Street: not far to go.

'My reception was slightly cantankerous. He wasn't alone and hadn't been expecting me and wasn't in the mood for playing amateur proctologist – not with a straight old drunk, in any case. But I do believe that I may have cried at him and even gone down on my knees. They're suckers for kneeling, these dominant types, very reminiscent of my second wife.

'Anyway, Oscar relented and let me come in, packed away his current, unsavoury, little friend and got down to business. Or *up* to business, one never quite knows with enemas . . . Both, I suppose. I asked him for a stronger solution than we'd used before, because these things always have to escalate: that's their nature, it can't be helped. And he obliged me.' Jack swallowed, pursed his lips. 'But he wanted an increase in payment – for the general inconvenience and the lateness of the hour.' His eyes widened slightly and, for a moment, he looked almost painfully childlike and, somehow, surprised or disappointed.

435

'See?' J. D. opened his mouth, yawned it wide, exposing the naked line of his gums. Barring his incisors, all Jack's teeth were gone. His multiple extractions had left their mark in ruddy puckers, a black fraying of stitches – Nathan hoped from hospital intervention – and the unpleasant dark of what might be either clots, or unhealed sockets, Nathan didn't wish to guess. His own mouth began to wash with anxious saliva.

'Christ, Jack. What were you thinking?'

'That I no longer wished to think. Besides which, it wasn't *bad*, didn't even especially go *wrong*. I had an entirely satisfactory dip into oblivion and then I was sent on my way. The sending on the way, that was the problem. Old Oscar was a little too anxious to see me go. Which unfortunately left me to provide one of the West End's more lurid pavement spectacles. I can see the headlines in the *Bookseller* now – *Editor Found Slush-Piled Near Soho Square* – '*He was bleeding from the mouth, unconscious, subject to alcoholic seizures and (upon close and expert examination) also had a recently penetrated and Vaseline'd arse. We are currently at a loss to guess what unnatural doings may have been done,*' *says baffled Inspector Bollock of the Yard.*

'I have told them I remember nothing, but that I may have been Mickey Finned.'

'And they believe you?'

'I shouldn't think so. Would you?' He gave a faintly shamefaced cough and leaned back. 'And that, Best Beloved, is the story of How The Editor Lost His Teeth. And I am a disgrace to my vocation. I do know. Nate?'

'Yes?'

'Come here and shake my hand.' An arm was extended, a vague tremble setting in, once it had halted in midair.

'What?'

'Shake my hand, Sport – there's a good man. Be here for me. Tangibly.'

And Nathan could do nothing but shuffle up and grip Jack's palm. Then, finding himself held startlingly tight, 'Steady, Jack. No need to break my fingers.'

'Oh, but there might be. If you don't agree.' Jack fixed Nathan with his firmest hard-bargaining stare.

'Jack. Don't fuck about.'

436

'You see, we aren't just being friendly, Nate. We're shaking on a deal.'

Nathan angled his head aslant, so that he didn't catch Jack's breath. 'You can't do this, Jack. For one thing, there's no need for it. Don't we generally agree?'

'Just an agreement won't be enough. This has to be a *complete understanding.*'

'We already have a contract, Jack.'

'Mm hm.' J. D. was breathing faster, beginning to sweat as his fist closed more urgently on Nathan's already throbbing knuckles. 'But that's business – that's not *us.* I want your absolute promise to *me*, not the company.'

'Jack, really . . .'

'Promise.'

'Promise what?' Nathan's remaining supplies of calm were seeping lumpily away.

'All right, I'll tell you two out of three. They're not bad things, Nate. They're for your own good.'

'Altruism, Jack. That isn't like you.' The joke didn't work, didn't make either one of them smile.

'They're all for your own good and one of them's also for mine. Will you listen?' Jack's voice shifted a little in his throat, made him halt, blinking at Nathan, eyes asking to be excused any further argument.

'I'm listening.'

'About time. I want you to tell your daughter who you are –'

'I'm going to, I'm going to. For fuck's sake, just allow me the dignity of picking my own time.' He controlled a glower, relented, met Jack's continuing gaze. 'And the next?'

'The proper novel. The one that breaks your heart. Do it.'

'Bearing in mind that nobody can break what's already broken . . . Yes, OK. I've told you, I'm already working on it – I'll get it done – but if you want a promise, then I promise. I promise. OK? And?'

'I'll tell you the last one later. It's for me. So allow me the dignity of picking my own time.'

'You want a blind promise?'

'I want you to trust me.'

'Jack, I –'

437

'I want you to trust me.'

'I do.'

They both swallowed while the instant held and folded round them. Neither man had anticipated the contract would be made completely with two words, that it would lock in their intentions, almost before they could recognise its key. Nathan slowly slipped his free hand over Jack's, then felt Jack fit the last hand moistly over that. They faced each other.

'Well, Nathan.'

'Well, Jack.'

'You'll be there for me, won't you?'

'I, uh –'

'Mm hm, mm hm. I know.' Jack nodded, leaned his head back and, for a moment, closed his eyes. 'That's good.' And then he looked at Nathan. 'That's us now. Isn't it?'

And Nathan looked back at him. 'Yes. Yes, that's us.'

What are we doing, Jack? What have we done?

Nathan's scalp tingled with a soft unease. He thought that he ought to feel foolish, clinging to another grown man like this, but he couldn't quite break away. Without knowing why, he leaned forward and gently, cleanly, kissed Jack on the forehead and then withdrew.

'Bloody hell, Nathan.' Quietly, almost a whisper, 'Was that really called for?'

'Yes, I would say so.' Whispering back.

'You're just taking advantage of a dying man.'

'Don't say that.' The air seeming to shiver now, making it difficult to see.

'Well, as it happens, Nate, if I actually had the choice, I would rather not.'

It really was getting quite ridiculously difficult to see.

'Don't worry, Nathan. I'll write to you. I'll write.'

D*ear Nate,*

The Christmas decorations are getting nearer. So far, my room can boast everything festive but mistletoe. I don't think they're going to offer me any of that.

First week of December and the decor can only get worse. I blame the staff. I believe that a number of them have been transferred into my orbit from a children's ward, hence their nervous fiddling with baubles and their air of asexual cheer. I am determined to be out of here before they ring me round with trees. I will not be a party to trimming, I am adamant.

Which brings me to a rather tricky editorial point. Here I am, writing to you: present and even future tense, first person and all that. But, in fact, if – or rather when – they send you this, I'll already be past.

So there it is. Has to be said. Sorry.

I've already written up a respectable stack of letters – too many dependants, you see. You're the last and then I'll settle down to dying. They say to keep cheerful, but most things about me aren't working any more. I think I have two or three days. During which I may be rather busy.

I think we didn't do too badly by each other, although you may disagree. By now I obviously won't care much if you do. But, at the time of writing, I hope you think that I did well by you.

And I hope that you'll take my advice when you pick my replacement. I feel, as your former partner, that I may have the right to suggest your next suitable mate. Certainly, I wouldn't want to think of you pining alone. Although, of course, I am assuming that you will find me to be quite irreplaceable. I'm enclosing the name and address of my choice for you. You should like him, he looks very like that acid bath murderer, Haigh.

Naturally, in the end, it's up to you.

But, talking of free will – that third promise, I am going to hold you to it. I've sealed up the relevant details inside the other envelope – I hope you

439

didn't open that one first. It would be just like you to fuck up the proper sequence of events. Anyway, please think of it as a final little gift. And something that you can do for me, something no one else could. Frankly, I wouldn't want anyone else to try. Only you.

All of the needful arrangements have been made.

Please, Nathan. I would like you to do it. For me.

And I do detest maudlin goodbyes, so this is it.

You were the near friend of my heart. But you know that, don't you?

Yours,

Jack Dowd Grace, Literary Editor

Nathan wasn't feeling the cold. That morning, he'd taken the launch across to Ancw and bought six half-bottles of whisky – the comfortable, inside-pocket-filling size. Now he sat on the cliff grass and stared at the Seven Brothers and the rising swing of water in his bay, his back to the wind, his cap on his head and his gloved hands resting snug around one of the bottles which was, by this point, almost drained.

To the west, a blue bank of cloud was thickening and he could smell a coming rain, a shower that would catch him, long before he made it home. He didn't mind. Back at the cottage, Eckless was probably still fretting, upset at not being in company, unsettled by the hard mood of the day, and Nathan didn't mind that either, especially. A splinter of irritation with himself, of guilt, would prick him dumbly, now and then, but it didn't matter, not a bit.

For the most part, his skull was simply filled with music, with Glenn Gould and the Goldberg Variations creeping and then bursting in mercury scatters, the mumble and fuss of the pianist occasionally nudging through. Ever since he'd got the letter, Mary's present had been earning its keep. He should have bought more batteries in Ancw. Stupid. Too late to go over again today. Too late and too drunk.

The final, oyster light was easing from the horizon and the rain had begun when he felt hands rest on his shoulders, the press of someone against his side. He didn't look, but knew it would be Mary.

She sat to his left, their bodies touching at the hip, and joined him in considering the sea.

By the time the last variation had played out, the sky was almost completely dark. Nathan swallowed, coughed, put away his little earphones in the pocket of his coat. He noticed he was shivering. 'I don't want to talk about it.'

441

'That's OK.'

'I don't want to think about it.'

'Fine.'

And he turned towards her dumbly, caught her in hard until his face was at her neck, the live heat of her neck. He wanted to cry, but couldn't.

1996

*O*ther people's quarrels, they never sound as sensible as your own. Not that I quarrel a lot. Not that **we** quarrel a lot.

Mary tried to think of how often she'd fallen out with Jonathan since they'd met.

Since we ever saw each other — since we were both at school, for heaven's sake — I think we've only really fought once, or maybe twice — five times at the most. Which either means that we're suited, or that we keep things bottled up. Probably that we're suited. And now . . .

She glanced off to the corner of the room, wanting to give herself a touch of privacy.

And now we've been fine since he came to Ancw — that's most of November, December and seven days of January. Nearly two months. All fine. Very fine.

The part of his lips, that neat, opening sound, brushed through her.

Across the table from her, Louis was waving his left hand, pinkly, while his other pressed a daintily curled finger to his lips and he tried to swallow a mouthful of chocolate mousse more rapidly than he'd intended. Richard smiled at him benignly and then smiled with equal warmth at Lynda, who was currently preoccupied with a screeching argument. That is to say, she was screeching as her contribution to the afternoon's argument.

'Bloody hell, this is so fucking childish.'

Mary sometimes couldn't work out why the Fellowship even tried to hold Business Meetings: proper, business-related business meetings. Joe had taken to holding them downstairs, away from the meditation room in what he hoped would be a more informal, round-the-dining-table atmosphere. But, half the time, they still ended in something not terribly far from a brawl. And the first meeting of the New Year was already mutating into something predictably venomous.

Lynda continued, rising half a tone. 'Just open the sodding thing. Or are you scared you'll spoil your game. Christ, you're like a mound of little boys.'

Mary, who never could take these performances seriously, failed to resist the temptation to join in. 'Is *mound* the correct collective noun for little boys?'

Finally freed from his pudding, Louis pushed back his chair and brought both his hands down against his knees with a vicious-sounding slap. He twitched at the impact, but still managed a respectable frown round the table, laden with a schoolboy's naked dismay and a schoolmaster's distaste. Having established a painful silence, he began, 'With the greatest respect to everyone, I do still have to say that we have this discussion about the jar really far too often. Joe and I have been around long enough to remember a number of jars and I would suggest that you take our words on what happens to them. Either we do this thing properly, or we don't bother doing it at all. The agreement is that we seal up the jar with the Fellowship's statements, predictions, promises, whatever, and then we keep it that way until seven years have absolutely, fully elapsed and, I'm afraid, they quite simply haven't done that yet. Mary's contribution was added at the end of 1990 when she,' he nodded to her, almost undermining his serious tone with a grin, 'when she decided to delight us with her company. The official sealing date was the first of November 1989. This is simply the New Year – we cannot open the jar until the first of November 1996, the Day of the Dead 1996. As usual. I do hope that satisfies everyone.' His lips pursed disappointedly. 'And I cannot imagine why this has all had to be so acrimonious. Very unnecessary. *Pueri inter sese quam pro levibus noxiis iras gerunt*, as I believe Terence once wrote.'

He gave Mary another, more expectant nod and she tried her best to translate for him, as she usually did. It was a matter of honour – hers and the Uncles'. And, in any case, the hardest thing in the world to resist was, as ever, an utterly innocent request.

Or an utterly loving one. Same difference.

'Ahm . . . Boys easily . . . How lightly boys squabble amongst themselves?'

Louis beamed. '*Squabble* – I like that. Better than *disagree*. Good.'

Lynda rolled her eyes. 'Correct me if I'm wrong, but I think I just said much the same thing myself and never mind fucking Terence. *Jesus.'*

'Never mind fucking Terence? That's not like you. Even if he *is* dead. What's the matter – something spoil your appetite?' Nathan had been quiet until then, morosely reducing a piece of bread to flattened pills. These he now swept on to the floor, before standing and stalking out of the dining room. He hadn't been in the best of tempers for a while.

'One day, he'll get the kicking he deserves.' Lynda had quietened, dragged her vowels back to something more convincingly middle class. 'Bloody drama queen. He just has to be the only one who's ever had a problem. And all of his precious suffering is supposed to mean he can act like a total shit.'

'He's not so bad.' Ruth flushed mildly. '*Well*, he's not.'

Lynda was having none of it. 'And well, we all know what *you're* after, don't we, dear?'

Here we go. Here we bloody go. Mary tried to catch Joe's eye. He had leaned himself back in his chair with his arms firmly folded and was studying the ceiling, apparently beyond all reach of communications. But, as she looked, he bowed gently forward and met her eye. Until he blinked, it seemed she could feel his attention in her mind, like the touch of a cool, clean hand. She shivered.

'Ladies and gentlemen,' Joe didn't shout, barely raised his voice, 'it's a cold day,' but, as he continued, he eased a wary calm around the table. 'Before dinner I lit a good fire upstairs in the Meeting Room.' Lynda and Richard found each other's hands and held on, watching him. 'And I'm sure that, in a moment, we'll go and be more comfortable together there. Once we've re-established our dignity.'

He inhaled and, Mary could have sworn, the room seemed to shimmer very slightly and then recoil when he sighed. This was only her imagination, she understood, a trick of her emotions, playing out over the facts.

'But first, gentlemen and ladies, I would like to mention a matter which may recently have proved disturbing for a few of us. On our island we try to keep apart from the world's news, but it comes to us, nevertheless. And I think that we are all now aware that on the twenty-third of December the bodies of sixteen members of the Solar Temple sect were found in a clearing near Grenoble. It is supposed that fourteen of those people were murdered by two of their fellows who, in turn, killed themselves.'

Joe gently reached across and scooped up Mary's fist, the customary heat in his surrounding fingers making her realise how chilled she'd become. He tilted his head briefly to one side, considering her, and then – satisfied by whatever he'd seen – continued.

His voice was careful, smooth, low. 'Naturally, we are, ourselves, a kind of sect. When I was moved to begin our Fellowship, my intention was to make a place where writers could stay for as long as they wished in order to find, or to rediscover, their calling. Although I tend to speak about them very little, our foundations are formed in part from a kind of spiritual discipline. We come here to uncover the privileges and the rights which permit our lives to speak. Naturally, we must, therefore, seek to understand our lives and this means that we must also consider our deaths. But we work towards creation, not destruction. We look for truth, not death.'

'We look for truth, not death.' Nathan, leaning on the doorway, back with them all again. 'We look for truth, not death,' and reciting, as if he were remembering a prayer: 'In writing, as in love, we die to ourselves and yet still live. We become immortality and less than nothingness. We make ourselves fit to hear truths. We make ourselves fit to tell them. Our hearts speak.'

And, when he seemed unwilling, or unable, to continue, Joe stepped in to take up the refrain. 'We are words in the mind of God and we are free.'

*So do we say **Amen** now, or what?*

Mary glanced gingerly around, a prickle of something unidentifiable rising in her neck.

But no one seemed especially surprised by the outburst. Louis, Ruth, Lynda, Richard: they all simply looked moderately content. Joe still held her hand, but was keeping his eye on Nathan who – after a small yawn and a casual scratch at one arm – began to stroll towards the table. He winked broadly at Mary. 'That's us told, then.'

Everyone took this as their cue to rearrange hands, clear throats, scuffle back chairs and prepare to move elsewhere. Joe stayed where he was, still gripping Mary. 'Glad you could join us again, Nathan.'

'I know you have a soft spot for sevens, Joe. Didn't want to let you down.'

This brought a punch of laughter from Joe, who unhanded Mary and stood. 'Ready to come upstairs?'

Nathan braced both arms on the back of an emptied chair and stretched his back, experimentally. 'We'll be there. We'll be there.'

He didn't kneel in close and look up at Mary until everyone else had gone.

'Are you all right?'

'I think so. I'm not sure. Everything he said *felt*,' she fumbled for a suitable word and then compromised, 'felt good, I suppose. But I'm not convinced I know what it meant.'

'What it meant? Nothing complicated – only that we're all of us after our own little piece of Grail. Which is hardly unusual – most people believe they have one thing they still need, one they have to get. It's what moves them.' He broke into a grin and attempted a grim kind of chuckle. 'Never mind all of that, anyway. You know what *you* have to remember. Hm?'

'No, but I'm sure you're going to tell me.'

'Too fucking right.' He loomed in at her and whispered. 'Rule Six, then. Ready?'

'Yes. Go on.'

'*There are no rules.*' Smiling flatly, he paused for her response. 'There are no fucking rules. Not a single one.'

She tried to keep it light. 'Now he tells me.'

'Now is when you're ready to know.' The skin at the corner of one of his eyes twitched very slightly and she thought he seemed weary. 'Look,' Nathan scratched at his stubble absently. He'd taken to shaving only every week or so and his face, that afternoon, was whitened with a haze of bristles. Mary didn't like to see him this way – as if he were giving in to getting old. 'I may not agree with everything Joe says. In fact, I may not agree with *anything* Joe says, but he's –' he stood again and prodded the tabletop with one forefinger, 'he is a man of faith. And he does his very best to make his faith contagious. Because he knows that no one can write without it. The author of the story must be the first to believe in what it says.' He suddenly seemed to notice the disarray left behind after the Lunch, 'Fuck,' and started slamming dirty bowls together into a stack, 'shower of clarty wasters.'

Mary felt she ought to join him, following on behind and

gathering up a handful of used spoons, two side plates and a serving dish. 'It's not our turn to do this.'

'Doesn't matter. Like I said – there are no rules.'

'No rules – more work.'

'Correct. Absolutely.' He preceded her into the kitchen, where they each clattered down their respective loads. 'Of course, Joe would say that no one can *live* without faith. But he'd be wrong.' Nathan snapped a look to her, apparently expecting contradiction. 'I live without it all the time.'

Christ, Nathan – what the hell do you want me to tell you? That you're wrong? That you're right? Nothing's going to please you, even if I want it to.

So she didn't say anything to him beyond, 'Come on, they'll be waiting for us upstairs.' She was surprised when he let her take his arm and then she felt him lean in against her lightly as they started to walk. She couldn't help noticing that he smelt much more than usual of dog and also of stale linen and unconcern.

In the Meeting Room Joe's promised fire was well established, pale salt flames rising randomly from driftwood. The rest of the group was waiting, everyone suitably chastened and arranged to either side of Joe, who sat, somehow energetically at peace, his fingers laced and tranquil across his stomach, but his eyes at their most frightening, active blue.

Two empty chairs had been left beside each other in the customary ring of seats and Mary edged in to settle herself ahead of Nathan. Her eyes were already closed when she heard him join her, the sigh of cloth as he folded his arms and the odd, small intake of air, as if dipping into silence was much the same as dipping into water, as if the shock of it had made him catch his breath.

If I tell him I'm having trouble with my novel – maybe not trouble, not as big a thing as that, but a difficult patch, maybe, something like that . . . If I tell him, then he's the one who's meant to help me. I can't ask now, though. Not when he's the way he is.

God, half the time I spend on the bloody island, I'm worrying about Nathan. He's too much by himself. Even when he's with people. And he never really says, never says what's wrong.

And 'There are no rules.' Well, what the bloody hell is that supposed to mean?

450

That he's in another funny mood.

She sighed before she could stop herself, disturbing the peace.

God, I give up. He's old enough to take care of himself. I'm just not sure if he knows that . . .

All right, though, enough now. Enough.

Every month she tried this, she hoped she would be better at it and still found that her thinking unravelled into pretty much the same unedifying mess. First her worries would rise to the surface and then would come a passage of calm, followed by a spasm of sexual recollection, another, more forced, hiatus and then a dwindling into haphazard fragments of imagination and incoherent memories. On a couple of afternoons, she'd found herself surprised by a bolt of irresistible sadness, or joy, but, more often, she had ended the session feeling that she would have got more benefit from slipping off and taking a walk, or perhaps a nap.

These thoughts idled by while the fire subsided gently into clinking embers, and a breeze nudged the window panes. Her concentration skipped to a little blank, almost dozing, and then she noticed that her breath was coming rather faster than usual, as if she were a little nervous, just slightly alarmed. At the same time, she realised the rise and turn of breathing round the room was matching, or even governing her own. Initially, the thought of this was mildly suffocating and she tried to break step, to stall her small regular hunger for air.

She tugged her concentration in and set herself to form and measure her own beat. Her throat seemed to smooth, to open and, in her solar plexus, she started to feel the wordless murmur and shine of something like anticipated sex – almost that ache, that tug, that anxious friction in the blood.

And then the ache broke like a split meniscus, flowed, and she felt, for a blink of her heart, a kind of towering possibility. She recognised it, this terrible expansion of reality. The same monstrous buzz and slap and suck and fluster had surrounded her that night in the wood and had made her really want to go and begin *writing*. That had been the first time that she realised she genuinely *could*.

And this was the second.

When Joe patted his hands together to mark the end of the hour,

Mary's imagination staggered back to her. When she opened her eyes, even the muted colours in the Meeting Room leaped and blared. She was enormously tired and muzzy, but also exhilarated. When she stood, the floor tipped at her gently and she swayed back to bump at Nathan.

'Steady.' He caught and then slowly turned her until they were face to face. 'You OK?'

Mary frowned quietly while he brushed the hair from her forehead. 'I think so. Good session today.'

'Ah.' He offered her a cautious, but entirely unironic smile. 'I see. Joe's finally put the 'fluence on you, has he?'

'Oh, don't be so cynical. You know you're really not that way at all.'

It had been a long time since they'd had a proper, amicable bicker between themselves.

'And how would you know the way I am?'

'Because I've had to put up with you for God knows how many years.'

He beamed and prodded at her upper arm, 'And, of course, it would never have occurred to you that I've had to show extraordinary tolerance in all of my dealings with you and your bloody moods and eccentricities. I am the most forbearing and enduring man I know.'

'Don't get out much, do you?' She prodded him back.

'I continue to be amazed that anyone so revoltingly insolent could have survived for so long in the world without serious injury. And, I might enquire, does the abuse of your elder and better really constitute the best use of your time when you have a leprous novel to cough up?'

'I could say much the same to you.' She was aware that the rest of the Fellowship was hovering, unsure of whether to withdraw discreetly, or to stay and observe the fun. 'Don't *you* have a novel to write, Mr Staples?'

'I've been busy.'

'Doing what?'

Nathan's expression blanked and the bounce dropped out of their conversation. 'I don't know.'

She surprised herself by tenderly grabbing his jacket lapels and leaning forward until her forehead rested on his chest. She spoke to the third button on his shirt, 'Well, whatever it was, don't do it again.'

She felt his voice, small in his chest, tense. 'I'll try.'

'I mean it.'

'And so do I.'

Eckless was snow-mad, steam-engining over the whitened grass, bounding as he never had, even when a modestly incautious puppy: crouching and then springing forward to root in the little drifts until his muzzle sported a permanent cocaine spill of astonishment.

He cantered up to Nathan yet again with a volley of smoky barks.

SEE BOSS SEE BOSS SEE BOSS SEE THIS DIFFERENT THIS GOOD DIFFERENT YES

His tail thrashed at Nathan's calves and then he raced off with a slithering yelp.

Nathan shook his head and kept watching the greenfinch. It was hunched in a birch tree, a bright knot of feathers towards the centre of a branch. Every five or six seconds a thick paring of snow would impact between its shoulders and, each time, it would shrug and shudder off the little weight. Nathan admired its patience. Although he also supposed that it didn't have much choice.

And how long is a greenfinch's memory, anyway. Four seconds? Ten? It probably hasn't the first idea that it's being stoical.

*It's all a sign of strange times, in any case. I don't think I've ever seen one before on the island, to say nothing of fucking **snow**. I mean, we're surrounded by salt water, for fuck's sake, snow shouldn't happen here. God knows, we have to put up with everything else – with the possible exception of tornadoes and tsunami – the least we can expect is exemption from blizzards, I'd say.*

The finch lobbed itself up into the thick, white air, hung, flurried and then rose to light on another, higher branch. Nathan wished he'd happened to bring some bread.

Not that bread is strictly a suitable food for birds, but I'm buggered if I'm trotting round the landscape with my pockets full of mealworms and seeds . . .

He was trying to take things gently, to creep up on his state of

454

mind with a delicate and wholly unintrusive care, but – even palping only very softly round his ragged, interior self – he couldn't help but notice that everything there had seemed almost jovial for several days. The first emotion he met on waking was no longer dismay. And he couldn't deny that, like Eckless, he'd been lifted by the happy accident of snow. Its icicle jab at his lung was invigorating and he'd already spent at least an hour this morning mesmerised by the padded descent of another shower. And as for the smoothing of the island to one big ripple of blameless white – that could only seduce every Calvinist muscle in his soul.

It's just nice. You can't help thinking that. It's just nice.

Eckless pelted back from some private treasury of grit and leaf mould.

Of course. I should have realised. This is the poor bastard's first snow. And he's already – what? – about fifty in dog years.

Nathan slowly produced an impressive spout of condensed breath, trying to recall if there'd ever been a time when he'd done that schoolboy thing of lurking outdoors and pretending he was smoking, as soon as the temperature had fallen low enough to make imitation smoke. On reflection, he'd probably always *been* smoking outdoors and sod the pretence.

And they only ever said it would stunt my growth. Lying bastards. If I'd had a boy child, I'd have told him – lie and blaspheme and drink and wank all you like, but skip the tobacco, or you'll end up with a hollow chest. Look at me.

But I didn't have a boy child, I had a girl.

The pleasure of this flexed in the pit of his stomach and softly tousled his brain.

Before Eckless charged again, spinning and baying, and eloquently indicating – only Lassie could have done more – that people he was fond of were coming this way.

'Hello, Nathan.' He leaned round towards the voice and was rewarded with a snowball to the hip. Sophie had halted, perhaps four yards away, and was struggling to catch her breath and laugh. She eyed him once, with a little snap of wariness, and then bent over to giggle more effectively. Now she was older, Nathan noticed, she sometimes faltered this way, had to check that any signs of relaxation, or enjoyment on her part, weren't leaving her, in some way, exposed.

All part of growing up.

He did his best to beam as if the very thing he'd wanted was one chilled and dampened kidney. 'Good shot.'

*Christ, go on, just fuck about, for heaven's sake, be a kid. Just **play** – no caution required. Take it from me, once you step over that line and get adolescent it's nothing but ugliness and embarrassment for a decade. For life.*

Joe now puffed over the rise, suitably rustic walking stick in hand. 'Is she attacking you?'

'Only a little. But I think that one of us should warn her that once I am roused to return her fire, I will take no prisoners.'

This announcement was welcomed with a palm full of slush from Sophie that managed to spatter his shoulder and drop a few clots of ice down the side of his neck.

Joe ambled forward to swoop Sophie up in a hug. 'That's probably enough, though, now. Poor old Nathan's done you no harm. Go on and have a scramble with Eckless if you like.'

The dog always wanted to be restrained with Sophie. He was already performing a kind of involuntary dressage in his efforts to restrain the urge to romp and leap.

Nathan crouched and scrambled around with his hands in the grass until he could find a piece of stick. He then launched this, with shameful inaccuracy, and suggested, 'Fetch.' Eckless thought about this and then consented to trot off. Nathan smiled at Sophie. 'Go on if you want. You know how much he loves you.' She looked very slightly discomfited. Eckless's adoration wasn't quite the appropriate thing to mention in front of a female person of such undoubted maturity. Nevertheless, Sophie rose above it and even allowed herself a look of satisfaction as she marched off, following her greatest canine admirer.

Then Joe closed on Nathan, halting to land an avuncular palm on his remaining dry shoulder. 'How's life? If you don't mind my asking.'

'No, I don't mind.'

'Must be not bad, then.'

'I suppose it must.'

Joe, Nathan noticed, was wearing a Bedouin keffiyeh instead of a scarf – the black and white check of it was visible under the collar of his coat.

You can take Joe out of the Holy Land, but you can't take the fucking

456

Holy Land out of Joe. And possibly I'm being picky, but I did think such things were intended to keep off the **sun** *and not the* **snow***.*

Joe raised an eyebrow amiably. 'You're glowering at my choice of scarf. But, really, it makes perfect sense. Very cold at night in the desert. If this kept me warm there, it'll keep me warm here. And it reminds me of the sun.' He slipped his arm through the crook of Nathan's and tugged him into a slow walk. 'It makes me happy. What makes you happy, Nathan?'

'I don't remember.'

'That's not true.'

'I don't want to say, then.' He halted their progress with a jerk. 'Look, I'm not uncheerful. I'm adjusting to my situation and everything's fine. You don't have to steer me about like a hospital patient. Mary's doing well, she's in love and so on and scribbling away. I have no editor, but that's not so bad, it's how I started out, after all.' He tried to swallow while his throat suddenly locked with something uncomfortably close to a sob.

Bollocks, bollocks, bollocks, change the subject, you dozy fuck.

He swabbed the snowflakes off his eyebrows. 'I was just watching that greenfinch. Funny, it being here.'

'They do sometimes come.' Joe allowed him to slip his arm free, but then took care to meet his eyes. 'And you were thinking?'

'Yes.' Nathan surrendered, rather than be wheedled at further. 'All right. I was thinking how I *did* start out. I was remembering that I wrote because it made me happy. Or I wrote because I wrote and it so happened that made me happy. And then I found out I could still write if I was sad. And then I found out that being happy was far less common than being sad and I decided that I would be satisfied with that, because, as long as I still wrote, it meant that even the very worst things in my life could have a purpose. It meant that pain would keep me eloquent. Just nature, isn't it? Pain is always supposed to make you howl.' He closed his eyes. 'But, right now, I hurt too much, Joe – too much to say anything at all. For the first time in my life, I'm nothing but quiet inside.'

'Which could be no bad thing.'

'Bad, or good – it's here.' The finch bounced up into flight, hovered blurrily and then settled again in a different, slightly more sheltering tree.

Well done, wee man. Good choice.

Nathan avoided saying more, occupying the silence by stamping to ease the growing cold in his feet. Somewhere to the left, Eckless had started to bark.

God, I wish Joe would just go away.

Then again, why not talk? Why not jabber away at him, if the person who used to listen isn't there. I still have to speak, don't I? I still have to get my voice out somehow, I still have to hear it. How else will I know I'm still here?

Nathan sniffed, rubbed his face where it was starting to numb in the cold. 'It's odd, though, in all of this silence – perhaps because I have more room for them now – I've got whole squads of new memories roaring about. And it's not as if you wouldn't think I had enough. But these are weird – details and whole incidents I haven't come across since I first met them. I even – and this is the finch's fault – I remembered, just now, that I found a gull once, with a broken leg. It heard me coming and was flagging its wings flat in the mud and limping and trailing all over the place. I was ten or eleven, probably eleven, and terrified of it and fascinated. Anyway, I took off my jacket and threw it over the bird, bundled it up and walked with it home. Its feet were extraordinarily cold, I recall, like dead things, and it tried to peck me once or twice.

'When I got to the house, I took the gull inside and unwrapped it. For a moment it lay on the table and then it slowly tried to move away. The surface made it slip and when its weight dropped on the injured leg, it screamed. Then it looked at me.

'And I knew I had to kill it. The sound it made explained everything. I had to kill it as soon as I could.

'So I ran and grabbed a hand towel from the bathroom and swaddled up the bird again. I carried it outside like that and set it down on one slab of the path. It blinked and clacked its beak before I covered over its head with the towel. I remember that was when the life or the will seemed to leave it and not when I brought my heel down on its head.

'I struck harder than I needed to. I wanted to be sure than one blow was enough.'

Joe nodded, but didn't attempt a comment of any kind. Eckless kept up his barking – playing hard.

'Of course, a couple of hours later, I caught myself running over

458

the incident and beginning to be excited by the poem it might make. Just the stuff poetry takes to: gull's heads crumpling like eggs, the soft feel of that. Which was when I found I had to throw up. Not when the bird died, but then.

'And I made sure to never write about it. And I gave up verse. Not to stop myself from being parasitic – from stealing the life out of life – but because something in it drew me to do wrong. I had a ridiculous presentiment that, if I kept on with the poems, they would make me do much worse things to feed the words. They seemed to suggest that kind of appetite.

'Whereas my current medium has always kept me much more virtuous. Or much more contained. All prose has ever brought out in me is *self*-abuse. It's been both generous and imaginative with that.' Nathan thought he'd put that rather well and wondered why Joe wasn't showing the slightest sign of approval.

Probably takes offence at the negativity of my tone. Pompous old tosser. Still, he's not so bad at . . .

*What the fuck is that bloody dog complaining about? Yapping on. I can't imagine he's actually **caught** something – he wouldn't know what to do with a rabbit if it dropped down dead at his feet.*

'Nathan?'

Joe was holding Nathan by both elbows, yanking his attention back into place. 'Uh?'

'Nathan, what is the matter with your dog?'

And before they understood they must, they were running, heading for the sound of barking and trying not to think the bad thought, which came anyway, overtook them, solidified as they breasted the slope and saw and saw and saw the black dog leaping and pawing and barking at the air, its breath in sheets, and the broken white of the lochan, a long shard of darkness tongued into it, fragments of ice in the charcoal-coloured water at the broad stub of its base. And the blue of her coat there also, the blue of Sophie's coat in a soft, small mound, barely clear of the surface and motionless.

And then they were down at the pool's side in a slip of sick time and Joe said her name, didn't call it, only spoke it, like a promise or a prayer, as he slewed out over the squealing ice on his feet and then his knees and then on his belly and reaching both arms down into the water as if he might dive in after her, but instead holding and clawing and scrambling the gleam of her up. She was floating with her face down, with her face down, and Nathan was here to help now and the two men hauling and hearing themselves bleating with the effort and the fear they were too preoccupied to feel.

And they had her out now, finally, and all of them lay together for a moment on the dangerous surface and next they were dragging her to the bank, where they looked at her face for the first time and the turning of the day around them stopped.

Her skin was a porcelain, violet white, her lips the colour of new bruises and gently parted to show good teeth. Her hat was gone, was deep and cold somewhere beyond reach, and her hair was a naked, black weight and heavy. Her eyes were closed.

Oh, God. Dear God.

Nathan crouched in the grass, cradling one hand in the other, observing vaguely that he'd lost one of his gloves, and he stared at Joe who, face as still as a sleeper's, kneeled beside his child's body and began to perform the correct procedures for feeding breath into empty lungs, for pressing blood through a stalled heart.

'There's no –' Nathan broke the sentence. Whatever he said, there would be no stopping Joe. He would repeat the kneading at her breastbone, the methodical kisses at her lips until his hopes were exhausted and he always had been a man with a quite remarkable store of hopes.

Eckless whined quietly, lying by Sophie's feet.

She was wearing newish trainers, their laces sensibly tied with a double knot.

Five minutes passed and then seven. The snow thinned to a halt and the breeze dropped. It was very much colder now. Nathan's arms, soaked to the shoulder, seemed to have lost all sensation and still Joe worked and still he watched.

At eleven minutes, 'Joe. She's gone. Please, now. She's gone.'

Silence arched above the men and Nathan wondered if Joe had even heard him, but, perhaps another minute later, back came the reply, jerking out with the dogged rhythm of the pumping at her chest.

'The cold. The cold will save her. She isn't dead. Not dead. Speak to her. For me.'

'Speak to her?'

'Yes.'

So, because he did almost believe his friend, because he wanted to believe him, Nathan huddled round to kneel at Sophie's other side, facing Joe. Then leaned his face so close to hers that he could feel the recoil of his breath when it touched her cheek and he spoke to her. He told her about the supper she'd have waiting, and the island full of people who needed her, he invented information about finches. He described to her the intricate coral beauty of resin casts taken from the airways that filament, miraculous, through lungs. He told her that Ibn Arabi once wrote that all being was one and that Al Kindi once wrote that all intellect was one and that she couldn't leave them because she was part of them – all one. He began – stumbling at subjects – to explain Syme's modification of the circular method of amputation. He tried to recite, to remember anything, anything, anything at all, until he was surprised to resurrect, 'My father and my mother uttered my name, and they hid it in my body when I was born, so that none of those who would use against me words of power might succeed in making enchantments to have dominion over me,' which was Egyptian, but he couldn't think what, and

that was when she moved her head and coughed.

For several days the island swam and fluttered with relief. Joe and Nathan had gone with Sophie all the convoluted way to the nearest hospital (not near) and hovered and mumbled nonsense to each other while she was tested for signs of damage (none present). Then they took charge of their miracle and they brought her back home.

'Is she sleeping?'

'Yes.' Joe, in stocking feet, edging his study door shut behind him. 'I keep on expecting her still to be cold. Not that it isn't chilly up there . . . we should think of central heating, I suppose.'

Nathan set down his emptied whisky glass. 'Whoever heard of central heating in a lighthouse?'

'Well, exactly.' Joe sank into his armchair and stretched, his voice drowsy with contentment, with the good satisfactions of care. 'But meanwhile I've layered the poor child under so many quilts and blankets, it's a wonder she can even turn.'

Nathan spoke gently, looking into the fire. 'Still, everything about her is a wonder, isn't it?'

They considered the absolute truth of this statement while the whole house rested, surrounded by the stillness of fallen snow, the moon-reflecting nature of geometric ice lapping light, up behind the curtains, bright as day.

Nathan felt the heat from the fireplace prickling his cheeks, but still kept leaning forward, anxious for more. Ever since the day at the lochan, he'd been craving warmth. And soft things, too, almost childish comforts: his gentlest shirts, rice pudding and toffees and custard and books he hadn't owned in years containing stories of great adventures, each one ending happily.

He guessed Joe might be feeling much the same.

'Shall I put another log on your fire, Joe?'

462

'Wouldn't mind if you did, Nate. More whisky?'

'I'll not say no.'

They pottered comfortably about the room, performing their little tasks without a sound, and then settled again, beginning to slide towards sleep. Joe squinted at the fireglow through his upheld glass. 'It's so good.'

'What, the whisky?'

'The everything.'

'Mm.'

'Nathan?'

'Yes?'

'I'm sorry I didn't let you read to her. I know you wanted to.'

'But you wanted to more.'

'You can do it tomorrow.'

'If you like.'

Nathan contemplated turning in soon, tried curling his mind in the improvised bed he'd been made here on the couch, with the fire easing down in the dark and nothing but peace and books around him – like all of those other times when he was younger, just after the divorce, when he'd slept in all of those other friends' studies, had borrowed the normalities of their households, their children, their ornaments, the presence of their wives, had let them help him to hide away all of his wants, responsibilities, recollections. He let a smile overtake him. 'It is good, isn't it?'

'What?'

'The everything.'

'Oh, yes.'

'And having a daughter.'

'That's good.'

'That is so very good.'

Nathan tried, in the cab, to think of Other Things.

All right, then, all right – something engaging, something distracting, something . . .

Stepping up on to the quay – yes, that'll do – stepping up on to the quay at Ancw and seeing Mary with Jonathan, walking: the two of them there.

His mind dashed ahead, unwary, simply anxious for a safe release.

And they weren't holding hands, linking arms, they weren't actually, physically touching in any way, but you still would have known absolutely that they were together, a couple, a pair – I think, because of their pace, the way they moved in time with each other without any effort, quite naturally. And their expressions – they're beginning to slip into nice resemblances. She has her smiles and he has his and now they have the way they smile when each is echoing the other – something new.

Which is a good thing to consider, nothing threatening or unusual in that.

He knew he was sweating: an almost shivery, anticipatory kind of damp creeping over him. Not a good sign.

Something else, then, something else.

The last thing he wanted this morning was to end up alone with himself.

Or alone with what I'm doing. Or, more accurately, with what I'm being forced to do.

He searched his thinking for a further firm handhold, a suitably involving grip.

Jonno wasn't meant to stay this long – Mary said he would be in Ancw until the summer. And this is the autumn and he's still here. Another six months on the contract – so they can fuck some more.

Found it. A good, raw point of contact.

*Not **fuck** her – sleep with her. They sleep together. As well as the other stuff.*

No matter how much of an everyday truth this was, the idea of it

464

still sliced and winked uncomfortably, somewhere on the underside of his brain.

Not that they shouldn't. Do the other stuff.

Nevertheless, there were many far worse things he might consider – like the way he was going to spend this next half-hour.

*Christ, they **ought** to be doing that. If they're both normal, healthy and young and normal. Which they are. Which she is. Which I'm sure they both are.*

It's all fine.

Nobody could have any objections.

Nobody normal, or open-minded. Or healthy, or young. Nobody who was, in these and other ways, quite completely fucking different from me.

He was inhaling gently, slowly, and thus avoiding any dizzying overuse of breath – an unmistakable sign of nervousness. But this attempt at discipline and common sense was making him, in itself, feel harried and panicked and short of air. He noticed the taxi was rancidly overheated: he should pull the window down.

Maybe Jonno's only getting what he wants from her and then, when he's bored again and horny, he'll just move on. Men are shits, really. Complete pigs. We can justify every brand of bad behaviour.

Then again, so can bloody women.

And, in any case, I would say, would guess –

His stomach, already anxious, gave an unpleasant, intimate skip. He drummed on with his train of thought in any case.

I would guess that Mary probably also is pretty generally in favour of what they're doing. Of the sex.

Ach, bollocks – she's bound to like it. She's bound to be a good, sensual woman, because that runs in the family and there's no harm in it – or only the usual.

Another skip.

And she looks well on it: easier about herself: a pound or two of tension just completely lifted out of her: gone. It'll do that, getting what you want. It'll make you feel better.

He tried to steer himself away from themes that might turn morbid, while his window darkened momentarily as the taxi passed under the shadow of a gate. The road narrowed and began to wind between high and disturbingly purposeful late Victorian blocks.

Fuck. Almost there.

And I was almost beginning to wonder why I'd been putting this off.
Come on, some other picture, any other picture, any other thought.

Mary and Jonathan on the quayside, having their stroll and asking me
where I was going, what I'd be up to in London, was it the usual kind of trip
– business? And then Mary, because she is a lovely person, snibbed her hand
into mine, nudged my elbow, and let me feel that she'd remembered that my
business isn't usual any more, because I am conducting it alone. And I
nudged her back and told her, told them both –

He clutched his hands together for the want of more meaningful
touch and found the clasp of his skin against his skin seemed terribly
wooden and chill.

I told them I was going to do a favour for a friend. Which was an evasion,
but not a lie. I **have** *come here to do a favour for a friend.*

And he kept that last sentence turning through his mind while he
left the cab, went into the building, gave in his name at reception and
waited and waited some more behind what he dearly, dearly hoped
was a feasible grin.

Although grinning in here might be thought inappropriate.

Something ticked in his left eyebrow and he sternly reminded
himself that there could be no chance, this afternoon, of his losing
the slightest fragment of control over anything, especially his face.

'Ah, Mr Staples, how very good to meet you.' A tidily muscular
man with downy grey hair had hurried up, apparently out of
nowhere, and now stood far too close to Nathan. 'Delighted to think
we might be able to aid your research.' He extended his hand,
'Although I have to say that your work is already really very
accurate,' the opened gesture, perfectly placed, inviting a response.
Nathan found he could do no more than stare at it.

The man tried again, energetically patient. 'I'm Professor Cairn.'

'Ah,' Nathan managed, and then, 'thanks,' while brushing his
hand dry on his sleeve, 'Yes. Good,' before his palm was snatched up
into a very thorough shake. 'Oh, thanks. Good to meet you. And to
. . . to . . . to be here.'

'Splendid. I always enjoy it when we have, shall we say, outsiders
visiting – not than anyone is genuinely an outsider, in a way.' He
paused long enough for Nathan to nod a queasily baffled agreement
and then went on, 'The artist's perspective – that's something we
often lack.' The professor began to pad along an innocent-looking

corridor, academic bookshelves here and there: nothing remotely alarming to catch the eye. 'Although, usually, we have *visual* artists, of course.' He went at a fair pace, the professor, had an unmistakable air of intelligent, physical strength – the type of man who might take vitamins and prefer his sports to be slightly dangerous.

Nathan's throat coughed out, 'Visual. Of course,' as he was trotted in through a set of double doors, restraining, all the while, the tremendous thought of what he might have to see beyond them.

But there was only more corridor lying in wait, lined with what seemed to be elderly deep-freezes. The professor stopped abruptly beside one.

Surely not. Not opening the lid. Not reaching in and plucking out.

Cairn tutted at himself, suddenly turning faintly coquettish. 'Now here I am, hurrying you along, and I've quite forgotten – this is for you.'

Nathan flinched mildly as what he had taken to be a vaguely ominous towel, tucked in the crook of Cairn's arm, was now thrust in his direction. He gripped it and watched the cloth unfurl between his hands into a lab coat of startling white. The one the professor sported was a much more placid magnolia.

Worn in, I suppose.

Nathan duly donned the pristine garment, glancing about in an effort to resist the placid fascination of Cairn's breast pocket. Nathan had only just noticed its neatly arrayed load of narrow, clever instruments and the reddish-brown stains rubbed in above them.

Greasy with use.

The air was starting to smell aggressively dry and, somehow, bitter.

'In a way, you know, you couldn't have timed this more perfectly.' The professor tucked one meaty hand into the other behind his back.

*No, actually, I couldn't have timed this any worse. But it wasn't my choice. If it **had** been my choice, I would have come here at any other fucking time. Believe me, there would be days when I would love this, pay to gain entry, break down your door. But now is not the hour and these are not the circumstances and I hope you will never know this, I hope I will make it through your tour without giving myself away – without giving my friend away.*

Nathan managed a whine of quizzical interest, his stomach

467

pitching, his feet jogging him on to fuck knew what, brain churning away maliciously, predicting his imminent future with jittery glee.

Cairn strode ever forward. 'They're trying to cut us back, you see, and only use computers. If they have their way, very little of this will be here soon. Which would, of course, be quite ridiculous. The presence, the *reality*, the quiddity – that always teaches so much more. It could be argued that it coarsens experience, it could, it could. But I would, quite probably, not agree. And our students are going to be *doctors*, for heaven's sake. They do have to be used to this. They also have to understand that their patients may, despite their best efforts –'

Nathan listened with a tiny proportion of his attention and nodded approximately when he should, as Professor Cairn slipped him carefully into the world of the fabric and the structure of their own selves, their own making. Nathan grew used to the headachy tang of acetone and the sharper edge of formalin and phenol and became, in spite of all misgivings, entranced.

What he knew to be his nature – his conscienceless, basic, inquisitive nature – asserted its appetites and hungrily investigated his species' construction. When he was offered things to look at, he looked. When he was presented with the complicated beauty of matter built for motion, for holding life, he couldn't help but love it, couldn't avoid succumbing also to a giddy admiration of his personal, individual, private form.

'Here, we've impregnated this with resin.' Cairn proffered a mildly glistening knot of flesh, rounded and crimson, neat in his palm. 'What would otherwise be a wet specimen is far more manageable like this.'

Nathan accepted the little weight of a whole human heart, preserved, and resisted the lunatic urge to stroke it, to keep hold of it, take it away. Anything would serve him better than the uneasy organ, currently fidgeting in his chest. 'Very nice.'

'Isn't it?' The professor plucked it back, delicately, almost affectionately proud.

'Ah, I was wondering, in fact . . .'

*I wasn't wondering, I do not, fucking **do not**, want to know.*

'I was wondering how long you could keep them for.'

'Organs like that?'

'No. No, the, the people.'

468

'The bodies we are permitted by law to keep for three years. It would be possible to keep them for much longer. But after three years we return them to *their* people, send them home.'

'Three years.'

'They're preserved quite differently, of course.'

'Oh, of course. Three years . . . That's longer than I'd thought.'

A long time to be here, without the proper company.

The afternoon continued, Nathan now darting from room to room, examining bottles and pictures and slides until a pleasant intoxication settled in. He was beginning to feel delighted, or at least more than satisfied, with the facts of his life, his livingness. When he noticed the turn of his wrist beneath its scar, the articulation of his fingers, his ability to observe them, to hear the shift of skin against his cuff, this all seemed both remarkable and lovely. *He* all seemed both remarkable and lovely.

Jesus fuck, I really have sunk to this – a building filled with bits of dead people is what it takes to make me feel OK.

*And even if I **do** feel OK, I still shouldn't be here. I have still lied to the good professor in order to get myself inside. I still have the worst to come.*

He handed back an inch-thick section – suitably preserved – taken through the skull of an adult male: here a fraction of bone, here a little of the jaw, here a portion of the tongue and here a close-trimmed hazing of soft hair, still rooted in the skin that once covered the nape of a neck. Nathan felt the gentle bristles tickling the ball of his thumb.

Shit. No, that's too close to life. Too close to having her touch you there, to her cupping the heat of your neck, your living neck.

He watched the section as Cairn carefully returned it to its drawer.

I hope you knew all about touching. I hope you got plenty – far more than your fair share. I hope you lived like fuck. Although that's the kind of living that can kill you, the kind that could lose you a friend. Even so, I hope you had good times.

Night, night.

And then, once again, they were moving, Cairn leading Nathan deeper inside the building. He was used now to the rhythm of disclosures, the leap and shine of body secrets – secrets his particular substance must also conceal. He was also accustomed to the absence of any shock.

So I should be all right for what's coming, shouldn't I? Acclimatised? Prepared?

He never liked it when he asked himself questions and had no replies.

The pair paused in a tight, square hallway they had crossed before. Just out of sight to the left, Nathan knew, a fresh body was curled on the table in the steely embalming room, its back to the door in a posture of easy sleep.

They must all look that way – everything about them, from a distance, seeming almost natural. Every body they bring here will have lain in that room, resting, being slowly taken by its next change.

To the right was a nest of laboratories, all bracketed and busied round each other. And then there was another door directly ahead, the one they hadn't yet passed through. Nathan was already close enough to hear, coming from it, the sound of comfortable chatter in a high, broad space.

The professor grinned, fatherly. 'I'm so glad you could come when the term time's started – with the students here and working – they make such a difference. Our ladies and gentlemen.' He softly ushered Nathan in.

An anteroom first, lined with empty metal tables, each with a metal bucket hooked at its foot. Nathan had already fixed his eyes on the back of Cairn's head. He already felt he knew too clearly what would be inside it: flush to the bone; but, even so, that particular mental image was something quite solid and calm to counteract the blasphemous slapstick that was capering in his own brain, his imagination lurching forward with threats he couldn't contemplate.

*Jack, you fuck. You can't really have meant this. Not this. You can't really have wanted this. For me to see **this**. I can't stop you being lonely **here**.*

*Jesus, Jack, I miss **you** – not whatever kind of fucking **experience** you've turned into.*

You always were a sick, fucking bastard. And I'd say that to your face.

But I don't want to. Not here. Not now. You shouldn't make me.

But already the main room, without his consent, had rushed up around him and he was taking the first breath in of nothing too ugly, or – by now – strange, only a firmly chemical scent, a heady demonstration of the force required to halt decay. On all sides there were tables, figures in lab coats grouped together round them, leaning, working in. There was too much information here to understand and too many variables fluctuating to allow him to make a plan. Nathan simply wasn't sure if he could do what Jack had asked him to – or even if he'd manage to try.

Cairn had turned and was speaking.

'We couldn't do any of this, of course, without people choosing to give us themselves. At one point, paupers, unclaimed cadavers, would be used without permission, but now we only work with gifts. Quite often the donors have been ill for long periods and are quite old . . . they want to give themselves to medicine, in gratitude for the care it's given them.'

And some of them want to trap those who survive them. Some of them are control freaks in death as in life.

Cairn seemed restless now, happily anxious to join in the currents of studious activity. Somewhere behind him, Nathan heard the sticky peel of what could only be skin, lifted quickly away from naked muscle.

'You'll want to move around and observe now. So I won't interfere. Do feel free to come and ask me anything. Or you could even speak to the students, a few of them are exceptional this year. A potential prosector among them.'

And what exactly would I say to them? That I'm looking for my friend?

As Cairn started to leave him, Nathan let himself survey the tables properly. His eyes followed the fall and rise of inquisitive fingers, the turn and smile of living heads, and then dropped to examine the subjects of such focused enquiry: the bodies, of course the bodies, of course the suddenly slow-motioned puzzlement of the bodies, of the way they were. He couldn't understand the way they were.

'Professor?' Nathan watched his hand reach out and catch Cairn by the arm. The movement seemed to take minutes to complete. 'Professor?' He wasn't panicking, he knew that, he didn't feel frightened at all. But if anyone had asked him what he *was* doing, he also knew he couldn't have said.

Cairn was facing him now, extremely animate, unmistakably competent and sturdy. 'Yes?'

It was clear to Nathan that the professor would be more than happy to answer almost anything he'd ask.

Except the proper questions, the big ones.

471

He began to form his mouth around the most appropriate words, while Cairn waited, jovial, encouraging him to speak. 'There's something I haven't covered?'

'Yes.' Nathan listened to his voice, its unlikely calm, its unlikely question. A cool blade seemed to open in his skull, slitting speech apart from thought.

The real questions, you can't answer – the ones like fucking walls, like standing stones in the head, something brainlessly hard and unavoidable, quiet but always there – somewhere in the head – the questions of my personal dying and the dying of those loves particular to me – all here in the head.

Nathan became aware that he had finished speaking and that Cairn's reply had already skipped a few phrases ahead, faded out by a little fugue of disorientation. It occurred to Nathan that he understood why someone might describe himself as staggered and mean exactly what he said – that something about him had lost its footing in the world.

The professor rounded off his final sentence with a smile. 'It's the only thing that seems to worry them.'

Nathan swallowed stupidly and stared, his gaze drawn for the eighth or ninth or God-knew-what-number time to a flat, transected surface, a raw core of bone. Too adrift to even know what further query he could make, he simply frowned, willing his expression to imply that he couldn't quite understand *worry* in this context – or that he had, perhaps, a problem with *them*.

Cairn took the hint. 'They still have to work with them, of course, but in a separate series of sessions. So, as far as the students are concerned, the body is always presented without the head. And, naturally, the head without the body.'

I won't know him – which seemed far worse – *how will I know him? –* than having to face Jack – *I won't know him –* having to recognise him here, in whatever disarray he might have reached.

Cairn, by this time, had tucked himself into one small, white-backed crowd, grouped off to the right. So Nathan was finally left to himself and the promise his editor had made him part of.

He began to walk, soft-shoeing between tables, trying to be a writer – always his very last line of defence – attempting to be peaceably filled with the details of it all. Observation was not involvement, was not guilt or strangeness, was only his vocation, his job.

Stripped to the waist, to bared muscle, to the clear-cut line where the body
fat's left in an inches-deep rind the rich colour of something sweet . . . of, Jesus
fuck it, marron glacé, just that and nothing else — and embalmed flesh, dark
as a cooked meat, you realise — something of the after-dinner, after-carving
mess here and the shame of hunger starting, in amongst the black plastic bags
and the pale, naked, vulnerable feet and the skin that looks pressed already,
buried already, prematurely underground.

In the end, his observations faltered, baffled, and retreated to the
hands: their relatively harmless resting curl; the unscathed, upturned
palms; the cyan blue or the milkiness of fingernails.

And, when he'd already given up searching, this was how Nathan
found him. He found Jack by recognising one of his hands. The right
hand. It was his, it could only be his. The slightly large knuckles and
nicotine staining were irreversibly eloquent, both part of the small
identity of the perfect instrument for jabbing out faulty typing,
miming gunfire, raising glasses, red-inking corrections, pointing out
cretins, building joints, producing a signature of surprising elegance
and drumming bar tops, turning pages, patting shoulders, shaking
hands, shaking Nathan's hand, shaking Nathan's hand.

Just fucking like you, leaving me here with all of this.

Nathan let his fingers close hard around nothing.

Just fucking like you, Jack.

'Just fucking like you.'

Mary was watching Nathan work. 'What is?' Not watching him writing, watching him doing proper work.

'"What is?" she says. "What is?"' He paused for a moment, breathless, hugging the tall roll of chicken wire he'd been waltzing and frogmarching over the increasingly muddied grass. 'It is just like you to stand by while I rip my sodding arms open with this stuff.' He had, indeed, managed to score both his forearms with fine, bloody lines from the wire.

Mary had been trying not to notice the marks – they made her squeamish. Anything involving pain in conjunction with Nathan always did. 'You said you didn't want me to help you. And I don't know what you're doing, in any case.' He blinked at that, she noticed, and twitched a mournful smile. She leaned over the border of what would soon be a finished fence and tapped at the back of his hand. 'You could, of course, roll down your sleeves.'

'And then I'd rip my shirt.'

'Your arms are probably worth more than your shirt.' She kept trying to meet his eye, but today he was having none of it.

'Shirts don't heal. And I do.'

He said this so completely unconvincingly that she wanted to give him a shake.

Jesus, man, I know you're upset about something. I know you're usually upset about something. I know you're an emotional fucking haemophiliac, but if you won't say what's the matter, I can't help. I am sympathetic, but I can't help. Subtext is all very well, but it isn't the same as communication.

Nathan folded his arms across the flat top of the roll and then rested his chin on them. 'What are you thinking?' His stare was firmly set at the edge of the trees behind her. Ever since he'd come back from London he'd been gently avoiding contacts, anything that might lead to questions he didn't want asked. 'Hm? Mary?' Now he was evading examination again by quizzing her.

She decided to abandon subtlety. 'I was thinking that subtext was no replacement for conversation.'

His mouth tightened. 'Are you referring to a theory, or a fact?' The voice almost too quiet to be heard now – which, with Nathan, was not a good sign.

'A fact.'

'A fact relating to what?'

He'd obviously decided to be angry, which was unreasonable of him, because she was doing nothing wrong and wouldn't be bullied into feeling that she was. 'A fact relating to this conversation.'

He closed his eyes for a breath or two, then lifted his head, faced her and said nothing, only stared: one long, inarticulate look which she met and dumbly returned. She couldn't understand what he was trying to tell her and had no idea of what her reply might appear to be.

This is ridiculous.

'Mary?'

The sound of his voice broke the moment, let her discover that her pulse was jolting high. 'Yes?'

'There's nothing wrong here.' He was focused on a point beyond her head again. 'There's nothing wrong with me.' This in his gentlest way of speaking, now: the one he used when they'd been working late at her manuscripts, the one he used with Eckless when he thought no one was listening. 'There's nothing wrong at all. I went away and attended to something for Jack Grace. I'd promised I would. It upset me, but now it's done. I've said my goodbyes.

'And now I'm building my little fence here, setting a part of the wood aside for some research I have to do. I'll probably use what I find out in the novel – depending on how things go. I'll see. Partly, I just feel like some strenuous exercise – an excuse to be active. If you have no objections, of course.'

'You run every day, how much more active do you need to be?'

'This much more. Please, Mary, this is nothing to concern you.'

'You mean that it's none of my business.'

'I mean you have no need to be concerned.'

'This is an island where people have accidents. I have noticed.'

Nathan slipped her an enquiring look and it was her turn to glance away. He sighed. 'I am not going to have an accident. Not as far as I know. As far as I'm concerned, I am going to take a very great deal of care. And, meanwhile, I have work to do. Everything in here has to be sealed off, so that it won't be disturbed. Even Eckless won't be coming in here once the fence is up. In fact, particularly Eckless. That's why he's at home just now. He'll give me hell when I get back — *what time of day do I call this and where have I been and why couldn't* **he** *come and were there any other dogs there* — you know what he's like.' Nathan made a fair attempt at a grin.

She tried her thumbnail against the post, it was good, hard wood, something to support a very serious fence. 'So everything's fine, then, is it, Nathan?'

'That's right.' He wiped his mouth with one hand, as if he didn't like the taste of what he'd said.

He's such a terrible liar, he really shouldn't even try.

She waited, although she could guess that he'd rather she didn't, that he'd hoped the conversation might be over with. 'Nathan —' but she stopped herself from going on.

He doesn't even want me here. Whatever it is he means to do, it's all decided, in any case, no matter what I say. That was the change in him when he came back — you could tell that he'd made a decision, that something had been fixed.

Mary was about to go, 'Well, I'll see you arou—' when Nathan pushed the roll of wire forward, let it thump into the grass while he watched her face and stepped forward and took hold of her wrist.

He lifted her hand in both of his and bent his head to meet it, set a kiss on her palm, and then folded her fingers over, as if she should keep what he'd given her: the brief press of soft heat. For a moment, he smiled at her — slightly apologetic, slightly surprised — and for the first time she really believed that he'd been a husband, had gone out courting, had quietly secured a wife.

Nathan let her go, buried one hand quickly in his pocket and used the other to scrub at his neck. 'There's something I'll have to tell you soon . . . that is, I'd like you to . . . know . . .' He frowned at the chicken wire, as if he couldn't recall how it came to be lying at his feet. 'When I've finished the book I'm writing, I'd like you to read it. I mean, I'd like it if you could read it *first*, before anyone else.'

476

'Yes, of course.'

'I wouldn't ask, but it's a real . . . you know. . . a *serious* . . . Jack would have called it a proper novel. I haven't really written one of those in years . . .'

'I'll do it.'

'All that slashing and premature burial stuff – not to mention the fast-seller/best-seller/genre-fiction amounts of money it tends to make – it all rather led me astray, so I don't know if I've still got the knack of . . .'

'I'd be glad to read it.' And without entirely intending to, she added, 'I'd be proud,' which made him look simultaneously happy and alarmed.

'Ah, well now, you shouldn't say that – you haven't read it yet.' Nathan tugging at one eyebrow and then the other for no obvious reason. 'And I haven't finished it yet.'

'We could swap.'

'Mm?'

'When I've finished mine, you'll see it. And then when you've finished yours . . .'

'That would be . . . yes, that would be . . .' he stooped and wrestled the chicken wire back up into a manageable embrace, 'fine. If everything works out. We'll see. But you'll be finished before me – you're practically done now, aren't you?' He halted and allowed himself a full smile. 'Practically a novelist – our Mary Lamb.'

'Hardly that.' She smiled back.

'*Exactly* that. But bugger off now, will you? I'm busy.'

Still smiling, 'All right, all right. I know when I'm not wanted.'

And as she walked away down the hill, she undoubtedly heard him shout, 'Thanks for agreeing. Means a lot,' but when she stopped to look up at him, his back was turned and he seemed, to Mary, completely preoccupied with his hammer and his staples and his wire, doing proper work alone, with his secrets still secret, his decisions still made.

I should call her back.

Nathan unrolled some of the chicken wire, started anchoring it to a post. His shoulders were aching in a way that made his arms seem twice their normal weight.

I should just call her back, it would be no bother and would make us both glad.

This was a fiddly business – fencing – it called for concentration and a weirdly precise kind of strength, both of which he lacked.

She would hear me, if I yelled.

Sneaking a look round, he could still see her, the dissatisfied tilt of her shoulders, the signs of concern. He bent to his work again.

I'm making her worried. I should call her back and tell all, tell some, tell a fraction, just –

Fuck.

He watched as the hammer calmly recoiled after battering on to his hand.

Fuck. You stupid, stupid wank.

He sucked his breath in hard while he waited for the first ugly slap of pain.

This is, of course, what will happen if you do not concentrate – the rattling of the hand bones with the fucking hammer. Working out here is supposed to completely fill the mind with the sunny preoccupations of the artisan. It is supposed to make you focus, but not think. So, naturally, you do the reverse, you fuck.

*Oh, **shite**, that hurts. No wonder I type for a living. I have the craft skills of a rubber plant.*

Still, he was relieved to see, he hadn't actually broken the skin: only kicked off a line of increasingly angry bruising across his knuckles. It hurt to work on, but he did so anyway.

Still, when I've done this, I'll be ready to really make a start. I can do the digging somewhere over past the beech and I'll think about the rest of the arrangements nearer the time. No need to be under pressure. There's enough young hazel for supple wood, enough load-bearing branches for everything else. I can set up whatever I like.

*And I didn't lie to Mary – this **is** research. If all goes well, it'll help me to finish my fucking book. And when the book's finished, I can tell Mary everything, do what I should have done years ago, and – coincidentally – work through my sodding promises to Jack. Christ, you'd think he would have had the decency to leave me the fuck alone once he was dead. But then, decency never was his speciality.*

Which didn't mean that Nathan didn't miss him, didn't mean he wouldn't have been glad to pick up the phone and call London, talk through all the things he planned to do, talk for the sake of talking, for the sake and the satisfaction of making words. They'd both liked words: Jack and Nathan, Nathan and Jack.

A thin rain came and went and Nathan sank, as he'd hoped, into the smooth and unreflecting rhythms of activity. He was fixing in the last of the hinges and tramping down the earth at the base of the wire as the day began to turn grainy and monochrome. Then he opened – for the first, most satisfying time – his newly hung gate and then chained it and padlocked it shut as if there were something behind it which might be precious, or at least worth hiding. This was not yet the case, of course, but might be, whenever he thought the time was right.

He came within sight of his cottage before the night was fully in, enjoying the drag of tiredness in his thinking, the mumble of worthy muscular discomforts as he walked. Nathan even liked the look of the lamplight, cast across the grass from his windows and drawing him on towards home. Then he remembered that he'd left on none of his lights and realised there was someone inside waiting for him. One of the better things that ever happened in this world.

Might be Mary.

Which would be nice – she'd see he was knackered and possibly make him a cup of tea, not push any more questions, just be friendly and domestic in a way she hadn't been in a while – Jonno and all that, intervening.

Naturally, he's got first call on her, of course.

Still, the fucker needn't begrudge me the odd cup of tea. Mary is still in training, she does still have to concentrate on developing her craft.

And making me tea would aid her development as a novelist, no end.

He shook his head at himself and stamped the mud off his boots before he opened the door. 'Hello. Anyone there?' Eckless trotted up dolefully, doing his best impression of a dog worn down with worry over its erring and incomprehensible master. Nathan set about breaking the animal's will with vigorous ear scratching until Eckless couldn't help but grunt and wag his tail, all sins forgiven.

From the next room, Nathan heard the shunt of chair legs and solid, measured footfalls; a polite, introductory clearing of the throat. He needed no more clues than that. 'Good evening, Joe. What can I do you for?'

479

Joe leaned against the kitchen door frame, head tilted enquiringly, and Nathan fought the immediate, irresistible urge to trust in him, to confide. The teapot was cosied and steaming on the kitchen table and, doubtless, the fire had been lit in the living room and the whole building suffused, one way or another, with the type of serenity that would unbutton the sternest resolve and have Nathan setting out his heart's small secrets as if they were a handful of spare change. He nodded and shrugged. 'Tea in the pot for me, is there, Joe?'

'Oh, yes.'

'And then we'll go through and talk, will we?'

'While I'm here, Nate. Might as well.'

'Mary said you should come and see me, then, did she?'

'And I'd been thinking that I might in any case – while I was passing.'

'We'd better get on with it, then, if that suits you?'

'That suits me fine.'

Joe disappeared back into the living room while Nathan poured a cup of tea and then trudged in after him with the air of a man heading off to the dentist's chair.

'No need to be quite so glum, though, Nathan. I'm only here to say hello.'

'In your capacity as Chairman of the Fellowship.'

'And in my capacity as your friend. And Mary's friend. What did you do in London?'

'I viewed the body.' Nathan felt himself grin and wondered why. 'That's what I did. All right? Jack's body – I went and saw it, because he wanted me to. And it didn't tell me a thing. I already knew that dead is dead.'

'It must have had some effect, though, surely. It filled you with the urge to start fencing as soon as you got back.'

Nathan pressed himself into his chair and folded his arms. He was too tired to be doing this and too tired to resist it. He knew that he could stay silent for as long as he liked, but Joe would still sit and be patient and ready to hear. It wasn't even that Nathan might not have chosen to talk to Joe eventually, he simply objected to being steamrollered like this.

Joe nipped in with an opening before Nathan was quite ready. 'I know you'd rather speak to Jack. I realise that.'

'That's . . .'

'Below the belt?'

'Yes. Something like that, anyway. Look, I just . . .' Nathan could feel it: the sad, little crumple of his resistance, the vaguely masochistic fumbling for comfort. God, sometimes he made himself sick. 'I don't have a problem with death. No more than anyone else has. My problem is living. That's what I saw when I looked at Jack – that's the kind of total selfishness I have. I look at my dead friend and all I want to do is understand why, if his death is so absolute, my life can't be absolute, too. I want to know why I can't be wholly living. Christ, it would take so little, so fucking little to do it, to let me *be* here properly. Joe, it would only take her. Just her. After all of this time, it's still her.

'And don't say that I shouldn't look for contentment outside myself. Don't fucking say it, because no one who fucking suggests that knows the first fucking thing about being lonely. A human fucking being cannot do everything entirely fucking alone, we're not made to be sealed units, we're *meant* to look outside ourselves, we're *meant* to find joy in that. If there's a God, he fucking *made* us that way. And don't even start to tell me that was a loving act.

'Joe, one hour with her – one hour with Maura – I would still give – I would give everything I have for that. That's the kind of fucking cliché I've been for all these years. Jack asked me to write this bloody novel, so I'm doing it – but you know why I stopped in the first place, why I gave it up, stopped writing books I believed in? Because those ones had to be for her, because I simply couldn't make them happen without her. Even the pulp I wrote . . . because it was aimed at women, because it got me into magazines, into the colour supplements, I always thought *well, maybe she'll read **something** – maybe she'll hear about me, see my photograph, maybe she will just fucking come back and visit me, only visit me once, nothing more than that.*

'But I'm doing what I said I would because that's all that I have left of myself – that I keep my fucking word. I'm writing this new thing and I'm trying to believe in it and I'm trying to make it good, but nothing has changed. I might as well never have stopped. Every page that I write of it, all I do is think about her. Doing this isn't worth it without her. Nothing is.

'I went into that anatomy room, Joe, and I understood how

wonderful I am, what a beautiful fucking thing. I know that. And I know that I have no purpose, I have no point.'

'Mary would disagree.'

Nathan was going to cry. 'I love Mary.' He could feel the sick cloy of betrayal as he spoke, 'I do love her,' and understood that his love for his daughter and her love for him were not enough. 'She's made these last years more possible than I could ever have imagined and I wish that I could have been her father earlier, I wish I could have been there when she genuinely needed me, but now she doesn't.'

'That's ridiculous. And you know it.'

By this time he *was* crying, could feel the tears, had to blink the room into focus, tasted salt when he licked his lips. 'She's a grown woman now and she's a writer. I'm not exactly indispensable any more. And she has Jonno.'

'You and Jonathan are not mutually exclusive.'

'Joe. You know what I mean. Leave it. I feel the way I feel and I know what I know. Anyway, you've said it yourself – Mary will be all right, whatever happens: she's special. She was in a car crash in the womb and she didn't die, she was born prematurely and she didn't die, she choked on – if I remember – a butter bean and I spun her round by the heels like a fucking lamb and forced it out of her and she didn't die, only looked at me with more trust than I'd thought I could tolerate and then there was the bee sting in her throat and . . . and . . . she's survived everything. You know and I know that she's already been through all seven of our steps without even thinking about it. Without any planning and without any doubt, she has her life absolutely. So either you believe what you've been preaching all these years, or you think she needs me.'

'Nathan, when you're like this, there's no persuading you of anything. She's certainly a remarkable young woman, very blessed, but she still needs a whole variety of things, including you. *I* need you, for that matter.'

Something about this cracked a sob through Nathan, set him clinging and wheezing around each breath. He could no longer speak.

'Nate, I know that you won't want to hear this, but there are other people who have other misfortunes. To take one example, you can see your daughter almost every day – every time I want to bring my daughter out here I have to enter into negotiations with her mother. The bargaining hasn't exactly got any easier since Sophie's accident at the pool. And I can't say that I especially long for my ex-wife, but I do remember what having the physical love of a woman was like. I do recall the giving and receiving of consensual delight. I do miss that. I may live a meditative life, but I'm not a saint, Nathan, I'm not anything approaching that.'

Joe got to his feet and began to pace, obviously finding it difficult to talk about this and stay still. 'You say you're finding the book hard; well, I do feel for you in that. But try to remember, Nate, I gave up writing completely. And I loved it as much as my daughter, as much as my wife. But I gave it up. Everyone round here acts as if that was an easy decision, as if it's all in the past now and gone. And yes, in a way, I do still write in my mind – in a way, I simply forgo the setting down of words. And I have my prayers and I have the joy of seeing other writers come here and rediscover their abilities and then leave me, better able to create, or stay with me and help make a community. But I have seen writers die here. And, however much it was their own decision to try the risk of that, I cannot help but feel responsible. I live with that. I live with that and I live with the knowledge that I can't ever write for them – for anyone – that I can't ever write about or for anything. All of my words die within sight of me, all of them are transient. You *want* to be dead, Nathan? Almost everyone thinks I *am* dead. Because I don't write. And a writer who doesn't write – what's that if it's not dead?

'So when you're considering your miseries, Nate, maybe take a pause to consider mine.' Joe walked to the window and halted, his back to the room. Nathan could hear the tensed rush of his breathing.

Nathan, still crying, 'I'm sorry,' trying his best to make sense, 'I'm so sorry,' weeping now with shame and self-disgust. 'Sometimes I don't think.'

Joe stayed at the window, motionless.

'Almost always, I don't think.' Nathan pushed himself out of his chair and went to stand behind his friend, to hold his shoulders, to rest his forehead against his back. 'Almost always, I don't think. You said I should come here to get things right with myself and I haven't, I haven't changed at all.'

For a space that Nathan couldn't judge, they said and did nothing more. Then slowly Nathan moved to look over Joe's shoulder, to see the night through the glass and their faces shining on it, both of them looking less than their best – two tired men, not happy, and the dark. He hoped that this wasn't the whole of the truth, he hoped this wasn't all there was to them.

Joe patted him on the hand and then shifted to the side, faced him. 'No need to be worried about me, Nathan. Not really.' Again a pat, this time at Nathan's arm. 'Thank you for listening.'

'Don't be so fucking reasonable.'

'You know me, I see no point in being otherwise: it just wastes so much time.'

Nathan gave a little huff, approaching a laugh, 'That's one explanation, yes,' and went towards the kitchen. 'You want some more tea now?'

'If you feel like tea yourself.'

'I feel like a drink myself.'

'We'll have a drink then.'

Nathan, already veering towards the whisky shelf, 'Yes, why not.' It surprised him that his hands were shaking slightly when he poured the measures out and that he felt, in some degree, lighter, but also more bereft.

'Nate, could I ask you something?'

'If you absolutely must.'

'Would you say that you were, in any way, a desperate man?'

'I would say, fuck off.' Nathan, not having lost it thus far, briefly wondered if he soon might.

'No, tell me, Nathan, it's important. Would you say you were a desperate man?'

'Of course I fucking would.'

'And that would, naturally, mean you are aware that desperation can create a kind of freedom, a certain strength: acknowledged, accepted, it can lead to almost anything.'

'What are you telling me, Joe?'

'Perhaps something you wanted to hear.'

They drank together gently after that: enjoying the drowse of each other's silences, or discussing harmless things until a couple of hours had passed and Joe set off back to the Lighthouse with a quiet goodbye and a short, hard hug. Then Nathan sat on alone, cradling the balance of his future in the light of another glass.

A desperate man – eh, Joe? A desperate fucking man. Just like on the wanted posters. **Approach with extreme caution – a desperate man.** *I should get that printed on a T-shirt, or maybe a badge for my lapel: more age-appropriate. Then again, anyone with any sense can simply read it in my face.*

And something must be done about it.

He frowned laboriously: whisky had slowed the muscles in his face, really rather soothingly, he thought.

Something must, very definitely, be done.

Bed now, though – go to bed first. And then possibly even sleep.

Nathan *said this would happen and I didn't believe him. Christ.*

Mary rolled carefully on to her side and decided not to examine the alarm clock – it was the middle of the night, that was all that she needed to know. To her left Jonno was still and sleeping, the shape of his weight a completely familiar pattern tugged softly into her half of the mattress. And she knew his breathing, knew his resting heat, knew that if she inched out her hand, she would find the smooth small of his back, the angle above his hip, the need to turn and work her way to fit against him, wake him up. And she knew she wouldn't reach and wouldn't touch him and hadn't woken with a thought of him in her head.

I honestly thought Nate was joking, being metaphorical, or something.

She'd snapped back into consciousness, a patter of excitement already disturbing her blood: a particular, private kind of happiness.

It would work. It would bloody work. I'd just have to put in another section before the last and then I could get away with it. The whole thing might even look as if I'd planned it.

It was the novel. When she'd got into bed, she hadn't known how to end it and now she did. The solution would be tricky, but not impossible, by any means. In fact, it had a surprising elegance – something she'd never suspected of herself.

God, this is appalling.

She absolutely needed to write. The desire to just get up and do it ached and rubbed in her as firmly and seductively as Jonno had ever done. So, as Nathan had predicted, she lay as motionless as she could beside the person she probably loved most in the world, certainly wanted most in the world, while her nerves seethed with the lack of an altogether different type of love.

It is good, though. He didn't say it was this good.

She resisted the urge to get up and work, to make even a single note.

That's the kind of thing Nathan would do – run away from a person and on to the page. But I won't. This is OK. It's just a writing thing, a writer's thing. It doesn't necessarily mean something bad – only that I've started to be a writer, even in my sleep.

The idea of this made her smile.

And I can at least share the feeling, because that would be the proper thing to do. We can both have a nice time with it.

Which meant that she tumbled Jonathan on to his back.

'Mm?'

'Ssh.'

Then she dived down and kissed him close to his navel while he mumbled awake and his hands found her neck, her hair, her head as it nuzzled in to let her sigh between his hips: brush, lick and lift where he was soft, suck him free from every dream until he straightened for her, borrowed her beat and pushed back at her, thick.

They didn't take long and were, perhaps, unusually fierce. Then Mary let him be with a final, tiny purse of her lips, made him shudder in a way she liked.

'What was all that about?' He stroked her shoulders, waited until she surfaced again. 'Mary?'

'Oh, I don't know.'

'Mm, well. It's practically time to wake up . . .' Kissing her mouth and smiling at the taste of himself there. 'Work in the morning.'

'Same thing for me.' She turned and let him fold himself against her back, his arms already gently clumsy again with drowsiness.

Yes, indeed, work in the morning. Back to the island and get right down to it, take it all the way.

The memory of his sweat pressed to her face, of him braced and pinned against her, fluttered in the pit of her stomach and sleeked in beside the raw tick of syllables, waiting: the anxious flex of ready words.

And if it hadn't seemed overly intimate to mention, Nathan could have told her about this, too – the author's unique capacity to commit almost entirely invisible infidelities.

Mary had news that wouldn't wait. 'Nathan.' News he'd be just the man to understand. She'd wanted to tell him on Sunday at the Lunch, but he'd been called away again to London, Joe said: business.

He's not away now, though. He came back yesterday, I saw him on the path.

It had taken her a week, which she hadn't expected – seven days of bouncing around off the Nissen hut walls, of taking fast walks in the middle of the night, of feeling her train of thought dismembered by even the simplest conversation and of giving the whole fucking manuscript up in disgust and then sitting back down, face to face with it again, in even more disgust, and of bullying and begging and dreaming awake ferociously until it was done, all done. She was finished and he'd want to know. 'Nathan?'

God, I'm tired. I should just go home and get some sleep, tell him later.

No. I don't want to sleep.

I want to tell him now.

'Are you there?' She hadn't even called Jonno, not yet: partly because it was probably too early, but also because it was Nathan who should be the first to know. ' Come on, Nate, it's me.'

'Nathan?' When he didn't answer, Mary tried his door. Not that Nathan ever locked it, even when he went away.

He's not out with the dog, his music's playing – bloody Bach again.

'Nathan?' She moved inside. The kitchen was as orderly as ever, except for the Thermos flask on the table, surrounded by a colourful litter of vaguely medical packages. Eckless padded up, quietly dishevelled, from an unaccustomed resting place near the stove and nudged against her while she prodded through boxes of various painkillers, sticking plasters, antiseptic ointments.

'Nathan? Are you awake?' Bach's familiar patterns clambered and fell behind the closed living-room door. 'I'm sorry it's so early, but you know . . .' The dog sniffed at his empty water bowl and then left her, took himself soundlessly outside.

She found Nathan on the floor of the living room, a cushion from one of the armchairs under his head. 'Christ.' The air numbed and slipped away from her as she ran and knelt beside him. 'Nathan?'

'Hmn? Fuck, what? What?' When he turned over she could see the imprint of the cushion fabric, pressed into his cheek. 'Mary?'

'You bloody –' She'd slapped at his shoulder before she could stop herself and before his hands could paddle up to shield his face.

'Mary, what the fuck are you . . . ? What time is it?'

'I don't bloody know what time it is. Half six. Something like that. What's the matter with you?'

He sat up gingerly. 'Ow. Christ. Nothing is the matter with me beyond what would be the matter with anyone who'd slept half the night on the floor.' Nathan stared up at her, pink-eyed. 'This couldn't have waited, love?'

'I, uh.' She felt – now that it seemed he was all right – embarrassed and clumsy. 'Well, no, I didn't think it could have waited.' She helped him to stand and watched while he limped up and down, rubbed at his knees, sighed. Only then did it occur to her that she might ask. 'Why did you sleep on the floor?'

'I wanted to hear the music better.' He clenched his eyes shut and bent his head back, blinked at the ceiling. 'And sometimes I don't feel like sleeping in my bed. Could you . . . do you . . .' He turned to study her, his look softer than usual and a little baffled. 'I wouldn't mind hugging something – since the dog seems unavailable, do you think . . . ?'

'Are you OK?' She walked forward, suddenly self-conscious, and hooped her arms lightly round him.

'Mm hm. Yes, I'm fine.' He leaned into her, a dead weight, arms at his sides and his chin heavy on her shoulder, 'That's fine, thank you,' and then slipped away into the kitchen. When she joined him, the table was clear, the dog's food and water bowls both full and he was loading up the percolator with coffee grounds. 'Caffeine. What we need. Caffeine. Why exactly are you here, by the way?'

And she told him that her novel was finished, that her first draft was done and he clattered his teaspoon of coffee down into the sink

489

and punched one hand into the other with a small, hot smile and then trotted over to hug her powerfully, lift her briefly off her feet. 'That's my girl. That's my grand, wee girl. My Mary.'

'Ow.'

'Sorry.' He set her down at once and stumbled back. 'Sorry. Did I squash something?'

'Most things. But I think I'll live.' Mary tried a giggle to reassure him as he watched her, increasingly crestfallen, but all that emerged was a kind of sob. She caught hold of his hands and then let him tug her in close again as a full, hard spasm of weeping took her.

'God, I'm sorry, love, I'm so sorry. Did I hurt you?'

She shook her head against his chest.

'Lamb, what's the matter?'

An ache peeled the length of her spine and she buckled inside the crush of her own breath, tightened her arms round his back until they shivered and lost their strength.

'Tell me what I've done?'

'No, nothing. You haven't done anything. I'm just tired.'

'Just tired.' He breathed a little laugh into her hair. 'I haven't heard that from a woman in years. But I still know what it means. You come back through now and tell me what's the matter, all right?'

'All right.'

He cupped her face in his hands, solemn, and then, with the crook of one forefinger, very lightly brushed at both her cheeks. This started her crying again.

'Sorry. Sorry, I'll stop. That was a bad idea. Sorry.' Nathan backed out of her reach and wandered gently through to the living room. 'Sorry.'

She followed him, sat in the chair that he'd moved and set tight beside his own. Eckless came back from wherever he'd been, looking slightly less despondent, stared at the pair of them appraisingly and then moved to his usual corner of the living room where he fell asleep in his basket with a sigh. And Mary watched the whole canine performance with more attention than it deserved, buying herself thinking time, but then did finally tell Nathan how long it had taken to finish her book and how hard she'd been working and how worried she had been when she came in and saw him, just lying there on the floor and that this was not how she'd expected to start telling her mentor her news.

Nathan listened and set his hand over hers. 'Anything else? Beyond that you haven't slept properly in days.'

'No.'

'You're sure?'

'Yes.'

'Really?'

'No.'

'Then tell me.'

She stared at the back of his hand, trying to think.

'Mary? You can tell me anything. You do know that, don't you? Because it's true.'

'Yes, I . . .' Tiredness was making it difficult to focus properly on words now, but she did want to speak to him – it seemed that she would hurt him if she tried to do anything else. 'It's the letters. The ones I used to get from my father. The person who said he was my father.'

His fingers tensed slightly against hers. 'Yes?'

'They've stopped coming. I mean, they never were very regular . . . but about every few months one would appear. I've had nothing since last year.'

'That could be for lots of reasons.'

'Like he's lost interest again.'

'That wouldn't be one of them, I'm sure.'

'The last time he wrote, he said he would try and see me.'

'He what?'

'He said we might meet. And I didn't really think it was a great idea, but then I got used to it and I might have, I might have given it a go. You could have come with me.'

'I –'

'Wouldn't you?'

'I could have been there.' He folded his hands together in his lap. 'Yes.'

'You called me Lamb.'

'What?'

'You called me Lamb. In the kitchen, just now.'

'I didn't, did I? I didn't notice. I mean, it's your name.'

'The way you said it – it felt . . . I think he called me that. I mean,

491

my father – I think that he called me . . . No. I don't know. I'm being stupid. It's because I'm tired. I'm sorry.'

'No, no. Not at all.' He folded his arms and leaned forward. 'These things are very difficult.' He spoke to the floor. 'I always find them very difficult. I think if – you know, I'm really too tired myself to be making much sense – but I think that you've, you've . . . you've got me, you know. There's a great deal wrong with me, of course, and there are – I have things I need to do, just a few things I need to do and then I'll be much more *here* for you and I'll, um, there's an order to what has to be done. And I do have to do it – what has to be done – but then – or even now – I'm . . . I'm . . .'

Mary rubbed at his back, 'I know,' thinking, once again, that she didn't really know him. She quite often understood him, but that wasn't the same thing at all. Whole areas of his identity were no more open than when they'd first met, although, sometimes, traces of his larger, untidier self would show as numbed intervals, inarticulate spaces in the image of the man that he intended to present.

She let her hand rest near the back of his neck. 'I know you're here.' Which seemed an absurdly insubstantial kind of endorsement, but then he hardly ever gave her the space to say anything more. Not that she didn't occasionally – in spite of his very obvious discomfort – try. 'And if anyone's like a . . . I mean, for me, you're as good as . . . well, you understand.'

She wasn't sure why the comparison failed her. It wasn't so terribly inappropriate, after all, he *was* like a father to her. And she couldn't mistake that he quite often wanted to be.

Mary thought of the lost child he never talked about, and then found that she had to lean in and kiss Nathan's cheek. He didn't move, only kept peering ahead of himself, looking wearily puzzled and, she thought, bleak.

He covered his eyes with one hand. 'This conversation – we should have it again soon. Right now is not the best time, but soon . . .'

'Yes, OK. You're probably right.' And she heard herself saying, 'I'll go,' although she wanted to stay with Nathan: to keep him, and herself, tucked up in the cottage together for a while, safe from any threat of feral loneliness.

'Well, if you must, that's maybe,' Nathan coughed, 'for the best.'

He looked up at her when she stood as if he were newly woken into a strange day. 'Still, I . . . I wouldn't really mind company – there's this piece I have to write and I don't really want to – not at all – it's one of those bits of work that I'd really be very much happier putting off. You know the way . . .' Taking her hand, his thumb rubbing at her wrist.

'Oh, I know the way.' She tried to make him smile. 'Usually it happens with the things *you've* made me write.'

He gave a little grimace of embarrassment. 'Doesn't surprise me.'

She pressed at his back, smoothing his shirt, 'Joke,' and waited until he looked a touch convinced. 'I can stay if you like. *I* would like.'

'That's nice of you to say. Better not, though. If I don't write this bloody thing now, it'll just lie in wait for me – I should get it done.'

'OK, then. Walk me to the door.'

Nathan nodded and they slowly escorted each other into the kitchen, only halting at the final doorway where they hovered, talking harmless nonsense, remembering little points they had to clarify, delaying their parting.

'I'll have another look at the manuscript, Nate, and then, if you don't mind, I'll pass it on to you.'

'I'd mind if you did anything else. Are you OK? To go home?' He peered past her at the weather, which was gloomy but docile.

'It's not exactly far.' She backed out over the step and on to the grass, leaving. 'I'll see you tomorrow.'

'Um, why not. Why not. You take care of yourself.' He scrambled a rushed hug in around her, kissed the top of her head and then withdrew just as quickly, nodded to her and, in a bolt of nervous motion, closed his door. Mary stared for a moment at its uncommunicative wood and then set off home to the Nissen hut.

The distance between their two houses seemed uneasy as she crossed it.

Nathan didn't stand in his kitchen window and watch her go, instead he walked through to the living room and woke up his dog and sat next to him on the floor, held him round the neck. Eckless grumbled and sneezed as a token complaint and then rested against his master, patient. Nathan had a headache: one of the panicky, blurry kind,

493

flywheeling behind the sockets of his eyes.

Which means I shouldn't do this now – it means I won't be able to.

Even so, he rubbed at his dog's ears, got up and left him, went to work.

This is insane. Just fucking insane.

He picked out a pen from the jar on the window ledge, found a fresh pad of paper – he didn't want to take one he'd used before.

I can't. And if I believe I can't, then that's all it takes to stop me.

But he came and sat at his table, as if he'd been ordered to, and he set down the unimpressive small tools of his trade.

I can't.

He cupped his hands to his face – they still had a touch of Mary's scent.

I can't.

No. You can. You can and you will do this.

If this is all you fucking have, if this is all you'll ever be allowed to have, if this is all you will fucking allow yourself, then this is what you fucking do, you cunt, this is what you fucking do until it's done. This is what you are for. This is all that you were ever fucking for, so write.

Paradise

I'm taking the Underground for luck. I'm liking the jig and nudge and wriggle of communal motion as we consent to be barrelled along, each one of us readied for Friday night. Not too many people yet, but already the carriage air is endearingly thick with aftershave and breath mints, adrenalin, Dutch courage doubles, Immac and sweat.

I do love it – I'd forgotten, but I do – I adore that weird, nude thrum that stays with your skin when you've showered and shaved and dressed again straight away – fresh clothes that little bit rigorous against flesh that you've made so warmed now, so stripped – and then you step out in the evening and find that you fit it, nicely tight.

Oh, fuck.

I manage – barely – to not miss my stop and change trains for the Piccadilly Line. Going into town. Ten, or fifteen minutes, I'll be there.

I shouldn't have drunk so much coffee. The caffeine's just making me rattled – filthy stuff's practically lifting my hair. What there is of my hair. Next thing, I'll need to piss. Although actually, now that I think of it, I already need to piss.

Shit, what a sorry specimen – dodgy bladder and wild but inadequate hair. Like a refugee from a sodding old folk's home.

*But drinking **drink**, instead of coffee, would have been bound to turn out worse. That kind of thing could easily lead to her getting the wrong impression.*

Oh, fuck.

I've done it – what I really shouldn't have – I've thought of her. Waiting on the platform and having to lean back against the wall while anticipation milks me out: a little squeeze of pain, then one of panic, one of sex, and all because I've thought of her. When the train comes I'll be emptied enough to simply blow away.

Christ, it wasn't even hard to find her number – she was in the fucking book: Maura Lamb, simple as that.

'Hello, Maura?'

The name of her springing in me, and then the whole sound of her voice being just exactly, exactly, exactly the same.

'Yes? Who is this?'

I couldn't answer.

'Who is this? Is it . . .? It's not . . . Nathan? Is that you?'

And everything started to work then – the conversation, the outcome, even my one little try at a joke – worked exactly as I'd imagined: effortless and lovely and better than my best hope. And part of me, quite a large part of me, wanted to fucking scream **WHY IS THIS ALL SO EASY NOW WHEN FOR PRACTICALLY TWO FUCKING DECADES IT HAS BEEN NOTHING BUT FUCKING HARD?**

And then I wondered when I first could have called her and found her gentle, kind. Five years ago? Fifteen? Only ten? I could feel myself starting to smother in wasted time.

But that doesn't matter, *cannot* matter, now, because I've passed through Piccadilly Circus and I'm already standing and anxious for Leicester Square.

I should maybe have caught a cab, though. The idea of having been here with her, of all of those other times – that afternoon when both her hands were up above her head, holding on, momentum teasing through her beautifully – me watching the stretch and give of her and saying that I was about to run amok and take perverse advantage of her hands being occupied. Maura was standing and looking right at me and then she smiled.

I wish, not for the first time, that I'd brought along my personal stereo – something to stop the head from incautious racing. It would also be great, I feel, to be able to batter up the station steps and into the outside air, held round with music, kept safe inside of that.

R.E.M. would be nice. Or, no . . . No, I do believe that I'd prefer the Kinks.

And, at once, one of their lyrics gets me, scythes and clatters in the mind, insensitively.

Well, once we had an easy ride and always felt the same. Time was on my side and I had everything to gain.

Which rather guarantees that the Kinks would have been a bad choice after all. I attempt to think of something else entirely.

Up and out in the fading day, it's chilly but not too bad: garish skeins of tourists maunder simple-mindedly over the square, an open invitation to pickpockets and recreational snipers.

And, as the last of the natural light is pared away, the cinemas begin to shine.

Going to the pictures. It's the sensible thing to do – a way of spending time together without too much responsibility.

Not that we're meeting to spend time together at all. We're meeting to talk about Mary. That's why we're meeting. No other reason. None.

The wailing of nerves in my stomach proves how very large and unaccepted a truth this is.

Minimum pressure, no expectations: I'll just buy us coffees somewhere, we can have a little chat, then go on in and watch a film.

I realise I haven't the slightest idea of what she'll want to see.

There's one from a Hardy novel – all sad romance and bad weather. But I couldn't watch a romance, not with her. Not with anyone.

Or there's a film about Flipper the friendly fucking dolphin. Nearly as bad as that one about the talking pig. Jesus, the things they think of. Didn't see that,

497

*either – a **flying** pig and I'd be interested – my clan
crest should show one rampant, or the space where my
forebears had hoped that a pig might eventually fly –
not that I actually even have a clan . . . Anyway –*

Striptease *– badly simulated fucking and horny dancing, I presume – I would go mad . . .*

Oh, Jesus, I can't do this. I just can't.

And my tongue's turned to cartridge paper and my heart
has apparently stopped, or is screaming so fast in my
torso that I can't even feel it any more and I am sweating too much sweat.

*Altogether too much sweat, soaking into the good, new
shirt – black: even I look good in black and it makes
me feel at home – and the nice pair of jeans because a
suit would be trying too hard, but, equally, I don't
want to look as if I couldn't give a fuck.*

If you see what I mean.

*If **she** sees what I mean.*

*And the flying jacket sort of sheepskin that I found
in the flat – which surprised me because I did think that
I'd thrown it away – I'm only wearing **that** because it's
quite like one I had when she still knew me.*

When we were married.

*Properly married, rather than being technically not
divorced.*

Let it be like yesterday.

Please let me have happy days.

I wore it all through our last winter.

Which probably makes it a dreadful idea for tonight.

*But still, it's something she might recognise, unlike
me. I am so ridiculously older. Back then, I wasn't even
balding and my hair was black and I had a bit of a belly
starting which wasn't attractive, but at least I also
had a softer face – I wasn't so drawn that I couldn't
seem to be anything other than intense.*

**Won't you tell me, where have all the good times gone,
where have all the good times gone?**

I decide I would give quite a lot to stop thinking my

way through that fucking song. Not that the alternative mental din isn't worse.

Why am I always so bastarding early? No one else ever is. It simply means that I turn up and then have to hang around for ages until it feels as if whoever I'm meet- ing is late and so I'm already pissed off with them, even if, when they arrive, they're precisely on time.

She's never on time.

Unless she's changed.

I don't want her to have changed.

Other than in a few particulars.

Like that I would like her to like me.

Liking – it's not a big thing, it isn't excessive or overly meaningful. It isn't unlikely.

I stand under the awning of the cinema and then, as I promised myself I would not, I check my watch. I am aware that I now look like all of the other sad shits, hovering miserably to either side of me, eyes thumbing through the crowd for a sight of that anticipated face. Not one of us is managing to look as if this might be any fun.

I really do need a piss.

But if I nip in and take one, Maura might come by. She might see that I'm not here and go away again.

Or, equally, I might be wise to fuck off, take a leak and, meanwhile, imagine that she really is outside and trying to meet me and yet – due to this one unfortunate happenstance – she will be destined to fail completely. That would be better than standing and watching and having to realise she isn't coming, that she will not come, that everything we agreed to was so easy because she never intended to come.

I consider leaving, waiting, pissing, putting my head through the glass pane in one of the doors, but actu- ally do nothing which looks very much like waiting, but isn't the same thing in any way.

'Nathan?'

She's everything, you know? She is everything.

'It is you, isn't it?'

All of my life.

'I know your face from the . . . um . . . magazines. Sometimes.'

She was why it made sense.

'And, anyway, you look like you. You always have.'

Maura leans in quickly, breathes a kiss near my cheek and steps away again before I understand that she's truly here, that she's kissed me, that I have gooseflesh suddenly.

She's here.

She's here.

She's here.

She's here.

She's here.

'Nathan, are you all right?'

'Yes.'

I am quite completely all right.

And then we walk together, in each other's company, side by side, as a pair, and find a café and then sit and drink grotesquely expensive coffee in varnished surroundings and watch fat rain begin falling and talk about Mary Lamb, our daughter.

'I'm glad she's found something to do that she believes in.'

I can only look at Maura in snatches, 'Really?' hoping to ease my way into longer views, 'even if it's writing?' while my trembling, restrained, gives way to a deep-seated rocking, a long ripple of motion that swipes me a little colder and more needy with every stroke.

'It's what she wants to do.' Maura keeps going through most of the motions required to light a cigarette, but then stopping before the moment of ignition. 'She was – that time she came to see me – she was obviously very fond of you. You've impressed her.'

'I didn't mean to.'

Maura smiles and half shakes her head. 'Don't be

silly, of course you did.' The memory of the gesture and its quick reality shudder in both of my lungs: the true one and the ghost.

I'm unsure of my focus on what we're saying, some phrases lunge at me and, somehow, penetrate, while others skate by, leaving me virtually intact.

Must be careful of the legs and feet under the table – I mustn't touch her by accident. Not when I want so much to touch her purposely.

Want is digging in my chest and I'm sure I'm being overbearing, far too loud, but it is really very difficult not to shout when she's sitting there, so many years away.

I tell her how thoroughly wonderful our Mary has turned out to be, entirely neglecting to mention how much she resembles her mother. And Maura suggests that we may not have failed her quite as badly as we have probably both thought.

'Either that, or she's simply resilient.'

'And a lot of it must be down to Bryn and Morgan. I couldn't go to either one of their funerals. Just couldn't do it.'

The conversation is dipping badly, Maura beginning to look very plainly depressed, and I wonder if she thinks I blame her for abandoning the child. I don't. I *genuinely* don't. We all only do what we can at the time. I know I had my faults, too.

Of course, I can't tell her any of this – it would be inappropriately intimate – and I opt instead for the mildly strangled effort, 'What d'you want to see? At the pictures.'

Maura is blank for a breath and then shrugs. 'I hadn't thought.'

'If you don't want to . . .'

Please want to, please want to, then you won't have to go yet. Don't go.

'No, I'd like to see something, I just wasn't sure of what. Have your tastes changed?'

This slaps me in the heart so badly that I cough. 'My . . .?'

'Tastes.'

'They're exactly the same.' I try to say this without undue emphasis.

'Well, then, there's one about a kidnapping that goes wrong – it's meant to be very clever and very dark. And funny.'

I nod, feeling very dark and very stupid and not funny at all, while the back of my head is yowling with delight.

She remembers my tastes.

First she says she's looked at me in magazines and now she remembers my tastes.

The tastes that prove I'm still predictably sick and sad.

I manage, 'Clever and dark, eh?' almost as if this were jolly news. 'But *you* wouldn't necessarily enjoy that. If I remember your tastes. Not that you're not clever, obviously, you always were very . . . I would just want to . . . Would you like to see that?'

'I wouldn't mind.'

'But what would you like?'

'There's *Breaking the Waves*. It's, maybe . . . something about a couple and he ends up . . . he can't . . . People say it's good, but it might not be. For us.'

'Sounds great.' *Not a couple, not a couple. No.* 'We'll see that, then. Let's go.'

'I'll just pay for this.' She lifts up a handbag that looks, in some way, middle-aged, not like her. She's still young – always was, factually, younger than me – but, even bearing that in mind, she *is* hardly changed. Still Maura, still beautiful.

'I've already paid.'

'Then let me give you something.' She searches in her purse for something.

'No. I've already paid.' *And paid and paid and paid.*

★

The dark of the cinema clasps about me and the advertisements gush by, all of them slightly too nubile, too knowing, hingeing too heavily on things I mustn't contemplate. Not that the film is any better, in that respect.

Shit, I can't watch this. It's going to be sad, I can tell. And it's going to be . . . all of the things I can't watch. **Shit***.*

I face strictly forward, but look at my knees, don't lean on her armrest, and feel thoroughly ashamed, while the scent of her shimmers beside me: the limited notes of her perfume and the other fuller, more complicated melody of her self.

God have mercy, this is what I used to live in, sleep in, what I wore under my clothes, what I spent lunatic months searching out once she'd made us be apart. I kept that scarf of hers and the blouse, tied up in a carrier bag, and, almost every morning, I'd decide to get rid of it and, almost every evening, I'd take it out from my bottom drawer and open it and breathe her in: one breath each time, exactly enough to make me weep.

In the end, it faded. In the end, it went away.

And I know that, in this close, synthetic, indoor night, I wouldn't be able to see myself and may conceivably be able to ignore the total lunacy of reaching out to find her hand.

Don't.

And don't look at the screen. Not while, not while they're . . .

Christ, she smells gorgeous, smells of what I thought was **us***, although really it was only ever her.* I never was properly part of **us** – never the genuine family man.

I make the attempt to coax myself from thoughts I shouldn't start on. My thinking, naturally, punches back.

I'm going to miss her. At the end of the night. Dear God, I am.

And I feel myself fall in the chill of this, brace my

legs and back against the soft plush of the seat and still keep falling while the screen blares out its patterns of terrible light.

This shouldn't be happening. These aren't new emotions, they can't be, they've just kept on fucking growing in their grave like the fucking nails and hair on a fucking corpse. They are not new and so they cannot make me feel this way. I will not give them my consent.

But they still take it, anyway.

Then Maura gets up, dips in to murmur like brimstone close at my neck, 'I won't be a minute,' and goes away.

The space she leaves in the darkness sings beside me, burns, and I haven't any words left and I know that I am lost. In the movie, I watch an actress and an actor both doing their jobs, pretending quite convincingly, moving into the shapes of unhappiness and sex, and I cry, the tears rolling back to my temples because of the angle of my head.

I'm glad Maura isn't here to notice this. She's already seen more than enough of my weaknesses.

I don't understand how this happened and I'd say it was deeply unwise, but I'm putting up no resistance: in fact, I haven't one word of complaint. Tucked up in a taxi with Maura and rocking along, there is no complaint I could possibly wish to make.

And this was her idea, her suggestion, she never got a hint towards it out of me.

We just shared a couple of drinks after the film – we'd both had a bit of a difficult time with it and were trying to close the evening gently in an equally bad choice of bar. I was going to lose my temper, I know, with all of the being jostled and having to shout, but then Maura suddenly asked me – almost yelling, her breath against my cheek – asked me if I wanted to come back now, to come back and talk, to come back to her place and open a bottle of wine and make this a more comfortable night.

'Why not? There's nothing to stop us. Is there,

really? Is there, Nate?'

And while my whole nervous system hooted and con-
vulsed, I gave only a wide-eyed shake of my head, my
tiniest smile, 'No reason I can think of.' Then I
drained the last sip of my drink, an ice fragment darting electrically in at my gum and, of course, this was
no time to flinch, what with both of us sitting there,
ready to leave, and slightly surprised at ourselves,
but still quite happy, quite recklessly unguarded
against the rush of hours ahead.

*And, after all, it's still fairly early. Or still not
too late.*

'You're sure you don't mind this?' The lock and jumble of city traffic is greasing against the cab windows,
the rain still pressing down. 'I mean, it's . . .' I'm
going to say, 'very nice of you,' but she stops me with
a look: very straight and pensive in the fractions of
passing light. There's something else there too, it
gives me the shifting impression that she is, in some
way, uncertain, or perhaps preoccupied.

'Of course I don't mind: that's why I asked you.' I
imagine I can hear a frailty in her voice, although this
might be nothing but an echo of the undoubted frailty
in my brain. 'The place is a bit of a mess, though.
You'll have to forgive me.'

'Of course I will. I'd have to give you much the same
warning if we went back to mine.' *The more warnings,
the better, if you ever came back to mine.*

'You still have somewhere in London?'

'Oh, yes.' *And so that you know,* 'It's in Dolphin
Square.' *So that you can find me.*

'Very swish.'

'And about to get slightly fashionable, I'm afraid.'
*Fuck, I sound like an utter wank. Look at her: smil-
ing, but not in a good way: only giving that seeping
grin you do when you tolerate a prat.*

And I am that prat.

'Maura?' Trying to change the subject and not wonder

in any way which side of the bed she sleeps on, whether it's still the left.

Christ.

The sheer idea of her, ice-picking, scorchingly in.

Oh, Christ.

She's looking at me, puzzled because I'm not speaking, because - probably - I am quite visibly coming unstitched.

'Nathan?'

'Uh, yes, I was just wondering . . . wondering if I could ask you a question. Hm?'

And she reaches out her hand and takes mine, takes me, as gently and totally as death by drowning. 'Of course you can.'

Maura sets a squeeze round my knuckles now, one that I can't help returning, although I don't know what I mean by this, what *we* mean by this.

'I'd have hoped you could ask me. . .' and I realise she wants to say 'anything' but stops herself, reconsiders, 'ask me whatever you want.' She's being careful with her phrasing, but is also a little tipsy, I can hear it in her voice, and this raises in me several sleazy hopes. 'Just ask.'

'Yes. Yes, OK. I will then.'

'Well, go on.' Another squeeze, before she frees me, leaves me cold where I've lost her touch.

Her hands are the same, precisely: they can still turn all my muscles to fucking sand. Sand and the beginnings of hot lead.

'Right, I'm going to.' *If you only take my hand once more, once more before we finish the night, then, God, it'll be enough - enough for the rest of my life.*

Liar. Fucking liar.

'And?'

'Mm hm. Really. The thing is . . .' I'm easing towards *her* hand now, searching my fingers out across the vaguely tacky undulations of the seat. 'God, well . . . I shouldn't . . . no, forget it.'

506

'What?' And her fingers soothe in around mine again, a good, concerned pressure, neat against me. Both my vocabulary and my breath have gone, but she stays insistent. 'Come on, what?'

'Would you, would you – it's your decision and I would abide by it. But if I could ask.' My eyes are wet, but don't quite pass the point of tears, for which I am thankful. 'Maura, I want to tell her who I am.' I am both frowning and swallowing, but this gains me no self-control.

'You?'

'I want to tell Mary who I am.'

'Christ, Nathan . . .'

And now Maura seems angry – as I knew she would be – and I shut my eyes and wait for whatever sort of impact must now come and perhaps my next inhalation isn't managed all that well, perhaps it breaks, I'm not really sure. But then I find that I'm leaning further and further down towards my left and then her arm catches hold, quick around me, pulling in, and the side of my head lands awkwardly against her in a way that very slightly hurts my neck and she pats at me, awkwardly, near my ear and, all this time, I can hear her saying, 'Christ, I thought you'd already done that. I really . . . I thought you must have. God, you didn't have to ask permission. You're so . . . sometimes.'

She sighs and the heat, the motion of her sighing, this does things to my stomach and my scalp, the inside edges of my arms and thighs.

'I'm sorry.'

'For what, Nate?'

'I don't know. Everything. I don't know.'

And I make the mistake of shifting my head on her shoulder, only easing that tick in my neck, not meaning to nuzzle or to be affectionate, but – whatever my intentions – I've muddied the atmosphere.

We struggle apart, ungainly, any accidental contacts seeming faintly ugly and abashed. For longer than I'd like, there is silence. Then, 'Nathan, you can tell her whatever you want to. She was always more fond of you than she was of me.'

'No, tha-'

'Well, however it was in the beginning, that's how it is now.' She sighs once more, the sound parting and stroking the air. 'I'd assumed that you'd told her. I thought that was why she'd not come to see me again – because I'd made you go away and then left her myself. And those are two very good reasons for her to hate me. But now you're saying she just couldn't be bothered.'

'I'm no-'

'Shit, simply meeting me one last time was enough to stop her doing it again. No more reasons needed. You know, that really makes me feel like a thoroughly attractive person.'

She breathes a kind of shaken laugh, tired sounding, and if I were any other man, I would be a comfort to her, I would kiss and reassure. Instead, I bleat, 'If I'd told her, I wouldn't have said it was your fault – any of it.'

'No. No, I know that. You're not malicious.' She says this as if it's an absolute fact. I find this astonishing. 'Look, Nathan – if you don't mind my saying, you should have done something about this a long time ago. Not that I should lecture, but I do know how badly wrong things can go when you leave them. It's going to be very difficult. She'll want to know -'

'Why I haven't mentioned it before – my being her father. Why I never got around to it.'

'And?'

I don't want to think about this. I don't. I want to think of, I want to-

Shut up, shut up, shut up.

'I've tried to tell her.' I sound angry and don't want to. 'I have tried.' The cab turns a corner and tilts me nowhere near enough to Maura. 'I got scared. She's older now, she's got a boyfriend, she's well on her way to leaving, whatever I do – but,' it's my turn to sigh, 'in the beginning, when she first came, when we didn't know each other, I got scared that I would make her go – that if she knew who I really was, it would make her go. This way, at least I've had a . . .' And any sense this ever made dwindles in the grainy yellow of the street lamps and burns away.

'Oh, Nathan.' Maura nudges herself nearer, sets a small, rather formal kiss against my cheek. 'Poor old you.' And I sit in this new hopeless, pointless proximity.

Sympathy. I could have borne anything from her but that.

We are close enough to brush shoulders, hips, at each stiff corner, dunting together and nursing our separate miseries. We say nothing more, attempt no further expressions of tenderness.

Congratulations, Nathan – fucked it up again. Poor old you.

I realise that I am currently slightly drunk.

This is fine, though, no need for alarm. In fact, quite the reverse. Just take this easy and things could be relatively fine. I am in control.

Because I am not remotely inebriated. I am only nicely, definitely, deeply and unthreateningly relaxed. Even here, in a house full of Maura, in her home, I am relaxed. Even now, when Maura is with me, her feet up on the sofa – shoes off, almost lying, shoes off, that small, domestic nakedness – I am still relaxed. Even when we talk about nothing and manage both our first and our second unforced laugh and are together in something so piercingly like the old, old way, I am relaxed.

*I'm not really **feeling** any more, that's the point to point out, pointedly. None of this hurts any more, none of this does **anything** any more.*

*I can't feel **me**. I've gone. All gone. It's always so wonderful when I've left me. So safe.*

We've already been in the kitchen for a while – about

509

half a bottle – but now we're in the living room with
only the light from one lamp and a cosy amount of central heating.

*A bit too warm, really, but that's probably only me
and my share of the rest of the bottle, glowing away.*

She fibbed about the mess. Maura clearly keeps the
place neat – none of that middle-class London leave-it-
to-the-cleaner sort of squalor. And I always did like
her taste, the way she could build up a room into somewhere agreeable.

Of course, I'm not being foolish, not looking about
too closely, in case I catch sight of a this or a that
I might recognise. I am equally anxious not to see any
traces of somebody else. Although I couldn't help but
notice that none are terribly apparent. I'm glad, if
surprised, that she seems to have no bookshelves, in
fact, no books – no chances for me to go searching out
my titles.

She won't have them.

You don't know that.

Yes, I do.

No, what you do is you like her taste.

The slick voice from the dark edge of the head.

She knows yours and you like hers. You like her taste.

'Nathan, can I tell you something – something
stupid?' She's half grinning, biting softly at her lip.
'This being the time of the evening when I might.'

'Please do.' *Might what?* 'Surely. Tell away.'

'You always got it wrong and I never . . . wanted to
say.'

'But now?'

'Now it seems more appropriate.' She fusses at her
fringe and I could almost swear that she is nervous –
that, or something even nicer. 'You see,' and now she
rushes this, but nevertheless does say, 'every time we
talked about it – not that we did a lot – you'd always
say that you were fond of *The Story of O* – "especially
the bit about the egg", but there isn't a bit about an

egg in *The Story of O* – that's in *Story of the Eye*. She breathes out audibly and slaps more wine down into her glass, not unshaky. 'Just thought I'd say.'

Jesus, where the fuck did that come from and if I say . . . do I follow that with . . . what does she want me to . . . Jesus.

I try, 'The bit with the . . .' *raw egg broken between the naked buttocks, the licking of yolk close to the cunt, Jesuschristalmighty.* 'Well, fancy getting that wrong.' Lust wallowing in the stomach. 'Not as sophisticated as I'd thought, eh. Darn it.'

Darn it? **Darn it?** *Are you sui-fucking-cidal?*

*Move it along, dear God, just think of a dirty – no, of an **erotic** something, something subtle, something –*

Maura lights a cigarette, hands confident again, assured. 'Anyway.' It's too late, she's already retreated. 'It doesn't matter now, does it?' And maybe she never did really advance. 'I don't know why I mentioned it.'

Fuck your eyes, Nathan Staples, fuck your fucking eyes, you had it on a plate.

I try to watch her smoking. I don't like smoking, but I have discovered that I can't mind it when it's hers.

I can't mind anything that's hers. Surely that means that I'm safe here, that I could even come back, now and then, and visit her with no ill effects.

And with no sign of current competition.

Ssh.

It would not be impossible for me to form a friendship with my separated wife. I can believe it would not be beyond us to grow accustomed to the tentative equation we already seem to make.

And I won't try for anything more. I won't.

Maura's watching me, quizzical. 'You're staring, Nathan.' She smiles – also relaxed – taking time with her words. 'But what can it be that you are staring at?' Everything she says sounds both wine-softened and meticulous. 'Mm?'

'I, ahm, was just staring.'

'Which means you were thinking. About what?'

'About this all being . . .' *Oh, fuck it, why not? – I'm relaxed, she's relaxed . . .* 'About how nice this was: seeing . . . well, seeing you.'

'That's . . .' She stops, looks briefly at a point somewhere between my feet.

And then I feel it: that sweetest, sweetest, airless moment when it happens, the slip into clear water, the change.

God, God, please.

The pulse in you ripping up from a standing start and you looking at her and her looking at you and then you can't help swallowing – that cartoon, nervous-tension type of gulp that might be funny at another time, but currently feels simply hideous and uncool – before the stillness between you takes that one hot step and fixes you by the bone, lays you bare and makes you want it, makes you need her to *see* you, really see you – muscle parted, veins unzipped, right into the sad, little shiver of your cells where, Jesus God, she already is, she already is, she already is.

Oh, shit, I'm too drunk, I can't stop, I won't be able to stop. This is . . . I've got no . . . there's no **defence.**

She stands, a brief unsteadiness making her grab at the table top and shudder the lamp's light between us, while the room and my ribcage swing.

'It's good,' she closes to lean a hand on each arm of my chair and has me wonderfully trapped, 'it's been good to see you,' and I catch her legs between my knees and I lift my face, as I know I should do, and watch her while she bends and then kisses me. Then I close my eyes while she kisses me and then open my lips while she kisses me and I am so hard and so living and so sick for more.

But Maura keeps her own kisses closed, dabs one at my forehead and then stops, leaves my thoughts staggering,

my hands twitchy on her hips. She considers me, grazes
my heart with a blink. 'But this is really very –'

'I know, I know.' I fold my arms and close my legs as
she slips from in between them with the best part of my
soul in tow. 'And I didn't expect –'

'Of course, you didn't.' She kneels, dizzyingly, next
to my chair and I turn, because she allows this, and
hold her head to, once again, kiss. And now we do open,
push, taste: the hard glide of her in my mouth and turning, trembling, drawing me forward to the edge of pain.
This is the hungriness I remember, our hungriness.

She's wet by now. Ready. For me.

Which would be fucking crazy, Nathan. Absolutely.

And wonderful.

I let her ease back, kiss the end of her nose to make
her smile. 'Thanks.'

Slowly, be slow, take it easy, be OK.

She frowns the way she sometimes does when she is
actually happy, but thinking on towards something else.

Please make everything be OK.

She must be actually happy: her fingertips tracing,
doing something light in the hair just beside my ear,
making a shiver come in my throat.

Fuck, I could just . . . I would so much like . . .

I notice I've caught hold of one of her hands, I kiss
that, too. 'That was lovely.' My hard-on isn't dying,
not at all, and I am glad, for the very first time, to
be over forty. If I was one second younger I would have
died, by now, of metastasised self-control. 'Really.'

'Nathan.' I've made her out of breath. Myself, too.
'Nathan, this is . . .' She frowns again, then softens.
'Yes, it was. Lovely.'

I stroke her cheek and, while she looks away, grin
like a bastard, a lucky bastard.

But don't push it, not yet, be sensible. Think of the
future, invest.

Fuck, I want to come. In my whole fucking life, I have
*never wanted so fucking much to just **come**.*

'Do you, I mean . . .' my words have a shake in them, but I continue in any case, 'it's really late . . . quite late.' And it drags at all of my vertebrae to say so, but I do, 'I should really go, because we're both a bit - with the wine and . . . I would do the same thing stone-cold sober in the middle of the day, but . . . I should go. Do you think I should go?'

She doesn't answer. I lean far over, rather uncomfortably, and kiss at the top of her head. I have always liked kissing, it is such a good thing. I could spend many days, perhaps weeks, doing nothing but.

'Should I go? Are there cabs?'

Yes, naturally there are cabs, you fuckwit. There are Manson-eyed, religious-maniac, all-night-healing-on-the-radio and asking-after-your-sins cabs, or seat-beltless-MOT-in-your-dreams cabs, or late-night, drunken, dope-fiend, axe-murderer, couldn't-find-the-Houses-of-Parliament-with-a-fucking-map cabs. And I am really going to ask her to get me one?

Oh, yes, I really am.

The first time she speaks, I don't hear her, I only catch the press of the one word like a punch under my belt.

And then she clears her throat, says it again. 'Stay.' She doesn't look at me. 'If you'd like to.'

'I –' A new flush of aching sweat.

'I have a spare room.'

And then the bang of disappointed blood and the babble to cover my tracks, fill in the time I need to think. 'Oh, yes, of course. Thanks. Very . . . very good of you. I appreciate . . . Thanks.'

'I'll make up the bed.'

Bed.

Fuck. **Bed**.

And why bother making it up, when I can just hang from your mantelpiece – it'll make me feel less tense.

Bed.

'Nate?' I glance up, brain still grinding, and Maura

is standing in front of me. 'I'll go and do that now,
then.' She doesn't move. 'Will I?'

'Ah, if you . . . yes. That would be best. It is about
time to turn in. Thanks.'

'The bathroom's at the top of the stairs on the left,
if you want to . . . And your room would be next door.'

'OK. Thanks.'

'There isn't much time, Nathan. I'm sorry.'

It puzzles me when she says this and she doesn't
explain, but I do understand when she holds out her arms
quite gently and lets me stand up into them: holds me,
while I hold her, my hips tucked back to keep her from
pressing against my prick and knowing about its condition – not that she couldn't guess. I mouth at her ear
and breathe, 'Thanks.'

'Stop saying thanks – you don't need to.' And she fas-
tens her arms at the small of my back, fits to me, all
of me.

I will not scream, not out loud.

One hug in, no more, and then she's walking and out
through the door and I don't see her face, can't tell
how she read me, or what she thought.

At least I didn't come.

I allow her a decent interval to climb the stairs and
set about things before I follow. On the landing,
although I try not to, I can hear the lovely, dry disturbance of a blanket being smartly unfurled. There is
also, of course, the working give and take of her
breath. I can hear that, too.

*I could go in and help her: the old mutual stretch
and fold and tuck.*

Which is why I shouldn't go in and do anything.

'Nathan?'

'Yes.' *Unless she calls me in, wants me in.*

'Your towel's the grey one – it's over the side of
the bath.'

'Fine, great.' *Shit.* 'Mm hm.' *Shit.* 'Mm hm.' *Shit.* I
mumble off into the bathroom, sporting a plastic smile.

515

Find the light switch, flick it, bolt the door.

So.

OK.

And, perhaps, one more step forward.

*And get the fucker **out**. God, Jesusgod, Jesus, oh, that's it, that's the boy.*

*We can at least, I can at least – even if she is next door. **Especially** if she **is** next door.*

Oh, Christ.

Oh, Maura.

Darling.

Very much. Yes, very much. Indeed.

Not that she'll know – although she might suppose it.

Ah, yes. She might. Nice.

But not that she'll hear me, I'll be quiet. I always am.

Out of the corner of my eye – this madman is standing side-on to the mirror, need cording in his neck.

Oh.

Ohfu, ohfu, ohfu, ohf.

The one blank moment.

The first wince in of breath.

And then again.

Ssth hhaa oh. Oh.

And the last of her, the last of me, spent in my palm, a cower of exhausted meat and a thick kiss spilt between my knuckles, something salt I'd had in mind for someone else.

Well, I'll sleep after that, though. Maybe.

Maybe, in your fucking dreams.

Washing my hands in her sink with her soap. I should splash my face also: not looking my best at the moment: bad eyes and a drinker's flush, red-wine tongue.

In my fucking dreams. I have a great deal of them.

She's downstairs somewhere now.

Must have passed by the door while I . . . must have.

I can hear her, locking up. I think, locking up. One of those homely, night noises, comforting.

516

Head's rushing. My blood pressure's screwed. Should sit.

All night with her here. Same house. Same floor.

You never know.

And she's drunker than I am.

Dousing the face again.

And I'm drunk enough for anything.

My interest in life is firming again. Not like me to be so vigorous.

God, thank you.

Maura's turned on the radio somewhere. She used to like to hear it while she did the washing-up: never music, always talk. I should go down and help her.

Like I used to.

When I wasn't too busy, or off somewhere touring, or pissed.

I wasn't so bad. Was I so bad? So awful?

I glower at my reflection, punchy, and then notice the shelf beside it, the contents of the shelf – the male shaving gear, the aftershave, the toothbrushes paired in the glass. The wall skips and hits me on the cheek.

She's with,

with

she's.

She's.

No.

No, she's obviously not.

She's not with anyone – he's not here. I'm here. It's me who's fucking here. It's me she fucking asked to stay and me she kissed.

I slip down the mirror for comfort, settle to squat on the floor. As I sink, I pass through a layer of her perfume, it hurts me in my teeth.

He isn't here, has maybe gone, really totally gone, but she hasn't got around to throwing out his things.

And, fuck it, I don't care.

*Even if he hasn't **gone for good**, but is simply absent*

– I am here and he is not. And my being here is that much more serious. It must have been a big decision to ask me back – a line crossed. That's good.

That's fucking wonderful.

If he's not here, he doesn't get her. I do. Because she's mine.

My wife.

Never did divorce me.

Still mine.

So now I step into the breach. Right in.

And I spruce whatever can be spruced, brush at the jeans and tuck the shirt in better, feel glad of the modestly stylish clean underpants – I'm equally well prepared for road accidents or sex. Dry the hands again on my towel: and the face, and the back of the neck: don't want to seem clammy for her. My cheek's slightly red where I hit it, but I think I'll be fine.

*I **know** I'll be fine.*

My brain throbbing gently against my balls.

I will have a backbone, a genuine spine, and I will walk downstairs and love her, because she is my darling, darling. She is my love.

I rummage carefully round for *his* comb, steady down *my* hair with it.

And fuck you, mate.

I leave the bathroom as I found it and lean over the banister, intending to call down something friendly, soft, perhaps only her name. That would be a start, our introduction to the rest of the night.

The radio is grumbling away still, louder – actually, surprisingly pin sharp.

'Sometimes I don't understand you. You asked him *back*?'

'Well, why not?'

'Well, I would have thought it was obvious why not.'

'It wasn't obvious.'

'He's gone now, though, right? Hm? Oh, no you di–'

'It was too late and he'd drunk too mu–'

518

'He was too pissed to leave?'

'No. But I said he should stay. So he's in the bath-room and keep your voice down.'

'Keep my –'

'He's harmless, a bit boring. Good at what he does. Come on. That's all.'

I hear her laugh. The tiny impact of a kiss.

And I think

That's it, the sound of my death: a small laugh and a stranger's kiss. How ridiculous.

And they stroll out into the hallway beneath me and Maura glances – of course, quite naturally, why not? – up and she sees me and I see her and I know from her look that she is sorry and that I am nothing, nothing at all.

Nothing that stamps its way to the foot of her stairs and nods and grins, more ludicrous than ever, and can tell – even so – that her other man has been out at his own brand of party, lager on his breath and smoking when Maura says that she wants to give up and I never did tell her about the cancer, there didn't seem to be an opportunity – it would have felt like special pleading – and perhaps I might mention it now to pass the time and keep as utterly civil as I must, for fear of, for fear of...

I want to kill him, to kill him the way he's killed me.

Except that I'm nothing and, besides, I have already told them – or, really told her, I can't quite look at him – already told her that I'll just head on up and get some rest, although this is impossible and will not happen and instead I will lie in the dark of a room I will never remember, curled in my clothes on the bed she has made me and I will listen to the shifting of dirt behind my eyes and will never have felt so unclean, so utterly unclean, and I will listen to the house and the shake of me on the mattress and I will listen and, in the end, because they must, I will hear them come up and settle themselves for the night, I will hear them go to bed.

And then, because I am nothing, I do not feel and have no words and I can move to my door and beyond it, crawl those few feet along the landing to sit and shudder by their wall and listen and listen and listen to their undressing, their mediocre little dialogue, their shifting and trying to connect and then the beat of him in her, too fast, the beat of him in her, he is too fast, the beat of him in her, the beat of him in her, the beat of him.

I don't know when I slipped from her house and started walking for the Square. I don't know how long the journey took. I wanted it to be longer, I'm sure of that.

The light was still on in the room, although it was morning. Nathan had worked through a day and its night, writing himself all out. He let his arms fall to his sides and rolled his shoulders, went through the usual moves for easing his pains when a piece was over. Not that he felt especially tired, or anything that he could put a name to.

He'd expected that, at this point, he might cry, but instead he was only peaceful and far away. The island was silent, too, crouched around him under the autumn dawn. He ran himself a drink from the tap, let out the dog and stood in the doorway, taking in the cool air, the cool water.

*You never do exorcise anything. You don't even manage that other thing: the making of the silk purse from the pig's shit, from the wreckage of yourself. It doesn't work. In the end, you only put things down to say they happened, to say **you** happened, and to hope you have a chance of making it all less real. Even if you never manage, even if you always still remember, anyway.*

Nathan poured a little of his water over his fingertips and then baptised his forehead, his eyes, the back of his neck. The feathering breeze felt especially live where the liquid had dampened his skin. One peaceable, merciful thought turned and locked in place.

It's a good day – right for getting things done.

A^{*h.*}
Bad head. Bad pains in the head.

I don't think I've had enough milk. Milk is the missing element here —
milk for the prevention of pains in the head — this I know. Jack told me. A
quality, professional drinker, Jack Grace — knew his stuff. Gave me the tip
about the milk. Can't remember when precisely, but he did. Good old Jack.

Too sad to think of him now. Don't want to be sad.

More milk, Nathan, and you won't pass out — you will stay the course
and you will get as drunk as it is possible for a mortal thing to be. Mortal
drunkenness — this is the first part of the plan.

Milk, then.

Don't like the look of it.

Half a glass?

Don't think I could manage half a glass. A quarter glass, that'll be enough
to see me right. Or wrong. Whichever.

Unless this is actually a proper headache, a migraine or something like that,
and not in any way connected with the drink.

Migraine — funny word. And it is, I happen to know, also the name of a
vineyard, down somewhere in France. At least, I'm almost sure it is. Fucking
stupid name for a vineyard — someone should have told them. Still, in French,
it might not mean the same.

Or maybe that's where the word comes from — you never know — it might
be the name for the headache you get from drinking Migraine wine.

Not sure about the French for anything, just at this point. Not sure. No.
Nobody gives a fuck in any case.

Except the French.

So. Mouthful of milk. A mouthful'll do. No need to go overboard.

Good lad, Nathan. God loves a trier, which would definitely mean that
God loves you.

And next the brandy. Down it goes and keep it down. Yes.

Not ready for action yet, though, not by a long way. Still, I don't have to hurry – everything's waiting, all safe behind the fence, all prepared – by me and for me – and a neat job, if I do say so myself. Want a thing doing, you do it yourself, because no fucker else will. Too right, too fucking right.

And now for a drop of the Lagavulin. Good.

I've been to where they make this – Port Ellen – lovely, lovely whisky from a fairly lovely place. But I won't go back there.

Burny stuff, the drink. You forget how uncomfy it was when you started at first – when you were young and only wanted to be older, to do old things – when you coughed yourself into adulthood with fly wee packs of Woodbine and bottles of fortified wine.

Then, eventually, the burn seems to be natural and you get used to it – but, really, there's no change – every mouthful keeps on tasting like a little bit of hell. Which is what being adult is all about – learning how to swallow your own damnation. How to keep it down.

Only my opinion, of course. But quite an unsuitable subject for right now. Shouldn't mention hell now, not even purgatory – limbo maybe – see how I feel.

Another go at the whisky, Nathan, another good swig, come on and take your medicine. Then we'll start in again with the lager and the milk.

And so, and so, and so.

And I am – yes, indeedy – starting to seed ouble. No. To see double. Yes. That's nice. Doublethevalue, doublethefun.

Hm.

Talking of fun.

Deadfall *– that's a grand word. It practically fucking perfectly tells you the nature of itself. The toggle trip-release and the spear deadfalls – poetry in those names, you can't deny it. Affy footery contraptions to build, though – all those toggles – pain in the arse – far more whittling involved than I would like.*

And the spring spear trap, also requiring a carefully hand-crafted toggle.

Where the fuck would we be without toggles?

Up shit creek without a toggle, that's where we'd be.

But I am a man who has toggles. Sufficient, a sufficiency, almost a superfluity of toggles. And they're all there, waiting just for me: the toggles and pits and trips and traps and even a couple of wee spring leg snares for a laugh – do you no harm, those, not a bit.

Fff. Getting sleepy. Tha won' do.

Lager.

Right.

Yes.

This lager's pish. No point in it, either – doesn't do the business – no fucking use. Want only the stuff to take the head: to confuse, bemuse, excuse. Stuff like that.

Fucking lager. Can't think why I bought it.

Odd deal, that. Take Mary over to Ancw, bring the booze back. Not a good swap. But the one I needed.

And she knew, looking at me like that all the way – she knew there was something up. Sweet girl. Sweet girl to worry. Wish I didn't worry her. Don't ever mean to. I won't do it again.

Enough of that.

It's the lager talking – depressing bloody swill at the best of times and these are not the best of my times.

Ah, but I do remember – yes – exactly why I bought it now. That's right, I was pretending to be about to be having a party and lager seemed convincing as a detail to add in. Six pack asacover story.

Donthink I've drunk this much since –

Cunt.

Go on, then, say it.

Since the night before my wedding night.

Cunt.

Night we don't mention.

Cunt.

*And then there's the **other** night we don't mention.*

The one that we walked right fucking into. Grinning all the way to the fuckingslaughter. But let's not mention it.

Cunt.

Nomention.

Cunt.

Nowife.

Cunt.

Nolife.

Cunt.

No.

Nocunt, neither.

Cunt.

Brandy.

Brandy better and whisky wetter. Fuck me – practically a poet. 'Magine that, dying a poet – who'd've thought.

This thing, glass, glass thing, tumbler – getting slippery.

Bugger. Gotto be able to walk. Still have to walk.

Night we don't mention – that night – didn't tell her – wanted to – would've made the difference – had it all prepared – wee bit of poem – Gaelic old poem. Women are suckers for that. Gaelic old shit. Remember it –

> **But the time has passed**
> **and I will not see your like,**
> **your like**
> **your like**

Fuck it – think

> **until I am put in the ground,**
> **I will love you without ceasing.**
> **My young, white love.**

See? Hardly drunk atll – could be able to walk, nobother.

Found the poem somwhere, somewere – put it in the notebook like a good boy – just in case – just in case – if I ever would see her again.

Never used it.

Stupid fuck. You never used it.

My youngwhitelove.

Somepoor fucking woman wrote it forher man – buut same fucking difference. If the love fits . . .

Glad Mary's away. Off with Jonno again. Can't keep them apart.

Fucking like bunnies. Donblame them.

Christ.

She won't see this. Shouldn' see this. This me.

Christ.

Thing is not to cry because it stops me swallowing.

Stay solid. Act the man. Like usual.

Badact.

Best I can do, though.

Verybest. And. And I'll fucking behere, be heer, be here for me like I always have been here for me, like every fucking allthetime when no cunt ever else has beenheer for me.

My father told me — **born alone, die alone, livealone inbetween. Find one fucking friend, you'rebloody lucky.**

Well, I did, I found him, lliked him, luky me. Looked at himdying. Sawhimontheslab. Lucky me. Jacky the man my fucking friend. Mr J. Dowd bastard Grace. Here is to you, you fuck.

In pishy lager.

And in brandy.

And in our favrite. Islay's finest. Heerstoyou.

Good at dying, aren'twe, Jack?

Yes. About ime nowtoo. About ready.

Yes.

Here's to me, then, Nathan Staples, who
was not a very good husband and
was not a very good father but
who always fucking wished that he could be.

I did.

Just did.

I just did wish.

To love my people. Only ever wanted that.

A nd then Nathan went out.
He staggered the door shut, already feeling breathless, sticky, and made the small climb to the wood, the fence, the gate. Then, whisky-slowed, he stooped and finally tumbled, both hands busy with his laces, intent on removing his boots. He frowned, twisted where he lay and persevered with his unfastening, stripping his feet to the skin.

Heat and breath clouded round him while he rolled over to right himself, crouched and knelt and trembled up on to his bared feet and then struggled for balance before attempting to move forward over the cold and suddenly terribly distant rocking turf. The grass was wet, harsher than he'd imagined and, at each step, he wondered if he'd reach it.

Nathan made it to the gate, which then took a week or two to open, and stood at the edge of the trees with his plan already fixed, politely hidden in the golden green ahead of him, primed to strike. A will he did not recognise started him swaying numbly on, the swoop and dart of small lights swarming close, the kiss of dying leaves against his face.

He hugged his arms in around his shoulders, closed his eyes and was no longer sure whether he was walking inside or outside his mind. The safe way through had escaped him, he knew that. He'd drunk it all away – part of the plan.

Four steps on and he felt a rush, the screamed white of an impact and then nothing, merciful nothing, the world gone.

A magpie.
        Laughing.

Nathan blinked. A band of chill hurt cupped his head and the magpie flew, sheathed and unsheathed the sore white of its wings, and dropped up out of sight, still laughing.

Before he could prevent himself, he rolled from his back to his side, unable to rise, and was sick. A kick of pain wrenched his right shoulder, spiked and spidered behind his ear. He was sick again.

If he moved his eyes too quickly a tremor started in his jaw, but, working very gently, he could show himself which particular device had hit him, which one he'd wandered into, which one had only half caught him, had failed to finish up the job.

At the base of the tree trunk were the neat little pegs that once held the bar that once held the line that once held the deadfall's weight. Somewhere at his back would be the other peg, the one where he'd tied down the trip at ankle height, so as to catch the ankle, to jerk the line, to shift the bar, to loose the line, to drop down the deadfall and crack out the life that Nate built. If everything had gone as he'd intended.

A low noise was raking in him under the hack of his breath, probably something to do with concussion, and he certainly had a fractured or a broken collarbone, which hurt like fuck but was not enough damage, nowhere near enough.

Serve you right for playing at it.

Next time, make it easy. Take the booze and then take pills. Just do it right. Too tired for anything else. Pills and then fuck it, fuck everything.

The noise needled at him, louder, while he tried to think if he could manage to stand up. Across the grass, the shadows were racked out, the light bloody: it must be evening, then, he must have lain that long. A fraction of him wished that he could want to be home before dark and safe and licking his wounds, but he understood in his heart that it no longer mattered to him where or when he was.

A fierce desire to leave the island hooked him, a need to be away from what he knew and what knew him. If he kept moving long enough, if he burnt up his pointless money round the world and ran just enough ahead of himself as the time zones fell away, he might finally blur to an adequate peace, get as close to death as made no difference. Pills or perpetual motion – such a wealth of choice.

Nathan heard himself laugh and then held steady beneath the ache this lashed across his skull. Then he heard the noise again, that continual noise: it rose and answered him. It was something like the scream of metal tearing metal: a high, almost mineral sound, but sticky with horrified muscle, with the unwelcome persistence of life.

The sound was impossible, coming from nowhere, twisting in the air behind him and above. He tried to scramble up and find it, understand it, to just stop it from going on, but his legs were stupid, his one good arm worse, as it scrabbled to support him while his balance Ferris-wheeled inside his skull. He looked down to see the dark shine where he'd bled into the grass. He looked up and saw a shadow, hung up against the last of the sun.

There was a pitching silence. Nathan finally stood. And then the shadow breathed and looked at him and a twitch of what he knew at once was happiness moved its length and ripped out another cry from the soft dark of its throat.

'Jesus, Eckless. Oh, my wee man. Jesus Christ.'

The dog had been caught by his hind leg, hauled aloft by a spring trap and held with no choice but to suffer his own weight.

I can't reach to get him down. Shit, I can't reach him – even if I could, my one arm's fucked. God, his hip – oh, Jesus.

'Wee man, sssh. Don't move, though. Please.' Not knowing whether to touch him or not. 'Wee man, you'll be, you'll be fine. I'll get you better. I'll get you down.' Steadying the body against his dead shoulder and stroking the dog's head, 'Sssh. Sssh.' Vertigo whenever he looks up, whenever he thinks of the displaced hip, the tearing, 'Wee man,' and the sick turn of his heart when Eckless nudges at his hand, whimpers.

Can't do anything. Fuck. Must be something. No way to get up, no way to lift him — loop's too tight around his paw, I'd have to cut the line. No fucking knife.

'Be easy now, be still. Please. Be still. I'll think of something.'

This is my fault, this is my fucking fault. I should have checked, checked he was safely in the house, shut the fucking gate behind me, just made fucking sure that he couldn't get in here, couldn't follow me.

Stupid, self-obsessed fuck.

'Brave boy. You are. You'll make it.' The dog's muzzle comfortable in his palm, familiarly soft.

Oh God, and I've been shitty to him all this week.

'Wee man, I'm going to have to leave you and you mustn't bark and you mustn't cry. Please.' Feeling the eyes move, gentle, through the warmth of their closed lids. 'Keep still. Please, keep still. I have to go and get help.'

He's a fucking dog, he doesn't understand, he'll just think I'm leaving.

God, you fucker, why are you doing this to me? He's all I've got. And he doesn't deserve it. And he's all I had that was really mine.

'You be a good boy. You be a good boy.'

And Nathan leaves his dog, carefully, gently, and runs now, as best he can, nausea sweating him to the bone, and no turning back to stare up at the stretch of that body, at the pain he can't stand to look at any longer and he's praying there won't be any more sound, more crying, although this might mean the whole thing's over, that he's already murdered his fucking dog.

Don't you take him, God, don't you fucking dare.

Yelling as he staggers, half falls, and his vision softens for a second and then drifts back, 'Here I am! I'm still here! You're OK!' and not a murmur comes to him from Eckless while he lurches beyond the fence and down the hill, thin-headed with panic and driving to stay with this first burst of his horror, the one that will keep him conscious and of use. 'I'm still here!'

Richard and Lynda, they're the closest, but they're still not close.

What if he can't walk again — if he loses his paw.

Shit, I'm so stupid, so fucking stupid. I don't take care.

'I'm still here!' Nathan's voice shearing off now and his strength slipping, his speed very difficult to judge. He runs on, head down and lolling beyond his control. He tries not to watch his naked feet, not

530

to see where they're bleeding and where any hurt might be. 'I'm still here.'

His progress drags and surges, sickens him, eats away the possibility of an arrival until he is flailing and juddering forward like a man caught in a looping dream.

'I'm still here. I'm still here.'

'I know you are.' Lynda knew better than to touch him.

'I'm still here.'

'I know you are, Nathan. Come in and tell me what's wrong.' She stepped carefully to the side and let him buffet past her into the cottage.

'Christ, he's bleeding.' Richard loped forward from his chair, throwing his newspaper down with a rattle of pages which seemed, to Nathan, almost unbearably loud.

'I can see he's bleeding – just give me a hand with him, he's going to faint.'

And the two of them closed on him from left and right and, as he faltered – baffled by his lack of progress, by the marvellous warmth and brightness of the room – they caught their arms around him. He could not recall ever feeling so secure, or so powerless, so likely to disappear.

They steered him to the sofa while he struggled, fought to focus on Lynda's face. 'Please, it's Eckless, it's my fault.'

She nodded, not understanding. 'You need to get some rest.'

'Eckless, he's hurt and I can't help him. You have to go and get him. You'll need a knife, a knife and a ladder and a . . . a . . .'

He could feel Lynda muttering over his head, 'He must have tried another step.'

'Obviously. But why's he going on about the dog?'

Nathan focused on the fireplace ahead of him, watched its right angles bow and melt and its fire splay to his feet like brassy water. It didn't hurt, didn't even seem warm. Voices bubbled beside his ears.

'He's not with us.'

'Christ, look at his head.'

'You phone Joe, tell him to have the boat ready – we'll get him over to a doctor.'

'Nate? Try to keep awake, will you? Can you do that?'

Nathan grabbed at a last coherent breath and made all he could of it. 'MY DOG IS HANGING BY HIS FOOT FROM A TREE BEHIND MY FENCE FROM A TREE HE IS DYING DO SOMETHING.'

The fire lapped thickly across the floor and started to climb the walls, paler and paler as it rose, until it closed the room in one hard snap of white.

That he was taken off the island, mumbling and holding his dog, Nathan forgot.

That he was loaded, beside Eckless, into the back of Radio Stevens's only available vehicle, Nathan forgot.

That the back of the vehicle had been padded with cushions from a three-piece suite but was, nevertheless, the glass-panelled rear of a second-hand hearse, Nathan forgot.

That he cried out and spoke the names of two women, Nathan forgot.

That only the pain in his shoulder let them prise Eckless away from him, Nathan forgot.

That he came to in Accident and Emergency, slapped a nurse and swore himself hoarse before passing out again, Nathan forgot.

He was set in his bed empty-headed: for the first time in his life, entirely ignorant of distressing events in which he had taken part.

He slept relatively well.

Of course, they all came to see him in hospital: Lynda and Richard cooing and smirking as if they'd both given birth to him, instead of just saving his life.

'Well, don't thank us.' Richard took a swig of Nathan's Lucozade and grimaced, then comforted himself with a rub at Lynda's knee. They were turning, Nathan reflected, into an even more hideous couple than before. Having each begun to sag equally and grow scared of a lonely future they were now – like phlegm and a chest infection – almost entirely inseparable. 'I said –'

'I know – *don't thank you*. I won't, then. Tell me about my dog.'

He asked every one of his visitors the same question.

Louis appeared alone with a packet of gipsy creams and a stack of entertaining paperbacks.

'Great.' An ache gnawed in Nathan's right shoulder every time he took a breath. 'Thomas à Kempis, Epicurus and – Louis, you surprise me – Louis Aragon?'

'My namesake. I thought you might like it.'

'So, all of this time, we've been calling you Lou-iss and it should have been Lou-ee. Even so – *Le Con d'Irene*? Wouldn't have imagined it was quite your cup of tea – a French dirty book.'

'A French surrealist book. I thought you'd like it. Particularly because it's dirty.'

'Thank you for thinking so highly of me. What about my dog?'

He asked again when Ruth had finished hovering at his bed's foot. She looked tearful and underslept.

'I was so worried.'

'There was no need.'

'You don't look . . .' she eased into the chair beside him, her perfume more overwhelming than usual. He prayed he wouldn't have to sneeze – the stitches in his head wouldn't take it.

'I don't look what? Healthy? Especially clean this morning? Happy enough to see you . . .?'

She pursed her lips, but her eyes glinted with hurt. 'I was going to say that you don't look as if you've done a step.'

Her voice had become unmistakably frail and he became unmistakably guilty, in spite of himself. 'You mean I don't look as though I'm delighted to still be alive. Well, no, I'm not.' He sighed gingerly. 'But I didn't mean to give you a hard time about it – it's hardly your fault. Sorry.' He noticed she was quick to pat at his one free wrist, damply forgiving. 'And will you tell me, or get someone else to tell me what has happened to my dog. I want to know about Eckless. Please.'

For two days, no one would give him any answer. They stared at his pillow or his lamp and then fell silent. Or else they tried to lead his thoughts elsewhere until the conversation broke and they could shuffle and mumble their way through another unwieldy leave-taking. Nathan would watch after them until they were gone and then ease his head forward, shield his hand across his eyes and try to weep. Nothing ever came of it.

'Nathan. Nathan, are you awake?'

Joe was leaning in close over Nathan's face, he smelled of the island, its particular brand of outdoors, and also of soup.

'I was just passing,' he lowered the startling heat of his palm over Nathan's fingers, 'so I had a nasty snack downstairs and then decided I'd come up to see you.' He inspected Nathan's head, 'Impressive bandage,' then sat down, unsmiling. 'Sorry I couldn't make it before – I was busy.'

'Yeah, I've been a bit tied up myself.'

Nathan yawned cautiously, coming to, and examined the ward – four of the other beds were empty, occupants off watching telly in the lounge, no doubt. The two stroke victims lay, as ever, staring silently at the wall above Nathan's bed, expressions caught in two separate moments of horror, mouths slackened and overly wet. He tried to think of them with sympathy, but still wished they were somewhere different and faced towards somebody else.

'There are some ways you wouldn't want to end up, eh, Nate?'

Nathan hissed back, restrained by the attentions of his audience, those two pairs of milky eyes, not quite convincingly beyond reach. 'Yes, all right – worse things do happen at sea – and I'll get back the use of my right arm and I can still speak and I don't piss myself or drool and I'm really not grateful enough for everything I've got. I should think myself lucky.'

His vision was hazing in and out of a throb of red, but he continued, 'Save your energy, I've heard it. I've said it to myself so often that I can't even find it funny any more and it never did fucking help in any case. Just, for Christ's sake, tell me when Eckless died. Those other cunts wouldn't say. They didn't have the fucking decency to tell me. Did they get to him? Did they make him comfortable? Did they –' He realised that he had, absurdly, been about to ask if they'd explained to the dog why his master hadn't come back to save him. Nathan's forehead stung and now, when he didn't want to, he knew he might easily cry.

Joe shook his head faintly and waited for Nathan to settle, to calm, to finally meet his eyes. 'Nathan, I said I was busy. That's what I was busy with.'

'You took care of him?'

Joe slowly bent forward and growled into Nathan's ear so that he shivered while, under his scalp, a weird kind of rasping set in. 'Nathan, I know you and I know what you are like, but there must be limits to even your maudlin self-obsession. Don't roll your eyes, it'll hurt you. Just listen. Your dog is alive and will, eventually, be quite well. At least, the vet has high hopes. I and the rest of your friends, who – quite inexplicably – care about you, have lied a number of times in a number of places to prevent your committal to a psychiatric ward and your prosecution by the RSPCA.'

'You were just covering your backs.' Even Nathan felt a little sickened when he said this – he probably didn't entirely mean it and he knew that Joe would let it pass to shame him. He was right.

'No, Nathan, we were covering yours. You went to see her, didn't you? Didn't you? You went to see Mau–'

'All right.' He couldn't hear her name, not now. 'All right.'

'You didn't tell anyone, didn't ask any advice – you just went off and put yourself in that kind of danger.'

'I wanted to be happy.' A slicing ache pressed between his temples and he began to cry, lost his vision, struggled to even out his breath so that it wouldn't jar. Joe took hold of his hand again and Nathan hated him for it and hated himself for feeling grateful, for needing the touch.

'Nathan, your dog's fine and – I would say – is missing you. Mary is coming back at the end of the week and called me because she was worried about you – said you had seemed to be in a very black mood. I haven't told her anything about this.

'Nathan, she needs you. *We* need you. I am even assured that you will get better and probably be put out with the unwanted limbs tomorrow, or perhaps the day after that, at which point we will all take you – that's Lynda and Richard and Ruth and Louis and myself – all of the friends that you don't want – we will take you back to your home. What more could you ask for?'

Nathan swallowed thickly and found that he was unable to say *everything*. He tried to glower round at Joe, but only twisted slightly and then produced a retching cough, a sob. He was past the point of self-control now, crying.

'Your dog's alive, Nathan. You wanted to be happy – now you can.'

Nathan kept on weeping, each new jerk of his breath clawing in his shoulder and the solid glow of Joe's grip, still fastened around his free hand, nagging away, insistently protective. Nathan only wanted to be left alone.

And also he wanted to never be left alone again. And he wanted to be loved by those he loved and to be set free from them, every one. And he wanted to be able to love those he loved and able to hate them, too. And he wanted to rest at ease in his skin and in his time and place, while he wished to abandon them completely and be gone. And he wanted to die of wanting and he wanted to be properly alive. And he wanted to be thought of fondly and never to be thought of at all.

'Nathan, come on now, that's enough. You're still here. Remember? No choice about it.'

Nathan had known that was coming, but the idea of it still locked round him, fastened a soft, cold numbness over his shoulders and down. 'I know. No fucking choice.'

'You won't try again, though, will you, Nathan? You've done enough steps. More than enough.'

'I wasn't doing a step. I was —'

'You won't do it again.'

'All right, all right. Of course I won't, it just, it just . . . fucks things up. Eckless is really, he's — you're not lying to me? He's all right?'

'Yes. And you'll see each other soon. Back on the island. As long as you promise me.'

'Christ, what? I spend my fucking life promising people things. What? Want me to visit you when you're dead? Hm?'

'I would certainly like you to outlive me. Promise me you won't try anything again.'

'You know I won't.'

'Promise me.'

'OK. Fuck. I promise. He's going to be all right?'

Joe nodded and finally smiled. 'Yes. Now you should get some rest.'

'Now?'

'Why not now?'

'Because I'm . . .'

'What?' Joe was smiling again and Nathan was hating him for it. 'Because you're what?'

'Because I am happy that Eckless isn't dead. So I don't want to go to sleep yet. I would rather be happy for a little while longer, thanks. I would rather feel it for as long as it lasts.'

'Do you want me to stay with you?'

'You can stay if you want to: I won't be good company.'

'Well, naturally, Nathan, but then I'm used to that.'

Mary was dozing, cheek propped against one fist and her personal stereo sending Glenn Gould's Salzburg Recital sneaking and loping and leafing through her dream – if it was good enough for Nathan, she'd thought she might try it herself. The fat autumn sun began pouring itself on the sea and burning in the grass outside the Nissen hut, while she peered through a forest in her sleep.

The branches were hung with a felty, brownish foliage, heavy and slightly clammy to the touch – she didn't like to push through it, but it seemed that she should.

'Ah, Mary.' She'd squeezed out into a clearing, thick with extraordinary fruit: some brittle and fine as coral, others pendulous, swollen in folds of glossy flesh. 'You've made it this far, then.' In the clearing Joe stood waiting, much taller than usual, his white hair brilliant with light, his eyes an impossible blue and penetrating as ever. 'I never really doubted that you would.'

'I –' Behind Joe's head a massive blade, curved like a scythe, swung in and out of nowhere, lopping off limbs and pods, slicing through rind and pulp, severing curtains of leaves. Blood seeped unmistakably from each cut surface, each raw edge, and misted gently in the air. Mary watched without alarm. 'Does this happen often?'

'It's part of the forest.' Joe smiled far too broadly and winked. 'You can't go back now, though.'

'No. I suppose not.' She felt a hot fall of liquid against her cheek, a sweet, strong smell. 'Am I safe?' This seemed an unnecessary question, but she heard herself ask it anyway and was – she supposed – quite interested in the answer.

'Safe? No, of course not. But you know that doesn't matter – being in danger, being safe. Being here isn't about that, not at all. You've come this far and you'll go further. This is your place. This is all your place.'

Joe grinned and reached down to grip her by the shoulders, spin her smoothly round to face the way she'd come. The forest wall shimmered and flickered, as if it were painted silk. She watched while the whole, broad tissue of it bellied out towards her, tightening and swelling until she could almost feel it tensed against her.

'All your place.'

The fabric paused and then broke into powder, into dust. 'Mine?' The powder shone like a turn in a school of fish and then vanished, left her staring at a plain of sand, at meat-coloured rocks and the writhing of baked air.

'All yours. And no going back.'

'Will I like it?'

'No. You'll love it. Cross the desert and you'll be in the forest again.'

'And then I'll be home.'

'You will find your way home.' A cloud of small, iridescent birds fountained up out of a hollow and spattered the heat with looping melodies.

'But will I get home?'

'You will find your way home. You will make your way home. Your way has always been your home.' The birds were slowly forming themselves into a column above him, their music growing more elegant, more mathematically complex. 'We don't ever arrive. We only find our way.'

Joe was elongating, stretching up into the open heart of the column until he began to be obscured by the rushing birds. 'You do understand that you're dreaming?' he called down to her, still jovial.

'I think so.'

'But dreams are a serious matter, of course.'

'Of course.'

Joe's feet had left the sand and he was gradually ascending, disappearing in the drum of wings. Mary shielded her eyes from the sun to watch him rise and couldn't stop herself from shouting, 'And what about Nathan?'

'In a bad way.' His voice was shimmering and broken with silences.

'What?' She couldn't see him any longer, not even the soles of his shoes.

'Needs care. A lot of care.'

The birds let their music lace and mesh above her while they span into a blur of oiled steel blue, which – in its turn – rubbed darker and darker until it was the dull red glow of her own closed eyelids, shut over her waking eyes.

She stirred, rubbed her cheek, her head still full of lunging and tickling notes – Gould working through the Goldberg Variations, sighing and tapping his feet. It was good, but she thought that she might not listen to it again.

Nathan was lying next to Eckless. Since they'd both come back from the mainland this was the way they preferred to be, matching each other, breath for breath, the dog's head tucked in close to Nathan's chin and Nathan's left arm around the dog. Joe had lent them his sofa for the purpose, carried it from the Lighthouse to Nathan's cottage. Even with Richard and Ruth helping, it had taken the better part of an afternoon.

'Nathan?' There was always a certain wariness about them, a sense of their keeping alert. Mary couldn't tell if both of them were sleeping, or if each was only pretending to rest in order to calm the other and still keep a proper watch. There was something defensive about their closeness, something fierce. 'Nathan?' She didn't exactly like to disturb them, but equally, watching them lying seemed a much greater intrusion and always left her staring, trying not to think about their pain. 'Na –'

'Sssh. I think he really is asleep this time.' Nathan was whispering, his eyes still shut. Eckless gave a wakeful little sigh of contradiction.' Or maybe not. Still, he should be tired. We walked twice round the cottage this afternoon.' He rubbed very softly at the dog's back, 'The boy done good,' and then yawned. 'Put the light on, could you – might as well.'

Mary did as she was asked and then watched the pair on the sofa shift and peer into life. This was when she always wanted to kiss them, or pat them – whatever would be more appropriate. Instead, she simply stood while they eased through small degrees of hurt, looked at her softly, became more like themselves, the two creatures on the island that she loved most. 'You seem, ah, seem a bit better.'

541

I still can't see those sodding bandages without feeling sick. And I'm feeling sick enough already.

Today's the day. When I show him.

God, I'm going to throw up.

Nathan squinted at her, enquiring, 'Better? Well, I'll look a lot better than this once I've stopped having to shave myself with my left hand. Another week of this and I'll have cut my throat.'

'Don't say that.' She couldn't help the sharpness in her voice.

'I mean inadvertently.' He scratched between Eckless's ears and muttered, 'There's no way I could actually cut my throat with a safety razor, anyway.'

'Well, you would know.'

Now why say that to him – you know there'll just be an awkward silence. He wants to keep his secrets and you just have to let him. Bugger it, I don't want a fight today. Not today.

Mary headed back to the kitchen and changed the subject. 'I brought some fresh bread and Ruth sends her regards and I'll, ah, put the kettle on.' She could hear him behind her, making the careful effort to move Eckless, to get up and follow her through.

I should just let him be.

I can't, though, can I? Not when h–

'Mary.' He rested his good arm on her shoulder. She noticed that he smelt powerfully of dog. 'Mary, I fenced off the wood and I built all those things.'

'The man traps.'

'All right, yes, man traps – that's what they were. I built them because . . . I'm going to write about them – I'm going to put them in my new book.'

'Mm hm. Did you want tea?'

'If you'd like to give me some.' He sighed, tiredly exasperated and she thought he might raise his voice. Instead, he only went on quietly. 'I didn't mean to go in there and for, for Eckless to follow. It was all . . . I'm too old to do this stuff any more – research, risks . . . I'm going to finish this book and then that'll be that.'

'None of my business.'

He took away his arm, slipped round to try and catch her eye while she kept busy with the tea caddy, the water, warming the pot.

'I would think it would be your business, *will* be your business,

542

when you read – if you would like to – the book.'

A blade of panic turned in her while she thought of her own book, nakedly and inappropriately there on the table top behind her where she'd left it. This hadn't been the day to bring it over.

Nathan murmured on. 'I'll finish it soon. Quite soon. I should think. Once my arm gets usable again.'

Mary put down her teaspoon and, because she could think of nothing to say, hugged him carefully while his patchy stubble grated slightly at her ear. 'Nathan.'

'Mm?'

She could feel his body, thinner than usual, give a little nervous flinch against her.

'Oh, I don't know.'

'Well, no. Neither do I. But here we are.'

They leaned gently against each other, Nathan relaxing a little, setting down part of his guard. 'I had an odd dream.' His voice in her hair, warm, comfortable. 'I don't remember it all, but it ended with a woman looking up at me as if she was sorry – a woman I loved.'

Mary could only hold him a fraction tighter and feel the usual twist of unease for him, the customary bafflement. 'Sssh.' Sometimes she wondered if bullying Nathan might work better than sympathy, might be more practically helpful. But she realised she'd never find out – there was no way on earth she could look in his face and even begin to be stern. 'I had an odd dream, too. Joe was in the middle of it – saying that somebody ought to take care of you.'

Nathan breathed a laugh. 'Just like him – interfering, even when we're both asleep.' He moved to kiss her forehead and then her crown. 'I am taken care of. It's OK.'

They rubbed each other's backs and then stood away. Nathan frowned at something behind her. 'What's that pile of waste paper doing on my nice, clean kitchen table?'

Every nerve in her stomach kicked. 'Oh, shit, I forgot again – it's the . . . it's my . . . you said . . .'

Nathan nodded while she stammered. He was grinning and wincing and pressing his knuckles to his lips in some kind of effort at restraint. She met his gaze and let him catch her with a raw, bright look. 'Mmhm?'

'It's my novel.'

543

'Yes.'

'It's as finished as I can make it.'

'Yes, I know that.' He sounded hoarse. 'I do know. I really do know.' He stopped and held out his hand to her. 'It wouldn't be anything else – not from you.'

She completed the grip. 'If you wouldn't mind –'

'Reading it. No, I wouldn't mind. In fact, I can't do much else in my current state.' He crunched in a burst of pressure round her fingers. 'Of course, if it's just so dreadful that it makes me feel even iller than I am, I shall have to sue you.'

'I don't think *iller* is a proper word.'

'There's no such thing as an *im*proper word.' He tugged her towards him, almost giggling. 'Haven't taught you anything, have I?'

He gets happy so easily – it ought to be easy for him to be happy for most of the time.

She consented to be tugged. 'No, you haven't really taught me anything.'

They halted, toe to toe, Nathan composing himself, becoming more serious. 'Congratulations.'

'On being poorly taught?'

He squeezed at her fingers again, 'Don't push your luck, all right?' and kissed her cheek. 'Well done. I will read it as fast as I can, given my packed schedule, and then we'll see how things go. My agent wouldn't be any use to you – she's only good for flogging the dreadful toss I usually produce – doesn't do literary fiction.'

'Oh, but it's not literary fiction – it's all about cowboys and large-breasted women from outer space. They hunt the world together looking for children's kidneys they can use to power their rocket ship. I wrote it in rhyming couplets.' She was close to giggling herself, but in a way she didn't think would be controllable once she'd started.

He left her, paced over to the table and scooped up the manuscript, flashing her his best psychopathic smile. 'I will read this and tell you what I think.' Eckless limped into the doorway and gave a little yelp of concern. Nathan spun at once to see what was wrong, 'OK, OK. No need to fret. Here I am. Yes, good lad. Here I am.' He made half an apologetic shrug to Mary. 'Must have dozed off and then woken up without me. Something which nobody else in the world would find disturbing.' One hand still strapped to his chest and the other full of novel, he could only very lightly dunt his shin against Eckless's side. 'Come on, then – all the cripples go back to the living room and then the nice lady might bring me a cup of tea.'

'If you're lucky.'

Mary had sugared Nathan's mug when he called to her, 'That dream I had.'

'Yes?'

'It's because . . . the woman, she sent me a letter. Joe came over with it yesterday.'

Mary walked in with the tea tray to find dog and master, sitting up together. She waited, but Nathan only took his mug from her, said nothing more. She settled in an armchair, drank, waited some more. Then, 'If you trusted me, you might tell me what it said.'

He turned to her, genuinely puzzled. 'Trust . . .? Of course, I do. Christ, I trust you more than anyone else on earth.' He paused, as if he'd then had to consider the sound of that. 'I do trust you. There's just nothing else I can tell you.'

'What do you mean?'

'I don't know what the letter said. I saw who it was from and I burned it. That was the safest thing to do.'

'But maybe –'

'It was the safest thing to do.'

Mary watched him: the angles of his body; the cautious, gentle way he drank, gentle-mouthed; the patterns of wear and creasing in these particular overalls.

Whenever he's after comfort he always gets out the overalls – bloody things – frayed seams and patches and Christ knows what. They make him look worn out himself, sagging, and he's not. He's not even that old.

She'd supposed that she knew him as well as anybody could. His patterns and rhythms and shapes were all quite familiar to her but now, she saw, they had always been coloured by something more, an involuntary signal, bleeding its constant light.

He's in love. He's always been in love.

Mary wasn't going to shave him. 'I am not going to shave you.'

'Ach, why not? Come on. Please. I look like a rat's arse.'

'No, you don't – a rat's arse is covered in hair. You look like a *mangy* rat's arse.' Normally, when Nathan pleaded, she gave in to him. But he'd been getting his way too much lately and – even when he was trying his best to seem plaintive – he couldn't avoid looking better than he had been, like someone on the mend.

In fact, he was actually rather dapper this afternoon: good jeans, a freshly, if rather clumsily, pressed shirt and his dark tweed jacket – the one he liked. He'd taken his final dressing off and his stitches had finally melted away into whatever place old stitches melted away to. He had a scar, naturally – a crooked, pinkish Y set in a down of regrowing hair, above and behind his right ear. Mary didn't look at it, unless she had to. 'Anyway, you can shave yourself. You can use your right arm again – you're using it now.'

'To keep my right hand in my right trouser pocket. It hurts when I use it for anything strenuous.' Nathan raised his eyebrows as appealingly as he could, then gave up and strolled about, pondering his shelves. Mary wondered if punching him would set his convalescence back.

Eckless watched them both, sitting at peace, his tail thumping softly – both of his favourite people in the one room.

Mary closed her eyes and pinched at the bridge of her nose, thinking loudly.

I knew he'd do this. He'll string this out until the last possible minute. Bastard. I don't know why I gave it to him, I really don't.

Nathan had called by that morning at the Nissen hut, partly to show her how Eckless was doing, how well he was getting about. Then, as far as she'd known, the intention had been for them all to make their way, at a suitably easy pace, up to the Lighthouse. There, they were meant to join everyone for the *Dia de los Muertos* and the unsealing of Louis's precious jar. But Nathan had led the way back to his house instead and Mary knew why.

He's finished reading it, I know he has. He's no good at lying so he isn't even making the attempt – he just can't look at me. He's finished and he can't deny it, but he doesn't want to say.

Nathan reached down a book, frowned into it, then glanced at her. He pursed his lips. When he kept his expression this still, it was impossible to guess what he might be thinking.

*Jesus wept, I've had to come round by here every day and clean up after him and bring him his fresh sodding loaves and his bloody cups of tea while he's sat with his bloody feet up and turned pages at me – my pages – and sighed now and then and laughed now and then and shaken his head now and then and never fucking **said a word**. I get more and more amazed that I haven't killed him. I really haven't killed him yet, not even threatened to. Miraculous.*

But I know he's finished – yesterday he only had a handful of pages left. He must be done by now.

Nathan had given her his back and was staring out of the window. 'I really do need *someone* to shave my head. I've got to even everything up. I may not have much hair, but I would like it all the same length.'

'I can't shave your head.'

'Well, don't sound so horrified. All right, you can't.'

'I mean, it won't suit you. And I might hurt you. Quite easily. Look, shouldn't we be going.'

He'll have to say something before we leave. He'll have to. Why else would he have got me over here?

'Yes, I suppose we should get under way. I'd forgotten we might have to carry Eckless for a bit, so I came back for a coat – don't want to get my decent jacket muddy.'

He doesn't like it. It didn't work and it's no good and he doesn't like it. That's why he can't even mention it. Fuck.

I tried. I tried to make it good. I tried to make it something that he'd like. Waste of bloody time.

'You wouldn't mind taking one end, if we have to lift him? If it comes to that?' Nathan had turned and was considering her, intent.

'Comes to . . .?'

'Lifting the dog. If it's necessary. We have to take him with us. I don't want to leave him alone – he wouldn't like it.'

'Sure, fine.' *Bugger it.* 'Let's go.'

'Because I realise that novelists can get really fucking picky about that kind of thing – refusing to do manual labour, denying their elders and betters a decent haircut. They get stroppy. And the better the novel, the stroppier the writer.' He clicked his tongue, sighed theatrically. 'So I'd expect you to be quite considerably awkward.'

Mary knew this was when she should say something, when she should show that she'd understood and was happy right into the lining of her veins.

Nathan began a smile. 'It's beginner's luck, obviously. And there are some things you really should think about again.' He checked her eyes. 'But not many.'

'You,' her breath was surprisingly unpredictable, 'bastard,' and she sounded too loud.

'Now, now.' Nathan beamed, irritatingly. 'That's no way to encourage me to help you out with an agent and advice –'

'You utter bastard. You could have told me this an hour ago. Two hours ago. Bastard.' She stood, inconveniently unsure of what to do with her arms.

'Well, yes, I could have, but it's not that easy. I'm a naturally humble person and I find it difficult to admit how well I've done with you.'

'What? How well *you* –'

Nathan held up his hands, placating, studiously looking anything but smug, and came to stand beside her. He elbowed her delicately in the ribs. 'This isn't the time to say too much, but I am extremely, really extremely proud of you. Your Uncles would have been proud, too. If you don't mind my saying.'

She nodded, a hot swing of sadness taking her for a moment. Mary wondered if they should hug now, or keep standing, or get ready to go. There didn't seem to be an obvious option available. Still beside her, Nathan was pensive.

Eckless ambled quietly over and offered himself as a distraction. They both knelt, relieved, and made a fuss of him.

★

548

Walking over the island with his daughter and his dog, Nathan could feel an echo, an aftershock breaking against him from every side. Colours persisted, sounds dragged and bounced, each step he took would then take him, would murmur and linger in his joints. He seemed to himself more tender than he should be, more breakable. Mary beside him simply shone.

She's pleased, then. She knows that I like her book and that I'm not lying.

An old, insoluble ache parted in him again.

*Jesus, Jesus, Jesus, look at her — I know women who'd kill to move that well — I know women who **ought** to kill to move that well — and she does it without a thought and she always will, it's in her bones, in her self, in her DN fucking A.*

Her hair's better like that, a bit longer, a bit more full, it means she gets highlights without trying. And somebody should tell her, fucking Jonathan should tell her, or any other even halfway sane man should tell her to be out of doors in sunsets, should pray on their fucking knees to see her like this: the pale skin in the glory light and the gold in the hair and the eyes, the eyes to take your soul.

Runs in the family, that look. I'll still forgive it anything.

His memory showed him a stairwell and a woman's upturned face.

Sorry.

We were always sorry when we made each other hurt — we always did it all the same.

For perhaps the twentieth time that day, he blinked and kicked the image shut.

Far to his right and barely visible was the hill with the wood at its top, the slashes in the grass where his fence posts had been plucked, the cut and broken branches where his plans had been dismantled and, further on, the dark mound where all that could be was carefully burned. Joe was nothing if not thorough when he set about putting things straight.

Nathan checked on Eckless, the falter in his gait — the dog was managing, had forgiven, was still faithful.

'What are you thinking?' Mary shook his good arm lightly to get his attention.

'Oh, nothing especially printable, I'm afraid.'

The sunset was at its best when they arrived, Eckless hammocked regally between them in Nathan's coat. He acted the wounded

549

soldier with perfect aplomb as Ruth lowered over him like a ripe cloud of cellulite. 'Poor baby. You're such a poor, brave baby. But you're looking much better.' She squinted up at Nathan, who was trying his best not to smile – she'd only take it as an encouragement when he knew, deep in his antisocial heart, that he really couldn't help his amusement having just a little to do with contempt.

'Yes, he is looking much better. But I don't know about the baby part. Factually, we're both in quite advanced middle age.'

I'm a bad man. I am a very bad man. She can't help it that she reeks of desperation.

It's not as if I don't, myself.

We're neither of us any different, even after all these years. Christ.

'And is your head . . . ?' She simpered sympathetically and he dutifully angled his neck to let her get a good view of his scar.

'Oh, Nathan. You poor . . . thing.'

So my dog's a baby and I'm a thing. Well, that's about right, I suppose.

'I'm fine.' Under the circumstances, there was no way to say this without sounding brave, so he added a brief, stiff manly grin to please her and then dodged aside, feeling nothing like a hero, more like every inch a shit.

*I know I should be grateful, I know I **am** grateful –*

Lynda kissed him with chaste enthusiasm while Richard watched, approving.

But I can't stomach this – everyone being kind to me at once – not when all I actually did was fuck up and hurt my dog.

'How are you doing?' Mary steered him towards a seat.

'Not great.'

'I know, you've started doing that thing with your eyes. You hate it, don't you – people being nice.' Her voice dropped slightly. 'But people quite often want to be nice to you. They find it annoying when you won't let them.'

He stared at her, caught. 'Don't make me feel more ashamed of myself than I already do. Please.'

She shook her head and brushed something from his lapel, pressing briefly across the wrong shoulder. An interesting, silvery pain trickled down his arm and he had to wince.

'Oh, God, I'm sorry, Nate. I didn't mean it.'

'It's all right.'

'But I must have hurt you.'

'Ssh. You'll have them all round, commiserating. I'm fine.'

'Are you sure?'

'Mm.' He nodded, neck rigid, determined not to whimper. 'Jesus, woman, there's no need to be *that* worried, you'll get me . . . Go and find me a drink. If you don't mind.'

'OK, if you'd like.'

He made a point of squeezing at her hand as she left him.

No, of course I don't like – I want you to stay, I want to sit here and fucking bask in your concern. It fits better than anyone else's. Almost anyone , else's.

It was about to be a long evening, he could tell. He called after her as unobtrusively as he could. 'Um – get me something large, Mary. In fact, two glasses of something very large.'

Eckless had worked his way through his admirers and now halted in front of Nathan with a ruminative tilt of the head.

'No. Sorry. You wouldn't fit up here. You'll have to lie down on the floor like a normal dog – you remember? – the way we used to do it.' The animal seemed to consider this for a moment before duly slumping across both of Nathan's feet. 'Good man, we'll keep ourselves company – this'll be fine.'

'Dip?' Lynda was at his side with one of her threatening side plates of vegetable batons. Nathan wondered, momentarily, how many tons of roots and shoots she'd gone through since they first met.

Or how many tons have gone through her.

'I said *dip*.' She met his eyes with a touch of her old, libidinous ferocity.

'Yes, I heard what you said, but I couldn't be certain if that was a question, or just an admission on your part.'

She set her haunch against his shoulder – his bad shoulder.

This is obviously the day for making that particular mistake. I should have worn my sling again – it might at least have warned them off.

Still, he forgave her – he even couldn't help liking her for trying the old nonsense now. It was enough to make him feel almost close to being something like a man. And was much better than sympathy.

'You know, Nate, no matter how often you hit yourself over the head, you'll still be a prick.'

'Talking of which, is that your snatch in my ear, or are you just pleased to see me?' Not his best ever line.

She giggled, which spoiled the mood of the whole pretence, but was still quite endearing. 'Ah, Nathan, Nathan . . .' She perched on the arm of his chair, nudging an ache in all the way from his bad side to his sound one. 'Why didn't we?'

'Why didn't we what?' He eased away, but she followed.

'Screw.'

'Charmingly put, as ever. I would say it was because . . .' He picked up a piece of carrot and ate it in one – no horseradish – meeting her eye while he munched.

You are a good woman, sometimes. Fuck saving my life – a minor grope and a bit of banter, that's what's needed. Just sometimes, just today.

He swallowed his mouthful – the flavour wasn't especially suspect. 'Do you want a serious answer?'

'Yes, OK, but hurry up – Mary's coming back with your drink and you won't want to talk about fucking in front of her – will you, *Dad*?'

He refused the bait. 'No, I wouldn't want that, actually – it would show a lack of respect. But, to be serious and truthful, I didn't screw you . . .' He endured a small spasm of discomfort and leaned closer to continue, softly, in the way she would find amusing. 'I didn't put my cock up your cunt and ride you witless, because I never met you when someone else wasn't on my mind. Otherwise . . . otherwise, I would have banged you till your ears rang.'

She'll like that – one good turn deserves another.

But she stood up immediately. 'Christ, Nathan – do I really seem as safe as all that?' She could be baffling sometimes.

'Uh, wha . . .?' He was aware of Mary standing and observing his confusion. Watching him beautifully closely – all curiosity, no shame. She made him feel proud – and intensely uncomfortable, of course.

Lynda continued, 'You've really depressed me now. You'd never have said something like that if you took me seriously – if you didn't think I was past it. I don't frighten you any more, do I?'

'Well, I w–'

'And I was trying to cheer you up, you fuck.'

She stalked off, leaving Nathan to accept his drinks. 'Don't ask – I don't think that I could explain.'

552

Mary was stifling a grin. 'But I could guess. You're not good at women, are you?'

'Thanks for reminding me.'

She caught his eye and winced. 'I'm sorry, Nate.'

'Don't be sorry. I don't need people to be sorry.' He was messing this up, he could see – making Mary look uneasy, sad.

Shit, this is her day – finishes the novel, hears it's OK – Christ, leave her the fuck alone.

He constructed a careful frown of affection and concern, let it lift into something more calm, a plain affection. 'I need people – as you've mentioned – to be nice to me. And you're perfectly nice.'

'Even if *nice* is a dreadful word.'

'We know what we mean.'

She nodded and sat, to his surprise, at the side of his chair: legs curled under her neatly, wonderfully, and the back of her head quite close to his good hand. It seemed an appropriate thing, an all right thing he could do, to glance a touch against her hair and simply stroke once over the curve of her skull.

You always had a lovely shape of head. I never saw another baby with such a perfect shape of head. You were fucking gorgeous.

She leaned back against his fingers once, but didn't turn round, or look up.

Nathan, trying to relax, let his eyes wander and found his attention running headlong into Joe's. The Chairman of the Fellowship was leaning against the mantelpiece, looking on with an almost offensive degree of content.

You can watch me if you want to, I don't mind. You can like the way we are together, that's fine. You can ask yourself if I've told her yet – I don't mind that either, OK? Even if it's none of your business in any way.

And we're fine as we are, me and Mary, and she's going to be great – a real writer – a real human being, too. The way her father never was.

And I have everything planned. My last plan, Joe – the good plan that lets me tell her every fucking thing. Not long now.

Joe met his stare gently for a moment and then broke off to address the room. 'Well, ladies and gentlemen.' The ambient chatter ignored him. 'Ladies and gentlemen!' Everyone had heard him the first time, of course, but it wouldn't do to be called to order so easily. A hush gradually fell, the sound of Lynda, hissing something vehemently to

553

Richard, the last voice to fade.

Joe sighed, paternal. 'Thank you, and if we could take our seats . . . that would be excellent. Thank you again.

'Now, as we all know –'

'I have an announcement.' Nathan hadn't expected himself to interrupt, but here he was, all the same – interrupting, heart pattering near his throat, as if he was back in the schoolroom and rashly volunteering an answer to something involving trigonometry. 'Yes, I . . .' The silence in the room was, all of a sudden, exemplary.

Joe, blazingly amiable, grinned at him with frightening interest. 'This isn't exactly the time and place, but would you like to take the floor?'

'Well, no, I wouldn't.' Nathan waited while Louis shifted in his seat, impatient, arms already hugged round his jar full of promises to the future. 'It won't take long. And it's not about me. It's about the writer whose work we all first read at – I suppose – around the time we put our little thoughts about 1996 in Louis's jar. It's about Mary.' Nathan knew that she'd kneeled up beside him in concern, but was trying not to pay any attention.

You've been spared more that twenty years of embarrassing paternal tributes – just be glad you're only getting your first one now.

'I thought this would be an appropriate time to tell the Fellowship that Mary has completed her first novel and –' A small din of applause broke out. 'And you shouldn't clap just because it's finished – fuck, anyone can *finish* a novel. She's finished a *good* novel.' The clapping started again, along with a scatter of well-intended laughter – the sort of indulgent, self-referential noise that groups make for others of their kind. Nathan had never heard it made for him.

But it's for Mary, really – that's the difference.

She prodded him in the elbow until he had to face her and then glared at him, 'You . . .' but also seemed not unhappy and able to tell the room, 'yes, thanks. All right. Thanks. We'll see.'

He leaned towards her. 'Couldn't help myself. And it's good practice.'

'For being humiliated?'

'For being congratulated.'

'Same difference.'

That coughed a laugh out of him. 'Well, as I said – good practice.'

'I'm just going to wait until you're well before I hit you.' But she kissed near the root of his jaw and didn't look angry in any way.

She blushes too much, though, just like me.

'If that's all you have to say . . .' Joe patiently began again, reminding everyone of what they already knew – that the jar Louis was embracing held their promises to their future and that their future had arrived. Nathan thought he did the job quite well, given the oddly unceremonious nature of the ceremony.

Then Louis stood – not quite so frail that he couldn't still enjoy a flirtation with authority. 'Well now, before I break the jar it is my responsibility, as your historian, to say a few words. And, like the alchemists of old, I would begin with the reminder that *many have perished in the work*. We are the living and we keep the words alive, we keep their purpose alive. We are the living, but this is the Day of the Dead: our words are for the dead, all of the dead: the dead who made us and the dead we loved; the dead moments, passed from time; the dead passions spent; and all of the dead possibilities, the things that never were. We make them live and speak, we have that privilege.

'In a variety of archaic stories – the kind of which you know I'm fond – one, final question would be asked of those who were following the ultimate way and seeking the ultimate prize – "Whom does the Grail serve?" Their answer would win them all they had ever desired or destroy their hopes completely. This is traditionally when I ask members of the Fellowship: "Whom does the word serve?" If we take what we are offered and we use it, friends, "Whom does the word serve?"' Louis closed his eyes, as if he might be considering his own answer, while the room paused, perhaps embarrassed, perhaps not. Still blind, and arms very slightly unsteady, he lifted the jar above his head, and then dashed it down. It broke open on the carpet, making a dull, small sound.

Nathan considered the mess of shards at Louis's feet, the dust and little fragments of clay and, of course, the cards: all seven of them scattered through the heap. Louis knelt slowly and stirred the wreckage here and there with his finger, touching an edge or a corner of this or that card, somebody's message to a year they could only imagine. Then he smiled, reached and lifted out his own white rectangle, studiously covered with his own black printing. 'Perhaps if we each came forward and picked our card, we could then move on to reading out our contributions, before concluding the formal part of the evening and, perhaps, becoming appropriately inebriated. I'm sure Joe wouldn't mind if, as usual, a few of us spend the night here, rather than having to weave our ways home.'

Good man, yourself, Louis – a real tearaway, aren't you, quite the bold old boy.

Louis began to ease himself upright, his duties complete. Nathan slipped his feet out from under Eckless and moved forward to take the old man's arm. He regretted the gesture immediately as minor agonies ground down the length of his back.

'Perhaps *I* should be helping *you*.' Louis winked, his hold on Nathan's forearm delicate but precise. 'Mm?'

'Yes. Perhaps.' Nathan delivered his charge to the appropriate easy chair and then nipped in quickly to find his card and fold it away in his jacket pocket.

He sat and stared at the clay dust on his hands while others trooped up and did what they had to, Mary going last, and he spoke and spoke over again in his head the five words that he'd written and allowed to be sealed away – one sentence to prove himself the stupidest fucker in creation. One sentence was all it took.

Joe was making another announcement, his suggestions sounding distant, vaguely absurd, '. . . this moment to think about what we . . .' Nathan couldn't seem to focus, '. . . draw lots, or go round the room, or just read aloud as we feel we . . .' He stroked Eckless. Meanwhile, claustrophobia oozed easily into his lung and made him instantly, hugely, defensively, comfortingly angry.

All right. That's it. That's it.

On his feet, it seemed, shockingly quickly, he then marched to the fireplace, took out his card and threw it hard into the fire. The flames crouched momentarily and then swung back into place. For a moment, the pale shape containing his self-deluding, unfulfilling prophecy seemed to rest in the blaze unscathed, but then it buckled, darkened and, mercifully, began to disappear.

'Nathan?' Joe was close behind him, sounding concerned, but understanding in his customary, saintly fucking way.

'Piss off.'

'Nathan, this isn't –'

'I don't care. I'm not reading what I wrote and I'm going outside now. OK?' He spun to face them all – why not be hung for a sheep, for a bull in a china shop? 'Anyone have any problems with that?'

And he charged out through the chairs and bewildered faces and stamped across the moonlit grass, feeling nauseous with rage, and wishing them all to go and fuck themselves – apart from Mary – in front of whom he had made a cunt of himself, a total cunt, when everything had been going not too badly and still he jogged on, catching his feet on unseen projections, stumbling, jarring the sore points in his shoulder and his head, until the sea breeze began to steady him and he could slow and breathe and slow again and finally sit on a rock looking down to the glow of the surf where it feathered up and curled and dipped at the base of the cliffs.

Ach bollocks. Cunt. Fuck. Nathan, you fuckwit, shithead, fuck.

'Nathan?'

'Wha– ?'

It was Mary, the dim shape of Mary, breathless and carrying his coat, calling his name as she closed on him, flopping down at his side with an involuntary shove that stung him to the base of his brain but was still lovely.

'What on earth are you . . .? He sounded ludicrously high-pitched, silly. He coughed and tried again, 'What are you doing?'

'Obviously, I followed you.' She draped the coat around his shoulders and made him notice that he had been cold. 'What were *you* doing?'

'Oh, I don't know. I didn't want to get involved with it all.'

'Well, I could see that.'

This seemed to put an end to their conversation for a time and they leaned together in the dark, listening to the wide rush and turn of water far below them and the easing of Mary's breath. After a while, Nathan shifted, opened his coat and let it rest around Mary, too.

'Thanks.'

'It's covered in dog hairs and mud, if you remember.'

'Thanks anyway.' She laughed quietly. 'You do like to stir things up. What an exit. Fuck.'

'Don't say *fuck*. I fucking say it all the time – it's a terribly bad habit. Doesn't befit a lady.'

'Fuck off.'

'Then again, you're not a lady, you're a novelist.' He felt her tense slightly at the idea of that and then give in to it. 'And one day soon, you'll be photographed in your darling little flat in Bloomsbury, or Hampstead, or maybe Chelsea that goes with your country place in . . . um . . .'

'The Conwy valley.'

'Yes, that'll do – eccentric, but why not? And you'll be there with your cats and your original watercolours and your adoring husband.'

She tensed again for a breath, then settled back. 'Adoring, you say.'

'Mm hm. It's compulsory. Authoresses' husbands always have to be adoring and very quiet. As do your incredibly talented, ah . . . talented children.'

Not that it isn't insane to even mention them.

'I think I'll just settle for Jonno and we'll see about the rest.'

'OK.'

'I would have to do that, though, wouldn't I, if anybody liked the book – all of that *being published* stuff?'

'It's a burden that you may well have to bear.' *Don't sound scared, please. I don't know what to do if you get scared.* 'We'll get through it together. You'll do fine. It's horrible crap with an occasional sweetie to relieve the bitterness, but we'll get through.' *And anyone who does you wrong, I will simply beat to death.*

'Nathan, can I ask you . . . ?'

'Anything.'

'What did you write?'

He hadn't expected that, but it was dark and he was tired and she was close and so the chill flux of blood in his heart only punched once or twice and then dissipated. She could know, he could tell her. Anything. 'I wrote *Nathan Staples is still married.*' He swallowed, went on. 'And I was right. Just not very right.' She squeezed her arm at his waist and he clenched his jaw, kept himself coherent, under control. 'Mm hm. Not to worry. You remind me now – what did you write?'

'Mary Lamb will be a writer.'

He smiled into the night, 'Couldn't be anything else,' and then gingerly stretched out both his legs. 'Come on, we'd better get back, so I can face the music. And thanks for coming to get me.'

'You'd do the same for me.'

They both stood, but then waited together, facing the black of the sea, the beat of its lights, the island like a great ship beneath them, drifting them safe away from shore.

And whom does the word serve, Nathan? You won't tell her that. You won't tell her that the card was your answer, that you were writing for your wife, that even when you didn't think it, you were writing for your wife: your wife, the one who thinks you're boring, the one who couldn't give a fuck. You won't tell her there's no point to it any more, that one more book and you're finished, no more bottle, no more heart. The word serves fucking no one. No one at all.

1997

It was a kind of remission, he supposed. Now that it didn't matter and he didn't care, or was, at least, determined not to, Nathan's work progressed quite easily, almost without him. He'd been a good boy through the worst of the winter and kept his head down, handwriting and then typing, then correcting, then typing again – a chapter forward, a chapter back, the familiar swing between loathing and the coming of little lights. He'd even sneaked away from the Lighthouse New Year party and welcomed the first hours of January with an especially gratuitous, but relatively literary description.

And he did forget her sometimes – that was a possibility. A good run of phrases, a day where he really set the pace, and he could lose himself and Maura, too. Although there were, of course, the bleak days, the raw ones when he let himself edge near the joy of her taking him in, drawing his voice up tight inside her own, reading him, having him. Then he would spend taut hours at the edge of a sweat, beginning to need her, almost feel her, and finally have to part himself from the page and go to an aching bed. He'd watched the dawn a good deal, these past months.

But he'd promised Jack that he'd produce it, the proper novel, and he would: he would honour his dead, himself amongst them, the writer who no longer wished to write.

Nearly there, now. It'll be strange to stop. Not like losing a limb, more like losing my name.

But, just at this minute, he wasn't attending to the novel, or even thinking of it. He was brushing Eckless and being rewarded for his efforts with a wad of compacted hairs, some mud and a series of appreciative grunts.

'Yes, I'd probably like it, too, if somebody did it to me. Ah, look at you there – handsome devil, you are. All smart for Mary. Yes, indeed. What a dog, what a fine, fine dog. There you go.'

Eckless, released, stood up and shook himself back into order, before trotting off to the kitchen. He was unsettled, picking up on Nathan's nervousness.

She should be home by now. Joe went to pick her up, ages ago. Then she'll find my note and she'll come over and that'll be that – all to plan.

Not that I put any faith in my plans.

He went to his wardrobe, picked out another shirt and changed for the second time this afternoon. It was difficult to know what he should wear to welcome his only daughter back from her very first publishing lunch.

Maybe I should have gone with her. Let the fucker know he couldn't take advantage – they always try. Skimming the advances, clipping off rights.

No. Best she does it herself.

Well, maybe not best, but necessary.

His manuscript was waiting for her on the shelf – a rather more substantial stack than he'd expected.

I wouldn't have thought I had that much to say.

And all but the last few pages were done. He'd get them polished off and give her the lot today – the whole of his proper novel. Fear elbowed him in the stomach again and he went and sat down in the living room, slapped at his forehead, rubbed his eyes. He wasn't sure what rattled him most: the old, old terror of submitting work, the flat horizon that was all he could picture beyond the end of his career, the panic when he thought of his daughter, reading and thinking of him.

'What's up?' She'd crept in and caught him unawares.

He could only hope he hadn't looked too anguished. 'Jesus fuck, don't do that. I'm an old man.'

'Nonsense. Ask me how it went.' She, on the other hand, looked wonderful, still in her business ensemble, hair undeniably wild after the crossing, but still impressive.

He could tell by her face that it had gone just fine. 'How did what go?'

'The lunch.'

'Oh, the lunch. Well, that surely went like most lunches – you'll have eaten stuff and talked a bit and then buggered off.'

'Nathan . . .' She growled at him, delighted.

'OK, tell me.'

So she did: the price of the meal and the cut of the suit and the whiteness of the tablecloth, the highs and small hitches in the conversation and, of course, naturally, unavoidably after all that, the considered, in person, professional opinion, given with convincing care, that a significant proportion of her paragraphs were not too bad.

'Don't let it go to your head, though.'

'Even if I do, you won't.'

Am I a killjoy? Does she mean I'm a killjoy?

'Do you mean I'm a killjoy?'

'No. Daft bugger. Of course not. Give us a hug. Nobody's hugged me for *days*.'

'Jonno's back from Cardiff tomorrow, I'm sure he could manage something.'

'But I'll have one of *your* hugs now. Thank you.'

He obliged, 'Not at all, thank *you*,' aware that he was vaguely shaky, but hoping she wouldn't notice if he was quick.

'Your note said you had a surprise for me. It's not your book, is it? Is it? Is it your book?' She held him by the shoulders and searched about the room for signs of a manuscript. 'Ah, you've moved it to the shelf. What does that mean?'

All in good time, all in good time.

'It means it's away from prying eyes.' He gulped in a swift breath, 'I sent you the note, because tonight I will cook you a celebration dinner.'

'Oh, my God.'

'Shut up – it will be good. Then, when it's fully dark, we can go out and watch the comet – I've been able to see it really clearly, the last two nights. It's weird, makes the sky look bigger, I'm not quite sure why.'

'Shit, I'd forgotten about that. What's it like?'

'A little fire, far away – you seem to see the smoke – one smudge above it and one to the side. But before all that, before I . . . there's . . . well, you know.'

'No, I don't – you'll have to tell me.' She was grinning.

He sighed, blinked, couldn't meet her eye. 'Before we do all of that – all the cooking and watching and so on – I am going to sit down and finish my novel.' He heard her let out a tiny breath, but carried on as if he hadn't. 'I am already very near the end. Really very near. Then, when you go off to Jonno tomorrow morning, you can take it with you. If you want.' He examined his shadow, almost smiling, horribly close to feeling proud, glad, at least satisfied. 'If you happened to want.'

'Yes, I probably wouldn't mind.' She hugged him again, kissed his ear. 'Good work, Nathan Staples.'

'Certainly work, anyway.'

'Then, in that case − look − I'll go over by the hut and get changed, because I haven't yet − obviously − and I'll come back feeling more comfortable and we'll help ourselves celebrate in − what − two hours?'

'Less, if you like.'

It won't take me that long to finish. Don't leave me alone when I've finished. Please. I won't know what to do.

'No, two hours would be best, because by then you'll have the dinner ready − that's what I'm aiming for.'

'Then two hours it is.'

If I was foolish, I would ask her for another hug to bring me luck.

But he let her leave him.

Maybe later. Perhaps. I can wait. I do know how to wait.

And then Nathan went to the shelf and he fetched his papers down and he set them on the table beside his typewriter and his pad.

I would quite like it if this last little bit was in longhand. I'm sure she wouldn't mind.

I'd like my hand to be on it. Old-fashioned of me.

But she'll get it typed, she'll get it proper. Not just the first draft.

God.

So close now, so close.

He sat and waited for his head to clear.

Oh, God. Please let her understand. Please let her understand me.

Gradually, a couple of pages came clear and he worked his way through them slowly, keeping calm.

Oh, God. Dear God. Please, God.

He fed his paper softly between the rollers of his machine. He typed out a title, underlined it, the way he always did.

And then he began.

Thinking the World

I'm writing.

Really, I'm too tired to do it, but I'm writing, all the same. The whole place is falling still, getting ready for evening and that last big burst of bird song we both like. And outside, a comet is rising.

But then, I've already told you that. I've already written the way that you came to me an hour ago, I've already written out everything I know.

Almost.

Here's one last Rule for you: Rule Seven. I think that I have tried to follow it and not done well, but I do still believe this to be the most useful and beautiful Rule of all, the one that is most true: *do it for love.*

And.

If you can, forgive me.

And.

I didn't intend to mention it, but I love you.

Of course.

I do love you.

And.

You know now as well as I do how this works. You understand what happens here.

This is where I'm in your hands completely.

Please, my darling, have need of me.

A. L. Kennedy

NOW THAT YOU'RE BACK

WINNER OF A
SOMERSET MAUGHAM AWARD

'Funny, deadpan, angry, tender and despairing'
Elle

Tender, precise, comic and chilling by turn, the stories in this collection confirm A. L. Kennedy's reputation as one of the most exciting new writers to have appeared in the past decade.

'Kennedy has now proved that she is one of the few young writers to have found a distinctive voice, one that we could recognise even from a couple of sentences; and that in itself is already a considerable achievement'
Mail on Sunday

'Powerful, acute and wholly convincing'
Sunday Times

'Great short stories are as rare if not rarer than great poems and the fact that a handful here possesses great magical quality is remarkable...A. L. Kennedy is a writer of original and beguiling diction'
Scotland on Sunday

V

VINTAGE